The Editor

CLARE VIRGINIA EBY is a professor of English at the University of Connecticut. She is the author of *Until Choice Do Us Part: Marriage Reform in the Progressive Era* and *Dreiser and Veblen, Saboteurs of the Status Quo*; editor of the Dreiser Edition of Theodore Dreiser's *The Genius*; and coeditor of *The Cambridge History of the American Novel.*

NORTON CRITICAL EDITIONS
AMERICAN REALISM & REFORM

For a complete list of Norton Critical Editions, visit
wwnorton.com/nortoncriticals

A NORTON CRITICAL EDITION

Upton Sinclair
THE JUNGLE

AN AUTHORITATIVE TEXT
CONTEXTS AND BACKGROUNDS
UPTON SINCLAIR AND LITERARY
PROGRESSIVISM

SECOND EDITION

Edited by

CLARE VIRGINIA EBY
UNIVERSITY OF CONNECTICUT

W. W. NORTON & COMPANY
Independent Publishers Since 1923

Copyright © 2022, 2003 by W. W. Norton & Company, Inc.

All rights reserved
Printed in the United States of America

Manufacturing by Maple Press
Book design by Antonina Krass
Production manager: Brenda Manzanedo

Library of Congress Cataloging-in-Publication Data

Names: Sinclair, Upton, 1878–1968, author. | Eby, Clare Virginia, editor.
Title: The jungle : an authoritative text, contexts and backgrounds, criticism /
    Upton Sinclair; edited by Clare Virginia Eby, University of Connecticut.
Description: Second edition. | New York : W. W. Norton & Company, [2022] |
    Series: A Norton critical edition | Includes bibliographical references.
Identifiers: LCCN 2020056671 | ISBN 9780393420364 (paperback)
Subjects: LCSH: Sinclair, Upton, 1878–1968. Jungle. | Political fiction.
Classification: LCC PS3537.I85 J85 2022 | DDC 813/.52—dc23
LC record available at https://lccn.loc.gov/2020056671

W. W. Norton & Company, Inc., 500 Fifth Avenue, New York, N.Y. 10110
www.wwnorton.com
W. W. Norton & Company Ltd., 15 Carlisle Street, London W1D 3BS

1 2 3 4 5 6 7 8 9 0

Contents

Upton Sinclair and Literary Progressivism 473

Introduction

A larger-than-life figure, Upton Sinclair cannily kept himself in the public eye even while railing against what he saw as journalistic snooping into his private life. In an early effort to secure national attention in the United States before his name became a household word, he made up a story about a writer who committed suicide—and then planted a fake obituary for this writer in *The New York Times*. Having created an advance market for the pretend author's books, Sinclair then published his own novel, *The Journal of Arthur Stirling* (1903), reputedly written by the fictitious suicide. Two decades later, when Sinclair's novel *Oil!* was banned in Boston for referring to sex and abortion, he produced what he called a "Fig Leaf Edition," with the offending passages covered by images of fig leaves. He then advertised the book by taking two large fig leaf posters, draping them front and back over his body like a sandwich board, marching to Boston Common, and offering to sell the novel directly to the public. The stunt made the front page of newspapers around the country, and sales of *Oil!* (1927) spiked. (Eighty years later, *Oil!* got a second life, as the inspiration of the Academy Award–winning film *There Will Be Blood* [2007].)

Sinclair wrote nearly ninety books, but *The Jungle* (1906) is unquestionably the one that secured his international renown. While the novel's historical importance has never been in doubt, the current moment seems right for a reappraisal, and perhaps even for *The Jungle* to enjoy a second life. The 2020–21 coronavirus pandemic focused attention on what we now call essential workers, who put their lives at risk—often for minimum wage—so the rest of the population can continue to, for example, eat meat and buy toilet paper. *The Jungle* centers on low-paid essential workers in a meat processing plant in Chicago's Packingtown district. In fact, Sinclair boasted that *The Jungle* "mark[ed] the beginning of a proletarian literature in America."[1] If he were still with us, he might have predicted that during the early months of the COVID-19 pandemic, meat processing plants would be among the virus's hot spots. A direct

---

1. Upton Sinclair, "What Life Means to Me," *Cosmopolitan* 41 (October 1906): 594 (part of this essay is reprinted below, pp. 478–83).

line can be drawn between the threats to individual health and to public health, from the time of *The Jungle* to our own.

While *The Jungle* is legendary for galvanizing public attention on the dangerous and often disgusting practices of meat processing plants—even playing a starring role in the passage of the Pure Food and Drug Act, in June 1906—neither consumer protection nor hygienic food was Sinclair's objective. Rather, he wrote *The Jungle* as an obscure young author who had recently discovered socialism and passionately believed that "wage slavery" in the North recapitulated chattel slavery in the South.[2] After Sinclair published an article in the popular socialist periodical *Appeal to Reason* supporting the 1904 meat workers' strike, the editor invited him to write a novel demonstrating his thesis about the evils of wage slavery, to be published serially. After months of intensive on-site research in Chicago, the first chapter of *The Jungle* appeared in the *Appeal* in February 1905. Published in book form by Doubleday, Page & Company in February 1906, it was translated within months into seventeen languages, and Sinclair became a celebrity practically overnight.[3] But to his chagrin, the buzz was not over wage slavery. As Sinclair famously described the distance between his intention for the book and its reception, "I aimed at the public's heart, and by accident I hit it in the stomach."[4]

While readers' stomachs still churn over *The Jungle*'s revelations about sausage, we might pause to reflect on what Sinclair intended as the novel's heart. *The Jungle* appeared during a time of extreme economic inequality—vividly displayed in the novel when the impoverished protagonist spends a day in the mansion of a very spoiled, very rich, very drunken young man—and also during what has been called the golden age of socialism in America. In 1904, Sinclair joined the Socialist Party of America (SPA), which at its peak had 100,000 members. Indeed, the charismatic Eugene Debs, SPA presidential candidate in five elections, won over 900,000 votes in 1920. *The Jungle* culminates in an optimistic reading of the 1904 election—in which Debs garnered 400,000 votes—as a sign that a socialist America was on the horizon.

Throughout his career, Sinclair recognized no distance between literature and politics. As he says in his literary manifesto, *Mammonart*, "*All art is propaganda*."[5] That was not a limitation for Sinclair, who believed the whole point of art was to change minds or, more precisely, hearts. *The Jungle* is not a delicately crafted or

---

2. See, for instance, "What Life Means to Me" (below, p. 481).
3. For further discussion of the publication history, see "A Note on the Text" (below, p. xiii). For a comparison of the endings of the two versions, see below, pp. 520–21.
4. "What Life Means to Me" (below, p. 481).
5. Sinclair, *Mammonart* (below, p. 486).

formally inventive novel, but it is one of those rare works of literature that have had an enormous impact on the public sphere.[6] (Harriet Beecher Stowe's *Uncle Tom's Cabin* [1852] is another, and Sinclair often compared his "wage slavery" novel to his predecessor's famous antislavery novel.) In any case, *The Jungle*'s beef (pun intended) for socialism, delivered from that political theory's golden age, merits attention today, as large swaths of Americans, especially young ones, ask if there are alternatives to capitalism—and once again, even vote in significant numbers for socialist candidates. Equally true, conservatives still brandish the word "socialism" to label a program or policy as un-American. Sinclair, who commented in 1951 that "[t]he American People will take Socialism, but they won't take the label,"[7] would probably interpret the recent openness on the part of at least some Americans to the socialist "label" as progress.

The overt politics of *The Jungle* have been roundly criticized and can present an obstacle for some readers. Yet it is certainly true that the socialism of the novel is, just as Daniel Aaron said of Sinclair overall, "*sui generis*,"[8] impossible to classify. That verdict can help make sense of the extended debate between two very different socialists at the end of *The Jungle*; however political the novel is, it is not doctrinaire. Moreover, there have been provocative suggestions that Sinclair's socialism is driven by something other than political fervor. The Russian leader Vladimir Lenin, for one, called Sinclair "an emotional socialist without theoretic grounding."[9] Biographer Anthony Arthur aptly pronounces Sinclair "the most conservative of revolutionaries" and describes him as approaching socialism from the standpoint of moralism, not political theory.[1]

Sinclair's moralism ran deep. Influenced by his devout mother (and by his father's alcoholism), Sinclair was a passionate teetotaler all his life. Many who knew him well, including his first wife, called him hopelessly puritanical. Most revealingly, among his personal heroes was no less than Jesus, and yet Sinclair admired him less as a religious icon than as a deeply principled man and misunderstood radical. Sinclair's moralism leaves a deep imprint on *The Jungle*,

---

6. As Jason Pickavance puts it, "No other American novel has been the subject of a presidential commission formed to assess the truth-value of its depictions" (95). "Gastronomic Realism: Upton Sinclair's *The Jungle*, the Fight for Pure Food, and the Magic of Mastication," *Food and Foodways* 11: 2–3 (2003): 87–112.
7. Upton Sinclair, 1951 letter to Norman Thomas.
8. Daniel Aaron, *Writers on the Left: Episodes in American Literary Communism* (New York: Harcourt, Brace & World, 1961), p. 159.
9. Vladimir Lenin quoted in Leon Harris, *Upton Sinclair: American Rebel* (New York: Thomas Y. Crowell, 1975), p. 159.
1. Anthony Arthur, *Radical Innocent: Upton Sinclair* (New York: Random House, 2006), pp. xii, 38. The different strains of socialism in Sinclair's time are discussed by Mark W. Van Wienen in this volume (pp. 506–12).

perhaps most notably in how its trajectory tracks what has been described as the conversion experience of the protagonist.[2]

The moral fervor of the novel makes it the preeminent example of muckraking, or the literature of exposure. The term was coined by President Teddy Roosevelt (TR) in a speech referencing the Christian allegory *Pilgrim's Progress* by the seventeenth-century English writer John Bunyan.[3] In *Pilgrim's Progress* (one of Sinclair's favorite books in childhood), a man with a muck rake turns down the offer of a celestial crown because he can't take his eyes off the filth of the world—the muck on his rake. Due to the public outcry over issues raised by *The Jungle*, TR invited Sinclair to the White House, but the president also denounced as "muckrakers" those investigative writers who went, he believed, too far in uncovering filth. While TR did not name any names, he obviously had *The Jungle* in mind, along with contemporaneous exposés such as Ida Tarbell's *A History of the Standard Oil Company* (1902), David Graham Phillips's *The Treason of the Senate* (1906), and Lincoln Steffens's *The Shame of the Cities* (1904). These examples are brilliant, meticulously researched, influential muckraking texts, but they lack the compelling narrative form of *The Jungle*. To borrow the words of a novelist quite different from Sinclair, sometimes fiction can seem truer than fact.[4]

The Jungle is also timely in demonstrating that workers who perform the most dangerous and thankless jobs for very little pay are disproportionately minorities. Many of Sinclair's racial views, particularly his disdain for Black Americans, will strike twenty-first-century readers as bigoted. Without apologizing for such views, we can place them in historical context and observe that Sinclair was writing in a time when Americans recognized a number of *different* white races—and subjected them all to a hierarchical ranking, according to which *The Jungle*'s Lithuanian protagonists fell quite low on the totem pole.[5] Consequently, the Lithuanian characters perform the most menial labors.

In this Norton Critical Edition, selected readings after the text of *The Jungle* illuminate the novel's immediate historical context and its continuing relevance. The eminent critic Edmund Wilson remarked during the Great Depression that "[p]ractically alone of the American writers of his generation, [Sinclair] put to the American public the fundamental questions raised by capitalism in such

---

2. See Walter Rideout's classic interpretation of *The Jungle*, in his book *The Radical Novel in the United States 1900–1954* (Cambridge, MA: Harvard UP, 1956), pp. 34–36; on the conversion motif, also see below, pp. 494–95, 499, and 520.
3. For an excerpt of this famous speech, see below, p. 504.
4. Virginia Woolf, *A Room of One's Own* (San Diego: Harcourt, Brace, 1929), p. 4.
5. See Matthew Frye Jacobson for further discussion of this point (below, pp. 392–96).

a way that they could not escape them."[6] Accordingly, the first section of readings following the novel focuses on capitalism as seen from multiple perspectives, including those of businessmen, medical investigators, muckrakers, and modern historians and economists. The second group of readings takes up two very different topics that are impossible to pry apart in *The Jungle*: labor and immigration. These readings range from studies by social scientists who were Sinclair's contemporaries to the nineteenth-century German socialist Karl Marx to twenty-first-century scholars who show how food production still relies on immigrant labor. The third section, "Nature," includes readings about the treatment of animals, the development of CAFOs (Concentrated Animal Feeding Operations), also known as factory farming, in the latter part of the twentieth century, and the environmental and public health consequences of a meat-based diet. The final section, "Upton Sinclair and Literary Progressivism," includes revealing writings by the novelist himself, early responses to *The Jungle*, and modern studies that position Sinclair as a literary progressive, as a muckraker, and as a socialist novelist, as well as an examination of what his novel can teach us about democracy in a divided era.

---

6. Edmund Wilson, "Lincoln Steffens and Upton Sinclair," *The New Republic* 72 (September 28, 1932): 174.

A Note on the Text

The text used is the Doubleday, Page & Company edition published on February 26, 1906. Italicization of foreign phrases has been regularized, but otherwise the text follows the first edition.

The compositional and publication history of *The Jungle* is unusually complicated. Before it appeared in the Doubleday, Page edition, Sinclair had published installments in the *Appeal to Reason*, a socialist weekly of wide circulation founded by Julius Augustus Wayland. In fact, it was the interest of the *Appeal*'s editor that prompted Sinclair to write *The Jungle*. In September 1904 the *Appeal* had published Sinclair's challenge to the Packingtown workers after the failure of their 1904 strike. Managing Editor Fred D. Warren then read Sinclair's Civil War novel, *Manassas* (1904), which led him to invite the author to compose a novel about present-day wage slavery for serial publication. Most important, Warren agreed to advance the impoverished novelist $500. Sinclair quickly settled on the Chicago stockyards as his subject, and after conducting seven weeks of on-site research he began writing on Christmas Day, 1904. Installments first appeared in the February 25, 1905, issue of the *Appeal* and ran through November 4, 1905; some installments appeared simultaneously in Wayland's related magazine, *One-Hoss Philosophy*.

Sinclair then quickly sought to publish *The Jungle* as a book. After failing to come to terms with five commercial publishers—many of whom demanded changes that he refused to make—Sinclair made an unsuccessful attempt to bypass the capitalist press by securing sufficient advance subscriptions to finance publishing it on his own, in what would be called a "Sustainers' Edition." But in December 1905, Sinclair reported, "I have received an offer from a publishing house of the highest standing, which is willing to bring out the book on my own terms."[1] This publisher was the commercial house of Doubleday, Page & Company. Sinclair used the same plates to publish his own edition (called the Jungle Publishing Company version) concurrently, which also suggests his satisfaction with the Doubleday, Page trade edition. Furthermore, as Ronald Gottesman

---

1. Quoted in Gene DeGruson, introduction. *The Lost First Edition of Upton Sinclair's "The Jungle"* (Memphis: Peachtree, 1988), p. xxiii.

points out, only one change—involving the color of an inspector's buttons—was ever introduced after this initial book publication.[2]

Since the manuscript was destroyed in a fire, the texts available for determining an authoritative edition are the *Appeal* serialization and the Doubleday, Page first edition. Approximately two-thirds the length of the serial version, the Doubleday, Page novel is more concise, and its prose is tighter and smoother. Installment writing can breed sloppiness as well as wordiness, as an author rushes to complete individual chapters for deadlines and pads others to make them long enough. These limitations are clearly evident in the *Appeal* version of *The Jungle,* which has been called the "unexpurgated" edition but might be better termed the unedited version. While the serial version has chronological primacy and contains some fascinating material discussed by Michael Folsom and others, most readers would agree that the Doubleday, Page edition is preferable.[3] It is also the version that has been discussed by the vast majority of commentators, from literary critics to policy makers to historians. Given the extraordinary impact *The Jungle* has had in the public sphere, the influence of the Doubleday, Page text is no small consideration.

The *Appeal* version comprises, of course, an essential part of the history of *The Jungle,* and we are fortunate to have it readily available, published in book form in 1988 as *The Lost First Edition of Upton Sinclair's "The Jungle,"* edited and introduced by Gene DeGruson.

2. Ronald Gottesman, "A Note on the Text," *The Jungle,* by Upton Sinclair (New York: Penguin, 1985), p. xxxvii.
3. Michael Brewster Folsom, "Upton Sinclair's Escape from *The Jungle:* The Narrative Strategy and Suppressed Conclusion of America's First Proletarian Novel," *Prospects* 4 (1979): 237–66.

The Text of
THE JUNGLE

TO THE WORKINGMEN OF AMERICA

The Jungle

Chapter I

It was four o'clock when the ceremony was over and the carriages began to arrive. There had been a crowd following all the way, owing to the exuberance of Marija Berczynskas. The occasion rested heavily upon Marija's broad shoulders—it was her task to see that all things went in due form, and after the best home traditions; and, flying wildly hither and thither, bowling every one out of the way, and scolding and exhorting all day with her tremendous voice, Marija was too eager to see that others conformed to the proprieties to consider them herself. She had left the church last of all, and, desiring to arrive first at the hall, had issued orders to the coachman to drive faster. When that personage had developed a will of his own in the matter, Marija had flung up the window of the carriage, and, leaning out, proceeded to tell him her opinion of him, first in Lithuanian, which he did not understand, and then in Polish, which he did. Having the advantage of her in altitude, the driver had stood his ground and even ventured to attempt to speak; and the result had been a furious altercation, which, continuing all the way down Ashland Avenue, had added a new swarm of urchins to the cortège at each side street for half a mile.

This was unfortunate, for already there was a throng before the door. The music had started up, and half a block away you could hear the dull "broom, broom" of a 'cello, with the squeaking of two fiddles which vied with each other in intricate and altitudinous gymnastics. Seeing the throng, Marija abandoned precipitately the debate concerning the ancestors of her coachman, and, springing from the moving carriage, plunged in and proceeded to clear a way to the hall. Once within, she turned and began to push the other way, roaring, meantime, *"Eik! Eik! Uzdaryk-duris!"*[1] in tones which made the orchestral uproar sound like fairy music.

---

1. "Go! Go! Close the doors!" All translations are from Lithuanian unless otherwise noted. Marija's comment about the coachman's ancestors follows a path familiar in the insults of many languages.

"Z. Graiczunas, Pasilinksminimams darzas. Vynas. Sznapsas. Wines and Liquors. Union Headquarters"[2]—that was the way the signs ran. The reader, who perhaps has never held much converse in the language of far-off Lithuania, will be glad of the explanation that the place was the rear-room of a saloon in that part of Chicago known as "back of the yards."[3] This information is definite and suited to the matter of fact; but how pitifully inadequate it would have seemed to one who understood that it was also the supreme hour of ecstasy in the life of one of God's gentlest creatures, the scene of the wedding-feast and the joy-transfiguration of little Ona Lukoszaite!

She stood in the doorway, shepherded by Cousin Marija, breathless from pushing through the crowd, and in her happiness painful to look upon. There was a light of wonder in her eyes and her lids trembled, and her otherwise wan little face was flushed. She wore a muslin dress, conspicuously white, and a stiff little veil coming to her shoulders. There were five pink paper-roses twisted in the veil, and eleven bright green rose-leaves. There were new white cotton gloves upon her hands, and as she stood staring about her she twisted them together feverishly. It was almost too much for her—you could see the pain of too great emotion in her face, and all the tremor of her form. She was so young—not quite sixteen—and small for her age, a mere child; and she had just been married—and married to Jurgis,[4] of all men, to Jurgis Rudkus, he with the white flower in the buttonhole of his new black suit, he with the mighty shoulders and the giant hands.

Ona was blue-eyed and fair, while Jurgis had great black eyes with beetling brows, and thick black hair that curled in waves about his ears—in short, they were one of those incongruous and impossible married couples with which Mother Nature so often wills to confound all prophets, before and after. Jurgis could take up a two-hundred-and-fifty-pound quarter of beef and carry it into a car without a stagger, or even a thought; and now he stood in a far corner, frightened as a hunted animal, and obliged to moisten his lips with his tongue each time before he could answer the congratulations of his friends.

Gradually there was effected a separation between the spectators and the guests—a separation at least sufficiently complete for

2. In immigrant communities, back rooms of saloons were used as meeting halls for unions and other activities. Z. Graiczunas is the proprietor's name.
3. Overcrowded area, littered with filth and lacking adequate sewage, where workers lived. In sight and smell of the stockyards and city dump, this section had the highest death rate in Chicago. *Lithuania*: a Baltic nation. From the 14th century through the 16th, the Grand Duchy of Lithuania (which included what are now Belarus and western Ukraine) had been one of the largest powers in eastern Europe. At the time of *The Jungle*, Lithuania was annexed by the Russian Empire, and it remained so until 1918, right after the Russian Revolution.
4. Pronounced *Yoorghis* [*Sinclair's note*].

working purposes. There was no time during the festivities which ensued when there were not groups of onlookers in the doorways and the corners; and if any one of these onlookers came sufficiently close, or looked sufficiently hungry, a chair was offered him, and he was invited to the feast. It was one of the laws of the *veselija*[5] that no one goes hungry; and, while a rule made in the forests of Lithuania is hard to apply in the stock-yards district of Chicago,[6] with its quarter of a million inhabitants, still they did their best, and the children who ran in from the street, and even the dogs, went out again happier. A charming informality was one of the characteristics of this celebration. The men wore their hats, or, if they wished, they took them off, and their coats with them; they ate when and where they pleased, and moved as often as they pleased. There were to be speeches and singing, but no one had to listen who did not care to; if he wished, meantime, to speak or sing himself, he was perfectly free. The resulting medley of sound distracted no one, save possibly alone the babies, of which there were present a number equal to the total possessed by all the guests invited. There was no other place for the babies to be, and so part of the preparations for the evening consisted of a collection of cribs and carriages in one corner. In these the babies slept, three or four together, or wakened together, as the case might be. Those who were still older, and could reach the tables, marched about munching contentedly at meat-bones and bologna sausages.

The room is about thirty feet square, with whitewashed walls, bare save for a calendar, a picture of a race-horse, and a family tree in a gilded frame. To the right there is a door from the saloon, with a few loafers in the doorway, and in the corner beyond it a bar, with a presiding genius clad in soiled white, with waxed black mustaches and a carefully oiled curl plastered against one side of his forehead. In the opposite corner are two tables, filling a third of the room and laden with dishes and cold viands, which a few of the hungrier guests are already munching. At the head, where sits the bride, is a snow-white cake, with an Eiffel tower of constructed decoration, with sugar roses and two angels upon it, and a generous sprinkling of pink and green and yellow candies. Beyond opens a door into the kitchen, where there is a glimpse to be had of a range with much steam ascending from it, and many women, old and young, rushing hither and thither. In the corner to the left are the three musicians, upon a little platform, toiling heroically to make some impression upon the hubbub; also the babies, similarly occupied, and an open

5. Wedding feast, part of traditional Lithuanian celebration.
6. Livestock was bought, sold, and slaughtered in the southwestern area of the city, part of an industrial belt that included railroad freight yards, the McCormick plant, and blast furnaces.

window whence the populace imbibes the sights and sounds and odors.

Suddenly some of the steam begins to advance, and, peering through it, you discern Aunt Elizabeth, Ona's step-mother—Teta Elzbieta, as they call her—bearing aloft a great platter of stewed duck. Behind her is Kotrina, making her way cautiously, staggering beneath a similar burden; and half a minute later there appears old Grandmother Majauszkiene, with a big yellow bowl of smoking potatoes, nearly as big as herself. So, bit by bit, the feast takes form— there is a ham and a dish of sauerkraut, boiled rice, macaroni, bologna sausages, great piles of penny buns, bowls of milk, and foaming pitchers of beer. There is also, not six feet from your back, the bar, where you may order all you please and do not have to pay for it. "*Eiksz! Graicziau!*"[7] screams Marija Berczynskas, and falls to work herself—for there is more upon the stove inside that will be spoiled if it be not eaten.

So, with laughter and shouts and endless badinage and merriment, the guests take their places. The young men, who for the most part have been huddled near the door, summon their resolution and advance; and the shrinking Jurgis is poked and scolded by the old folks until he consents to seat himself at the right hand of the bride. The two bridesmaids, whose insignia of office are paper wreaths, come next, and after them the rest of the guests, old and young, boys and girls. The spirit of the occasion takes hold of the stately bartender, who condescends to a plate of stewed duck; even the fat policeman—whose duty it will be, later in the evening, to break up the fights—draws up a chair to the foot of the table. And the children shout and the babies yell, and every one laughs and sings and chatters—while above all the deafening clamor Cousin Marija shouts orders to the musicians.

The musicians—how shall one begin to describe them? All this time they have been there, playing in a mad frenzy—all of this scene must be read, or said, or sung, to music. It is the music which makes it what it is; it is the music which changes the place from the rear-room of a saloon in back of the yards to a fairy place, a wonderland, a little corner of the high mansions of the sky.

The little person who leads this trio is an inspired man. His fiddle is out of tune, and there is no rosin on his bow, but still he is an inspired man—the hands of the muses[8] have been laid upon him. He plays like one possessed by a demon, by a whole horde of demons. You can feel them in the air round about him, capering frenetically; with their invisible feet they set the pace, and the hair of the leader

---

7. "Come! Hurry up!"
8. In Greek mythology, nine sister goddesses believed to bring inspiration.

of the orchestra rises on end, and his eyeballs start from their sockets, as he toils to keep up with them.

Tamoszius Kuszleika is his name, and he has taught himself to play the violin by practising all night, after working all day on the "killing beds."[9] He is in his shirt-sleeves, with a vest figured with faded gold horseshoes, and a pink-striped shirt, suggestive of peppermint candy. A pair of military trousers, light blue with a yellow stripe, serve to give that suggestion of authority proper to the leader of a band. He is only about five feet high, but even so these trousers are about eight inches short of the ground. You wonder where he can have gotten them—or rather you would wonder, if the excitement of being in his presence left you time to think of such things.

For he is an inspired man. Every inch of him is inspired—you might almost say inspired separately. He stamps with his feet, he tosses his head, he sways and swings to and fro; he has a wizened-up little face, irresistibly comical; and, when he executes a turn or a flourish, his brows knit and his lips work and his eyelids wink—the very ends of his necktie bristle out. And every now and then he turns upon his companions, nodding, signalling, beckoning frantically—with every inch of him appealing, imploring, in behalf of the muses and their call.

For they are hardly worthy of Tamoszius, the other two members of the orchestra. The second violin is a Slovak, a tall, gaunt man with black-rimmed spectacles and the mute and patient look of an overdriven mule; he responds to the whip but feebly, and then always falls back into his old rut. The third man is very fat, with a round, red, sentimental nose, and he plays with his eyes turned up to the sky and a look of infinite yearning. He is playing a bass part upon his 'cello, and so the excitement is nothing to him; no matter what happens in the treble, it is his task to saw out one long-drawn and lugubrious note after another, from four o'clock in the afternoon until nearly the same hour next morning, for his third of the total income of one dollar per hour.

Before the feast has been five minutes under way, Tamoszius Kuszleika has risen in his excitement; a minute or two more and you see that he is beginning to edge over toward the tables. His nostrils are dilated and his breath comes fast—his demons are driving him. He nods and shakes his head at his companions, jerking at them with his violin, until at last the long form of the second violinist also rises up. In the end all three of them begin advancing, step by step, upon the banqueters, Valentinavyczia, the 'cellist, bumping along with his instrument between notes. Finally all three are gathered at the foot of the tables, and there Tamoszius mounts upon a stool.

9. Where livestock is slaughtered.

Now he is in his glory, dominating the scene. Some of the people are eating, some are laughing and talking—but you will make a great mistake if you think there is one of them who does not hear him. His notes are never true, and his fiddle buzzes on the low ones and squeaks and scratches on the high; but these things they heed no more than they heed the dirt and noise and squalor about them—it is out of this material that they have to build their lives, with it that they have to utter their souls. And this is their utterance; merry and boisterous, or mournful and wailing, or passionate and rebellious, this music is their music, music of home. It stretches out its arms to them, they have only to give themselves up. Chicago and its saloons and its slums fade away—there are green meadows and sunlit rivers, mighty forests and snow-clad hills. They behold home landscapes and childhood scenes returning; old loves and friendships begin to waken, old joys and griefs to laugh and weep. Some fall back and close their eyes, some beat upon the table. Now and then one leaps up with a cry and calls for this song or that; and then the fire leaps brighter in Tamoszius's eyes, and he flings up his fiddle and shouts to his companions, and away they go in mad career.[1] The company takes up the choruses, and men and women cry out like all possessed; some leap to their feet and stamp upon the floor, lifting their glasses and pledging each other. Before long it occurs to some one to demand an old wedding-song, which celebrates the beauty of the bride and the joys of love. In the excitement of this masterpiece Tamoszius Kuszleika begins to edge in between the tables, making his way toward the head, where sits the bride. There is not a foot of space between the chairs of the guests, and Tamoszius is so short that he pokes them with his bow whenever he reaches over for the low notes; but still he presses in, and insists relentlessly that his companions must follow. During their progress, needless to say, the sounds of the 'cello are pretty well extinguished; but at last the three are at the head, and Tamoszius takes his station at the right hand of the bride and begins to pour out his soul in melting strains.

Little Ona is too excited to eat. Once in a while she tastes a little something, when Cousin Marija pinches her elbow and reminds her; but, for the most part, she sits gazing with the same fearful eyes of wonder. Teta Elzbieta is all in a flutter, like a humming-bird; her sisters, too, keep running up behind her, whispering, breathless. But Ona seems scarcely to hear them—the music keeps calling, and the far-off look comes back, and she sits with her hands pressed together over her heart. Then the tears begin to come into her eyes; and as she is ashamed to wipe them away, and ashamed to let them run down her cheeks, she turns and shakes her head a little, and then

1. Gallop, fast pace.

flushes red when she sees that Jurgis is watching her. When in the end Tamoszius Kuszleika has reached her side, and is waving his magic wand above her, Ona's cheeks are scarlet, and she looks as if she would have to get up and run away.

In this crisis, however, she is saved by Marija Berczynskas, whom the muses suddenly visit. Marija is fond of a song, a song of lovers' parting; she wishes to hear it, and, as the musicians do not know it, she has risen, and is proceeding to teach them. Marija is short, but powerful in build. She works in a canning factory, and all day long she handles cans of beef that weigh fourteen pounds. She has a broad Slavic face, with prominent red cheeks. When she opens her mouth, it is tragical, but you cannot help thinking of a horse. She wears a blue flannel shirt-waist, which is now rolled up at the sleeves, disclosing her brawny arms; she has a carving-fork in her hand, with which she pounds on the table to mark the time. As she roars her song, in a voice of which it is enough to say that it leaves no portion of the room vacant, the three musicians follow her, laboriously and note by note, but averaging one note behind; thus they toil through stanza after stanza of a love-sick swain's lamentation:—

> "Sudiev' kvietkeli, tu brangiausis;
> Sudiev' ir laime, man biednam,
> Matau—paskyre teip Aukszcziausis,
> Jog vargt ant svieto reik vienam!"[2]

When the song is over, it is time for the speech, and old Dede Antanas rises to his feet. Grandfather Anthony, Jurgis's father, is not more than sixty years of age, but you would think that he was eighty. He has been only six months in America, and the change has not done him good. In his manhood he worked in a cotton-mill, but then a coughing fell upon him, and he had to leave; out in the country the trouble disappeared, but he has been working in the pickle-rooms[3] at Durham's, and the breathing of the cold, damp air all day has brought it back. Now as he rises he is seized with a coughing-fit, and holds himself by his chair and turns away his wan and battered face until it passes.

Generally it is the custom for the speech at a *veselija* to be taken out of one of the books and learned by heart; but in his youthful

---

2. Popular Lithuanian folk song by Antanas Vienazindys:

> "Good-bye little flower, thou dearest one;
> Good-bye also happiness,
> I see that the Highest Power has appointed
> For me, poor fellow, to suffer on earth alone."
>   (Translation courtesy of William R. Schmalstieg)

3. Preserving or "pickling" meats in brine or vinegar remained common after the development of refrigeration.

days Dede Antanas used to be a scholar, and really make up all the love-letters of his friends. Now it is understood that he has composed an original speech of congratulation and benediction, and this is one of the events of the day. Even the boys, who are romping about the room, draw near and listen, and some of the women sob and wipe their aprons in their eyes. It is very solemn, for Antanas Rudkus has become possessed of the idea that he has not much longer to stay with his children. His speech leaves them all so tearful that one of the guests, Jokubas Szedvilas, who keeps a delicatessen store on Halsted Street,[4] and is fat and hearty, is moved to rise and say that things may not be as bad as that, and then to go on and make a little speech of his own, in which he showers congratulations and prophecies of happiness upon the bride and groom, proceeding to particulars which greatly delight the young men, but which cause Ona to blush more furiously than ever. Jokubas possesses what his wife complacently describes as "*poetiszka vaidintuve*"—a poetical imagination.

Now a good many of the guests have finished, and, since there is no pretence of ceremony, the banquet begins to break up. Some of the men gather about the bar; some wander about, laughing and singing; here and there will be a little group, chanting merrily, and in sublime indifference to the others and to the orchestra as well. Everybody is more or less restless—one would guess that something is on their minds. And so it proves. The last tardy diners are scarcely given time to finish, before the tables and the débris are shoved into the corner, and the chairs and the babies piled out of the way, and the real celebration of the evening begins. Then Tamoszius Kuszleika, after replenishing himself with a pot of beer, returns to his platform, and, standing up, reviews the scene; he taps authoritatively upon the side of his violin, then tucks it carefully under his chin, then waves his bow in an elaborate flourish, and finally smites the sounding strings and closes his eyes, and floats away in spirit upon the wings of a dreamy waltz. His companion follows, but with his eyes open, watching where he treads, so to speak; and finally Valentinavyczia, after waiting for a little and beating with his foot to get the time, casts up his eyes to the ceiling and begins to saw—"Broom! broom! broom!"

The company pairs off quickly, and the whole room is soon in motion. Apparently nobody knows how to waltz, but that is nothing of any consequence—there is music, and they dance, each as he pleases, just as before they sang. Most of them prefer the "two-step,"[5] especially the young, with whom it is the fashion. The older people have dances from home, strange and complicated steps which they

4. Major thoroughfare forming the eastern border of stockyards and Packingtown, the surrounding district, which included living quarters.
5. A folk dance step; or, since Sinclair links it to the younger generation, he could have in mind a new move by this name, a precursor to a jazz step that appeared in 1902.

execute with grave solemnity. Some do not dance anything at all, but simply hold each other's hands and allow the undisciplined joy of motion to express itself with their feet. Among those are Jokubas Szedvilas and his wife, Lucija, who together keep the delicatessen store, and consume nearly as much as they sell; they are too fat to dance, but they stand in the middle of the floor, holding each other fast in their arms, rocking slowly from side to side and grinning seraphically, a picture of toothless and perspiring ecstasy.

Of these older people many wear clothing reminiscent in some detail of home—an embroidered waistcoat or stomacher,[6] or a gayly colored handkerchief, or a coat with large cuffs and fancy buttons. All these things are carefully avoided by the young, most of whom have learned to speak English and to affect the latest style of clothing. The girls wear ready-made dresses or shirt-waists,[7] and some of them look quite pretty. Some of the young men you would take to be Americans, of the type of clerks, but for the fact that they wear their hats in the room. Each of these younger couples affects a style of its own in dancing. Some hold each other tightly, some at a cautious distance. Some hold their arms out stiffly, some drop them loosely at their sides. Some dance springily, some glide softly, some move with grave dignity. There are boisterous couples, who tear wildly about the room, knocking every one out of their way. There are nervous couples, whom these frighten, and who cry, "*Nustok! Kas yra?*"[8] at them as they pass. Each couple is paired for the evening—you will never see them change about. There is Alena Jasaityte, for instance, who has danced unending hours with Juozas Raczius, to whom she is engaged. Alena is the beauty of the evening, and she would be really beautiful if she were not so proud. She wears a white shirt-waist, which represents, perhaps, half a week's labor painting cans.[9] She holds her skirt with her hand as she dances, with stately precision, after the manner of the *grandes dames*.[1] Juozas is driving one of Durham's wagons, and is making big wages. He affects a "tough" aspect, wearing his hat on one side and keeping a cigarette in his mouth all the evening. Then there is Jadvyga Marcinkus, who is also beautiful, but humble. Jadvyga likewise paints cans, but then she has an invalid mother and three little sisters to support by it, and so she does not spend her wages for shirt-waists. Jadvyga is small and delicate, with jet-black eyes and hair, the latter twisted into a little knot and tied on the top of her head. She wears an old white

---

6. Waist or bodice piece, heavily embroidered or jeweled: a traditional garment.
7. Americanized clothing: *shirtwaists* were women's tailored garments, and *ready-made* clothing was purchased in stores or by mail order rather than being sewed at home.
8. "Stop! What is this?"
9. Before stamping machinery was developed, cans were painted by hand. Three-quarters of cannery workers were women.
1. Elegant ladies (French).

dress which she has made herself and worn to parties for the past five years; it is high-waisted—almost under her arms, and not very becoming,—but that does not trouble Jadvyga, who is dancing with her Mikolas. She is small, while he is big and powerful; she nestles in his arms as if she would hide herself from view, and leans her head upon his shoulder. He in turn has clasped his arms tightly around her, as if he would carry her away; and so she dances, and will dance the entire evening, and would dance forever, in ecstasy of bliss. You would smile, perhaps, to see them—but you would not smile if you knew all the story. This is the fifth year, now, that Jadvyga has been engaged to Mikolas, and her heart is sick. They would have been married in the beginning, only Mikolas has a father who is drunk all day, and he is the only other man in a large family. Even so they might have managed it (for Mikolas is a skilled man) but for cruel accidents which have almost taken the heart out of them. He is a beef-boner, and that is a dangerous trade, especially when you are on piece-work[2] and trying to earn a bride. Your hands are slippery, and your knife is slippery, and you are toiling like mad, when somebody happens to speak to you, or you strike a bone. Then your hand slips up on the blade, and there is a fearful gash. And that would not be so bad, only for the deadly contagion. The cut may heal, but you never can tell. Twice now, within the last three years, Mikolas has been lying at home with blood-poisoning—once for three months and once for nearly seven. The last time, too, he lost his job, and that meant six weeks more of standing at the doors of the packing-houses,[3] at six o'clock on bitter winter mornings, with a foot of snow on the ground and more in the air. There are learned people who can tell you out of the statistics that beef-boners make forty cents an hour, but, perhaps, these people have never looked into a beef-boner's hands.

When Tamoszius and his companions stop for a rest, as perforce they must, now and then, the dancers halt where they are and wait patiently. They never seem to tire; and there is no place for them to sit down if they did. It is only for a minute, anyway, for the leader starts up again, in spite of all the protests of the other two. This time it is another sort of a dance, a Lithuanian dance. Those who prefer to, go on with the two-step, but the majority go through an intricate series of motions, resembling more fancy skating than a dance. The climax of it is a furious *prestissimo*, at which the couples seize hands and begin a mad whirling. This is quite irresistible, and every one

2. Method of payment, especially common for immigrants and women; the worker is paid by unit produced rather than for time worked. Intended to encourage rapid labor, piece-work often results in accidents.
3. "Packing" originally referred to curing, salting, and packing pork in barrels, but by this time it had assumed the broader meaning of slaughtering and preparing animals for food.

in the room joins in, until the place becomes a maze of flying skirts and bodies, quite dazzling to look upon. But the sight of sights at this moment is Tamoszius Kuszleika. The old fiddle squeaks and shrieks in protest, but Tamoszius has no mercy. The sweat starts out on his forehead, and he bends over like a cyclist on the last lap of a race. His body shakes and throbs like a runaway steam-engine, and the ear cannot follow the flying showers of notes—there is a pale blue mist where you look to see his bowing arm. With a most wonderful rush he comes to the end of the tune, and flings up his hands and staggers back exhausted; and with a final shout of delight the dancers fly apart, reeling here and there, bringing up against the walls of the room.

After this there is beer for every one, the musicians included, and the revellers take a long breath and prepare for the great event of the evening, which is the *acziavimas*. The *acziavimas* is a ceremony which, once begun, will continue for three or four hours, and it involves one uninterrupted dance. The guests form a great ring, locking hands, and, when the music starts up, begin to move around in a circle. In the centre stands the bride, and, one by one, the men step into the enclosure and dance with her. Each dances for several minutes—as long as he pleases; it is a very merry proceeding, with laughter and singing, and when the guest has finished, he finds himself face to face with Teta Elzbieta, who holds the hat. Into it he drops a sum of money—a dollar, or perhaps five dollars, according to his power, and his estimate of the value of the privilege. The guests are expected to pay for this entertainment; if they be proper guests, they will see that there is a neat sum left over for the bride and bridegroom to start life upon.

Most fearful they are to contemplate, the expenses of this entertainment. They will certainly be over two hundred dollars, and may be three hundred; and three hundred dollars is more than the year's income of many a person in this room. There are able-bodied men here who work from early morning until late at night, in ice-cold cellars with a quarter of an inch of water on the floor—men who for six or seven months in the year never see the sunlight from Sunday afternoon till the next Sunday morning—and who cannot earn three hundred dollars in a year. There are little children here, scarce in their teens, who can hardly see the top of the work benches—whose parents have lied to get them their places—and who do not make the half of three hundred dollars a year, and perhaps not even the third of it.[4]

---

4. Following an ineffective 1891 Illinois child labor law, an 1893 provision requiring factory inspectors kept children out of factories, although many continued to work elsewhere. Illinois strengthened the law in 1897 and again in 1903, eventually requiring children aged seven to fourteen to attend school 110 days a year. But compulsory school attendance remained poorly enforced, and sixteen was the legal age for working at this time.

And then to spend such a sum, all in a single day of your life, at a wedding-feast! (For obviously it is the same thing, whether you spend it at once for your own wedding, or in a long time, at the weddings of all your friends.)

It is very imprudent, it is tragic—but, ah, it is so beautiful! Bit by bit these poor people have given up everything else; but to this they cling with all the power of their souls—they cannot give up the *veselija*! To do that would mean, not merely to be defeated, but to acknowledge defeat—and the difference between these two things is what keeps the world going. The *veselija* has come down to them from a far-off time; and the meaning of it was that one might dwell within the cave and gaze upon shadows, provided only that once in his lifetime he could break his chains, and feel his wings, and behold the sun; provided that once in his lifetime he might testify to the fact that life, with all its cares and its terrors, is no such great thing after all, but merely a bubble upon the surface of a river, a thing that one may toss about and play with as a juggler tosses his golden balls, a thing that one may quaff, like a goblet of rare red wine. Thus having known himself for the master of things, a man could go back to his toil and live upon the memory all his days.

Endlessly the dancers swung round and round—when they were dizzy they swung the other way. Hour after hour this had continued—the darkness had fallen and the room was dim from the light of two smoky oil lamps. The musicians had spent all their fine frenzy by now, and played only one tune, wearily, ploddingly. There were twenty bars or so of it, and when they came to the end they began again. Once every ten minutes or so they would fail to begin again, but instead would sink back exhausted; a circumstance which invariably brought on a painful and terrifying scene, that made the fat policeman stir uneasily in his sleeping-place behind the door.

It was all Marija Berczynskas. Marija was one of those hungry souls who cling with desperation to the skirts of the retreating muse. All day long she had been in a state of wonderful exaltation; and now it was leaving—and she would not let it go. Her soul cried out in the words of Faust, "Stay, thou art fair!"[5] Whether it was by beer, or by shouting, or by music, or by motion, she meant that it should not go. And she would go back to the chase of it—and no sooner be fairly started than her chariot would be thrown off the track, so to speak, by the stupidity of those thrice-accursed musicians. Each time, Marija would emit a howl and fly at them, shaking her fists in their

5. Exclamation of deep satisfaction. Alludes to *Faust* (1808, 1832), the version of the legendary tale by the German writer Johann Wolfgang von Goethe (1749–1832), in which the scholar Faust wages that the devil, Mephistopheles, cannot make him so satisfied that he would cry out "O Stay! Thou [this moment] art so fair."

faces, stamping upon the floor, purple and incoherent with rage. In vain the frightened Tamoszius would attempt to speak, to plead the limitations of the flesh; in vain would the puffing and breathless *ponas*[6] Jokubas insist, in vain would Teta Elzbieta implore. "*Szalin!*" Marija would scream. "*Palauk! isz kelio!*[7] What are you paid for, children of hell?" And so, in sheer terror, the orchestra would strike up again, and Marija would return to her place and take up her task.

She bore all the burden of the festivities now. Ona was kept up by her excitement, but all of the women and most of the men were tired—the soul of Marija was alone unconquered. She drove on the dancers—what had once been the ring had now the shape of a pear, with Marija at the stem, pulling one way and pushing the other, shouting, stamping, singing, a very volcano of energy. Now and then some one coming in or out would leave the door open, and the night air was chill; Marija as she passed would stretch out her foot and kick the door-knob, and *slam* would go the door! Once this procedure was the cause of a calamity of which Sebastijonas Szedvilas was the hapless victim. Little Sebastijonas, aged three, had been wandering about oblivious to all things, holding turned up over his mouth a bottle of liquid known as "pop," pink-colored, ice-cold, and delicious. Passing through the doorway the door smote him full, and the shriek which followed brought the dancing to a halt. Marija, who threatened horrid murder a hundred times a day, and would weep over the injury of a fly, seized little Sebastijonas in her arms and bid fair to smother him with kisses. There was a long rest for the orchestra, and plenty of refreshments, while Marija was making her peace with her victim, seating him upon the bar, and standing beside him and holding to his lips a foaming schooner of beer.

In the meantime there was going on in another corner of the room an anxious conference between Teta Elzbieta and Dede Antanas, and a few of the more intimate friends of the family. A trouble was come upon them. The *veselija* is a compact, a compact not expressed, but therefore only the more binding upon all. Every one's share was different—and yet every one knew perfectly well what his share was, and strove to give a little more. Now, however, since they had come to the new country, all this was changing; it seemed as if there must be some subtle poison in the air that one breathed here—it was affecting all the young men at once. They would come in crowds and fill themselves with a fine dinner, and then sneak off. One would throw another's hat out of the window, and both would go out to get it, and neither would be seen again. Or now and then half a dozen of them would get together and march out openly, staring at you,

6. Mister.
7. "Get away!"; "Wait! Out of the way!"

and making fun of you to your face. Still others, worse yet, would crowd about the bar, and at the expense of the host drink themselves sodden, paying not the least attention to any one, and leaving it to be thought that either they had danced with the bride already, or meant to later on.

All these things were going on now, and the family was helpless with dismay. So long they had toiled, and such an outlay they had made! Ona stood by, her eyes wide with terror. Those frightful bills—how they had haunted her, each item gnawing at her soul all day and spoiling her rest at night. How often she had named them over one by one and figured on them as she went to work—fifteen dollars for the hall, twenty-two dollars and a quarter for the ducks, twelve dollars for the musicians, five dollars at the church,[8] and a blessing of the Virgin besides—and so on without an end! Worst of all was the frightful bill that was still to come from Graiczunas for the beer and liquor that might be consumed. One could never get in advance more than a guess as to this from a saloon-keeper—and then, when the time came he always came to you scratching his head and saying that he had guessed too low, but that he had done his best—your guests had gotten so very drunk. By him you were sure to be cheated unmercifully, and that even though you thought your-self the dearest of the hundreds of friends he had. He would begin to serve your guests out of a keg that was half full, and finish with one that was half empty, and then you would be charged for two kegs of beer. He would agree to serve a certain quality at a certain price, and when the time came you and your friends would be drinking some horrible poison that could not be described. You might com-plain, but you would get nothing for your pains but a ruined eve-ning; while, as for going to law about it, you might as well go to heaven at once. The saloon-keeper stood in with all the big politics men in the district;[9] and when you had once found out what it meant to get into trouble with such people, you would know enough to pay what you were told to pay and shut up.

What made all this the more painful was that it was so hard on the few that had really done their best. There was poor old *ponas* Jokubas, for instance—he had already given five dollars, and did not every one know that Jokubas Szedvilas had just mortgaged his delicates-sen store for two hundred dollars[1] to meet several months' overdue rent? And then there was withered old *poni*[2] Aniele—who was a

---

8. One dollar in 1904 was worth about $30.51 in 2021 dollars. Adjusted for inflation, the hall cost about $458, the ducks $680, the musicians $366, and the church $153.
9. The stockyards district had over 500 saloons, most financed by wealthy brewers with political connections.
1. About $6,100 in 2021 dollars.
2. Lady.

widow, and had three children, and the rheumatism besides, and did washing for the tradespeople on Halsted Street at prices it would break your heart to hear named. Aniele had given the entire profit of her chickens for several months. Eight of them she owned, and she kept them in a little place fenced around on her backstairs. All day long the children of Aniele were raking in the dump for food for these chickens; and sometimes, when the competition there was too fierce, you might see them on Halsted Street, walking close to the gutters, and with their mother following to see that no one robbed them of their finds.[3] Money could not tell the value of these chickens to old Mrs. Jukniene—she valued them differently, for she had a feeling that she was getting something for nothing by means of them—that with them she was getting the better of a world that was getting the better of her in so many other ways. So she watched them every hour of the day, and had learned to see like an owl at night to watch them then. One of them had been stolen long ago, and not a month passed that some one did not try to steal another. As the frustrating of this one attempt involved a score of false alarms, it will be understood what a tribute old Mrs. Jukniene brought, just because Teta Elzbieta had once loaned her some money for a few days and saved her from being turned out of her house.

More and more friends gathered round while the lamentation about these things was going on. Some drew nearer, hoping to overhear the conversation, who were themselves among the guilty—and surely that was a thing to try the patience of a saint. Finally there came Jurgis, urged by some one, and the story was retold to him. Jurgis listened in silence, with his great black eyebrows knitted. Now and then there would come a gleam underneath them and he would glance about the room. Perhaps he would have liked to go at some of those fellows with his big clenched fists; but then, doubtless, he realized how little good it would do him. No bill would be any less for turning out any one at this time; and then there would be the scandal—and Jurgis wanted nothing except to get away with Ona and to let the world go its own way. So his hands relaxed and he merely said quietly: "It is done, and there is no use in weeping, Teta Elzbieta." Then his look turned toward Ona, who stood close to his side, and he saw the wide look of terror in her eyes. "Little one," he said, in a low voice, "do not worry—it will not matter to us. We will pay them all somehow. I will work harder." That was always what Jurgis said. Ona had grown used to it as the solution of all difficulties—"I will work harder!" He had said that in Lithuania when one official had taken his passport from him, and another had arrested him for being without it, and the two had divided a third of his belongings. He had said it again in New York, when the smooth-spoken

---

3. Children scavenged to supplement their families' meager incomes.

agent had taken them in hand and made them pay such high prices, and almost prevented their leaving his place, in spite of their paying. Now he said it a third time, and Ona drew a deep breath; it was so wonderful to have a husband, just like a grown woman—and a husband who could solve all problems, and who was so big and strong!

The last sob of little Sebastijonas has been stifled, and the orchestra has once more been reminded of its duty. The ceremony begins again—but there are few now left to dance with, and so very soon the collection is over and promiscuous dances once more begin. It is now after midnight, however, and things are not as they were before. The dancers are dull and heavy—most of them have been drinking hard, and have long ago passed the stage of exhilaration. They dance in monotonous measure, round after round, hour after hour, with eyes fixed upon vacancy, as if they were only half conscious, in a constantly growing stupor. The men grasp the women very tightly, but there will be half an hour together when neither will see the other's face. Some couples do not care to dance, and have retired to the corners, where they sit with their arms enlaced. Others, who have been drinking still more, wander about the room, bumping into everything; some are in groups of two or three, singing, each group its own song. As time goes on there is a variety of drunkenness, among the younger men especially. Some stagger about in each other's arms, whispering maudlin words—others start quarrels upon the slightest pretext, and come to blows and have to be pulled apart. Now the fat policeman wakens definitely, and feels of his club to see that it is ready for business. He has to be prompt—for these two-o'clock-in-the-morning fights, if they once get out of hand, are like a forest fire, and may mean the whole reserves at the station. The thing to do is to crack every fighting head that you see, before there are so many fighting heads that you cannot crack any of them. There is but scant account kept of cracked heads in back of the yards, for men who have to crack the heads of animals all day seem to get into the habit, and to practise on their friends, and even on their families, between times. This makes it a cause for congratulation that by modern methods a very few men can do the painfully necessary work of head-cracking for the whole of the cultured world.

There is no fight that night—perhaps because Jurgis, too, is watchful—even more so than the policeman. Jurgis has drunk a great deal, as any one naturally would on an occasion when it all has to be paid for, whether it is drunk or not; but he is a very steady man, and does not easily lose his temper. Only once there is a tight shave—and that is the fault of Marija Berczynskas. Marija has apparently concluded about two hours ago that if the altar in the corner, with the deity in soiled white, be not the true home of the muses, it is, at any rate, the nearest substitute on earth attainable. And Marija is just fighting drunk when there come to her ears the facts about the villains who have not paid that night. Marija goes on the warpath straight off, without even the preliminary of a good cursing, and when she is pulled off it is with the coat collars of two villains in her hands. Fortunately, the policeman is disposed to be reasonable, and so it is not Marija who is flung out of the place.

All this interrupts the music for not more than a minute or two. Then again the merciless tune begins—the tune that has been played for the last half-hour without one single change. It is an American tune this time, one which they have picked up on the streets; all seem to know the words of it—or, at any rate, the first line of it, which they hum to themselves, over and over again without rest: "In the good old summer time—in the good old summer time! In the good old summer time—in the good old summer time!"[4] There seems to be something hypnotic about this, with its endlessly-recurring dominant. It has put a stupor upon every one who hears it, as well as upon the men who are playing it. No one can get away from it, or even think of getting away from it; it is three o'clock in the morning, and they have danced out all their joy, and danced out all their strength, and all the strength that unlimited drink can lend them— and still there is no one among them who has the power to think of stopping. Promptly at seven o'clock this same Monday morning they will every one of them have to be in their places at Durham's or Brown's or Jones's,[5] each in his working clothes. If one of them be a minute late, he will be docked an hour's pay, and if he be many minutes late, he will be apt to find his brass check turned to the wall,[6] which will send him out to join the hungry mob that waits every morning at the gates of the packing-houses, from six o'clock until nearly half-past eight. There is no exception to this rule, not even little Ona—who has asked for a holiday the day after her wedding-day, a holiday without pay, and been refused. While there are so many who are anxious to work as you wish, there is no occasion for incommoding yourself with those who must work otherwise.

Little Ona is nearly ready to faint—and half in a stupor herself, because of the heavy scent in the room. She has not taken a drop, but every one else there is literally burning alcohol, as the lamps are burning oil; some of the men who are sound asleep in their chairs

---

4. Popular 1902 song by George Evans (music) and Ren Shields (lyrics).
5. In the serial version of the novel, Sinclair retained the initials of Chicago's "Big Three" meatpackers, Armour, Swift, and Morris, calling them Anderson, Smith, and Morton. The term "Big Four" includes the packer Hammond, and "Big Five," Cudahy.
6. To find he had lost his job. Sinclair expressed his view of the prostitution of the press by titling a book about journalism *The Brass Check*, in reference to a token purchased at a brothel and exchanged for sexual favors, but here the token is one picked up by a laborer each day of work and tallied by clerks who made the rounds four times a day.

or on the floor are reeking of it so that you cannot go near them. Now and then Jurgis gazes at her hungrily—he has long since forgotten his shyness; but then the crowd is there, and he still waits and watches the door, where a carriage is supposed to come. It does not, and finally he will wait no longer, but comes up to Ona, who turns white and trembles. He puts her shawl about her and then his own coat. They live only two blocks away, and Jurgis does not care about the carriage.

There is almost no farewell—the dancers do not notice them, and all of the children and many of the old folks have fallen asleep of sheer exhaustion. Dede Antanas is asleep, and so are the Szedvilases, husband and wife, the former snoring in octaves. There is Teta Elzbieta, and Marija, sobbing loudly; and then there is only the silent night, with the stars beginning to pale a little in the east. Jurgis, without a word, lifts Ona in his arms, and strides out with her, and she sinks her head upon his shoulder with a moan. When he reaches home he is not sure whether she has fainted or is asleep, but when he has to hold her with one hand while he unlocks the door, he sees that she has opened her eyes.

"You shall not go to Brown's to-day, little one," he whispers, as he climbs the stairs; and she catches his arm in terror, gasping: "No! No! I dare not! It will ruin us!"

But he answers her again: "Leave it to me; leave it to me. I will earn more money—I will work harder."

Chapter II

Jurgis talked lightly about work, because he was young. They told him stories about the breaking down of men, there in the stockyards of Chicago, and of what had happened to them afterwards—stories to make your flesh creep, but Jurgis would only laugh. He had only been there four months, and he was young, and a giant besides. There was too much health in him. He could not even imagine how it would feel to be beaten. "That is well enough for men like you," he would say, "*silpnas*,[1] puny fellows—but my back is broad."

Jurgis was like a boy, a boy from the country. He was the sort of man the bosses like to get hold of, the sort they make it a grievance they cannot get hold of. When he was told to go to a certain place, he would go there on the run. When he had nothing to do for the moment, he would stand round fidgeting, dancing, with the overflow of energy that was in him. If he were working in a line of men, the line always moved too slowly for him, and you could pick him out by his impatience and restlessness. That was why he had been picked out on one important occasion; for Jurgis had stood outside of Brown and Company's "Central Time Station" not more than half an hour,[2] the second day of his arrival in Chicago, before he had been beckoned by one of the bosses. Of this he was very proud, and it made him more disposed than ever to laugh at the pessimists. In vain would they all tell him that there were men in that crowd from which he had been chosen who had stood there a month—yes, many months—and not been chosen yet. "Yes," he would say, "but what sort of men? Broken-down tramps and good-for-nothings, fellows who have spent all their money drinking, and want to get more for it. Do you want me to believe that with these arms"—and he would clench his fists and hold them up in the air, so that you might see the rolling muscles—"that with these arms people will ever let me starve?"

"It is plain," they would answer to this, "that you have come from the country, and from very far in the country." And this was the fact, for Jurgis had never seen a city, and scarcely even a fair-sized town, until he had set out to make his fortune in the world and earn his right to Ona. His father, and his father's father before him, and as many ancestors back as legend could go, had lived in that part of Lithuania known as *Brelovicz*, the Imperial Forest. This is a great tract of a hundred thousand acres, which from time immemorial has been a hunting preserve of the nobility. There are a very few

---

1. Weak.
2. Job seekers applied at the time station, often waiting months for a chance to work.

peasants settled in it, holding title from ancient times; and one of these was Antanas Rudkus, who had been reared himself, and had reared his children in turn, upon half a dozen acres of cleared land in the midst of a wilderness. There had been one son besides Jurgis, and one sister. The former had been drafted into the army; that had been over ten years ago, but since that day nothing had ever been heard of him. The sister was married, and her husband had bought the place when old Antanas had decided to go with his son.

It was nearly a year and a half ago that Jurgis had met Ona, at a horse-fair a hundred miles from home. Jurgis had never expected to get married—he had laughed at it as a foolish trap for a man to walk into; but here, without ever having spoken a word to her, with no more than the exchange of half a dozen smiles, he found himself, purple in the face with embarrassment and terror, asking her parents to sell her to him for his wife—and offering his father's two horses he had been sent to the fair to sell. But Ona's father proved as a rock— the girl was yet a child, and he was a rich man, and his daughter was not to be had in that way. So Jurgis went home with a heavy heart, and that spring and summer toiled and tried hard to forget. In the fall, after the harvest was over, he saw that it would not do, and tramped the full fortnight's journey that lay between him and Ona.

He found an unexpected state of affairs—for the girl's father had died, and his estate was tied up with creditors; Jurgis's heart leaped as he realized that now the prize was within his reach. There was Elzbieta Lukoszaite, Teta, or Aunt, as they called her, Ona's stepmother, and there were her six children, of all ages. There was also her brother Jonas, a dried-up little man who had worked upon the farm. They were people of great consequence, as it seemed to Jurgis, fresh out of the woods; Ona knew how to read, and knew many other things that he did not know; and now the farm had been sold, and the whole family was adrift—all they owned in the world being about seven hundred roubles, which is half as many dollars. They would have had three times that, but it had gone to court, and the judge had decided against them, and it had cost the balance to get him to change his decision.

Ona might have married and left them, but she would not, for she loved Teta Elzbieta. It was Jonas who suggested that they all go to America, where a friend of his had gotten rich. He would work, for his part, and the women would work, and some of the children, doubtless—they would live somehow. Jurgis, too, had heard of America. That was a country where, they said, a man might earn three roubles a day; and Jurgis figured what three roubles a day would mean, with prices as they were where he lived, and decided forthwith that he would go to America and marry, and be a rich man in the bargain. In that country, rich or poor, a man was free, it was said; he did not have to go into the army, he did not have to pay out his money to rascally officials,—he might do as he pleased, and count himself as good as any other man. So America was a place of which lovers and young people dreamed. If one could only manage to get the price of a passage, he could count his troubles at an end.

It was arranged that they should leave the following spring, and meantime Jurgis sold himself to a contractor for a certain time, and tramped nearly four hundred miles from home with a gang of men to work upon a railroad in Smolensk.[3] This was a fearful experience, with filth and bad food and cruelty and overwork; but Jurgis stood it and came out in fine trim, and with eighty roubles sewed up in his coat. He did not drink or fight, because he was thinking all the time of Ona; and for the rest, he was a quiet, steady man, who did what he was told to, did not lose his temper often, and when he did lose it made the offender anxious that he should not lose it again. When they paid him off he dodged the company gamblers and dramshops, and so they tried to kill him;[4] but he escaped, and tramped it home, working at odd jobs, and sleeping always with one eye open.

So in the summer time they had all set out for America. At the last moment there joined them Marija Berczynskas, who was a cousin of Ona's. Marija was an orphan, and had worked since childhood for a rich farmer of Vilna,[5] who beat her regularly. It was only at the age of twenty that it had occurred to Marija to try her strength, when she had risen up and nearly murdered the man, and then come away.

There were twelve in all in the party, five adults and six children— and Ona, who was a little of both. They had a hard time on the passage; there was an agent who helped them, but he proved a scoundrel, and got them into a trap with some officials, and cost them a good deal of their precious money, which they clung to with such horrible fear. This happened to them again in New York—for, of course, they knew nothing about the country, and had no one to tell them, and it was easy for a man in a blue uniform to lead them away, and to take them to a hotel and keep them there, and make them pay enormous charges to get away. The law says that the rate-card shall be on the door of a hotel, but it does not say that it shall be in Lithuanian.

It was in the stockyards that Jonas's friend had gotten rich, and so to Chicago the party was bound. They knew that one word, Chicago,—and that was all they needed to know, at least, until they

---

3. City in western Russia, commercial center and port on the Dneiper River; also the name of a province.
4. Jurgis contracted out his labor for a fixed period, an arrangement that could end with the worker losing his wages either to company gamblers or to spending the earnings on drinking at "dramshops."
5. Russian name for Vilnius, largest city in Lithuania and its capital.

reached the city. Then, tumbled out of the cars without ceremony, they were no better off than before; they stood staring down the vista of Dearborn Street,[6] with its big black buildings towering in the distance, unable to realize that they had arrived, and why, when they said "Chicago," people no longer pointed in some direction, but instead looked perplexed, or laughed, or went on without paying any attention. They were pitiable in their helplessness; above all things they stood in deadly terror of any sort of person in official uniform, and so whenever they saw a policeman they would cross the street and hurry by.[7] For the whole of the first day they wandered about in the midst of deafening confusion, utterly lost; and it was only at night that, cowering in the doorway of a house, they were finally discovered and taken by a policeman to the station. In the morning an interpreter was found, and they were taken and put upon a car, and taught a new word—"stockyards." Their delight at discovering that they were to get out of this adventure without losing another share of their possessions, it would not be possible to describe.

They sat and stared out of the window. They were on a street which seemed to run on forever, mile after mile—thirty-four of them, if they had known it—and each side of it one uninterrupted row of wretched little two-story frame buildings. Down every side street they could see, it was the same,—never a hill and never a hollow, but always the same endless vista of ugly and dirty little wooden buildings. Here and there would be a bridge crossing a filthy creek, with hard-baked mud shores and dingy sheds and docks along it; here and there would be a railroad crossing, with a tangle of switches, and locomotives puffing, and rattling freight-cars filing by; here and there would be a great factory, a dingy building with innumerable windows in it, and immense volumes of smoke pouring from the chimneys, darkening the air above and making filthy the earth beneath. But after each of these interruptions, the desolate procession would begin again—the procession of dreary little buildings.

A full hour before the party reached the city they had begun to note the perplexing changes in the atmosphere. It grew darker all the time, and upon the earth the grass seemed to grow less green. Every minute, as the train sped on, the colors of things became dingier; the fields were grown parched and yellow, the landscape hideous and bare. And along with the thickening smoke they began to notice another circumstance, a strange, pungent odor. They were not sure that it was unpleasant, this odor; some might have called it

---

6. The family has arrived at the Dearborn Station, on the south edge of the Loop (the city's central business district, once encircled by an elevated rail); they are probably staring north toward commercial buildings.
7. The immigrants avoid police not because of any wrongdoing but because of bad experiences with Russian officials in Lithuania.

sickening, but their taste in odors was not developed, and they were only sure that it was curious. Now, sitting in the trolley car, they realized that they were on their way to the home of it—that they had travelled all the way from Lithuania to it. It was now no longer something far-off and faint, that you caught in whiffs; you could literally taste it, as well as smell it—you could take hold of it, almost, and examine it at your leisure. They were divided in their opinions about it. It was an elemental odor, raw and crude; it was rich, almost rancid, sensual, and strong. There were some who drank it in as if it were an intoxicant; there were others who put their handkerchiefs to their faces. The new emigrants were still tasting it, lost in wonder, when suddenly the car came to a halt, and the door was flung open, and a voice shouted—"Stockyards!"

They were left standing upon the corner, staring; down a side street there were two rows of brick houses, and between them a vista: half a dozen chimneys, tall as the tallest of buildings, touching the very sky—and leaping from them half a dozen columns of smoke, thick, oily, and black as night. It might have come from the centre of the world, this smoke, where the fires of the ages still smoulder. It came as if self-impelled, driving all before it, a perpetual explosion. It was inexhaustible; one stared, waiting to see it stop, but still the great streams rolled out. They spread in vast clouds overhead, writhing, curling; then, uniting in one giant river, they streamed away down the sky, stretching a black pall as far as the eye could reach.

Then the party became aware of another strange thing. This, too, like the odor, was a thing elemental; it was a sound, a sound made up of ten thousand little sounds. You scarcely noticed it at first—it sunk into your consciousness, a vague disturbance, a trouble. It was like the murmuring of the bees in the spring, the whisperings of the forest; it suggested endless activity, the rumblings of a world in motion. It was only by an effort that one could realize that it was made by animals, that it was the distant lowing of ten thousand cattle, the distant grunting of ten thousand swine.

They would have liked to follow it up, but, alas, they had no time for adventures just then. The policeman on the corner was beginning to watch them; and so, as usual, they started up the street. Scarcely had they gone a block, however, before Jonas was heard to give a cry, and began pointing excitedly across the street. Before they could gather the meaning of his breathless ejaculations he had bounded away, and they saw him enter a shop, over which was a sign: "J. Szedvilas, Delicatessen." When he came out again it was in company with a very stout gentleman in shirt sleeves and an apron, clasping Jonas by both hands and laughing hilariously. Then Teta Elzbieta recollected suddenly that Szedvilas had been the name of the mythical friend who had made his fortune in America. To find that he had been making it in the delicatessen business was an extraordinary piece of good fortune at this juncture; though it was well on in the morning, they had not breakfasted, and the children were beginning to whimper.

Thus was the happy ending of a woeful voyage. The two families literally fell upon each other's necks—for it had been years since Jokubas Szedvilas had met a man from his part of Lithuania. Before half the day they were lifelong friends. Jokubas understood all the pitfalls of this new world, and could explain all of its mysteries; he could tell them the things they ought to have done in the different emergencies—and what was still more to the point, he could tell them what to do now. He would take them to *poni* Aniele, who kept a boarding-house the other side of the yards; old Mrs. Jukniene, he explained, had not what one would call choice accommodations, but they might do for the moment. To this Teta Elzbieta hastened to respond that nothing could be too cheap to suit them just then; for they were quite terrified over the sums they had had to expend. A very few days of practical experience in this land of high wages had been sufficient to make clear to them the cruel fact that it was also a land of high prices, and that in it the poor man was almost as poor as in any other corner of the earth; and so there vanished in a night all the wonderful dreams of wealth that had been haunting Jurgis. What had made the discovery all the more painful was that they were spending, at American prices, money which they had earned at home rates of wages—and so were really being cheated by the world! The last two days they had all but starved themselves—it made them quite sick to pay the prices that the railroad people asked them for food.

Yet, when they saw the home of the Widow Jukniene they could not but recoil, even so. In all their journey they had seen nothing so bad as this. *Poni* Aniele had a four-room flat in one of that wilderness of two-story frame tenements that lie "back of the yards." There were four such flats in each building, and each of the four was a "boarding-house" for the occupancy of foreigners—Lithuanians, Poles, Slovaks, or Bohemians. Some of these places were kept by private persons, some were cooperative. There would be an average of half a dozen boarders to each room—sometimes there were thirteen or fourteen to one room, fifty or sixty to a flat. Each one of the occupants furnished his own accommodations—that is, a mattress and some bedding. The mattresses would be spread upon the floor in rows—and there would be nothing else in the place except a stove. It was by no means unusual for two men to own the same mattress in common, one working by day and using it by night, and the other working at night and using it in the daytime. Very frequently a lodging-house keeper would rent the same beds to double shifts of men.

Mrs. Jukniene was a wizened-up little woman, with a wrinkled face. Her home was unthinkably filthy; you could not enter by the front door at all, owing to the mattresses, and when you tried to go up the backstairs you found that she had walled up most of the porch with old boards to make a place to keep her chickens. It was a standing jest of the boarders that Aniele cleaned house by letting the chickens loose in the rooms. Undoubtedly this did keep down the vermin, but it seemed probable, in view of all the circumstances, that the old lady regarded it rather as feeding the chickens than as cleaning the rooms. The truth was that she had definitely given up the idea of cleaning anything, under pressure of an attack of rheumatism, which had kept her doubled up in one corner of her room for over a week; during which time eleven of her boarders, heavily in her debt, had concluded to try their chances of employment in Kansas City. This was July, and the fields were green. One never saw the fields, nor any green thing whatever, in Packingtown;[8] but one could go out on the road and "hobo it," as the men phrased it, and see the country, and have a long rest, and an easy time riding on the freight-cars.

Such was the home to which the new arrivals were welcomed. There was nothing better to be had—they might not do so well by looking further, for Mrs. Jukniene had at least kept one room for herself and her three little children, and now offered to share this with the women and the girls of the party. They could get bedding at a second-hand store, she explained; and they would not need any, while the weather was so hot—doubtless they would all sleep on the sidewalk such nights as this, as did nearly all of her guests. "To-morrow," Jurgis said, when they were left alone, "to-morrow I will get a job, and perhaps Jonas will get one also; and then we can get a place of our own."

Later that afternoon he and Ona went out to take a walk and look about them, to see more of this district which was to be their home. In back of the yards the dreary two-story frame houses were scattered farther apart, and there were great spaces bare—that seemingly had been overlooked by the great sore of a city as it spread itself over the surface of the prairie. These bare places were grown up with dingy, yellow weeds, hiding innumerable tomato-cans; innumerable children played upon them, chasing one another here and there, screaming and fighting. The most uncanny thing about this neighborhood was the number of the children; you thought there must be a school just out, and it was only after long acquaintance that you were able to realize that there was no school, but that these were

8. Section of industrialized southwest Chicago where 40,000 meatpacking workers lived with their families. The living quarters comprised about one square mile, surrounded by dumps, stockyards, meatpacking plants, and railroad tracks.

the children of the neighborhood—that there were so many children to the block in Packingtown that nowhere on its streets could a horse and buggy move faster than a walk!

It could not move faster anyhow, on account of the state of the streets. Those through which Jurgis and Ona were walking resembled streets less than they did a miniature topographical map. The road-way was commonly several feet lower than the level of the houses, which were sometimes joined by high board walks; there were no pavements—there were mountains and valleys and rivers, gullies and ditches, and great hollows full of stinking green water. In these pools the children played, and rolled about in the mud of the streets; here and there one noticed them digging in it, after trophies which they had stumbled on. One wondered about this, as also about the swarms of flies which hung about the scene, literally blackening the air, and the strange, fetid odor which assailed one's nostrils, a ghastly odor, of all the dead things of the universe. It impelled the visitor to questions—and then the residents would explain, quietly, that all this was "made" land, and that it had been "made" by using it as a dumping-ground for the city garbage. After a few years the unpleasant effect of this would pass away, it was said; but meantime, in hot weather—and especially when it rained—the flies were apt to be annoying. Was it not unhealthful? the stranger would ask, and the residents would answer, "Perhaps; but there is no telling."

A little way further on, and Jurgis and Ona, staring open-eyed and wondering, came to the place where this "made" ground was in process of making. Here was a great hole, perhaps two city blocks square, and with long files of garbage wagons creeping into it. The place had an odor for which there are no polite words; and it was sprinkled over with children, who raked in it from dawn till dark. Sometimes visitors from the packing-houses would wander out to see this "dump," and they would stand by and debate as to whether the children were eating the food they got, or merely collecting it for the chickens at home. Apparently none of them ever went down to find out.

Beyond this dump there stood a great brick-yard, with smoking chimneys. First they took out the soil to make bricks, and then they filled it up again with garbage, which seemed to Jurgis and Ona a felicitous arrangement, characteristic of an enterprising country like America. A little way beyond was another great hole, which they had emptied and not yet filled up. This held water, and all summer it stood there, with the near-by soil draining into it, festering and stewing in the sun; and then, when winter came, somebody cut the ice on it, and sold it to the people of the city. This, too, seemed to the newcomers an economical arrangement; for they did not read the newspapers, and their heads were not full of trouble-some thoughts about "germs."[9]

They stood there while the sun went down upon this scene, and the sky in the west turned blood-red, and the tops of the houses shone like fire. Jurgis and Ona were not thinking of the sunset, however—their backs were turned to it, and all their thoughts were of Packingtown, which they could see so plainly in the distance. The line of the buildings stood clear-cut and black against the sky; here and there out of the mass rose the great chimneys, with the river of smoke streaming away to the end of the world. It was a study in colors now, this smoke; in the sunset light it was black and brown and gray and purple. All the sordid suggestions of the place were gone—in the twilight it was a vision of power. To the two who stood watching while the darkness swallowed it up, it seemed a dream of wonder, with its tale of human energy, of things being done, of employment for thousands upon thousands of men, of opportunity and freedom, of life and love and joy. When they came away, arm in arm, Jurgis was saying, "To-morrow I shall go there and get a job!"

9. In the third quarter of the 19th century, bacteriologists led by Louis Pasteur (1822–1895) and Joseph Lister (1827–1912) proved the germ theory of disease causation, one of the foundations of modern medicine. Because American physicians had been slow to embrace this discovery, it was still newsworthy in the early 20th century.

Chapter III

In his capacity as delicatessen vender, Jokubas Szedvilas had many acquaintances. Among these was one of the special policemen employed by Durham, whose duty it frequently was to pick out men for employment. Jokubas had never tried it, but he expressed a certainty that he could get some of his friends a job through this man. It was agreed, after consultation, that he should make the effort with old Antanas and with Jonas. Jurgis was confident of his ability to get work for himself, unassisted by any one.

As we have said before, he was not mistaken in this. He had gone to Brown's and stood there not more than half an hour before one of the bosses noticed his form towering above the rest, and signalled to him. The colloquy which followed was brief and to the point:—

"Speak English?"

"No; Lit-uanian." (Jurgis had studied this word carefully.)

"Job?"

"*Je.*" (A nod.)

"Worked here before?"

"No 'stand."

(Signals and gesticulations on the part of the boss. Vigorous shakes of the head by Jurgis.)

"Shovel guts?"

"No 'stand." (More shakes of the head.)

"*Zarnos. Pagaiksztis. Szluota!*"[1] (Imitative motions.)

"Je."

"See door. *Durys?*" (Pointing.)

"Je."

"To-morrow, seven o'clock. Understand? *Rytoj! Prieszpietys! Septyni!*"[2]

"*Dekui, tamistai!*" (Thank you, sir.) And that was all. Jurgis turned away, and then in a sudden rush the full realization of his triumph swept over him, and he gave a yell and a jump, and started off on a run. He had a job! He had a job! And he went all the way home as if upon wings, and burst into the house like a cyclone, to the rage of the numerous lodgers who had just turned in for their daily sleep.

Meantime Jokubas had been to see his friend the policeman, and received encouragement, so it was a happy party. There being no more to be done that day, the shop was left under the care of Lucija, and her husband sallied forth to show his friends the sights of Packingtown.

---

1. "Guts. Rake. Broom!" Unskilled laborers such as Jurgis had little job security and were frequently hired and fired. Skilled laborers with defined jobs fared somewhat better.
2. English instructions repeated in Lithuanian.

Jokubas did this with the air of a country gentleman escorting a party of visitors over his estate; he was an old-time resident, and all these wonders had grown up under his eyes, and he had a personal pride in them. The packers might own the land, but he claimed the landscape, and there was no one to say nay to this.

They passed down the busy street that led to the yards. It was still early morning, and everything was at its high tide of activity. A steady stream of employees was pouring through the gate—employees of the higher sort, at this hour, clerks and stenographers and such. For the women there were waiting big two-horse wagons, which set off at a gallop as fast as they were filled. In the distance there was heard again the lowing of the cattle, a sound as of a far-off ocean calling. They followed it, this time, as eager as children in sight of a circus menagerie—which, indeed, the scene a good deal resembled. They crossed the railroad tracks, and then on each side of the street were the pens full of cattle; they would have stopped to look, but Jokubas hurried them on, to where there was a stairway and a raised gallery, from which everything could be seen. Here they stood, staring, breathless with wonder.

There is over a square mile of space in the yards, and more than half of it is occupied by cattle-pens; north and south as far as the eye can reach there stretches a sea of pens. And they were all filled—so many cattle no one had ever dreamed existed in the world. Red cattle, black, white, and yellow cattle; old cattle and young cattle; great bellowing bulls and little calves not an hour born; meek-eyed milch cows[3] and fierce, long-horned Texas steers. The sound of them here was as of all the barnyards of the universe; and as for counting them— it would have taken all day simply to count the pens. Here and there ran long alleys, blocked at intervals by gates; and Jokubas told them that the number of these gates was twenty-five thousand. Jokubas had recently been reading a newspaper article which was full of statistics such as that, and he was very proud as he repeated them and made his guests cry out with wonder. Jurgis too had a little of this sense of pride. Had he not just gotten a job, and become a sharer in all this activity, a cog in this marvellous machine?

Here and there about the alleys galloped men upon horseback, booted, and carrying long whips; they were very busy, calling to each other, and to those who were driving the cattle. They were drovers and stock-raisers, who had come from far states, and brokers and commission-merchants, and buyers for all the big packing-houses.[4]

3. Milk cows.
4. Middlemen between raisers and buyers, drovers conducted livestock on overland "drives" to centers such as Chicago. Although Sinclair concentrates on packing, the buying and selling of livestock was also big business. In 1884 the Chicago Live Stock

Here and there they would stop to inspect a bunch of cattle, and there would be a parley, brief and businesslike. The buyer would nod or drop his whip, and that would mean a bargain; and he would note it in his little book, along with hundreds of others he had made that morning. Then Jokubas pointed out the place where the cattle were driven to be weighed, upon a great scale that would weigh a hundred thousand pounds at once and record it automatically. It was near to the east entrance that they stood, and all along this east side of the yards ran the railroad tracks, into which the cars were run, loaded with cattle. All night long this had been going on, and now the pens were full; by to-night they would all be empty, and the same thing would be done again.

"And what will become of all these creatures?" cried Teta Elzbieta.

"By to-night," Jokubas answered, "they will all be killed and cut up; and over there on the other side of the packing-houses are more railroad tracks, where the cars come to take them away."

There were two hundred and fifty miles of track within the yards, their guide went on to tell them. They brought about ten thousand head of cattle every day, and as many hogs, and half as many sheep— which meant some eight or ten million live creatures turned into food every year. One stood and watched, and little by little caught the drift of the tide, as it set in the direction of the packing-houses. There were groups of cattle being driven to the chutes, which were roadways about fifteen feet wide, raised high above the pens. In these chutes the stream of animals was continuous; it was quite uncanny to watch them, pressing on to their fate, all unsuspicious—a very river of death.[5] Our friends were not poetical, and the sight suggested to them no metaphors of human destiny; they thought only of the wonderful efficiency of it all. The chutes into which the hogs went climbed high up—to the very top of the distant buildings; and Jokubas explained that the hogs went up by the power of their own legs, and then their weight carried them back through all the processes necessary to make them into pork.[6]

"They don't waste anything here," said the guide, and then he laughed and added a witticism, which he was pleased that his unsophisticated friends should take to be his own: "They use everything about the hog except the squeal."[7] In front of Brown's General

---

Exchange was formed to systematize trading, but buyers for large packing houses tampered with the market by setting prices. As trade became more complex and prices more volatile, commission merchants helped finance large purchases.

5. In Greek mythology, Charon ferried souls of the dead across Styx, one of the five rivers in Hades.

6. Pork-packing factories were built in three or four floors. Pigs were run up to the top for slaughtering, and gravity moved the carcasses down chutes into scalding tubs. Other chutes sent meat into curing and pickling divisions.

7. Generally attributed to Philip D. Armour (1832–1901), who began packing pork in Milwaukee in 1862 and settled in Chicago in 1875. He allegedly told this jest to

Office building there grows a tiny plot of grass, and this, you may learn, is the only bit of green thing in Packingtown; likewise this jest about the hog and his squeal, the stock in trade of all the guides, is the one gleam of humor that you will find there.

After they had seen enough of the pens, the party went up the street, to the mass of buildings which occupy the centre of the yards. These buildings, made of brick and stained with innumerable layers of Packingtown smoke, were painted all over with advertising signs, from which the visitor realized suddenly that he had come to the home of many of the torments of his life. It was here that they made those products with the wonders of which they pestered him so—by placards that defaced the landscape when he travelled, and by staring advertisements in the newspapers and magazines—by silly little jingles that he could not get out of his mind, and gaudy pictures that lurked for him around every street corner. Here was where they made Brown's Imperial Hams and Bacon, Brown's Dressed Beef, Brown's Excelsior Sausages! Here was the headquarters of Durham's Pure Leaf Lard, of Durham's Breakfast Bacon, Durham's Canned Beef, Potted Ham, Devilled Chicken, Peerless Fertilizer!

Entering one of the Durham buildings, they found a number of other visitors waiting; and before long there came a guide, to escort them through the place. They make a great feature of showing strangers through the packing-plants, for it is a good advertisement. But *ponas* Jokubas whispered maliciously that the visitors did not see any more than the packers wanted them to.

They climbed a long series of stairways outside of the building, to the top of its five or six stories. Here were the chute, with its river of hogs, all patiently toiling upward; there was a place for them to rest to cool off, and then through another passageway they went into a room from which there is no returning for hogs.

It was a long, narrow room, with a gallery along it for visitors. At the head there was a great iron wheel, about twenty feet in circumference, with rings here and there along its edge. Upon both sides of this wheel there was a narrow space, into which came the hogs at the end of their journey; in the midst of them stood a great burly negro, bare-armed and bare-chested. He was resting for the moment, for the wheel had stopped while men were cleaning up. In a minute or two, however, it began slowly to revolve, and then the men upon each side of it sprang to work. They had chains which they fastened about the leg of the nearest hog, and the other end of the chain they hooked into one of the rings upon the wheel. So, as the wheel turned, a hog was suddenly jerked off his feet and borne aloft.

---

visitors, often with the punchline "and they are building a machine now to can that for Fourth of July celebrations."

At the same instant the ear was assailed by a most terrifying shriek; the visitors started in alarm, the women turned pale and shrank back. The shriek was followed by another, louder and yet more agonizing—for once started upon that journey, the hog never came back; at the top of the wheel he was shunted off upon a trolley, and went sailing down the room. And meantime another was swung up, and then another, and another, until there was a double line of them, each dangling by a foot and kicking in frenzy—and squealing. The uproar was appalling, perilous to the eardrums; one feared there was too much sound for the room to hold—that the walls must give way or the ceiling crack. There were high squeals and low squeals, grunts, and wails of agony; there would come a momentary lull, and then a fresh outburst, louder than ever, surging up to a deafening climax. It was too much for some of the vistors—the men would look at each other, laughing nervously, and the women would stand with hands clenched, and the blood rushing to their faces, and the tears starting in their eyes.

Meantime, heedless of all these things, the men upon the floor were going about their work. Neither squeals of hogs nor tears of visitors made any difference to them; one by one they hooked up the hogs, and one by one with a swift stroke they slit their throats. There was a long line of hogs, with squeals and life-blood ebbing away together; until at last each started again, and vanished with a splash into a huge vat of boiling water.

It was all so very businesslike that one watched it fascinated. It was pork-making by machinery, pork-making by applied mathematics. And yet somehow the most matter-of-fact person could not help thinking of the hogs; they were so innocent, they came so very trustingly; and they were so very human in their protests—and so perfectly within their rights! They had done nothing to deserve it; and it was adding insult to injury, as the thing was done here, swinging them up in this cold-blooded, impersonal way, without a pretence at apology, without the homage of a tear. Now and then a visitor wept, to be sure; but this slaughtering-machine ran on, visitors or no visitors. It was like some horrible crime committed in a dungeon, all unseen and unheeded, buried out of sight and of memory.

One could not stand and watch very long without becoming philosophical, without beginning to deal in symbols and similes, and to hear the hog-squeal of the universe. Was it permitted to believe that there was nowhere upon the earth, or above the earth, a heaven for hogs, where they were requited for all this suffering? Each one of these hogs was a separate creature. Some were white hogs, some were black; some were brown, some were spotted; some were old, some were young; some were long and lean, some were monstrous. And each of them had an individuality of his own, a will of his own, a hope and a heart's desire; each was full of self-confidence, of self-importance, and a sense of dignity. And trusting and strong in faith he had gone about his business, the while a black shadow hung over him and a horrid Fate waited in his pathway. Now suddenly it had swooped upon him, and had seized him by the leg. Relentless, remorseless, it was; all his protests, his screams, were nothing to it— it did its cruel will with him, as if his wishes, his feelings, had simply no existence at all; it cut his throat and watched him gasp out his life. And now was one to believe that there was nowhere a god of hogs, to whom this hog-personality was precious, to whom these hog-squeals and agonies had a meaning? Who would take this hog into his arms and comfort him, reward him for his work well done, and show him the meaning of his sacrifice? Perhaps some glimpse of all this was in the thoughts of our humble-minded Jurgis, as he turned to go on with the rest of the party, and muttered: "*Dieve*—[8] but I'm glad I'm not a hog!"

The carcass hog was scooped out of the vat by machinery, and then it fell to the second floor, passing on the way through a wonderful machine with numerous scrapers, which adjusted themselves to the size and shape of the animal, and sent it out at the other end with nearly all of its bristles removed. It was then again strung up by machinery, and sent upon another trolley ride; this time passing between two lines of men, who sat upon a raised platform, each doing a certain single thing to the carcass as it came to him. One scraped the outside of a leg; another scraped the inside of the same leg. One with a swift stroke cut the throat; another with two swift strokes severed the head, which fell to the floor and vanished through a hole. Another made a slit down the body; a second opened the body wider; a third with a saw cut the breast-bone; a fourth loosened the entrails; a fifth pulled them out—and they also slid through a hole in the floor. There were men to scrape each side and men to scrape the back; there were men to clean the carcass inside, to trim it and wash it. Looking down this room, one saw, creeping slowly, a line of dangling hogs a hundred yards in length; and for every yard there was a man, working as if a demon were after him. At the end of this hog's progress every inch of the carcass had been gone over several times; and then it was rolled into the chilling-room, where it stayed for twenty-four hours, and where a stranger might lose himself in a forest of freezing hogs.

Before the carcass was admitted here, however, it had to pass a government inspector, who sat in the doorway and felt of the glands in the neck for tuberculosis. This government inspector did not have

---

8. "God." In *The Autobiography of Upton Sinclair* (New York: Harcourt, Brace & World, 1962), the author expresses surprise that so many readers took this passage seriously when he had intended it as "hilarious farce."

the manner of a man who was worked to death; he was apparently
not haunted by a fear that the hog might get by him before he had
finished his testing. If you were a sociable person, he was quite willing to enter into conversation with you, and to explain to you the
deadly nature of the ptomaines[9] which are found in tubercular pork;
and while he was talking with you you could hardly be so ungrateful
as to notice that a dozen carcasses were passing him untouched. This
inspector wore a blue uniform, with brass buttons, and he gave an
atmosphere of authority to the scene, and, as it were, put the stamp of
official approval upon the things which were done in Durham's.

Jurgis went down the line with the rest of the visitors, staring
open-mouthed, lost in wonder. He had dressed hogs himself in the
forest of Lithuania; but he had never expected to live to see one hog
dressed by several hundred men. It was like a wonderful poem to
him, and he took it all in guilelessly—even to the conspicuous signs
demanding immaculate cleanliness of the employees. Jurgis was
vexed when the cynical Jokubas translated these signs with sarcastic comments, offering to take them to the secret-rooms where the
spoiled meats went to be doctored.

The party descended to the next floor, where the various waste
materials were treated. Here came the entrails, to be scraped and
washed clean for sausage-casings; men and women worked here in
the midst of a sickening stench, which caused the visitors to hasten
by, gasping. To another room came all the scraps to be "tanked,"
which meant boiling and pumping off the grease to make soap and
lard; below they took out the refuse, and this, too, was a region in
which the visitors did not linger. In still other places men were
engaged in cutting up the carcasses that had been through the
chilling-rooms. First there were the "splitters," the most expert workmen in the plant, who earned as high as fifty cents an hour, and did
not a thing all day except chop hogs down the middle. Then there
were "cleaver men," great giants with muscles of iron; each had two
men to attend him—to slide the half carcass in front of him on the
table, and hold it while he chopped it, and then turn each piece so
that he might chop it once more. His cleaver had a blade about two
feet long, and he never made but one cut; he made it so neatly, too,
that his implement did not smite through and dull itself—there was
just enough force for a perfect cut, and no more. So through various yawning holes there slipped to the floor below—to one room
hams, to another fore-quarters, to another sides of pork. One might

---

9. Term coined in the 1870s for nitrogen compounds resulting from putrefaction of food and
   believed to cause sickness. Tuberculosis is an infectious disease usually centering in the
   lungs and transferred by breathing exhalations from an infected party. Poor ventilation in
   factories contributed to the disease, often deadly for humans as well. Tuberculosis was
   one of the biggest killers in urban areas, and Packingtown had among the highest rates.

go down to this floor and see the pickling-rooms, where the hams were put into vats, and the great smoke-rooms, with their air-tight iron doors. In other rooms they prepared salt-pork—there were whole cellars full of it, built up in great towers to the ceiling. In yet other rooms they were putting up meat in boxes and barrels, and wrapping hams and bacon in oiled paper, sealing and labelling and sewing them. From the doors of these rooms went men with loaded trucks, to the platform where freight-cars were waiting to be filled; and one went out there and realized with a start that he had come at last to the ground floor of this enormous building.

Then the party went across the street to where they did the killing of beef—where every hour they turned four or five hundred cattle into meat. Unlike the place they had left, all this work was done on one floor; and instead of there being one line of carcasses which moved to the workmen, there were fifteen or twenty lines, and the men moved from one to another of these. This made a scene of intense activity, a picture of human power wonderful to watch. It was all in one great room, like a circus amphitheatre, with a gallery for visitors running over the centre.

Along one side of the room ran a narrow gallery, a few feet from the floor; into which gallery the cattle were driven by men with goads which gave them electric shocks. Once crowded in here, the creatures were prisoned, each in a separate pen, by gates that shut, leaving them no room to turn around; and while they stood bellowing and plunging, over the top of the pen there leaned one of the "knockers,"[1] armed with a sledge-hammer, and watching for a chance to deal a blow. The room echoed with the thuds in quick succession, and the stamping and kicking of the steers. The instant the animal had fallen, the "knocker" passed on to another; while a second man raised a lever, and the side of the pen was raised, and the animal, still kicking and struggling, slid out to the "killing-bed." Here a man put shackles about one leg, and pressed another lever, and the body was jerked up into the air. There were fifteen or twenty such pens, and it was a matter of only a couple of minutes to knock fifteen or twenty cattle and roll them out. Then once more the gates were opened, and another lot rushed in; and so out of each pen there rolled a steady stream of carcasses, which the men upon the killing-beds had to get out of the way.

The manner in which they did this was something to be seen and never forgotten. They worked with furious intensity, literally upon the run—at a pace with which there is nothing to be compared except a football game. It was all highly specialized labor, each man

1. Part of a killing team, knockers stood above the cattle on a boardwalk and stunned them with a heavy sledge. Another worker slit the animals' throats.

having his task to do; generally this would consist of only two or three specific cuts, and he would pass down the line of fifteen or twenty carcasses, making these cuts upon each. First there came the "butcher," to bleed them; this meant one swift stroke, so swift that you could not see it—only the flash of the knife; and before you could realize it, the man had darted on to the next line, and a stream of bright red was pouring out upon the floor. This floor was half an inch deep with blood, in spite of the best efforts of men who kept shovelling it through holes; it must have made the floor slippery, but no one could have guessed this by watching the men at work.

The carcass hung for a few minutes to bleed; there was no time lost, however, for there were several hanging in each line, and one was always ready. It was let down to the ground, and there came the "headsman," whose task it was to sever the head, with two or three swift strokes. Then came the "floorsman," to make the first cut in the skin; and then another to finish ripping the skin down the centre; and then half a dozen more in swift succession, to finish the skinning. After they were through, the carcass was again swung up; and while a man with a stick examined the skin, to make sure that it had not been cut, and another rolled it up and tumbled it through one of the inevitable holes in the floor, the beef proceeded on its journey. There were men to cut it, and men to split it, and men to gut it and scrape it clean inside. There were some with hose which threw jets of boiling water upon it, and others who removed the feet and added the final touches. In the end, as with the hogs, the finished beef was run into the chilling-room, to hang its appointed time.

The visitors were taken there and shown them, all neatly hung in rows, labelled conspicuously with the tags of the government inspectors—and some, which had been killed by a special process, marked with the sign of the "kosher" rabbi, certifying that it was fit for sale to the orthodox.[2] And then the visitors were taken to the other parts of the building, to see what became of each particle of the waste material that had vanished through the floor; and to the pickling-rooms, and the salting-rooms, the canning-rooms, and the packing-rooms, where choice meat was prepared for shipping in refrigerator-cars, destined to be eaten in all the four corners of civilization. Afterward they went outside, wandering about among the mazes of buildings in which was done the work auxiliary to this great industry. There was scarcely a thing needed in the business that Durham and Company did not make for themselves. There was a great steam-power plant and an electricity plant. There was a barrel

---

2. A rabbi ensures that meat intended for consumption by Orthodox Jews is kosher (Yiddish, meaning proper, fit for use). In conformance with dietary laws of the Hebrew Bible (see especially Leviticus 17:10–14), special methods are followed for killing animals as well as for inspection, hanging and repeated washing, and blessing of meats.

factory, and a boiler-repair shop. There was a building to which the grease was piped, and made into soap and lard; and then there was a factory for making lard cans, and another for making soap boxes. There was a building in which the bristles were cleaned and dried, for the making of hair cushions and such things; there was a building where the skins were dried and tanned, there was another where heads and feet were made into glue, and another where bones were made into fertilizer. No tiniest particle of organic matter was wasted in Durham's. Out of the horns of the cattle they made combs, buttons, hair-pins, and imitation ivory; out of the shin bones and other big bones they cut knife and tooth-brush handles, and mouthpieces for pipes; out of the hoofs they cut hair-pins and buttons, before they made the rest into glue. From such things as feet, knuckles, hide clippings, and sinews came such strange and unlikely products as gelatin, isinglass, and phosphorus, bone-black, shoe-blacking, and bone-oil. They had curled-hair works for the cattle tails, and a "wool-pullery" for the sheep skins; they made pepsin from the stomachs of the pigs, and albumen from the blood, and violin strings from the ill-smelling entrails. When there was nothing else to be done with a thing, they first put it into a tank and got out of it all the tallow and grease, and then they made it into fertilizer.[3] All these industries were gathered into buildings near by, connected by galleries and railroads with the main establishment; and it was estimated that they had handled nearly a quarter of a billion of animals since the founding of the plant by the elder Durham a generation and more ago.[4] If you counted with it the other big plants—and they were now really all one—it was, so Jokubas informed them, the greatest aggregation of labor and capital ever gathered in one place. It employed thirty thousand men; it supported directly two hundred and fifty thousand people in its neighborhood, and indirectly it supported half a million. It sent its products to every country in the civilized world, and it furnished the food for no less than thirty million people!

3. Because 60 percent of livestock is inedible, meatpacking produced colossal wastes until by-products industries such as these became highly lucrative. *Gelatin:* technically an edible glue, made from fibers of connective tissue formed into jelly and then dried; *isinglass:* a form of gelatin; *phosphorus:* an organic product used in match heads and fertilizer; *bone-black:* fine charcoal made from animal bones, used as coloring in products including *shoe-blacking; bone-oil:* a beef fat made from bone marrow and feet, often used in tankage (foodstuffs and fertilizer), glue, and gelatin; *curled hair:* usually clipped from cow tails, used for stuffing upholstery; *wool-pullery:* area of factory where wool was separated from sheep skins; *pepsin:* one of the earliest pharmaceuticals manufactured by the packing industry, made from the glandular part of hog stomachs, mixed with water and hydrochloric acid, filtered, purified, and dried; after *blood* was separated into serum and fibrous substance, the clarified serum was sold as *albumen,* and the remainder was made into *fertilizer.*
4. Based on Philip D. Armour (see above, p. 34, n. 7), who in 1867 formed Armour & Co. with his brothers.

To all of these things our friends would listen open-mouthed—it seemed to them impossible of belief that anything so stupendous could have been devised by mortal man. That was why to Jurgis it seemed almost profanity to speak about the place as did Jokubas, sceptically; it was a thing as tremendous as the universe—the laws and ways of its working no more than the universe to be questioned or understood. All that a mere man could do, it seemed to Jurgis, was to take a thing like this as he found it, and do as he was told; to be given a place in it and a share in its wonderful activities was a blessing to be grateful for, as one was grateful for the sunshine and the rain. Jurgis was even glad that he had not seen the place before meeting with his triumph, for he felt that the size of it would have overwhelmed him. But now he had been admitted—he was a part of it all! He had the feeling that this whole huge establishment had taken him under its protection, and had become responsible for his welfare. So guileless was he, and ignorant of the nature of business, that he did not even realize that he had become an employee of Brown's, and that Brown and Durham were supposed by all the world to be deadly rivals—were even required to be deadly rivals by the law of the land, and ordered to try to ruin each other under penalty of fine and imprisonment![5]

5. "Ruin each other" by competition. A 1903 court injunction had dissolved packers' collusive pools as a restraint of trade.

Chapter IV

Promptly at seven the next morning Jurgis reported for work. He came to the door that had been pointed out to him, and there he waited for nearly two hours. The boss had meant for him to enter, but had not said this, and so it was only when on his way out to hire another man that he came upon Jurgis. He gave him a good cursing, but as Jurgis did not understand a word of it he did not object. He followed the boss, who showed him where to put his street clothes, and waited while he donned the working clothes he had bought in a second-hand shop and brought with him in a bundle; then he led him to the "killing-beds." The work which Jurgis was to do here was very simple, and it took him but a few minutes to learn it. He was provided with a stiff besom,[1] such as is used by street sweepers, and it was his place to follow down the line the man who drew out the smoking entrails from the carcass of the steer; this mass was to be swept into a trap, which was then closed, so that no one might slip into it. As Jurgis came in, the first cattle of the morning were just making their appearance; and so, with scarcely time to look about him, and none to speak to any one, he fell to work. It was a sweltering day in July, and the place ran with steaming hot blood—one waded in it on the floor. The stench was almost overpowering, but to Jurgis it was nothing. His whole soul was dancing with joy—he was at work at last! He was at work and earning money! All day long he was figuring to himself. He was paid the fabulous sum of seventeen and a half cents an hour; and as it proved a rush day and he worked until nearly seven o'clock in the evening, he went home to the family with the tidings that he had earned more than a dollar and a half in a single day!

At home, also, there was more good news; so much of it at once that there was quite a celebration in Aniele's hall bedroom. Jonas had been to have an interview with the special policeman to whom Szedvilas had introduced him, and had been taken to see several of the bosses, with the result that one had promised him a job the beginning of the next week. And then there was Marija Berczynskas, who, fired with jealousy by the success of Jurgis, had set out upon her own responsibility to get a place. Marija had nothing to take with her save her two brawny arms and the word "job," laboriously learned; but with these she had marched about Packingtown all day, entering every door where there were signs of activity. Out of some she had been ordered with curses; but Marija was not afraid of man or devil, and asked every one she saw—visitors and strangers, or work-people

---

1. Broom, likely made of twig.

like herself, and once or twice even high and lofty office personages, who stared at her as if they thought she was crazy. In the end, however, she had reaped her reward. In one of the smaller plants she had stumbled upon a room where scores of women and girls were sitting at long tables preparing smoked beef in cans; and wandering through room after room, Marija came at last to the place where the sealed cans were being painted and labelled, and here she had the good fortune to encounter the "forelady." Marija did not understand then, as she was destined to understand later, what there was attractive to a "forelady" about the combination of a face full of boundless good nature and the muscles of a dray horse; but the woman had told her to come the next day and she would perhaps give her a chance to learn the trade of painting cans. The painting of cans being skilled piece work, and paying as much as two dollars a day, Marija burst in upon the family with the yell of a Comanche Indian,[2] and fell to capering about the room so as to frighten the baby almost into convulsions.

Better luck than all this could hardly have been hoped for; there was only one of them left to seek a place. Jurgis was determined that Teta Elzbieta should stay at home to keep house, and that Ona should help her. He would not have Ona working—he was not that sort of a man, he said, and she was not that sort of a woman. It would be a strange thing if a man like him could not support the family, with the help of the board of Jonas and Marija. He would not even hear of letting the children go to work—there were schools here in America for children, Jurgis had heard, to which they could go for nothing. That the priest would object to these schools[3] was something of which he had as yet no idea, and for the present his mind was made up that the children of Teta Elzbieta should have as fair a chance as any other children. The oldest of them, little Stanislovas, was but thirteen, and small for his age at that; and while the oldest son of Szedvilas was only twelve, and had worked for over a year at Jones's, Jurgis would have it that Stanislovas should learn to speak English, and grow up to be a skilled man.

So there was only old Dede Antanas; Jurgis would have had him rest too, but he was forced to acknowledge that this was not possible, and, besides, the old man would not hear it spoken of—it was his whim to insist that he was as lively as any boy. He had come to America as full of hope as the best of them; and now he was the chief problem that worried his son. For every one that Jurgis spoke to assured him that it was a waste of time to seek employment for the old man in

2. American Indian tribe (now nation), dominant in the northern Great Plains during the 18th and 19th centuries. They adopted horses and were skilled warriors, taking as captives members of weaker tribes as well as Europeans and Mexicans.
3. Because they were not Catholic. Packingtown had both public and parochial schools, the latter charging tuition. Lithuanian parishes maintained schools of their own, providing instruction in the native language.

Packingtown. Szedvilas told him that the packers did not even keep the men who had grown old in their own service—to say nothing of taking on new ones. And not only was it the rule here, it was the rule everywhere in America, so far as he knew. To satisfy Jurgis he had asked the policeman, and brought back the message that the thing was not to be thought of. They had not told this to old Anthony, who had consequently spent the two days wandering about from one part of the yards to another, and had now come home to hear about the triumph of the others, smiling bravely and saying that it would be his turn another day.

Their good luck, they felt, had given them the right to think about a home; and sitting out on the doorstep that summer evening, they held consultation about it, and Jurgis took occasion to broach a weighty subject. Passing down the avenue to work that morning he had seen two boys leaving an advertisement from house to house; and seeing that there were pictures upon it, Jurgis had asked for one, and had rolled it up and tucked it into his shirt. At noontime a man with whom he had been talking had read it to him and told him a little about it, with the result that Jurgis had conceived a wild idea.

He brought out the placard, which was quite a work of art. It was nearly two feet long, printed on calendered paper, with a selection of colors so bright that they shone even in the moonlight. The centre of the placard was occupied by a house, brilliantly painted, new, and dazzling. The roof of it was of a purple hue, and trimmed with gold; the house itself was silvery, and the doors and windows red. It was a two-story building, with a porch in front, and a very fancy scrollwork around the edges; it was complete in every tiniest detail, even the door-knob, and there was a hammock on the porch and white lace curtains in the windows. Underneath this, in one corner, was a picture of a husband and wife in loving embrace; in the opposite corner was a cradle, with fluffy curtains drawn over it, and a smiling cherub hovering upon silver-colored wings. For fear that the significance of all this should be lost, there was a label, in Polish, Lithuanian, and German—"*Dom. Namai. Heim.*"[4] "Why pay rent?" the linguistic circular went on to demand. "Why not own your own home? Do you know that you can buy one for less than your rent? We have built thousands of homes which are now occupied by happy families."—So it became eloquent, picturing the blissfulness of married life in a house with nothing to pay. It even quoted "Home, Sweet Home," and made bold to translate it into Polish—though for some reason it omitted the Lithuanian of this. Perhaps the translator found it a difficult matter to be sentimental in a language in which a sob is known as a "*gukcziojimas*" and a smile as a "*nusiszypsojimas.*"

4. "Home."

Over this document the family pored long, while Ona spelled out its contents. It appeared that this house contained four rooms, besides a basement, and that it might be bought for fifteen hundred dollars, the lot and all. Of this, only three hundred dollars had to be paid down, the balance being paid at the rate of twelve dollars a month. These were frightful sums, but then they were in America, where people talked about such without fear. They had learned that they would have to pay a rent of nine dollars a month for a flat, and there was no way of doing better, unless the family of twelve was to exist in one or two rooms, as at present. If they paid rent, of course, they might pay forever, and be no better off; whereas, if they could only meet the extra expense in the beginning, there would at last come a time when they would not have any rent to pay for the rest of their lives.

They figured it up. There was a little left of the money belonging to Teta Elzbieta, and there was a little left to Jurgis. Marija had about fifty dollars pinned up somewhere in her stockings, and Grandfather Anthony had part of the money he had gotten for his farm. If they all combined, they would have enough to make the first payment; and if they had employment, so that they could be sure of the future, it might really prove the best plan. It was, of course, not a thing even to be talked of lightly; it was a thing they would have to sift to the bottom. And yet, on the other hand, if they were going to make the venture, the sooner they did it the better; for were they not paying rent all the time, and living in a most horrible way besides? Jurgis was used to dirt—there was nothing could scare a man who had been with a railroad-gang,[5] where one could gather up the fleas off the floor of the sleeping-room by the handful. But that sort of thing would not do for Ona. They must have a better place of some sort very soon—Jurgis said it with all the assurance of a man who had just made a dollar and fifty-seven cents in a single day. Jurgis was at a loss to understand why, with wages as they were, so many of the people of this district should live the way they did.

The next day Marija went to see her "forelady," and was told to report the first of the week, and learn the business of can-painter. Marija went home, singing out loud all the way, and was just in time to join Ona and her stepmother as they were setting out to go and make inquiry concerning the house. That evening the three made their report to the men—the thing was altogether as represented in the circular, or at any rate so the agent had said. The houses lay to the south, about a mile and a half from the yards; they were wonderful

---

5. Lacking connotations of criminal activity, "gang" denotes a group of laborers, especially strong and unskilled. Unskilled workers are also called common laborers, not in a pejorative sense but to distinguish them from workers with a particular skill.

bargains, the gentleman had assured them—personally, and for their own good. He could do this, so he explained to them, for the reason that he had himself no interest in their sale—he was merely the agent for a company that had built them. These were the last, and the company was going out of business, so if any one wished to take advantage of this wonderful no-rent plan, he would have to be very quick. As a matter of fact there was just a little uncertainty as to whether there was a single house left; for the agent had taken so many people to see them, and for all he knew the company might have parted with the last. Seeing Teta Elzbieta's evident grief at this news, he added, after some hesitation, that if they really intended to make a purchase, he would send a telephone message at his own expense, and have one of the houses kept. So it had finally been arranged—and they were to go and make an inspection the following Sunday morning.

That was Thursday; and all the rest of the week the killing-gang at Brown's worked at full pressure, and Jurgis cleared a dollar seventy-five every day. That was at the rate of ten and one-half dollars a week, or forty-five a month; Jurgis was not able to figure, except it was a very simple sum, but Ona was like lightning at such things, and she worked out the problem for the family. Marija and Jonas were each to pay sixteen dollars a month board, and the old man insisted that he could do the same as soon as he got a place—which might be any day now. That would make ninety-three dollars. Then Marija and Jonas were between them to take a third share in the house, which would leave only eight dollars a month for Jurgis to contribute to the payment. So they would have eighty-five dollars a month,—or, supposing that Dede Antanas did not get work at once, seventy dollars a month—which ought surely to be sufficient for the support of a family of twelve.

An hour before the time on Sunday morning the entire party set out. They had the address written on a piece of paper, which they showed to some one now and then. It proved to be a long mile and a half, but they walked it, and half an hour or so later the agent put in an appearance. He was a smooth and florid personage, elegantly dressed, and he spoke their language freely, which gave him a great advantage in dealing with them. He escorted them to the house, which was one of a long row of the typical frame dwellings of the neighborhood, where architecture is a luxury that is dispensed with. Ona's heart sank, for the house was not as it was shown in the picture; the color-scheme was different, for one thing, and then it did not seem quite so big. Still, it was freshly painted, and made a considerable show. It was all brand-new, so the agent told them, but he talked so incessantly that they were quite confused, and did not have time to ask many questions. There were all sorts of things they had made up their minds to inquire about, but when the time came, they either forgot them or lacked the courage. The other houses in the row did not seem to be new, and few of them seemed to be occupied. When they ventured to hint at this, the agent's reply was that the purchasers would be moving in shortly. To press the matter would have seemed to be doubting his word, and never in their lives had any one of them ever spoken to a person of the class called "gentleman" except with deference and humility.

The house had a basement, about two feet below the street line, and a single story, about six feet above it, reached by a flight of steps. In addition there was an attic, made by the peak of the roof, and having one small window in each end. The street in front of the house was unpaved and unlighted, and the view from it consisted of a few exactly similar houses, scattered here and there upon lots grown up with dingy brown weeds. The house inside contained four rooms, plastered white; the basement was but a frame, the walls being unplastered and the floor not laid. The agent explained that the houses were built that way, as the purchasers generally preferred to finish the basements to suit their own taste. The attic was also unfinished—the family had been figuring that in case of an emergency they could rent this attic, but they found that there was not even a floor, nothing but joists, and beneath them the lath and plaster of the ceiling below. All of this, however, did not chill their ardor as much as might have been expected, because of the volubility of the agent. There was no end to the advantages of the house, as he set them forth, and he was not silent for an instant; he showed them everything, down to the locks on the doors and the catches on the windows, and how to work them. He showed them the sink in the kitchen, with running water and a faucet, something which Teta Elzbieta had never in her wildest dreams hoped to possess. After a discovery such as that it would have seemed ungrateful to find any fault, and so they tried to shut their eyes to other defects.

Still, they were peasant people, and they hung on to their money by instinct; it was quite in vain that the agent hinted at promptness— they would see, they would see, they told him, they could not decide until they had had more time. And so they went home again, and all day and evening there was figuring and debating. It was an agony to them to have to make up their minds in a matter such as this. They never could agree all together; there were so many arguments upon each side, and one would be obstinate, and no sooner would the rest have convinced him than it would transpire that his arguments had caused another to waver. Once, in the evening, when they were all in harmony, and the house was as good as bought, Szedvilas came in and upset them again. Szedvilas had no use for property-owning. He told them cruel stories of people who had been done to death in this "buying a home" swindle. They would be almost sure to get into a tight place and lose all their money; and there was no end of expense that one could never foresee; and the house might be good-for-nothing from top to bottom—how was a poor man to know? Then, too, they would swindle you with the contract—and how was a poor man to understand anything about a contract? It was all nothing but robbery, and there was no safety but in keeping out of it. And pay rent? asked Jurgis. Ah, yes, to be sure, the other answered, that too was robbery. It was all robbery, for a poor man. After half an hour of such depressing conversation, they had their minds quite made up that they had been saved at the brink of a precipice; but then Szedvilas went away, and Jonas, who was a sharp little man, reminded them that the delicatessen business was a failure, according to its proprietor, and that this might account for his pessimistic views. Which, of course, reopened the subject!

The controlling factor was that they could not stay where they were—they had to go somewhere. And when they gave up the house plan and decided to rent, the prospect of paying out nine dollars a month forever they found just as hard to face. All day and all night for nearly a whole week they wrestled with the problem, and then in the end Jurgis took the responsibility. Brother Jonas had gotten his job, and was pushing a truck in Durham's; and the killing-gang at Brown's continued to work early and late, so that Jurgis grew more confident every hour, more certain of his mastership. It was the kind of thing the man of the family had to decide and carry through, he told himself. Others might have failed at it, but he was not the failing kind—he would show them how to do it. He would work all day, and all night, too, if need be; he would never rest until the house was paid for and his people had a home. So he told them, and so in the end the decision was made.

They had talked about looking at more houses before they made the purchase; but then they did not know where any more were, and they did not know any way of finding out. The one they had seen held the sway in their thoughts; whenever they thought of themselves in a house, it was this house that they thought of. And so they went and told the agent that they were ready to make the agreement. They knew, as an abstract proposition, that in matters of business all men are to be accounted liars; but they could not but have been influenced by all they had heard from the eloquent agent, and were quite persuaded that the house was something they had run a risk of losing by their delay. They drew a deep breath when he told them that they were still in time.

They were to come on the morrow, and he would have the papers all drawn up. This matter of papers was one in which Jurgis understood to the full the need of caution; yet he could not go himself—every one told him that he could not get a holiday, and that he might lose his job by asking. So there was nothing to be done but to trust it to the women, with Szedvilas, who promised to go with them. Jurgis spent a whole evening impressing upon them the seriousness of the occasion—and then finally, out of innumerable hiding-places about their persons and in their baggage, came forth the precious wads of money, to be done up tightly in a little bag and sewed fast in the lining of Teta Elzbieta's dress.

Early in the morning they sallied forth. Jurgis had given them so many instructions and warned them against so many perils, that the women were quite pale with fright, and even the imperturbable delicatessen vender, who prided himself upon being a business man, was ill at ease. The agent had the deed all ready, and invited them to sit down and read it; this Szedvilas proceeded to do—a painful and laborious process, during which the agent drummed upon the desk. Teta Elzbieta was so embarrassed that the perspiration came out upon her forehead in beads; for was not this reading as much as to say plainly to the gentleman's face that they doubted his honesty? Yet Jokubas Szedvilas read on and on; and presently there developed that he had good reason for doing so. For a horrible suspicion had begun dawning in his mind; he knitted his brows more and more as he read. This was not a deed of sale at all, so far as he could see—it provided only for the renting of the property! It was hard to tell, with all this strange legal jargon, words he had never heard before; but was not this plain—"the party of the first part hereby covenants and agrees to *rent* to the said party of the second part!" And then again—"a monthly *rental* of twelve dollars, for a period of eight years and four months!" Then Szedvilas took off his spectacles, and looked at the agent, and stammered a question.

The agent was most polite, and explained that that was the usual formula; that it was always arranged that the property should be merely rented. He kept trying to show them something in the next paragraph; but Szedvilas could not get by the word "rental"—and when he translated it to Teta Elzbieta, she too was thrown into a fright. They would not own the home at all, then, for nearly nine years! The agent, with infinite patience, began to explain again; but no explanation would do now. Elzbieta had firmly fixed in her mind the last solemn warning of Jurgis: "If there is anything wrong, do not give him the money, but go out and get a lawyer." It was an agonizing moment, but she sat in the chair, her hands clenched like death, and made a fearful effort, summoning all her powers, and gasped out her purpose.

Jokubas translated her words. She expected the agent to fly into a passion, but he was, to her bewilderment, as ever imperturbable; he even offered to go and get a lawyer for her, but she declined this. They went a long way, on purpose to find a man who would not be a confederate. Then let any one imagine their dismay, when, after half an hour, they came in with a lawyer, and heard him greet the agent by his first name!

They felt that all was lost; they sat like prisoners summoned to hear the reading of their death-warrant. There was nothing more that they could do—they were trapped! The lawyer read over the deed, and when he had read it he informed Szedvilas that it was all perfectly regular, that the deed was a blank deed such as was often used in these sales. And was the price as agreed? the old man asked—three hundred dollars down, and the balance at twelve dollars a month, till the total of fifteen hundred dollars had been paid? Yes, that was correct. And it was for the sale of such and such a house—the house and lot and everything? Yes,—and the lawyer showed him where that was all written. And it was all perfectly regular—there were no tricks about it of any sort? They were poor people, and this was all they had in the world, and if there was anything wrong they would be ruined. And so Szedvilas went on, asking one trembling question after another, while the eyes of the women folks were fixed upon him in mute agony. They could not understand what he was saying, but they knew that upon it their fate depended. And when at last he had questioned until there was no more questioning to be done, and the time came for them to make up their minds, and either close the bargain or reject it, it was all that poor Teta Elzbieta could do to keep from bursting into tears. Jokubas had asked her if she wished to sign; he had asked her twice—and what could she say? How did she know if this lawyer were telling the truth—that he was not in the conspiracy? And yet, how could she say so—what excuse could she give? The eyes of every one in the room were upon her, awaiting her decision; and at last, half blind with her tears, she began fumbling in her jacket, where she had pinned the precious money. And she brought it out and unwrapped it before the men. All of this Ona sat watching, from a corner of the room, twisting her hands together, meantime, in a fever of fright. Ona longed to cry out and tell her stepmother to stop, that it was all a trap; but there seemed to be something clutching her by the throat, and she could not make a sound. And so Teta Elzbieta laid the money on the table, and the agent picked it up and counted it, and then wrote them a receipt for it and passed them the deed. Then he gave a sigh of satisfaction, and rose and shook hands with them all, still as smooth and polite as at the beginning. Ona had a dim recollection of the lawyer telling Szedvilas that his charge was a dollar, which occasioned some debate, and more agony; and then, after they had paid that, too, they went out into the street, her stepmother clutching the deed in her hand. They were so weak from fright that they could not walk, but had to sit down on the way.

So they went home, with a deadly terror gnawing at their souls; and that evening Jurgis came home and heard their story, and that was the end. Jurgis was sure that they had been swindled, and were ruined; and he tore his hair and cursed like a madman, swearing that he would kill the agent that very night. In the end he seized the paper and rushed out of the house, and all the way across the yards to Halsted Street. He dragged Szedvilas out from his supper, and together they rushed to consult another lawyer. When they entered his office the lawyer sprang up, for Jurgis looked like a crazy person, with flying hair and bloodshot eyes. His companion explained the situation, and the lawyer took the paper and began to read it, while Jurgis stood clutching the desk with knotted hands, trembling in every nerve.

Once or twice the lawyer looked up and asked a question of Szedvilas; the other did not know a word that he was saying, but his eyes were fixed upon the lawyer's face, striving in an agony of dread to read his mind. He saw the lawyer look up and laugh, and he gave a gasp; the man said something to Szedvilas, and Jurgis turned upon his friend, his heart almost stopping.

"Well?" he panted.

"He says it is all right," said Szedvilas.

"All right!"

"Yes, he says it is just as it should be." And Jurgis, in his relief, sank down into a chair.

"Are you sure of it?" he gasped, and made Szedvilas translate question after question. He could not hear it often enough; he could not ask with enough variations. Yes, they had bought the house, they had really bought it. It belonged to them, they had only to pay the money and it would be all right. Then Jurgis covered his face with his hands, for there were tears in his eyes, and he felt like a fool. But he had had such a horrible fright; strong man as he was, it left him almost too weak to stand up.

The lawyer explained that the rental was a form—the property was said to be merely rented until the last payment had been made, the purpose being to make it easier to turn the party out if he did not make the payments. So long as they paid, however, they had nothing to fear, the house was all theirs.

Jurgis was so grateful that he paid the half dollar the lawyer asked without winking an eyelash, and then rushed home to tell the news to the family. He found Ona in a faint and the babies screaming, and the whole house in an uproar—for it had been believed by all that he had gone to murder the agent. It was hours before the excitement could be calmed; and all through that cruel night Jurgis would wake up now and then and hear Ona and her stepmother in the next room, sobbing softly to themselves.

Chapter V

They had bought their home. It was hard for them to realize that the wonderful house was theirs to move into whenever they chose. They spent all their time thinking about it, and what they were going to put into it. As their week with Aniele was up in three days, they lost no time in getting ready. They had to make some shift to furnish it, and every instant of their leisure was given to discussing this.

A person who had such a task before him would not need to look very far in Packingtown—he had only to walk up the avenue and read the signs, or get into a street-car, to obtain full information as to pretty much everything a human creature could need. It was quite touching, the zeal of people to see that his health and happiness were provided for. Did the person wish to smoke? There was a little discourse about cigars, showing him exactly why the Thomas Jefferson Five-cent Perfecto was the only cigar worthy of the name. Had he, on the other hand, smoked too much? Here was a remedy for the smoking habit, twenty-five doses for a quarter, and a cure absolutely guaranteed in ten doses. In innumerable ways such as this, the traveller found that somebody had been busied to make smooth his paths through the world, and to let him know what had been done for him. In Packingtown the advertisements had a style all of their own, adapted to the peculiar population. One would be tenderly solicitous. "Is your wife pale?" it would inquire. "Is she discouraged, does she drag herself about the house and find fault with everything? Why do you not tell her to try Dr. Lanahan's Life Preservers?" Another would be jocular in tone, slapping you on the back, so to speak. "Don't be a chump!" it would exclaim. "Go and get the Goliath Bunion Cure." "Get a move on you!" would chime in another. "It's easy, if you wear the Eureka Two-fifty Shoe."

Among these importunate signs was one that had caught the attention of the family by its pictures. It showed two very pretty little birds building themselves a home; and Marija had asked an acquaintance to read it to her, and told them that it related to the furnishing of a house. "Feather your nest," it ran—and went on to say that it could furnish all the necessary feathers for a four-room nest for the ludicrously small sum of seventy-five dollars. The particularly important thing about this offer was that only a small part of the money need be had at once—the rest one might pay a few dollars every month.[1] Our friends had to have some furniture, there was no getting away from that; but their little fund of money had sunk so

---

1. Installment purchases, often carrying exorbitant interest charges, were common before modern forms of credit became available.

low that they could hardly get to sleep at night, and so they fled to this as their deliverance. There was more agony and another paper for Elzbieta to sign, and then one night when Jurgis came home, he was told the breathless tidings that the furniture had arrived and was safely stowed in the house: a parlor set of four pieces, a bed-room set of three pieces, a dining-room table and four chairs, a toilet-set with beautiful pink roses painted all over it, an assortment of crockery, also with pink roses—and so on. One of the plates in the set had been found broken when they unpacked it, and Ona was going to the store the first thing in the morning to make them change it; also they had promised three sauce-pans, and there had only two come, and did Jurgis think that they were trying to cheat them?

The next day they went to the house; and when the men came from work they ate a few hurried mouthfuls at Aniele's, and then set to work at the task of carrying their belongings to their new home. The distance was in reality over two miles, but Jurgis made two trips that night, each time with a huge pile of mattresses and bedding on his head, with bundles of clothing and bags and things tied up inside. Anywhere else in Chicago he would have stood a good chance of being arrested; but the policemen in Packingtown were apparently used to these informal movings, and contented themselves with a cursory examination now and then. It was quite wonderful to see how fine the house looked, with all the things in it, even by the dim light of a lamp: it was really home, and almost as exciting as the plac-ard had described it. Ona was fairly dancing, and she and Cousin Marija took Jurgis by the arm and escorted him from room to room, sitting in each chair by turns, and then insisting that he should do the same. One chair squeaked with his great weight, and they screamed with fright, and woke the baby and brought everybody running. Alto-gether it was a great day; and tired as they were, Jurgis and Ona sat up late, contented simply to hold each other and gaze in rapture about the room. They were going to be married as soon as they could get everything settled, and a little spare money put by; and this was to be their home—that little room yonder would be theirs!

It was in truth a never-ending delight, the fixing up of this house. They had no money to spend for the pleasure of spending, but there were a few absolutely necessary things, and the buying of these was a perpetual adventure for Ona. It must always be done at night, so that Jurgis could go along; and even if it were only a pepper-cruet,[2] or half a dozen glasses for ten cents, that was enough for an expedi-tion. On Saturday night they came home with a great basketful of things, and spread them out on the table, while every one stood round, and the children climbed up on the chairs, or howled to be

2. A glass-bottle pepper shaker.

lifted up to see. There were sugar and salt and tea and crackers, and a can of lard and a milk-pail, and a scrubbing-brush, and a pair of shoes for the second oldest boy, and a can of oil, and a tack-hammer, and a pound of nails. These last were to be driven into the walls of the kitchen and the bedrooms, to hang things on; and there was a family discussion as to the place where each one was to be driven. Then Jurgis would try to hammer, and hit his fingers because the hammer was too small, and get mad because Ona had refused to let him pay fifteen cents more and get a bigger hammer; and Ona would be invited to try it herself, and hurt her thumb, and cry out, which necessitated the thumb's being kissed by Jurgis. Finally, after every one had had a try, the nails would be driven, and something hung up. Jurgis had come home with a big packing-box on his head, and he sent Jonas to get another that he had bought. He meant to take one side out of these to-morrow, and put shelves in them, and make them into bureaus and places to keep things for the bedrooms. The nest which had been advertised had not included feathers for quite so many birds as there were in this family.

They had, of course, put their dining-table in the kitchen, and the dining-room was used as the bedroom of Teta Elzbieta and five of her children. She and the two youngest slept in the only bed, and the other three had a mattress on the floor. Ona and her cousin dragged a mattress into the parlor and slept at night, and the three men and the oldest boy slept in the other room, having nothing but the very level floor to rest on for the present. Even so, however, they slept soundly—it was necessary for Teta Elzbieta to pound more than once on the door at a quarter past five every morning. She would have ready a great pot full of steaming black coffee, and oatmeal and bread and smoked sausages; and then she would fix them their dinner pails with more thick slices of bread with lard between them—they could not afford butter—and some onions and a piece of cheese, and so they would tramp away to work.

This was the first time in his life that he had ever really worked, it seemed to Jurgis; it was the first time that he had ever had anything to do which took all he had in him. Jurgis had stood with the rest up in the gallery and watched the men on the killing-beds, marvelling at their speed and power as if they had been wonderful machines; it somehow never occurred to one to think of the flesh-and-blood side of it—that is, not until he actually got down into the pit and took off his coat. Then he saw things in a different light, he got at the inside of them. The pace they set here, it was one that called for every faculty of a man—from the instant the first steer fell till the sounding of the noon whistle, and again from half-past twelve till heaven only knew what hour in the late afternoon or evening, there was never one instant's rest for a man, for his hand or his eye or his brain.

Jurgis saw how they managed it; there were portions of the work which determined the pace of the rest, and for these they had picked men whom they paid high wages, and whom they changed frequently. You might easily pick out these pace-makers,[3] for they worked under the eye of the bosses, and they worked like men possessed. This was called "speeding up the gang," and if any man could not keep up with the pace, there were hundreds outside begging to try.

Yet Jurgis did not mind it; he rather enjoyed it. It saved him the necessity of flinging his arms about and fidgeting as he did in most work. He would laugh to himself as he ran down the line, darting a glance now and then at the man ahead of him. It was not the pleasantest work one could think of, but it was necessary work; and what more had a man the right to ask than a chance to do something useful, and to get good pay for doing it?

So Jurgis thought, and so he spoke, in his bold, free way; very much to his surprise, he found that it had a tendency to get him into trouble. For most of the men here took a fearfully different view of the thing. He was quite dismayed when he first began to find it out—that most of the men *hated* their work. It seemed strange, it was even terrible, when you came to find out the universality of the sentiment; but it was certainly the fact—they hated their work. They hated the bosses and they hated the owners; they hated the whole place, the whole neighborhood—even the whole city, with an all-inclusive hatred, bitter and fierce. Women and little children would fall to cursing about it; it was rotten, rotten as hell—everything was rotten. When Jurgis would ask them what they meant, they would begin to get suspicious, and content themselves with saying, "Never mind, you stay here and see for yourself."

One of the first problems that Jurgis ran upon was that of the unions. He had had no experience with unions, and he had to have it explained to him that the men were banded together for the purpose of fighting for their rights. Jurgis asked them what they meant by their rights, a question in which he was quite sincere, for he had not any idea of any rights that he had, except the right to hunt for a job, and do as he was told when he got it. Generally, however, this harmless question would only make his fellow-workingmen lose their tempers and call him a fool. There was a delegate of the butcher-helpers' union who came to see Jurgis to enroll him; and when Jurgis found that this meant that he would have to part with some of his money, he froze up directly, and the delegate, who was an Irishman and only knew a few words of Lithuanian, lost his temper and began to threaten him.[4] In the end Jurgis got into a fine rage, and made it sufficiently plain that

3. Fast workers, also called "pacesetters," were used to speed production.
4. Sinclair places Jurgis in the midst of a union organizing drive.

it would take more than one Irishman to scare him into a union. Little by little he gathered that the main thing the men wanted was to put a stop to the habit of "speeding-up"; they were trying their best to force a lessening of the pace, for there were some, they said, who could not keep up with it, whom it was killing. But Jurgis had no sympathy with such ideas as this—he could do the work himself, and so could the rest of them, he declared, if they were good for anything. If they couldn't do it, let them go somewhere else. Jurgis had not studied the books, and he would not have known how to pronounce "laissez-faire";[5] but he had been round the world enough to know that a man has to shift for himself in it, and that if he gets the worst of it, there is nobody to listen to him holler.

Yet there have been known to be philosophers and plain men who swore by Malthus in the books, and would, nevertheless, subscribe to a relief fund in time of a famine. It was the same with Jurgis, who consigned the unfit to destruction,[6] while going about all day sick at heart because of his poor old father, who was wandering somewhere in the yards begging for a chance to earn his bread. Old Antanas had been a worker ever since he was a child; he had run away from home when he was twelve, because his father beat him for trying to learn to read.[7] And he was a faithful man, too; he was a man you might leave alone for a month, if only you had made him understand what you wanted him to do in the meantime. And now here he was, worn out in soul and body, and with no more place in the world than a sick dog. He had his home, as it happened, and some one who would care for him if he never got a job; but his son could not help thinking, suppose this had not been the case. Antanas Rudkus had been into every building in Packingtown by this time, and into nearly every room; he had stood mornings among the crowd of applicants till the very policemen had come to know his face and to tell him to go home and give it up. He had been likewise

---

5. Literally, "let it be" (French); doctrine that the market operates best without government regulation or intervention.
6. Thomas *Malthus* (1766–1834), English political economist, theorized that population inevitably increases more quickly than food supply. The theories of natural selection, formulated by the English naturalist Charles Darwin (1809–1882), were influenced by Malthusian ideas of population. Jurgis's belief that *consigned the unfit to destruction*, however, suggests more the social Darwinism of the English philosopher Herbert Spencer (1820–1903) than it does Darwinian science. The notion of survival of the fittest—very popular in Sinclair's time—is commonly misattributed to Darwin, but in fact comes from Spencer, who extended Darwin's biological theories to human society. Advocates of *laissez-faire* often express social Darwinist beliefs, such as that one person's financial success demonstrates fitness, while another person's poverty demonstrates unfitness. Humane intervention such as a *relief fund* to assist the poor—or recognition of structural inequities in capitalism, such as socialism provides—are alternatives to the winner-take-all premise of social Darwinism.
7. To preempt more serious punishment. From 1865 to 1904, occupying Russians forbade Lithuanian publications, deporting to the remote lands of Siberia anyone caught reading contraband material.

to all the stores and saloons for a mile about, begging for some little thing to do; and everywhere they had ordered him out, sometimes with curses, and not once even stopping to ask him a question.

So, after all, there was a crack in the fine structure of Jurgis's faith in things as they are. The crack was wide while Dede Antanas was hunting a job—and it was yet wider when he finally got it. For one evening the old man came home in a great state of excitement, with the tale that he had been approached by a man in one of the corridors of the pickle-rooms of Durham's, and asked what he would pay to get a job. He had not known what to make of this at first; but the man had gone on with matter-of-fact frankness to say that he could get him a job, provided that he were willing to pay one-third of his wages for it. Was he a boss?[8] Antanas had asked; to which the man had replied that that was nobody's business, but that he could do what he said.

Jurgis had made some friends by this time, and he sought one of them and asked what this meant. The friend, who was named Tamoszius Kuszleika, was a sharp little man who folded hides on the killing-beds, and he listened to what Jurgis had to say without seeming at all surprised. They were common enough, he said, such cases of petty graft. It was simply some boss who proposed to add a little to his income. After Jurgis had been there awhile he would know that the plants were simply honeycombed with rottenness of that sort— the bosses grafted off the men, and they grafted off each other; and some day the superintendent would find out about the boss, and then he would graft off the boss. Warming to the subject, Tamoszius went on to explain the situation. Here was Durham's, for instance, owned by a man who was trying to make as much money out of it as he could, and did not care in the least how he did it; and underneath him, ranged in ranks and grades like an army, were managers and superintendents and foremen, each one driving the man next below him and trying to squeeze out of him as much work as possible. And all the men of the same rank were pitted against each other; the accounts of each were kept separately, and every man lived in terror of losing his job, if another made a better record than he. So from top to bottom the place was simply a seething cauldron of jealousies and hatreds; there was no loyalty or decency anywhere about it, there was no place in it where a man counted for anything against a dollar. And worse than there being no decency, there was not even any honesty. The reason for that? Who could say? It must have been old Durham in the beginning; it was a heritage which the self-made merchant had left to his son,[9] along with his millions.

8. Foremen ("bosses") received money from job seekers for the opportunity to work.
9. J. Ogden Armour (1863–1927) assumed control of the company after his father's death in 1901.

Jurgis would find out these things for himself, if he stayed there long enough; it was the men who had to do all the dirty jobs, and so there was no deceiving them; and they caught the spirit of the place, and did like all the rest. Jurgis had come there, and thought he was going to make himself useful, and rise and become a skilled man; but he would soon find out his error—for nobody rose in Packingtown by doing good work. You could lay that down for a rule—if you met a man who was rising in Packingtown, you met a knave. That man who had been sent to Jurgis's father by the boss, *he* would rise; the man who told tales and spied upon his fellows would rise; but the man who minded his own business and did his work—why, they would "speed him up" till they had worn him out, and then they would throw him into the gutter.

Jurgis went home with his head buzzing. Yet he could not bring himself to believe such things—no, it could not be so. Tamoszius was simply another of the grumblers. He was a man who spent all his time fiddling; and he would go to parties at night and not get home till sunrise, and so of course he did not feel like work. Then, too, he was a puny little chap; and so he had been left behind in the race, and that was why he was sore. And yet so many strange things kept coming to Jurgis's notice every day!

He tried to persuade his father to have nothing to do with the offer. But old Antanas had begged until he was worn out, and all his courage was gone; he wanted a job, any sort of a job. So the next day he went and found the man who had spoken to him, and promised to bring him a third of all he earned; and that same day he was put to work in Durham's cellars. It was a "pickle-room," where there was never a dry spot to stand upon, and so he had to take nearly the whole of his first week's earnings to buy him a pair of heavy-soled boots. He was a "squeedgie" man; his job was to go about all day with a long-handled mop, swabbing up the floor. Except that it was damp and dark, it was not an unpleasant job, in summer.

Now Antanas Rudkus was the meekest man that God ever put on earth; and so Jurgis found it a striking confirmation of what the men all said, that his father had been at work only two days before he came home as bitter as any of them, and cursing Durham's with all the power of his soul. For they had set him to cleaning out the traps; and the family sat round and listened in wonder while he told them what that meant. It seemed that he was working in the room where the men prepared the beef for canning, and the beef had lain in vats full of chemicals, and men with great forks speared it out and dumped it into trucks, to be taken to the cooking-room. When they had speared out all they could reach, they emptied the vat on the floor, and then with shovels scraped up the balance and dumped it into the truck. This floor was filthy, yet they set Antanas with his mop slopping the "pickle" into a hole that connected with a sink, where it was caught and used over again forever; and if that were not enough, there was a trap in the pipe, where all the scraps of meat and odds and ends of refuse were caught, and every few days it was the old man's task to clean these out, and shovel their contents into one of the trucks with the rest of the meat!

This was the experience of Antanas; and then there came also Jonas and Marija with tales to tell. Marija was working for one of the independent packers, and was quite beside herself and outrageous with triumph over the sums of money she was making as a painter of cans. But one day she walked home with a pale-faced little woman who worked opposite to her, Jadvyga Marcinkus by name, and Jadvyga told her how she, Marija, had chanced to get her job. She had taken the place of an Irish woman who had been working in that factory ever since any one could remember, for over fifteen years, so she declared. Mary Dennis was her name, and a long time ago she had been seduced, and had a little boy; he was a cripple, and an epileptic, but still he was all that she had in the world to love, and they had lived in a little room alone somewhere back of Halsted Street, where the Irish were.[1] Mary had had consumption,[2] and all day long you might hear her coughing as she worked; of late she had been going all to pieces, and when Marija came, the "forelady" had suddenly decided to turn her off. The forelady had to come up to a certain standard herself, and could not stop for sick people, Jadvyga explained. The fact that Mary had been there so long had not made any difference to her—it was doubtful if she even knew that, for both the forelady and the superintendent were new people, having only been there two or three years themselves. Jadvyga did not know what had become of the poor creature; she would have gone to see her, but had been sick herself. She had pains in her back all the time, Jadvyga explained, and feared that she had womb trouble. It was not fit work for a woman, handling fourteen-pound cans all day.[3]

It was a striking circumstance that Jonas, too, had gotten his job by the misfortune of some other person. Jonas pushed a truck loaded with hams from the smoke-rooms on to an elevator, and thence to the packing-rooms. The trucks were all of iron, and heavy, and they put about threescore hams on each of them, a load of more than a quarter of a ton. On the uneven floor it was a task for a man to start one of these trucks, unless he was a giant; and when it was once started he

1. An Irish neighborhood known as Bridgeport began east of Halsted.
2. Tuberculosis, called consumption before the discovery of tubercle bacillus because bodily tissues wasted away as if consumed.
3. Many women's health problems were lumped under the catchall term "womb trouble," for the uterus was believed to determine women's physical and mental health. In his *Autobiography*, Sinclair describes his first wife's taking a nostrum for "womb trouble." Doctors believed menstrual and uterine dysfunctions were caused by overwork, particularly routine labor such as demanded in a factory.

naturally tried his best to keep it going. There was always the boss prowling about, and if there was a second's delay he would fall to cursing; Lithuanians and Slovaks and such, who could not understand what was said to them, the bosses were wont to kick about the place like so many dogs. Therefore these trucks went for the most part on the run; and the predecessor of Jonas had been jammed against the wall by one and crushed in a horrible and nameless manner.

All of these were sinister incidents; but they were trifles compared to what Jurgis saw with his own eyes before long. One curious thing he had noticed, the very first day, in his profession of shoveller of guts; which was the sharp trick of the floor-bosses whenever there chanced to come a "slunk" calf. Any man who knows anything about butchering knows that the flesh of a cow that is about to calve, or has just calved, is not fit for food. A good many of these came every day to the packing-houses—and, of course, if they had chosen, it would have been an easy matter for the packers to keep them till they were fit for food. But for the saving of time and fodder, it was the law that cows of that sort came along with the others, and whoever noticed it would tell the boss, and the boss would start up a conversation with the government inspector, and the two would stroll away. So in a trice the carcass of the cow would be cleaned out, and the entrails would have vanished; it was Jurgis's task to slide them into the trap, calves and all, and on the floor below they took out these "slunk" calves, and butchered them for meat, and used even the skins of them.

One day a man slipped and hurt his leg; and that afternoon, when the last of the cattle had been disposed of, and the men were leaving, Jurgis was ordered to remain and do some special work which this injured man had usually done. It was late, almost dark, and the government inspectors had all gone, and there were only a dozen or two of men on the floor. That day they had killed about four thousand cattle, and these cattle had come in freight trains from far states, and some of them had got hurt. There were some with broken legs, and some with gored sides; there were some that had died, from what cause no one could say; and they were all to be disposed of, here in darkness and silence. "Downers," the men called them; and the packing-house had a special elevator upon which they were raised to the killing-beds, where the gang proceeded to handle them, with an air of businesslike nonchalance which said plainer than any words that it was a matter of everyday routine. It took a couple of hours to get them out of the way, and in the end Jurgis saw them go into the chilling-rooms with the rest of the meat, being carefully scattered here and there so that they could not be identified. When he came home that night he was in a very sombre mood, having begun to see at last how those might be right who had laughed at him for his faith in America.

Chapter VI

Jurgis and Ona were very much in love; they had waited a long time—it was now well into the second year, and Jurgis judged everything by the criterion of its helping or hindering their union. All his thoughts were there; he accepted the family because it was a part of Ona, and he was interested in the house because it was to be Ona's home. Even the tricks and cruelties he saw at Durham's had little meaning for him just then, save as they might happen to affect his future with Ona.

The marriage would have been at once, if they had had their way; but this would mean that they would have to do without any wedding-feast, and when they suggested this they came into conflict with the old people. To Teta Elzbieta especially the very suggestion was an affliction. What! she would cry. To be married on the roadside like a parcel of beggars! No! No!—Elzbieta had some traditions behind her; she had been a person of importance in her girlhood—had lived on a big estate and had servants, and might have married well and been a lady, but for the fact that there had been nine daughters and no sons in the family. Even so, however, she knew what was decent, and clung to her traditions with desperation. They were not going to lose all caste,[1] even if they had come to be unskilled laborers in Packingtown; and that Ona had even talked of omitting a *veselija* was enough to keep her stepmother lying awake all night. It was in vain for them to say that they had so few friends; they were bound to have friends in time, and then the friends would talk about it. They must not give up what was right for a little money—if they did, the money would never do them any good, they could depend upon that. And Elzbieta would call upon Dede Antanas to support her; there was a fear in the souls of these two, lest this journey to a new country might somehow undermine the old home virtues of their children. The very first Sunday they had all been taken to mass; and poor as they were, Elzbieta had felt it advisable to invest a little of her resources in a representation of the babe of Bethlehem, made in plaster, and painted in brilliant colors. Though it was only a foot high, there was a shrine with four snow-white steeples, and the Virgin standing with her child in her arms, and the kings and shepherds and wise men bowing down before him. It had cost fifty cents; but Elzbieta had a feeling that money spent for such things was not to be counted too closely, it would come back in hidden ways. The piece was beautiful on the parlor mantel, and one could not have a home without some sort of ornament.

---

1. Social standing.

The cost of the wedding-feast would, of course be returned to them; but the problem was to raise it even temporarily. They had been in the neighborhood so short a time that they could not get much credit, and there was no one except Szedvilas from whom they could borrow even a little. Evening after evening Jurgis and Ona would sit and figure the expenses, calculating the term of their separation. They could not possibly manage it decently for less than two hundred dollars, and even though they were welcome to count in the whole of the earnings of Marija and Jonas, as a loan, they could not hope to raise this sum in less than four or five months. So Ona began thinking of seeking employment herself, saying that if she had even ordinarily good luck, she might be able to take two months off the time. They were just beginning to adjust themselves to this necessity, when out of the clear sky there fell a thunderbolt upon them—a calamity that scattered all their hopes to the four winds.

About a block away from them there lived another Lithuanian family, consisting of an elderly widow and one grown son; their name was Majauszkis, and our friends struck up an acquaintance with them before long. One evening they came over for a visit, and naturally the first subject upon which the conversation turned was the neighborhood and its history; and then Grandmother Majauszkiene, as the old lady was called, proceeded to recite to them a string of horrors that fairly froze their blood. She was a wrinkled-up and wizened personage—she must have been eighty—and as she mumbled the grim story through her toothless gums, she seemed a very old witch to them. Grandmother Majauszkiene had lived in the midst of misfortune so long that it had come to be her element, and she talked about starvation, sickness, and death as other people might about weddings and holidays.

The thing came gradually. In the first place as to the house they had bought, it was not new at all, as they had supposed; it was about fifteen years old, and there was nothing new upon it but the paint, which was so bad that it needed to be put on new every year or two. The house was one of a whole row that was built by a company which existed to make money by swindling poor people. The family had paid fifteen hundred dollars for it, and it had not cost the builders five hundred, when it was new—Grandmother Majauszkiene knew that because her son belonged to a political organization with a contractor who put up exactly such houses. They used the very flimsiest and cheapest material; they built the houses a dozen at a time, and they cared about nothing at all except the outside shine. The family could take her word as to the trouble they would have, for she had been through it all—she and her son had bought their house in exactly the same way. They had fooled the company, however, for her son was a skilled man, who made as high as a hundred dollars a month, and as he had had sense enough not to marry, they had been able to pay for the house.

Grandmother Majauszkiene saw that her friends were puzzled at this remark; they did not quite see how paying for the house was "fooling the company." Evidently they were very inexperienced. Cheap as the houses were, they were sold with the idea that the people who bought them would not be able to pay for them. When they failed— if it were only by a single month—they would lose the house and all that they had paid on it, and then the company would sell it over again. And did they often get a chance to do that? *Dieve!* (Grandmother Majauszkiene raised her hands.) They did it—how often no one could say, but certainly more than half of the time. They might ask any one who knew anything at all about Packingtown as to that; she had been living here ever since this house was built, and she could tell them all about it. And had it ever been sold before? *Susimilkie!*[2] Why, since it had been built, no less than four families that their informant could name had tried to buy it and failed. She would tell them a little about it.

The first family had been Germans. The families had all been of different nationalities—there had been a representative of several races[3] that had displaced each other in the stockyards. Grandmother Majauszkiene had come to America with her son at a time when so far as she knew there was only one other Lithuanian family in the district; the workers had all been Germans then—skilled cattle-butchers that the packers had brought from abroad to start the business. Afterward, as cheaper labor had come, these Germans had moved away. The next were the Irish—there had been six or eight years when Packingtown had been a regular Irish city. There were a few colonies of them still here, enough to run all the unions and the police force and get all the graft; but the most of those who were working in the packing-houses had gone away at the next drop in wages—after the big strike. The Bohemians[4] had come then, and after them the Poles. People said that old man Durham himself was responsible for these immigrations; he had sworn that he would fix the people of Packingtown so that they would never again call a strike on him, and so he had sent his agents into every city and village in Europe to spread the tale of the chances of work and high wages at the stockyards. The people had come in hordes; and old Durham had squeezed them tighter and tighter, speeding them up

2. Heaven have mercy!
3. As seen by assimilated white Americans, most of whom considered more recent immigrants, including Caucasians, "racially" different from themselves.
4. Immigrants from Bohemia, a duchy of Great Moravia that became Czechoslovakia after World War I. In 1990, the name was changed to the Czech Republic.

and grinding them to pieces, and sending for new ones. The Poles, who had come by tens of thousands, had been driven to the wall by the Lithuanians, and now the Lithuanians were giving way to the Slovaks.[5] Who there was poorer and more miserable than the Slovaks, Grandmother Majauszkiene had no idea, but the packers would find them, never fear. It was easy to bring them, for wages were really much higher, and it was only when it was too late that the poor people found out that everything else was higher too. They were like rats in a trap, that was the truth; and more of them were piling in every day. By and by they would have their revenge, though, for the thing was getting beyond human endurance, and the people would rise and murder the packers. Grandmother Majauszkiene was a socialist, or some such strange thing; another son of hers was working in the mines of Siberia, and the old lady herself had made speeches in her time—which made her seem all the more terrible[6] to her present auditors.

They called her back to the story of the house. The German family had been a good sort. To be sure there had been a great many of them, which was a common failing in Packingtown; but they had worked hard, and the father had been a steady man, and they had a good deal more than half paid for the house. But he had been killed in an elevator accident in Durham's.

Then there had come the Irish, and there had been lots of them, too; the husband drank and beat the children—the neighbors could hear them shrieking any night. They were behind with their rent all the time, but the company was good to them; there was some politics back of that, Grandmother Majauszkiene could not say just what, but the Laffertys had belonged to the "War Whoop League,"[7] which was a sort of political club of all the thugs and rowdies in the district; and if you belonged to that, you could never be arrested for anything. Once upon a time old Lafferty had been caught with a gang that had stolen cows from several of the poor people of the neighborhood and butchered them in an old shanty back of the yards and sold them. He had been in jail only three days for it, and had come out laughing, and had not even lost his place in the packing-house. He

---

5. Immigration to Packingtown had proceeded in waves from different areas, Lithuanians and Slovaks being the most recent arrivals. As newer arrivals accepted less pay, the stream of immigrants kept packers' labor costs down.

6. Inspiring terror; a *socialist* advocates collective rather than private ownership, particularly of the means of production, and believes that socialism offers an equitable and humane alternative to capitalism. When Sinclair first learned about socialism, he called it a "wonderful discovery . . . for it gave me the key to all my problems" ("What Life Means to Me," 1906; reprinted below, pp. 478–83). The broad term, however, encompasses many variations; in a 1924 *Dictionary of Socialism* (London: T. F. Unwin), A. S. Rappoport enumerated forty different definitions.

7. Democratic political machine.

had gone all to ruin with the drink, however, and lost his power; one of his sons, who was a good man, had kept him and the family up for a year or two, but then he had got sick with consumption.

That was another thing, Grandmother Majauzskiene interrupted herself—this house was unlucky. Every family that lived in it, some one was sure to get consumption. Nobody could tell why that was; there must be something about a house, or the way it was built—some folks said it was because the building had been begun in the dark of the moon. There were dozens of houses that way in Packingtown. Sometimes there would be a particular room that you could point out—if anybody slept in that room he was just as good as dead. With this house it had been the Irish first; and then a Bohemian family had lost a child of it—though, to be sure, that was uncertain, since it was hard to tell what was the matter with children who worked in the yards. In those days there had been no law about the age of children—the packers had worked all but the babies. At this remark the family looked puzzled, and Grandmother Majauszkiene again had to make an explanation—that it was against the law for children to work before they were sixteen. What was the sense of that? they asked. They had been thinking of letting little Stanislovas go to work. Well, there was no need to worry, Grandmother Majauszkiene said—the law made no difference except that it forced people to lie about the ages of their children. One would like to know what the lawmakers expected them to do; there were families that had no possible means of support except the children, and the law provided them no other way of getting a living. Very often a man could get no work in Packingtown for months, while a child could go and get a place easily; there was always some new machine, by which the packers could get as much work out of a child as they had been able to get out of a man, and for a third of the pay.

To come back to the house again, it was the woman of the next family that had died. That was after they had been there nearly four years, and this woman had had twins regularly every year—and there had been more than you could count when they moved in. After she died the man would go to work all day and leave them to shift for themselves—the neighbors would help them now and then, for they would almost freeze to death. At the end there were three days that they were alone, before it was found out that the father was dead. He was a "floorsman" at Jones's, and a wounded steer had broken loose and mashed him against a pillar. Then the children had been taken away, and the company had sold the house that very same week to a party of emigrants.

So this grim old woman went on with her tale of horrors. How much of it was exaggeration—who could tell? It was only too plausible. There was that about consumption, for instance. They knew nothing about consumption whatever, except that it made people cough; and for two weeks they had been worrying about a coughing-spell of Antanas. It seemed to shake him all over, and it never stopped; you could see a red stain wherever he had spit upon the floor.

And yet all these things were as nothing to what came a little later. They had begun to question the old lady as to why one family had been unable to pay, trying to show her by figures that it ought to have been possible; and Grandmother Majauszkiene had disputed their figures—"You say twelve dollars a month; but that does not include the interest."

Then they stared at her. "Interest!" they cried.

"Interest on the money you still owe," she answered.

"But we don't have to pay any interest!" they exclaimed, three or four at once. "We only have to pay twelve dollars each month."

And for this she laughed at them. "You are like all the rest," she said; "they trick you and eat you alive. They never sell the houses without interest. Get your deed, and see."

Then, with a horrible sinking of the heart, Teta Elzbieta unlocked her bureau and brought out the paper that had already caused them so many agonies. Now they sat round, scarcely breathing, while the old lady, who could read English, ran over it. "Yes," she said, finally, "here it is, of course: 'With interest thereon monthly, at the rate of seven per cent per annum.'"

And there followed a dead silence. "What does that mean?" asked Jurgis finally, almost in a whisper.

"That means," replied the other, "that you have to pay them seven dollars next month, as well as the twelve dollars."

Then again there was not a sound. It was sickening, like a night-mare, in which suddenly something gives way beneath you, and you feel yourself sinking, sinking, down into bottomless abysses. As if in a flash of lightning they saw themselves—victims of a relentless fate, cornered, trapped, in the grip of destruction. All the fair struc-ture of their hopes came crashing about their ears.—And all the time the old woman was going on talking. They wished that she would be still; her voice sounded like the croaking of some dismal raven.[8] Jurgis sat with his hands clenched and beads of perspira-tion on his forehead, and there was a great lump in Ona's throat, choking her. Then suddenly Teta Elzbieta broke the silence with a wail, and Marija began to wring her hands and sob, "*Ai! Ai! Beda man!*"[9]

---

8. Believed to be a bird of ill omen.
9. "Oh! Oh! Problem mine!"

All their outcry did them no good, of course. There sat Grandmother Majauszkiene, unrelenting, typifying fate. No, of course it
was not fair, but then fairness had nothing to do with it. And of
course they had not known it. They had not been intended to know
it. But it was in the deed, and that was all that was necessary, as
they would find when the time came.

Somehow or other they got rid of their guest, and then they passed
a night of lamentation. The children woke up and found out that
something was wrong, and they wailed and would not be comforted.
In the morning, of course, most of them had to go to work, the
packing-houses would not stop for their sorrows; but by seven o'clock
Ona and her stepmother were standing at the door of the office of
the agent. Yes, he told them, when he came, it was quite true that
they would have to pay interest. And then Teta Elzbieta broke forth
into protestations and reproaches, so that the people outside stopped
and peered in at the window. The agent was as bland as ever. He
was deeply pained, he said. He had not told them, simply because
he had supposed they would understand that they had to pay interest upon their debt, as a matter of course.

So they came away, and Ona went down to the yards, and at
noon-time saw Jurgis and told him. Jurgis took it stolidly—he had
made up his mind to it by this time. It was part of fate; they would
manage it somehow—he made his usual answer, "I will work harder."
It would upset their plans for a time; and it would perhaps be necessary for Ona to get work after all. Then Ona added that Teta Elzbieta
had decided that little Stanislovas would have to work too. It was
not fair to let Jurgis and her support the family—the family would
have to help as it could. Previously Jurgis had scouted this idea, but
now knit his brows and nodded his head slowly—yes, perhaps it
would be best; they would all have to make some sacrifices now.

So Ona set out that day to hunt for work; and at night Marija came
home saying that she had met a girl named Jasaityte who had a friend
that worked in one of the wrapping-rooms in Brown's, and might get
a place for Ona there; only the forelady was the kind that takes presents—it was no use for any one to ask her for a place unless at the
same time they slipped a ten-dollar bill into her hand. Jurgis was
not in the least surprised at this now—he merely asked what the
wages of the place would be. So negotiations were opened, and after
an interview Ona came home and reported that the forelady seemed
to like her, and had said that, while she was not sure, she thought
she might be able to put her at work sewing covers on hams, a job at
which she could earn as much as eight or ten dollars a week. That
was a bid, so Marija reported, after consulting her friend; and then
there was an anxious conference at home. The work was done in one

of the cellars, and Jurgis did not want Ona to work in such a place; but then it was easy work, and one could not have everything. So in the end Ona, with a ten-dollar bill burning a hole in her palm, had another interview with the forelady.

Meantime Teta Elzbieta had taken Stanislovas to the priest and gotten a certificate to the effect that he was two years older than he was; and with it the little boy now sallied forth to make his fortune in the world. It chanced that Durham had just put in a wonderful new lard-machine, and when the special policeman in front of the time-station saw Stanislovas and his document, he smiled to himself and told him to go—"*Czia! Czia!*"[1] pointing. And so Stanislovas went down a long stone corridor, and up a flight of stairs, which took him into a room lighted by electricity, with the new machines for filling lard-cans at work in it. The lard was finished on the floor above, and it came in little jets, like beautiful, wriggling, snow-white snakes of unpleasant odor. There were several kinds and sizes of jets, and after a certain precise quantity had come out, each stopped automatically, and the wonderful machine made a turn, and took the can under another jet, and so on, until it was filled neatly to the brim, and pressed tightly, and smoothed off. To attend to all this and fill several hundred cans of lard per hour, there were necessary two human creatures, one of whom knew how to place an empty lard-can on a certain spot every few seconds, and the other of whom knew how to take a full lard-can off a certain spot every few seconds and set it upon a tray.

And so, after little Stanislovas had stood gazing timidly about him for a few minutes, a man approached him, and asked what he wanted, to which Stanislovas said, "Job." Then the man said "How old?" and Stanislovas answered, "Sixtin." Once or twice every year a state inspector would come wandering through the packing-plants, asking a child here and there how old he was; and so the packers were very careful to comply with the law, which cost them as much trouble as was now involved in the boss's taking the document from the little boy, and glancing at it, and then sending it to the office to be filed away. Then he set some one else at a different job, and showed the lad how to place a lard-can every time the empty arm of the remorseless machine came to him; and so was decided the place in the universe of little Stanislovas, and his destiny till the end of his days. Hour after hour, day after day, year after year, it was fated that he should stand upon a certain square foot of floor from seven in the morning until noon, and again from half-past twelve till half-past five, making never a motion and thinking never a thought, save

---

1. "Here! Here!"

for the setting of lard-cans. In summer the stench of the warm lard would be nauseating, and in winter the cans would all but freeze to his naked little fingers in the unheated cellar. Half the year it would be dark as night when he went in to work, and dark as night again when he came out, and so he would never know what the sun looked like on week-days. And for this, at the end of the week, he would carry home three dollars to his family, being his pay at the rate of five cents per hour[2]—just about his proper share of the total earnings of the million and three-quarters of children who are now engaged in earning their livings in the United States.

And meantime, because they were young, and hope is not to be stifled before its time, Jurgis and Ona were again calculating; for they had discovered that the wages of Stanislovas would a little more than pay the interest, which left them just about as they had been before! It would be but fair to them to say that the little boy was delighted with his work, and at the idea of earning a lot of money; and also that the two were very much in love with each other.

2. Jurgis's weekly pay would be about $92 in 2021 dollars; his hourly rate would be around $1.53.

Chapter VII

All summer long the family toiled, and in the fall they had money enough for Jurgis and Ona to be married according to home traditions of decency. In the latter part of November they hired a hall, and invited all their new acquaintances, who came and left them over a hundred dollars in debt.

It was a bitter and cruel experience, and it plunged them into an agony of despair. Such a time, of all times, for them to have it, when their hearts were made tender! Such a pitiful beginning it was for their married life; they loved each other so, and they could not have the briefest respite! It was a time when everything cried out to them that they ought to be happy; when wonder burned in their hearts, and leaped into flame at the slightest breath. They were shaken to the depths of them, with the awe of love realized—and was it so very weak of them that they cried out for a little peace? They had opened their hearts, like flowers to the springtime, and the merciless winter had fallen upon them. They wondered if ever any love that had blossomed in the world had been so crushed and trampled!

Over them, relentless and savage, there cracked the lash of want; the morning after the wedding it sought them as they slept, and drove them out before daybreak to work. Ona was scarcely able to stand with exhaustion; but if she were to lose her place they would be ruined, and she would surely lose it if she were not on time that day. They all had to go, even little Stanislovas, who was ill from overindulgence in sausages and sarsaparilla.[1] All that day he stood at his lard-machine, rocking unsteadily, his eyes closing in spite of him; and he all but lost his place even so, for the foreman booted him twice to waken him.

It was fully a week before they were all normal again, and meantime, with whining children and cross adults, the house was not a pleasant place to live in. Jurgis lost his temper very little, however, all things considered. It was because of Ona; the least glance at her was always enough to make him control himself. She was so sensitive—she was not fitted for such a life as this; and a hundred times a day, when he thought of her, he would clench his hands and fling himself again at the task before him. She was too good for him, he told himself, and he was afraid, because she was his. So long he had hungered to possess her, but now that the time had come he knew that he had not earned the right; that she trusted him so was all her own simple goodness, and no virtue of his. But he was resolved

---

1. Soft drink similar to root beer.

that she should never find this out, and so was always on the watch
to see that he did not betray any of his ugly self; he would take care
even in little matters, such as his manners, and his habit of swearing when things went wrong. The tears came so easily into Ona's
eyes, and she would look at him so appealingly—it kept Jurgis quite
busy making resolutions, in addition to all the other things he had
on his mind. It was true that more things were going on at this time
in the mind of Jurgis than ever had in all his life before.

He had to protect her, to do battle for her against the horror he
saw about them. He was all that she had to look to, and if he failed
she would be lost; he would wrap his arms about her, and try to hide
her from the world. He had learned the ways of things about him
now. It was a war of each against all, and the devil take the hind-
most.[2] You did not give feasts to other people, you waited for them to
give feasts to you. You went about with your soul full of suspicion and
hatred; you understood that you were environed by hostile powers
that were trying to get your money, and who used all the virtues to
bait their traps with. The storekeepers plastered up their windows
with all sorts of lies to entice you; the very fences by the wayside, the
lamp-posts and telegraph-poles, were pasted over with lies. The great
corporation which employed you lied to you, and lied to the whole
country—from top to bottom it was nothing but one gigantic lie.

So Jurgis said that he understood it; and yet it was really pitiful,
for the struggle was so unfair—some had so much the advantage!
Here he was, for instance, vowing upon his knees that he would save
Ona from harm, and only a week later she was suffering atrociously,
and from the blow of an enemy that he could not possibly have
thwarted. There came a day when the rain fell in torrents; and it
being December, to be wet with it and have to sit all day long in one
of the cold cellars of Brown's was no laughing matter. Ona was a
working-girl, and did not own waterproofs and such things, and so
Jurgis took her and put her on the street-car. Now it chanced that
this car-line was owned by gentlemen who were trying to make
money. And the city having passed an ordinance requiring them to
give transfers, they had fallen into a rage; and first they had made a
rule that transfers could be had only when the fare was paid; and
later, growing still uglier, they had made another—that the passenger must ask for the transfer, the conductor was not allowed to offer
it. Now Ona had been told that she was to get a transfer; but it was
not her way to speak up, and so she merely waited, following the conductor about with her eyes, wondering when he would think of her.

2. This sentence combines a social Darwinist idea of "war of each against all" with a
  medieval adage about the devil that had been popularized by a Renaissance tragicomedy,
  Philaster (first produced ca. 1608–10), by Francis Beaumont (1585–1616) and John
  Fletcher (1579–1625).

When at last the time came for her to get out, she asked for the transfer, and was refused. Not knowing what to make of this, she began to argue with the conductor, in a language of which he did not understand a word. After warning her several times, he pulled the bell and the car went on—at which Ona burst into tears. At the next corner she got out, of course; and as she had no more money, she had to walk the rest of the way to the yards in the pouring rain. And so all day long she sat shivering, and came home at night with her teeth chattering and pains in her head and back. For two weeks afterward she suffered cruelly—and yet every day she had to drag herself to her work. The forewoman was especially severe with Ona, because she believed that she was obstinate on account of having been refused a holiday the day after her wedding. Ona had an idea that her "forelady" did not like to have her girls marry—perhaps because she was old and ugly and unmarried herself.

There were many such dangers, in which the odds were all against them. Their children were not as well as they had been at home; but how could they know that there was no sewer to their house, and that the drainage of fifteen years was in a cesspool under it? How could they know that the pale blue milk that they bought around the corner was watered, and doctored with formaldehyde besides?[3] When the children were not well at home, Teta Elzbieta would gather herbs and cure them; now she was obliged to go to the drug-store and buy extracts—and how was she to know that they were all adulterated? How could they find out that their tea and coffee, their sugar and flour, had been doctored; that their canned peas had been colored with copper salts, and their fruit jams with aniline dyes? And even if they had known it, what good would it have done them, since there was no place within miles of them where any other sort was to be had? The bitter winter was coming, and they had to save money to get more clothing and bedding; but it would not matter in the least how much they saved, they could not get anything to keep them warm. All the clothing that was to be had in the stores was made of cotton and shoddy, which is made by tearing old clothes to pieces and weaving the fibre again. If they paid higher prices, they might get frills and fanciness, or be cheated; but genuine quality they could not obtain for love nor money. A young friend of Szedvilas's, recently come from abroad, had become a clerk in a store on Ashland Avenue, and he narrated with glee a trick that had been played upon an unsuspecting countryman by his boss. The customer had desired to purchase an alarm-clock, and the boss had shown him two exactly

3. Adulterated milk had been identified as early as the 1820s, the consequence of feeding distillery waste to cattle. The resulting "swill milk," thin and bluish, was sold to the urban poor. Formaldehyde was a common preservative: its advocates maintained its presence in milk reduced infant mortality rates.

similar, telling him that the price of one was a dollar and of the other a dollar seventy-five. Upon being asked what the difference was the man had wound up the first half-way and the second all the way, and showed the customer how the latter made twice as much noise; upon which the customer remarked that he was a sound sleeper, and had better take the more expensive clock!

There is a poet who sings that

> "Deeper their heart grows and nobler their bearing,
> Whose youth in the fires of anguish hath died."[4]

But it is not likely that he had reference to the kind of anguish that comes with destitution, that is so endlessly bitter and cruel, and yet so sordid and petty, so ugly, so humiliating—unredeemed by the slightest touch of dignity or even of pathos. It is a kind of anguish that poets have not commonly dealt with; its very words are not admitted into the vocabulary of poets—the details of it cannot be told in polite society at all. How, for instance, could any one expect to excite sympathy among lovers of good literature by telling how a family found their home alive with vermin, and of all the suffering and inconvenience and humiliation they were put to, and the hard-earned money they spent, in efforts to get rid of them? After long hesitation and uncertainty they paid twenty-five cents for a big package of insect-powder—a patent preparation which chanced to be ninety-five per cent gypsum,[5] a harmless earth which had cost about two cents to prepare. Of course it had not the least effect, except upon a few roaches which had the misfortune to drink water after eating it, and so got their inwards set in a coating of plaster of Paris. The family, having no idea of this, and no more money to throw away, had nothing to do but give up and submit to one more misery for the rest of their days.

Then there was old Antanas. The winter came, and the place where he worked was a dark, unheated cellar, where you could see your breath all day, and where your fingers sometimes tried to freeze. So the old man's cough grew every day worse, until there came a time when it hardly ever stopped, and he had become a nuisance about the place. Then, too, a still more dreadful thing happened to him; he worked in a place where his feet were soaked in chemicals, and it was not long before they had eaten through his new boots. Then sores began to break out on his feet, and grow worse and worse.

---

4. A slight misquotation, suggesting Sinclair recalls from memory "A Modern Sappho" (1849), by the English writer Matthew Arnold (1822–1888). The line actually reads, "But deeper their voice grows. . . ."
5. A hydrated sulfate of calcium found in sedimentary rocks and used for making *plaster of Paris.*

Whether it was that his blood was bad, or there had been a cut, he could not say; but he asked the men about it, and learned that it was a regular thing—it was the saltpetre.[6] Every one felt it, sooner or later, and then it was all up with him, at least for that sort of work. The sores would never heal—in the end his toes would drop off, if he did not quit. Yet old Antanas would not quit; he saw the suffering of his family, and he remembered what it had cost him to get a job. So he tied up his feet, and went on limping about and coughing, until at last he fell to pieces, all at once and in a heap, like the One-Horse Shay.[7] They carried him to a dry place and laid him on the floor, and that night two of the men helped him home. The poor old man was put to bed, and though he tried it every morning until the end, he never could get up again. He would lie there and cough and cough, day and night, wasting away to a mere skeleton. There came a time when there was so little flesh on him that the bones began to poke through—which was a horrible thing to see or even to think of. And one night he had a choking fit, and a little river of blood came out of his mouth. The family, wild with terror, sent for a doctor, and paid half a dollar to be told that there was nothing to be done. Mercifully the doctor did not say this so that the old man could hear, for he was still clinging to the faith that to-morrow or next day he would be better, and could go back to his job. The company had sent word to him that they would keep it for him—or rather Jurgis had bribed one of the men to come one Sunday afternoon and say they had. Dede Antanas continued to believe it, while three more hemorrhages came; and then at last one morning they found him stiff and cold. Things were not going well with them then, and though it nearly broke Teta Elzbieta's heart, they were forced to dispense with nearly all the decencies of a funeral; they had only a hearse, and one hack for the women and children; and Jurgis, who was learning things fast, spent all Sunday making a bargain for these, and he made it in the presence of witnesses, so that when the man tried to charge him for all sorts of incidentals, he did not have to pay. For twenty-five years old Antanas Rudkus and his son had dwelt in the forest together, and it was hard to part in this way; perhaps it was just as well that Jurgis had to give all his attention to the task of having a funeral without being bankrupted, and so had no time to indulge in memories and grief.

Now the dreadful winter was come upon them. In the forests, all summer long, the branches of the trees do battle for light, and some

<hr/>

6. A nitrate commonly used in packing to preserve the color of meat.
7. In the 1858 poem "The Deacon's Masterpiece Or, the Wonderful 'One-Hoss Shay': A Logical Story," by the American physician and writer Oliver Wendell Holmes Sr. (1809–1894), a perfectly built carriage collapses during an earthquake.

of them lose and die; and then come the raging blasts, and the storms of snow and hail, and strew the ground with these weaker branches. Just so it was in Packingtown; the whole district braced itself for the struggle that was an agony, and those whose time was come died off in hordes. All the year round they had been serving as cogs in the great packing-machine; and now was the time for the renovating of it, and the replacing of damaged parts. There came pneumonia and grippe,[8] stalking among them, seeking for weakened constitutions; there was the annual harvest of those whom tuberculosis had been dragging down. There came cruel, cold, and biting winds, and blizzards of snow, all testing relentlessly for failing muscles and impoverished blood. Sooner or later came the day when the unfit one did not report for work; and then, with no time lost in waiting, and no inquiries or regrets, there was a chance for a new hand.

The new hands were here by the thousands. All day long the gates of the packing-houses were besieged by starving and penniless men; they came, literally, by the thousands every single morning, fighting with each other for a chance for life. Blizzards and cold made no difference to them, they were always on hand; they were on hand two hours before the sun rose, an hour before the work began. Sometimes their faces froze, sometimes their feet and their hands; sometimes they froze all together—but still they came, for they had no other place to go. One day Durham advertised in the paper for two hundred men to cut ice; and all that day the homeless and starving of the city came trudging through the snow from all over its two hundred square miles. That night forty score of them crowded into the station-house of the stock-yards district—they filled the rooms, sleeping in each other's laps, toboggan-fashion, and they piled on top of each other in the corridors, till the police shut the doors and left some to freeze outside. On the morrow, before daybreak, there were three thousand at Durham's, and the police-reserves had to be sent for to quell the riot. Then Durham's bosses picked out twenty of the biggest; the "two hundred" proved to have been a printer's error.

Four or five miles to the eastward lay the lake, and over this the bitter winds came raging.[9] Sometimes the thermometer would fall to ten or twenty degrees below zero at night, and in the morning the streets would be piled with snowdrifts up to the first-floor windows. The streets through which our friends had to go to their work were all unpaved and full of deep holes and gullies; in summer, when it rained hard, a man might have to wade to his waist to get to his house; and now in winter it was no joke getting through these places,

---

8. *Pneumonia*: acute infection of the lungs, causing fever, chills, chest pain, difficulty breathing, and coughing; *grippe*: common name for influenza, an infectious respiratory disease caused by a virus.
9. Chilling winds off Lake Michigan make Chicago winters particularly cold.

before light in the morning and after dark at night. They would wrap up in all they owned, but they could not wrap up against exhaustion; and many a man gave out in these battles with the snowdrifts, and lay down and fell asleep.

And if it was bad for the men, one may imagine how the women and children fared. Some would ride in the cars,[1] if the cars were running; but when you are making only five cents an hour, as was little Stanislovas, you do not like to spend that much to ride two miles. The children would come to the yards with great shawls about their ears, and so tied up that you could hardly find them—and still there would be accidents. One bitter morning in February the little boy who worked at the lard-machine with Stanislovas came about an hour late, and screaming with pain. They unwrapped him, and a man began vigorously rubbing his ears; and as they were frozen stiff, it took only two or three rubs to break them short off. As a result of this, little Stanislovas conceived a terror of the cold that was almost a mania. Every morning, when it came time to start for the yards, he would begin to cry and protest. Nobody knew quite how to manage him, for threats did no good—it seemed to be something that he could not control, and they feared sometimes that he would go into convulsions. In the end it had to be arranged that he always went with Jurgis, and came home with him again; and often, when the snow was deep, the man would carry him the whole way on his shoulders. Sometimes Jurgis would be working until late at night, and then it was pitiful, for there was no place for the little fellow to wait, save in the doorways or in a corner of the killing-beds, and he would all but fall asleep there, and freeze to death.

There was no heat upon the killing-beds; the men might exactly as well have worked out of doors all winter. For that matter, there was very little heat anywhere in the building, except in the cooking-rooms and such places—and it was the men who worked in these who ran the most risk of all, because whenever they had to pass to another room they had to go through ice-cold corridors, and sometimes with nothing on above the waist except a sleeveless undershirt. On the killing-beds you were apt to be covered with blood, and it would freeze solid; if you leaned against a pillar, you would freeze to that, and if you put your hand upon the blade of your knife, you would run a chance of leaving your skin on it. The men would tie up their feet in newspapers and old sacks, and these would be soaked in blood and frozen, and then soaked again, and so on, until by night-time a man would be walking on great lumps the size of the feet of an elephant. Now and then, when the bosses were not looking, you would see them plunging their feet and ankles into the steaming hot

1. Public transportation, street railway cars, by this time mostly electric.

carcass of the steer, or darting across the room to the hot-water jets. The cruelest thing of all was that nearly all of them—all of those who used knives—were unable to wear gloves, and their arms would be white with frost and their hands would grow numb, and then of course there would be accidents. Also the air would be full of steam, from the hot water and the hot blood, so that you could not see five feet before you; and then, with men rushing about at the speed they kept up on the killing-beds, and all with butcher-knives, like razors, in their hands—well, it was to be counted as a wonder that there were not more men slaughtered than cattle.

And yet all this inconvenience they might have put up with, if only it had not been for one thing—if only there had been some place where they might eat. Jurgis had either to eat his dinner amid the stench in which he had worked, or else to rush, as did all his companions, to any one of the hundreds of liquor stores which stretched out their arms to him. To the west of the yards ran Ashland Avenue, and here was an unbroken line of saloons—"Whiskey Row," they called it; to the north was Forty-seventh Street, where there were half a dozen to the block, and at the angle of the two was "Whiskey Point," a space of fifteen or twenty acres, and containing one glue-factory and about two hundred saloons.[2]

One might walk among these and take his choice: "Hot pea-soup and boiled cabbage to-day." "Sauerkraut and hot frankfurters. Walk in." "Bean-soup and stewed lamb. Welcome." All of these things were printed in many languages, as were also the names of the resorts, which were infinite in their variety and appeal. There was the "Home Circle" and the "Cosey Corner"; there were "Firesides" and "Hearth-stones" and "Pleasure Palaces" and "Wonderlands" and "Dream Castles" and "Love's Delights." Whatever else they were called, they were sure to be called "Union Headquarters," and to hold out a welcome to workingmen; and there was always a warm stove, and a chair near it, and some friends to laugh and talk with. There was only one condition attached,—you must drink. If you went in not intending to drink, you would be put out in no time, and if you were slow about going, like as not you would get your head split open with a beer-bottle in the bargain. But all of the men understood the convention and drank; they believed that by it they were getting something for nothing—for they did not need to take more than one drink, and upon the strength of it they might fill themselves up with a good hot dinner. This did not always work out in practice, however, for there was pretty sure to be a friend who would treat you,

2. Clustered near plant entrances, saloons such as those at Whiskey Point were among the few places where workers could cash paychecks. A 1911 observer counted forty-six saloons on Whiskey Row, which ran across from the main packing plants on Ashland Avenue.

and then you would have to treat him. Then some one else would come in—and, anyhow, a few drinks were good for a man who worked hard. As he went back he did not shiver so, he had more courage for his task; the deadly brutalizing monotony of it did not afflict him so,—he had ideas while he worked, and took a more cheerful view of his circumstances. On the way home, however, the shivering was apt to come on him again; and so he would have to stop once or twice to warm up against the cruel cold. As there were hot things to eat in this saloon too, he might get home late to his supper, or he might not get home at all. And then his wife might set out to look for him, and she too would feel the cold; and perhaps she would have some of the children with her—and so a whole family would drift into drinking, as the current of a river drifts downstream. As if to complete the chain, the packers all paid their men in checks, refusing all requests to pay in coin; and where in Packingtown could a man go to have his check cashed but to a saloon, where he could pay for the favor by spending a part of the money?

From all of these things Jurgis was saved because of Ona. He never would take but the one drink at noon-time; and so he got the reputation of being a surly fellow, and was not quite welcome at the saloons, and had to drift about from one to another. Then at night he would go straight home, helping Ona and Stanislovas, or often putting the former on a car. And when he got home perhaps he would have to trudge several blocks, and come staggering back through the snowdrifts with a bag of coal upon his shoulder. Home was not a very attractive place—at least not this winter. They had only been able to buy one stove, and this was a small one, and proved not big enough to warm even the kitchen in the bitterest weather. This made it hard for Teta Elzbieta all day, and for the children when they could not get to school. At night they would sit huddled round this stove, while they ate their supper off their laps; and then Jurgis and Jonas would smoke a pipe, after which they would all crawl into their beds to get warm, after putting out the fire to save the coal. Then they would have some frightful experiences with the cold. They would sleep with all their clothes on, including their overcoats, and put over them all the bedding and spare clothing they owned; the children would sleep all crowded into one bed, and yet even so they could not keep warm. The outside ones would be shivering and sobbing, crawling over the others and trying to get down into the centre, and causing a fight. This old house with the leaky weather-boards was a very different thing from their cabins at home, with great thick walls plastered inside and outside with mud; and the cold which came upon them was a living thing, a demon-presence in the room. They would waken in the midnight hours, when everything was black; perhaps they would hear it yelling outside, or perhaps there would be deathlike stillness—and that would be worse yet. They could feel the cold as it crept in through the cracks, reaching out for them with its icy, death-dealing fingers; and they would crouch and cower, and try to hide from it, all in vain. It would come, and it would come; a grisly thing, a spectre born in the black caverns of terror; a power primeval, cosmic, shadowing the tortures of the lost souls flung out to chaos and destruction. It was cruel, iron-hard; and hour after hour they would cringe in its grasp, alone, alone. There would be no one to hear them if they cried out; there would be no help, no mercy. And so on until morning—when they would go out to another day of toil, a little weaker, a little nearer to the time when it would be their turn to be shaken from the tree.

Chapter VIII

Yet even by this deadly winter the germ of hope was not to be kept from sprouting in their hearts. It was just at this time that the great adventure befell Marija.

The victim was Tamoszius Kuszleika, who played the violin. Everybody laughed at them, for Tamoszius was petite and frail, and Marija could have picked him up and carried him off under one arm. But perhaps that was why she fascinated him; the sheer volume of Marija's energy was overwhelming. That first night at the wedding Tamoszius had hardly taken his eyes off her; and later on, when he came to find that she had really the heart of a baby, her voice and her violence ceased to terrify him, and he got the habit of coming to pay her visits on Sunday afternoons. There was no place to entertain company except in the kitchen, in the midst of the family, and Tamoszius would sit there with his hat between his knees, never saying more than half a dozen words at a time, and turning red in the face before he managed to say those; until finally Jurgis would clap him upon the back, in his hearty way, crying, "Come now, brother, give us a tune." And then Tamoszius's face would light up and he would get out his fiddle, tuck it under his chin, and play. And forthwith the soul of him would flame up and become eloquent—it was almost an impropriety, for all the while his gaze would be fixed upon Marija's face, until she would begin to turn red and lower her eyes. There was no resisting the music of Tamoszius, however; even the children would sit awed and wondering, and the tears would run down Teta Elzbieta's cheeks. A wonderful privilege it was to be thus admitted into the soul of a man of genius, to be allowed to share the ecstasies and the agonies of his inmost life.

Then there were other benefits accruing to Marija from this friendship—benefits of a more substantial nature. People paid Tamoszius big money to come and make music on state occasions; and also they would invite him to parties and festivals, knowing well that he was too good-natured to come without his fiddle, and that having brought it, he could be made to play while others danced. Once he made bold to ask Marija to accompany him to such a party, and Marija accepted, to his great delight—after which he never went anywhere without her, while if the celebration were given by friends of his, he would invite the rest of the family also. In any case Marija would bring back a huge pocketful of cakes and sandwiches for the children, and stories of all the good things she herself had managed to consume. She was compelled, at these parties, to spend most of her time at the refreshment table, for she could not dance with anybody except other women and very old men; Tamoszius was of an excitable temperament, and afflicted with a frantic jealousy, and any unmarried man who ventured to put his arm about the ample waist of Marija would be certain to throw the orchestra out of tune.

It was a great help to a person who had to toil all the week to be able to look forward to some such relaxation as this on Saturday nights. The family were too poor and too hardworked to make many acquaintances; in Packingtown, as a rule, people know only their near neighbors and shopmates, and so the place is like a myriad of little country villages. But now there was a member of the family who was permitted to travel and widen her horizon; and so each week there would be new personalities to talk about,—how so-and-so was dressed, and where she worked, and what she got, and whom she was in love with; and how this man had jilted his girl, and how she had quarrelled with the other girl, and what had passed between them; and how another man beat his wife, and spent all her earnings upon drink, and pawned her very clothes. Some people would have scorned this talk as gossip; but then one has to talk about what one knows.

It was one Saturday night, as they were coming home from a wedding, that Tamoszius found courage, and set down his violin-case in the street and spoke his heart; and then Marija clasped him in her arms. She told them all about it the next day, and fairly cried with happiness, for she said that Tamoszius was a lovely man. After that he no longer made love to her[1] with his fiddle, but they would sit for hours in the kitchen, blissfully happy in each other's arms; it was the tacit convention of the family to know nothing of what was going on in that corner.

They were planning to be married in the spring, and have the garret of the house fixed up, and live there. Tamoszius made good wages; and little by little the family were paying back their debt to Marija, so she ought soon to have enough to start life upon—only, with her preposterous soft-heartedness, she would insist upon spending a good part of her money every week for things which she saw they needed. Marija was really the capitalist of the party, for she had become an expert can-painter by this time—she was getting fourteen cents for every hundred and ten cans, and she could paint more than two cans every minute. Marija felt, so to speak, that she had her hand on the throttle, and the neighborhood was vocal with her rejoicings.

Yet her friends would shake their heads and tell her to go slow; one could not count upon such good fortune forever—there were accidents that always happened. But Marija was not to be prevailed upon, and went on planning and dreaming of all the treasures she was going to have for her home; and so, when the crash did come, her grief was painful to see.

---

1. Lacking modern connotations of sexual intercourse; meaning to court, to woo.

For her canning-factory shut down! Marija would about as soon have expected to see the sun shut down—the huge establishment had been to her a thing akin to the planets and the seasons. But now it was shut! And they had not given her any explanation, they had not even given her a day's warning; they had simply posted a notice one Saturday that all hands would be paid off that afternoon, and would not resume work for at least a month! And that was all that there was to it—her job was gone!

It was the holiday rush that was over, the girls said in answer to Marija's inquiries; after that there was always a slack. Sometimes the factory would start up on half-time after a while, but there was no telling—it had been known to stay closed until way into the summer. The prospects were bad at present, for truckmen who worked in the store-rooms said that these were piled up to the ceilings, so that the firm could not have found room for another week's output of cans. And they had turned off three-quarters of these men, which was a still worse sign, since it meant that there were no orders to be filled. It was all a swindle, can-painting, said the girls—you were crazy with delight because you were making twelve or fourteen dollars a week, and saving half of it; but you had to spend it all keeping alive while you were out, and so your pay was really only half what you thought.

Marija came home, and because she was a person who could not rest without danger of explosion, they first had a great house-cleaning, and then she set out to search Packingtown for a job to fill up the gap. As nearly all the canning-establishments were shut down, and all the girls hunting work, it will be readily understood that Marija did not find any. Then she took to trying the stores and saloons, and when this failed she even travelled over into the far-distant regions near the lake front, where lived the rich people in great palaces, and begged there for some sort of work that could be done by a person who did not know English.

The men upon the killing-beds felt also the effects of the slump which had turned Marija out; but they felt it in a different way, and a way which made Jurgis understand at last all their bitterness. The big packers did not turn their hands off and close down, like the canning-factories; but they began to run for shorter and shorter hours. They had always required the men to be on the killing-beds and ready for work at seven o'clock, although there was almost never any work to be done till the buyers out in the yards had gotten to work, and some cattle had come over the chutes. That would often be ten or eleven o'clock, which was bad enough, in all conscience; but now, in the slack season, they would perhaps not have a thing for their men to do till late in the afternoon. And so they would have to loaf around, in a place where the thermometer might be twenty degrees below zero! At first one would see them running about, or skylarking with each other, trying to keep warm; but before the day was over they would become quite chilled through and exhausted, and, when the cattle finally came, so near frozen that to move was an agony. And then suddenly the place would spring into activity, and the merciless "speeding-up" would begin!

There were weeks at a time when Jurgis went home after such a day as this with not more than two hours' work to his credit—which meant about thirty-five cents. There were many days when the total was less than half an hour, and others when there was none at all. The general average was six hours a day, which meant for Jurgis about six dollars a week; and this six hours of work would be done after standing on the killing-bed till one o'clock, or perhaps even three or four o'clock, in the afternoon. Like as not there would come a rush of cattle at the very end of the day, which the men would have to dispose of before they went home, often working by electric light till nine or ten, or even twelve or one o'clock, and without a single instant for a bite of supper. The men were at the mercy of the cattle. Perhaps the buyers would be holding off for better prices—if they could scare the shippers into thinking that they meant to buy nothing that day, they could get their own terms. For some reason the cost of fodder for cattle in the yards was much above the market price—and you were not allowed to bring your own fodder! Then, too, a number of cars were apt to arrive late in the day, now that the roads were blocked with snow, and the packers would buy their cattle that night, to get them cheaper, and then would come into play their iron-clad rule, that all cattle must be killed the same day they were bought. There was no use kicking about this—there had been one delegation after another to see the packers about it, only to be told that it was the rule, and that there was not the slightest chance of its ever being altered. And so on Christmas Eve Jurgis worked till nearly one o'clock in the morning, and on Christmas Day he was on the killing-bed at seven o'clock.

All this was bad; and yet it was not the worst. For after all the hard work a man did, he was paid for only part of it. Jurgis had once been among those who scoffed at the idea of these huge concerns cheating; and so now he could appreciate the bitter irony of the fact that it was precisely their size which enabled them to do it with impunity. One of the rules on the killing-beds was that a man who was one minute late was docked an hour; and this was economical, for he was made to work the balance of the hour—he was not allowed to stand round and wait. And on the other hand if he came ahead of time he got no pay for that—though often the bosses would start up the gang ten or fifteen minutes before the whistle. And this same custom they carried over to the end of the day; they did not pay for any fraction of an hour—for "broken time." A man might work full fifty minutes, but if there was no work to fill out the hour, there was no pay for him. Thus the end of every day was a sort of lottery—a struggle, all but breaking into open war between the bosses and the men, the former trying to rush a job through and the latter trying to stretch it out. Jurgis blamed the bosses for this, though the truth to be told it was not always their fault; for the packers kept them frightened for their lives—and when one was in danger of falling behind the standard, what was easier than to catch up by making the gang work awhile "for the church"? This was a savage witticism the men had, which Jurgis had to have explained to him. Old man Jones was great on missions and such things, and so whenever they were doing some particularly disreputable job, the men would wink at each other and say, "Now we're working for the church!"[2]

One of the consequences of all these things was that Jurgis was no longer perplexed when he heard men talk of fighting for their rights. He felt like fighting now himself; and when the Irish delegate of the butcher-helpers' union came to him a second time, he received him in a far different spirit. A wonderful idea it now seemed to Jurgis, this of the men—that by combining they might be able to make a stand and conquer the packers! Jurgis wondered who had first thought of it; and when he was told that it was a common thing for men to do in America, he got the first inkling of a meaning in the phrase "a free country." The delegate explained to him how it depended upon their being able to get every man to join and stand by the organization, and so Jurgis signified that he was willing to do his share. Before another month was by, all the working members of his family had union cards, and wore their union buttons conspicuously and with pride. For fully a week they were quite blissfully happy, thinking that belonging to a union meant an end of all their troubles.

But only ten days after she had joined, Marija's canning-factory closed down, and that blow quite staggered them. They could not understand why the union had not prevented it, and the very first time she attended a meeting Marija got up and made a speech about it. It was a business meeting, and was transacted in English, but that made no difference to Marija; she said what was in her, and all the pounding of the chairman's gavel and all the uproar and confusion in the room could not prevail. Quite apart from her own troubles she was boiling over with a general sense of the injustice of it, and she told what she thought of the packers, and what she thought of a world where such things were allowed to happen; and then, while the echoes of the hall rang with the shock of her terrible voice,

2. For charity; in other words, working for no pay (slang).

she sat down again and fanned herself, and the meeting gathered itself together and proceeded to discuss the election of a recording secretary.

Jurgis too had an adventure the first time he attended a union meeting, but it was not of his own seeking. Jurgis had gone with the desire to get into an inconspicuous corner and see what was done; but this attitude of silent and open-eyed attention had marked him out for a victim. Tommy Finnegan was a little Irishman, with big staring eyes and a wild aspect, a "hoister" by trade, and badly cracked.[3] Somewhere back in the far-distant past Tommy Finnegan had had a strange experience, and the burden of it rested upon him. All the balance of his life he had done nothing but try to make it understood. When he talked he caught his victim by the buttonhole, and his face kept coming closer and closer—which was trying, because his teeth were so bad. Jurgis did not mind that, only he was frightened. The method of operation of the higher intelligences was Tom Finnegan's theme, and he desired to find out if Jurgis had ever considered that the representation of things in their present similarity might be altogether unintelligible upon a more elevated plane. There were assuredly wonderful mysteries about the developing of these things; and then, becoming confidential, Mr. Finnegan proceeded to tell of some discoveries of his own. "If ye have iver had onything to do wid shperrits," said he, and looked inquiringly at Jurgis, who kept shaking his head. "Niver mind, niver mind," continued the other, "but their influences may be operatin' upon ye; it's shure as I'm tellin' ye, it's them that has the reference to the immejit surroundin's that has the most of power. It was vouchsafed to me in me youthful days to be acquainted with shperrits"—and so Tommy Finnegan went on, expounding a system of philosophy, while the perspiration came out on Jurgis's forehead, so great was his agitation and embarrassment. In the end one of the men, seeing his plight, came over and rescued him; but it was some time before he was able to find any one to explain things to him, and meanwhile his fear lest the strange little Irishman should get him cornered again was enough to keep him dodging about the room the whole evening.

He never missed a meeting, however. He had picked up a few words of English by this time, and friends would help him to understand. They were often very turbulent meetings, with half a dozen men declaiming at once, in as many dialects of English; but the speakers were all desperately in earnest, and Jurgis was in earnest too, for he understood that a fight was on, and that it was his fight. Since the time of his disillusionment, Jurgis had sworn to trust no

---

3. Crazy, eccentric (slang); *"hoister" by trade*: worker who hoists cow carcasses onto overhead trolleys for further processing.

man, except in his own family; but here he discovered that he had brothers in affliction, and allies. Their one chance for life was in union, and so the struggle became a kind of crusade. Jurgis had always been a member of the church, because it was the right thing to be, but the church had never touched him, he left all that for the women. Here, however, was a new religion—one that did touch him, that took hold of every fibre of him; and with all the zeal and fury of a convert he went out as a missionary. There were many non-union men among the Lithuanians, and with these he would labor and wrestle in prayer, trying to show them the right. Sometimes they would be obstinate and refuse to see it, and Jurgis, alas, was not always patient! He forgot how he himself had been blind, a short time ago—after the fashion of all crusaders since the original ones, who set out to spread the gospel of Brotherhood by force of arms.[4]

---

4. Medieval Christian crusaders, Roman Catholic fighters in religious wars directed against Muslims and those perceived as heretics.

Chapter IX

One of the first consequences of the discovery of the union was that Jurgis became desirous of learning English. He wanted to know what was going on at the meetings, and to be able to take part in them; and so he began to look about him, and to try to pick up words. The children, who were at school, and learning fast, would teach him a few; and a friend loaned him a little book that had some in it, and Ona would read them to him. Then Jurgis became sorry that he could not read himself; and later on in the winter, when some one told him that there was a night-school that was free, he went and enrolled. After that, every evening that he got home from the yards in time, he would go to the school; he would go even if he were in time for only half an hour. They were teaching him both to read and to speak English—and they would have taught him other things, if only he had had a little time.

Also the union made another great difference with him—it made him begin to pay attention to the country. It was the beginning of democracy with him. It was a little state, the union, a miniature republic; its affairs were every man's affairs, and every man had a real say about them. In other words, in the union Jurgis learned to talk politics. In the place where he had come from there had not been any politics—in Russia one thought of the government as an affliction like the lightning and the hail. "Duck, little brother, duck," the wise old peasants would whisper; "everything passes away." And when Jurgis had first come to America he had supposed that it was the same. He had heard people say that it was a free country—but what did that mean? He found that here, precisely as in Russia, there were rich men who owned everything; and if one could not find any work, was not the hunger he began to feel the same sort of hunger?

When Jurgis had been working about three weeks at Brown's, there had come to him one noon-time a man who was employed as a night-watchman, and who asked him if he would not like to take out naturalization papers and become a citizen. Jurgis did not know what that meant, but the man explained the advantages. In the first place, it would not cost him anything, and it would get him half a day off, with his pay just the same; and then when election time came he would be able to vote—and there was something in that. Jurgis was naturally glad to accept, and so the night-watchman said a few words to the boss, and he was excused for the rest of the day. When, later on, he wanted a holiday to get married he could not get it; and as for a holiday with pay just the same—what power had wrought that miracle heaven only knew! However, he went with the man, who picked up several other newly landed immigrants, Poles,

Lithuanians, and Slovaks, and took them all outside, where stood a great four-horse tally-ho coach,[1] with fifteen or twenty men already in it. It was a fine chance to see the sights of the city, and the party had a merry time, with plenty of beer handed up from inside. So they drove down-town and stopped before an imposing granite building, in which they interviewed an official, who had the papers all ready, with only the names to be filled in. So each man in turn took an oath of which he did not understand a word, and then was presented with a handsome ornamented document with a big red seal and the shield of the United States upon it, and was told that he had become a citizen of the Republic and the equal of the President himself.

A month or two later Jurgis had another interview with this same man, who told him where to go to "register." And then finally, when election day came, the packing-houses posted a notice that men who desired to vote might remain away until nine that morning, and the same night-watchman took Jurgis and the rest of his flock into the back room of a saloon, and showed each of them where and how to mark a ballot, and then gave each two dollars, and took them to the polling place, where there was a policeman on duty especially to see that they got through all right. Jurgis felt quite proud of this good luck till he got home and met Jonas, who had taken the leader aside and whispered to him, offering to vote three times for four dollars, which offer had been accepted.

And now in the union Jurgis met men who explained all this mystery to him; and he learned that America differed from Russia in that its government existed under the form of a democracy. The officials who ruled it, and got all the graft, had to be elected first; and so there were two rival sets of grafters, known as political parties, and the one got the office which bought the most votes. Now and then the election was very close, and that was the time the poor man came in. In the stockyards this was only in national and state elections, for in local elections the democratic party always carried everything. The ruler of the district was therefore the democratic boss, a little Irishman named Mike Scully. Scully held an important party office in the state, and bossed even the mayor of the city, it was said; it was his boast that he carried the stockyards in his pocket.[2] He was an enormously rich man—he had a hand in all the big graft in the neighborhood. It was Scully, for instance, who owned that dump which Jurgis and Ona had seen the first day of their arrival. Not only did he own the dump, but he owned the brick-factory as well; and first he took out the clay and made it into bricks, and then

1. Fast pleasure coach drawn by four horses.
2. Elected officials, representing sections or wards of the city, controlled Chicago. Tom Carey, Democratic alderman from 1893 to 1906 and leader of the Twenty-ninth Ward, owned many of the houses where workers lived and controlled many stockyards jobs.

he had the city bring garbage to fill up the hole, so that he could build houses to sell to the people. Then, too, he sold the bricks to the city, at his own price, and the city came and got them in its own wagons. And also he owned the other hole near by, where the stagnant water was; and it was he who cut the ice and sold it; and what was more, if the men told truth, he had not had to pay any taxes for the water, and he had built the ice-house out of city lumber, and had not had to pay anything for that. The newspapers had got hold of that story, and there had been a scandal; but Scully had hired somebody to confess and take all the blame, and then skip the country. It was said, too, that he had built his brick-kiln in the same way, and that the workmen were on the city pay-roll while they did it; however, one had to press closely to get these things out of the men, for it was not their business, and Mike Scully was a good man to stand in with. A note signed by him was equal to a job any time at the packing-houses; and also he employed a good many men himself, and worked them only eight hours a day, and paid them the highest wages. This gave him many friends—all of whom he had gotten together into the "War-Whoop League," whose club-house you might see just outside of the yards. It was the biggest club-house, and the biggest club, in all Chicago; and they had prize-fights every now and then, and cock-fights and even dog-fights. The policemen in the district all belonged to the league, and instead of suppressing the fights, they sold tickets for them. The man that had taken Jurgis to be naturalized was one of these "Indians,"[3] as they were called; and on election day there would be hundreds of them out, and all with big wads of money in their pockets and free drinks at every saloon in the district. That was another thing, the men said— all the saloon-keepers had to be "Indians," and to put up on demand, otherwise they could not do business on Sundays, nor have any gambling at all. In the same way Scully had all the jobs in the fire department at his disposal, and all the rest of the city graft in the stockyards district; he was building a block of flats somewhere up on Ashland Avenue, and the man who was overseeing it for him was drawing pay as a city inspector of sewers. The city inspector of water-pipes had been dead and buried for over a year, but somebody was still drawing his pay. The city inspector of sidewalks was a bar-keeper at the War-Whoop café—and maybe he could not make it uncomfortable for any tradesman who did not stand in with Scully!

Even the packers were in awe of him, so the men said. It gave them pleasure to believe this, for Scully stood as the people's man, and boasted of it boldly when election day came. The packers had wanted

---

3. "Back of the yards" district was also known as "the Reservation" and Carey's followers as "Indians."

a bridge at Ashland Avenue, but they had not been able to get it till they had seen Scully; and it was the same with "Bubbly Creek," which the city had threatened to make the packers cover over, till Scully had come to their aid. "Bubbly Creek" is an arm of the Chicago River, and forms the southern boundary of the yards; all the drainage of the square mile of packing-houses empties into it, so that it is really a great open sewer a hundred or two feet wide. One long arm of it is blind, and the filth stays there forever and a day. The grease and chemicals that are poured into it undergo all sorts of strange transformations, which are the cause of its name; it is constantly in motion, as if huge fish were feeding in it, or great leviathans disporting themselves in its depths. Bubbles of carbonic acid gas will rise to the surface and burst, and make rings two or three feet wide. Here and there the grease and filth have caked solid, and the creek looks like a bed of lava; chickens walk about on it, feeding, and many times an unwary stranger has started to stroll across, and vanished temporarily. The packers used to leave the creek that way, till every now and then the surface would catch on fire and burn furiously, and the fire department would have to come and put it out. Once, however, an ingenious stranger came and started to gather this filth in scows, to make lard out of; then the packers took the cue, and got out an injunction to stop him, and afterwards gathered it themselves. The banks of "Bubbly Creek" are plastered thick with hairs, and this also the packers gather and clean.

And there were things even stranger than this, according to the gossip of the men. The packers had secret mains, through which they stole billions of gallons of the city's water. The newspapers had been full of this scandal—once there had even been an investigation, and an actual uncovering of the pipes; but nobody had been punished, and the thing went right on. And then there was the condemned meat industry, with its endless horrors. The people of Chicago saw the government inspectors in Packingtown, and they all took that to mean that they were protected from diseased meat; they did not understand that these hundred and sixty-three inspectors had been appointed at the request of the packers, and that they were paid by the United States government to certify that all the diseased meat was kept in the state.[4] They had no authority beyond that; for the inspection of meat to be sold in the city and state the whole force in Packingtown consisted of three henchmen of the local political machine![5] And shortly afterward one of these, a physician, made the

4. In 1890, at the urging of packers worried about decreasing European sales, Congress passed the first act requiring inspection of some exports. In 1891, inspection was extended to other exported meats as well as to some slaughtered for interstate trade.
5. "Rules and Regulations for the Inspection of Live Stock and their Products." United States Department of Agriculture, Bureau of Animal Industries, Order No. 125:—

discovery that the carcasses of steers which had been condemned as tubercular by the government inspectors, and which therefore contained ptomaines, which are deadly poisons, were left upon an open platform and carted away to be sold in the city; and so he insisted that these carcasses be treated with an injection of kerosene—and was ordered to resign the same week![6] So indignant were the packers that they went farther, and compelled the mayor to abolish the whole bureau of inspection; so that since then there has not been even a pretence of any interference with the graft. There was said to be two thousand dollars a week hush-money from the tubercular steers alone; and as much again from the hogs which had died of cholera on the trains, and which you might see any day being loaded into box-cars and hauled away to a place called Globe, in Indiana, where they made a fancy grade of lard.

Jurgis heard of these things little by little, in the gossip of those who were obliged to perpetrate them. It seemed as if every time you met a person from a new department, you heard of new swindles and new crimes. There was, for instance, a Lithuanian who was a cattle-butcher for the plant where Marija had worked, which killed meat for canning only; and to hear this man describe the animals which came to his place would have been worth while for a Dante or a Zola.[7] It seemed that they must have agencies all over the country, to hunt out old and crippled and diseased cattle to be canned. There were cattle which had been fed on "whiskey-malt," the refuse of the breweries, and had become what the men called "steerly"— which means covered with boils. It was a nasty job killing these, for when you plunged your knife into them they would burst and splash foul-smelling stuff into your face; and when a man's sleeves were smeared with blood, and his hands steeped in it, how was he ever to wipe his face, or to clear his eyes so that he could see? It was stuff

---

SECTION 1. Proprietors of slaughterhouses, canning, salting, packing, or rendering establishments engaged in the slaughtering of cattle, sheep, or swine, or the packing of any of their products, *the carcasses or products of which are to become subjects of interstate or foreign commerce*, shall make application to the Secretary of Agriculture for inspection of said animals and their products. . . .

SECTION 15. Such rejected or condemned animals shall at once be removed by the owners from the pens containing animals which have been inspected and found to be free from disease and fit for human food, and *shall be disposed of in accordance with the laws, ordinances, and regulations of the state and municipality in which said rejected or condemned animals are located.* . . .

SECTION 25. A microscopic examination for trichinæ shall be made of all swine products exported to countries requiring such examination. *No microscopic examination will be made of hogs slaughtered for interstate trade, but this examination shall be confined to those intended for the export trade* [Sinclair's note].

6. Dr. W. K. Jacques, formerly head of meat inspection at the stockyards, was forced to resign for insisting on careful scrutiny of meat and condemnation of bad product. He later testified that *The Jungle* was substantially accurate.

7. *Dante* Alighieri (1265–1321), Italian author of *The Divine Comedy*, which recounts the poet's epic journey through Hell, Purgatory, and Heaven; Emile *Zola* (1840–1902), French naturalist author of novels distinguished by detailed descriptions, quasi-scientific precision, and social themes.

such as this that made the "embalmed beef" that had killed several times as many United States soldiers as all the bullets of the Spaniards;[8] only the army beef, besides, was not fresh canned, it was old stuff that had been lying for years in the cellars.

Then one Sunday evening, Jurgis sat puffing his pipe by the kitchen stove, and talking with an old fellow whom Jonas had introduced, and who worked in the canning-rooms at Durham's; and so Jurgis learned a few things about the great and only Durham canned goods, which had become a national institution. They were regular alchemists at Durham's;[9] they advertised a mushroom-catsup, and the men who made it did not know what a mushroom looked like. They advertised "potted chicken,"—and it was like the boarding-house soup of the comic papers, through which a chicken had walked with rubbers on.[1] Perhaps they had a secret process for making chickens chemically—who knows? said Jurgis's friend; the things that went into the mixture were tripe, and the fat of pork, and beef suet, and hearts of beef, and finally the waste ends of veal, when they had any. They put these up in several grades, and sold them at several prices; but the contents of the cans all came out of the same hopper.[2] And then there was "potted game" and "potted grouse," "potted ham," and "devilled ham"—de-vyled, as the men called it. "De-vyled" ham was made out of the waste ends of smoked beef that were too small to be sliced by the machines; and also tripe, dyed with chemicals so that it would not show white; and trimmings of hams and corned beef; and potatoes, skins and all; and finally the hard cartilaginous gullets of beef, after the tongues had been cut out. All this ingenious mixture was ground up and flavored with spices to make it taste like something. Anybody who could invent a new imitation had been sure of a fortune from old Durham, said Jurgis's informant; but it was hard to think of anything new in a place where so many sharp wits had been at work for so long; where men welcomed tuberculosis in the cattle they were feeding, because it made them fatten more quickly; and where they bought up all the old rancid butter left over in the grocery-stores of a continent, and "oxidized" it by a forced-air process, to take away the odor, rechurned it with skim-milk, and sold it in bricks in the cities! Up to a year or two ago it had been the custom to kill horses in the yards—ostensibly for fertilizer; but after long agitation

8. In the Spanish-American War (1898), 280 U.S. soldiers were lost to battle and 2,630 to other causes. Most scandalously, a number of deaths were attributed to the consumption of rations of nauseating canned beef and supposedly fresh meat "embalmed" in boric or salicylic acid.
9. Medieval alchemists sought to change base metals into gold; "alchemy" here refers ironically to the process of turning animal waste products into palatable food.
1. *Rubbers* are thin boots worn over shoes to keep feet dry, so in this joke, "chicken soup" is concocted with little if any poultry. A 1902 federal study had shown that some cans labeled "potted chicken" contained mostly beef or pork.
2. Large tank, usually with a pipe at the bottom for releasing contents.

the newspapers had been able to make the public realize that the
horses were being canned. Now it was against the law to kill horses
in Packingtown, and the law was really complied with—for the present, at any rate. Any day, however, one might see sharp-horned and
shaggy-haired creatures running with the sheep—and yet what a
job you would have to get the public to believe that a good part of
what it buys for lamb and mutton is really goat's flesh!

There was another interesting set of statistics that a person might
have gathered in Packingtown—those of the various afflictions of
the workers. When Jurgis had first inspected the packing-plants with
Szedvilas, he had marvelled while he listened to the tale of all the
things that were made out of the carcasses of animals, and of all
the lesser industries that were maintained there; now he found that
each one of these lesser industries was a separate little inferno, in
its way as horrible as the killing-beds, the source and fountain of
them all. The workers in each of them had their own peculiar diseases. And the wandering visitor might be sceptical about all the
swindles, but he could not be sceptical about those, for the worker
bore the evidence of them about on his own person—generally he
had only to hold out his hand.

There were the men in the pickle-rooms, for instance, where old
Antanas had gotten his death; scarce a one of these that had not some
spot of horror on his person. Let a man so much as scrape his finger
pushing a truck in the pickle-rooms, and he might have a sore that
would put him out of the world; all the joints in his fingers might be
eaten by the acid, one by one. Of the butchers and floorsmen, the
beef-boners and trimmers, and all those who used knives, you could
scarcely find a person who had the use of his thumb; time and time
again the base of it had been slashed, till it was a mere lump of flesh
against which the man pressed the knife to hold it. The hands of
these men would be criss-crossed with cuts, until you could no longer
pretend to count them or to trace them. They would have no nails,—
they had worn them off pulling hides; their knuckles were swollen so
that their fingers spread out like a fan. There were men who worked
in the cooking-rooms, in the midst of steam and sickening odors, by
artificial light; in these rooms the germs of tuberculosis might live for
two years, but the supply was renewed every hour. There were the
beef-luggers, who carried two-hundred-pound quarters into the
refrigerator-cars; a fearful kind of work, that began at four o'clock in
the morning, and that wore out the most powerful men in a few years.
There were those who worked in the chilling-rooms, and whose special disease was rheumatism;[3] the time-limit that a man could work

---

3. General term designating pain in muscles, joints, and bones; includes rheumatoid
   arthritis and, in Sinclair's time, rheumatic fever.

in the chilling-rooms was said to be five years. There were the wool-pluckers, whose hands went to pieces even sooner than the hands of the pickle-men; for the pelts of the sheep had to be painted with acid to loosen the wool, and then the pluckers had to pull out this wool with their bare hands, till the acid had eaten their fingers off. There were those who made the tins for the canned-meat; and their hands, too, were a maze of cuts, and each cut represented a chance for blood-poisoning. Some worked at the stamping-machines, and it was very seldom that one could work long there at the pace that was set, and not give out and forget himself, and have a part of his hand chopped off. There were the "hoisters," as they were called, whose task it was to press the lever which lifted the dead cattle off the floor. They ran along upon a rafter, peering down through the damp and the steam; and as old Durham's architects had not built the killing-room for the convenience of the hoisters, at every few feet they would have to stoop under a beam, say four feet above the one they ran on; which got them into the habit of stooping, so that in a few years they would be walking like chimpanzees. Worst of any, however, were the fertilizer-men, and those who served in the cooking-rooms. These people could not be shown to the visitor,—for the odor of a fertilizer-man would scare any ordinary visitor at a hundred yards, and as for the other men, who worked in tank-rooms full of steam, and in some of which there were open vats near the level of the floor, their peculiar trouble was that they fell into the vats; and when they were fished out, there was never enough of them left to be worth exhibiting,—sometimes they would be overlooked for days, till all but the bones of them had gone out to the world as Durham's Pure Leaf Lard![4]

---

4. In his *Autobiography*, Sinclair claims this is the only passage not confirmed by government inspection.

Chapter X

During the early part of the winter the family had had money enough
to live and a little over to pay their debts with; but when the earnings of Jurgis fell from nine or ten dollars a week to five or six, there
was no longer anything to spare. The winter went, and the spring
came, and found them still living thus from hand to mouth, hanging on day by day, with literally not a month's wages between them
and starvation. Marija was in despair, for there was still no word
about the reopening of the canning-factory, and her savings were
almost entirely gone. She had had to give up all idea of marrying
then; the family could not get along without her—though for that
matter she was likely soon to become a burden even upon them, for
when her money was all gone, they would have to pay back what they
owed her in board. So Jurgis and Ona and Teta Elzbieta would hold
anxious conferences until late at night, trying to figure how they
could manage this too without starving.

Such were the cruel terms upon which their life was possible, that
they might never have nor expect a single instant's respite from worry,
a single instant in which they were not haunted by the thought of
money. They would no sooner escape, as by a miracle, from one difficulty, than a new one would come into view. In addition to all their
physical hardships, there was thus a constant strain upon their minds;
they were harried all day and nearly all night by worry and fear. This
was in truth not living; it was scarcely even existing, and they felt that
it was too little for the price they paid. They were willing to work all
the time; and when people did their best, ought they not to be able to
keep alive?

There seemed never to be an end to the things they had to buy and
to the unforeseen contingencies. Once their water-pipes froze and
burst; and when, in their ignorance, they thawed them out, they had
a terrifying flood in their house. It happened while the men were
away, and poor Elzbieta rushed out into the street screaming for
help, for she did not even know whether the flood could be stopped,
or whether they were ruined for life. It was nearly as bad as the latter,
they found in the end, for the plumber charged them seventy-five
cents an hour, and seventy-five cents for another man who had stood
and watched him, and included all the time the two had been going
and coming, and also a charge for all sorts of material and extras.
And then again, when they went to pay their January's instalment on
the house, the agent terrified them by asking them if they had had the
insurance attended to yet. In answer to their inquiry he showed them
a clause in the deed which provided that they were to keep the house
insured for one thousand dollars, as soon as the present policy ran

out, which would happen in a few days. Poor Elzbieta, upon whom again fell the blow, demanded how much it would cost them. Seven dollars, the man said; and that night came Jurgis, grim and determined, requesting that the agent would be good enough to inform him, once for all, as to all the expenses they were liable for. The deed was signed now, he said, with sarcasm proper to the new way of life he had learned—the deed was signed, and so the agent had no longer anything to gain by keeping quiet. And Jurgis looked the fellow squarely in the eye, and so he did not waste any time in conventional protests, but read him the deed. They would have to renew the insurance every year; they would have to pay the taxes, about ten dollars a year; they would have to pay the water-tax, about six dollars a year— (Jurgis silently resolved to shut off the hydrant). This, besides the interest and the monthly instalments, would be all—unless by chance the city should happen to decide to put in a sewer or to lay a sidewalk. Yes, said the agent, they would have to have these, whether they wanted them or not, if the city said so. The sewer would cost them about twenty-two dollars, and the sidewalk fifteen if it were wood, twenty-five if it were cement.

So Jurgis went home again; it was a relief to know the worst, at any rate, so that he could no more be surprised by fresh demands. He saw now how they had been plundered; but they were in for it, there was no turning back. They could only go on and make the fight and win—for defeat was a thing that could not even be thought of.

When the springtime came, they were delivered from the dreadful cold, and that was a great deal; but in addition they had counted on the money they would not have to pay for coal—and it was just at this time that Marija's board began to fail. Then, too, the warm weather brought trials of its own; each season had its trials, as they found. In the spring there were cold rains, that turned the streets into canals and bogs; the mud would be so deep that wagons would sink up to the hubs, so that half a dozen horses could not move them. Then, of course, it was impossible for any one to get to work with dry feet; and this was bad for men that were poorly clad and shod, and still worse for women and children. Later came midsummer, with the stifling heat, when the dingy killing-beds of Durham's became a very purgatory; one time, in a single day, three men fell dead from sunstroke. All day long the rivers of hot blood poured forth, until, with the sun beating down, and the air motionless, the stench was enough to knock a man over; all the old smells of a generation would be drawn out by this heat—for there was never any washing of the walls and rafters and pillars, and they were caked with the filth of a lifetime. The men who worked on the killing-beds would come to reek with foulness, so that you could smell one of them fifty feet away; there was simply no such thing as keeping decent, the most careful man gave it up in the end, and wallowed in uncleanness. There was not even a place where a man could wash his hands, and the men ate as much raw blood as food at dinner-time. When they were at work they could not even wipe off their faces—they were as helpless as newly born babes in that respect; and it may seem like a small matter, but when the sweat began to run down their necks and tickle them, or a fly to bother them, it was a torture like being burned alive. Whether it was the slaughter-houses or the dumps that were responsible, one could not say, but with the hot weather there descended upon Packingtown a veritable Egyptian plague of flies;[1] there could be no describing this—the houses would be black with them. There was no escaping; you might provide all your doors and windows with screens, but their buzzing outside would be like the swarming of bees, and whenever you opened the door they would rush in as if a storm of wind were driving them.

Perhaps the summer-time suggests to you thoughts of the country, visions of green fields and mountains and sparkling lakes. It had no such suggestion for the people in the yards. The great packing-machine ground on remorselessly, without thinking of green fields; and the men and women and children who were part of it never saw any green thing, not even a flower. Four or five miles to the east of them lay the blue waters of Lake Michigan; but for all the good it did them it might have been as far away as the Pacific Ocean. They had only Sundays, and then they were too tired to walk. They were tied to the great packing-machine, and tied to it for life. The managers and superintendents and clerks of Packingtown were all recruited from another class, and never from the workers; they scorned the workers, the very meanest of them. A poor devil of a bookkeeper who had been working in Durham's for twenty years at a salary of six dollars a week, and might work there for twenty more and do no better, would yet consider himself a gentleman, as far removed as the poles from the most skilled worker on the killing-beds; he would dress differently, and live in another part of the town, and come to work at a different hour of the day, and in every way make sure that he never rubbed elbows with a laboring-man. Perhaps this was due to the repulsiveness of the work; at any rate, the people who worked with their hands were a class apart, and were made to feel it.

In the late spring the canning-factory started up again, and so once more Marija was heard to sing, and the love-music of Tamoszius took on a less melancholy tone. It was not for long, however; for a month or two later a dreadful calamity fell upon Marija. Just one year and three days after she had begun work as a can-painter, she lost her job.

1. In Exodus 7:11, God punishes Egypt with a series of plagues for keeping the Israelites in bondage.

It was a long story. Marija insisted that it was because of her activity in the union. The packers, of course, had spies in all the unions, and in addition they made a practice of buying up a certain number of the union officials, as many as they thought they needed. So every week they received reports as to what was going on, and often they knew things before the members of the union knew them. Any one who was considered to be dangerous by them would find that he was not a favorite with his boss; and Marija had been a great hand for going after the foreign people and preaching to them. However that might be, the known facts were that a few weeks before the factory closed, Marija had been cheated out of her pay for three hundred cans. The girls worked at a long table, and behind them walked a woman with pencil and notebook, keeping count of the number they finished. This woman was, of course, only human, and sometimes made mistakes; when this happened, there was no redress—if on Saturday you got less money than you had earned, you had to make the best of it. But Marija did not understand this, and made a disturbance. Marija's disturbances did not mean anything, and while she had known only Lithuanian and Polish, they had done no harm, for people only laughed at her and made her cry. But now Marija was able to call names in English, and so she got the woman who made the mistake to disliking her. Probably, as Marija claimed, she made mistakes on purpose after that; at any rate, she made them, and the third time it happened Marija went on the war-path and took the matter first to the forelady, and when she got no satisfaction there, to the superintendent. This was unheard-of presumption, but the superintendent said he would see about it, which Marija took to mean that she was going to get her money; after waiting three days, she went to see the superintendent again. This time the man frowned, and said that he had not had time to attend to it; and when Marija, against the advice and warning of every one, tried it once more, he ordered her back to her work in a passion. Just how things happened after that Marija was not sure, but that afternoon the forelady told her that her services would not be any longer required. Poor Marija could not have been more dumfounded had the woman knocked her over the head; at first she could not believe what she heard, and then she grew furious and swore that she would come anyway, that her place belonged to her. In the end she sat down in the middle of the floor and wept and wailed.

It was a cruel lesson; but then Marija was headstrong—she should have listened to those who had had experience. The next time she would know her place, as the forelady expressed it; and so Marija went out, and the family faced the problem of an existence again.

It was especially hard this time, for Ona was to be confined before long,[2] and Jurgis was trying hard to save up money for this. He had heard dreadful stories of the midwives, who grow as thick as fleas in Packingtown; and he had made up his mind that Ona must have a man-doctor. Jurgis could be very obstinate when he wanted to, and he was in this case, much to the dismay of the women, who felt that a man-doctor was an impropriety, and that the matter really belonged to them. The cheapest doctor they could find would charge them fifteen dollars, and perhaps more when the bill came in; and here was Jurgis, declaring that he would pay it, even if he had to stop eating in the meantime!

Marija had only about twenty-five dollars left. Day after day she wandered about the yards begging a job, but this time without hope of finding it. Marija could do the work of an able-bodied man, when she was cheerful, but discouragement wore her out easily, and she would come home at night a pitiable object. She learned her lesson this time, poor creature; she learned it ten times over. All the family learned it along with her—that when you have once got a job in Packingtown, you hang on to it, come what will.

Four weeks Marija hunted, and half of a fifth week. Of course she stopped paying her dues to the union. She lost all interest in the union, and cursed herself for a fool that she had ever been dragged into one. She had about made up her mind that she was a lost soul, when somebody told her of an opening, and she went and got a place as a "beef-trimmer."[3] She got this because the boss saw that she had the muscles of a man, and so he discharged a man and put Marija to do his work, paying her a little more than half what he had been paying before.

When she first came to Packingtown, Marija would have scorned such work as this. She was in another canning-factory, and her work was to trim the meat of those diseased cattle that Jurgis had been told about not long before. She was shut up in one of the rooms where the people seldom saw the daylight; beneath her were the chilling-rooms, where the meat was frozen, and above her were the cooking-rooms; and so she stood on an ice-cold floor, while her head was often so hot that she could scarcely breathe. Trimming beef off the bones by the hundred-weight, while standing up from early morning till late at night with heavy boots on and the floor always damp and full of puddles, liable to be thrown out of work indefinitely

2. Ona is "confined" because she is in late pregnancy. Although the professionalization of medicine had elevated doctors practicing obstetrics and gynecology (almost all of them men) over midwives, these traditional attendants at the birth process remained common among working classes, the urban poor, and rural and immigrant populations.
3. Trimmers worked at various specialized tasks, including trimming bruised flesh or removing offal.

because of a slackening in the trade, liable again to be kept over-time in rush seasons, and be worked till she trembled in every nerve and lost her grip on her slimy knife, and gave herself a poisoned wound—that was the new life that unfolded itself before Marija. But because Marija was a human horse she merely laughed and went at it; it would enable her to pay her board again, and keep the family going. And as for Tamoszius—well, they had waited a long time, and they could wait a little longer. They could not possibly get along upon his wages alone, and the family could not live without hers. He could come and visit her, and sit in the kitchen and hold her hand, and he must manage to be content with that. But day by day the music of Tamoszius's violin became more passionate and heart-breaking; and Marija would sit with her hands clasped and her cheeks wet and all her body a-tremble, hearing in the wailing melodies the voices of the unborn generations which cried out in her for life.

Marija's lesson came just in time to save Ona from a similar fate. Ona, too, was dissatisfied with her place, and had far more reason than Marija. She did not tell half of her story at home, because she saw it was a torment to Jurgis, and she was afraid of what he might do. For a long time Ona had seen that Miss Henderson, the fore-lady in her department, did not like her. At first she thought it was the old-time mistake she had made in asking for a holiday to get mar-ried. Then she concluded it must be because she did not give the forelady a present occasionally—she was the kind that took presents from the girls, Ona learned, and made all sorts of discriminations in favor of those who gave them. In the end, however, Ona discov-ered that it was even worse than that. Miss Henderson was a new-comer, and it was some time before rumor made her out; but finally it transpired that she was a kept-woman, the former mistress of the superintendent of a department in the same building. He had put her there to keep her quiet, it seemed—and that not altogether with success, for once or twice they had been heard quarrelling. She had the temper of a hyena, and soon the place she ran was a witch's cal-dron. There were some of the girls who were of her own sort, who were willing to toady to her and flatter her; and these would carry tales about the rest, and so the furies[4] were unchained in the place. Worse than this, the woman lived in a bawdy-house[5] down-town, with a coarse, red-faced Irishman named Connor, who was the boss of the loading-gang outside, and would make free with the girls as they went to and from their work. In the slack seasons some of them would go with Miss Henderson to this house down-town—in fact,

4. In Greek mythology, spirits of punishment.
5. House of prostitution.

it would not be too much to say that she managed her department at Brown's in conjunction with it. Sometimes women from the house would be given places alongside of decent girls, and after other decent girls had been turned off to make room for them. When you worked in this woman's department the house down-town was never out of your thoughts all day—there were always whiffs of it to be caught, like the odor of the Packingtown rendering-plants at night, when the wind shifted suddenly. There would be stories about it going the rounds; the girls opposite you would be telling them and winking at you. In such a place Ona would not have stayed a day, but for starvation; and, as it was, she was never sure that she could stay the next day. She understood now that the real reason that Miss Henderson hated her was that she was a decent married girl; and she knew that the talebearers and the toadies hated her for the same reason, and were doing their best to make her life miserable.

But there was no place a girl could go in Packingtown, if she was particular about things of this sort; there was no place in it where a prostitute could not get along better than a decent girl. Here was a population, low-class and mostly foreign, hanging always on the verge of starvation, and dependent for its opportunities of life upon the whim of men every bit as brutal and unscrupulous as the old-time slave-drivers; under such circumstances immorality was exactly as inevitable, and as prevalent, as it was under the system of chattel slavery. Things that were quite unspeakable went on there in the packing-houses all the time, and were taken for granted by every-body; only they did not show, as in the old slavery times, because there was no difference in color between master and slave.

One morning Ona stayed home, and Jurgis had the man-doctor, according to his whim, and she was safely delivered of a fine baby. It was an enormous big boy, and Ona was such a tiny creature herself, that it seemed quite incredible. Jurgis would stand and gaze at the stranger by the hour, unable to believe that it had really happened.

The coming of this boy was a decisive event with Jurgis. It made him irrevocably a family man; it killed the last lingering impulse that he might have had to go out in the evenings and sit and talk with the men in the saloons. There was nothing he cared for now so much as to sit and look at the baby. This was very curious, for Jurgis had never been interested in babies before. But then, this was a very unusual sort of a baby. He had the brightest little black eyes, and little black ringlets all over his head; he was the living image of his father, everybody said—and Jurgis found this a fascinating circum-stance. It was sufficiently perplexing that this tiny mite of life should have come into the world at all in the manner that it had; that it should have come with a comical imitation of its father's nose was simply uncanny.

Perhaps, Jurgis thought, this was intended to signify that it was his baby; that it was his and Ona's, to care for all its life. Jurgis had never possessed anything nearly so interesting—a baby was, when you came to think about it, assuredly a marvellous possession. It would grow up to be a man, a human soul, with a personality all its own, a will of its own! Such thoughts would keep haunting Jurgis, filling him with all sorts of strange and almost painful excitements. He was wonderfully proud of little Antanas; he was curious about all the details of him—the washing and the dressing and the eating and the sleeping of him, and asked all sorts of absurd questions. It took him quite a while to get over his alarm at the incredible short-ness of the little creature's legs.

Jurgis had, alas, very little time to see his baby; he never felt the chains about him more than just then. When he came home at night, the baby would be asleep, and it would be the merest chance if he awoke before Jurgis had to go to sleep himself. Then in the morning there was no time to look at him, so really the only chance the father had was on Sundays. This was more cruel yet for Ona, who ought to have stayed home and nursed him, the doctor said, for her own health as well as the baby's; but Ona had to go to work, and leave him for Teta Elzbieta to feed upon the pale blue poison that was called milk at the corner-grocery. Ona's confinement lost her only a week's wages—she would go to the factory the second Monday, and the best that Jurgis could persuade her was to ride in the car, and let him run along behind and help her to Brown's when she alighted. After that it would be all right, said Ona, it was no strain sitting still sewing hams all day; and if she waited longer she might find that her dreadful forelady had put some one else in her place. That would be a greater calamity than ever now, Ona continued, on account of the baby. They would all have to work harder now on his account. It was such a responsibility—they must not have the baby grow up to suffer as they had. And this indeed had been the first thing that Jur-gis had thought of himself—he had clenched his hands and braced himself anew for the struggle, for the sake of that tiny mite of human possibility.

And so Ona went back to Brown's and saved her place and a week's wages; and so she gave herself some one of the thousand ailments that women group under the title of "womb-trouble," and was never again a well person as long as she lived. It is difficult to convey in words all that this meant to Ona; it seemed such a slight offence, and the punishment was so out of all proportion, that neither she nor any one else ever connected the two. "Womb-trouble" to Ona did not mean a specialist's diagnosis, and a course of treatment, and perhaps an operation or two; it meant simply headaches and pains in the back, and depression and heartsickness, and neuralgia[6] when she had to go to work in the rain. The great majority of the women who worked in Packingtown suffered in the same way, and from the same cause, so it was not deemed a thing to see the doctor about; instead Ona would try patent medicines,[7] one after another, as her friends told her about them. As these all contained alcohol, or some other stimulant, she found that they all did her good while she took them; and so she was always chasing the phantom of good health, and losing it because she was too poor to continue.

6. Pain caused by compression or disease of the nerve.
7. A misnomer in that such proprietary remedies were not under patent, which would have required disclosure of their contents. Some nostrums contained such dangerous substances as morphine, alcohol, and opium; others contained innocuous ingredients; and most made fraudulent claims about their restorative powers.

Chapter XI

During the summer the packing-houses were in full activity again, and Jurgis made more money. He did not make so much, however, as he had the previous summer, for the packers took on more hands. There were new men every week, it seemed—it was a regular system; and this number they would keep over to the next slack season, so that every one would have less than ever. Sooner or later, by this plan, they would have all the floating labor of Chicago trained to do their work. And how very cunning a trick was that! The men were to teach new hands, who would some day come and break their strike; and meantime they were kept so poor that they could not prepare for the trial!

But let no one suppose that this superfluity of employees meant easier work for any one! On the contrary, the speeding-up seemed to be growing more savage all the time; they were continually inventing new devices to crowd the work on—it was for all the world like the thumb-screw of the mediæval torture-chamber. They would get new pace-makers and pay them more; they would drive the men on with new machinery—it was said that in the hog-killing rooms the speed at which the hogs moved was determined by clock-work, and that it was increased a little every day. In piece-work they would reduce the time, requiring the same work in a shorter time, and paying the same wages; and then, after the workers had accustomed themselves to this new speed, they would reduce the rate of payment to correspond with the reduction in time![1] They had done this so often in the canning establishments that the girls were fairly desperate; their wages had gone down by a full third in the past two years, and a storm of discontent was brewing that was likely to break any day. Only a month after Marija had become a beef-trimmer the canning-factory that she had left posted a cut that would divide the girls' earnings almost squarely in half; and so great was the indignation at this that they marched out without even a parley, and organized in the street outside. One of the girls had read somewhere that a red flag was the proper symbol for oppressed workers,[2] and so they mounted one, and paraded all about the yards, yelling with rage. A new union was the result of this outburst, but the impromptu strike went to pieces in three days, owing to the rush of new labor. At the end of it the girl who had carried the red flag went down-town and got a position in a great department store, at a salary of two dollars and a half a week.

1. Practices such as this suggest why unions opposed the piecework system.
2. International symbol of socialist revolution. Here Sinclair draws details from a 1900 strike of Irish-American women over cuts in labor rates.

Jurgis and Ona heard these stories with dismay, for there was no telling when their own time might come. Once or twice there had been rumors that one of the big houses was going to cut its unskilled men to fifteen cents an hour, and Jurgis knew that if this was done, his turn would come soon. He had learned by this time that Packingtown was really not a number of firms at all, but one great firm, the Beef Trust. And every week the managers of it got together and compared notes, and there was one scale for all the workers in the yards and one standard of efficiency. Jurgis was told that they also fixed the price they would pay for beef on the hoof and the price of all dressed meat in the country;[3] but that was something he did not understand or care about.

The only one who was not afraid of a cut was Marija, who congratulated herself, somewhat naïvely, that there had been one in her place only a short time before she came. Marija was getting to be a skilled beef-trimmer, and was mounting to the heights again. During the summer and fall Jurgis and Ona managed to pay her back the last penny they owed her, and so she began to have a bank account. Tamoszius had a bank account also, and they ran a race, and began to figure upon household expenses once more.

The possession of vast wealth entails cares and responsibilities, however, as poor Marija found out. She had taken the advice of a friend and invested her savings in a bank on Ashland Avenue. Of course she knew nothing about it, except that it was big and imposing—what possible chance has a poor foreign working-girl to understand the banking business, as it is conducted in this land of frenzied finance?[4] So Marija lived in continual dread lest something should happen to her bank, and would go out of her way mornings to make sure that it was still there. Her principal thought was of fire, for she had deposited her money in bills, and was afraid that if they were burned up the bank would not give her any others. Jurgis made fun of her for this, for he was a man and was proud of his superior

---

3. Following the "pool" and superseded by the "holding company," the "trust" was an organizational structure that, technically, assigned stock of competing firms to a group of trustees who functioned as board of directors; practically, it allowed one firm or alliance to control an industry. When the 1890 Sherman Anti-Trust Act outlawed trusts as in restraint of trade, similar organizations remained, often incorporated under the lax laws of New Jersey or Delaware. After a pool of Chicago meatpackers was disbanded under a Department of Justice injunction in May 1902, the National Packing Company was incorporated in 1903, with Swift owning 46 percent, Armour 40 percent, and Morris 14 percent of the stock. Actually a holding company (in which one company holds stock in another, thus maintaining discreet product lines and corporate identities), the National Packing Company was reviled as the "Beef Trust," for "trust" remained the commonplace term for any oligopoly or monopoly. Chicago packers colluded in setting prices for living animals ("on the hoof") and butchered ("dressed") meat, as well as workers' wages.
4. Boston financier Thomas W. Lawson (1857–1925) published a series of muckraking articles about insurance and stock market fraud, "Frenzied Finance" (1904–05), in *Everybody's Magazine*. He later published the series as the book *Frenzied Finance: The Crime of Amalgamated* (1906).

knowledge, telling her that the bank had fire-proof vaults, and all its millions of dollars hidden safely away in them.

However, one morning Marija took her usual detour, and, to her horror and dismay, saw a crowd of people in front of the bank, filling the avenue solid for half a block. All the blood went out of her face for terror. She broke into a run, shouting to the people to ask what was the matter, but not stopping to hear what they answered, till she had come to where the throng was so dense that she could no longer advance. There was a "run on the bank,"[5] they told her then, but she did not know what that was, and turned from one person to another, trying in an agony of fear to make out what they meant. Had something gone wrong with the bank? Nobody was sure, but they thought so. Couldn't she get her money? There was no telling; the people were afraid not, and they were all trying to get it. It was too early yet to tell anything—the bank would not open for nearly three hours. So in a frenzy of despair Marija began to claw her way toward the doors of this building, through a throng of men, women, and children, all as excited as herself. It was a scene of wild confusion, women shrieking and wringing their hands and fainting, and men fighting and trampling down everything in their way. In the midst of the mêlée Marija recollected that she did not have her bank-book, and could not get her money anyway, so she fought her way out and started on a run for home. This was fortunate for her, for a few minutes later the police-reserves arrived.

In half an hour Marija was back, Teta Elzbieta with her, both of them breathless with running and sick with fear. The crowd was now formed in a line, extending for several blocks, with half a hundred policemen keeping guard, and so there was nothing for them to do but to take their places at the end of it. At nine o'clock the bank opened and began to pay the waiting throng; but then, what good did that do Marija, who saw three thousand people before her— enough to take out the last penny of a dozen banks?

To make matters worse a drizzling rain came up, and soaked them to the skin; yet all the morning they stood there, creeping slowly toward the goal—all the afternoon they stood there, heart-sick, seeing that the hour of closing was coming, and that they were going to be left out. Marija made up her mind that, come what might, she would stay there and keep her place; but as nearly all did the same, all through the long, cold night, she got very little closer to the bank for that. Toward evening Jurgis came; he had heard the story from the children, and he brought some food and dry wraps, which made it a little easier.

5. Occurring when depositors rushed to withdraw money, behavior that could exacerbate the very financial panic that they feared.

The next morning, before daybreak, came a bigger crowd than ever, and more policemen from down-town. Marija held on like grim death, and toward afternoon she got into the bank and got her money—all in big silver dollars, a handkerchief full. When she had once got her hands on them her fear vanished, and she wanted to put them back again; but the man at the window was savage, and said that the bank would receive no more deposits from those who had taken part in the run. So Marija was forced to take her dollars home with her, watching to right and left, expecting every instant that some one would try to rob her; and when she got home she was not much better off. Until she could find another bank there was nothing to do but sew them up in her clothes, and so Marija went about for a week or more, loaded down with bullion,[6] and afraid to cross the street in front of the house, because Jurgis told her she would sink out of sight in the mud. Weighted this way she made her way to the yards, again in fear, this time to see if she had lost her place; but fortunately about ten per cent of the working-people of Packingtown had been depositors in that bank, and it was not convenient to discharge that many at once. The cause of the panic had been the attempt of a policeman to arrest a drunken man in a saloon next door, which had drawn a crowd at the hour the people were on their way to work, and so started the "run."

About this time Jurgis and Ona also began a bank-account. Besides having paid Jonas and Marija, they had almost paid for their furniture, and could have that little sum to count on. So long as each of them could bring home nine or ten dollars a week, they were able to get along finely. Also election day came round again, and Jurgis made half a week's wages out of that, all net profit. It was a very close election that year, and the echoes of the battle reached even to Packingtown. The two rival sets of grafters hired halls and set off fireworks and made speeches, to try to get the people interested in the matter. Although Jurgis did not understand it all, he knew enough by this time to realize that it was not supposed to be right to sell your vote. However, as every one did it, and his refusal to join would not have made the slightest difference in the results, the idea of refusing would have seemed absurd, had it ever come into his head.

Now chill winds and shortening days began to warn them that the winter was coming again. It seemed as if the respite had been too short—they had not had time enough to get ready for it; but still it came, inexorably, and the hunted look began to come back into the eyes of little Stanislovas. The prospect struck fear to the heart of Jurgis also, for he knew that Ona was not fit to face the cold and the

6. Precious metal, in this case silver, usually bars or ingots.

snow-drifts this year. And suppose that some day when a blizzard struck them and the cars were not running, Ona should have to give it up, and should come the next day to find that her place had been given to some one who lived nearer and could be depended on?

It was the week before Christmas that the first great storm came, and then the soul of Jurgis rose up within him like a sleeping lion. There were four days that the Ashland Avenue cars were stalled, and in those days, for the first time in his life, Jurgis knew what it was to be really opposed. He had faced difficulties before, but they had been child's play; now there was a death struggle, and all the furies were unchained within him. The first morning they set out two hours before dawn, Ona wrapped all in blankets and tossed upon his shoulder like a sack of meal, and the little boy, bundled nearly out of sight, hanging by his coat-tails. There was a raging blast beating in his face, and the thermometer stood below zero; the snow was never short of his knees, and in some of the drifts it was nearly up to his armpits. It would catch his feet and try to trip him; it would build itself into a wall before him to beat him back; and he would fling himself into it, plunging like a wounded buffalo, puffing and snorting in rage. So foot by foot he drove his way, and when at last he came to Durham's he was staggering and almost blind, and leaned against a pillar, gasping, and thanking God that the cattle came late to the killing-beds that day. In the evening the same thing had to be done again; and because Jurgis could not tell what hour of the night he would get off, he got a saloon-keeper to let Ona sit and wait for him in a corner. Once it was eleven o'clock at night, and black as the pit, but still they got home.

That blizzard knocked many a man out, for the crowd outside begging for work was never greater, and the packers would not wait long for any one. When it was over, the soul of Jurgis was a song, for he had met the enemy and conquered, and felt himself the master of his fate.—So it might be with some monarch of the forest that has vanquished his foes in fair fight, and then falls into some cowardly trap in the night-time.

A time of peril on the killing-beds was when a steer broke loose. Sometimes, in the haste of speeding-up, they would dump one of the animals out on the floor before it was fully stunned, and it would get upon its feet and run amuck. Then there would be a yell of warning—the men would drop everything and dash for the nearest pillar, slipping here and there on the floor, and tumbling over each other. This was bad enough in the summer, when a man could see; in winter-time it was enough to make your hair stand up, for the room would be so full of steam that you could not make anything out five feet in front of you. To be sure, the steer was generally blind and frantic, and not especially bent on hurting any one; but think of the chances of running upon a knife, while nearly every man had one in his hand! And then, to cap the climax, the floor-boss would come rushing up with a rifle and begin blazing away!

It was in one of these mêlées that Jurgis fell into his trap. That is the only word to describe it; it was so cruel, and so utterly not to be foreseen. At first he hardly noticed it, it was such a slight accident—simply that in leaping out of the way he turned his ankle. There was a twinge of pain, but Jurgis was used to pain, and did not coddle himself. When he came to walk home, however, he realized that it was hurting him a great deal; and in the morning his ankle was swollen out nearly double its size, and he could not get his foot into his shoe. Still, even then, he did nothing more than swear a little, and wrapped his foot in old rags, and hobbled out to take the car. It chanced to be a rush day at Durham's,[7] and all the long morning he limped about with his aching foot; by noon-time the pain was so great that it made him faint, and after a couple of hours in the afternoon he was fairly beaten, and had to tell the boss. They sent for the company doctor, and he examined the foot and told Jurgis to go home to bed, adding that he had probably laid himself up for months by his folly. The injury was not one that Durham and Company could be held responsible for, and so that was all there was to it, so far as the doctor was concerned.[8]

Jurgis got home somehow, scarcely able to see for the pain, and with an awful terror in his soul. Elzbieta helped him into bed and bandaged his injured foot with cold water, and tried hard not to let him see her dismay; when the rest came home at night she met them outside and told them, and they, too, put on a cheerful face, saying it would only be for a week or two, and that they would pull him through.

When they had gotten him to sleep, however, they sat by the kitchen fire and talked it over in frightened whispers. They were in for a siege, that was plainly to be seen. Jurgis had only about sixty dollars in the bank, and the slack season was upon them. Both Jonas and Marija might soon be earning no more than enough to pay their board, and besides that there were only the wages of Ona and the pittance of the little boy. There was the rent to pay, and still some on the furniture; there was the insurance just due, and every month there was sack after sack of coal. It was January, midwinter, an awful time to have to face privation. Deep snows would come again, and who would carry Ona to her work now? She might lose her place—she

---

7. Buyers for large firms often waited until desperate sellers would sell livestock at a loss; workers then had to rush to prepare meats.
8. Despite its inferior working conditions and more frequent accidents, the United States lacked virtually any federal provisions for injured workers such as were extensive in European nations.

was almost certain to lose it. And then little Stanislovas began to
whimper—who would take care of him?

It was dreadful that an accident of this sort, that no man can help,
should have meant such suffering. The bitterness of it was the daily
food and drink of Jurgis. It was of no use for them to try to deceive
him; he knew as much about the situation as they did, and he knew
that the family might literally starve to death. The worry of it fairly
ate him up—he began to look haggard the first two or three days of
it. In truth, it was almost maddening for a strong man like him, a
fighter, to have to lie there helpless on his back. It was for all the
world the old story of Prometheus bound.[9] As Jurgis lay on his bed,
hour after hour, there came to him emotions that he had never
known before. Before this he had met life with a welcome—it had
its trials, but none that a man could not face. But now, in the night-
time, when he lay tossing about, there would come stalking into his
chamber a grisly phantom, the sight of which made his flesh to curl
and his hair to bristle up. It was like seeing the world fall away from
underneath his feet; like plunging down into a bottomless abyss, into
yawning caverns of despair. It might be true, then, after all, what
others had told him about life, that the best powers of a man might
not be equal to it! It might be true that, strive as he would, toil as
he would, he might fail, and go down and be destroyed! The thought
of this was like an icy hand at his heart; the thought that here, in
this ghastly home of all horror, he and all those who were dear to
him might lie and perish of starvation and cold, and there would be
no ear to hear their cry, no hand to help them! It was true, it was
true,—that here in this huge city, with its stores of heaped-up wealth,
human creatures might be hunted down and destroyed by the wild-
beast powers of nature, just as truly as ever they were in the days of
the cave-men!

Ona was now making about thirty dollars a month, and Stanislovas about thirteen. To add to this there was the board of Jonas and
Marija, about forty-five dollars. Deducting from this the rent,
interest, and instalments on the furniture, they had left sixty dollars, and deducting the coal, they had fifty. They did without everything that human beings could do without; they went in old and
ragged clothing, that left them at the mercy of the cold, and when
the children's shoes wore out, they tied them up with string. Half

9. In Greek mythology, Prometheus the titan incurs the anger of Zeus, the chief god, by
    championing humankind, giving them fire and the arts, for which he is bound to a
    mountain in punishment. The figure appears in many literary works, including the
    ancient Greek playwright Aeschylus's tragedy *Prometheus Bound* and the English
    Romantic poet Percy Bysshe Shelley's poem "Prometheus Unbound," which Sinclair
    called "the distilled essence of revolt" in *Mammonart* (1925).

invalid as she was, Ona would do herself harm by walking in the rain and cold when she ought to have ridden; they bought literally nothing but food—and still they could not keep alive on fifty dollars a month. They might have done it, if only they could have gotten pure food, and at fair prices; or if only they had known what to get—if they had not been so pitifully ignorant! But they had come to a new country, where everything was different, including the food. They had always been accustomed to eat a great deal of smoked sausage, and how could they know that what they bought in America was not the same—that its color was made by chemicals, and its smoky flavor by more chemicals, and that it was full of "potato-flour" besides? Potato-flour is the waste of potato after the starch and alcohol have been extracted; it has no more food value than so much wood, and as its use as a food adulterant is a penal offence in Europe, thousands of tons of it are shipped to America every year. It was amazing what quantities of food such as this were needed every day, by eleven hungry persons. A dollar sixty-five a day was simply not enough to feed them, and there was no use trying; and so each week they made an inroad upon the pitiful little bank-account that Ona had begun. Because the account was in her name, it was possible for her to keep this a secret from her husband, and to keep the heart-sickness of it for her own.

It would have been better if Jurgis had been really ill; if he had not been able to think. For he had no resources such as most invalids have; all he could do was to lie there and toss about from side to side. Now and then he would break into cursing, regardless of everything; and now and then his impatience would get the better of him, and he would try to get up, and poor Teta Elzbieta would have to plead with him in frenzy. Elzbieta was all alone with him the greater part of the time. She would sit and smooth his forehead by the hour, and talk to him and try to make him forget. Sometimes it would be too cold for the children to go to school, and they would have to play in the kitchen, where Jurgis was, because it was the only room that was half warm. These were dreadful times, for Jurgis would get as cross as any bear; he was scarcely to be blamed, for he had enough to worry him, and it was hard when he was trying to take a nap to be kept awake by noisy and peevish children.

Elzbieta's only resource in those times was little Antanas; indeed, it would be hard to say how they could have gotten along at all if it had not been for little Antanas. It was the one consolation of Jurgis's long imprisonment that now he had time to look at his baby. Teta Elzbieta would put the clothes-basket in which the baby slept alongside of his mattress, and Jurgis would lie upon one elbow and watch him by the hour, imagining things. Then little Antanas would open his eyes—he was beginning to take notice of things now; and he would smile—how he would smile! So Jurgis would begin to forget and be happy, because he was in a world where there was a thing so beautiful as the smile of little Antanas, and because such a world could not but be good at the heart of it. He looked more like his father every hour, Elzbieta would say, and said it many times a day, because she saw that it pleased Jurgis; the poor little terror-stricken woman was planning all day and all night to soothe the prisoned giant who was intrusted to her care. Jurgis, who knew nothing about the age-long and everlasting hypocrisy of woman, would take the bait and grin with delight; and then he would hold his finger in front of little Antanas's eyes, and move it this way and that, and laugh with glee to see the baby follow it. There is no pet quite so fascinating as a baby; he would look into Jurgis's face with such uncanny seriousness, and Jurgis would start and cry: "*Palauk!* Look, Muma, he knows his papa! He does, he does! *Tu mano szirdele,*[1] the little rascal!"

---

1. "Wait! . . . You are my dear one."

Chapter XII

For three weeks after his injury Jurgis never got up from bed. It was a very obstinate sprain; the swelling would not go down, and the pain still continued. At the end of that time, however, he could contain himself no longer, and began trying to walk a little every day, laboring to persuade himself that he was better. No arguments could stop him, and three or four days later he declared that he was going back to work. He limped to the cars and got to Brown's, where he found that the boss had kept his place—that is, was willing to turn out into the snow the poor devil he had hired in the meantime. Every now and then the pain would force Jurgis to stop work, but he stuck it out till nearly an hour before closing. Then he was forced to acknowledge that he could not go on without fainting; it almost broke his heart to do it, and he stood leaning against a pillar and weeping like a child. Two of the men had to help him to the car, and when he got out he had to sit down and wait in the snow till some one came along.

So they put him to bed again, and sent for the doctor, as they ought to have done in the beginning. It transpired that he had twisted a tendon out of place, and could never have gotten well without attention. Then he gripped the sides of the bed, and shut his teeth together, and turned white with agony, while the doctor pulled and wrenched away at his swollen ankle. When finally the doctor left, he told him that he would have to lie quiet for two months, and that if he went to work before that time he might lame himself for life.

Three days later there came another heavy snow-storm, and Jonas and Marija and Ona and little Stanislovas all set out together, an hour before daybreak, to try to get to the yards. About noon the last two came back, the boy screaming with pain. His fingers were all frosted, it seemed. They had had to give up trying to get to the yards, and had nearly perished in a drift. All that they knew how to do was to hold the frozen fingers near the fire, and so little Stanislovas spent most of the day dancing about in horrible agony, till Jurgis flew into a passion of nervous rage and swore like a madman, declaring that he would kill him if he did not stop. All that day and night the family was half-crazed with fear that Ona and the boy had lost their places; and in the morning they set out earlier than ever, after the little fellow had been beaten with a stick by Jurgis. There could be no trifling in a case like this, it was a matter of life and death; little Stanislovas could not be expected to realise that he might a great deal better freeze in the snow-drift than lose his job at the lard-machine. Ona was quite certain that she would find her place gone, and was all unnerved when she finally got to Brown's, and found that the forelady herself had failed to come, and was therefore compelled to be lenient.

One of the consequences of this episode was that the first joints of three of the little boy's fingers were permanently disabled, and another that thereafter he always had to be beaten before he set out to work, whenever there was fresh snow on the ground. Jurgis was called upon to do the beating, and as it hurt his foot he did it with a vengeance; but it did not tend to add to the sweetness of his temper. They say that the best dog will turn cross if he be kept chained all the time, and it was the same with the man; he had not a thing to do all day but lie and curse his fate, and the time came when he wanted to curse everything.

This was never for very long, however, for when Ona began to cry, Jurgis could not stay angry. The poor fellow looked like a homeless ghost, with his cheeks sunken in and his long black hair straggling into his eyes; he was too discouraged to cut it, or to think about his appearance. His muscles were wasting away, and what were left were soft and flabby. He had no appetite, and they could not afford to tempt him with delicacies. It was better, he said, that he should not eat, it was a saving. About the end of March he had got hold of Ona's bank-book, and learned that there was only three dollars left to them in the world.

But perhaps the worst of the consequences of this long siege was that they lost another member of their family; Brother Jonas disappeared. One Saturday night he did not come home, and thereafter all their efforts to get trace of him were futile. It was said by the boss at Durham's that he had gotten his week's money and left there. That might not be true, of course, for sometimes they would say that when a man had been killed; it was the easiest way out of it for all concerned. When, for instance, a man had fallen into one of the rendering tanks and had been made into pure leaf lard and peerless fertilizer, there was no use letting the fact out and making his family unhappy. More probable, however, was the theory that Jonas had deserted them, and gone on the road, seeking happiness. He had been discontented for a long time, and not without some cause. He paid good board, and was yet obliged to live in a family where nobody had enough to eat. And Marija would keep giving them all her money, and of course he could not but feel that he was called upon to do the same. Then there were crying brats, and all sorts of misery; a man would have had to be a good deal of a hero to stand it all without grumbling, and Jonas was not in the least a hero—he was simply a weather-beaten old fellow who liked to have a good supper and sit in the corner by the fire and smoke his pipe in peace before he went to bed. Here there was not room by the fire, and through the winter the kitchen had seldom been warm enough for comfort. So, with the springtime, what was more likely than that the wild idea of escaping had come to him? Two years he had been yoked like a horse to a half-ton truck in Durham's dark cellars, with never a rest, save on Sundays and four holidays in the year, and with never a word of thanks—only kicks and blows and curses, such as no decent dog would have stood. And now the winter was over, and the spring winds were blowing—and with a day's walk a man might put the smoke of Packingtown behind him forever, and be where the grass was green and the flowers all the colors of the rainbow!

But now the income of the family was cut down more than one-third, and the food-demand was cut only one-eleventh, so that they were worse off than ever. Also they were borrowing money from Marija, and eating up her bank-account, and spoiling once again her hopes of marriage and happiness. And they were even going into debt to Tamoszius Kuszleika and letting him impoverish himself. Poor Tamoszius was a man without any relatives, and with a wonderful talent besides, and he ought to have made money and prospered; but he had fallen in love, and so given hostages to fortune, and was doomed to be dragged down too.

So it was finally decided that two more of the children would have to leave school. Next to Stanislovas, who was now fifteen, there was a girl, little Kotrina, who was two years younger, and then two boys, Vilimas, who was eleven, and Nikalojus, who was ten. Both of these last were bright boys, and there was no reason why their family should starve when tens of thousands of children no older were earning their own livings. So one morning they were given a quarter apiece and a roll with a sausage in it, and, with their minds top-heavy with good advice, were sent out to make their way to the city and learn to sell newspapers. They came back late at night in tears, having walked the five or six miles to report that a man had offered to take them to a place where they sold newspapers, and had taken their money and gone into a store to get them, and nevermore been seen. So they both received a whipping, and the next morning set out again. This time they found the newspaper place, and procured their stock; and after wandering about till nearly noontime, saying "Paper?" to every one they saw, they had all their stock taken away and received a thrashing besides from a big newsman upon whose territory they had trespassed. Fortunately, however, they had already sold some papers, and came back with nearly as much as they started with.

After a week of mishaps such as these, the two little fellows began to learn the ways of the trade,—the names of the different papers, and how many of each to get, and what sort of people to offer them to, and where to go and where to stay away from. After this, leaving home at four o'clock in the morning, and running about the streets, first with morning papers and then with evening, they might come home late at night with twenty or thirty cents apiece—possibly as much as forty cents. From this they had to deduct their car-fare, since the distance was so great; but after a while they made friends, and learned still more, and then they would save their car-fare. They would get on a car when the conductor was not looking, and hide in the crowd; and three times out of four he would not ask for their fares, either not seeing them, or thinking they had already paid; or if he did ask, they would hunt through their pockets, and then begin to cry, and either have their fares paid by some kind old lady, or else try the trick again on a new car. All this was fair play, they felt. Whose fault was it that at the hours when workingmen were going to their work and back, the cars were so crowded that the conductors could not collect all the fares? And besides, the companies were thieves, people said—had stolen all their franchises with the help of scoundrelly politicians![1]

Now that the winter was by, and there was no more danger of snow, and no more coal to buy, and another room warm enough to put the children into when they cried, and enough money to get along from week to week with, Jurgis was less terrible than he had been. A man can get used to anything in the course of time, and Jurgis had gotten used to lying about the house. Ona saw this, and was very careful not to destroy his peace of mind, by letting him know how very much pain she was suffering. It was now the time of the spring rains, and Ona had often to ride to her work, in spite of the expense; she was getting paler every day, and sometimes, in spite of her good resolutions, it pained her that Jurgis did not notice it. She wondered if he cared for her as much as ever, if all this misery was not wearing out his love. She had to be away from him all the time, and bear her own troubles while he was bearing his; and then, when she came home, she was so worn out; and whenever they talked they had only their worries to talk of—truly it was hard, in such a life, to keep any sentiment alive. The woe of this would flame up in Ona sometimes— at night she would suddenly clasp her big husband in her arms and break into passionate weeping, demanding to know if he really loved her. Poor Jurgis, who had in truth grown more matter-of-fact, under the endless pressure of penury, would not know what to make of these things, and could only try to recollect when he had last been cross; and so Ona would have to forgive him and sob herself to sleep.

The latter part of April Jurgis went to see the doctor, and was given a bandage to lace about his ankle, and told that he might go back to work. It needed more than the permission of the doctor, however, for when he showed up on the killing-floor of Brown's, he was told by the foreman that it had not been possible to keep his job for him. Jurgis knew that this meant simply that the foreman had found some one

1. See below, p. 185, n. 8.

else to do the work as well and did not want to bother to make a change. He stood in the doorway, looking mournfully on, seeing his friends and companions at work, and feeling like an outcast. Then he went out and took his place with the mob of the unemployed.

This time, however, Jurgis did not have the same fine confidence, nor the same reason for it. He was no longer the finest-looking man in the throng, and the bosses no longer made for him; he was thin and haggard, and his clothes were seedy, and he looked miserable. And there were hundreds who looked and felt just like him, and who had been wandering about Packingtown for months begging for work. This was a critical time in Jurgis's life, and if he had been a weaker man he would have gone the way the rest did. Those out-of-work wretches would stand about the packing-houses every morning till the police drove them away, and then they would scatter among the saloons. Very few of them had the nerve to face the rebuffs that they would encounter by trying to get into the buildings to interview the bosses; if they did not get a chance in the morning, there would be nothing to do but hang about the saloons the rest of the day and night. Jurgis was saved from all this—partly, to be sure, because it was pleasant weather, and there was no need to be indoors; but mainly because he carried with him always the pitiful little face of his wife. He must get work, he told himself, fighting the battle with despair every hour of the day. He must get work! He must have a place again and some money saved up, before the next winter came.

But there was no work for him. He sought out all the members of his union—Jurgis had stuck to the union through all this—and begged them to speak a word for him. He went to every one he knew, asking for a chance, there or anywhere. He wandered all day through the buildings; and in a week or two, when he had been all over the yards, and into every room to which he had access, and learned that there was not a job anywhere, he persuaded himself that there might have been a change in the places he had first visited, and began the round all over; till finally the watchmen and the "spotters"[2] of the companies came to know him by sight and to order him out with threats. Then there was nothing more for him to do but go with the crowd in the morning, and keep in the front row and look eager, and when he failed, go back home, and play with little Kotrina and the baby.

The peculiar bitterness of all this was that Jurgis saw so plainly the meaning of it. In the beginning he had been fresh and strong, and he had gotten a job the first day; but now he was second-hand, a damaged article, so to speak, and they did not want him. They had got the best out of him,—they had worn him out, with their speeding-up and their carelessness, and now they had thrown him away!

2. Company detectives or spies.

And Jurgis would make the acquaintance of others of these unemployed men and find that they had all had the same experience. There were some, of course, who had wandered in from other places, who had been ground up in other mills; there were others who were out from their own fault—some, for instance, who had not been able to stand the awful grind without drink. The vast majority, however, were simply the worn-out parts of the great merciless packing-machine; they had toiled there, and kept up with the pace, some of them for ten or twenty years, until finally the time had come when they could not keep up with it any more. Some had been frankly told that they were too old, that a sprier man was needed; others had given occasion, by some act of carelessness or incompetence; with most, however, the occasion had been the same as with Jurgis. They had been overworked and underfed so long, and finally some disease had laid them on their backs; or they had cut themselves, and had blood-poisoning, or met with some other accident. When a man came back after that, he would get his place back only by the courtesy of the boss. To this there was no exception, save when the accident was one for which the firm was liable; in that case they would send a slippery lawyer to see him, first to try to get him to sign away his claims, but if he was too smart for that, to promise him that he and his should always be provided with work. This promise they would keep, strictly and to the letter—for two years. Two years was the "statute of limitations," and after that the victim could not sue.

What happened to a man after any of these things, all depended upon the circumstances. If he were of the highly skilled workers, he would probably have enough saved up to tide him over. The best-paid men, the "splitters,"[3] made fifty cents an hour, which would be five or six dollars a day in the rush seasons, and one or two in the dullest. A man could live and save on that; but then there were only half a dozen splitters in each place, and one of them that Jurgis knew had a family of twenty-two children, all hoping to grow up to be splitters like their father. For an unskilled man, who made ten dollars a week in the rush seasons and five in the dull, it all depended upon his age and the number he had dependent upon him. An unmarried man could save, if he did not drink, and if he was absolutely selfish— that is, if he paid no heed to the demands of his old parents, or of his little brothers and sisters, or of any other relatives he might have, as well as of the members of his union, and his chums, and the people who might be starving to death next door.

3. Each of the 78 specialized occupations in a cattle-killing gang received its own wage. Splitting the steer in half through the backbone required considerable strength and dexterity, making it one of the better-paying Packingtown jobs in 1904.

Chapter XIII

During this time that Jurgis was looking for work occurred the death of little Kristoforas, one of the children of Teta Elzbieta. Both Kristoforas and his brother, Juozapas, were cripples, the latter having lost one leg by having it run over, and Kristoforas having congenital dislocation of the hip, which made it impossible for him ever to walk. He was the last of Teta Elzbieta's children, and perhaps he had been intended by nature to let her know that she had had enough. At any rate he was wretchedly sick and undersized; he had the rickets,[1] and though he was over three years old, he was no bigger than an ordinary child of one. All day long he would crawl around the floor in a filthy little dress, whining and fretting; because the floor was full of draughts he was always catching cold, and snuffling because his nose ran. This made him a nuisance, and a source of endless trouble in the family. For his mother, with unnatural perversity, loved him best of all her children, and made a perpetual fuss over him—would let him do anything undisturbed, and would burst into tears when his fretting drove Jurgis wild.

And now he died. Perhaps it was the smoked sausage he had eaten that morning—which may have been made out of some of the tubercular pork that was condemned as unfit for export. At any rate, an hour after eating it, the child had begun to cry with pain, and in another hour he was rolling about on the floor in convulsions. Little Kotrina, who was all alone with him, ran out screaming for help, and after a while a doctor came, but not until Kristoforas had howled his last howl. No one was really sorry about this except poor Elzbieta, who was inconsolable. Jurgis announced that so far as he was concerned the child would have to be buried by the city, since they had no money for a funeral; and at this the poor woman almost went out of her senses, wringing her hands and screaming with grief and despair. Her child to be buried in a pauper's grave! And her stepdaughter to stand by and hear it said without protesting! It was enough to make Ona's father rise up out of his grave to rebuke her! If it had come to this, they might as well give up at once, and be buried all of them together! . . . In the end Marija said that she would help with ten dollars; and Jurgis being still obdurate, Elzbieta went in tears and begged the money from the neighbors, and so little Kristoforas had a mass and a hearse with white plumes on it, and a tiny plot in a graveyard with a wooden cross to mark the place. The poor mother was not the same for months after that; the mere sight of the floor

---

1. Bone disease deforming skeletal growth in children, caused by a deficiency of vitamin D (often due to inadequate exposure to sunlight), common in smoggy industrial cities in the early 20th century, especially among the poor.

where little Kristoforas had crawled about would make her weep. He had never had a fair chance, poor little fellow, she would say. He had been handicapped from his birth. If only she had heard about it in time, so that she might have had that great doctor to cure him of his lameness! . . . Some time ago, Elzbieta was told, a Chicago billionnaire had paid a fortune to bring a great European surgeon over to cure his little daughter of the same disease from which Kristoforas had suffered. And because this surgeon had to have bodies to demonstrate upon, he announced that he would treat the children of the poor, a piece of magnanimity over which the papers became quite eloquent. Elzbieta, alas, did not read the papers, and no one had told her; but perhaps it was as well, for just then they would not have had the car-fare to spare to go every day to wait upon the surgeon, nor for that matter anybody with the time to take the child.

All this while that he was seeking for work, there was a dark shadow hanging over Jurgis; as if a savage beast were lurking somewhere in the pathway of his life, and he knew it, and yet could not help approaching the place. There are all stages of being out of work in Packingtown, and he faced in dread the prospect of reaching the lowest. There is a place that waits for the lowest man—the fertilizer-plant!

The men would talk about it in awe-stricken whispers. Not more than one in ten had ever really tried it; the other nine had contented themselves with hearsay evidence and a peep through the door. There were some things worse than even starving to death. They would ask Jurgis if he had worked there yet, and if he meant to; and Jurgis would debate the matter with himself. As poor as they were, and making all the sacrifices that they were, would he dare to refuse any sort of work that was offered to him, be it as horrible as ever it could? Would he dare to go home and eat bread that had been earned by Ona, weak and complaining as she was, knowing that he had been given a chance, and had not had the nerve to take it?—And yet he might argue that way with himself all day, and one glimpse into the fertilizer-works would send him away again shuddering. He was a man, and he would do his duty; he went and made application— but surely he was not also required to hope for success!

The fertilizer-works of Durham's lay away from the rest of the plant. Few visitors ever saw them, and the few who did would come out looking like Dante, of whom the peasants declared that he had been into hell. To this part of the yards came all the "tankage," and the waste products of all sorts;[2] here they dried out the bones,—and in

---

2. Wastes left after extracting grease and tallow from meat scraps, along with condemned carcasses, were thrown into a carcass destructor or "tank." According to a 1904 Department of Agriculture notice, "A sufficient quantity of low-grade offal (uteri, floor scrapings, trimmings from gutters' benches, skimmings from catch basins, unemptied intestines,

suffocating cellars where the daylight never came you might see men and women and children bending over whirling machines and sawing bits of bone into all sorts of shapes,[3] breathing their lungs full of the fine dust, and doomed to die, every one of them, within a certain definite time. Here they made the blood into albumen, and made other foul-smelling things into things still more foul-smelling. In the corridors and caverns where it was done you might lose yourself as in the great caves of Kentucky.[4] In the dust and the steam the electric lights would shine like far-off twinkling stars— red and blue, green and purple stars, according to the color of the mist and the brew from which it came. For the odors in these ghastly charnel-houses[5] there may be words in Lithuanian, but there are none in English. The person entering would have to summon his courage as for a cold-water plunge. He would go on like a man swimming under water; he would put his handkerchief over his face, and begin to cough and choke; and then, if he were still obstinate, he would find his head beginning to ring, and the veins in his forehead to throb, until finally he would be assailed by an overpowering blast of ammonia fumes,[6] and would turn and run for his life, and come out half-dazed.

On top of this were the rooms where they dried the "tankage," the mass of brown stringy stuff that was left after the waste portions of the carcasses had had the lard and tallow tried out of them. This dried material they would then grind to a fine powder, and after they had mixed it up well with a mysterious but inoffensive brown rock which they brought in and ground up by the hundreds of car-loads for that purpose, the substance was ready to be put into bags and sent out to the world as any one of a hundred different brands of standard bone-phosphate. And then the farmer in Maine or California or Texas would buy this, at say twenty-five dollars a ton, and plant it with his corn; and for several days after the operation the fields would have a strong odor, and the farmer and his wagon and the very horses that had hauled it would all have it too. In Packingtown the fertilizer is pure, instead of being a flavoring, and instead of a ton or so spread out on several acres under the open sky, there are

---

omasa, paunches emptied but not washed, &c.) shall be tanked with all condemned carcasses (except those tanked for lard) to effectually render the ultimate product unfit for human food" (quoted in A. [Adolphe] Smith, "Chicago: The Dark and Insanitary Premises Used for the Slaughtering of Cattle and Hogs—The Government Inspection," *The Lancet*, January 14, 1905, 122). See below, pp. 343–44, for one of Smith's related writings about Packingtown.

3. The bone-cutting department (a branch of the fertilizer works at Armour's) made buttons, dice, and handles for knives and razors.
4. Mammoth Cave, now known to be at least 350 miles long, is the home of unusual species such as eyeless fish and blind beetles that have evolved to survive in the absolute darkness of the environment.
5. Depositories for dead bodies or bones.
6. Given off by the decomposition of flesh.

hundreds and thousands of tons of it in one building, heaped here and there in haystack piles, covering the floor several inches deep, and filling the air with a choking dust that becomes a blinding sand-storm when the wind stirs.

It was to this building that Jurgis came daily, as if dragged by an unseen hand. The month of May was an exceptionally cool one, and his secret prayers were granted; but early in June there came a record-breaking hot spell, and after that there were men wanted in the fertilizer-mill.

The boss of the grinding room had come to know Jurgis by this time, and had marked him for a likely man; and so when he came to the door about two o'clock this breathless hot day, he felt a sudden spasm of pain shoot through him—the boss beckoned to him! In ten minutes more Jurgis had pulled off his coat and over-shirt, and set his teeth together and gone to work. Here was one more difficulty for him to meet and conquer!

His labor took him about one minute to learn. Before him was one of the vents of the mill in which the fertilizer was being ground—rushing forth in a great brown river, with a spray of the finest dust flung forth in clouds. Jurgis was given a shovel, and along with half a dozen others it was his task to shovel this fertilizer into carts. That others were at work he knew by the sound, and by the fact that he sometimes collided with them; otherwise they might as well not have been there, for in the blinding dust-storm a man could not see six feet in front of his face. When he had filled one cart he had to grope around him until another came, and if there was none on hand he continued to grope till one arrived. In five minutes he was, of course, a mass of fertilizer from head to feet; they gave him a sponge to tie over his mouth, so that he could breathe, but the sponge did not pre-vent his lips and eyelids from caking up with it and his ears from fill-ing solid. He looked like a brown ghost at twilight—from hair to shoes he became the color of the building and of everything in it, and for that matter a hundred yards outside it. The building had to be left open, and when the wind blew Durham and Company lost a great deal of fertilizer.

Working in his shirt-sleeves, and with the thermometer at over a hundred, the phosphates soaked in through every pore of Jurgis's skin, and in five minutes he had a headache, and in fifteen was almost dazed. The blood was pounding in his brain like an engine's throb-bing; there was a frightful pain in the top of his skull, and he could hardly control his hands. Still, with the memory of his four months' siege behind him, he fought on, in a frenzy of determination; and half an hour later he began to vomit—he vomited until it seemed as if his inwards must be torn into shreds. A man could get used to the fertilizer-mill, the boss had said, if he would only make up his mind to it; but Jurgis now began to see that it was a question of making up his stomach.

At the end of that day of horror, he could scarcely stand. He had to catch himself now and then, and lean against a building and get his bearings. Most of the men, when they came out, made straight for a saloon—they seemed to place fertilizer and rattlesnake poison[7] in one class. But Jurgis was too ill to think of drinking—he could only make his way to the street and stagger on to a car. He had a sense of humor, and later on, when he became an old hand, he used to think it fun to board a street-car and see what happened. Now, however, he was too ill to notice it—how the people in the car began to gasp and sputter, to put their handkerchiefs to their noses, and transfix him with furious glances. Jurgis only knew that a man in front of him immediately got up and gave him a seat; and that half a minute later the two people on each side of him got up; and that in a full minute the crowded car was nearly empty—those passengers who could not get room on the platform having gotten out to walk.

Of course Jurgis had made his home a miniature fertilizer-mill a minute after entering. The stuff was half an inch deep in his skin—his whole system was full of it, and it would have taken a week not merely of scrubbing, but of vigorous exercise, to get it out of him. As it was, he could be compared with nothing known to men, save that newest discovery of the savants, a substance which emits energy for an unlimited time, without being itself in the least diminished in power.[8] He smelt so that he made all the food at the table taste, and set the whole family to vomiting; for himself it was three days before he could keep anything upon his stomach—he might wash his hands, and use a knife and fork, but were not his mouth and throat filled with the poison?

And still Jurgis stuck it out! In spite of splitting headaches he would stagger down to the plant and take up his stand once more, and begin to shovel in the blinding clouds of dust. And so at the end of the week he was a fertilizer-man for life—he was able to eat again, and though his head never stopped aching, it ceased to be so bad that he could not work.

So there passed another summer. It was a summer of prosperity, all over the country, and the country ate generously of packing-house products, and there was plenty of work for all the family, in spite of the packers' efforts to keep a superfluity of labor. They were again able to pay their debts and to begin to save a little sum but there were one or two sacrifices they considered too heavy to be made for long—it was too bad that the boys should have to sell papers at their age. It was

7. Alcohol (slang).
8. Probably radium, which has a half-life of 1,600 years, discovered by 1900.

utterly useless to caution them and plead with them; quite without knowing it, they were taking on the tone of their new environment. They were learning to swear in voluble English; they were learning to pick up cigar-stumps and smoke them, to pass hours of their time gambling with pennies and dice and cigarette-cards; they were learning the location of all the houses of prostitution on the "Lêvée,"[9] and the names of the "madames" who kept them, and the days when they gave their state banquets, which the police captains and the big politicians all attended. If a visiting "country-customer" were to ask them, they could show him which was "Hinkydink's" famous saloon,[1] and could even point out to him by name the different gamblers and thugs and "hold-up men" who made the place their headquarters. And worse yet, the boys were getting out of the habit of coming home at night. What was the use, they would ask, of wasting time and energy and a possible car-fare riding out to the stockyards every night when the weather was pleasant and they could crawl under a truck or into an empty doorway and sleep exactly as well? So long as they brought home a half dollar for each day, what mattered it when they brought it? But Jurgis declared that from this to ceasing to come at all would not be a very long step, and so it was decided that Vilimas and Nikalojus should return to school in the fall, and that instead Elzbieta should go out and get some work, her place at home being taken by her younger daughter.

Little Kotrina was like most children of the poor, prematurely made old; she had to take care of her little brother, who was a cripple, and also of the baby; she had to cook the meals and wash the dishes and clean house, and have supper ready when the workers came home in the evening. She was only thirteen, and small for her age, but she did all this without a murmur; and her mother went out, and after trudging a couple of days about the yards, settled down as a servant of a "sausage-machine."

Elzbieta was used to working, but she found this change a hard one, for the reason that she had to stand motionless upon her feet from seven o'clock in the morning till half-past twelve, and again from one till half-past five. For the first few days it seemed to her that she could not stand it—she suffered almost as much as Jurgis had from the fertilizer, and would come out at sundown with her head fairly reeling. Besides this, she was working in one of the dark holes, by electric light, and the dampness, too, was deadly—there were always puddles of water on the floor, and a sickening odor of moist flesh in the room. The people who worked here followed the ancient custom of nature, whereby the ptarmigan is the color of dead

9. Chicago's First Ward, the Levee of the near South Side, a red-light district of gambling and prostitution.
1. See below, p. 233, n. 7

leaves in the fall and of snow in the winter, and the chameleon, who is black when he lies upon a stump and turns green when he moves to a leaf. The men and women who worked in this department were precisely the color of the "fresh country sausage" they made.

The sausage-room was an interesting place to visit, for two or three minutes, and provided that you did not look at the people; the machines were perhaps the most wonderful things in the entire plant. Presumably sausages were once chopped and stuffed by hand, and if so it would be interesting to know how many workers had been displaced by these inventions. On one side of the room were the hoppers, into which men shovelled loads of meat and wheelbarrows full of spices; in these great bowls were whirling knives that made two thousand revolutions a minute, and when the meat was ground fine and adulterated with potato-flour, and well mixed with water, it was forced to the stuffing-machines on the other side of the room. The latter were tended by women; there was a sort of spout, like the nozzle of a hose, and one of the women would take a long string of "casing" and put the end over the nozzle and then work the whole thing on, as one works on the finger of a tight glove. This string would be twenty or thirty feet long, but the woman would have it all on in a jiffy; and when she had several on, she would press a lever, and a stream of sausage-meat would be shot out, taking the casing with it as it came. Thus one might stand and see appear, miraculously born from the machine, a wriggling snake of sausage of incredible length. In front was a big pan which caught these creatures, and two more women who seized them as fast as they appeared and twisted them into links. This was for the uninitiated the most perplexing work of all; for all that the woman had to give was a single turn of the wrist; and in some way she contrived to give it so that instead of an endless chain of sausages, one after another, there grew under her hands a bunch of strings, all dangling from a single centre. It was quite like the feat of a prestidigitator,—for the woman worked so fast that the eye could literally not follow her, and there was only a mist of motion, and tangle after tangle of sausages appearing. In the midst of the mist, however, the visitor would suddenly notice the tense set face, with the two wrinkles graven in the forehead, and the ghastly pallor of the cheeks; and then he would suddenly recollect that it was time he was going on. The woman did not go on; she stayed right there—hour after hour, day after day, year after year, twisting sausage-links and racing with death. It was piece-work, and she was apt to have a family to keep alive; and stern and ruthless economic laws had arranged it that she could only do this by working just as she did, with all her soul upon her work, and with never an instant for a glance at the well-dressed ladies and gentlemen who came to stare at her, as at some wild beast in a menagerie.

Chapter XIV

With one member trimming beef in a cannery, and another working in a sausage factory, the family had a first-hand knowledge of the great majority of Packingtown swindles. For it was the custom, as they found, whenever meat was so spoiled that it could not be used for anything else, either to can it or else to chop it up into sausage. With what had been told them by Jonas, who had worked in the pickle-rooms, they could now study the whole of the spoiled-meat industry on the inside, and read a new and grim meaning into that old Packingtown jest,—that they use everything of the pig except the squeal.

Jonas had told them how the meat that was taken out of pickle would often be found sour, and how they would rub it up with soda to take away the smell, and sell it to be eaten on free-lunch counters;[1] also of all the miracles of chemistry which they performed, giving to any sort of meat, fresh or salted, whole or chopped, any color and any flavor and any odor they chose. In the pickling of hams they had an ingenious apparatus, by which they saved time and increased the capacity of the plant—a machine consisting of a hollow needle attached to a pump; by plunging this needle into the meat and work-ing with his foot, a man could fill a ham with pickle in a few sec-onds. And yet, in spite of this, there would be hams found spoiled, some of them with an odor so bad that a man could hardly bear to be in the room with them. To pump into these the packers had a second and much stronger pickle which destroyed the odor—a process known to the workers as "giving them thirty per cent."[2] Also, after the hams had been smoked, there would be found some that had gone to the bad. Formerly these had been sold as "Number Three Grade,"[3] but later on some ingenious person had hit upon a new device, and now they would extract the bone, about which the bad part generally lay, and insert in the hole a white-hot iron. After this invention there was no longer Number One, Two, and Three Grade—there was only Number One Grade. The packers were always originating such schemes—they had what they called "boneless hams," which were all the odds and ends of pork stuffed into casings; and "California hams," which were the shoulders, with big knuckle-joints, and nearly all the

1. Perhaps at the nearby saloons, where a "free" lunch could be had in exchange for buy-ing a beer, as above, pp. 78–79.
2. While pickling with brine was a common practice for preserving meat, using "stronger pickle" to mask the smell of meat that had spoiled was unethical and hazardous to the health of consumers.
3. Lowest grade of ham—as one commentator said, "like charity, [number three grade] covers a multitude of sins" (Joseph W. Grand, *Illustrated History of the Union Stock Yards* [Chicago: T. Knapp, 1896], p. 242).

meat cut out; and fancy "skinned hams," which were made of the oldest hogs, whose skins were so heavy and coarse that no one would buy them—that is, until they had been cooked and chopped fine and labelled "head cheese"!

It was only when the whole ham was spoiled that it came into the department of Elzbieta. Cut up by the two-thousand-revolutions-a-minute flyers, and mixed with half a ton of other meat, no odor that ever was in a ham could make any difference. There was never the least attention paid to what was cut up for sausage; there would come all the way back from Europe old sausage that had been rejected, and that was mouldy and white—it would be dosed with borax and glycerine,[4] and dumped into the hoppers, and made over again for home consumption. There would be meat that had tumbled out on the floor, in the dirt and sawdust, where the workers had tramped and spit uncounted billions of consumption germs. There would be meat stored in great piles in rooms; and the water from leaky roofs would drip over it, and thousands of rats would race about on it. It was too dark in these storage places to see well, but a man could run his hand over these piles of meat and sweep off handfuls of the dried dung of rats. These rats were nuisances, and the packers would put poisoned bread out for them; they would die, and then rats, bread, and meat would go into the hoppers together. This is no fairy story and no joke; the meat would be shovelled into carts, and the man who did the shovelling would not trouble to lift out a rat even when he saw one—there were things that went into the sausage in comparison with which a poisoned rat was a tidbit. There was no place for the men to wash their hands[5] before they ate their dinner, and so they made a practice of washing them in the water that was to be ladled into the sausage. There were the butt-ends of smoked meat, and the scraps of corned beef, and all the odds and ends of the waste of the plants, that would be dumped into old barrels in the cellar and left there. Under the system of rigid economy which the packers enforced, there were some jobs that it only paid to do once in a long time, and among these was the cleaning out of the waste-barrels. Every spring they did it; and in the barrels would be dirt and rust and old nails and stale water—and cart load after cart load of it would be taken up and dumped into the hoppers with fresh meat, and sent out to the public's breakfast. Some of it they would make into "smoked" sausage—but as the smoking took time, and was therefore expensive, they would call upon their chemistry department, and preserve it with borax and color it with gelatine to make it brown.

---

4. *Borax:* used as a cleansing agent and preservative, toxic in large doses; *glycerine* (or glycerol): used as solvent and softener.
5. Besides its literal meaning, a euphemism for no toilets available; workers relieved themselves in the same rooms where meats were processed.

All of their sausage came out of the same bowl, but when they came to wrap it they would stamp some of it "special," and for this they would charge two cents more a pound.

Such were the new surroundings in which Elzbieta was placed, and such was the work she was compelled to do. It was stupefying, brutalizing work; it left her no time to think, no strength for anything. She was part of the machine she tended, and every faculty that was not needed for the machine was doomed to be crushed out of existence. There was only one mercy about the cruel grind—that it gave her the gift of insensibility. Little by little she sank into a torpor— she fell silent. She would meet Jurgis and Ona in the evening, and the three would walk home together, often without saying a word. Ona, too, was falling into a habit of silence—Ona, who had once gone about singing like a bird. She was sick and miserable, and often she would barely have strength enough to drag herself home. And there they would eat what they had to eat, and afterwards, because there was only their misery to talk of, they would crawl into bed and fall into a stupor and never stir until it was time to get up again, and dress by candle-light, and go back to the machines. They were so numbed that they did not even suffer much from hunger, now; only the children continued to fret when the food ran short.

Yet the soul of Ona was not dead—the souls of none of them were dead, but only sleeping; and now and then they would waken, and these were cruel times. The gates of memory would roll open—old joys would stretch out their arms to them, old hopes and dreams would call to them, and they would stir beneath the burden that lay upon them, and feel its forever immeasurable weight. They could not even cry out beneath it; but anguish would seize them, more dreadful than the agony of death. It was a thing scarcely to be spoken—a thing never spoken by all the world, that will not know its own defeat.

They were beaten; they had lost the game, they were swept aside. It was not less tragic because it was so sordid, because that it had to do with wages and grocery bills and rents. They had dreamed of freedom; of a chance to look about them and learn something; to be decent and clean, to see their child grow up to be strong. And now it was all gone—it would never be! They had played the game and they had lost. Six years more of toil they had to face before they could expect the least respite, the cessation of the payments upon the house; and how cruelly certain it was that they could never stand six years of such a life as they were living! They were lost, they were going down—and there was no deliverance for them, no hope; for all the help it gave them the vast city in which they lived might have been an ocean waste, a wilderness, a desert, a tomb. So often this mood would come to Ona, in the night-time, when something wakened her; she would lie, afraid of the beating of her own heart, fronting the blood-red eyes of the old primeval terror of life. Once she cried aloud, and woke Jurgis, who was tired and cross. After that she learned to weep silently—their moods so seldom came together now! It was as if their hopes were buried in separate graves.

Jurgis, being a man, had troubles of his own. There was another spectre following him. He had never spoken of it, nor would he allow any one else to speak of it—he had never acknowledged its existence to himself. Yet the battle with it took all the manhood that he had—and once or twice, alas, a little more. Jurgis had discovered drink.

He was working in the steaming pit of hell; day after day, week after week—until now there was not an organ of his body that did its work without pain, until the sound of ocean breakers echoed in his head day and night, and the buildings swayed and danced before him as he went down the street. And from all the unending horror of this there was a respite, a deliverance—he could drink! He could forget the pain, he could slip off the burden; he would see clearly again, he would be master of his brain, of his thoughts, of his will. His dead self would stir in him, and he would find himself laughing and cracking jokes with his companions—he would be a man again, and master of his life.

It was not an easy thing for Jurgis to take more than two or three drinks. With the first drink he could eat a meal, and he could persuade himself that that was economy; with the second he could eat another meal—but there would come a time when he could eat no more, and then to pay for a drink was an unthinkable extravagance, a defiance of the age-long instincts of his hunger-haunted class. One day, however, he took the plunge, and drank up all that he had in his pockets, and went home half "piped," as the men phrase it. He was happier than he had been in a year; and yet, because he knew that the happiness would not last, he was savage, too—with those who would wreck it, and with the world, and with his life; and then again, beneath this, he was sick with the shame of himself. Afterward, when he saw the despair of his family, and reckoned up the money he had spent, the tears came into his eyes, and he began the long battle with the spectre.

It was a battle that had no end, that never could have one. But Jurgis did not realize that very clearly; he was not given much time for reflection. He simply knew that he was always fighting. Steeped in misery and despair as he was, merely to walk down the street was to be put upon the rack. There was surely a saloon on the corner—perhaps on all four corners, and some in the middle of the block as well; and each one stretched out a hand to him—each one had a personality of its own, allurements unlike any other. Going and coming—before sunrise and after dark—there was warmth and a glow of light, and the steam of hot food, and perhaps music, or a friendly face, and a word of good cheer. Jurgis developed a fondness for having Ona on his arm whenever he went out on the street, and he would hold her tightly, and walk fast. It was pitiful to have Ona know of this—it drove him wild to think of it; the thing was not fair, for Ona had never tasted drink, and so could not understand. Sometimes, in desperate hours, he would find himself wishing that she might learn what it was, so that he need not be ashamed in her presence. They might drink together, and escape from the horror— escape for a while, come what would.

So there came a time when nearly all the conscious life of Jurgis consisted of a struggle with the craving for liquor. He would have ugly moods, when he hated Ona and the whole family, because they stood in his way. He was a fool to have married; he had tied himself down, had made himself a slave. It was all because he was a married man that he was compelled to stay in the yards; if it had not been for that he might have gone off like Jonas, and to hell with the packers. There were few single men in the fertilizer-mill—and those few were working only for a chance to escape. Meantime, too, they had something to think about while they worked,—they had the memory of the last time they had been drunk, and the hope of the time when they would be drunk again. As for Jurgis, he was expected to bring home every penny; he could not even go with the men at noon-time—he was supposed to sit down and eat his dinner on a pile of fertilizer dust.

This was not always his mood, of course; he still loved his family. But just now was a time of trial. Poor little Antanas, for instance— who had never failed to win him with a smile—little Antanas was not smiling just now, being a mass of fiery red pimples. He had had all the diseases that babies are heir to, in quick succession, scarlet fever, mumps, and whooping-cough in the first year, and now he was down with the measles. There was no one to attend him but Kotrina; there was no doctor to help him, because they were too poor, and children did not die of the measles—at least not often. Now and then Kotrina would find time to sob over his woes, but for the greater part of the time he had to be left alone, barricaded upon the bed. The floor was full of draughts, and if he caught cold he would die. At night he was tied down, lest he should kick the covers off him, while the family lay in their stupor of exhaustion. He would lie and scream for hours, almost in convulsions; and then, when he was worn out, he would lie whimpering and wailing in his torment. He was burning up with fever, and his eyes were running sores; in the daytime he was a thing uncanny and impish to behold, a plaster of pimples and sweat, a great purple lump of misery.

Yet all this was not really as cruel as it sounds, for, sick as he was, little Antanas was the least unfortunate member of that family. He was quite able to bear his sufferings—it was as if he had all these complaints to show what a prodigy of health he was. He was the child of his parents' youth and joy; he grew up like the conjurer's rose bush, and all the world was his oyster.[6] In general, he toddled around the kitchen all day with a lean and hungry look—the portion of the family's allowance that fell to him was not enough, and he was unrestrainable in his demand for more. Antanas was but little over a year old, and already no one but his father could manage him.

It seemed as if he had taken all of his mother's strength—had left nothing for those that might come after him. Ona was with child again now, and it was a dreadful thing to contemplate; even Jurgis, dumb and despairing as he was, could not but understand that yet other agonies were on the way, and shudder at the thought of them.

For Ona was visibly going to pieces. In the first place she was developing a cough, like the one that had killed old Dede Antanas. She had had a trace of it ever since that fatal morning when the greedy street-car corporation had turned her out into the rain; but now it was beginning to grow serious, and to wake her up at night. Even worse than that was the fearful nervousness from which she suffered; she would have frightful headaches and fits of aimless weeping; and sometimes she would come home at night shuddering and moaning, and would fling herself down upon the bed and burst into tears. Several times she was quite beside herself and hysterical; and then Jurgis would go half mad with fright. Elzbieta would explain to him that it could not be helped, that a woman was subject to such things when she was pregnant; but he was hardly to be persuaded, and would beg and plead to know what had happened. She had never been like this before, he would argue—it was monstrous and unthinkable. It was the life she had to live, the accursed work she had to do, that was killing her by inches. She was not fitted for it—no woman was fitted for it, no woman ought to be allowed to do such work; if the world could not keep them alive any other way it ought to kill them at once and be done with it. They ought not to marry, to have children; no working-man ought to marry—if he, Jurgis, had known what a woman was like, he would have had his eyes torn out first. So he would carry on, becoming half hysterical himself, which was an unbearable thing to see in a big man; Ona would pull herself together and fling herself into his arms, begging him to stop, to be still, that she would be better, it would be all right. So she would lie and sob out her grief upon his shoulder, while he gazed at her, as helpless as a wounded animal, the target of unseen enemies.

6. One of the celebrated routines of renowned magician Karl Germain (1878–1959) was making a rose bush bloom before audiences; "world's mine oyster" from Shakespeare's *The Merry Wives of Windsor* II.ii.2.

Chapter XV

The beginning of these perplexing things was in the summer; and each time Ona would promise him with terror in her voice that it would not happen again—but in vain. Each crisis would leave Jurgis more and more frightened, more disposed to distrust Elzbieta's consolations, and to believe that there was some terrible thing about all this that he was not allowed to know. Once or twice in these outbreaks he caught Ona's eye, and it seemed to him like the eye of a hunted animal; there were broken phrases of anguish and despair now and then, amid her frantic weeping. It was only because he was so numb and beaten himself that Jurgis did not worry more about this. But he never thought of it, except when he was dragged to it—he lived like a dumb beast of burden, knowing only the moment in which he was.

The winter was coming on again, more menacing and cruel than ever. It was October, and the holiday rush had begun. It was necessary for the packing-machines to grind till late at night to provide food that would be eaten at Christmas breakfasts; and Marija and Elzbieta and Ona, as part of the machine, began working fifteen or sixteen hours a day. There was no choice about this—whatever work there was to be done they had to do, if they wished to keep their places; besides that, it added another pittance to their incomes, so they staggered on with the awful load. They would start work every morning at seven, and eat their dinners at noon, and then work until ten or eleven at night without another mouthful of food. Jurgis wanted to wait for them, to help them home at night, but they would not think of this; the fertilizer-mill was not running overtime, and there was no place for him to wait save in a saloon. Each would stagger out into the darkness, and make her way to the corner, where they met; or if the others had already gone, would get into a car, and begin a painful struggle to keep awake. When they got home they were always too tired either to eat or to undress; they would crawl into bed with their shoes on, and lie like logs. If they should fail, they would certainly be lost; if they held out, they might have enough coal for the winter.

A day or two before Thanksgiving Day there came a snow-storm. It began in the afternoon, and by evening two inches had fallen. Jurgis tried to wait for the women, but went into a saloon to get warm, and took two drinks, and came out and ran home to escape from the demon; there he lay down to wait for them, and instantly fell asleep. When he opened his eyes again he was in the midst of a nightmare, and found Elzbieta shaking him and crying out. At first he could not realize what she was saying—Ona had not come home. What time was it, he asked. It was morning—time to be up. Ona had not been home that night! And it was bitter cold, and a foot of snow on the ground.

Jurgis sat up with a start. Marija was crying with fright and the children were wailing in sympathy—little Stanislovas in addition, because the terror of the snow was upon him. Jurgis had nothing to put on but his shoes and his coat, and in half a minute he was out of the door. Then, however, he realized that there was no need of haste, that he had no idea where to go. It was still dark as midnight, and the thick snowflakes were sifting down—everything was so silent that he could hear the rustle of them as they fell. In the few seconds that he stood there hesitating he was covered white.

He set off at a run for the yards, stopping by the way to inquire in the saloons that were open. Ona might have been overcome on the way; or else she might have met with an accident in the machines. When he got to the place where she worked he inquired of one of the watchmen—there had not been any accident, so far as the man had heard. At the time-office, which he found already open, the clerk told him that Ona's check had been turned in the night before, showing that she had left her work.

After that there was nothing for him to do but wait, pacing back and forth in the snow, meantime, to keep from freezing. Already the yards were full of activity; cattle were being unloaded from the cars in the distance, and across the way the "beef-luggers" were toiling in the darkness, carrying two-hundred-pound quarters of bullocks into the refrigerator-cars.[1] Before the first streaks of daylight there came the crowding throngs of workingmen, shivering, and swinging their dinner pails as they hurried by. Jurgis took up his stand by the time-office window, where alone there was light enough for him to see; the snow fell so thick that it was only by peering closely that he could make sure that Ona did not pass him.

Seven o'clock came, the hour when the great packing-machine began to move. Jurgis ought to have been at his place in the fertilizer-mill; but instead he was waiting, in an agony of fear, for Ona. It was fifteen minutes after the hour when he saw a form emerge from the snow-mist, and sprang toward it with a cry. It was she, running swiftly; as she saw him, she staggered forward, and half fell into his outstretched arms.

"What has been the matter?" he cried, anxiously. "Where have you been?"

It was several seconds before she could get breath to answer him. "I couldn't get home," she exclaimed. "The snow—the cars had stopped."

---

1. Strong workers loaded sides of beef onto refrigerated train cars, technology initially developed by Gustavus F. Swift (1839–1903) in the 1870s that contributed significantly to Chicago packers' market dominance.

"But where were you then?" he demanded.

"I had to go home with a friend," she panted—"with Jadvyga."

Jurgis drew a deep breath; but then he noticed that she was sobbing and trembling—as if in one of those nervous crises that he dreaded so. "But what's the matter?" he cried. "What has happened?"

"Oh, Jurgis, I was so frightened!" she said, clinging to him wildly. "I have been so worried!"

They were near the time-station window, and people were staring at them. Jurgis led her away. "How do you mean?" he asked, in perplexity.

"I was afraid—I was just afraid!" sobbed Ona. "I knew you wouldn't know where I was, and I didn't know what you might do. I tried to get home, but I was so tired. Oh, Jurgis, Jurgis!"

He was so glad to get her back that he could not think clearly about anything else. It did not seem strange to him that she should be so very much upset; all her fright and incoherent protestations did not matter since he had her back. He let her cry away her fears; and then, because it was nearly eight o'clock, and they would lose another hour if they delayed, he left her at the packing-house door, with her ghastly white face and her haunted eyes of terror.

There was another brief interval. Christmas was almost come; and because the snow still held, and the searching cold, morning after morning Jurgis half carried his wife to her post, staggering with her through the darkness; until at last, one night, came the end.

It lacked but three days of the holidays. About midnight Marija and Elzbieta came home, exclaiming in alarm when they found that Ona had not come. The two had agreed to meet her; and, after waiting, had gone to the room where she worked, only to find that the ham-wrapping girls had quit work an hour before, and left. There was no snow that night, nor was it especially cold; and still Ona had not come! Something more serious must be wrong this time.

They aroused Jurgis, and he sat up and listened crossly to the story. She must have gone home again with Jadvyga, he said; Jadvyga lived only two blocks from the yards, and perhaps she had been tired. Nothing could have happened to her—and even if there had, there was nothing could be done about it until morning. Jurgis turned over in his bed, and was snoring again before the two had closed the door.

In the morning, however, he was up and out nearly an hour before the usual time. Jadvyga Marcinkus lived on the other side of the yards, beyond Halsted Street, with her mother and sisters, in a single basement room—for Mikolas had recently lost one hand from blood-poisoning, and their marriage had been put off forever. The door of the room was in the rear, reached by a narrow court, and

Jurgis saw a light in the window and heard something frying as he passed; he knocked, half expecting that Ona would answer.

Instead there was one of Jadvyga's little sisters, who gazed at him through a crack in the door. "Where's Ona?" he demanded; and the child looked at him in perplexity. "Ona?" she said.

"Yes," said Jurgis, "isn't she here?"

"No," said the child, and Jurgis gave a start. A moment later came Jadvyga, peering over the child's head. When she saw who it was, she slid around out of sight, for she was not quite dressed. Jurgis must excuse her, she began, her mother was very ill——

"Ona isn't here?" Jurgis demanded, too alarmed to wait for her to finish.

"Why, no," said Jadvyga. "What made you think she would be here? Had she said she was coming?"

"No," he answered. "But she hasn't come home—and I thought she would be here the same as before."

"As before?" echoed Jadvyga, in perplexity.

"The time she spent the night here," said Jurgis.

"There must be some mistake," she answered, quickly. "Ona has never spent the night here."

He was only half able to realize her words. "Why—why—" he exclaimed. "Two weeks ago, Jadvyga! She told me so—the night it snowed, and she could not get home."

"There must be some mistake," declared the girl, again; "she didn't come here."

He steadied himself by the door-sill; and Jadvyga in her anxiety—for she was fond of Ona—opened the door wide, holding her jacket across her throat. "Are you sure you didn't misunderstand her?" she cried. "She must have meant somewhere else. She——"

"She said here," insisted Jurgis. "She told me all about you, and how you were, and what you said. Are you sure? You haven't forgotten? You weren't away?"

"No, no!" she exclaimed—and then came a peevish voice— "Jadvyga, you are giving the baby a cold. Shut the door!" Jurgis stood for half a minute more, stammering his perplexity through an eighth of an inch of crack; and then, as there was really nothing more to be said, he excused himself and went away.

He walked on half dazed, without knowing where he went. Ona had deceived him! She had lied to him! And what could it mean— where had she been? Where was she now? He could hardly grasp the thing—much less try to solve it; but a hundred wild surmises came to him, a sense of impending calamity overwhelmed him.

Because there was nothing else to do, he went back to the time-office to watch again. He waited until nearly an hour after seven, and then went to the room where Ona worked to make inquiries of

Ona's "forelady." The "forelady," he found, had not yet come; all the lines of cars that came from down-town were stalled—there had been an accident in the power-house, and no cars had been running since last night. Meantime, however, the ham-wrappers were working away, with some one else in charge of them. The girl who answered Jurgis was busy, and as she talked she looked to see if she were being watched. Then a man came up, wheeling a truck; he knew Jurgis for Ona's husband, and was curious about the mystery.

"Maybe the cars had something to do with it," he suggested—"maybe she had gone down-town."

"No," said Jurgis, "she never went down-town."

"Perhaps not," said the man.

Jurgis thought he saw him exchange a swift glance with the girl as he spoke, and he demanded quickly, "What do you know about it?"

But the man had seen that the boss was watching him; he started on again, pushing his truck. "I don't know anything about it," he said, over his shoulder. "How should I know where your wife goes?"

Then Jurgis went out again, and paced up and down before the building. All the morning he stayed there, with no thought of his work. About noon he went to the police station to make inquiries, and then came back again for another anxious vigil. Finally, toward the middle of the afternoon, he set out for home once more.

He was walking out Ashland Avenue. The street-cars had begun running again, and several passed him, packed to the steps with people. The sight of them set Jurgis to thinking again of the man's sarcastic remark; and half involuntarily he found himself watching the cars—with the result that he gave a sudden startled exclamation, and stopped short in his tracks.

Then he broke into a run. For a whole block he tore after the car, only a little ways behind. That rusty black hat with the drooping red flower, it might not be Ona's, but there was very little likelihood of it. He would know for certain very soon, for she would get out two blocks ahead. He slowed down, and let the car go on.

She got out; and as soon as she was out of sight on the side street Jurgis broke into a run. Suspicion was rife in him now, and he was not ashamed to shadow her; he saw her turn the corner near their home, and then he ran again, and saw her as she went up the porch-steps of the house. After that he turned back, and for five minutes paced up and down, his hands clenched tightly and his lips set, his mind in a turmoil. Then he went home and entered.

As he opened the door, he saw Elzbieta, who had also been looking for Ona, and had come home again. She was now on tiptoe, and had a finger on her lips. Jurgis waited until she was close to him.

"Don't make any noise," she whispered, hurriedly.

"What's the matter?" he asked.

"Ona is asleep," she panted. "She's been very ill. I'm afraid her mind's been wandering, Jurgis. She was lost on the street all night, and I've only just succeeded in getting her quiet."

"When did she come in?" he asked.

"Soon after you left this morning," said Elzbieta.

"And has she been out since?"

"No, of course not. She's so weak, Jurgis, she——"

And he set his teeth hard together. "You are lying to me," he said.

Elzbieta started, and turned pale. "Why!" she gasped. "What do you mean?"

But Jurgis did not answer. He pushed her aside, and strode to the bedroom door and opened it.

Ona was sitting on the bed. She turned a startled look upon him as he entered. He closed the door in Elzbieta's face, and went toward his wife. "Where have you been?" he demanded.

She had her hands clasped tightly in her lap, and he saw that her face was as paper, and drawn with pain. She gasped once or twice as she tried to answer him, and then began, speaking low, and swiftly, "Jurgis, I—I think I have been out of my mind. I started to come last night, and I could not find the way. I walked—I walked all night, I think, and—and I only got home—this morning."

"You needed a rest," he said, in a hard tone. "Why did you go out again?"

He was looking her fairly in the face, and he could read the sudden fear and wild uncertainty that leaped into her eyes. "I—I had to go to—to the store," she gasped, almost in a whisper, "I had to go——"

"You are lying to me," said Jurgis.

Then he clenched his hands and took a step toward her. "Why do you lie to me?" he cried, fiercely. "What are you doing that you have to lie to me?"

"Jurgis!" she exclaimed, starting up in fright. "Oh, Jurgis, how can you?"

"You have lied to me, I say!" he cried. "You told me you had been to Jadvyga's house that other night, and you hadn't. You had been where you were last night—somewheres down-town, for I saw you get off the car. Where were you?"

It was as if he had struck a knife into her. She seemed to go all to pieces. For half a second she stood, reeling and swaying, staring at him with horror in her eyes; then, with a cry of anguish, she tottered forward, stretching out her arms to him.

But he stepped aside, deliberately, and let her fall. She caught herself at the side of the bed, and then sank down, burying her face in her hands and bursting into frantic weeping.

There came one of those hysterical crises that had so often dismayed him. Ona sobbed and wept, her fear and anguish building themselves up into long climaxes. Furious gusts of emotion would come sweeping over her, shaking her as the tempest shakes the trees upon the hills; all her frame would quiver and throb with them—it was as if some dreadful thing rose up within her and took possession of her, torturing her, tearing her. This thing had been wont to set Jurgis quite beside himself; but now he stood with his lips set tightly and his hands clenched—she might weep till she killed herself, but she should not move him this time—not an inch, not an inch. Because the sounds she made set his blood to running cold and his lips to quivering in spite of himself, he was glad of the diversion when Teta Elzbieta, pale with fright, opened the door and rushed in; yet he turned upon her with an oath. "Go out!" he cried, "go out!" And then, as she stood hesitating, about to speak, he seized her by the arm, and half flung her from the room, slamming the door and barring it with a table. Then he turned again and faced Ona, crying— "Now, answer me!"

Yet she did not hear him—she was still in the grip of the fiend. Jurgis could see her outstretched hands, shaking and twitching, roaming here and there over the bed at will, like living things; he could see convulsive shudderings start in her body and run through her limbs. She was sobbing and choking—it was as if there were too many sounds for one throat, they came chasing each other, like waves upon the sea. Then her voice would begin to rise into screams, louder and louder until it broke in wild, horrible peals of laughter. Jurgis bore it until he could bear it no longer, and then he sprang at her, seizing her by the shoulders and shaking her, shouting into her ear: "Stop it, I say! Stop it!"

She looked up at him, out of her agony; then she fell forward at his feet. She caught them in her hands, in spite of his efforts to step aside, and with her face upon the floor lay writhing. It made a choking in Jurgis's throat to hear her, and he cried again, more savagely than before: "Stop it, I say!"

This time she heeded him, and caught her breath and lay silent, save for the gasping sobs that wrenched all her frame. For a long minute she lay there, perfectly motionless, until a cold fear seized her husband, thinking that she was dying. Suddenly, however, he heard her voice, faintly: "Jurgis! Jurgis!"

"What is it?" he said.

He had to bend down to her, she was so weak. She was pleading with him, in broken phrases, painfully uttered: "Have faith in me! Believe me!"

"Believe what?" he cried.

"Believe that I—that I know best—that I love you! And do not ask me—what you did. Oh, Jurgis, please, please! It is for the best—it is——"

He started to speak again, but she rushed on frantically, heading him off. "If you will only do it! If you will only—only believe me! It wasn't my fault—I couldn't help it—it will be all right—it is nothing—it is no harm. Oh, Jurgis—please, please!"

She had hold of him, and was trying to raise herself to look at him; he could feel the palsied shaking of her hands and the heaving of the bosom she pressed against him. She managed to catch one of his hands and gripped it convulsively, drawing it to her face, and bathing it in her tears. "Oh, believe me, believe me!" she wailed again; and he shouted in fury, "I will not!"

But still she clung to him, wailing aloud in her despair: "Oh, Jurgis, think what you are doing! It will ruin us—it will ruin us! Oh, no, you must not do it! No, don't, don't do it. You must not do it! It will drive me mad—it will kill me—no, no, Jurgis, I am crazy—it is nothing. You do not really need to know. We can be happy—we can love each other just the same. Oh, please, please, believe me!"

Her words fairly drove him wild. He tore his hands loose, and flung her off. "Answer me," he cried. "God damn it, I say—answer me!"

She sank down upon the floor, beginning to cry again. It was like listening to the moan of a damned soul, and Jurgis could not stand it. He smote his fist upon the table by his side, and shouted again at her, "Answer me!"

She began to scream aloud, her voice like the voice of some wild beast: "Ah! Ah! I can't! I can't do it!"

"Why can't you do it?" he shouted.

"I don't know how!"

He sprang and caught her by the arm, lifting her up, and glaring into her face. "Tell me where you were last night!" he panted. "Quick, out with it!"

Then she began to whisper, one word at a time: "I—was in—a house—down-town——"

"What house? What do you mean?"

She tried to hide her eyes away, but he held her. "Miss Henderson's house," she gasped.

He did not understand at first. "Miss Henderson's house," he echoed. And then suddenly, as in an explosion, the horrible truth burst over him, and he reeled and staggered back with a scream. He caught himself against the wall, and put his hand to his forehead, staring about him, and whispering, "Jesus! Jesus!"

An instant later he leaped at her, as she lay grovelling at his feet. He seized her by the throat. "Tell me!" he gasped, hoarsely. "Quick! Who took you to that place?"

She tried to get away, making him furious; he thought it was fear, or the pain of his clutch—he did not understand that it was the agony of her shame. Still she answered him, "Connor."

"Connor," he gasped. "Who is Connor?"

"The boss," she answered. "The man——"

He tightened his grip, in his frenzy, and only when he saw her eyes closing did he realize that he was choking her. Then he relaxed his fingers, and crouched, waiting, until she opened her lids again. His breath beat hot into her face.

"Tell me," he whispered, at last, "tell me about it."

She lay perfectly motionless, and he had to hold his breath to catch her words. "I did not want—to do it," she said; "I tried—I tried not to do it. I only did it—to save us. It was our only chance."

Again, for a space, there was no sound but his panting. Ona's eyes closed and when she spoke again she did not open them. "He told me—he would have me turned off. He told me he would—we would all of us lose our places. We could never get anything to do—here—again. He—he meant it—he would have ruined us."

Jurgis's arms were shaking so that he could scarcely hold himself up, and lurched forward now and then as he listened. "When—when did this begin?" he gasped.

"At the very first," she said. She spoke as if in a trance. "It was all—it was their plot—Miss Henderson's plot. She hated me. And he—he wanted me. He used to speak to me—out on the platform. Then he began to—to make love to me. He offered me money. He begged me—he said he loved me. Then he threatened me. He knew all about us, he knew we would starve. He knew your boss—he knew Marija's. He would hound us to death, he said—then he said if I would—if I—we would all of us be sure of work—always. Then one day he caught hold of me—he would not let go—he—he——"

"Where was this?"

"In the hallway—at night—after every one had gone. I could not help it. I thought of you—of the baby—of mother and the children. I was afraid of him—afraid to cry out."

A moment ago her face had been ashen gray, now it was scarlet. She was beginning to breathe hard again. Jurgis made not a sound.

"That was two months ago. Then he wanted me to come—to that house. He wanted me to stay there. He said all of us—that we would not have to work. He made me come there—in the evenings. I told you—you thought I was at the factory. Then—one night it snowed, and I couldn't get back. And last night—the cars were stopped. It was such a little thing—to ruin us all. I tried to walk, but I couldn't. I didn't want you to know. It would have—it would have been all right. We could have gone on—just the same—you need never have known about it. He was getting tired of me—he would have let me alone soon. I am going to have a baby—I am getting ugly. He told me that—twice, he told me, last night. He kicked me—last night—too. And now you will kill him—you—you will kill him—and we shall die."

All this she had said without a quiver; she lay still as death, not an eyelid moving. And Jurgis, too, said not a word. He lifted himself by the bed, and stood up. He did not stop for another glance at her, but went to the door and opened it. He did not see Elzbieta, crouching terrified in the corner. He went out, hatless, leaving the street door open behind him. The instant his feet were on the side-walk he broke into a run.

He ran like one possessed, blindly, furiously, looking neither to the right nor left. He was on Ashland Avenue before exhaustion compelled him to slow down, and then, noticing a car, he made a dart for it and drew himself aboard. His eyes were wild and his hair flying, and he was breathing hoarsely, like a wounded bull; but the people on the car did not notice this particularly—perhaps it seemed natural to them that a man who smelt as Jurgis smelt should exhibit an aspect to correspond. They began to give way before him as usual. The conductor took his nickel gingerly, with the tips of his fingers, and then left him with the platform to himself. Jurgis did not even notice it—his thoughts were far away. Within his soul it was like a roaring furnace; he stood waiting, waiting, crouching as if for a spring.

He had some of his breath back when the car came to the entrance of the yards, and so he leaped off and started again, racing at full speed. People turned and stared at him, but he saw no one—there was the factory, and he bounded through the doorway and down the corridor. He knew the room where Ona worked, and he knew Connor, the boss of the loading-gang outside. He looked for the man as he sprang into the room.

The truckmen were hard at work, loading the freshly packed boxes and barrels upon the cars. Jurgis shot one swift glance up and down the platform—the man was not on it. But then suddenly he heard a voice in the corridor, and started for it with a bound. In an instant more he fronted the boss.

He was a big, red-faced Irishman, coarse-featured, and smelling of liquor. He saw Jurgis as he crossed the threshold, and turned white. He hesitated one second, as if meaning to run; and in the next his assailant was upon him. He put up his hands to protect his face, but Jurgis, lunging with all the power of his arm and body, struck him fairly between the eyes and knocked him backward. The next moment he was on top of him, burying his fingers in his throat.

To Jurgis this man's whole presence reeked of the crime he had committed; the touch of his body was madness to him—it set every nerve of him a-tremble, it aroused all the demon in his soul. It had worked its will upon Ona, this great beast—and now he had it, he had it! It was his turn now! Things swam blood before him, and he screamed aloud in his fury, lifting his victim and smashing his head upon the floor.

The place, of course, was in an uproar; women fainting and shrieking, and men rushing in. Jurgis was so bent upon his task that he knew nothing of this, and scarcely realized that people were trying to interfere with him; it was only when half a dozen men had seized him by the legs and shoulders and were pulling at him, that he understood that he was losing his prey. In a flash he had bent down and sunk his teeth into the man's cheek; and when they tore him away he was dripping with blood, and little ribbons of skin were hanging in his mouth.

They got him down upon the floor, clinging to him by his arms and legs, and still they could hardly hold him. He fought like a tiger, writhing and twisting, half flinging them off, and starting toward his unconscious enemy. But yet others rushed in, until there was a little mountain of twisted limbs and bodies, heaving and tossing, and working its way about the room. In the end, by their sheer weight, they choked the breath out of him, and then they carried him to the company police-station, where he lay still until they had summoned a patrol wagon to take him away.

Chapter XVI

When Jurgis got up again he went quietly enough. He was exhausted and half dazed, and besides he saw the blue uniforms of the policemen. He drove in a patrol wagon with half a dozen of them watching him; keeping as far away as possible, however, on account of the fertilizer. Then he stood before the sergeant's desk and gave his name and address, and saw a charge of assault and battery entered against him. On his way to his cell a burly policeman cursed him because he started down the wrong corridor, and then added a kick when he was not quick enough; nevertheless, Jurgis did not even lift his eyes—he had lived two years and a half in Packingtown, and he knew what the police were. It was as much as a man's very life was worth to anger them, here in their inmost lair; like as not a dozen would pile on to him at once, and pound his face into a pulp. It would be nothing unusual if he got his skull cracked in the mêlée—in which case they would report that he had been drunk and had fallen down, and there would be no one to know the difference or to care.

So a barred door clanged upon Jurgis and he sat down upon a bench and buried his face in his hands. He was alone; he had the afternoon and all of the night to himself.

At first he was like a wild beast that has glutted itself; he was in a dull stupor of satisfaction. He had done up the scoundrel pretty well—not as well as he would have if they had given him a minute more, but pretty well, all the same; the ends of his fingers were still tingling from their contact with the fellow's throat. But then, little by little, as his strength came back and his senses cleared, he began to see beyond his momentary gratification; that he had nearly killed the boss would not help Ona—not the horrors that she had borne, nor the memory that would haunt her all her days. It would not help to feed her and her child; she would certainly lose her place, while he—what was to happen to him God only knew.

Half the night he paced the floor, wrestling with this nightmare; and when he was exhausted he lay down, trying to sleep, but finding instead, for the first time in his life, that his brain was too much for him. In the cell next to him was a drunken wife-beater and in the one beyond a yelling maniac. At midnight they opened the station-house to the homeless wanderers who were crowded about the door, shivering in the winter blast, and they thronged into the corridor outside of the cells. Some of them stretched themselves out on the bare stone floor and fell to snoring; others sat up, laughing and talking, cursing and quarrelling. The air was fetid with their breath, yet in spite of this some of them smelt Jurgis and called down the torments of hell upon him, while he lay in a far corner of his cell, counting the throbbings of the blood in his forehead.

They had brought him his supper, which was "duffers and dope"—being hunks of dry bread on a tin plate, and coffee, called "dope" because it was drugged to keep the prisoners quiet. Jurgis had not known this, or he would have swallowed the stuff in desperation; as it was, every nerve of him was a-quiver with shame and rage. Toward morning the place fell silent, and he got up and began to pace his cell; and then within the soul of him there rose up a fiend, red-eyed and cruel, and tore out the strings of his heart.

It was not for himself that he suffered—what did a man who worked in Durham's fertilizer-mill care about anything that the world might do to him! What was any tyranny of prison compared with the tyranny of the past, of the thing that had happened and could not be recalled, of the memory that could never be effaced! The horror of it drove him mad; he stretched out his arms to heaven, crying out for deliverance from it—and there was no deliverance, there was no power even in heaven that could undo the past. It was a ghost that would not down; it followed him, it seized upon him and beat him to the ground. Ah, if only he could have foreseen it—but then, he would have foreseen it, if he had not been a fool! He smote his hands upon his forehead, cursing himself because he had ever allowed Ona to work where she had, because he had not stood between her and a fate which every one knew to be so common. He should have taken her away, even if it were to lie down and die of starvation in the gutters of Chicago's streets! And now—oh, it could not be true; it was too monstrous, too horrible.

It was a thing that could not be faced; a new shuddering seized him every time he tried to think of it. No, there was no bearing the load of it, there was no living under it. There would be none for her—he knew that he might pardon her, might plead with her on his knees, but she would never look him in the face again, she would never be his wife again. The shame of it would kill her—there could be no other deliverance, and it was best that she should die.

This was simple and clear, and yet, with cruel inconsistency, whenever he escaped from this nightmare it was to suffer and cry out at the vision of Ona starving. They had put him in jail, and they would keep him here a long time, years maybe. And Ona would surely not go to work again, broken and crushed as she was. And Elzbieta and Marija, too, might lose their places—if that hell-fiend Connor chose to set to work to ruin them, they would all be turned out. And even if he did not, they could not live—even if the boys left school again, they could surely not pay all the bills without him and Ona. They had only a few dollars now—they had just paid the rent of the house a week ago, and that after it was two weeks overdue. So it would be due again in a week!

They would have no money to pay it then—and they would lose the house, after all their long, heart-breaking struggle. Three times now the agent had warned him that he would not tolerate another delay. Perhaps it was very base of Jurgis to be thinking about the house when he had the other unspeakable thing to fill his mind; yet, how much he had suffered for this house, how much they had all of them suffered! It was their one hope of respite, as long as they lived; they had put all their money into it—and they were working-people, poor people, whose money was their strength, the very substance of them, body and soul, the thing by which they lived and for lack of which they died.

And they would lose it all; they would be turned out into the streets, and have to hide in some icy garret, and live or die as best they could! Jurgis had all the night—and all of many more nights— to think about this, and he saw the thing in its details; he lived it all, as if he were there. They would sell their furniture, and then run into debt at the stores, and then be refused credit; they would borrow a little from the Szedvilases, whose delicatessen store was tottering on the brink of ruin; the neighbors would come and help them a little—poor, sick Jadvyga would bring a few spare pennies, as she always did when people were starving, and Tamoszius Kusleika would bring them the proceeds of a night's fiddling. So they would struggle to hang on until he got out of jail—or would they know that he was in jail, would they be able to find out anything about him? Would they be allowed to see him—or was it to be part of his punishment to be kept in ignorance about their fate?

His mind would hang upon the worst possibilities; he saw Ona ill and tortured, Marija out of her place, little Stanislovas unable to get to work for the snow, the whole family turned out on the street. God Almighty! would they actually let them lie down in the street and die? Would there be no help even then—would they wander about in the snow till they froze? Jurgis had never seen any dead bodies in the streets, but he had seen people evicted and disappear, no one knew where; and though the city had a relief-bureau, though there was a charity organization society in the stockyards district, in all his life there he had never heard of either of them. They did not advertise their activities, having more calls than they could attend to without that.

—So on until morning. Then he had another ride in the patrol wagon, along with the drunken wife-beater and the maniac, several "plain drunks" and "saloon fighters," a burglar, and two men who had been arrested for stealing meat from the packing-houses. Along with them he was driven into a large, white-walled room, stale-smelling and crowded. In front, upon a raised platform behind a rail, sat a stout, florid-faced personage, with a nose broken out in purple blotches.

Our friend realized vaguely that he was about to be tried. He wondered what for—whether or not his victim might be dead, and if so, what they would do with him. Hang him, perhaps, or beat him to death—nothing would have surprised Jurgis, who knew little of the laws. Yet he had picked up gossip enough to have it occur to him that the loud-voiced man upon the bench might be the notorious Justice Callahan, about whom the people of Packingtown spoke with bated breath.

"Pat" Callahan—"Growler" Pat,[1] as he had been known before he ascended the bench—had begun life as a butcher-boy and a bruiser of local reputation; he had gone into politics almost as soon as he had learned to talk, and had held two offices at once before he was old enough to vote. If Scully was the thumb, Pat Callahan was the first finger of the unseen hand whereby the packers held down the people of the district. No politician in Chicago ranked higher in their confidence; he had been at it a long time—had been the business agent in the city council of old Durham, the self-made merchant, way back in the early days, when the whole city of Chicago had been up at auction. "Growler" Pat had given up holding city offices very early in his career—caring only for party power, and giving the rest of his time to superintending his dives and brothels. Of late years, however, since his children were growing up, he had begun to value respectability, and had had himself made a magistrate; a position for which he was admirably fitted, because of his strong conservatism and his contempt for "foreigners."

Jurgis sat gazing about the room for an hour or two; he was in hopes that some one of the family would come, but in this he was disappointed. Finally, he was led before the bar, and a lawyer for the company appeared against him. Connor was under the doctor's care, the lawyer explained briefly, and if his Honor would hold the prisoner for a week—"Three hundred dollars," said his Honor, promptly.

Jurgis was staring from the judge to the lawyer in perplexity. "Have you any one to go on your bond?" demanded the judge, and then a clerk who stood at Jurgis's elbow explained to him what this meant. The latter shook his head, and before he realized what had happened the policemen were leading him away again. They took him to a room where other prisoners were waiting, and here he stayed until court adjourned, when he had another long and bitterly cold ride in a patrol wagon to the country jail, which is on the north side of the city, and nine or ten miles from the stockyards.

Here they searched Jurgis, leaving him only his money, which consisted of fifteen cents. Then they led him to a room and told him to strip for a bath; after which he had to walk down a long gallery, past

---

1. Perhaps inspired by Johnny Powers (1852–1930), locally known as "De Pow." An Irish immigrant who became a Chicago Nineteenth Ward alderman (1888–1903, 1904–27), infamous as "Prince of the Boodlers," Powers is one of the three "gray wolves" mentioned below (233), who used their political influence to prey on the public.

the grated cell-doors of the inmates of the jail. This was a great event
to the latter—the daily review of the new arrivals, all stark naked,
and many and diverting were the comments. Jurgis was required to
stay in the bath longer than any one, in the vain hope of getting out
of him a few of his phosphates and acids. The prisoners roomed two
in a cell, but that day there was one left over, and he was the one.

The cells were in tiers, opening upon galleries. His cell was about
five feet by seven in size, with a stone floor and a heavy wooden bench
built into it. There was no window—the only light came from windows near the roof at one end of the court outside. There were two
bunks, one above the other, each with a straw mattress and a pair of
gray blankets—the latter stiff as boards with filth, and alive with
fleas, bed-bugs, and lice. When Jurgis lifted up the mattress he discovered beneath it a layer of scurrying roaches, almost as badly frightened as himself.

Here they brought him more "duffers and dope," with the addition of a bowl of soup. Many of the prisoners had their meals brought
in from a restaurant, but Jurgis had no money for that. Some had
books to read and cards to play, with candles to burn by night, but
Jurgis was all alone in darkness and silence. He could not sleep
again; there was the same maddening procession of thoughts that
lashed him like whips upon his naked back. When night fell he was
pacing up and down his cell like a wild beast that breaks its teeth
upon the bars of its cage. Now and then in his frenzy he would fling
himself against the walls of the place, beating his hands upon them.
They cut him and bruised him—they were cold and merciless as the
men who had built them.

In the distance there was a church-tower bell that tolled the hours
one by one. When it came to midnight Jurgis was lying upon the
floor with his head in his arms, listening. Instead of falling silent at
the end, the bell broke into a sudden clangor. Jurgis raised his head;
what could that mean—a fire? God! suppose there were to be a fire
in this jail! But then he made out a melody in the ringing; there were
chimes. And they seemed to waken the city—all around, far and
near, there were bells, ringing wild music; for fully a minute Jurgis
lay lost in wonder, before, all at once, the meaning of it broke over
him—that this was Christmas Eve!

Christmas Eve—he had forgotten it entirely! There was a breaking
of flood-gates, a whirl of new memories and new griefs rushing into
his mind. In far Lithuania they had celebrated Christmas; and it
came to him as if it had been yesterday—himself a little child, with
his lost brother and his dead father in the cabin in the deep black
forest, where the snow fell all day and all night and buried them from
the world. It was too far off for Santa Claus in Lithuania, but it was
not too far for peace and good will to men, for the wonder-bearing
vision of the Christ-child. And even in Packingtown they had

not forgotten it—some gleam of it had never failed to break their darkness. Last Christmas Eve and all Christmas Day Jurgis had toiled on the killing-beds, and Ona at wrapping hams, and still they had found strength enough to take the children for a walk upon the avenue, to see the store windows all decorated with Christmas trees and ablaze with electric lights. In one window there would be live geese, in another marvels in sugar—pink and white canes big enough for ogres, and cakes with cherubs upon them; in a third there would be rows of fat yellow turkeys, decorated with rosettes, and rabbits and squirrels hanging; in a fourth would be a fairy-land of toys— lovely dolls with pink dresses, and woolly sheep and drums and sol- dier hats. Nor did they have to go without their share of all this, either. The last time they had had a big basket with them and all their Christmas marketing to do—a roast of pork and a cabbage and some rye-bread, and a pair of mittens for Ona, and a rubber doll that squeaked, and a little green cornucopia full of candy to be hung from the gas jet and gazed at by half a dozen pairs of longing eyes.

Even half a year of the sausage-machines and the fertilizer-mill had not been able to kill the thought of Christmas in them; there was a choking in Jurgis's throat as he recalled that the very night Ona had not come home Teta Elzbieta had taken him aside and shown him an old valentine that she had picked up in a paper store for three cents—dingy and shop-worn, but with bright colors, and figures of angels and doves. She had wiped all the specks off this, and was going to set it on the mantel, where the children could see it. Great sobs shook Jurgis at this memory—they would spend their Christmas in misery and despair, with him in prison and Ona ill and their home in desolation. Ah, it was too cruel! Why at least had they not left him alone—why, after they had shut him in jail, must they be ringing Christmas chimes in his ears!

But no, their bells were not ringing for him—their Christmas was not meant for him, they were simply not counting him at all. He was of no consequence—he was flung aside, like a bit of trash, the car- cass of some animal. It was horrible, horrible! His wife might be dying, his baby might be starving, his whole family might be perish- ing in the cold—and all the while they were ringing their Christmas chimes! And the bitter mockery of it—all this was punishment for him! They put him in a place where the snow could not beat in, where the cold could not eat through his bones; they brought him food and drink—why, in the name of heaven, if they must punish him, did they not put his family in jail and leave him outside—why could they find no better way to punish him than to leave three weak women and six helpless children to starve and freeze?

That was their law, that was their justice! Jurgis stood upright, trembling with passion, his hands clenched and his arms upraised, his whole soul ablaze with hatred and defiance. Ten thousand curses upon them and their law! Their justice—it was a lie, it was a lie, a hideous, brutal lie, a thing too black and hateful for any world but a world of nightmares. It was a sham and a loathsome mockery. There was no justice, there was no right, anywhere in it—it was only force, it was tyranny, the will and the power, reckless and unrestrained! They had ground him beneath their heel, they had devoured all his substance; they had murdered his old father, they had broken and wrecked his wife, they had crushed and cowed his whole family; and now they were through with him, they had no further use for him—and because he had interfered with them, had gotten in their way, this was what they had done to him! They had put him behind bars, as if he had been a wild beast, a thing without sense or reason, without rights, without affections, without feelings. Nay, they would not even have treated a beast as they had treated him! Would any man in his senses have trapped a wild thing in its lair, and left its young behind to die?

These midnight hours were fateful ones to Jurgis; in them was the beginning of his rebellion, of his outlawry and his unbelief. He had no wit to trace back the social crime to its far sources—he could not say that it was the thing men have called "the system" that was crushing him to the earth; that it was the packers, his masters, who had bought up the law of the land, and had dealt out their brutal will to him from the seat of justice. He only knew that he was wronged, and that the world had wronged him; that the law, that society, with all its powers, had declared itself his foe. And every hour his soul grew blacker, every hour he dreamed new dreams of vengeance, of defiance, of raging, frenzied hate.

> "The vilest deeds, like poison weeds,
>   Bloom well in prison air;
> It is only what is good in Man
>   That wastes and withers there;
> Pale Anguish keeps the heavy gate,
>   And the Warder is Despair."

So wrote a poet, to whom the world had dealt its justice—

> "I know not whether Laws be right,
>   Or whether Laws be wrong;
> All that we know who lie in gaol
>   Is that the wall is strong.
> And they do well to hide their hell,
>   For in it things are done
> That Son of God nor son of Man
>   Ever should look upon!"[2]

2. From Part V, stanzas 5 and 1 of "The Ballad of Reading Gaol" (1898), written by the Irish writer Oscar Wilde (1854–1900) after his own incarceration. The poem recounts the horror of inmates over the hanging of a fellow prisoner who had murdered his wife.

Chapter XVII

At seven o'clock the next morning Jurgis was let out to get water to
wash his cell—a duty which he performed faithfully, but which most
of the prisoners were accustomed to shirk, until their cells became
so filthy that the guards interposed. Then he had more "duffers and
dope," and afterward was allowed three hours for exercise, in a long,
cement-walled court roofed with glass. Here were all the inmates of
the jail crowded together. At one side of the court was a place for
visitors, cut off by two heavy wire screens, a foot apart, so that nothing could be passed in to the prisoners; here Jurgis watched anxiously, but there came no one to see him.

Soon after he went back to his cell, a keeper opened the door to
let in another prisoner. He was a dapper young fellow, with a light
brown mustache and blue eyes, and a graceful figure. He nodded to
Jurgis, and then, as the keeper closed the door upon him, began gazing critically about him.

"Well, pal," he said, as his glance encountered Jurgis again, "good
morning."

"Good morning," said Jurgis.

"A rum go[1] for Christmas, eh?" added the other.

Jurgis nodded.

The new-comer went to the bunks and inspected the blankets; he
lifted up the mattress, and then dropped it with an exclamation. "My
God!" he said, "that's the worst yet."

He glanced at Jurgis again. "Looks as if it hadn't been slept in last
night. Couldn't stand it, eh?"

"I didn't want to sleep last night," said Jurgis.

"When did you come in?"

"Yesterday."

The other had another look round, and then wrinkled up his nose.
"There's the devil of a stink in here," he said, suddenly. "What is it?"

"It's me," said Jurgis.

"You?"

"Yes, me."

"Didn't they make you wash?"

"Yes, but this don't wash."

"What is it?"

"Fertilizer."

"Fertilizer! The deuce![2] What are you?"

"I work in the stockyards—at least I did until the other day. It's in
my clothes."

---

1. A bad time (slang).
2. Exclamation of surprise or frustration, similar to "What the devil!" (slang).

"That's a new one on me," said the new-comer. "I thought I'd been up against 'em all. What are you in for?"

"I hit my boss."

"Oh—that's it. What did he do?"

"He—he treated me mean."

"I see. You're what's called an honest working-man!"

"What are you?" Jurgis asked.

"I?" The other laughed. "They say I'm a cracksman," he said.

"What's that?" asked Jurgis.

"Safes, and such things," answered the other.

"Oh," said Jurgis, wonderingly, and stared at the speaker in awe. "You mean you break into them—you—you—"

"Yes," laughed the other, "that's what they say."

He did not look to be over twenty-two or three, though, as Jurgis found afterward, he was thirty. He spoke like a man of education, like what the world calls a "gentleman."

"Is that what you're here for?" Jurgis inquired.

"No," was the answer. "I'm here for disorderly conduct. They were mad because they couldn't get any evidence."

"What's your name?" the young fellow continued after a pause. "My name's Duane—Jack Duane. I've more than a dozen, but that's my company one." He seated himself on the floor with his back to the wall and his legs crossed, and went on talking easily; he soon put Jurgis on a friendly footing—he was evidently a man of the world, used to getting on, and not too proud to hold conversation with a mere laboring man. He drew Jurgis out, and heard all about his life—all but the one unmentionable thing; and then he told stories about his own life. He was a great one for stories, not always of the choicest. Being sent to jail had apparently not disturbed his cheerfulness; he had "done time" twice before, it seemed, and he took it all with a frolic welcome. What with women and wine and the excitement of his vocation, a man could afford to rest now and then.

Naturally, the aspect of prison life was changed for Jurgis by the arrival of a cell-mate. He could not turn his face to the wall and sulk, he had to speak when he was spoken to; nor could he help being interested in the conversation of Duane—the first educated man with whom he had ever talked. How could he help listening with wonder while the other told of midnight ventures and perilous escapes, of feastings and orgies, of fortunes squandered in a night? The young fellow had an amused contempt for Jurgis, as a sort of working mule; he, too, had felt the world's injustice, but instead of bearing it patiently, he had struck back, and struck hard. He was striking all the time—there was war between him and society. He was a genial free-booter, living off the enemy, without fear or shame.

He was not always victorious, but then defeat did not mean annihilation, and need not break his spirit.

Withal he was a good-hearted fellow—too much so, it appeared. His story came out, not in the first day, nor the second, but in the long hours that dragged by, in which they had nothing to do but talk, and nothing to talk of but themselves. Jack Duane was from the East; he was a college-bred man—had been studying electrical engineering. Then his father had met with misfortune in business and killed himself; and there had been his mother and a younger brother and sister. Also, there was an invention of Duane's; Jurgis could not understand it clearly, but it had to do with telegraphing, and it was a very important thing—there were fortunes in it, millions upon millions of dollars. And Duane had been robbed of it by a great company, and got tangled up in lawsuits and lost all his money. Then somebody had given him a tip on a horse-race, and he had tried to retrieve his fortune with another person's money, and had to run away, and all the rest had come from that. The other asked him what had led him to safe-breaking—to Jurgis a wild and appalling occupation to think about. A man he had met, his cell-mate had replied—one thing leads to another. Didn't he ever wonder about his family, Jurgis asked. Sometimes, the other answered, but not often—he didn't allow it. Thinking about it would make it no better. This wasn't a world in which a man had any business with a family; sooner or later Jurgis would find that out also, and give up the fight and shift for himself.

Jurgis was so transparently what he pretended to be that his cell-mate was as open with him as a child; it was pleasant to tell him adventures, he was so full of wonder and admiration, he was so new to the ways of the country. Duane did not even bother to keep back names and places—he told all his triumphs and his failures, his loves and his griefs. Also he introduced Jurgis to many of the other prisoners, nearly half of whom he knew by name. The crowd had already given Jurgis a name—they called him "the stinker." This was cruel, but they meant no harm by it, and he took it with a good-natured grin.

Our friend had caught now and then a whiff from the sewers over which he lived, but this was the first time that he had ever been splashed by their filth. This jail was a Noah's ark of the city's crime—there were murderers, "hold-up men" and burglars, embezzlers, counterfeiters and forgers, bigamists, "shoplifters," "confidence-men," petty thieves and pickpockets, gamblers and procurers,[3] brawlers, beggars, tramps and drunkards; they were black and white, old and young, Americans and natives of every nation under the sun. There were hardened criminals and innocent men too poor to give bail; old men, and boys literally not yet in their teens. They were the

3. Pimps.

drainage of the great festering ulcer of society; they were hideous to look upon, sickening to talk to. All life had turned to rottenness and stench in them—love was a beastliness, joy was a snare, and God was an imprecation. They strolled here and there about the courtyard, and Jurgis listened to them. He was ignorant and they were wise; they had been everywhere and tried everything. They could tell the whole hateful story of it, set forth the inner soul of a city in which justice and honor, women's bodies and men's souls, were for sale in the market-place, and human beings writhed and fought and fell upon each other like wolves in a pit; in which lusts were raging fires, and men were fuel, and humanity was festering and stewing and wallowing in its own corruption. Into this wild-beast tangle these men had been born without their consent, they had taken part in it because they could not help it; that they were in jail was no disgrace to them, for the game had never been fair, the dice were loaded. They were swindlers and thieves of pennies and dimes, and they had been trapped and put out of the way by the swindlers and thieves of millions of dollars.

To most of this Jurgis tried not to listen. They frightened him with their savage mockery; and all the while his heart was far away, where his loved ones were calling. Now and then in the midst of it his thoughts would take flight; and then the tears would come into his eyes—and he would be called back by the jeering laughter of his companions.

He spent a week in this company, and during all that time he had no word from his home. He paid one of his fifteen cents for a postal card, and his companion wrote a note to the family, telling them where he was and when he would be tried. There came no answer to it, however, and at last, the day before New Year's, Jurgis bade good-by to Jack Duane. The latter gave him his address, or rather the address of his mistress, and made Jurgis promise to look him up. "Maybe I could help you out of a hole some day," he said, and added that he was sorry to have him go. Jurgis rode in the patrol wagon back to Justice Callahan's court for trial.

One of the first things he made out as he entered the room was Teta Elzbieta and little Kotrina, looking pale and frightened, seated far in the rear. His heart began to pound, but he did not dare to try to signal to them, and neither did Elzbieta. He took his seat in the prisoners' pen and sat gazing at them in helpless agony. He saw that Ona was not with them, and was full of foreboding as to what that might mean. He spent half an hour brooding over this—and then suddenly he straightened up and the blood rushed into his face. A man had come in—Jurgis could not see his features for the bandages that swathed him, but he knew the burly figure. It was Connor! A trembling seized him, and his limbs bent as if for a spring. Then suddenly he felt a hand on his collar, and heard a voice behind him: "Sit down, you son of a——!"

He subsided, but he never took his eyes off his enemy. The fellow was still alive, which was a disappointment, in one way; and yet it was pleasant to see him, all in penitential plasters. He and the company lawyer, who was with him, came and took seats within the judge's railing; and a minute later the clerk called Jurgis's name, and the policeman jerked him to his feet and led him before the bar, gripping him tightly by the arm, lest he should spring upon the boss.

Jurgis listened while the man entered the witness chair, took the oath, and told his story. The wife of the prisoner had been employed in a department near him, and had been discharged for impudence to him. Half an hour later he had been violently attacked, knocked down, and almost choked to death. He had brought witnesses—

"They will probably not be necessary," observed the judge, and he turned to Jurgis. "You admit attacking the plaintiff?" he asked.

"Him?" inquired Jurgis, pointing at the boss.

"Yes," said the judge.

"I hit him, sir," said Jurgis.

"Say 'your Honor,'" said the officer, pinching his arm hard.

"Your Honor," said Jurgis, obediently.

"You tried to choke him?"

"Yes, sir, your Honor."

"Ever been arrested before?"

"No, sir, your Honor."

"What have you to say for yourself?"

Jurgis hesitated. What had he to say? In two years and a half he had learned to speak English for practical purposes, but these had never included the statement that some one had intimidated and seduced his wife. He tried once or twice, stammering and balking, to the annoyance of the judge, who was gasping from the odor of fertilizer. Finally, the prisoner made it understood that his vocabulary was inadequate, and there stepped up a dapper young man with waxed mustaches, bidding him speak in any language he knew.

Jurgis began; supposing that he would be given time, he explained how the boss had taken advantage of his wife's position to make advances to her and had threatened her with the loss of her place. When the interpreter had translated this, the judge, whose calendar was crowded, and whose automobile was ordered for a certain hour, interrupted with the remark: "Oh, I see. Well, if he made love to your wife, why didn't she complain to the superintendent or leave the place?"

Jurgis hesitated, somewhat taken aback; he began to explain that they were very poor—that work was hard to get—

"I see," said Justice Callahan; "so instead you thought you would knock him down." He turned to the plaintiff, inquiring, "Is there any truth in this story, Mr. Connor?"

"Not a particle, your Honor," said the boss. "It is very unpleasant— they tell some such tale every time you have to discharge a woman—"

"Yes, I know," said the judge. "I hear it often enough. The fellow seems to have handled you pretty roughly. Thirty days and costs. Next case."

Jurgis had been listening in perplexity. It was only when the policeman who had him by the arm turned and started to lead him away that he realized that sentence had been passed. He gazed round him wildly. "Thirty days!" he panted—and then he whirled upon the judge. "What will my family do?" he cried, frantically. "I have a wife and baby, sir, and they have no money—my God, they will starve to death!"

"You would have done well to think about them before you committed the assault," said the judge, dryly, as he turned to look at the next prisoner.

Jurgis would have spoken again, but the policeman had seized him by the collar and was twisting it, and a second policeman was making for him with evidently hostile intentions. So he let them lead him away. Far down the room he saw Elzbieta and Kotrina, risen from their seats, staring in fright; he made one effort to go to them, and then, brought back by another twist at his throat, he bowed his head and gave up the struggle. They thrust him into a cell-room, where other prisoners were waiting; and as soon as court had adjourned they led him down with them into the "Black Maria,"[4] and drove him away.

This time Jurgis was bound for the "Bridewell,"[5] a petty jail where Cook County prisoners serve their time. It was even filthier and more crowded than the county jail; all the smaller fry out of the latter had been sifted into it—the petty thieves and swindlers, the brawlers and vagrants. For his cell-mate Jurgis had an Italian fruit-seller who had refused to pay his graft to the policeman, and been arrested for carrying a large pocket-knife; as he did not understand a word of English our friend was glad when he left. He gave place to a Norwegian sailor, who had lost half an ear in a drunken brawl, and who proved to be quarrelsome, cursing Jurgis because he moved in his bunk and caused the roaches to drop upon the lower one. It would have been quite intolerable, staying in a cell with this wild beast, but for the fact that all day long the prisoners were put at work breaking stone.

---

4. Patrol wagon for transporting prisoners.
5. For less serious crimes, such as fighting and public drunkenness, and officially known as the Chicago House of Corrections. Located at West 26th Street and California Avenue.

Ten days of his thirty Jurgis spent thus, without hearing a word from his family; then one day a keeper came and informed him that there was a visitor to see him. Jurgis turned white, and so weak at the knees that he could hardly leave his cell.

The man led him down the corridor and a flight of steps to the visitors' room, which was barred like a cell. Through the grating Jurgis could see some one sitting in a chair; and as he came into the room the person started up, and he saw that it was little Stanislovas. At the sight of some one from home the big fellow nearly went to pieces—he had to steady himself by a chair, and he put his other hand to his forehead, as if to clear away a mist. "Well?" he said, weakly.

Little Stanislovas was also trembling, and all but too frightened to speak. "They—they sent me to tell you—" he said, with a gulp.

"Well?" Jurgis repeated.

He followed the boy's glance to where the keeper was standing watching them. "Never mind that," Jurgis cried, wildly. "How are they?"

"Ona is very sick," Stanislovas said; "and we are almost starving. We can't get along; we thought you might be able to help us."

Jurgis gripped the chair tighter; there were beads of perspiration on his forehead, and his hand shook. "I—can't—help you," he said.

"Ona lies in her room all day," the boy went on, breathlessly. "She won't eat anything, and she cries all the time. She won't tell what is the matter and she won't go to work at all. Then a long time ago the man came for the rent. He was very cross. He came again last week. He said he would turn us out of the house. And then Marija—"

A sob choked Stanislovas, and he stopped. "What's the matter with Marija?" cried Jurgis.

"She's cut her hand!" said the boy. "She's cut it bad, this time, worse than before. She can't work, and it's all turning green,[6] and the company doctor says she may—she may have to have it cut off. And Marija cries all the time—her money is nearly all gone, too, and we can't pay the rent and the interest on the house; and we have no coal, and nothing more to eat, and the man at the store, he says—"

The little fellow stopped again, beginning to whimper. "Go on!" the other panted in frenzy—"Go on!"

"I—I will," sobbed Stanislovas. "It's so—so cold all the time. And last Sunday it snowed again—a deep, deep snow—and I couldn't—couldn't get to work."

"God!" Jurgis half shouted, and he took a step toward the child. There was an old hatred between them because of the snow—ever since that dreadful morning when the boy had had his fingers frozen and Jurgis had had to beat him to send him to work. Now he

---

6. Probably because of infection from an accident at the canning factory.

clenched his hands, looking as if he would try to break through the grating. "You little villain," he cried, "you didn't try!"

"I did—I did!" wailed Stanislovas, shrinking from him in terror. "I tried all day—two days. Elzbieta was with me, and she couldn't either. We couldn't walk at all, it was so deep. And we had nothing to eat, and oh, it was so cold! I tried, and then the third day Ona went with me—"

"Ona!"

"Yes. She tried to go to work, too. She had to. We were all starving. But she had lost her place—"

Jurgis reeled, and gave a gasp. "She went back to that place?" he screamed.

"She tried to," said Stanislovas, gazing at him in perplexity. "Why not, Jurgis?"

The man breathed hard, three or four times. "Go—on," he panted, finally.

"I went with her," said Stanislovas, "but Miss Henderson wouldn't take her back. And Connor saw her and cursed her. He was still bandaged up—why did you hit him, Jurgis?" (There was some fascinating mystery about this, the little fellow knew; but he could get no satisfaction.)

Jurgis could not speak; he could only stare, his eyes starting out. "She has been trying to get other work," the boy went on; "but she's so weak she can't keep up. And my boss would not take me back, either—Ona says he knows Connor, and that's the reason; they've all got a grudge against us now. So I've got to go down-town and sell papers with the rest of the boys and Kotrina—"

"Kotrina!"

"Yes, she's been selling papers, too. She does best, because she's a girl. Only the cold is so bad—it's terrible coming home at night, Jurgis. Sometimes they can't come home at all—I'm going to try to find them to-night and sleep where they do, it's so late, and it's such a long ways home. I've had to walk, and I didn't know where it was—I don't know how to get back, either. Only mother said I must come, because you would want to know, and maybe somebody would help your family when they had put you in jail so you couldn't work. And I walked all day to get here—and I only had a piece of bread for breakfast, Jurgis. Mother hasn't any work either, because the sausage department is shut down; and she goes and begs at houses with a basket, and people give her food. Only she didn't get much yesterday; it was too cold for her fingers, and to-day she was crying—"

So little Stanislovas went on, sobbing as he talked; and Jurgis stood, gripping the table tightly, saying not a word, but feeling that his head would burst; it was like having weights piled upon him, one after another, crushing the life out of him. He struggled and fought within himself—as if in some terrible nightmare, in which a man suffers an agony, and cannot lift his hand, nor cry out, but feels that he is going mad, that his brain is on fire—

Just when it seemed to him that another turn of the screw would kill him, little Stanislovas stopped. "You cannot help us?" he said, weakly.

Jurgis shook his head.

"They won't give you anything here?"

He shook it again.

"When are you coming out?"

"Three weeks yet," Jurgis answered.

And the boy gazed around him uncertainly. "Then I might as well go," he said.

Jurgis nodded. Then, suddenly recollecting, he put his hand into his pocket and drew it out, shaking. "Here," he said, holding out the fourteen cents. "Take this to them."

And Stanislovas took it, and after a little more hesitation, started for the door. "Good-by, Jurgis," he said, and the other noticed that he walked unsteadily as he passed out of sight.

For a minute or so Jurgis stood clinging to the chair, reeling and swaying; then the keeper touched him on the arm, and he turned and went back to breaking stone.

Chapter XVIII

Jurgis did not get out of the Bridewell quite as soon as he had expected. To his sentence there were added "court costs" of a dollar and a half—he was supposed to pay for the trouble of putting him in jail, and not having the money, was obliged to work it off by three days more of toil. Nobody had taken the trouble to tell him this—only after counting the days and looking forward to the end in an agony of impatience, when the hour came that he expected to be free he found himself still set at the stone-heap, and laughed at when he ventured to protest. Then he concluded he must have counted wrong; but as another day passed, he gave up all hope—and was sunk in the depths of despair, when one morning after breakfast a keeper came to him with the word that his time was up at last. So he doffed his prison garb, and put on his old fertilizer clothing, and heard the door of the prison clang behind him.

He stood upon the steps, bewildered; he could hardly believe that it was true,—that the sky was above him again and the open street before him; that he was a free man. But then the cold began to strike through his clothes, and he started quickly away.

There had been a heavy snow, and now a thaw had set in; a fine sleety rain was falling, driven by a wind that pierced Jurgis to the bone. He had not stopped for his overcoat when he set out to "do up" Connor, and so his rides in the patrol wagons had been cruel experiences; his clothing was old and worn thin, and it never had been very warm. Now as he trudged on the rain soon wet it through; there were six inches of watery slush on the sidewalks, so that his feet would soon have been soaked, even had there been no holes in his shoes.

Jurgis had had enough to eat in the jail, and the work had been the least trying of any that he had done since he came to Chicago; but even so, he had not grown strong—the fear and grief that had preyed upon his mind had worn him thin. Now he shivered and shrunk from the rain, hiding his hands in his pockets and hunching his shoulders together. The Bridewell grounds were on the outskirts of the city and the country around them was unsettled and wild—on one side was the big drainage canal, and on the other a maze of railroad tracks, and so the wind had full sweep.

After walking a ways, Jurgis met a little ragamuffin whom he hailed: "Hey, sonny!"

The boy cocked one eye at him—he knew that Jurgis was a "jail bird" by his shaven head. "Wot yer want?" he queried.

"How do you go to the stockyards?" Jurgis demanded.

"I don't go," replied the boy.

Jurgis hesitated a moment, nonplussed. Then he said, "I mean which is the way?"

"Why don't yer say so then?" was the response, and the boy pointed to the northwest, across the tracks. "That way."

"How far is it?" Jurgis asked.

"I dunno," said the other. "Mebby twenty miles or so."

"Twenty miles!" Jurgis echoed, and his face fell. He had to walk every foot of it, for they had turned him out of jail without a penny in his pockets.

Yet, when he once got started, and his blood had warmed with walking, he forgot everything in the fever of his thoughts. All the dreadful imaginations that had haunted him in his cell now rushed into his mind at once. The agony was almost over—he was going to find out; and he clenched his hands in his pockets as he strode, following his flying desire, almost at a run. Ona—the baby—the family—the house—he would know the truth about them all! And he was coming to the rescue—he was free again! His hands were his own, and he could help them, he could do battle for them against the world.

For an hour or so he walked thus, and then he began to look about him. He seemed to be leaving the city altogether. The street was turning into a country road, leading out to the westward; there were snow-covered fields on either side of him. Soon he met a farmer driving a two-horse wagon loaded with straw, and he stopped him.

"Is this the way to the stockyards?" he asked.

The farmer scratched his head. "I dunno jest where they be," he said. "But they're in the city somewhere, and you're going dead away from it now."

Jurgis looked dazed. "I was told this was the way," he said.

"Who told you?"

"A boy."

"Well, mebbe he was playing a joke on ye. The best thing ye kin do is to go back, and when ye git into town ask a policeman. I'd take ye in, only I've come a long ways an' I'm loaded heavy. Git up!"

So Jurgis turned and followed, and toward the end of the morning he began to see Chicago again. Past endless blocks of two-story shanties he walked, along wooden sidewalks and unpaved pathways treacherous with deep slush-holes. Every few blocks there would be a railroad crossing on the level with the sidewalk, a death-trap for the unwary; long freight-trains would be passing, the cars clanking and crashing together, and Jurgis would pace about waiting, burning up with a fever of impatience. Occasionally the cars would stop for some minutes, and wagons and street-cars would crowd together waiting, the drivers swearing at each other, or hiding beneath umbrellas out of the rain; at such times Jurgis would dodge under the gates and run across the tracks and between the cars, taking his life into his hands.

He crossed a long bridge over a river frozen solid and covered with slush. Not even on the river bank was the snow white—the rain which fell was a diluted solution of smoke, and Jurgis's hands and face were streaked with black. Then he came into the business part of the city, where the streets were sewers of inky blackness, with horses slipping and plunging, and women and children flying across in panic-stricken droves. These streets were huge cañons formed by towering black buildings, echoing with the clang of car-gongs and the shouts of drivers; the people who swarmed in them were as busy as ants—all hurrying breathlessly, never stopping to look at anything nor at each other. The solitary trampish-looking foreigner, with water-soaked clothing and haggard face and anxious eyes, was as much alone as he hurried past them, as much unheeded and as lost, as if he had been a thousand miles deep in a wilderness.

A policeman gave him his direction and told him that he had five miles to go. He came again to the slum-districts, to avenues of saloons and cheap stores, with long dingy red factory buildings, and coal-yards and railroad-tracks; and then Jurgis lifted up his head and began to sniff the air like a startled animal—scenting the far-off odor of home. It was late afternoon then, and he was hungry, but the dinner invitations hung out of the saloons were not for him.

So he came at last to the stockyards, to the black volcanoes of smoke and the lowing cattle and the stench. Then, seeing a crowded car, his impatience got the better of him and he jumped aboard, hiding behind another man, unnoticed by the conductor. In ten minutes more he had reached his street, and home.

He was half running as he came round the corner. There was the house, at any rate—and then suddenly he stopped and stared. What was the matter with the house?

Jurgis looked twice, bewildered; then he glanced at the house next door and at the one beyond—then at the saloon on the corner. Yes, it was the right place, quite certainly—he had not made any mistake. But the house—the house was a different color!

He came a couple of steps nearer. Yes; it had been gray and now it was yellow! The trimmings around the windows had been red, and now they were green! It was all newly painted! How strange it made it seem!

Jurgis went closer yet, but keeping on the other side of the street. A sudden and horrible spasm of fear had come over him. His knees were shaking beneath him, and his mind was in a whirl. New paint on the house, and new weatherboards, where the old had begun to rot off, and the agent had got after them! New shingles over the hole in the roof, too, the hole that had for six months been the bane of his soul—he having no money to have it fixed and no time to fix it himself, and the rain leaking in, and overflowing the pots and pans he put to catch it, and flooding the attic and loosening the plaster. And now it was fixed! And the broken window-pane replaced! And curtains in the windows! New, white curtains, stiff and shiny!

Then suddenly the front door opened. Jurgis stood, his chest heaving as he struggled to catch his breath. A boy had come out, a stranger to him; a big, fat, rosy-cheeked youngster, such as had never been seen in his home before.

Jurgis stared at the boy, fascinated. He came down the steps whistling, kicking off the snow. He stopped at the foot, and picked up some, and then leaned against the railing, making a snow-ball. A moment later he looked around and saw Jurgis, and their eyes met; it was a hostile glance, the boy evidently thinking that the other had suspicions of the snow-ball. When Jurgis started slowly across the street toward him, he gave a quick glance about, meditating retreat, but then he concluded to stand his ground.

Jurgis took hold of the railing of the steps, for he was a little unsteady. "What—what are you doing here?" he managed to gasp.

"Go on!" said the boy.

"You—" Jurgis tried again. "What do you want here?"

"Me?" answered the boy, angrily. "I live here."

"You live here!" Jurgis panted. He turned white, and clung more tightly to the railing. "You live here! Then where's my family?"

The boy looked surprised. "Your family!" he echoed.

And Jurgis started toward him. "I—this is my house!" he cried.

"Come off!" said the boy; then suddenly the door upstairs opened, and he called: "Hey, ma! Here's a fellow says he owns this house."

A stout Irish woman came to the top of the steps. "What's that?" she demanded.

Jurgis turned toward her. "Where is my family?" he cried, wildly. "I left them here! This is my home! What are you doing in my home?"

The woman stared at him in frightened wonder, she must have thought she was dealing with a maniac—Jurgis looked like one. "Your home!" she echoed.

"My home!" he half shrieked. "I lived here, I tell you."

"You must be mistaken," she answered him. "No one ever lived here. This is a new house. They told us so. They—"

"What have they done with my family?" shouted Jurgis, frantically.

A light had begun to break upon the woman; perhaps she had had doubts of what "they" had told her. "I don't know where your family is," she said. "I bought the house only three days ago, and there was nobody here, and they told me it was all new. Do you really mean you had ever rented it?"

"Rented it!" panted Jurgis. "I bought it! I paid for it! I own it! And they—my God, can't you tell me where my people went?"

She made him understand at last that she knew nothing. Jurgis's brain was so confused that he could not grasp the situation. It was as if his family had been wiped out of existence; as if they were proving to be dream people, who never had existed at all. He was quite lost—but then suddenly he thought of Grandmother Majauszkiene, who lived in the next block. She would know! He turned and started at a run.

Grandmother Majauszkiene came to the door herself. She cried out when she saw Jurgis, wild-eyed and shaking. Yes, yes, she could tell him. The family had moved; they had not been able to pay the rent and they had been turned out into the snow, and the house had been repainted and sold again the next week. No, she had not heard how they were, but she could tell him that they had gone back to Aniele Jukniene, with whom they had stayed when they first came to the yards. Wouldn't Jurgis come in and rest? It was certainly too bad—if only he had not got into jail—

And so Jurgis turned and staggered away. He did not go very far—round the corner he gave out completely, and sat down on the steps of a saloon, and hid his face in his hands, and shook all over with dry, racking sobs.

Their home! Their home! They had lost it! Grief, despair, rage, overwhelmed him—what was any imagination of the thing to this heart-breaking, crushing reality of it—to the sight of strange people living in his house, hanging their curtains in his windows, staring at him with hostile eyes! It was monstrous, it was unthinkable—they could not do it—it could not be true! Only think what he had suffered for that house—what miseries they had all suffered for it—the price they had paid for it!

The whole long agony came back to him. Their sacrifices in the beginning, their three hundred dollars that they had scraped together, all they owned in the world, all that stood between them and starvation! And then their toil, month by month, to get together the twelve dollars, and the interest as well, and now and then the taxes, and the other charges, and the repairs, and what not! Why, they had put their very souls into their payments on that house, they had paid for it with their sweat and tears—yes, more, with their very life-blood. Dede Antanas had died of the struggle to earn that money—he would have been alive and strong to-day if he had not had to work in Durham's dark cellars to earn his share. And Ona, too, had given her health and strength to pay for it—she was wrecked and ruined because of it; and so was he, who had been a big, strong man three years ago, and now sat here shivering, broken, cowed, weeping like a hysterical child. Ah! they had cast their all into the fight; and they had lost, they had lost!

All that they had paid was gone—every cent of it. And their house was gone—they were back where they had started from, flung out into the cold to starve and freeze!

Jurgis could see all the truth now—could see himself, through the whole long course of events, the victim of ravenous vultures that had torn into his vitals and devoured him;[1] of fiends that had racked and tortured him, mocking him, meantime, jeering in his face. Ah, God, the horror of it, the monstrous, hideous, demoniacal wickedness of it! He and his family, helpless women and children, struggling to live, ignorant and defenceless and forlorn as they were—and the enemies that had been lurking for them, crouching upon their trail and thirsting for their blood! That first lying circular, that smooth-tongued slippery agent! That trap of the extra payments, the interest, and all the other charges that they had not the means to pay, and would never have attempted to pay! And then all the tricks of the packers, their masters, the tyrants who ruled them,—the shut-downs and the scarcity of work, the irregular hours and the cruel speeding-up, the lowering of wages, the raising of prices! The mercilessness of nature about them, of heat and cold, rain and snow; the mercilessness of the city, of the country in which they lived, of its laws and customs that they did not understand! All of these things had worked together for the company that had marked them for its prey and was waiting for its chance. And now, with this last hideous injustice, its time had come, and it had turned them out bag and baggage, and taken their house and sold it again! And they could do nothing, they were tied hand and foot— the law was against them, the whole machinery of society was at their oppressors' command! If Jurgis so much as raised a hand against them, back he would go into that wild-beast pen from which he had just escaped!

To get up and go away was to give up, to acknowledge defeat, to leave the strange family in possession; and Jurgis might have sat shivering in the rain for hours before he could do that, had it not been for the thought of his family. It might be that he had worse things yet to learn—and so he got to his feet and started away, walking on, wearily, half-dazed.

To Aniele's house, in back of the yards, was a good two miles; the distance had never seemed longer to Jurgis, and when he saw the familiar dingy-gray shanty his heart was beating fast. He ran up the steps and began to hammer upon the door.

The old woman herself came to open it. She had shrunk all up with her rheumatism since Jurgis had seen her last, and her yellow parchment face stared up at him from a little above the level of the

---

1. An allusion to the Greek mythological figure Prometheus, tortured by a vulture feeding on his liver.

door-knob. She gave a start when she saw him. "Is Ona here?" he cried, breathlessly.

"Yes," was the answer, "she's here."

"How—" Jurgis began, and then stopped short, clutching convulsively at the side of the door. From somewhere within the house had come a sudden cry, a wild, horrible scream of anguish. And the voice was Ona's.

For a moment Jurgis stood half-paralyzed with fright; then he bounded past the old woman and into the room.

It was Aniele's kitchen, and huddled round the stove were half a dozen women, pale and frightened. One of them started to her feet as Jurgis entered; she was haggard and frightfully thin, with one arm tied up in bandages—he hardly realized that it was Marija. He looked first for Ona; then, not seeing her, he stared at the women, expecting them to speak. But they sat dumb, gazing back at him, panic-stricken; and a second later came another piercing scream.

It was from the rear of the house, and upstairs. Jurgis bounded to a door of the room and flung it open; there was a ladder leading through a trap-door to the garret, and he was at the foot of it, when suddenly he heard a voice behind him, and saw Marija at his heels. She seized him by the sleeve with her good hand, panting wildly, "No, no, Jurgis! Stop!"

"What do you mean?" he gasped.

"You mustn't go up," she cried.

Jurgis was half-crazed with bewilderment and fright. "What's the matter?" he shouted. "What is it?"

Marija clung to him tightly; he could hear Ona sobbing and moaning above, and he fought to get away and climb up, without waiting for her reply. "No, no," she rushed on. "Jurgis! You mustn't go up! It's—it's the child!"

"The child?" he echoed in perplexity. "Antanas?"

Marija answered him, in a whisper: "The new one!"

And then Jurgis went limp, and caught himself on the ladder. He stared at her as if she were a ghost. "The new one!" he gasped. "But it isn't time," he added, wildly.

Marija nodded. "I know," she said; "but it's come."

And then again came Ona's scream, smiting him like a blow in the face, making him wince and turn white. Her voice died away into a wail—then he heard her sobbing again, "My God—let me die, let me die!" And Marija flung her arms about him, crying: "Come out! Come away!"

She dragged him back into the kitchen, half carrying him, for he had gone all to pieces. It was as if the pillars of his soul had fallen in—he was blasted with horror. In the room he sank into a chair, trembling like a leaf, Marija still holding him, and the women staring at him in dumb, helpless fright.

And then again Ona cried out; he could hear it nearly as plainly here, and he staggered to his feet. "How long has this been going on?" he panted.

"Not very long," Marija answered, and then, at a signal from Aniele, she rushed on: "You go away, Jurgis—you can't help—go away and come back later. It's all right—it's—"

"Who's with her?" Jurgis demanded; and then, seeing Marija hesitating, he cried again, "Who's with her?"

"She's—she's all right," she answered. "Elzbieta's with her."

"But the doctor!" he panted. "Some one who knows!"

He seized Marija by the arm; she trembled, and her voice sank beneath a whisper as she replied. "We—we have no money." Then, frightened at the look on his face, she exclaimed: "It's all right, Jurgis! You don't understand—go away—go away! Ah, if you only had waited!"

Above her protests Jurgis heard Ona again; he was almost out of his mind. It was all new to him; raw and horrible—it had fallen upon him like a lightning stroke. When little Antanas was born he had been at work, and had known nothing about it until it was over; and now he was not to be controlled. The frightened women were at their wits' end; one after another they tried to reason with him, to make him understand that this was the lot of woman. In the end they half drove him out into the rain, where he began to pace up and down, bareheaded and frantic. Because he could hear Ona from the street, he would first go away to escape the sounds, and then come back because he could not help it. At the end of a quarter of an hour he rushed up the steps again, and for fear that he would break in the door they had to open it and let him in.

There was no arguing with him. They could not tell him that all was going well—how could they know, he cried—why, she was dying, she was being torn to pieces! Listen to her—listen! Why, it was monstrous—it could not be allowed—there must be some help for it! Had they tried to get a doctor? They might pay him afterwards—they could promise—

"We couldn't promise, Jurgis," protested Marija. "We had no money—we have scarcely been able to keep alive."

"But I can work," Jurgis exclaimed. "I can earn money!"

"Yes," she answered—"but we thought you were in jail. How could we know when you would return? They will not work for nothing."

Marija went on to tell how she had tried to find a midwife, and how they had demanded ten, fifteen, even twenty-five dollars, and that in cash. "And I had only a quarter," she said. "I have spent every cent of my money—all that I had in the bank; and I owe the doctor who has been coming to see me, and he has stopped because he thinks I don't mean to pay him. And we owe Aniele for two weeks' rent, and she is nearly starving, and is afraid of being turned out. We have been borrowing and begging to keep alive, and there is nothing more we can do—"

"And the children?" cried Jurgis.

"The children have not been home for three days, the weather has been so bad. They could not know what is happening—it came suddenly, two months before we expected it."

Jurgis was standing by the table, and he caught himself with his hands; his head sank and his arms shook—it looked as if he were going to collapse. Then suddenly Aniele got up and came hobbling toward him, fumbling in her skirt pocket. She drew out a dirty rag, in one corner of which she had something tied.

"Here, Jurgis!" she said, "I have some money *Palauk!* See!"

She unwrapped it and counted it out—thirty-four cents. "You go, now," she said, "and try and get somebody yourself. And maybe the rest can help—give him some money, you; he will pay you back some day, and it will do him good to have something to think about, even if he doesn't succeed. When he comes back, maybe it will be over."

And so the other women turned out the contents of their pocketbooks; most of them had only pennies and nickels, but they gave him all. Mrs. Olszewski, who lived next door, and had a husband who was a skilled cattle-butcher, but a drinking man, gave nearly half a dollar, enough to raise the whole sum to a dollar and a quarter. Then Jurgis thrust it into his pocket, still holding it tightly in his fist, and started away at a run.

Chapter XIX

"Madame Haupt, Hebamme,"[1] ran a sign, swinging from a second-story window over a saloon on the avenue; at a side door was another sign, with a hand pointing up a dingy flight of steps. Jurgis went up them, three at a time.

Madame Haupt was frying pork and onions, and had her door half open to let out the smoke. When he tried to knock upon it, it swung open the rest of the way, and he had a glimpse of her, with a black bottle turned up to her lips. Then he knocked louder, and she started and put it away. She was a Dutch woman, enormously fat—when she walked she rolled like a small boat on the ocean, and the dishes in the cupboard jostled each other. She wore a filthy blue wrapper, and her teeth were black.

"Vot is it?" she said, when she saw Jurgis.

He had run like mad all the way and was so out of breath he could hardly speak. His hair was flying and his eyes wild—he looked like a man that had risen from the tomb. "My wife!" he panted. "Come quickly!"

Madame Haupt set the frying pan to one side and wiped her hands on her wrapper. "You vant me to come for a case?" she inquired.

"Yes," gasped Jurgis.

"I haf yust come back from a case," she said. "I haf had no time to eat my dinner. Still—if it is so bad—"

"Yes—it is!" cried he.

"Vell, den, perhaps—vot you pay?"

"I—I—how much do you want?" Jurgis stammered.

"Twenty-five dollars."

His face fell. "I can't pay that," he said.

The woman was watching him narrowly. "How much do you pay?" she demanded.

"Must I pay now—right away?"

"Yes; all my customers do."

"I—I haven't much money," Jurgis began, in an agony of dread. "I've been in—in trouble—and my money is gone. But I'll pay you—every cent—just as soon as I can; I can work—"

"Vot is your work?"

"I have no place now. I must get one. But I—"

"How much haf you got now?"

He could hardly bring himself to reply. When he said "A dollar and a quarter," the woman laughed in his face.

"I vould not put on my hat for a dollar und a quarter," she said.

1. Midwife (German).

"It's all I've got," he pleaded, his voice breaking. "I must get some one—my wife will die. I can't help it—I—"

Madame Haupt had put back her pork and onions on the stove. She turned to him and answered, out of the steam and noise: "Git me ten dollars cash, und so you can pay me de rest next mont'."

"I can't do it—I haven't got it!" Jurgis protested. "I tell you I have only a dollar and a quarter."

The woman turned to her work. "I don't believe you," she said. "Dot is all to try to sheat me. Vot is de reason a big man like you has got only a dollar und a quarter?"

"I've just been in jail," Jurgis cried,—he was ready to get down upon his knees to the woman,—"and I had no money before, and my family has almost starved."

"Vere is your friends, dot ought to help you?"

"They are all poor," he answered. "They gave me this. I have done everything I can—"

"Haven't you got notting you can sell?"

"I have nothing, I tell you—I have nothing," he cried, frantically.

"Can't you borrow it, den? Don't your store people trust you?" Then, as he shook his head, she went on: "Listen to me—if you git me you vill be glad of it. I vill save your wife und baby for you, und it vill not seem like mooch to you in de end. If you loose dem now how you tink you feel den? Und here is a lady dot knows her business—I could send you to people in dis block, und dey vould tell you—"

Madame Haupt was pointing her cooking-fork at Jurgis persuasively; but her words were more than he could bear. He flung up his hands with a gesture of despair and turned and started away. "It's no use," he exclaimed—but suddenly he heard the woman's voice behind him again:—

"I vill make it five dollars for you."

She followed behind him, arguing with him. "You vill be foolish not to take such an offer," she said. "You von't find nobody to go out on a rainy day like dis for less. Vy, I haf never took a case in my life so sheap as dot. I couldn't pay mine room rent—"

Jurgis interrupted her with an oath of rage. "If I haven't got it," he shouted, "how can I pay it? Damn it, I would pay you if I could, but I tell you I haven't got it. I haven't got it! Do you hear me—*I haven't got it!*"

He turned and started away again. He was halfway down the stairs before Madame Haupt could shout to him: "Vait! I vill go mit you! Come back!"

He went back into the room again.

"It is not goot to tink of anybody suffering," she said, in a melancholy voice. "I might as vell go mit you for notting as vot you offer me, but I vill try to help you. How far is it?"

"Three or four blocks from here."

"Tree or four! Und so I shall get soaked! *Gott in Himmel*,[2] it ought to be vorth more! Vun dollar und a quarter, und a day like dis! But you understand now—you vill pay me de rest of twenty-five dollars soon?"

"As soon as I can."

"Some time dis mont'?"

"Yes, within a month," said poor Jurgis. "Anything! Hurry up!"

"Vere is de dollar und a quarter?" persisted Madame Haupt, relentlessly.

Jurgis put the money on the table and the woman counted it and stowed it away. Then she wiped her greasy hands again and proceeded to get ready, complaining all the time; she was so fat that it was painful for her to move, and she grunted and gasped at every step. She took off her wrapper without even taking the trouble to turn her back to Jurgis, and put on her corsets and dress. Then there was a black bonnet which had to be adjusted carefully, and an umbrella which was mislaid, and a bag full of necessaries which had to be collected from here and there—the man being nearly crazy with anxiety in the meantime. When they were on the street he kept about four paces ahead of her, turning now and then, as if he could hurry her on by the force of his desire. But Madame Haupt could only go so far at a step, and it took all her attention to get the needed breath for that.

They came at last to the house, and to the group of frightened women in the kitchen. It was not over yet, Jurgis learned—he heard Ona crying still; and meantime Madame Haupt removed her bonnet and laid it on the mantelpiece, and got out of her bag, first an old dress and then a saucer of goose-grease,[3] which she proceeded to rub upon her hands. The more cases this goose-grease is used in, the better luck it brings to the midwife, and so she keeps it upon her kitchen mantelpiece or stowed away in a cupboard with her dirty clothes, for months, and sometimes even for years.

Then they escorted her to the ladder, and Jurgis heard her give an exclamation of dismay. "*Gott in Himmel*, vot for haf you brought me to a place like dis? I could not climb up dot ladder. I could not git troo a trap-door! I vill not try it—vy, I might kill myself already. Vot sort of a place is dot for a woman to bear a child in—up in a garret, mit only a ladder to it? You ought to be ashamed of yourselves!" Jurgis stood in the doorway and listened to her scolding, half drowning out the horrible moans and screams of Ona.

At last Aniele succeeded in pacifying her, and she essayed the ascent; then, however, she had to be stopped while the old woman cautioned her about the floor of the garret. They had no real

2. God in Heaven (German).
3. Used as lubricant.

floor—they had laid old boards in one part to make a place for the family to live; it was all right and safe there, but the other part of the garret had only the joists of the floor, and the lath and plaster of the ceiling below, and if one stepped on this there would be a catastrophe. As it was half dark up above, perhaps one of the others had best go up first with a candle. Then there were more outcries and threatening, until at last Jurgis had a vision of a pair of elephantine legs disappearing through the trap-door, and felt the house shake as Madame Haupt started to walk. Then suddenly Aniele came to him and took him by the arm.

"Now," she said, "you go away. Do as I tell you—you have done all you can, and you are only in the way. Go away and stay away."

"But where shall I go?" Jurgis asked, helplessly.

"I don't know where," she answered. "Go on the street, if there is no other place—only go! And stay all night!"

In the end she and Marija pushed him out of the door and shut it behind him. It was just about sundown, and it was turning cold— the rain had changed to snow, and the slush was freezing. Jurgis shivered in his thin clothing, and put his hands into his pockets and started away. He had not eaten since morning, and he felt weak and ill; with a sudden throb of hope he recollected he was only a few blocks from the saloon where he had been wont to eat his dinner. They might have mercy on him there, or he might meet a friend. He set out for the place as fast as he could walk.

"Hello, Jack," said the saloon-keeper, when he entered—they call all foreigners and unskilled men "Jack" in Packingtown. "Where've you been?"

Jurgis went straight to the bar. "I've been in jail," he said, "and I've just got out. I walked home all the way, and I've not a cent, and had nothing to eat since this morning. And I've lost my home, and my wife's ill, and I'm done up."

The saloon-keeper gazed at him, with his haggard white face and his blue trembling lips. Then he pushed a big bottle toward him. "Fill her up!" he said.

Jurgis could hardly hold the bottle, his hands shook so.

"Don't be afraid," said the saloon-keeper; "fill her up!"

So Jurgis drank a huge glass of whiskey, and then turned to the lunch-counter, in obedience to the other's suggestion. He ate all he dared, stuffing it in as fast as he could; and then, after trying to speak his gratitude, he went and sat down by the big red stove in the middle of the room.

It was too good to last, however—like all things in this hard world. His soaked clothing began to steam, and the horrible stench of fertilizer to fill the room. In an hour or so the packing-houses would be closing and the men coming in from their work; and they would not come into a place that smelt of Jurgis. Also it was Saturday night, and in a couple of hours would come a violin and a cornet, and in the rear part of the saloon the families of the neighborhood would dance and feast upon wienerwurst and lager, until two or three o'clock in the morning. The saloon-keeper coughed once or twice, and then remarked, "Say, Jack, I'm afraid you'll have to quit."

He was used to the sight of human wrecks, this saloon-keeper; he "fired"[4] dozens of them every night, just as haggard and cold and forlorn as this one. But they were all men who had given up and been counted out, while Jurgis was still in the fight, and had reminders of decency about him. As he got up meekly, the other reflected that he had always been a steady man, and might soon be a good customer again. "You've been up against it, I see," he said. "Come this way."

In the rear of the saloon were the cellar-stairs. There was a door above and another below, both safely padlocked, making the stairs an admirable place to stow away a customer who might still chance to have money, or a political light whom it was not advisable to kick out of doors.

So Jurgis spent the night. The whiskey had only half warmed him, and he could not sleep, exhausted as he was; he would nod forward, and then start up, shivering with the cold, and begin to remember again. Hour after hour passed, until he could only persuade himself that it was not morning by the sounds of music and laughter and singing that were to be heard from the room. When at last these ceased, he expected that he would be turned out into the street; as this did not happen, he fell to wondering whether the man had forgotten him.

In the end, when the silence and suspense were no longer to be borne, he got up and hammered on the door; and the proprietor came, yawning and rubbing his eyes. He was keeping open all night, and dozing between customers.

"I want to go home," Jurgis said. "I'm worried about my wife—I can't wait any longer."

"Why the hell didn't you say so before?" said the man. "I thought you didn't have any home to go to."

Jurgis went outside. It was four o'clock in the morning, and as black as night. There were three or four inches of fresh snow on the ground, and the flakes were falling thick and fast. He turned toward Aniele's and started at a run.

There was a light burning in the kitchen window and the blinds were drawn. The door was unlocked and Jurgis rushed in.

4. Turned out (slang).

Aniele, Marija, and the rest of the women were huddled about the stove, exactly as before; with them were several new-comers, Jurgis noticed—also he noticed that the house was silent.

"Well?" he said.

No one answered him; they sat staring at him with their pale faces. He cried again: "Well?"

And then, by the light of the smoky lamp, he saw Marija, who sat nearest him, shaking her head slowly. "Not yet," she said.

And Jurgis gave a cry of dismay. "Not *yet?*"

Again Marija's head shook. The poor fellow stood dumfounded. "I don't hear her," he gasped.

"She's been quiet a long time," replied the other.

There was another pause—broken suddenly by a voice from the attic: "Hello, there!"

Several of the women ran into the next room, while Marija sprang toward Jurgis. "Wait here!" she cried, and the two stood, pale and trembling, listening. In a few moments it became clear that Madame Haupt was engaged in descending the ladder, scolding and exhorting again, while the ladder creaked in protest. In a moment or two she reached the ground, angry and breathless, and they heard her coming into the room. Jurgis gave one glance at her, and then turned white and reeled. She had her jacket off, like one of the workers on the killing-beds. Her hands and arms were smeared with blood, and blood was splashed upon her clothing and her face.

She stood breathing hard, and gazing about her; no one made a sound.

"I haf done my best," she began suddenly. "I can do notting more—dere is no use to try."

Again there was silence.

"It ain't my fault," she said. "You had ought to haf had a doctor, und not vaited so long—it vas too late already ven I come." Once more there was deathlike stillness. Marija was clutching Jurgis with all the power of her one well arm.

Then suddenly Madame Haupt turned to Aniele. "You haf not got something to drink, hey?" she queried. "Some brandy?"

Aniele shook her head.

"*Herr Gott!*"[5] exclaimed Madame Haupt. "Such people! Perhaps you vill give me something to eat den—I haf had notting since yesterday morning, und I haf vorked myself near to death here. If I could haf known it vas like dis, I vould never haf come for such money as you gif me."

At this moment she chanced to look round, and saw Jurgis. She shook her finger at him. "You understand me," she said, "you pays

---

5. Lord God! (German).

me dot money yust de same! It is not my fault dat you send for me so late I can't help you vife. It is not my fault if der baby comes mit one arm first, so dot I can't save it. I haf tried all night, und in dot place vere it is not fit for dogs to be born, und mit notting to eat only vot I brings in mine own pockets."

Here Madame Haupt paused for a moment to get her breath; and Marija, seeing the beads of sweat on Jurgis's forehead, and feeling the quivering of his frame, broke out in a low voice: "How is Ona?"

"How is she?" echoed Madame Haupt. "How do you tink she can be ven you leave her to kill herself so? I told dem dot ven dey send for de priest. She is young, und she might haf got over it, und been vell und strong, if she been treated right. She fight hard, dot girl—she is not yet quite dead."

And Jurgis gave a frantic scream. *"Dead!"*

"She vill die, of course," said the other, angrily.[6] "Der baby is dead now."

The garret was lighted by a candle stuck upon a board; it had almost burned itself out, and was sputtering and smoking as Jurgis rushed up the ladder. He could make out dimly in one corner a pallet of rags and old blankets, spread upon the floor; at the foot of it was a crucifix, and near it a priest muttering a prayer. In a far corner crouched Elzbieta, moaning and wailing. Upon the pallet lay Ona.

She was covered with a blanket, but he could see her shoulders and one arm lying bare; she was so shrunken he would scarcely have known her—she was all but a skeleton, and as white as a piece of chalk. Her eyelids were closed, and she lay still as death. He staggered toward her and fell upon his knees with a cry of anguish: "Ona! Ona!"

She did not stir. He caught her hand in his, and began to clasp it frantically, calling: "Look at me! Answer me! It is Jurgis come back—don't you hear me?"

There was the faintest quivering of the eyelids, and he called again in frenzy: "Ona! Ona!"

Then suddenly her eyes opened—one instant. One instant she looked at him—there was a flash of recognition between them, he saw her afar off, as through a dim vista, standing forlorn. He stretched out his arms to her, he called her in wild despair; a fearful yearning surged up in him, hunger for her that was agony, desire that was a new being born within him, tearing his heartstrings, torturing him. But it was all in vain—she faded from him, she slipped back and was gone. And a wail of anguish burst from him, great sobs shook all his

---

6. Throughout the second half of the 19th century, the filthiness of Chicago led to a surge in puerperal fever (also called childbed fever), an infection of the reproductive organs, increasing the mortality rates for women giving birth.

frame, and hot tears ran down his cheeks and fell upon her. He clutched her hands, he shook her, he caught her in his arms and pressed her to him; but she lay cold and still—she was gone—she was gone!

The word rang through him like the sound of a bell, echoing in the far depths of him, making forgotten chords to vibrate, old shadowy fears to stir—fears of the dark, fears of the void, fears of annihilation. She was dead! She was dead! He would never see her again, never hear her again! An icy horror of loneliness seized him; he saw himself standing apart and watching all the world fade away from him—a world of shadows, of fickle dreams. He was like a little child, in his fright and grief; he called and called, and got no answer, and his cries of despair echoed through the house, making the women down-stairs draw nearer to each other in fear. He was inconsolable, beside himself—the priest came and laid his hand upon his shoulder and whispered to him, but he heard not a sound. He was gone away himself, stumbling through the shadows, and groping after the soul that had fled.

So he lay. The gray dawn came up and crept into the attic. The priest left, the women left, and he was alone with the still, white figure—quieter now, but moaning and shuddering, wrestling with the grisly fiend. Now and then he would raise himself and stare at the white mask before him, then hide his eyes, because he could not bear it. Dead! *dead!* And she was only a girl, she was barely eighteen! Her life had hardly begun—and here she lay murdered—mangled, tortured to death!

It was morning when he rose up and came down into the kitchen—haggard and ashen gray, reeling and dazed. More of the neighbors had come in, and they stared at him in silence as he sank down upon a chair by the table and buried his face in his arms.

A few minutes later the front door opened; a blast of cold and snow rushed in, and behind it little Kotrina, breathless from running, and blue with the cold. "I'm home again!" she exclaimed. "I could hardly—"

And then, seeing Jurgis, she stopped with an exclamation. Looking from one to another she saw that something had happened, and she asked, in a lower voice "What's the matter?"

Before any one could reply, Jurgis started up; he went toward her, walking unsteadily. "Where have you been?" he demanded.

"Selling papers with the boys," she said. "The snow—"

"Have you any money?" he demanded.

"Yes."

"How much?"

"Nearly three dollars, Jurgis."

"Give it to me."

Kotrina, frightened by his manner, glanced at the others. "Give it to me!" he commanded again, and she put her hand into her pocket and pulled out a lump of coins tied in a bit of rag. Jurgis took it without a word, and went out of the door and down the street.

Three doors away was a saloon. "Whiskey," he said, as he entered, and as the man pushed him some, he tore at the rag with his teeth and pulled out half a dollar. "How much is the bottle?" he said. "I want to get drunk."

Chapter XX

But a big man cannot stay drunk very long on three dollars. That was Sunday morning, and Monday night Jurgis came home, sober and sick, realizing that he had spent every cent the family owned, and had not bought a single instant's forgetfulness with it.

Ona was not yet buried; but the police had been notified, and on the morrow they would put the body in a pine coffin and take it to the potter's field.[1] Elzbieta was out begging now, a few pennies from each of the neighbors, to get enough to pay for a mass for her; and the children were upstairs starving to death, while he, good-for-nothing rascal, had been spending their money on drink. So spoke Aniele, scornfully, and when he started toward the fire she added the information that her kitchen was no longer for him to fill with his phosphate stinks. She had crowded all her boarders into one room on Ona's account, but now he could go up in the garret where he belonged—and not there much longer, either, if he did not pay her some rent.

Jurgis went without a word, and, stepping over half a dozen sleeping boarders in the next room, ascended the ladder. It was dark up above; they could not afford any light; also it was nearly as cold as outdoors. In a corner, as far away from the corpse as possible, sat Marija, holding little Antanas in her one good arm and trying to soothe him to sleep. In another corner crouched poor little Juozapas, wailing because he had had nothing to eat all day. Marija said not a word to Jurgis; he crept in like a whipped cur, and went and sat down by the body.

Perhaps he ought to have meditated upon the hunger of the children, and upon his own baseness; but he thought only of Ona, he gave himself up again to the luxury of grief. He shed no tears, being ashamed to make a sound; he sat motionless and shuddering with his anguish. He had never dreamed how much he loved Ona, until now that she was gone; until now that he sat here, knowing that on the morrow they would take her away, and that he would never lay eyes upon her again—never all the days of his life. His old love, which had been starved to death, beaten to death, awoke in him again; the flood-gates of memory were lifted—he saw all their life together, saw her as he had seen her in Lithuania, the first day at the fair, beautiful as the flowers, singing like a bird. He saw her as he had married her, with all her tenderness, with her heart of wonder; the very words she had spoken seemed to ring now in his ears, the tears she had shed to be wet upon his cheek. The long, cruel battle with misery and

---

1. Burial ground for the poor, the unknown, and criminals.

hunger had hardened and embittered him, but it had not changed her—she had been the same hungry soul to the end, stretching out her arms to him, pleading with him, begging him for love and tenderness. And she had suffered—so cruelly she had suffered, such agonies, such infamies—ah, God, the memory of them was not to be borne. What a monster of wickedness, of heartlessness, he had been! Every angry word that he had ever spoken came back to him and cut him like a knife; every selfish act that he had done—with what torments he paid for them now! And such devotion and awe as welled up in his soul—now that it could never be spoken, now that it was too late, too late! His bosom was choking with it, bursting with it; he crouched here in the darkness beside her, stretching out his arms to her—and she was gone forever, she was dead! He could have screamed aloud with the horror and despair of it; a sweat of agony beaded his forehead, yet he dared not make a sound—he scarcely dared to breathe, because of his shame and loathing of himself.

Late at night came Elzbieta, having gotten the money for a mass, and paid for it in advance, lest she should be tempted too sorely at home. She brought also a bit of stale rye-bread that some one had given her, and with that they quieted the children and got them to sleep. Then she came over to Jurgis and sat down beside him.

She said not a word of reproach—she and Marija had chosen that course before; she would only plead with him, here by the corpse of his dead wife. Already Elzbieta had choked down her tears, grief being crowded out of her soul by fear. She had to bury one of her children—but then she had done it three times before, and each time risen up and gone back to take up the battle for the rest. Elzbieta was one of the primitive creatures: like the angleworm, which goes on living though cut in half; like a hen, which, deprived of her chickens one by one, will mother the last that is left her. She did this because it was her nature—she asked no questions about the justice of it, nor the worthwhileness of life in which destruction and death ran riot.

And this old common-sense view she labored to impress upon Jurgis, pleading with him with tears in her eyes. Ona was dead, but the others were left and they must be saved. She did not ask for her own children. She and Marija could care for them somehow, but there was Antanas, his own son. Ona had given Antanas to him—the little fellow was the only remembrance of her that he had; he must treasure it and protect it, he must show himself a man. He knew what Ona would have had him do, what she would ask of him at this moment, if she could speak to him. It was a terrible thing that she should have died as she had; but the life had been too hard for her, and she had to go. It was terrible that they were not able to bury her, that he could not even have a day to mourn her—but so it was. Their fate was pressing; they had not a cent, and the children would perish—some money must be had. Could he not be a man for Ona's sake, and pull himself together? In a little while they would be out of danger—now that they had given up the house they could live more cheaply, and with all the children working they could get along, if only he would not go to pieces. So Elzbieta went on, with feverish intensity. It was a struggle for life with her; she was not afraid that Jurgis would go on drinking, for he had no money for that, but she was wild with dread at the thought that he might desert them, might take to the road, as Jonas had done.

But with Ona's dead body beneath his eyes, Jurgis could not well think of treason to his child. Yes, he said, he would try, for the sake of Antanas. He would give the little fellow his chance—would get to work at once, yes, to-morrow, without even waiting for Ona to be buried. They might trust him, he would keep his word, come what might.

And so he was out before daylight the next morning, headache, heartache, and all. He went straight to Graham's fertilizer-mill, to see if he could get back his job. But the boss shook his head when he saw him—no, his place had been filled long ago, and there was no room for him.

"Do you think there will be?" Jurgis asked. "I may have to wait."

"No," said the other, "it will not be worth your while to wait— there will be nothing for you here."

Jurgis stood gazing at him in perplexity. "What is the matter?" he asked. "Didn't I do my work?"

The other met his look with one of cold indifference, and answered, "There will be nothing for you here, I said."

Jurgis had his suspicions as to the dreadful meaning of that incident, and he went away with a sinking at the heart. He went and took his stand with the mob of hungry wretches who were standing about in the snow before the time-station. Here he stayed, breakfastless, for two hours, until the throng was driven away by the clubs of the police. There was no work for him that day.

Jurgis had made a good many acquaintances in his long services at the yards—there were saloon-keepers who would trust him for a drink and a sandwich, and members of his old union who would lend him a dime at a pinch. It was not a question of life and death for him, therefore; he might hunt all day, and come again on the morrow, and try hanging on thus for weeks, like hundreds and thousands of others. Meantime, Teta Elzbieta would go and beg, over in the Hyde Park district,[2] and the children would bring home enough to pacify Aniele, and keep them all alive.

---

2. Respectable middle-class neighborhood in the midst of Chicago's industrial South Side, with wide boulevards and tree-lined streets. Just a few miles from Packingtown, Hyde Park was a world apart socially.

It was at the end of a week of this sort of waiting, roaming about in the bitter winds or loafing in saloons, that Jurgis stumbled on a chance in one of the cellars of Jones's big packing plant. He saw a foreman passing the open doorway, and hailed him for a job.

"Push a truck?" inquired the man, and Jurgis answered, "Yes, sir!" before the words were well out of his mouth.

"What's your name?" demanded the other.

"Jurgis Rudkus."

"Worked in the yards before?"

"Yes."

"Whereabouts?"

"Two places,—Brown's killing-beds and Durham's fertilizer-mill."

"Why did you leave there?"

"The first time I had an accident, and the last time I was sent up for a month."

"I see. Well, I'll give you a trial. Come early to-morrow and ask for Mr. Thomas."

So Jurgis rushed home with the wild tidings that he had a job—that the terrible siege was over. The remnants of the family had quite a celebration that night; and in the morning Jurgis was at the place half an hour before the time of opening. The foreman came in shortly afterward, and when he saw Jurgis he frowned.

"Oh," he said, "I promised you a job, didn't I?"

"Yes, sir," said Jurgis.

"Well, I'm sorry, but I made a mistake. I can't use you."

Jurgis stared, dumfounded. "What's the matter?" he gasped.

"Nothing," said the man, "only I can't use you."

There was the same cold, hostile stare that he had had from the boss of the fertilizer-mill. He knew that there was no use in saying a word, and he turned and went away.

Out in the saloons the men could tell him all about the meaning of it; they gazed at him with pitying eyes—poor devil, he was blacklisted![3] What had he done? they asked—knocked down his boss? Good heavens, then he might have known! Why, he stood as much chance of getting a job in Packingtown as of being chosen mayor of Chicago. Why had he wasted his time hunting? They had him on a secret list in every office, big and little, in the place. They had his name by this time in St. Louis and New York, in Omaha and Boston, in Kansas City and St. Joseph. He was condemned and sentenced, without trial and without appeal; he could never work for the packers again—he could not even clean cattle-pens or drive a truck in any place where they controlled. He might try it, if he

---

3. After the 1894 strike and riots, packers instituted blacklists to keep labor agitators out of plants, and they soon used the tactic against any worker they disliked.

chose, as hundreds had tried it, and found out for themselves. He would never be told anything about it; he would never get any more satisfaction than he had gotten just now; but he would always find when the time came that he was not needed. It would not do for him to give any other name, either—they had company "spotters" for just that purpose, and he wouldn't keep a job in Packingtown three days. It was worth a fortune to the packers to keep their blacklist effective, as a warning to the men and a means of keeping down union agitation and political discontent.

Jurgis went home, carrying these new tidings to the family council. It was a most cruel thing; here in this district was his home, such as it was, the place he was used to and the friends he knew—and now every possibility of employment in it was closed to him. There was nothing in Packingtown but packing-houses; and so it was the same thing as evicting him from his home.

He and the two women spent all day and half the night discussing it. It would be convenient, down-town, to the children's place of work; but then Marija was on the road to recovery, and had hopes of getting a job in the yards; and though she did not see her old-time lover once a month, because of the misery of their state, yet she could not make up her mind to go away and give him up forever. Then, too, Elzbieta had heard something about a chance to scrub floors in Durham's offices, and was waiting every day for word. In the end it was decided that Jurgis should go down-town to strike out for himself, and they would decide after he got a job. As there was no one from whom he could borrow there, and he dared not beg for fear of being arrested, it was arranged that every day he should meet one of the children and be given fifteen cents of their earnings, upon which he could keep going. Then all day he was to pace the streets with hundreds and thousands of other homeless wretches, inquiring at stores, warehouses, and factories for a chance; and at night he was to crawl into some doorway or underneath a truck, and hide there until midnight, when he might get into one of the station-houses,[4] and spread a newspaper upon the floor, and lie down in the midst of a throng of "bums" and beggars, reeking with alcohol and tobacco, and filthy with vermin and disease.

So for two weeks more Jurgis fought with the demon of despair. Once he got a chance to load a truck for half a day, and again he carried an old woman's valise and was given a quarter. This let him into a lodging-house on several nights when he might otherwise have frozen to death; and it also gave him a chance now and then to buy a newspaper in the morning and hunt up jobs while his rivals were

4. Police stations.

watching and waiting for a paper to be thrown away. This, however, was really not the advantage it seemed, for the newspaper advertisements were a cause of much loss of precious time and of many weary journeys. A full half of these were "fakes," put in by the endless variety of establishments which preyed upon the helpless ignorance of the unemployed. If Jurgis lost only his time, it was because he had nothing else to lose; whenever a smooth-tongued agent would tell him of the wonderful positions he had on hand, he could only shake his head sorrowfully and say that he had not the necessary dollar to deposit; when it was explained to him what "big money" he and all his family could make by coloring photographs, he could only promise to come in again when he had two dollars to invest in the outfit.

In the end Jurgis got a chance through an accidental meeting with an old-time acquaintance of his union days. He met this man on his way to work in the giant factories of the Harvester Trust;[5] and his friend told him to come along and he would speak a good word for him to his boss, whom he knew well. So Jurgis trudged four or five miles, and passed through a waiting throng of unemployed at the gate under the escort of his friend. His knees nearly gave way beneath him when the foreman, after looking him over and questioning him, told him that he could find an opening for him.

How much this accident meant to Jurgis he realized only by stages; for he found that the harvester-works were the sort of place to which philanthropists and reformers pointed with pride.[6] It had some thought for its employees; its workshops were big and roomy, it provided a restaurant where the workmen could buy good food at cost, it had even a reading-room, and decent places where its girl-hands could rest; also the work was free from many of the elements of filth and repulsiveness that prevailed at the stockyards. Day after day Jurgis discovered these things—things never expected nor dreamed of by him—until this new place came to seem a kind of a heaven to him.

It was an enormous establishment, covering a hundred and sixty acres of ground, employing five thousand people, and turning out over three hundred thousand machines every year—a good part of all the harvesting and mowing machines used in the country. Jurgis

5. One of the U.S.'s largest industrial corporations for much of the 20th century, International Harvester Corporation was created in 1902 when McCormick Harvesting Machine Company merged with several smaller firms. By 1910, it grossed $100 million in sales of agricultural equipment and employed 17,000 workers in the Chicago area, making it the region's largest employer.
6. International Harvester extended generous benefits, practicing what is known as welfare capitalism (pioneered in England and Germany), to instill employee loyalty and ramp up productivity—and also to deter unionization. Harvester's strategy of courting labor (and pleasing philanthropists) contrasts with the treatment of employees by one of its precursor firms. Under the second generation of ownership, McCormick Harvesting Machine Company's contempt for organized labor led to strikes in 1885 and 1886, the second of which was linked to a famous explosion of a bomb in Chicago's Haymarket Square.

saw very little of it, of course—it was all specialized work, the same as at the stockyards; each one of the hundreds of parts of a mowing-machine was made separately, and sometimes handled by hundreds of men. Where Jurgis worked there was a machine which cut and stamped a certain piece of steel about two square inches in size; the pieces came tumbling out upon a tray, and all that human hands had to do was to pile them in regular rows, and change the trays at intervals. This was done by a single boy, who stood with eyes and thought centred upon it, and fingers flying so fast that the sounds of the bits of steel striking upon each other was like the music of an express train as one hears it in a sleeping-car at night. This was "piece-work," of course; and besides it was made certain that the boy did not idle, by setting the machine to match the highest possible speed of human hands. Thirty thousand of these pieces he handled every day, nine or ten millions every year—how many in a lifetime it rested with the gods to say. Near by him men sat bending over whirling grindstones, putting the finishing touches to the steel knives of the reaper; picking them out of a basket with the right hand, pressing first one side and then the other against the stone and finally dropping them with the left hand into another basket. One of these men told Jurgis that he had sharpened three thousand pieces of steel a day for thirteen years. In the next room were won-derful machines that ate up long steel rods by slow stages, cutting them off, seizing the pieces, stamping heads upon them, grinding them and polishing them, threading them, and finally dropping them into a basket, all ready to bolt the harvesters together. From yet another machine came tens of thousands of steel burs to fit upon these bolts. In other places all these various parts were dipped into troughs of paint and hung up to dry, and then slid along on trolleys to a room where men streaked them with red and yellow, so that they might look cheerful in the harvest-fields.

Jurgis's friend worked upstairs in the casting-rooms, and his task was to make the moulds of a certain part. He shovelled black sand into an iron receptacle and pounded it tight and set it aside to harden; then it would be taken out, and molten iron poured into it.[7] This man, too, was paid by the mould—or rather for perfect castings, nearly half his work going for naught. You might see him, along with dozens of others, toiling like one possessed by a whole community of demons; his arms working like the driving rods of an engine, his long, black hair flying wild, his eyes starting out, the sweat rolling in rivers down his face. When he had shovelled the mould full of sand, and reached for the pounder to pound it with, it was after the manner of a canoeist running rapids and seizing a pole at sight of a

7. Jurgis's friend works in sand casting, a method of producing steel.

submerged rock. All day long this man would toil thus, his whole being centred upon the purpose of making twenty-three instead of twenty-two and a half cents an hour; and then his product would be reckoned up by the census-taker, and jubilant captains of industry would boast of it in their banquet-halls, telling how our workers are nearly twice as efficient as those of any other country. If we are the greatest nation the sun ever shone upon, it would seem to be mainly because we have been able to goad our wage-earners to this pitch of frenzy; though there are a few other things that are great among us, including our drink-bill, which is a billion and a quarter of dollars a year, and doubling itself every decade.

There was a machine which stamped out the iron plates, and then another which, with a mighty thud, mashed them to the shape of the sitting-down portion of the American farmer. Then they were piled upon a truck, and it was Jurgis's task to wheel them to the room where the machines were "assembled." This was child's play for him, and he got a dollar and seventy-five cents a day for it; on Saturday he paid Aniele the seventy-five cents a week he owed her for the use of her garret, and also redeemed his overcoat, which Elzbieta had put in pawn when he was in jail.

This last was a great blessing. A man cannot go about in midwinter in Chicago with no overcoat and not pay for it, and Jurgis had to walk or ride five or six miles back and forth to his work. It so happened that half of this was in one direction and half in another, necessitating a change of cars; the law required that transfers be given at all intersecting points, but the railway corporation had gotten round this by arranging a pretence at separate ownership. So whenever he wished to ride, he had to pay ten cents each way, or over ten per cent of his income to this power, which had gotten its franchises long ago by buying up the city council, in the face of popular clamor amounting almost to a rebellion. Tired as he felt at night, and dark and bitter cold as it was in the morning, Jurgis generally chose to walk; at the hours other workmen were travelling, the street-car monopoly saw fit to put on so few cars that there would be men hanging to every foot of the backs of them and often crouching upon the snow-covered roof.[8] Of course the doors could never be closed, and so the cars were as cold as outdoors; Jurgis, like many

---

8. The condition of Chicago streetcars was scandalous, as was their financial control by tycoons. Passengers needing to use two or more streetcar companies for a single trip had to pay multiple fares. American financier Charles Tyson Yerkes (1837–1905), who dominated Chicago streetcars through city franchises, cut corners and packed in passengers, claiming "the straphangers pay the dividends." In other words, profits come from crowding travelers in so tightly as to leave standing room only.

others, found it better to spend his fare for a drink and a free lunch, to give him strength to walk.

These, however, were all slight matters to a man who had escaped from Durham's fertilizer-mill. Jurgis began to pick up heart again and to make plans. He had lost his house, but then the awful load of the rent and interest was off his shoulders, and when Marija was well again they could start over and save. In the shop where he worked was a man, a Lithuanian like himself, whom the others spoke of in admiring whispers, because of the mighty feats he was performing. All day he sat at a machine turning bolts; and then in the evening he went to the public school to study English and learn to read. In addition, because he had a family of eight children to support and his earnings were not enough, on Saturdays and Sundays he served as a watchman; he was required to press two buttons at opposite ends of a building every five minutes, and as the walk only took him two minutes, he had three minutes to study between each trip. Jurgis felt jealous of this fellow; for that was the sort of thing he himself had dreamed of, two or three years ago. He might do it even yet, if he had a fair chance—he might attract attention and become a skilled man or a boss, as some had done in this place. Suppose that Marija could get a job in the big mill where they made binder-twine[9]—then they would move into this neighborhood, and he would really have a chance. With a hope like that, there was some use in living; to find a place where you were treated like a human being—by God! he would show them how he could appreciate it. He laughed to himself as he thought how he would hang on to this job!

And then one afternoon, the ninth of his work in the place, when he went to get his overcoat he saw a group of men crowded before a placard on the door, and when he went over and asked what it was, they told him that beginning with the morrow his department of the harvester works would be closed until further notice!

9. A cheap rope.

Chapter XXI

That was the way they did it! There was not half an hour's warning—
the works were closed! It had happened that way before, said the
men, and it would happen that way forever. They had made all the
harvesting-machines that the world needed, and now they had to
wait till some wore out! It was nobody's fault—that was the way of
it; and thousands of men and women were turned out in the dead of
winter, to live upon their savings if they had any, and otherwise to
die. So many tens of thousands already in the city, homeless and begging for work, and now several thousand more added to them!

Jurgis walked home with his pittance of pay in his pocket, heart-
broken, overwhelmed. One more bandage had been torn from his
eyes, one more pitfall was revealed to him! Of what help was kindness and decency on the part of employers—when they could not
keep a job for him, when there were more harvesting-machines
made than the world was able to buy! What a hellish mockery it
was, anyway, that a man should slave to make harvesting-machines
for the country, only to be turned out to starve for doing his duty
too well!

It took him two days to get over this heart-sickening disappointment.
He did not drink anything, because Elzbieta got his money for safe-
keeping, and knew him too well to be in the least frightened by his
angry demands. He stayed up in the garret, however, and sulked—
what was the use of a man's hunting a job when it was taken from
him before he had time to learn the work? But then their money was
going again, and little Antanas was hungry, and crying with the
bitter cold of the garret. Also Madame Haupt, the midwife, was after
him for some money. So he went out once more.

For another ten days he roamed the streets and alleys of the huge
city, sick and hungry, begging for any work. He tried in stores and
offices, in restaurants and hotels, along the docks and in the railroad-
yards, in warehouses and mills and factories where they made products that went to every corner of the world. There were often one or
two chances—but there were always a hundred men for every
chance, and his turn would not come. At night he crept into sheds
and cellars and doorways—until there came a spell of belated winter
weather, with a raging gale, and the thermometer five degrees below
zero at sundown and falling all night. Then Jurgis fought like a wild
beast to get into the big Harrison Street police-station, and slept
down in a corridor, crowded with two other men upon a single
step.

He had to fight often in these days—to fight for a place near the factory gates, and now and again with gangs on the street. He found, for instance, that the business of carrying satchels for railroad-passengers was a preëmpted one—whenever he essayed it, eight or ten men and boys would fall upon him and force him to run for his life. They always had the policeman "squared,"[1] and so there was no use in expecting protection.

That Jurgis did not starve to death was due solely to the pittance the children brought him. And even this was never certain. For one thing the cold was almost more than the children could bear; and then they, too, were in perpetual peril from rivals who plundered and beat them. The law was against them, too—little Vilimas, who was really eleven, but did not look to be eight, was stopped on the streets by a severe old lady in spectacles, who told him that he was too young to be working and that if he did not stop selling papers she would send a truant-officer after him. Also one night a strange man caught little Kotrina by the arm and tried to persuade her into a dark cellar-way, an experience which filled her with such terror that she was hardly to be kept at work.

At last, on a Sunday, as there was no use looking for work, Jurgis went home by stealing rides on the cars. He found that they had been waiting for him for three days—there was a chance of a job for him.

It was quite a story. Little Juozapas, who was near crazy with hunger these days, had gone out on the street to beg for himself. Juoza-pas had only one leg, having been run over by a wagon when a little child, but he had got himself a broomstick, which he put under his arm for a crutch. He had fallen in with some other children and found the way to Mike Scully's dump,[2] which lay three or four blocks away. To this place there came every day many hundreds of wagon-loads of garbage and trash from the lake-front, where the rich people lived; and in the heaps the children raked for food—there were hunks of bread and potato peelings and apple-cores and meat-bones, all of it half frozen and quite unspoiled. Little Juozapas gorged himself, and came home with a newspaper full, which he was feed-ing to Antanas when his mother came in. Elzbieta was horrified, for she did not believe that the food out of the dumps was fit to eat. The next day, however, when no harm came of it and Juozapas began to cry with hunger, she gave in and said that he might go again. And that afternoon he came home with a story of how while he had been digging away with a stick, a lady upon the street had called him. A real fine lady, the little boy explained, a beautiful lady, and she

---

1. Settled with, in this case by bribery (slang).
2. The garbage of wealthy residents was dumped "back of the yards," where poor residents picked through it. Tom Carey owned the dump and built houses on top of the trash.

wanted to know all about him, and whether he got the garbage for chickens, and why he walked with a broomstick, and why Ona had died, and how Jurgis had come to go to jail, and what was the matter with Marija, and everything. In the end she had asked where he lived, and said that she was coming to see him, and bring him a new crutch to walk with. She had on a hat with a bird upon it, Juozapas added, and a long fur snake around her neck.

She really came, the very next morning, and climbed the ladder to the garret, and stood and stared about her, turning pale at the sight of the blood stains on the floor where Ona had died. She was a "settlement-worker,"[3] she explained to Elzbieta—she lived around on Ashland Avenue. Elzbieta knew the place, over a feed-store; somebody had wanted her to go there, but she had not cared to, for she thought that it must have something to do with religion, and the priest did not like her to have anything to do with strange religions. They were rich people who came to live there to find out about the poor people; but what good they expected it would do them to know, one could not imagine. So spoke Elzbieta, naïvely, and the young lady laughed and was rather at a loss for an answer—she stood and gazed about her, and thought of a cynical remark that had been made to her, that she was standing upon the brink of the pit of hell and throwing in snow-balls to lower the temperature.

Elzbieta was glad to have somebody to listen, and she told all their woes,—what had happened to Ona, and the jail, and the loss of their home, and Marija's accident, and how Ona had died, and how Jurgis could get no work. As she listened the pretty young lady's eyes filled with tears, and in the midst of it she burst into weeping and hid her face on Elzbieta's shoulder, quite regardless of the fact that the woman had on a dirty old wrapper and that the garret was full of fleas. Poor Elzbieta was ashamed of herself for having told so woful a tale, and the other had to beg and plead with her to get her to go on. The end of it was that the young lady sent them a basket of things to eat, and left a letter that Jurgis was to take to a gentleman who was superintendent in one of the mills of the great steelworks in South Chicago. "He will get Jurgis something to do," the young lady had said, and added, smiling through her tears—"If he doesn't, he will never marry me."

The steel-works were fifteen miles away,[4] and as usual it was so contrived that one had to pay two fares to get there. Far and wide the

---

3. Settlement houses were distinctive reform projects that characterized the Progressive era (ca. 1890–1920). Staffed by middle-class white women volunteers, they were located in poor city neighborhoods and designed to assist with practical matters such as childcare as well as cultural assimilation, particularly for immigrants.
4. Steel mills on the far South Side, another industry dominated by a large trust.

sky was flaring with the red glare that leaped from rows of towering chimneys—for it was pitch dark when Jurgis arrived. The vast works, a city in themselves, were surrounded by a stockade; and already a full hundred men were waiting at the gate where new hands were taken on. Soon after daybreak whistles began to blow, and then suddenly thousands of men appeared, streaming from saloons and boarding-houses across the way, leaping from trolley-cars that passed—it seemed as if they rose out of the ground, in the dim gray light. A river of them poured in through the gate—and then gradually ebbed away again, until there were only a few late ones running, and the watchman pacing up and down, and the hungry strangers stamping and shivering.

Jurgis presented his precious letter. The gatekeeper was surly, and put him through a catechism, but he insisted that he knew nothing, and as he had taken the precaution to seal his letter, there was nothing for the gatekeeper to do but send it to the person to whom it was addressed. A messenger came back to say that Jurgis should wait, and so he came inside of the gate, perhaps not sorry enough that there were others less fortunate watching him with greedy eyes.

The great mills were getting under way—one could hear a vast stirring, a rolling and rumbling and hammering. Little by little the scene grew plain: towering, black buildings here and there, long rows of shops and sheds, little railways branching everywhere, bare gray cinders under foot and oceans of billowing black smoke above. On one side of the grounds ran a railroad with a dozen tracks, and on the other side lay the lake, where steamers came to load.

Jurgis had time enough to stare and speculate, for it was two hours before he was summoned. He went into the office-building, where a company time-keeper interviewed him. The superintendent was busy, he said, but he (the time-keeper) would try to find Jurgis a job. He had never worked in a steel-mill before? But he was ready for anything? Well, then, they would go and see.

So they began a tour, among sights that made Jurgis stare amazed. He wondered if ever he could get used to working in a place like this, where the air shook with deafening thunder, and whistles shrieked warnings on all sides of him at once; where miniature steam-engines came rushing upon him, and sizzling, quivering, white-hot masses of metal sped past him, and explosions of fire and flaming sparks dazzled him and scorched his face. The men in these mills were all black with soot, and hollow-eyed and gaunt; they worked with fierce intensity, rushing here and there, and never lifting their eyes from their tasks. Jurgis clung to his guide like a scared child to its nurse, and while the latter hailed one foreman after another to ask if they could use another unskilled man, he stared about him and marvelled.

He was taken to the Bessemer furnace,[5] where they made billets of steel—a dome-like building the size of a big theatre. Jurgis stood where the balcony of the theatre would have been, and opposite, by the stage, he saw three giant caldrons, big enough for all the devils of hell to brew their broth in, full of something white and blinding, bubbling and splashing, roaring as if volcanoes were blowing through it—one had to shout to be heard in the place. Liquid fire would leap from these caldrons and scatter like bombs below—and men were working there, seeming careless, so that Jurgis caught his breath with fright. Then a whistle would toot, and across the curtain of the theatre would come a little engine with a car-load of something to be dumped into one of the receptacles; and then another whistle would toot, down by the stage, and another train would back up—and suddenly, without an instant's warning, one of the giant kettles began to tilt and topple, flinging out a jet of hissing, roaring flame. Jurgis shrank back appalled, for he thought it was an accident; there fell a pillar of white flame, dazzling as the sun, swishing like a huge tree falling in the forest. A torrent of sparks swept all the way across the building, overwhelming everything, hiding it from sight; and then Jurgis looked through the fingers of his hands, and saw pouring out of the caldron a cascade of living, leaping fire, white with a whiteness not of earth, scorching the eyeballs. Incandescent rainbows shone above it, blue, red, and golden lights played about it; but the stream itself was white, ineffable. Out of regions of wonder it streamed, the very river of life; and the soul leaped up at the sight of it, fled back upon it, swift and resistless, back into far-off lands, where beauty and terror dwell.—Then the great caldron tilted back again, empty, and Jurgis saw to his relief that no one was hurt, and turned and followed his guide out into the sunlight.

They went through the blast-furnaces, through rolling-mills where bars of steel were tossed about and chopped like bits of cheese. All around and above giant machine-arms were flying, giant wheels were turning, giant hammers crashing; travelling cranes creaked and groaned overhead, reaching down iron hands and seizing iron prey— it was like standing in the centre of the earth, where the machinery of time was revolving.

By and by they came to the place where steel rails were made; and Jurgis heard a toot behind him, and jumped out of the way of a car with a white-hot ingot upon it, the size of a man's body. There was a sudden crash and the car came to a halt, and the ingot toppled out upon a moving platform, where steel fingers and arms seized hold of

5. Technological breakthrough based on the discovery that impurities could be removed from hot pig iron by forcing air through it.

it, punching it and prodding it into place, and hurrying it into the grip of huge rollers. Then it came out upon the other side, and there were more crashings and clatterings, and over it was flopped, like a pancake on a gridiron, and seized again and rushed back at you through another squeezer. So amid deafening uproar it clattered to and fro, growing thinner and flatter and longer. The ingot seemed almost a living thing; it did not want to run this mad course, but it was in the grip of fate, it was tumbled on, screeching and clanking and shivering in protest. By and by it was long and thin, a great red snake escaped from purgatory; and then, as it slid through the rollers, you would have sworn that it was alive—it writhed and squirmed, and wriggles and shudders passed out through its tail, all but flinging it off by their violence. There was no rest for it until it was cold and black—and then it needed only to be cut and straightened to be ready for a railroad.

It was at the end of this rail's progress that Jurgis got his chance. They had to be moved by men with crowbars, and the boss here could use another man. So he took off his coat and set to work on the spot.

It took him two hours to get to this place every day and cost him a dollar and twenty cents a week. As this was out of the question, he wrapped his bedding in a bundle and took it with him, and one of his fellow-working-men introduced him to a Polish lodging-house, where he might have the privilege of sleeping upon the floor for ten cents a night. He got his meals at free-lunch counters, and every Saturday night he went home—bedding and all—and took the greater part of his money to the family. Elzbieta was sorry for this arrangement, for she feared that it would get him into the habit of living without them, and once a week was not very often for him to see his baby; but there was no other way of arranging it. There was no chance for a woman at the steel-works, and Marija was now ready for work again, and lured on from day to day by the hope of finding it at the yards.

In a week Jurgis got over his sense of helplessness and bewilderment in the rail-mill. He learned to find his way about and to take all the miracles and terrors for granted, to work without hearing the rumbling and crashing. From blind fear he went to the other extreme; he became reckless and indifferent, like all the rest of the men, who took but little thought of themselves in the ardor of their work. It was wonderful, when one came to think of it, that these men should have taken an interest in the work they did; they had no share in it—they were paid by the hour, and paid no more for being interested. Also they knew that if they were hurt they would be flung aside and forgotten—and still they would hurry to their task by dangerous short-cuts, would use methods that were quicker and more effective in spite of the fact that they were also risky. His fourth day at his work Jurgis saw a man stumble while running in front of a car, and have his foot mashed off; and before he had been there three weeks he was witness of a yet more dreadful accident. There was a row of brick-furnaces, shining white through every crack with the molten steel inside. Some of these were bulging dangerously, yet men worked before them, wearing blue glasses[6] when they opened and shut the doors. One morning as Jurgis was passing, a furnace blew out, spraying two men with a shower of liquid fire. As they lay screaming and rolling upon the ground in agony, Jurgis rushed to help them, and as a result he lost a good part of the skin from the inside of one of his hands. The company doctor bandaged it up, but he got no other thanks from any one, and was laid up for eight working days without any pay.

Most fortunately, at this juncture, Elzbieta got the long-awaited chance to go at five o'clock in the morning and help scrub the office-floors of one of the packers. Jurgis came home and covered himself with blankets to keep warm, and divided his time between sleeping and playing with little Antanas. Juozapas was away raking in the dump a good part of the time, and Elzbieta and Marija were hunting for more work.

Antanas was now over a year and a half old, and was a perfect talking-machine. He learned so fast that every week when Jurgis came home it seemed to him as if he had a new child. He would sit down and listen and stare at him, and give vent to delighted exclamations,—"*Palauk! Muma! Tu mano szirdele!*"[7] The little fellow was now really the one delight that Jurgis had in the world—his one hope, his one victory. Thank God, Antanas was a boy! And he was as tough as a pine-knot, and with the appetite of a wolf. Nothing had hurt him, and nothing could hurt him; he had come through all the suffering and deprivation unscathed—only shriller-voiced and more determined in his grip upon life. He was a terrible child to manage, was Antanas, but his father did not mind that—he would watch him and smile to himself with satisfaction. The more of a fighter he was the better—he would need to fight before he got through.

Jurgis had got the habit of buying the Sunday paper whenever he had the money; a most wonderful paper could be had for only five cents, a whole armful, with all the news of the world set forth in big headlines, that Jurgis could spell out slowly, with the children to help him at the long words. There was battle and murder and sudden death—it was marvellous how they ever heard about so many entertaining and thrilling happenings; the stories must be all true, for surely no man could have made such things up, and besides, there were pictures of them all, as real as life. One of these papers was as

6. Protective eyewear to reduce the impact of yellow light and glare.
7. See above, p. 113, n. 1.

good as a circus, and nearly as good as a spree—certainly a most
wonderful treat for a working-man, who was tired out and stupe-
fied, and had never had any education, and whose work was one dull,
sordid grind, day after day, and year after year, with never a sight of
a green field nor an hour's entertainment, nor anything but liquor
to stimulate his imagination. Among other things, these papers had
pages full of comical pictures, and these were the main joy in life to
little Antanas. He treasured them up, and would drag them out and
make his father tell him about them; there were all sorts of animals
among them, and Antanas could tell the names of all of them, lying
upon the floor for hours and pointing them out with his chubby little
fingers. Whenever the story was plain enough for Jurgis to make out,
Antanas would have it repeated to him, and then he would remember it, prattling funny little sentences and mixing it up with other
stories in an irresistible fashion. Also his quaint pronunciation of
words was such a delight—and the phrases he would pick up and
remember, the most outlandish and impossible things! The first time
that the little rascal burst out with "God-damn," his father nearly
rolled off the chair with glee; but in the end he was sorry for this,
for Antanas was soon "God-damning" everything and everybody.

And then, when he was able to use his hands, Jurgis took his bedding again and went back to his task of shifting rails. It was now
April, and the snow had given place to cold rains, and the unpaved
street in front of Aniele's house was turned into a canal. Jurgis would
have to wade through it to get home, and if it was late he might easily get stuck to his waist in the mire. But he did not mind this much—
it was a promise that summer was coming. Marija had now gotten a
place as beef-trimmer in one of the smaller packing-plants; and he
told himself that he had learned his lesson now, and would meet
with no more accidents—so that at last there was prospect of an end
to their long agony. They could save money again, and when another
winter came they would have a comfortable place; and the children
would be off the streets and in school again, and they might set to
work to nurse back into life their habits of decency and kindness.
So once more Jurgis began to make plans and dream dreams.
    And then one Saturday night he jumped off the car and started
home, with the sun shining low under the edge of a bank of clouds
that had been pouring floods of water into the mud-soaked street.
There was a rainbow in the sky, and another in his breast—for he
had thirty-six hours' rest before him, and a chance to see his family.
Then suddenly he came in sight of the house, and noticed that there
was a crowd before the door. He ran up the steps and pushed his
way in, and saw Aniele's kitchen crowded with excited women. It
reminded him so vividly of the time when he had come home from

jail and found Ona dying, that his heart almost stood still. "What's the matter?" he cried.

A dead silence had fallen in the room, and he saw that every one was staring at him. "What's the matter?" he exclaimed again.

And then, up in the garret, he heard sounds of wailing, in Marija's voice. He started for the ladder—and Aniele seized him by the arm. "No, no!" she exclaimed. "Don't go up there!"

"What is it?" he shouted.

And the old woman answered him weakly: "It's Antanas. He's dead. He was drowned out in the street!"

Chapter XXII

Jurgis took the news in a peculiar way. He turned deadly pale, but he caught himself, and for half a minute stood in the middle of the room, clenching his hands tightly and setting his teeth. Then he pushed Aniele aside and strode into the next room and climbed the ladder.

In the corner was a blanket, with a form half showing beneath it; and beside it lay Elzbieta, whether crying or in a faint, Jurgis could not tell. Marija was pacing the room, screaming and wringing her hands. He clenched his hands tighter yet, and his voice was hard as he spoke.

"How did it happen?" he asked.

Marija scarcely heard him in her agony. He repeated the question, louder and yet more harshly. "He fell off the sidewalk!" she wailed. The sidewalk in front of the house was a platform made of half-rotten boards, about five feet above the level of the sunken street.

"How did he come to be there?" he demanded.

"He went—he went out to play," Marija sobbed, her voice choking her. "We couldn't make him stay in. He must have got caught in the mud!"

"Are you sure that he is dead?" he demanded.

"Ai! ai!" she wailed. "Yes; we had the doctor."

Then Jurgis stood a few seconds, wavering. He did not shed a tear. He took one glance more at the blanket with the little form beneath it, and then turned suddenly to the ladder and climbed down again. A silence fell once more in the room as he entered. He went straight to the door, passed out, and started down the street.

When his wife had died, Jurgis made for the nearest saloon, but he did not do that now, though he had his week's wages in his pocket. He walked and walked, seeing nothing, splashing through mud and water. Later on he sat down upon a step and hid his face in his hands and for half an hour or so he did not move. Now and then he would whisper to himself: "Dead! *Dead!*"

Finally, he got up and walked on again. It was about sunset, and he went on and on until it was dark, when he was stopped by a railroad-crossing. The gates were down, and a long train of freight-cars was thundering by. He stood and watched it; and all at once a wild impulse seized him, a thought that had been lurking within him, unspoken, unrecognized, leaped into sudden life. He started down the track, and when he was past the gate-keeper's shanty he sprang forward and swung himself on to one of the cars.

By and by the train stopped again, and Jurgis sprang down and ran under the car, and hid himself upon the truck. Here he sat, and when the train started again, he fought a battle with his soul. He gripped his hands and set his teeth together—he had not wept, and he would not—not a tear! It was past and over, and he was done with it—he would fling it off his shoulders, be free of it, the whole business, that night. It should go like a black, hateful nightmare, and in the morning he would be a new man. And every time that a thought of it assailed him—a tender memory, a trace of a tear—he rose up, cursing with rage, and pounded it down.

He was fighting for his life; he gnashed his teeth together in his desperation. He had been a fool, a fool! He had wasted his life, he had wrecked himself, with his accursed weakness; and now he was done with it—he would tear it out of him, root and branch! There should be no more tears and no more tenderness; he had had enough of them— they had sold him into slavery! Now he was going to be free, to tear off his shackles, to rise up and fight. He was glad that the end had come—it had to come some time, and it was just as well now. This was no world for women and children, and the sooner they got out of it the better for them. Whatever Antanas might suffer where he was, he could suffer no more than he would have had he stayed upon earth. And meantime his father had thought the last thought about him that he meant to; he was going to think of himself, he was going to fight for himself, against the world that had baffled him and tortured him!

So he went on, tearing up all the flowers from the garden of his soul, and setting his heel upon them. The train thundered deafeningly, and a storm of dust blew in his face; but though it stopped now and then through the night, he clung where he was—he would cling there until he was driven off, for every mile that he got from Packingtown meant another load from his mind.

Whenever the cars stopped a warm breeze blew upon him, a breeze laden with the perfume of fresh fields, of honeysuckle and clover. He snuffed it, and it made his heart beat wildly—he was out in the country again! He was going to *live* in the country! When the dawn came he was peering out with hungry eyes, getting glimpses of meadows and woods and rivers. At last he could stand it no longer, and when the train stopped again he crawled out. Upon the top of the car was a brakeman, who shook his fist and swore; Jurgis waved his hand derisively, and started across the country.

Only think that he had been a countryman all his life; and for three long years he had never seen a country sight nor heard a country sound! Excepting for that one walk when he left jail, when he was too much worried to notice anything, and for a few times that he had rested in the city parks in the winter time when he was out of work, he had literally never seen a tree! And now he felt like a bird lifted up and borne away upon a gale; he stopped and stared at each new sight of wonder,—at a herd of cows, and a meadow full of daisies, at hedgerows set thick with June roses, at little birds singing in the trees.

Then he came to a farm-house, and after getting himself a stick for protection, he approached it. The farmer was greasing a wagon in front of the barn, and Jurgis went to him. "I would like to get some breakfast, please," he said.

"Do you want to work?" said the farmer.

"No," said Jurgis, "I don't."

"Then you can't get anything here," snapped the other.

"I meant to pay for it," said Jurgis.

"Oh," said the farmer; and then added sarcastically, "We don't serve breakfast after 7 A.M."

"I am very hungry," said Jurgis, gravely; "I would like to buy some food."

"Ask the woman," said the farmer, nodding over his shoulder. The "woman" was more tractable, and for a dime Jurgis secured two thick sandwiches and a piece of pie and two apples. He walked off eating the pie, as the least convenient thing to carry. In a few minutes he came to a stream, and he climbed a fence and walked down the bank, along a woodland path. By and by he found a comfortable spot, and there he devoured his meal, slaking his thirst at the stream. Then he lay for hours, just gazing and drinking in joy; until at last he felt sleepy, and lay down in the shade of a bush.

When he awoke the sun was shining hot in his face. He sat up and stretched his arms, and then gazed at the water sliding by. There was a deep pool, sheltered and silent, below him, and a sudden wonderful idea rushed upon him. He might have a bath! The water was free, and he might get into it—all the way into it! It would be the first time that he had been all the way into the water since he left Lithuania!

When Jurgis had first come to the stockyards he had been as clean as any working-man could well be. But later on, what with sickness and cold and hunger and discouragement, and the filthiness of his work, and the vermin in his home, he had given up washing in winter, and in summer only as much of him as would go into a basin. He had had a shower-bath in jail, but nothing since—and now he would have a swim!

The water was warm, and he splashed about like a very boy in his glee. Afterward he sat down in the water near the bank, and proceeded to scrub himself—soberly and methodically, scouring every inch of him with sand. While he was doing it he would do it thoroughly, and see how it felt to be clean. He even scrubbed his head with sand, and combed what the men called "crumbs"[1] out of his long, black hair, holding his head under water as long as he could, to see if he could not kill them all. Then, seeing that the sun was

---

1. Lice. This was slang used by what were then called hobos (homeless people, especially men who traveled around seeking work). They were also called "tramps."

still hot, he took his clothes from the bank and proceeded to wash them, piece by piece; as the dirt and grease went floating off downstream he grunted with satisfaction and soused the clothes again, venturing even to dream that he might get rid of the fertilizer.

He hung them all up, and while they were drying he lay down in the sun and had another long sleep. They were hot and stiff as boards on top, and a little damp on the under-side, when he awakened; but being hungry, he put them on and set out again. He had no knife, but with some labor he broke himself a good stout club, and, armed with this, he marched down the road again.

Before long he came to a big farm-house, and turned up the lane that led to it. It was just supper-time, and the farmer was washing his hands at the kitchen-door. "Please, sir," said Jurgis, "can I have something to eat? I can pay." To which the farmer responded promptly, "We don't feed tramps here. Get out!"

Jurgis went without a word; but as he passed round the barn he came to a freshly ploughed and harrowed field, in which the farmer had set out some young peach-trees; and as he walked he jerked up a row of them by the roots, more than a hundred trees in all, before he reached the end of the field. That was his answer, and it showed his mood; from now on he was fighting, and the man who hit him would get all that he gave, every time.

Beyond the orchard Jurgis struck through a patch of woods, and then a field of winter-grain, and came at last to another road. Before long he saw another farm-house, and, as it was beginning to cloud over a little, he asked here for shelter as well as food. Seeing the farmer eying him dubiously, he added, "I'll be glad to sleep in the barn."

"Well, I dunno," said the other. "Do you smoke?"

"Sometimes," said Jurgis, "but I'll do it out of doors." When the man had assented, he inquired, "How much will it cost me? I haven't very much money."

"I reckon about twenty cents for supper," replied the farmer. "I won't charge ye for the barn."

So Jurgis went in, and sat down at the table with the farmer's wife and half a dozen children. It was a bountiful meal—there were baked beans and mashed potatoes and asparagus chopped and stewed, and a dish of strawberries, and great, thick slices of bread, and a pitcher of milk. Jurgis had not had such a feast since his wedding day, and he made a mighty effort to put in his twenty cents' worth.

They were all of them too hungry to talk; but afterward they sat upon the steps and smoked, and the farmer questioned his guest. When Jurgis had explained that he was a working-man from Chicago, and that he did not know just whither he was bound, the other said, "Why don't you stay here and work for me?"

"I'm not looking for work just now," Jurgis answered.

"I'll pay ye good," said the other, eying his big form—"a dollar a day and board ye. Help's terrible scarce round here."

"Is that winter as well as summer?" Jurgis demanded quickly.

"N—no," said the farmer; "I couldn't keep ye after November—I ain't got a big enough place for that."

"I see," said the other, "that's what I thought. When you get through working your horses this fall, will you turn them out in the snow?" (Jurgis was beginning to think for himself nowadays.)

"It ain't quite the same," the farmer answered, seeing the point. "There ought to be work a strong fellow like you can find to do, in the cities, or some place, in the winter time."

"Yes," said Jurgis, "that's what they all think; and so they crowd into the cities, and when they have to beg or steal to live, then people ask 'em why they don't go into the country, where help is scarce."

The farmer meditated awhile.

"How about when your money's gone?" he inquired, finally. "You'll have to, then, won't you?"

"Wait till she's gone," said Jurgis; "then I'll see."

He had a long sleep in the barn and then a big breakfast of coffee and bread and oatmeal and stewed cherries, for which the man charged him only fifteen cents, perhaps having been influenced by his arguments. Then Jurgis bade farewell, and went on his way.

Such was the beginning of his life as a tramp.[2] It was seldom he got as fair treatment as from this last farmer, and so as time went on he learned to shun the houses and to prefer sleeping in the fields. When it rained he would find a deserted building, if he could, and if not, he would wait until after dark and then, with his stick ready, begin a stealthy approach upon a barn. Generally he could get in before the dog got scent of him, and then he would hide in the hay and be safe until morning; if not, and the dog attacked him, he would rise up and make a retreat in battle order. Jurgis was not the mighty man he had once been, but his arms were still good, and there were few farm dogs he needed to hit more than once.

Before long there came raspberries, and then blackberries, to help him save his money; and there were apples in the orchards and potatoes in the ground—he learned to note the places and fill his pockets after dark. Twice he even managed to capture a chicken, and had a feast, once in a deserted barn and the other time in a lonely spot alongside of a stream. When all of these things failed him he used his money carefully, but without worry—for he saw that he could earn more whenever he chose. Half an hour's chopping wood in his lively fashion was enough to bring him a meal, and when the farmer had seen him working he would sometimes try to bribe him to stay.

2. See above, p. 198, n. 1.

But Jurgis was not staying. He was a free man now, a buccaneer. The old wanderlust had got into his blood, the joy of the unbound life, the joy of seeking, of hoping without limit. There were mishaps and discomforts—but at least there was always something new; and only think what it meant to a man who for years had been penned up in one place, seeing nothing but one dreary prospect of shanties and factories, to be suddenly set loose beneath the open sky, to behold new landscapes, new places, and new people every hour! To a man whose whole life had consisted of doing one certain thing all day, until he was so exhausted that he could only lie down and sleep until the next day—and to be now his own master, working as he pleased and when he pleased, and facing a new adventure every hour!

Then, too, his health came back to him, all his lost youthful vigor, his joy and power that he had mourned and forgotten! It came with a sudden rush, bewildering him, startling him; it was as if his dead childhood had come back to him, laughing and calling! What with plenty to eat and fresh air and exercise that was taken as it pleased him, he would waken from his sleep and start off not knowing what to do with his energy, stretching his arms, laughing, singing old songs of home that came back to him. Now and then, of course, he could not help but think of little Antanas, whom he should never see again, whose little voice he should never hear; and then he would have to battle with himself. Sometimes at night he would waken dreaming of Ona, and stretch out his arms to her, and wet the ground with his tears. But in the morning he would get up and shake himself, and stride away again to battle with the world.

He never asked where he was nor where he was going; the country was big enough, he knew, and there was no danger of his coming to the end of it. And of course he could always have company for the asking—everywhere he went there were men living just as he lived, and whom he was welcome to join. He was a stranger at the business, but they were not clannish, and they taught him all their tricks,—what towns and villages it was best to keep away from, and how to read the secret signs upon the fences,[3] and when to beg and when to steal, and just how to do both. They laughed at his ideas of paying for anything with money or with work—for they got all they wanted without either. Now and then Jurgis camped out with a gang of them in some woodland haunt, and foraged with them in the neighborhood at night. And then among them some one would "take a shine" to him, and they would go off together and travel for a week, exchanging reminiscences.

Of these professional tramps a great many had, of course, been shiftless and vicious all their lives. But the vast majority of them had

---

3. To help fellow travelers, hobos left hieroglyphic-like signs to pass along such important information as the disposition of the local residents.

been working-men, had fought the long fight as Jurgis had, and found that it was a losing fight, and given up. Later on he encountered yet another sort of men, those from whose ranks the tramps were recruited, men who were homeless and wandering, but still seeking work—seeking it in the harvest-fields. Of these there was an army, the huge surplus labor army of society; called into being under the stern system of nature, to do the casual work of the world, the tasks which were transient and irregular, and yet which had to be done. They did not know that they were such, of course; they only knew that they sought the job, and that the job was fleeting. In the early summer they would be in Texas, and as the crops were ready they would follow north with the season, ending with the fall in Manitoba. Then they would seek out the big lumber-camps, where there was winter work; or failing in this, would drift to the cities, and live upon what they had managed to save, with the help of such transient work as was there,—the loading and unloading of steamships and drays, the digging of ditches and the shovelling of snow. If there were more of them on hand than chanced to be needed, the weaker ones died off of cold and hunger, again according to the stern system of nature.

It was in the latter part of July, when Jurgis was in Missouri, that he came upon the harvest-work. Here were crops that men had worked for three or four months to prepare, and of which they would lose nearly all unless they could find others to help them for a week or two. So all over the land there was a cry for labor—agencies were set up and all the cities were drained of men, even college boys were brought by the car-load, and hordes of frantic farmers would hold up trains and carry off wagon-loads of men by main force. Not that they did not pay them well—any man could get two dollars a day and his board, and the best men could get two dollars and a half or three.

The harvest-fever was in the very air, and no man with any spirit in him could be in that region and not catch it. Jurgis joined a gang and worked from dawn till dark, eighteen hours a day, for two weeks without a break. Then he had a sum of money that would have been a fortune to him in the old days of misery—but what could he do with it now? To be sure he might have put it in a bank, and, if he were fortunate, get it back again when he wanted it. But Jurgis was now a homeless man, wandering over a continent; and what did he know about banking and drafts and letters of credit? If he carried the money about with him, he would surely be robbed in the end; and so what was there for him to do but enjoy it while he could? On a Saturday night he drifted into a town with his fellows; and because it was raining, and there was no other place provided for him, he went to a saloon. And there were some who treated him and whom he had to treat, and there was laughter and singing and good cheer; and then out of the rear part of the saloon a girl's face, red-cheeked and merry, smiled at Jurgis, and his heart thumped suddenly in his throat. He nodded to her, and she came and sat by him, and they had more drink, and then he went upstairs into a room with her, and the wild beast rose up within him and screamed, as it has screamed in the jungle from the dawn of time. And then because of his memories and his shame, he was glad when others joined them, men and women; and they had more drink and spent the night in wild rioting and debauchery. In the van of the surplus-labor army, there followed another, an army of women,[4] they also struggling for life under the stern system of nature. Because there were rich men who sought pleasure, there had been ease and plenty for them so long as they were young and beautiful; and later on, when they were crowded out by others younger and more beautiful, they went out to follow upon the trail of the working-men. Sometimes they came of themselves, and the saloon-keepers shared with them; or sometimes they were handled by agencies, the same as the labor army. They were in the towns in harvest-time, near the lumber-camps in the winter, in the cities when the men came there; if a regiment were encamped, or a railroad or canal being made, or a great exposition getting ready, the crowd of women were on hand, living in shanties or saloons or tenement-rooms, sometimes eight or ten of them together.

In the morning Jurgis had not a cent, and he went out upon the road again. He was sick and disgusted, but after the new plan of his life, he crushed his feelings down. He had made a fool of himself, but he could not help it now—all he could do was to see that it did not happen again. So he tramped on until exercise and fresh air banished his headache, and his strength and joy returned. This happened to him every time, for Jurgis was still a creature of impulse, and his pleasures had not yet become business. It would be a long time before he could be like the majority of these men of the road, who roamed until the hunger for drink and for women mastered them, and then went to work with a purpose in mind, and stopped when they had the price of a spree.

On the contrary, try as he would, Jurgis could not help being made miserable by his conscience. It was the ghost that would not down. It would come upon him in the most unexpected places—sometimes it fairly drove him to drink.

One night he was caught by a thunder-storm, and he sought shelter in a little house just outside of a town. It was a workingman's home, and the owner was a Slav like himself, a new emigrant from White Russia;[5] he bade Jurgis welcome in his home language, and

---

4. Women whose only means of support is prostitution.
5. Belarus, once part of Lithuania and later of Poland, conquered by Russia in the 18th century.

told him to come to the kitchen-fire and dry himself. He had no bed for him, but there was straw in the garret, and he could make out. The man's wife was cooking the supper, and their children were playing about on the floor. Jurgis sat and exchanged thoughts with him about the old country, and the places where they had been and the work they had done. Then they ate, and afterward sat and smoked and talked more about America, and how they found it. In the middle of a sentence, however, Jurgis stopped, seeing that the woman had brought a big basin of water and was proceeding to undress her youngest baby. The rest had crawled into the closet where they slept, but the baby was to have a bath, the working-man explained. The nights had begun to be chilly, and his mother, ignorant as to the climate in America, had sewed him up for the winter; then it had turned warm again, and some kind of a rash had broken out on the child. The doctor had said she must bathe him every night, and she, foolish woman, believed him.

Jurgis scarcely heard the explanation; he was watching the baby. He was about a year old, and a sturdy little fellow, with soft fat legs, and a round ball of a stomach, and eyes as black as coals. His pimples did not seem to bother him much, and he was wild with glee over the bath, kicking and squirming and chuckling with delight, pulling at his mother's face and then at his own little toes. When she put him into the basin he sat in the midst of it and grinned, splashing the water over himself and squealing like a little pig. He spoke in Russian, of which Jurgis knew some; he spoke it with the quaintest of baby accents—and every word of it brought back to Jurgis some word of his own dead little one, and stabbed him like a knife. He sat perfectly motionless, silent, but gripping his hands tightly, while a storm gathered in his bosom and a flood heaped itself up behind his eyes. And in the end he could bear it no more, but buried his face in his hands and burst into tears, to the alarm and amazement of his hosts. Between the shame of this and his woe, Jurgis could not stand it, and got up and rushed out into the rain.

He went on and on down the road, finally coming to a black woods, where he hid and wept as if his heart would break. Ah, what agony was that, what despair, when the tomb of memory was rent open and the ghosts of his old life came forth to scourge him! What terror to see what he had been and now could never be—to see Ona and his child and his own dead self stretching out their arms to him, calling to him across a bottomless abyss—and to know that they were gone from him forever, and he writhing and suffocating in the mire of his own vileness!

Chapter XXIII

Early in the fall Jurgis set out for Chicago again. All the joy went out of tramping as soon as a man could not keep warm in the hay; and, like many thousands of others, he deluded himself with the hope that by coming early he could avoid the rush. He brought fifteen dollars with him, hidden away in one of his shoes, a sum which had been saved from the saloon-keepers, not so much by his conscience, as by the fear which filled him at the thought of being out of work in the city in the winter-time.

He travelled upon the railroad with several other men, hiding in freight-cars at night, and liable to be thrown off at any time, regardless of the speed of the train. When he reached the city he left the rest, for he had money and they did not, and he meant to save himself in this fight. He would bring to it all the skill that practice had brought him, and he would stand, whoever fell. On fair nights he would sleep in the park or on a truck or an empty barrel or box, and when it was rainy or cold he would stow himself upon a shelf in a ten-cent lodging-house, or pay three cents for the privileges of a "squatter" in a tenement hallway. He would eat at free lunches, five cents a meal, and never a cent more—so he might keep alive for two months and more, and in that time he would surely find a job. He would have to bid farewell to his summer cleanliness, of course, for he would come out of the first night's lodging with his clothes alive with vermin. There was no place in the city where he could wash even his face, unless he went down to the lake-front—and there it would soon be all ice.

First he went to the steel-mill and the harvester-works, and found that his places there had been filled long ago. He was careful to keep away from the stockyards—he was a single man now, he told himself, and he meant to stay one, to have his wages for his own when he got a job. He began the long, weary round of factories and warehouses, tramping all day, from one end of the city to the other, finding everywhere from ten to a hundred men ahead of him. He watched the newspapers, too—but no longer was he to be taken in by smooth-spoken agents. He had been told of all those tricks while "on the road."

In the end it was through a newspaper that he got a job, after nearly a month of seeking. It was a call for a hundred laborers, and though he thought it was a "fake," he went because the place was near by. He found a line of men a block long, but as a wagon chanced to come out of an alley and break the line, he saw his chance and sprang to seize a place. Men threatened him and tried to throw him out, but he cursed and made a disturbance to attract a policeman, upon which they subsided, knowing that if the latter interfered it would be to "fire" them all.

An hour or two later he entered a room and confronted a big Irishman behind a desk.

"Ever worked in Chicago before?" the man inquired; and whether it was a good angel that put it into Jurgis's mind, or an intuition of his sharpened wits, he was moved to answer, "No, sir."

"Where do you come from?"

"Kansas City, sir."

"Any references?"

"No, sir. I'm just an unskilled man. I've got good arms."

"I want men for hard work—it's all underground, digging tunnels for telephones. Maybe it won't suit you."

"I'm willing, sir—anything for me. What's the pay?"

"Fifteen cents an hour."

"I'm willing, sir."

"All right; go back there and give your name."

So within half an hour he was at work, far underneath the streets of the city. The tunnel was a peculiar one for telephone-wires; it was about eight feet high, and with a level floor nearly as wide. It had innumerable branches—a perfect spider-web beneath the city; Jurgis walked over half a mile with his gang to the place where they were to work. Stranger yet, the tunnel was lighted by electricity, and upon it was laid a double-tracked, narrow-gauge railroad!

But Jurgis was not there to ask questions, and he did not give the matter a thought. It was nearly a year afterward that he finally learned the meaning of this whole affair. The City Council had passed a quiet and innocent little bill allowing a company to construct telephone conduits under the city streets; and upon the strength of this, a great corporation had proceeded to tunnel all Chicago with a system of railway freight-subways. In the city there was a combination of employers, representing hundreds of millions of capital, and formed for the purpose of crushing the labor unions. The chief union which troubled it was the teamsters'; and when these freight tunnels were completed, connecting all the big factories and stores with the railroad depots, they would have the teamsters' union by the throat. Now and then there were rumors and murmurs in the Board of Aldermen, and once there was a committee to investigate—but each time another small fortune was paid over, and the rumors died away; until at last the city woke up with a start to find the work completed. There was a tremendous scandal, of course; it was found that the city records had been falsified and other crimes committed, and some of Chicago's big capitalists got into jail—figuratively speaking. The aldermen declared that they had had no idea of it all, in spite of the fact that the main entrance to the work had been in the rear of the saloon of one of them.[1]

It was in a newly opened cut that Jurgis worked, and so he knew that he had an all-winter job. He was so rejoiced that he treated himself to a spree that night, and with the balance of his money he hired himself a place in a tenement-room,[2] where he slept upon a big home-made straw mattress along with four other workingmen. This was one dollar a week, and for four more he got his food in a boarding-house near his work. This would leave him four dollars extra each week, an unthinkable sum for him. At the outset he had to pay for his digging tools, and also to buy a pair of heavy boots, since his shoes were falling to pieces, and a flannel shirt, since the one he had worn all summer was in shreds. He spent a week meditating whether or not he should also buy an overcoat. There was one belonging to a Hebrew collar-button pedler, who had died in the room next to him, and which the landlady was holding for her rent; in the end, however, Jurgis decided to do without it, as he was to be underground by day and in bed at night.

This was an unfortunate decision, however, for it drove him more quickly than ever into the saloons. From now on Jurgis worked from seven o'clock until half-past five, with half an hour for dinner; which meant that he never saw the sunlight on week-days. In the evenings there was no place for him to go except a bar-room; no place where there was light and warmth, where he could hear a little music or sit with a companion and talk. He had now no home to go to; he had no affection left in his life—only the pitiful mockery of it in the *camaraderie* of vice. On Sundays the churches were open—but where was there a church in which an ill-smelling working-man, with vermin crawling upon his neck, could sit without seeing people edge away and look annoyed? He had, of course, his corner in a close though unheated room, with a window opening upon a blank wall two feet away; and also he had the bare streets, with the winter gales sweeping through them; besides this he had only the saloons—and, of course, he had to drink to stay in them. If he drank now and then he was free to make himself at home, to gamble with dice or a pack of greasy cards, to play at a dingy pool-table for money, or to look at a beer-stained pink "sporting paper," with pictures of murderers and

1. In 1899, the Illinois Telegraph and Telephone Company received a franchise to tunnel under the streets for telephone wires but instead installed a freight subway, part of an effort to decrease corporate dependence on the well-organized Chicago teamsters (those who transport freight by team or truck). One of the main investors in the scheme was J. Ogden Armour.
2. Tenements were cheap multi-unit urban housing, often with inadequate light, air, and plumbing; they were also used as workshops.

half-naked women.³ It was for such pleasures as these that he spent his money; and such was his life during the six weeks and a half that he toiled for the merchants of Chicago, to enable them to break the grip of their teamsters' union.

In a work thus carried out, not much thought was given to the welfare of the laborers. On an average, the tunnelling cost a life a day and several manglings; it was seldom, however, that more than a dozen or two men heard of any one accident. The work was all done by the new boring-machinery, with as little blasting as possible; but there would be falling rocks and crushed supports and premature explosions—and in addition all the dangers of railroading. So it was that one night, as Jurgis was on his way out with his gang, an engine and a loaded car dashed round one of the innumerable right-angle branches and struck him upon the shoulder, hurling him against the concrete wall and knocking him senseless.

When he opened his eyes again it was to the clanging of the bell of an ambulance. He was lying in it, covered by a blanket, and it was threading its way slowly through the holiday-shopping crowds. They took him to the county hospital, where a young surgeon set his arm; then he was washed and laid upon a bed in a ward with a score or two more of maimed and mangled men.

Jurgis spent his Christmas in this hospital, and it was the pleasantest Christmas he had had in America. Every year there were scandals and investigations in this institution, the newspapers charging that doctors were allowed to try fantastic experiments upon the patients; but Jurgis knew nothing of this—his only complaint was that they used to feed him upon tinned meat, which no man who had ever worked in Packingtown would feed to his dog. Jurgis had often wondered just who ate the canned corned beef and "roast beef" of the stockyards; now he began to understand—that it was what you might call "graft-meat,"⁴ put up to be sold to public officials and contractors, and eaten by soldiers and sailors, prisoners and inmates of institutions, "shanty-men" and gangs of railroad laborers.

Jurgis was ready to eave the hospital at the end of two weeks. This did not mean that his arm was strong and that he was able to go back to work, but simply that he could get along without further attention, and that his place was needed for some one worse off than

---

3. Unlike the Sunday paper Jurgis read to his son, this is a men's magazine such as the infamous *Police Gazette*, which featured crime, sports, and women of the demimonde.
4. Allusion to the embalmed beef scandal in the Spanish-American War; see above, p. 93, n. 8, and below, p. 354, n. 8. Jurgis is staying in Cook County Hospital, which serviced a large immigrant population and saw numerous *scandals and investigations* due to corruption. Staff positions "were obtained only through political influence or outright bribery," and the hospital budgeted more for liquor than for patient gowns (Thomas Neville Bonner, *Medicine in Chicago 1850–1950: A Chapter in the Social and Scientific Development of a City* [Madison, WI: American History Research Center, 1957], pp. 163, 162).

he. That he was utterly helpless, and had no means of keeping himself alive in the meantime, was something which did not concern the hospital authorities, nor any one else in the city.

As it chanced, he had been hurt on a Monday, and had just paid for his last week's board and his room rent, and spent nearly all the balance of his Saturday's pay. He had less than seventy-five cents in his pockets, and a dollar and a half due him for the day's work he had done before he was hurt. He might possibly have sued the company, and got some damages for his injuries, but he did not know this, and it was not the company's business to tell him. He went and got his pay and his tools, which he left in a pawnshop for fifty cents. Then he went to his landlady, who had rented his place and had no other for him; and then to his boarding-house keeper, who looked him over and questioned him. As he must certainly be helpless for a couple of months, and had boarded there only six weeks, she decided very quickly that it would not be worth the risk to keep him on trust.

So Jurgis went out into the streets, in a most dreadful plight. It was bitterly cold, and a heavy snow was falling, beating into his face. He had no overcoat, and no place to go, and two dollars and sixty-five cents in his pocket, with the certainty that he could not earn another cent for months. The snow meant no chance to him now; he must walk along and see others shovelling, vigorous and active—and he with his left arm bound to his side! He could not hope to tide himself over by odd jobs of loading trucks; he could not even sell newspapers or carry satchels, because he was now at the mercy of any rival. Words could not paint the terror that came over him as he realized all this. He was like a wounded animal in the forest; he was forced to compete with his enemies upon unequal terms. There would be no consideration for him because of his weakness—it was no one's business to help him in such distress, to make the fight the least bit easier for him. Even if he took to begging, he would be at a disadvantage, for reasons which he was to discover in good time.

In the beginning he could not think of anything except getting out of the awful cold. He went into one of the saloons he had been wont to frequent and bought a drink, and then stood by the fire shivering and waiting to be ordered out. According to an unwritten law, the buying a drink included the privilege of loafing for just so long; then one had to buy another drink or move on. That Jurgis was an old customer entitled him to a somewhat longer stop; but then he had been away two weeks, and was evidently "on the bum." He might plead and tell his "hard-luck story," but that would not help him much; a saloonkeeper who was to be moved by such means would soon have his place jammed to the doors with "hoboes" on a day like this.

So Jurgis went out into another place, and paid another nickel. He was so hungry this time that he could not resist the hot beef-stew, an indulgence which cut short his stay by a considerable time. When he was again told to move on, he made his way to a "tough" place in the "Lêvée" district, where now and then he had gone with a certain rat-eyed Bohemian working-man of his acquaintance, seeking a woman. It was Jurgis's vain hope that here the proprietor would let him remain as a "sitter." In low-class places, in the dead of winter, saloon-keepers would often allow one or two forlorn-looking bums who came in covered with snow or soaked with rain to sit by the fire and look miserable to attract custom.[5] A workingman would come in, feeling cheerful after his day's work was over, and it would trouble him to have to take his glass with such a sight under his nose; and so he would call out: "Hello, Bub, what's the matter? You look as if you'd been up against it!" And then the other would begin to pour out some tale of misery, and the man would say, "Come have a glass, and maybe that'll brace you up." And so they would drink together, and if the tramp was sufficiently wretched-looking, or good enough at the "gab," they might have two; and if they were to discover that they were from the same country, or had lived in the same city or worked at the same trade, they might sit down at a table and spend an hour or two in talk—and before they got through the saloon-keeper would have taken in a dollar. All of this might seem diabolical, but the saloon-keeper was in no wise to blame for it. He was in the same plight as the manufacturer who has to adulterate and misrepresent his product. If he does not, some one else will; and the saloon-keeper, unless he is also an alderman, is apt to be in debt to the big brewers, and on the verge of being sold out.

The market for "sitters" was glutted that afternoon, however, and there was no place for Jurgis. In all he had to spend six nickels in keeping a shelter over him that frightful day, and then it was just dark, and the station-houses would not open until midnight! At the last place, however, there was a bartender who knew him and liked him, and let him doze at one of the tables until the boss came back; and also, as he was going out, the man gave him a tip,—on the next block there was a religious revival of some sort, with preaching and singing, and hundreds of hoboes would go there for the shelter and warmth.

Jurgis went straightway, and saw a sign hung out, saying that the door would open at seven-thirty; then he walked, or half ran, a block, and hid awhile in a doorway and then ran again, and so on until the hour. At the end he was all but frozen, and fought his way in with the rest of the throng (at the risk of having his arm broken again), and got close to the big stove.

5. Customers, business.

By eight o'clock the place was so crowded that the speakers ought to have been flattered; the aisles were filled halfway up, and at the door men were packed tight enough to walk upon. There were three elderly gentlemen in black upon the platform, and a young lady who played the piano in front. First they sang a hymn, and then one of the three, a tall, smooth-shaven man, very thin, and wearing black spectacles, began an address. Jurgis heard smatterings of it, for the reason that terror kept him awake—he knew that he snored abominably, and to have been put out just then would have been like a sentence of death to him.

The evangelist was preaching "sin and redemption," the infinite grace of God and His pardon for human frailty. He was very much in earnest, and he meant well, but Jurgis, as he listened, found his soul filled with hatred. What did he know about sin and suffering—with his smooth, black coat and his neatly starched collar, his body warm, and his belly full, and money in his pocket—and lecturing men who were struggling for their lives, men at the death-grapple with the demon powers of hunger and cold!—This, of course, was unfair; but Jurgis felt that these men were out of touch with the life they discussed, that they were unfitted to solve its problems; nay, they themselves were part of the problem—they were part of the order established that was crushing men down and beating them! They were of the triumphant and insolent possessors; they had a hall, and a fire, and food and clothing and money, and so they might preach to hungry men, and the hungry men must be humble and listen! They were trying to save their souls—and who but a fool could fail to see that all that was the matter with their souls was that they had not been able to get a decent existence for their bodies?

At eleven the meeting closed, and the desolate audience filed out into the snow, muttering curses up on the few traitors who had got repentance and gone upon the platform. It was yet an hour before the station-house would open, and Jurgis had no overcoat—and was weak from a long illness. During that hour he nearly perished. He was obliged to run hard to keep his blood moving at all—and then he came back to the station-house and found a crowd blocking the street before the door! This was in the month of January, 1904, when the country was on the verge of "hard times," and the newspapers were reporting the shutting down of factories every day—it was estimated that a million and a half of men were thrown out of work before the spring.[6] So all the hiding-places of the city were crowded, and before that station-house door men fought and tore

6. Several events in 1901 sparked the 1902–04 recession, including a financial panic (followed by the first Stock Market crash) and the assassination of President William McKinley.

each other like savage beasts. When at last the place was jammed and they shut the doors, half the crowd was still outside; and Jurgis, with his helpless arm, was among them. There was no choice then but to go to a lodging-house and spend another dime. It really broke his heart to do this, at half-past twelve o'clock, after he had wasted the night at the meeting and on the street. He would be turned out of the lodging-house promptly at seven—they had the shelves which served as bunks so contrived that they could be dropped, and any man who was slow about obeying orders could be tumbled to the floor.

This was one day, and the cold spell lasted for fourteen of them. At the end of six days every cent of Jurgis's money was gone; and then he went out on the streets to beg for his life.

He would begin as soon as the business of the city was moving. He would sally forth from a saloon, and, after making sure there was no policeman in sight, would approach every likely-looking person who passed him, telling his woful story and pleading for a nickel or a dime. Then when he got one, he would dart round the corner and return to his base to get warm; and his victim, seeing him do this, would go away, vowing that he would never give a cent to a beggar again. The victim never paused to ask where else Jurgis could have gone under the circumstances—where he, the victim, would have gone. At the saloon Jurgis could not only get more food and better food than he could buy in any restaurant for the same money, but a drink in the bargain to warm him up. Also he could find a comfortable seat by a fire, and could chat with a companion until he was as warm as toast. At the saloon, too, he felt at home. Part of the saloon-keeper's business was to offer a home and refreshments to beggars in exchange for the proceeds of their foragings; and was there any one else in the whole city who would do this—would the victim have done it himself?

Poor Jurgis might have been expected to make a successful beggar. He was just out of the hospital, and desperately sick-looking, and with a helpless arm; also he had no overcoat, and shivered pitifully. But, alas, it was again the case of the honest merchant, who finds that the genuine and unadulterated article is driven to the wall by the artistic counterfeit. Jurgis, as a beggar, was simply a blundering amateur in competition with organized and scientific professionalism. He was just out of the hospital—but the story was worn threadbare, and how could he prove it? He had his arm in a sling—and it was a device a regular beggar's little boy would have scorned. He was pale and shivering—but they were made up with cosmetics, and had studied the art of chattering their teeth. As to his being without an overcoat, among them you would meet men you could swear had on nothing but a ragged linen duster and a pair of cotton trousers—so cleverly had they concealed the several suits of all-wool underwear beneath. Many of these professional mendicants had comfortable homes, and families, and thousands of dollars in the bank; some of them had retired upon their earnings, and gone into the business of fitting out and doctoring others, or working children at the trade. There were some who had both their arms bound tightly to their sides, and padded stumps in their sleeves, and a sick child hired to carry a cup for them. There were some who had no legs, and pushed themselves upon a wheeled platform—some who had been favored with blindness, and were led by pretty little dogs. Some less fortunate had mutilated themselves or burned themselves, or had brought horrible sores upon themselves with chemicals; you might suddenly encounter upon the street a man holding out to you a finger rotting and discolored with gangrene—or one with livid scarlet wounds half escaped from their filthy bandages. These desperate ones were the dregs of the city's cesspools, wretches who hid at night in the rain-soaked cellars of old ramshackle tenements, in "stale-beer dives" and opium joints, with abandoned women in the last stages of the harlot's progress[7]—women who had been kept by Chinamen and turned away at last to die.[8] Every day the police net would drag hundreds of them off the streets, and in the Detention Hospital you might see them, herded together in a miniature inferno, with hideous, beastly faces, bloated and leprous with disease, laughing, shouting, screaming in all stages of drunkenness, barking like dogs, gibbering like apes, raving and tearing themselves in delirium.

7. Allusion to *A Harlot's Progress*, six paintings (1731) and etchings (1732) about a young woman who moves from the country to London and becomes a prostitute, by the English artist William Hogarth (1697–1764).
8. At a time of considerable hostility to Chinese immigrants, many native-born whites believed the Chinese were predisposed to become pimps and engage in other criminal activity, such as selling opium. On the anti-Asian sentiment in this period, see below, p. 360.

Chapter XXIV

In the face of all his handicaps, Jurgis was obliged to make the price of a lodging, and of a drink every hour or two, under penalty of freezing to death. Day after day he roamed about in the arctic cold, his soul filled full of bitterness and despair. He saw the world of civilization then more plainly than ever he had seen it before; a world in which nothing counted but brutal might, an order devised by those who possessed it for the subjugation of those who did not. He was one of the latter; and all outdoors, all life, was to him one colossal prison, which he paced like a pent-up tiger, trying one bar after another, and finding them all beyond his power. He had lost in the fierce battle of greed, and so was doomed to be exterminated; and all society was busied to see that he did not escape the sentence. Everywhere that he turned were prison-bars, and hostile eyes following him; the well-fed, sleek policemen, from whose glances he shrank, and who seemed to grip their clubs more tightly when they saw him; the saloon-keepers, who never ceased to watch him while he was in their places, who were jealous of every moment he lingered after he had paid his money; the hurrying throngs upon the streets, who were deaf to his entreaties, oblivious of his very existence—and savage and contemptuous when he forced himself upon them. They had their own affairs, and there was no place for him among them. There was no place for him anywhere—every direction he turned his gaze, this fact was forced upon him. Everything was built to express it to him: the residences, with their heavy walls and bolted doors, and basement-windows barred with iron; the great warehouses filled with the products of the whole world, and guarded by iron shutters and heavy gates; the banks with their unthinkable billions of wealth, all buried in safes and vaults of steel.

And then one day there befell Jurgis the one adventure of his life. It was late at night, and he had failed to get the price of a lodging. Snow was falling, and he had been out so long that he was covered with it, and was chilled to the bone. He was working among the theatre crowds, flitting here and there, taking large chances with the police, in his desperation half hoping to be arrested. When he saw a blue-coat[1] start toward him, however, his heart failed him, and he dashed down a side street and fled a couple of blocks. When he stopped again he saw a man coming toward him, and placed himself in his path.

"Please, sir," he began, in the usual formula, "will you give me the price of a lodging? I've had a broken arm, and I can't work, and I've

1. Policeman.

not a cent in my pocket. I'm an honest working-man, sir, and I never begged before. It's not my fault, sir—"

Jurgis usually went on until he was interrupted, but this man did not interrupt, and so at last he came to a breathless stop. The other had halted, and Jurgis suddenly noticed that he stood a little unsteadily. "Whuzzat you say?" he queried suddenly, in a thick voice.

Jurgis began again, speaking more slowly and distinctly; before he was half through the other put out his hand and rested it upon his shoulder. "Poor ole chappie!" he said. "Been up—hic—up—against it, hey?"

Then he lurched toward Jurgis, and the hand upon his shoulder became an arm about his neck. "Up against it myself, ole sport," he said. "She's a hard ole world."

They were close to a lamp post, and Jurgis got a glimpse of the other. He was a young fellow—not much over eighteen, with a handsome boyish face. He wore a silk hat and a rich soft overcoat with a fur collar; and he smiled at Jurgis with benignant sympathy. "I'm hard up, too, my goo' fren'," he said. "I've got cruel parents, or I'd set you up. Whuzzamatter whizyer?"

"I've been in the hospital."

"Hospital!" exclaimed the young fellow, still smiling sweetly, "thass too bad! Same's my Aunt Polly—hic—my Aunt Polly's in the hospital, too—ole auntie's been havin' twins! Whuzzamatter whiz *you?*"

"I've got a broken arm—" Jurgis began.

"So," said the other, sympathetically. "That ain't so bad—you get over that. I wish somebody's break *my* arm, ole chappie—damfi-don't! Then they's treat me better—hic—hole me up, ole sport! Whuzzit you wamme do?"

"I'm hungry, sir," said Jurgis.

"Hungry! Why don't you hassome supper?"

"I've got no money, sir."

"No money! Ho, ho—less be chums, ole boy—jess like me! No money, either,—a'most busted! Why don't you go home, then, same's me?"

"I haven't any home," said Jurgis.

"No home! Stranger in the city, hey? Goo' God, thass bad! Better come home wiz me—yes, by Harry, thass the trick, you'll come home an' hassome supper—hic—wiz me! Awful lonesome—nobody home! Guv'ner[2] gone abroad—Bubby on's honeymoon—Polly havin' twins— every damn soul gone away! Nuff—hic—nuff to drive a feller to drink, I say! Only ole Ham standin' by, passin' plates—damfican eat like that, no sir! The club for me every time, my boy, I say. But then

2. Governor, slang for father.

they won't lemme sleep there—guv'ner's orders, by Harry—home every night, sir! Ever hear anythin' like that? 'Every mornin' do?' I asked him. 'No, sir, every night, or no allowance at all, sir.' Thass my guv'ner—hic—hard as nails, by Harry! Tole ole Ham to watch me, too—servants spyin' on me—whuzyer think that, my fren'? A nice, quiet—hic—good-hearted young feller like me, an' his daddy can't go to Europe—hup!—an' leave him in peace! Ain't that a shame, sir? An' I gotter go home every evenin' an' miss all the fun, by Harry! Thass whuzzamatter now—thass why I'm here! Hadda come away an' leave Kitty—hic—left her cryin', too—whujja think of that, ole sport? 'Lemme go, Kittens,' says I—'come early an' often—I go where duty—hic—calls me. Farewell, farewell, my own true love—farewell, fare-we-hell, my-own-true-love!'"

This last was a song, and the young gentleman's voice rose mournful and wailing, while he swung upon Jurgis's neck. The latter was glancing about nervously, lest some one should approach. They were still alone, however.

"But I came all right, all right," continued the youngster, aggressively. "I can—hic—I can have my own way when I want it, by Harry—Freddie Jones is a hard man to handle when he gets goin'! 'No, sir,' says I, 'by thunder, and I don't need anybody goin' home with me, either—whujja take me for, hey? Think I'm drunk, dontcha, hey?—I know you! But I'm no more drunk than you are, Kittens,' says I to her. And then says she, 'Thass true, Freddie dear' (she's a smart one, is Kitty), 'but I'm stayin' in the flat, an' you're goin' out into the cold, cold night!' 'Put it in a pome, lovely Kitty,' says I. 'No jokin', Freddie, my boy,' says she. 'Lemme call a cab now, like a good dear'—but I can call my own cabs, dontcha fool yourself—I know what I'm a-doin', you bet! Say, my fren', whatcha say—willye come home an' see me, an' hassome supper? Come 'long like a good feller—don't be haughty! You're up against it, same as me, an' you can unnerstan' a feller; your heart's in the right place, by Harry—come 'long, ole chappie, an' we'll light up the house, an' have some fizz, an' we'll raise hell, we will—whoop-la! S'long's I'm inside the house I can do as I please—the guv'ner's own very orders, b'God! Hip! hip!"

They had started down the street, arm in arm, the young man pushing Jurgis along, half dazed. Jurgis was trying to think what to do—he knew he could not pass any crowded place with his new acquaintance without attracting attention and being stopped. It was only because of the falling snow that people who passed here did not notice anything wrong.

Suddenly, therefore, Jurgis stopped. "Is it very far?" he inquired.

"Not very," said the other. "Tired, are you, though? Well, we'll ride—whatcha say? Good! Call a cab!"

And then, gripping Jurgis tight with one hand, the young fellow began searching his pockets with the other. "You call, ole sport, an' I'll pay," he suggested. "How's that, hey?"

And he pulled out from somewhere a big roll of bills. It was more money than Jurgis had ever seen in his life before, and he stared at it with startled eyes.

"Looks like a lot, hey?" said Master Freddie, fumbling with it. "Fool you, though, ole chappie—they're all little ones! I'll be busted[3] in one week more, sure thing—word of honor. An' not a cent more till the first—hic—guv'ner's orders—hic—not a *cent*, by Harry! Nuff to set a feller crazy, it is. I sent him a cable this af 'noon—thass one reason more why I'm goin' home. 'Hangin' on the verge of starvation,' I says—'for the honor of the family—hic—sen' me some bread. Hunger will compel me to join you.—Freddie.' Thass what I wired him, by Harry, an' I mean it—I'll run away from school, b'God, if he don't sen' me some."

After this fashion the young gentleman continued to prattle on—and meantime Jurgis was trembling with excitement. He might grab that wad of bills and be out of sight in the darkness before the other could collect his wits. Should he do it? What better had he to hope for, if he waited longer? But Jurgis had never committed a crime in his life, and now he hesitated half a second too long. "Freddie" got one bill loose, and then stuffed the rest back into his trousers' pocket.

"Here, ole man," he said, "you take it." He held it out fluttering. They were in front of a saloon; and by the light of the window Jurgis saw that it was a hundred-dollar bill!

"You take it," the other repeated. "Pay the cabbie an' keep the change—I've got—hic—no head for business! Guv'ner says so his self, an' the guv'ner knows—the guv'ner's got a head for business, you bet! 'All right, guv'ner,' I told him, 'you run the show, and I'll take the tickets!' An' so he set Aunt Polly to watch me—hic—an' now Polly's off in the hospital havin' twins, an' me out raisin' Cain![4] Hello, there! Hey! Call him!"

A cab was driving by; and Jurgis sprang and called, and it swung round to the curb. Master Freddie clambered in with some difficulty, and Jurgis had started to follow, when the driver shouted: "Hi, there! Get out—you!"

Jurgis hesitated, and was half obeying; but his companion broke out: "Whuzzat? Whuzzamatter wiz you, hey?"

And the cabbie subsided, and Jurgis climbed in. Then Freddie gave a number on the Lake Shore Drive,[5] and the carriage started

3. Broke.
4. Causing trouble. The phrase derives from the biblical story of Adam and Eve's son Cain, who killed his brother Abel (Genesis 4:1–9).
5. Exclusive address along Lake Michigan, known for beautiful and expensive homes.

away. The youngster leaned back and snuggled up to Jurgis, murmuring contentedly; in half a minute he was sound asleep. Jurgis sat shivering, speculating as to whether he might not still be able to get hold of the roll of bills. He was afraid to try to go through his companion's pockets, however; and besides, the cabbie might be on the watch. He had the hundred safe, and he would have to be content with that.

At the end of half an hour or so the cab stopped. They were out on the water-front, and from the east a freezing gale was blowing off the ice-bound lake. "Here we are," called the cabbie, and Jurgis awakened his companion.

Master Freddie sat up with a start.

"Hello!" he said. "Where are we? Whuzzis? Who are you, hey? Oh, yes, sure nuff! Mos' forgot you—hic—ole chappie! Home, are we? Lessee! Br-r-r—it's cold! Yes—come 'long—we're home—be it ever so—hic—humble!"

Before them there loomed an enormous granite pile, set far back from the street, and occupying a whole block. By the light of the driveway lamps Jurgis could see that it had towers and huge gables, like a mediæval castle. He thought that the young fellow must have made a mistake—it was inconceivable to him that any person could have a home like a hotel or the city hall. But he followed in silence, and they went up the long flight of steps, arm in arm.

"There's a button here, ole sport," said Master Freddie. "Hole my arm while I find her! Steady, now—oh, yes, here she is! Saved!"

A bell rang, and in a few seconds the door was opened. A man in blue livery stood holding it, and gazing before him, silent as a statue.

They stood for a moment blinking in the light. Then Jurgis felt his companion pulling, and he stepped in, and the blue automaton closed the door. Jurgis's heart was beating wildly; it was a bold thing for him to do—into what strange unearthly place he was venturing he had no idea. Aladdin entering his cave could not have been more excited.[6]

The place where he stood was dimly lighted; but he could see a vast hall, with pillars fading into the darkness above, and a great staircase opening at the far end of it. The floor was of tesselated marble, smooth as glass, and from the walls strange shapes loomed out, woven into huge portières in rich, harmonious colors, or gleaming from paintings, wonderful and mysterious-looking in the half-light, purple and red and golden, like sunset glimmers in a shadowy forest.

The man in livery had moved silently toward them; Master Freddie took off his hat and handed it to him, and then, letting go of Jurgis's arm, tried to get out of his overcoat. After two or three

---

6. In the Middle Eastern folk-tale collection *One Thousand and One Nights*, Aladdin goes into a cave for a magical lamp that, when rubbed, produces two genii who do his bidding.

attempts he accomplished this, with the lackey's help; and meantime a second man had approached, a tall and portly personage, solemn as an executioner. He bore straight down upon Jurgis, who shrank away nervously; he seized him by the arm without a word, and started toward the door with him. Then suddenly came Master Freddie's voice, "Hamilton! My fren' will remain wiz me."

The man paused and half released Jurgis. "Come 'long, ole chappie," said the other, and Jurgis started toward him.

"Master Frederick!" exclaimed the man.

"See that the cabbie—hic—is paid," was the other's response; and he linked his arm in Jurgis's. Jurgis was about to say, "I have the money for him," but he restrained himself. The stout man in uniform signalled to the other, who went out to the cab, while he followed Jurgis and his young master.

They went down the great hall, and then turned. Before them were two huge doors.

"Hamilton," said Master Freddie.

"Well, sir?" said the other.

"Whuzzamatter wizze dinin'-room doors?"

"Nothing is the matter, sir."

"Then why dontcha openum?"

The man rolled them back; another vista lost itself in the darkness. "Lights," commanded Master Freddie; and the butler pressed a button, and a flood of brilliant incandescence streamed from above, half blinding Jurgis. He stared; and little by little he made out the great apartment, with a domed ceiling from which the light poured, and walls that were one enormous painting—nymphs and dryads dancing in a flower-strewn glade—Diana[7] with her hounds and horses, dashing headlong through a mountain streamlet—a group of maidens bathing in a forest-pool—all life-size, and so real that Jurgis thought that it was some work of enchantment, that he was in a dream-palace. Then his eye passed to the long table in the centre of the hall, a table black as ebony, and gleaming with wrought silver and gold. In the centre of it was a huge carven bowl, with the glistening gleam of ferns and the red and purple of rare orchids, glowing from a light hidden somewhere in their midst.

"This's the dinin'-room," observed Master Freddie. "How you like it, hey, ole sport?"

He always insisted on having an answer to his remarks, leaning over Jurgis and smiling into his face. Jurgis liked it.

"Rummy ole place to feed in all 'lone, though," was Freddie's comment—"rummy's hell! Whuzya think, hey?" Then another idea

---

7. A favorite artistic subject, the ancient Greek goddess of wild nature, hunting, and childbirth; *nymphs*: female personifications of natural objects; *dryads*: tree nymphs.

occurred to him and he went on, without waiting: "Maybe you never saw anything—hic—like this 'fore? Hey, ole chappie?"

"No," said Jurgis.

"Come from country, maybe—hey?"

"Yes," said Jurgis.

"Aha! I thosso! Lossa folks from country never saw such a place. Guv'ner brings 'em—free show—hic—reg'lar circus! Go home tell folks about it. Ole man Jones's place—Jones the packer—beef-trust man. Made it all out of hogs, too, damn ole scoundrel. Now we see where our pennies go—rebates, an' private-car lines[8]—hic—by Harry! Bully[9] place, though—worth seein'! Ever hear of Jones the packer, hey, ole chappie?"

Jurgis had started involuntarily; the other, whose sharp eyes missed nothing, demanded: "Whuzzamatter, hey? Heard of him?"

And Jurgis managed to stammer out: "I have worked for him in the yards."

"What!" cried Master Freddie, with a yell. "*You!* In the yards? Ho, ho! Why, say, thass good! Shake hands on it, ole man—by Harry! Guv'ner ought to be here—glad to see you. Great fren's with the men, guv'ner—labor an' capital, commun'ty 'f int'rests, an' all that—hic! Funny things happen in this world, don't they, ole man? Hamilton, lemme interduce you—fren' the family—ole fren' the guv'ner's—works in the yards. Come to spend the night wiz me, Hamilton—have a hot time. My fren', Mr.—whuzya name, ole chappie? Tell us your name."

"Rudkus—Jurgis Rudkus."

"My fren', Mr. Rudnose, Hamilton—shake han's."

The stately butler bowed his head, but made not a sound; and suddenly Master Freddie pointed an eager finger at him. "I know whuzzamatter wiz you, Hamilton—lay you a dollar I know! You think—hic—you think I'm drunk! Hey, now?"

And the butler again bowed his head. "Yes, sir," he said, at which Master Freddie hung tightly upon Jurgis's neck and went into a fit of laughter. "Hamilton, you damn ole scoundrel," he roared, "I'll 'scharge you for impudence, you see 'f I don't! Ho, ho, ho! I'm drunk! Ho, ho!"

The two waited until his fit had spent itself, to see what new whim would seize him. "Whatcha wanta do?" he queried suddenly. "Wanta see the place, ole chappie? Wamme play the guv'ner—show you roun'? State parlors—Looee Cans—Looee Sez—chairs cost three thousand apiece. Tea-room—Maryanntnet—picture of shepherds

8. When railroads refused to provide refrigerator cars, packing companies built their own private cars, then demanded rebates for their use by fruit and other agricultural industries.

9. First-rate (slang).

dancing—Ruysdael—twenty-three thousan'! Ball-room—balc'ny pillars—hic—imported—special ship—sixty-eight thousan'! Ceilin' painted in Rome—whuzzat feller's name, Hamilton—Mattatoni? Macaroni? Then this place—silver bowl—Benvenuto Cellini— rummy ole Dago! An' the organ—thirty thousan' dollars, sir—starter up, Hamilton, let Mr. Rednose hear it. No—never mind—clean forgot—says he's hungry, Hamilton—less have some supper. Only— hic—don't less have it here—come up to my place, ole sport—nice an' cosy. This way—steady now, don't slip on the floor. Hamilton, we'll have a cole spread, an' some fizz—don't leave out the fizz, by Harry. We'll have some of the eighteen-thirty Madeira.[1] Hear me, sir?"

"Yes, sir," said the butler, "but, Master Frederick, your father left orders—"

And Master Frederick drew himself up to a stately height. "My father's orders were left to me—hic—an' not to you," he said. Then, clasping Jurgis tightly by the neck, he staggered out of the room; on the way another idea occurred to him, and he asked: "Any—hic— cable message for me, Hamilton?"

"No, sir," said the butler.

"Guv'ner must be travellin'. An' how's the twins, Hamilton?"

"They are doing well, sir."

"Good!" said Master Freddie; and added fervently: "God bless 'em, the little lambs!"

They went up the great staircase, one step at a time; at the top of it there gleamed at them out of the shadows the figure of a nymph crouching by a fountain, a figure ravishingly beautiful, the flesh warm and glowing with the hues of life. Above was a huge court, with domed roof, the various apartments opening into it. The butler had paused below but a few minutes to give orders, and then followed them; now he pressed a button, and the hall blazed with light. He opened a door before them, and then pressed another button, as they staggered into the apartment.

It was fitted up as a study. In the centre was a mahogany table, covered with books, and smokers' implements; the walls were decorated with college trophies and colors,—flags, posters, photographs and knickknacks—tennis-rackets, canoe-paddles, golf-clubs, and polo-sticks. An enormous moose head, with horns six feet across,

<hr>

1. A parade of leisure-class allusions presented by a drunk: Louis Quinze (Louis XV, 1643–1715), Louis Seize (Louis XVI, 1754–1793), kings of France after whom ornamental furniture styles were named, while entire rooms were decorated after the manner of Marie Antoinette (1755–1793), queen of France. Jacob van Ruisdael (1628–1682), Dutch landscape painter. *Mattatoni/Macaroni*, perhaps corruption of Carlo Maratti (1625–1713) or Giovanii Battista Mornoni (1520–1570), Italian painters, or even the famous Michelangelo Buonarroti (1475–1564). *Benvenuto Cellini* (1500–1571), Italian metalsmith, sculptor, and author; *dago* is a derogatory term for an Italian. *Madeira* is a fortified wine.

faced a buffalo head on the opposite wall, while bear and tiger skins covered the polished floor. There were lounging-chairs and sofas, window-seats covered with soft cushions of fantastic designs; there was one corner fitted in Persian fashion, with a huge canopy and a jewelled lamp beneath. Beyond, a door opened upon a bedroom, and beyond that was a swimming pool of the purest marble, that had cost about forty thousand dollars.

Master Freddie stood for a moment or two, gazing about him; then out of the next room a dog emerged, a monstrous bulldog, the most hideous object that Jurgis had ever laid eyes upon. He yawned, opening a mouth like a dragon's; and he came toward the young man, wagging his tail. "Hello, Dewey!" cried his master. "Been havin' a snooze, ole boy? Well, well—hello there, whuzzamatter?" (The dog was snarling at Jurgis.) "Why, Dewey—this' my fren', Mr. Rednose— ole fren' the guv'ner's! Mr. Rednose, Admiral Dewey;[2] shake han's— hic. Ain't he a daisy, though—blue ribbon at the New York show— eighty-five hundred at a clip! How's that, hey?"

The speaker sank into one of the big arm-chairs, and Admiral Dewey crouched beneath it; he did not snarl again, but he never took his eyes off Jurgis. He was perfectly sober, was the Admiral.

The butler had closed the door, and he stood by it, watching Jurgis every second. Now there came footsteps outside, and, as he opened the door a man in livery entered, carrying a folding-table, and behind him two men with covered trays. They stood like statues while the first spread the table and set out the contents of the trays upon it. There were cold patés, and thin slices of meat, tiny bread and butter sandwiches with the crust cut off, a bowl of sliced peaches and cream (in January),[3] little fancy cakes, pink and green and yellow and white, and half a dozen ice-cold bottles of wine.

"Thass the stuff for you!" cried Master Freddie, exultantly, as he spied them. "Come 'long, ole chappie, move up."

And he seated himself at the table; the waiter pulled a cork, and he took the bottle and poured three glasses of its contents in succession down his throat. Then he gave a long-drawn sigh, and cried again to Jurgis to seat himself.

The butler held the chair at the opposite side of the table, and Jurgis thought it was to keep him out of it; but finally he understood that it was the other's intention to put it under him, and so he sat down, cautiously and mistrustingly. Master Freddie perceived that the attendants embarrassed him, and he remarked, with a nod to them, "You may go."

They went, all save the butler.

2. The dog is named after George Dewey (1837–1917), U.S. naval officer who served in the American Civil War and the Spanish-American War.
3. Out-of-season fruit was a costly extravagance at this time.

"You may go too, Hamilton," he said.

"Master Frederick—" the man began.

"Go!" cried the youngster, angrily. "Damn you, don't you hear me?"

The man went out and closed the door; Jurgis, who was as sharp as he, observed that he took the key out of the lock, in order that he might peer through the key-hole.

Master Frederick turned to the table again. "Now," he said, "go for it."

Jurgis gazed at him doubtingly. "Eat!" cried the other. "Pile in, ole chappie!"

"Don't you want anything?" Jurgis asked.

"Ain't hungry," was the reply—"only thirsty. Kitty and me had some candy—you go on."

So Jurgis began, without further parley. He ate as with two shovels, his fork in one hand and his knife in the other; when he once got started his wolf-hunger got the better of him, and he did not stop for breath until he had cleared every plate. "Gee whiz!" said the other, who had been watching him in wonder.

Then he held Jurgis the bottle. "Lessee you drink now," he said; and Jurgis took the bottle and turned it up to his mouth, and a wonderful unearthly liquid ecstasy poured down his throat, tickling every nerve of him, thrilling him with joy. He drank the very last drop of it, and then he gave vent to a long-drawn "Ah!"

"Good stuff, hey?" said Freddie, sympathetically; he had leaned back in the big chair, putting his arm behind his head and gazing at Jurgis.

And Jurgis gazed back at him. He was clad in spotless evening-dress, was Freddie, and looked very handsome—he was a beautiful boy, with light golden hair and the head of an Antinous.[4] He smiled at Jurgis confidingly, and then started talking again, with his blissful insouciance. This time he talked for ten minutes at a stretch, and in the course of the speech he told Jurgis all of his family history. His big brother Charlie was in love with the guileless maiden who played the part of "Little Bright-Eyes" in "The Kaliph of Kamskatka." He had been on the verge of marrying her once, only "the guv'ner" had sworn to disinherit him, and had presented him with a sum that would stagger the imagination, and that had staggered the virtue of "Little Bright-Eyes." Now Charlie had got leave from college, and had gone away in his automobile on the next best thing to a honeymoon. "The guv'ner" had made threats to disinherit another of his children also, sister Gwendolen, who had married an Italian marquis with a string of titles and a duelling record. They lived in his chateau, or rather had, until he had taken to firing the

4. Paragon of masculine beauty (ca. 110–130), companion of Emperor Hadrian of Rome.

breakfast-dishes at her; then she had cabled for help, and the old gentleman had gone over to find out what were his Grace's terms. So they had left Freddie all alone, and he with less than two thousand dollars in his pocket. Freddie was up in arms and meant serious business, as they would find in the end—if there was no other way of bringing them to terms he would have his "Kittens" wire that she was about to marry him, and see what happened then.

So the cheerful youngster rattled on, until he was tired out. He smiled his sweetest smile at Jurgis, and then he closed his eyes, sleepily. Then he opened them again, and smiled once more, and finally closed them and forgot to open them.

For several minutes Jurgis sat perfectly motionless, watching him, and revelling in the strange sensations of the champagne. Once he stirred, and the dog growled; after that he sat almost holding his breath—until after a while the door of the room opened softly, and the butler came in.

He walked toward Jurgis upon tiptoe, scowling at him; and Jurgis rose up, and retreated, scowling back. So until he was against the wall, and then the butler came close, and pointed toward the door. "Get out of here!" he whispered.

Jurgis hesitated, giving a glance at Freddie, who was snoring softly. "If you do, you son of a——" hissed the butler, "I'll mash in your face for you before you get out of here!"

And Jurgis wavered but an instant more. He saw "Admiral Dewey" coming up behind the man and growling softly, to back up his threats. Then he surrendered and started toward the door.

They went out without a sound, and down the great echoing staircase, and through the dark hall. At the front door he paused, and the butler strode close to him.

"Hold up your hands," he snarled. Jurgis took a step back, clinching his one well fist.

"What for?" he cried; and then understanding that the fellow proposed to search him, he answered, "I'll see you in hell first."

"Do you want to go to jail?" demanded the butler, menacingly. "I'll have the police—"

"Have 'em!" roared Jurgis, with fierce passion. "But you won't put your hands on me till you do! I haven't touched anything in your damned house, and I'll not have you touch me!"

So the butler, who was terrified lest his young master should waken, stepped suddenly to the door, and opened it. "Get out of here!" he said; and then as Jurgis passed through the opening, he gave him a ferocious kick that sent him down the great stone steps at a run, and landed him sprawling in the snow at the bottom.

Chapter XXV

Jurgis got up, wild with rage; but the door was shut and the great castle was dark and impregnable. Then the icy teeth of the blast bit into him, and he turned and went away at a run.

When he stopped again it was because he was coming to frequented streets and did not wish to attract attention. In spite of that last humiliation, his heart was thumping fast with triumph. He had come out ahead on that deal! He put his hand into his trousers' pocket every now and then, to make sure that the precious hundred-dollar bill was still there.

Yet he was in a plight—a curious and even dreadful plight, when he came to realize it. He had not a single cent but that one bill! And he had to find some shelter that night—he had to change it!

Jurgis spent half an hour walking and debating the problem. There was no one he could go to for help—he had to manage it all alone. To get it changed in a lodging-house would be to take his life in his hands—he would almost certainly be robbed, and perhaps murdered, before morning. He might go to some hotel or railroad-depot and ask to have it changed; but what would they think, seeing a "bum" like him with a hundred dollars? He would probably be arrested if he tried it; and what story could he tell? On the morrow Freddie Jones would discover his loss, and there would be a hunt for him, and he would lose his money. The only other plan he could think of was to try in a saloon. He might pay them to change it, if it could not be done otherwise.

He began peering into places as he walked; he passed several as being too crowded—then finally, chancing upon one where the bartender was all alone, he gripped his hands in sudden resolution and went in.

"Can you change me a hundred-dollar bill?" he demanded.

The bartender was a big, husky fellow, with the jaw of a prize fighter, and a three weeks' stubble of hair upon it. He stared at Jurgis. "What's that youse say?" he demanded.

"I said, could you change me a hundred-dollar bill?"

"Where'd youse get it?" he inquired incredulously.

"Never mind," said Jurgis; "I've got it, and I want it changed. I'll pay you if you'll do it."

The other stared at him hard. "Lemme see it," he said.

"Will you change it?" Jurgis demanded, gripping it tightly in his pocket.

"How the hell can I know if it's good or not?" retorted the bartender. "Whatcher take me for, hey?"

Then Jurgis slowly and warily approached him; he took out the bill, and fumbled it for a moment, while the man stared at him with hostile eyes across the counter. Then finally he handed it over.

The other took it, and began to examine it; he smoothed it between his fingers, and he held it up to the light; he turned it over and upside down, and edgeways. It was new and rather stiff, and that made him dubious. Jurgis was watching him like a cat all the time.

"Humph," he said, finally, and gazed at the stranger, sizing him up—a ragged, ill-smelling tramp, with no overcoat and one arm in a sling—and a hundred-dollar bill! "Want to buy anything?" he demanded.

"Yes," said Jurgis, "I'll take a glass of beer."

"All right," said the other, "I'll change it." And he put the bill in his pocket, and poured Jurgis out a glass of beer, and set it on the counter. Then he turned to the cash-register, and punched up five cents, and began to pull money out of the drawer. Finally, he faced Jurgis, counting it out—two dimes, a quarter, and fifty cents. "There," he said.

For a second Jurgis waited, expecting to see him turn again. "My ninety-nine dollars," he said.

"What ninety-nine dollars?" demanded the bartender.

"My change!" he cried—"the rest of my hundred!"

"Go on," said the bartender, "you're nutty!"

And Jurgis stared at him with wild eyes. For an instant horror reigned in him—black, paralyzing, awful horror, clutching him at the heart; and then came rage, in surging, blinding floods—he screamed aloud, and seized the glass and hurled it at the other's head. The man ducked, and it missed him by half an inch; he rose again and faced Jurgis, who was vaulting over the bar with his one well arm, and dealt him a smashing blow in the face, hurling him backward upon the floor. Then, as Jurgis scrambled to his feet again and started round the counter after him, he shouted at the top of his voice, "Help! help!"

Jurgis seized a bottle off the counter as he ran; and as the bartender made a leap he hurled the missile at him with all his force. It just grazed his head, and shivered into a thousand pieces against the post of the door. Then Jurgis started back, rushing at the man again in the middle of the room. This time, in his blind frenzy, he came without a bottle, and that was all the bartender wanted—he met him halfway and floored him with a sledge-hammer drive between the eyes. An instant later the screen-doors flew open, and two men rushed in—just as Jurgis was getting to his feet again, foaming at the mouth with rage, and trying to tear his broken arm out of its bandages.

"Look out!" shouted the bartender. "He's got a knife!" Then, seeing that the two were disposed to join in the fray, he made another rush at Jurgis, and knocked aside his feeble defence and sent him tumbling again; and the three flung themselves upon him, rolling and kicking about the place.

A second later a policeman dashed in, and the bartender yelled once more—"Look out for his knife!" Jurgis had fought himself half to his knees, when the policeman made a leap at him, and cracked him across the face with his club. Though the blow staggered him, the wild beast frenzy still blazed in him, and he got to his feet, lunging into the air. Then again the club descended, full upon his head, and he dropped like a log to the floor.

The policeman crouched over him, clutching his stick, waiting for him to try to rise again; and meantime the barkeeper got up, and put his hand to his head. "Christ!" he said, "I thought I was done for that time. Did he cut me?"

"Don't see anything, Jake," said the policeman. "What's the matter with him?"

"Just crazy drunk," said the other. "A lame duck, too—but he 'most got me under the bar. Youse had better call the wagon, Billy."

"No," said the officer. "He's got no more fight in him, I guess—and he's only got a block to go." He twisted his hand in Jurgis's collar and jerked at him. "Git up here, you!" he commanded.

But Jurgis did not move, and the bartender went behind the bar, and, after stowing the hundred-dollar bill away in a safe hiding-place, came and poured a glass of water over Jurgis. Then, as the latter began to moan feebly, the policeman got him to his feet and dragged him out of the place. The station-house was just around the corner, and so in a few minutes Jurgis was in a cell.

He spent half the night lying unconscious, and the balance moaning in torment, with a blinding headache and a racking thirst. Now and then he cried aloud for a drink of water, but there was no one to hear him. There were others in that same station-house with split heads and a fever; there were hundreds of them in the great city, and tens of thousands of them in the great land, and there was no one to hear any of them.

In the morning Jurgis was given a cup of water and a piece of bread, and then hustled into a patrol wagon and driven to the nearest police-court. He sat in the pen with a score of others until his turn came.

The bartender—who proved to be a well-known bruiser—was called to the stand. He took the oath and told his story. The prisoner had come into his saloon after midnight, fighting drunk, and had ordered a glass of beer and tendered a dollar bill in payment. He had been given ninety-five cents' change, and had demanded ninety-nine dollars more, and before the plaintiff could even answer had hurled the glass at him and then attacked him with a bottle of bitters, and nearly wrecked the place.

Then the prisoner was sworn—a forlorn object, haggard and unshorn, with an arm done up in a filthy bandage, a cheek and head cut and bloody, and one eye purplish black and entirely closed. "What have you to say for yourself?" queried the magistrate.

"Your Honor," said Jurgis, "I went into his place and asked the man if he could change me a hundred-dollar bill. And he said he would if I bought a drink. I gave him the bill and then he wouldn't give me the change."

The magistrate was staring at him in perplexity. "You gave him a hundred-dollar bill!" he exclaimed.

"Yes, your Honor," said Jurgis.

"Where did you get it?"

"A man gave it to me, your Honor."

"A man? What man, and what for?"

"A young man I met upon the street, your Honor. I had been begging."

There was a titter in the court-room; the officer who was holding Jurgis put up his hand to hide a smile, and the magistrate smiled without trying to hide it. "It's true, your Honor!" cried Jurgis, passionately.

"You had been drinking as well as begging last night, had you not?" inquired the magistrate.

"No, your Honor—" protested Jurgis. "I—"

"You had not had anything to drink?"

"Why, yes, your Honor, I had—"

"What did you have?"

"I had a bottle of something—I don't know what it was—something that burned—"

There was again a laugh round the court-room, stopping suddenly as the magistrate looked up and frowned. "Have you ever been arrested before?" he asked abruptly.

The question took Jurgis aback. "I—I—" he stammered.

"Tell me the truth, now!" commanded the other, sternly.

"Yes, your Honor," said Jurgis.

"How often?"

"Only once, your Honor."

"What for?"

"For knocking down my boss, your Honor. I was working in the stockyards, and he—"

"I see," said his Honor; "I guess that will do. You ought to stop drinking if you can't control yourself. Ten days and costs. Next case."

Jurgis gave vent to a cry of dismay, cut off suddenly by the police-man, who seized him by the collar. He was jerked out of the way, into a room with the convicted prisoners, where he sat and wept like a child in his impotent rage. It seemed monstrous to him that police-men and judges should esteem his word as nothing in comparison with the bartender's; poor Jurgis could not know that the owner of the saloon paid five dollars each week to the policeman alone for Sunday privileges and general favors—nor that the pugilist bar-tender was one of the most trusted henchmen of the Democratic leader of the district, and had helped only a few months before to hustle out a record-breaking vote as a testimonial to the magistrate, who had been made the target of odious kid-gloved reformers.[1]

Jurgis was driven out to the Bridewell for the second time. In his tumbling around he had hurt his arm again, and so could not work, but had to be attended by the physician. Also his head and his eye had to be tied up—and so he was a pretty-looking object when, the second day after his arrival, he went out into the exercise-court and encountered—Jack Duane!

The young fellow was so glad to see Jurgis that he almost hugged him. "By God, if it isn't 'the Stinker'!" he cried. "And what is it—have you been through a sausage-machine?"

"No," said Jurgis, "but I've been in a railroad wreck and a fight." And then, while some of the other prisoners gathered round, he told his wild story; most of them were incredulous, but Duane knew that Jurgis could never have made up such a yarn as that.

"Hard luck, old man," he said, when they were alone; "but maybe it's taught you a lesson."

"I've learned some things since I saw you last," said Jurgis, mourn-fully. Then he explained how he had spent the last summer, "hobo-ing it," as the phrase was. "And you?" he asked, finally. "Have you been here ever since?"

"Lord, no!" said the other. "I only came in the day before yester-day. It's the second time they've sent me up on a trumped-up charge—I've had hard luck and can't pay them what they want. Why don't you quit Chicago with me, Jurgis?"

"I've no place to go," said Jurgis, sadly.

"Neither have I," replied the other, laughing lightly.—"But we'll wait till we get out and see."

In the Bridewell Jurgis met few who had been there the last time, but he met scores of others, old and young, of exactly the same sort.

---

1. Dismissive term for reformers, suggesting they are wealthy and out of touch. *Sunday privileges*: Despite being illegal in Illinois, Sunday openings of saloons were wide-spread in Chicago. *Trusted henchmen*: Many saloonkeepers were also politicians, and well-connected bartenders delivered votes for political favorites.

It was like breakers upon a beach; there was new water, but the wave looked just the same. He strolled about and talked with them, and the biggest of them told tales of their prowess, while those who were weaker, or younger and inexperienced, gathered round and listened in admiring silence. The last time he was there, Jurgis had thought of little but his family; but now he was free to listen to these men, and to realize that he was one of them,—that their point of view was his point of view, and that the way they kept themselves alive in the world was the way he meant to do it in future.

And so, when he was turned out of prison again, without a penny in his pocket, he went straight to Jack Duane. He went full of humility and gratitude; for Duane was a gentleman, and a man with a profession—and it was remarkable that he should be willing to throw in his lot with a humble working-man, one who had even been a beggar and a tramp. Jurgis could not see what help he could be to him; he did not understand that a man like himself—who could be trusted to stand by any one who was kind to him—was as rare among criminals as among any other class of men.

The address Jurgis had was a garret-room in the Ghetto district,[2] the home of a pretty little French girl, Duane's mistress, who sewed all day, and eked out her living by prostitution. He had gone elsewhere, she told Jurgis—he was afraid to stay there now, on account of the police. The new address was a cellar dive, whose proprietor said that he had never heard of Duane; but after he had put Jurgis through a catechism he showed him a back stairs which led to a "fence" in the rear of a pawnbroker's shop, and thence to a number of assignation-rooms,[3] in one of which Duane was hiding.

Duane was glad to see him; he was without a cent of money, he said, and had been waiting for Jurgis to help him get some. He explained his plan—in fact he spent the day in laying bare to his friend the criminal world of the city, and in showing him how he might earn himself a living in it. That winter he would have a hard time, on account of his arm, and because of an unwonted fit of activity of the police; but so long as he was unknown to them he would be safe if he were careful. Here at "Papa" Hanson's (so they called the old man who kept the dive) he might rest at ease, for "Papa" Hanson was "square"—would stand by him so long as he paid, and gave him an hour's notice if there were to be a police raid. Also

2. Originally referring to a section of a city where Jews were confined, at this time a ghetto could be a section occupied by any minority group or groups who lived in slumlike conditions because they were economically or socially marginalized. *Garret*: cramped attic room, difficult to access in the days before elevators.
3. Typically used for illicit romantic encounters; the proprietor's "catechism," or series of questions, ascertains Jurgis's underworld connections, not his religious faith; *fence*: can refer either to a place where stolen goods are taken or to the person who sells them.

Rosensteg, the pawnbroker, would buy anything he had for a third of its value, and guarantee to keep it hidden for a year.

There was an oil stove in the little cupboard of a room, and they had some supper; and then about eleven o'clock at night they sallied forth together, by a rear entrance to the place, Duane armed with a slung-shot. They came to a residence district, and he sprang up a lamp post and blew out the light, and then the two dodged into the shelter of an area-step and hid in silence.

Pretty soon a man came by, a working-man—and they let him go. Then after a long interval came the heavy tread of a policeman, and they held their breath till he was gone. Though half frozen, they waited a full quarter of an hour after that—and then again came footsteps, walking briskly. Duane nudged Jurgis, and the instant the man had passed they rose up. Duane stole out as silently as a shadow, and a second later Jurgis heard a thud and a stifled cry. He was only a couple of feet behind, and he leaped to stop the man's mouth, while Duane held him fast by the arms, as they had agreed. But the man was limp and showed a tendency to fall, and so Jurgis had only to hold him by the collar, while the other, with swift fingers, went through his pockets,—ripping open, first his overcoat, and then his coat, and then his vest, searching inside and outside, and transferring the contents into his own pockets. At last, after feeling of the man's fingers and in his neck-tie, Duane whispered, "That's all!" and they dragged him to the area and dropped him in. Then Jurgis went one way and his friend the other, walking briskly.

The latter arrived first, and Jurgis found him examining the "swag."[4] There was a gold watch, for one thing, with a chain and locket; there was a silver pencil, and a match-box, and a handful of small change, and finally a card-case. This last Duane opened feverishly—there were letters and checks, and two theatre-tickets, and at last, in the back part, a wad of bills. He counted them—there was a twenty, five tens, four fives, and three ones. Duane drew a long breath. "That lets us out!" he said.

After further examination, they burned the card-case and its contents, all but the bills, and likewise the picture of a little girl in the locket. Then Duane took the watch and trinkets downstairs, and came back with sixteen dollars. "The old scoundrel said the case was filled," he said. "It's a lie, but he knows I want the money."

They divided up the spoils, and Jurgis got as his share fifty-five dollars and some change. He protested that it was too much, but the other had agreed to divide even. That was a good haul, he said, better than the average.

---

4. Loot, stolen goods.

When they got up in the morning, Jurgis was sent out to buy a paper; one of the pleasures of committing a crime was the reading about it afterward. "I had a pal that always did it," Duane remarked, laughing—"until one day he read that he had left three thousand dollars in a lower inside pocket of his party's vest!"

There was a half-column account of the robbery—it was evident that a gang was operating in the neighborhood, said the paper, for it was the third within a week, and the police were apparently powerless. The victim was an insurance agent, and he had lost a hundred and ten dollars that did not belong to him. He had chanced to have his name marked on his shirt, otherwise he would not have been identified yet. His assailant had hit him too hard, and he was suffering from concussion of the brain; and also he had been half-frozen when found, and would lose three fingers of his right hand. The enterprising newspaper reporter had taken all this information to his family, and told how they had received it.

Since it was Jurgis's first experience, these details naturally caused him some worriment; but the other laughed coolly—it was the way of the game, and there was no helping it. Before long Jurgis would think no more of it than they did in the yards of knocking out a bullock. "It's a case of us or the other fellow, and I say the other fellow every time," he observed.

"Still," said Jurgis, reflectively, "he never did us any harm."

"He was doing it to somebody as hard as he could, you can be sure of that," said his friend.

Duane had already explained to Jurgis that if a man of their trade were known he would have to work all the time to satisfy the demands of the police.[5] Therefore it would be better for Jurgis to stay in hiding and never be seen in public with his pal. But Jurgis soon got very tired of staying in hiding. In a couple of weeks he was feeling strong and beginning to use his arm, and then he could not stand it any longer. Duane, who had done a job of some sort by himself, and made a truce with the powers, brought over Marie, his little French girl, to share with him; but even that did not avail for long, and in the end he had to give up arguing, and take Jurgis out and introduce him to the saloons and "sporting-houses" where the big crooks and "hold-up men" hung out.

And so Jurgis got a glimpse of the high-class criminal world of Chicago. The city, which was owned by an oligarchy of business men, being nominally ruled by the people, a huge army of graft was necessary for the purpose of effecting the transfer of power. Twice a year, in the spring and fall elections, millions of dollars were furnished by

5. To pay off the police.

the business men and expended by this army; meetings were held and clever speakers were hired, bands played and rockets sizzled, tons of documents and reservoirs of drinks were distributed, and tens of thousands of votes were bought for cash. And this army of graft had, of course, to be maintained the year round. The leaders and organizers were maintained by the business men directly,— aldermen and legislators by means of bribes, party officials out of the campaign funds, lobbyists and corporation lawyers in the form of salaries, contractors by means of jobs, labor union leaders by subsidies, and newspaper proprietors and editors by advertisements. The rank and file, however, were either foisted upon the city, or else lived off the populace directly. There was the police department, and the fire and water departments, and the whole balance of the civil list, from the meanest office-boy to the head of a city department; and for the horde who could find no room in these, there was the world of vice and crime, there was license to seduce, to swindle and plunder and prey. The law forbade Sunday drinking; and this had delivered the saloon-keepers into the hands of the police, and made an alliance between them necessary. The law forbade prostitution; and this had brought the "madames" into the combination. It was the same with the gambling-house keeper and the pool-room man, and the same with any other man or woman who had a means of getting "graft," and was willing to pay over a share of it; the green-goods man and the highwayman, the pickpocket and the sneak-thief, and the receiver of stolen goods, the seller of adulterated milk, of stale fruit and diseased meat, the proprietor of unsanitary tenements, the fake-doctor and the usurer, the beggar and the "push-cart man," the prize-fighter and the professional slugger, the race-track "tout," the procurer, the white-slave agent,[6] and the expert seducer of young girls. All of these agencies of corruption were banded together, and leagued in blood brotherhood with the politician and the police; more often than not they were one and the same person,—the police captain would own the brothel he pretended to raid, and the politician would open his headquarters in his saloon. "Hinkydink" or "Bath-house John," or others of that ilk, were proprietors of the most notorious dives in Chicago, and also the "gray wolves" of the city council,[7] who gave away the streets of the city to the business men; and those who

6. Who used false pretenses to lure girls and young women (of any race) into forced prostitution; green-goods man: handled counterfeit paper money; race-track "tout": provided gambling tips, solicited bets, or worked as a messenger stationed to secure early information on races.

7. Chicago aldermen who developed a Democratic political machine based on graft and protection money from saloons, brothels, and gambling halls; also delivered votes in exchange for favors. The gray wolves were led by First Ward aldermen Michael "Hinky Dink" Kenna (1857–1946) and "Bathhouse" John Coughlin (1860–1938) and by Johnny Powers (see above, p. 147, n. 1) from the Nineteenth Ward.

patronized their places were the gamblers and prize-fighters who set the law at defiance, and the burglars and hold-up men who kept the whole city in terror. On election day all these powers of vice and crime were one power; they could tell within one per cent what the vote of their district would be, and they could change it at an hour's notice.

A month ago Jurgis had all but perished of starvation upon the streets; and now suddenly, as by the gift of a magic key, he had entered into a world where money and all the good things of life came freely. He was introduced by his friend to an Irishman named "Buck" Halloran, who was a political "worker" and on the inside of things. This man talked with Jurgis for a while, and then told him that he had a little plan by which a man who looked like a working-man might make some easy money; but it was a private affair, and had to be kept quiet. Jurgis expressed himself as agreeable, and the other took him that afternoon (it was Saturday) to a place where city laborers were being paid off. The pay-master sat in a little booth, with a pile of envelopes before him, and two policemen standing by. Jurgis went, according to directions, and gave the name of "Michael O'Flaherty," and received an envelope, which he took around the corner and delivered to Halloran, who was waiting for him in a saloon. Then he went again, and gave the name of "Johann Schmidt," and a third time, and gave the name of "Serge Reminitsky." Halloran had quite a list of imaginary working-men, and Jurgis got an envelope for each one. For this work he received five dollars, and was told that he might have it every week, so long as he kept quiet. As Jurgis was excellent at keeping quiet, he soon won the trust of "Buck" Halloran, and was introduced to others as a man who could be depended upon.

This acquaintance was useful to him in another way, also; before long Jurgis made his discovery of the meaning of "pull," and just why his boss, Connor, and also the pugilist bartender, had been able to send him to jail. One night there was given a ball,[8] the "benefit" of "One-eyed Larry," a lame man who played the violin in one of the big "high-class" houses of prostitution on Clark Street, and was a wag and a popular character on the "Levée." This ball was held in a big dance-hall, and was one of the occasions when the city's powers of debauchery gave themselves up to madness. Jurgis attended and got half insane with drink, and began quarrelling over a girl; his arm was pretty strong by then, and he set to work to clean out the place, and ended in a cell in the police-station. The police-station being crowded to the doors, and stinking with "bums," Jurgis did not relish staying there to sleep off his liquor, and sent for Halloran, who called up the district leader and had Jurgis bailed out by

8. Possibly the notorious annual First Ward Ball organized by Kenna and Coughlin.

telephone at four o'clock in the morning. When he was arraigned that same morning, the district leader had already seen the clerk of the court and explained that Jurgis Rudkus was a decent fellow, who had been indiscreet; and so Jurgis was fined ten dollars and the fine was "suspended"—which meant that he did not have to pay it, and never would have to pay it, unless somebody chose to bring it up against him in the future.

Among the people Jurgis lived with now money was valued according to an entirely different standard from that of the people of Packingtown; yet, strange as it may seem, he did a great deal less drinking than he had as a working-man. He had not the same provocations of exhaustion and hopelessness; he had now something to work for, to struggle for. He soon found that if he kept his wits about him, he would come upon new opportunities; and being naturally an active man, he not only kept sober himself, but helped to steady his friend, who was a good deal fonder of both wine and women than he.

One thing led to another. In the saloon where Jurgis met "Buck" Halloran he was sitting late one night with Duane, when a "country customer" (a buyer for an out-of-town merchant) came in, a little more than half "piped." There was no one else in the place but the bartender, and as the man went out again Jurgis and Duane followed him; he went round the corner, and in a dark place made by a combination of the elevated railroad and an unrented building, Jurgis leaped forward and shoved a revolver under his nose, while Duane, with his hat pulled over his eyes, went through the man's pockets with lightning fingers. They got his watch and his "wad,"[9] and were round the corner again and into the saloon before he could shout more than once. The bartender, to whom they had tipped the wink,[1] had the cellar-door open for them, and they vanished, making their way by a secret entrance to a brothel next door. From the roof of this there was access to three similar places beyond. By means of these passages the customers of any one place could be gotten out of the way, in case a falling out with the police chanced to lead to a raid; and also it was necessary to have a way of getting a girl out of reach in case of an emergency. Thousands of them came to Chicago answering advertisements for "servants" and "factory hands," and found themselves trapped by fake employment agencies, and locked up in a bawdy-house. It was generally enough to take all their clothes away from them; but sometimes they would have to be "doped" and kept prisoners for weeks; and meantime their parents might be telegraphing the police, and even coming on to see why nothing was

9. Of cash.
1. Let in on a secret.

done. Occasionally there was no way of satisfying them but to let them search the place to which the girl had been traced.

For his help in this little job, the bartender received twenty out of the hundred and thirty odd dollars that the pair secured; and naturally this put them on friendly terms with him, and a few days later he introduced them to a little "sheeny" named Goldberger, one of the "runners" of the "sporting-house" where they had been hidden.[2] After a few drinks Goldberger began, with some hesitation, to narrate how he had had a quarrel over his best girl with a professional "card-sharp," who had hit him in the jaw. The fellow was a stranger in Chicago, and if he was found some night with his head cracked there would be no one to care very much. Jurgis, who by this time would cheerfully have cracked the heads of all the gamblers in Chicago, inquired what would be coming to him; at which the Jew became still more confidential, and said that he had some tips on the New Orleans races, which he got direct from the police captain of the district, whom he had got out of a bad scrape, and who "stood in" with a big syndicate of horse owners. Duane took all this in at once, but Jurgis had to have the whole race-track situation explained to him before he realized the importance of such an opportunity.

There was the gigantic Racing Trust. It owned the legislatures in every state in which it did business; it even owned some of the big newspapers, and made public opinion—there was no power in the land that could oppose it unless, perhaps, it were the Pool-room Trust. It built magnificent racing parks all over the country, and by means of enormous purses it lured the people to come, and then it organized a gigantic shell-game, whereby it plundered them of hundreds of millions of dollars every year. Horse-racing had once been a sport, but nowadays it was a business; a horse could be "doped" and doctored, undertrained or overtrained; it could be made to fall at any moment—or its gait could be broken by lashing it with the whip, which all the spectators would take to be a desperate effort to keep it in the lead. There were scores of such tricks; and sometimes it was the owners who played them and made fortunes, sometimes it was the jockeys and trainers, sometimes it was outsiders, who bribed them—but most of the time it was the chiefs of the trust. Now, for instance, they were having winter-racing in New Orleans, and a syndicate was laying out each day's programme in advance, and its agents in all the Northern cities were "milking" the pool-rooms. The word came by long-distance telephone in a cipher code, just a little while before each race; and any man who could get the secret had as good as a fortune. If Jurgis did not believe it, he could

---

2. *Sheeny:* derogatory slang for Jewish person; *runners* solicit patrons for a *sporting-house,* or brothel.

try it, said the little Jew—let them meet at a certain house on the morrow and make a test. Jurgis was willing, and so was Duane, and so they went to one of the high-class poolrooms where brokers and merchants gambled (with society women in a private room), and they put up ten dollars each upon a horse called "Black Beldame," a six to one shot, and won. For a secret like that they would have done a good many sluggings—but the next day Goldberger informed them that the offending gambler had got wind of what was coming to him, and had skipped the town.

There were ups and downs at the business; but there was always a living, inside of a jail, if not out of it. Early in April the city elections were due, and that meant prosperity for all the powers of graft. Jurgis, hanging round in dives and gambling-houses and brothels, met with the heelers of both parties, and from their conversation he came to understand all the ins and outs of the game, and to hear of a number of ways in which he could make himself useful about election time. "Buck" Halloran was a "Democrat," and so Jurgis became a Democrat also; but he was not a bitter one—the Republicans were good fellows, too, and were to have a pile of money in this next campaign. At the last election the Republicans had paid four dollars a vote to the Democrats' three; and "Buck" Halloran sat one night playing cards with Jurgis and another man, who told how Halloran had been charged with the job of voting a "bunch" of thirty-seven newly landed Italians, and how he, the narrator, had met the Republican worker who was after the very same gang, and how the three had effected a bargain, whereby the Italians were to vote half and half, for a glass of beer apiece, while the balance of the fund went to the conspirators!

Not long after this, Jurgis, wearying of the risks and vicissitudes of miscellaneous crime, was moved to give up the career for that of a politician. Just at this time there was a tremendous uproar being raised concerning the alliance between the criminals and the police. For the criminal graft was one in which the business men had no direct part—it was what is called a "side-line," carried by the police. "Wide-open" gambling and debauchery made the city pleasing to "trade," but burglaries and hold-ups did not. One night it chanced that while Jack Duane was drilling a safe in a clothing store he was caught red-handed by the night-watchman, and turned over to a policeman, who chanced to know him well, and who took the responsibility of letting him make his escape. Such a howl from the newspapers followed this that Duane was slated for a sacrifice, and barely got out of town in time.

And just at that juncture it happened that Jurgis was introduced to a man named Harper whom he recognized as the night-watchman at Brown's, who had been instrumental in making him an American citizen, the first year of his arrival at the yards. The other was interested in the coincidence, but did not remember Jurgis—he had handled too many "green ones" in his time, he said. He sat in a dance-hall with Jurgis and Halloran until one or two in the morning, exchanging experiences. He had a long story to tell of his quarrel with the superintendent of his department, and how he was now a plain working-man, and a good union man as well. It was not until some months afterward that Jurgis understood that the quarrel with the superintendent had been prearranged, and that Harper was in reality drawing a salary of twenty dollars a week from the packers for an inside report of his union's secret proceedings. The yards were seething with agitation just then, said the man, speaking as a unionist. The people of Packingtown had borne about all that they would bear, and it looked as if a strike might begin any week.

After this talk the man made inquiries concerning Jurgis, and a couple of days later he came to him with an interesting proposition. He was not absolutely certain, he said, but he thought that he could get him a regular salary if he would come to Packingtown and do as he was told, and keep his mouth shut. Harper—"Bush" Harper, he was called—was a right-hand man of Mike Scully, the Democratic boss of the stockyards; and in the coming election there was a peculiar situation. There had come to Scully a proposition to nominate a certain rich brewer who lived upon a swell boulevard that skirted the district, and who coveted the big badge and the "honorable" of an alderman. The brewer was a Jew, and had no brains, but he was harmless, and would put up a rare campaign fund. Scully had accepted the offer, and then gone to the Republicans with a proposition. He was not sure that he could manage the "sheeny," and he did not mean to take any chances with his district; let the Republicans nominate a certain obscure but amiable friend of Scully's, who was now setting ten-pins in the cellar of an Ashland Avenue saloon, and he, Scully, would elect him with the "sheeny's" money, and the Republicans might have the glory, which was more than they would get otherwise. In return for this the Republicans would agree to put up no candidate the following year, when Scully himself came up for reëlection as the other alderman from the ward. To this the Republicans had assented at once; but the hell of it was—so Harper explained—that the Republicans were all of them fools—a man had to be a fool to be a Republican in the stockyards, where Scully was king. And they didn't know how to work, and of course it would not do for the Democratic workers, the noble redskins of the War-Whoop League, to support the Republican openly. The difficulty would not have been so great except for another fact—there had been a curious development in stockyards politics in the last year or two, a new party having leaped into being. They were the Socialists; and it was a devil of a mess, said "Bush" Harper. The one image which the word "Socialist" brought to Jurgis was of poor little Tamoszius Kuszleika, who had called himself one, and would go out with a couple of other men and a soap-box, and shout himself hoarse on a street corner Saturday nights. Tamoszius had tried to explain to Jurgis what it was all about, but Jurgis, who was not of an imaginative turn, had never quite got it straight; at present he was content with his companion's explanation that the Socialists were the enemies of American institutions—could not be bought, and would not combine or make any sort of a "dicker." Mike Scully was very much worried over the opportunity which his last deal gave to them—the stockyards Democrats were furious at the idea of a rich capitalist for their candidate, and while they were changing they might possibly conclude that a Socialist firebrand was preferable to a Republican bum. And so right here was a chance for Jurgis to make himself a place in the world, explained "Bush" Harper; he had been a union man, and he was known in the yards as a working-man; he must have hundreds of acquaintances, and as he had never talked politics with them he might come out as a Republican now without exciting the least suspicion. There were barrels of money for the use of those who could deliver the goods; and Jurgis might count upon Mike Scully, who had never yet gone back on a friend. Just what could he do? Jurgis asked, in some perplexity, and the other explained in detail. To begin with, he would have to go to the yards and work, and he mightn't relish that; but he would have what he earned, as well as the rest that came to him. He would get active in the union again, and perhaps try to get an office, as he, Harper, had; he would tell all his friends the good points of Doyle, the Republican nominee, and the bad ones of the "sheeny"; and then Scully would furnish a meeting-place, and he would start the "Young Men's Republican Association," or something of that sort, and have the rich brewer's best beer by the hogshead, and fireworks and speeches, just like the War-Whoop League. Surely Jurgis must know hundreds of men who would like that sort of fun; and there would be the regular Republican leaders and workers to help him out, and they would deliver a big enough majority on election day.

When he had heard all this explanation to the end, Jurgis demanded: "But how can I get a job in Packingtown? I'm blacklisted."

At which "Bush" Harper laughed. "I'll attend to that all right," he said.

And the other replied, "It's a go, then; I'm your man."

So Jurgis went out to the stockyards again, and was introduced to the political lord of the district, the boss of Chicago's mayor. It was Scully who owned the brick-yards and the dump and the ice

pond—though Jurgis did not know it. It was Scully who was to blame
for the unpaved street in which Jurgis's child had been drowned; it
was Scully who had put into office the magistrate who had first sent
Jurgis to jail; it was Scully who was principal stockholder in the company which had sold him the ramshackle tenement, and then robbed
him of it. But Jurgis knew none of these things—any more than he
knew that Scully was but a tool and puppet of the packers. To him
Scully was a mighty power, the "biggest" man he had ever met.

He was a little, dried-up Irishman, whose hands shook. He had a
brief talk with his visitor, watching him with his rat-like eyes, and
making up his mind about him; and then he gave him a note to
Mr. Harmon, one of the head managers of Durham's:—

"The bearer, Jurgis Rudkus, is a particular friend of mine, and I
would like you to find him a good place, for important reasons. He was
once indiscreet, but you will perhaps be so good as to overlook that."

Mr. Harmon looked up inquiringly when he read this. "What does
he mean by 'indiscreet'?" he asked.

"I was blacklisted, sir," said Jurgis.

At which the other frowned. "Blacklisted?" he said. "How do you
mean?"

And Jurgis turned red with embarrassment. He had forgotten that
a blacklist did not exist. "I—that is—I had difficulty in getting a
place," he stammered.

"What was the matter?"

"I got into a quarrel with a foreman—not my own boss, sir—and
struck him."

"I see," said the other, and meditated for a few moments. "What
do you wish to do?" he asked.

"Anything, sir," said Jurgis—"only I had a broken arm this winter,
and so I have to be careful."

"How would it suit you to be a night-watchman?"

"That wouldn't do, sir. I have to be among the men at night."

"I see—politics. Well, would it suit you to trim hogs?"

"Yes, sir," said Jurgis.

And Mr. Harmon called a time-keeper and said, "Take this man
to Pat Murphy and tell him to find room for him somehow."

And so Jurgis marched into the hog-killing room, a place where,
in the days gone by, he had come begging for a job. Now he walked
jauntily, and smiled to himself, seeing the frown that came to the
boss's face as the time-keeper said, "Mr. Harmon says to put this
man on." It would overcrowd his department and spoil the record
he was trying to make—but he said not a word except "All right."

And so Jurgis became a working-man once more; and straightway
he sought out his old friends, and joined the union, and began to

"root" for "Scotty" Doyle. Doyle had done him a good turn once, he explained, and was really a bully chap; Doyle was a working-man himself, and would represent the working-men—why did they want to vote for a millionnaire "sheeny," and what the hell had Mike Scully ever done for them that they should back his candidates all the time? And meantime Scully had given Jurgis a note to the Republican leader of the ward, and he had gone there and met the crowd he was to work with. Already they had hired a big hall, with some of the brewer's money, and every night Jurgis brought in a dozen new members of the "Doyle Republican Association." Pretty soon they had a grand opening night; and there was a brass band, which marched through the streets, and fireworks and bombs and red lights in front of the hall; and there was an enormous crowd, with two overflow meetings—so that the pale and trembling candidate had to recite three times over the little speech which one of Scully's henchmen had written, and which he had been a month learning by heart. Best of all, the famous and eloquent Senator Spareshanks,[3] presidential candidate, rode out in an automobile to discuss the sacred privileges of American citizenship, and protection and prosperity for the American working-man. His inspiriting address was quoted to the extent of half a column in all the morning newspapers, which also said that it could be stated upon excellent authority that the unexpected popularity developed by Doyle, the Republican candidate for alderman, was giving great anxiety to Mr. Scully, the chairman of the Democratic City Committee.

The chairman was still more worried when the monster torchlight procession came off, with the members of the Doyle Republican Association all in red capes and hats, and free beer for every voter in the ward—the best beer ever given away in a political campaign, as the whole electorate testified. During this parade, and at innumerable cart-tail meetings[4] as well, Jurgis labored tirelessly. He did not make any speeches—there were lawyers and other experts for that—but he helped to manage things: distributing notices and posting placards and bringing out the crowds; and when the show was on he attended to the fireworks and the beer. Thus in the course of the campaign he handled many hundreds of dollars of the Hebrew brewer's money, administering it with naïve and touching fidelity. Toward the end, however, he learned that he was regarded with hatred by the rest of

3. The Republican candidate for president in 1904 was Theodore Roosevelt (see below, p. 342, n. 4 and pp. 500–05), who had become president in 1901 after the assassination of President William McKinley, whom Roosevelt had served as vice president. Sinclair might have in mind the 1904 vice presidential candidate, Senator Charles W. Fairbanks (1852–1918) of Indiana, more conservative than the progressive Republican Roosevelt.
4. Form of campaigning in which a cart filled with speakers was taken around, stopping wherever a group was gathered.

the "boys," because he compelled them either to make a poorer showing than he or to do without their share of the pie. After that Jurgis
did his best to please them, and to make up for the time he had lost
before he discovered the extra bung-holes of the campaign-barrel.

He pleased Mike Scully, also. On election morning he was out at
four o'clock, "getting out the vote"; he had a two-horse carriage to
ride in, and he went from house to house for his friends, and
escorted them in triumph to the polls. He voted half a dozen times
himself, and voted some of his friends as often; he brought bunch
after bunch of the newest foreigners—Lithuanians, Poles, Bohemians, Slovaks—and when he had put them through the mill he
turned them over to another man to take to the next polling-place.
When Jurgis first set out, the captain of the precinct gave him a
hundred dollars, and three times in the course of the day he came
for another hundred, and not more than twenty-five out of each lot
got stuck in his own pocket. The balance all went for actual votes,
and on a day of Democratic landslides they elected "Scotty" Doyle,
the ex-ten-pin setter, by nearly a thousand plurality—and beginning at five o'clock in the afternoon, and ending at three the next
morning, Jurgis treated himself to a most unholy and horrible "jag."
Nearly every one else in Packingtown did the same, however, for
there was universal exultation over this triumph of popular government, this crushing defeat of an arrogant plutocrat by the power of
the common people.

Chapter XXVI

After the elections Jurgis stayed on in Packingtown and kept his job. The agitation to break up the police protection of criminals was continuing, and it seemed to him best to "lay low" for the present. He had nearly three hundred dollars in the bank, and might have considered himself entitled to a vacation; but he had an easy job, and force of habit kept him at it. Besides, Mike Scully, whom he consulted, advised him that something might "turn up" before long.

Jurgis got himself a place in a boarding-house with some congenial friends. He had already inquired of Aniele, and learned that Elzbieta and her family had gone down-town, and so he gave no further thought to them. He went with a new set, now, young unmarried fellows who were "sporty." Jurgis had long ago cast off his fertilizer clothing, and since going into politics he had donned a linen collar and a greasy red necktie. He had some reason for thinking of his dress, for he was making about eleven dollars a week, and two-thirds of it he might spend upon his pleasures without ever touching his savings.

Sometimes he would ride down-town with a party of friends to the cheap theatres and the music halls and other haunts with which they were familiar. Many of the saloons in Packingtown had pool-tables, and some of them bowling-alleys, by means of which he could spend his evenings in petty gambling. Also, there were cards and dice. One time Jurgis got into a game on a Saturday night and won prodigiously, and because he was a man of spirit he stayed in with the rest and the game continued until late Sunday afternoon, and by that time he was "out" over twenty dollars. On Saturday nights, also, a number of balls were generally given in Packingtown; each man would bring his "girl" with him, paying half a dollar for a ticket, and several dollars additional for drinks in the course of the festivities, which continued until three or four o'clock in the morning, unless broken up by fighting. During all this time the same man and woman would dance together, half-stupefied with sensuality and drink.

Before long Jurgis discovered what Scully had meant by something "turning up." In May the agreement between the packers and the unions expired, and a new agreement had to be signed. Negotiations were going on, and the yards were full of talk of a strike. The old scale had dealt with the wages of the skilled men only; and of the members of the Meat Workers' Union about two-thirds were unskilled men. In Chicago these latter were receiving, for the most part, eighteen and a half cents an hour, and the unions wished to make this the general wage for the next year. It was not nearly so large a wage as it seemed—in the course of the negotiations the union officers examined time-checks to the amount of ten thousand dollars, and they found that the highest wages paid had been fourteen dollars a week, the lowest two dollars and five cents, and the average of the whole, six dollars and sixty-five cents. And six dollars and sixty-five cents was hardly too much for a man to keep a family on. Considering the fact that the price of dressed meat had increased nearly fifty per cent in the last five years, while the price of "beef on the hoof" had decreased as much, it would have seemed that the packers ought to be able to pay it; but the packers were unwilling to pay it—they rejected the union demand, and to show what their purpose was, a week or two after the agreement expired they put down the wages of about a thousand men to sixteen and a half cents, and it was said that old man Jones had vowed he would put them to fifteen before he got through. There were a million and a half of men in the country looking for work, a hundred thousand of them right in Chicago; and were the packers to let the union stewards march into their places and bind them to a contract that would lose them several thousand dollars a day for a year? Not much!

All this was in June; and before long the question was submitted to a referendum in the unions, and the decision was for a strike. It was the same in all the packing-house cities; and suddenly the newspapers and public woke up to face the grewsome spectacle of a meat famine. All sorts of pleas for a reconsideration were made, but the packers were obdurate; and all the while they were reducing wages, and heading off shipments of cattle, and rushing in wagonloads of mattresses and cots. So the men boiled over, and one night telegrams went out from the union headquarters to all the big packing centres,—to St. Paul, South Omaha, Sioux City, St. Joseph, Kansas City, East St. Louis, and New York,—and the next day at noon between fifty and sixty thousand men drew off their working clothes and marched out of the factories, and the great "Beef Strike" was on.[1]

Jurgis went to his dinner, and afterward he walked over to see Mike Scully, who lived in a fine house, upon a street which had been decently paved and lighted for his especial benefit. Scully had gone into semi-retirement, and looked nervous and worried. "What do you want?" he demanded, when he saw Jurgis.

"I came to see if maybe you could get me a place during the strike," the other replied.

---

1. At noon on July 12, 1904, 28,000 Chicago packinghouse workers cleaned their tools and machines and marched out of work, joined by thousands around the country. The striking point was the rejection of their demand for a minimum wage of 20 cents per hour (a demand later reduced to 18½ cents) for all unskilled workers. Although the Amalgamated Meat Cutters and Butcher Workmen's Union maintained order and discipline, the packers broke the strike.

And Scully knit his brows and eyed him narrowly. In that morning's papers Jurgis had read a fierce denunciation of the packers by Scully, who had declared that if they did not treat their people better the city authorities would end the matter by tearing down their plants. Now, therefore, Jurgis was not a little taken aback when the other demanded suddenly, "See here, Rudkus, why don't you stick by your job?"

Jurgis started. "Work as a scab?"[2] he cried.

"Why not?" demanded Scully. "What's that to you?"

"But—but—" stammered Jurgis. He had somehow taken it for granted that he should go out with his union.

"The packers need good men, and need them bad," continued the other, "and they'll treat a man right that stands by them. Why don't you take your chance and fix yourself?"

"But," said Jurgis, "how could I ever be of any use to you—in politics?"

"You couldn't be it anyhow," said Scully, abruptly.

"Why not?" asked Jurgis.

"Hell, man!" cried the other. "Don't you know you're a Republican? And do you think I'm always going to elect Republicans? My brewer has found out already how we served him, and there is the deuce to pay."

Jurgis looked dumfounded. He had never thought of that aspect of it before. "I could be a Democrat," he said.

"Yes," responded the other, "but not right away; a man can't change his politics every day. And besides, I don't need you—there'd be nothing for you to do. And it's a long time to election day, anyhow; and what are you going to do meantime?"

"I thought I could count on you," began Jurgis.

"Yes," responded Scully, "so you could—I never yet went back on a friend. But is it fair to leave the job I got you and come to me for another? I have had a hundred fellows after me to-day, and what can I do? I've put seventeen men on the city pay-roll to clean streets this one week, and do you think I can keep that up forever? It wouldn't do for me to tell other men what I tell you, but you've been on the inside, and you ought to have sense enough to see for yourself. What have you to gain by a strike?"

"I hadn't thought," said Jurgis.

"Exactly," said Scully, "but you'd better. Take my word for it, the strike will be over in a few days, and the men will be beaten; and meantime what you get out of it will belong to you. Do you see?"

And Jurgis saw. He went back to the yards, and into the workroom. The men had left a long line of hogs in various stages of preparation,

2. Person who works during a strike, seen by other workers as a traitor and thus often the object of verbal if not physical violence.

and the foreman was directing the feeble efforts of a score or two of clerks and stenographers and office-boys to finish up the job and get them into the chilling-rooms. Jurgis went straight up to him and announced, "I have come back to work, Mr. Murphy."

The boss's face lighted up. "Good man!" he cried. "Come ahead!"

"Just a moment," said Jurgis, checking his enthusiasm. "I think I ought to get a little more wages."

"Yes," replied the other, "of course. What do you want?"

Jurgis had debated on the way. His nerve almost failed him now, but he clenched his hands. "I think I ought to have three dollars a day," he said.

"All right," said the other, promptly; and before the day was out our friend discovered that the clerks and stenographers and office-boys were getting five dollars a day, and then he could have kicked himself!

So Jurgis became one of the new "American heroes," a man whose virtues merited comparison with those of the martyrs of Lexington and Valley Forge.[3] The resemblance was not complete, of course, for Jurgis was generously paid and comfortably clad, and was provided with a spring-cot and a mattress and three substantial meals a day; also he was perfectly at ease, and safe from all peril of life and limb, save only in the case that a desire for beer should lead him to venture outside of the stockyards gates. And even in the exercise of this privilege he was not left unprotected; a good part of the inadequate police force of Chicago was suddenly diverted from its work of hunting criminals, and rushed out to serve him.

The police, and the strikers also, were determined that there should be no violence; but there was another party interested which was minded to the contrary—and that was the press. On the first day of his life as a strike-breaker Jurgis quit work early, and in a spirit of bravado he challenged three men of his acquaintance to go outside and get a drink. They accepted, and went through the big Halsted Street gate,[4] where several policemen were watching, and also some union pickets, scanning sharply those who passed in and out. Jurgis and his companions went south on Halsted Street, past the hotel, and then suddenly half a dozen men started across the street toward them and proceeded to argue with them concerning the error of their ways. As the arguments were not taken in the proper spirit, they went on to threats; and suddenly one of them

3. Battle sites in the American Revolution (see below, p. 514, n. 6).
4. Probably the famous "Stone Gate" near Thirty-ninth and Halsted Streets, built by architects Burnham & Root in 1879, so widely recognized as to become practically a trademark of Union Stock Yard and Transit Company. In 1972, it was designated a Chicago landmark.

jerked off the hat of one of the four and flung it over the fence. The man started after it, and then, as a cry of "Scab!" was raised and a dozen people came running out of saloons and doorways, a second man's heart failed him and he followed. Jurgis and the fourth stayed long enough to give themselves the satisfaction of a quick exchange of blows, and then they, too, took to their heels and fled back of the hotel and into the yards again. Meantime, of course, policemen were coming on a run, and as a crowd gathered other police got excited and sent in a riot-call. Jurgis knew nothing of this, but went back to "Packers' Avenue," and in front of the "Central Time-Station" he saw one of his companions, breathless and wild with excitement, narrating to an ever growing throng how the four had been attacked and surrounded by a howling mob, and had been nearly torn to pieces. While he stood listening, smiling cynically, several dapper young men stood by with note-books in their hands, and it was not more than two hours later that Jurgis saw newsboys running about with armfuls of newspapers, printed in red and black letters six inches high:—

VIOLENCE IN THE YARDS!
STRIKE-BREAKERS SURROUNDED BY FRENZIED MOB!

If he had been able to buy all of the newspapers of the United States the next morning, he might have discovered that his beer-hunting exploit was being perused by some two score millions of people, and had served as a text for editorials in half the staid and solemn business men's newspapers in the land.

Jurgis was to see more of this as time passed. For the present, his work being over, he was free to ride into the city, by a railroad direct from the yards, or else to spend the night in a room where cots had been laid in rows. He chose the latter, but to his regret, for all night long gangs of strike-breakers kept arriving. As very few of the better class of working-men could be got for such work, these specimens of the new American hero contained an assortment of the criminals and thugs of the city, besides negroes and the lowest foreigners—Greeks, Roumanians, Sicilians, and Slovaks. They had been attracted more by the prospect of disorder than by the big wages; and they made the night hideous with singing and carousing, and only went to sleep when the time came for them to get up to work.

In the morning before Jurgis had finished his breakfast, "Pat" Murphy ordered him to one of the superintendents, who questioned him as to his experience in the work of the killing-room. His heart began to thump with excitement, for he divined instantly that his hour had come—that he was to be a boss!

Some of the foremen were union members, and many who were not had gone out with the men. It was in the killing department that the packers had been left most in the lurch, and precisely here that they could least afford it; the smoking and canning and salting of meat might wait, and all the by-products might be wasted—but fresh meats must be had, or the restaurants and hotels and brown-stone houses would feel the pinch, and then "public opinion" would take a startling turn.

An opportunity such as this would not come twice to a man; and Jurgis seized it. Yes, he knew the work, the whole of it, and he could teach it to others. But if he took the job and gave satisfaction he would expect to keep it—they would not turn him off at the end of the strike? To which the superintendent replied that he might safely trust Durham's for that—they proposed to teach these unions a lesson, and most of all those foremen who had gone back on them. Jurgis would receive five dollars a day during the strike, and twenty-five a week after it was settled.

So our friend got a pair of "slaughter-pen" boots and "jeans," and flung himself at his task. It was a weird sight, there on the killing-beds—a throng of stupid black negroes, and foreigners who could not understand a word that was said to them, mixed with pale-faced, hollow-chested bookkeepers and clerks, half-fainting for the tropical heat and the sickening stench of fresh blood—and all struggling to dress a dozen or two of cattle in the same place where, twenty-four hours ago, the old killing-gang had been speeding, with their marvellous precision, turning out four hundred carcasses every hour!

The negroes and the "toughs" from the Levée did not want to work, and every few minutes some of them would feel obliged to retire and recuperate. In a couple of days Durham and Company had electric fans up to cool off the rooms for them, and even couches for them to rest on; and meantime they could go out and find a shady corner and take a "snooze," and as there was no place for any one in particular, and no system, it might be hours before their boss discovered them. As for the poor office employees, they did their best, moved to it by terror; thirty of them had been "fired" in a bunch that first morning for refusing to serve, besides a number of women clerks and typewriters who had declined to act as waitresses.

It was such a force as this that Jurgis had to organize. He did his best, flying here and there, placing them in rows and showing them the tricks; he had never given an order in his life before, but he had taken enough of them to know, and he soon fell into the spirit of it, and roared and stormed like any old stager.[5] He had not the most tractable pupils, however. "See hyar, boss," a big black "buck" would begin, "ef you doan' like de way Ah does dis job, you kin git somebody else to do it." Then a crowd would gather and listen, muttering

5. Experienced person, veteran.

threats. After the first meal nearly all the steel knives had been missing, and now every negro had one, ground to a fine point, hidden in
his boots.

There was no bringing order out of such a chaos, Jurgis soon discovered; and he fell in with the spirit of the thing—there was no
reason why he should wear himself out with shouting. If hides and
guts were slashed and rendered useless there was no way of tracing
it to any one; and if a man lay off and forgot to come back there was
nothing to be gained by seeking him, for all the rest would quit in
the meantime. Everything went, during the strike, and the packers
paid. Before long Jurgis found that the custom of resting had suggested to some alert minds the possibility of registering at more than
one place and earning more than one five dollars a day. When he
caught a man at this he "fired" him, but it chanced to be in a quiet
corner, and the man tendered him a ten-dollar bill and a wink, and
he took them. Of course, before long this custom spread, and Jurgis
was soon making quite a good income from it.

In the face of handicaps such as these the packers counted themselves lucky if they could kill off the cattle that had been crippled
in transit and the hogs that had developed disease. Frequently, in
the course of a two or three days' trip, in hot weather and without
water, some hog would develop cholera,[6] and die; and the rest would
attack him before he had ceased kicking, and when the car was
opened there would be nothing of him left but the bones. If all the
hogs in this car-load were not killed at once, they would soon be
down with the dread disease, and there would be nothing to do but
make them into lard. It was the same with cattle that were gored
and dying, or were limping with broken bones stuck through their
flesh—they must be killed, even if brokers and buyers and superintendents had to take off their coats and help drive and cut and skin
them. And meantime, agents of the packers were gathering gangs
of negroes in the country districts of the far South, promising them
five dollars a day and board, and being careful not to mention there
was a strike; already car-loads of them were on the way, with special rates from the railroads, and all traffic ordered out of the way.
Many towns and cities were taking advantage of the chance to clear
out their jails and work-houses—in Detroit the magistrates would
release every man who agreed to leave town within twenty-four
hours, and agents of the packers were in the court-rooms to ship
them right. And meantime train-loads of supplies were coming in
for their accommodation, including beer and whiskey, so that they
might not be tempted to go outside. They hired thirty young girls in

6. Infectious epidemic disease, often spread by polluted water, caused by bacteria that
live in intestines, resulting in acute nausea and diarrhea.

Cincinnati to "pack fruit," and when they arrived put them at work canning corned-beef, and put cots for them to sleep in a public hall-way, through which the men passed. As the gangs came in day and night, under the escort of squads of police, they stowed them away in unused work-rooms and store-rooms, and in the car-sheds, crowded so closely together that the cots touched. In some places they would use the same room for eating and sleeping, and at night the men would put their cots upon the tables, to keep away from the swarms of rats.

But with all their best efforts, the packers were demoralized. Ninety per cent of the men had walked out; and they faced the task of completely remaking their labor force—and with the price of meat up thirty per cent, and the public clamoring for a settlement. They made an offer to submit the whole question at issue to arbitration; and at the end of ten days the unions accepted it, and the strike was called off.[7] It was agreed that all the men were to be reëmployed within forty-five days, and that there was to be "no discrimination against union men."

This was an anxious time for Jurgis. If the men were taken back "without discrimination," he would lose his present place. He sought out the superintendent, who smiled grimly and bade him "wait and see." Durham's strike-breakers were few of them leaving.

Whether or not the "settlement" was simply a trick of the packers to gain time, or whether they really expected to break the strike and cripple the unions by the plan, cannot be said; but that night there went out from the office of Durham and Company a telegram to all the big packing-centres, "Employ no union leaders." And in the morning, when the twenty thousand men thronged into the yards, with their dinner-pails and working-clothes, Jurgis stood near the door of the hog-trimming room, where he had worked before the strike, and saw a throng of eager men, with a score or two of police-men watching them; and he saw a superintendent come out and walk down the line, and pick out man after man that pleased him; and one after another came, and there were some men up near the head of the line who were never picked—they being the union stewards and delegates, and the men Jurgis had heard making speeches at the meetings. Each time, of course, there were louder murmurings and angrier looks. Over where the cattle-butchers were waiting, Jurgis heard shouts and saw a crowd, and he hurried there. One big butcher, who was president of the Packing Trades Council, had been passed over five times, and the men were wild with rage; they had appointed a committee of three to go in and see the superintendent, and the committee had made three attempts, and each time the police had

7. On July 21, 1904, the strike briefly ended.

clubbed them back from the door. Then there were yells and hoots, continuing until at last the superintendent came to the door. "We all go back or none of us do!" cried a hundred voices. And the other shook his fist at them, and shouted, "You went out of here like cattle, and like cattle you'll come back!"[8]

Then suddenly the big butcher president[9] leaped upon a pile of stones and yelled: "It's off, boys. We'll all of us quit again!" And so the cattle-butchers declared a new strike on the spot; and gathering their members from the other plants, where the same trick had been played, they marched down Packers' Avenue, which was thronged with a dense mass of workers, cheering wildly. Men who had already got to work on the killing-beds dropped their tools and joined them; some galloped here and there on horseback, shouting the tidings, and within half an hour the whole of Packingtown was on strike again, and beside itself with fury.

There was quite a different tone in Packingtown after this—the place was a seething caldron of passion, and the "scab" who ventured into it fared badly. There were one or two of these incidents each day, the newspapers detailing them, and always blaming them upon the unions. Yet ten years before, when there were no unions in Packingtown, there was a strike, and national troops had to be called, and there were pitched battles fought at night, by the light of blazing freight-trains.[1] Packingtown was always a centre of violence; in "Whiskey Point," where there were a hundred saloons and one glue-factory, there was always fighting, and always more of it in hot weather. Any one who had taken the trouble to consult the station-house blotter[2] would have found that there was less violence that summer than ever before—and this while twenty thousand men were out of work, and with nothing to do all day but brood upon bitter wrongs. There was no one to picture the battle the union leaders were fighting—to hold this huge army in rank, to keep it from straggling and pillaging, to cheer and encourage and guide a hundred thousand people, of a dozen different tongues, through six long weeks of hunger and disappointment and despair.

Meantime the packers had set themselves definitely to the task of making a new labor force. A thousand or two of strike-breakers were

---

8. Insults such as this one, attributed to an Armour superintendent, and the packers' violating their agreement not to discriminate against union workers provoked resumption of the strike on July 22.

9. Probably a nod to Michael Donnelly, president of the meat cutters' union, who came to Chicago in 1900 and within a year had organized most of the cattle butchers.

1. Unlike the 1904 strike, the 1894 event—beginning in sympathy with the Pullman strike (see below, p. 300, n. 6)—was a crowd action of unskilled laborers and characterized by widespread rioting. In 1897 an international union seeking uniformity in wages and working conditions had been organized, but Chicago was not represented until 1900.

2. Police blotter, record of events.

brought in every night, and distributed among the various plants. Some of them were experienced workers,—butchers, salesmen, and managers from the packers' branch stores, and a few union men who had deserted from other cities; but the vast majority were "green" negroes from the cotton districts of the far South, and they were herded into the packing-plants like sheep.[3] There was a law forbidding the use of buildings as lodging-houses unless they were licensed for the purpose, and provided with proper windows, stairways, and fire-escapes; but here, in a "paint-room," reached only by an enclosed "chute," a room without a single window and only one door, a hundred men were crowded upon mattresses on the floor.[4] Up on the third story of the "hog-house" of Jones's was a store-room, without a window, into which they crowded seven hundred men, sleeping upon the bare springs of cots, and with a second shift to use them by day. And when the clamor of the public led to an investigation into these conditions, and the mayor of the city was forced to order the enforcement of the law, the packers got a judge to issue an injunction forbidding him to do it!

Just at this time the mayor[5] was boasting that he had put an end to gambling and prize-fighting in the city; but here a swarm of professional gamblers had leagued themselves with the police to fleece the strike-breakers; and any night, in the big open space in front of Brown's, one might see brawny negroes stripped to the waist and pounding each other for money, while a howling throng of three or four thousand surged about, men and women, young white girls from the country rubbing elbows with big buck negroes with daggers in their boots, while rows of woolly heads peered down from every window of the surrounding factories. The ancestors of these black people had been savages[6] in Africa; and since then they had been chattel slaves, or had been held down by a community ruled by the traditions of slavery. Now for the first time they were free,—free to gratify every passion, free to wreck themselves. They were wanted to break a strike, and when it was broken they would be shipped away, and their present masters would never see them again; and so whiskey and women were brought in by the car-load and sold to them, and hell was let loose in the yards. Every night there were stabbings and shootings; it was said that the packers had blank permits, which

3. In an attempt to continue production and break the strike, packers brought in inexperienced ("green") workers, including many Black Americans, Italians, and Greeks, paying them $2.15 per day, higher than the going rate, which fanned hostilities further and provoked violence.
4. The men are living in a pork-packing factory.
5. Democrat Carter Henry Harrison IV (1860–1953), in office 1897–1905 and 1911–15, son of a former Chicago mayor by the same name.
6. The misconception held by many white people that Africans were "savages" perpetuated the erroneous belief that Black people were saved from their own worst instincts by, first, slavery and, later, Jim Crow policies of segregation.

enabled them to ship dead bodies from the city without troubling the authorities. They lodged men and women on the same floor; and with the night there began a saturnalia of debauchery—scenes such as never before had been witnessed in America. And as the women were the dregs from the brothels of Chicago, and the men were for the most part ignorant country negroes, the nameless diseases of vice were soon rife; and this where food was being handled which was sent out to every corner of the civilized world.

The "Union Stockyards"[7] were never a pleasant place; but now they were not only a collection of slaughter-houses, but also the camping-place of an army of fifteen or twenty thousand human beasts. All day long the blazing midsummer sun beat down upon that square mile of abominations: upon tens of thousands of cattle crowded into pens whose wooden floors stank and steamed contagion; upon bare, blistering, cinder-strewn railroad-tracks, and huge blocks of dingy meat-factories, whose labyrinthine passages defied a breath of fresh air to penetrate them; and there were not merely rivers of hot blood, and car-loads of moist flesh, and rendering-vats and soap-caldrons, glue-factories and fertilizer tanks, that smelt like the craters of hell—there were also tons of garbage festering in the sun, and the greasy laundry of the workers hung out to dry, and dining-rooms littered with food and black with flies, and toilet-rooms that were open sewers.

And then at night, when this throng poured out into the streets to play—fighting, gambling, drinking and carousing, cursing and screaming, laughing and singing, playing banjoes and dancing! They were worked in the yards all the seven days of the week, and they had their prize-fights and crap-games on Sunday nights as well; but then around the corner one might see a bonfire blazing, and an old, gray-headed negress, lean and witchlike, her hair flying wild and her eyes blazing, yelling and chanting of the fires of perdition and the blood of the "Lamb,"[8] while men and women lay down upon the ground and moaned and screamed in convulsions of terror and remorse.

Such were the stockyards during the strike; while the unions watched in sullen despair, and the country clamored like a greedy child for its food, and the packers went grimly on their way. Each day they added new workers, and could be more stern with the old ones—could put them on piece-work, and dismiss them if they did not keep

7. Union Stock Yard & Transit Company, built in 1865 to eliminate the necessity of driving animals through city streets and to coordinate trade, largely financed by the railroads and dominated by large packers. Adjacent to Packingtown and a town unto itself with its own hotel, town hall, police, banks, restaurants, and hundreds of miles of roads, the Union Stockyards were called "the eighth wonder of the world" by the *Chicago Tribune*.
8. The evangelist alludes to the Christian concept of Jesus as the sacrificial lamb of God.

up the pace. Jurgis was now one of their agents in this process; and he could feel the change day by day, like the slow starting up of a huge machine. He had gotten used to being a master of men; and because of the stifling heat and the stench, and the fact that he was a "scab" and knew it and despised himself, he was drinking, and developing a villainous temper, and he stormed and cursed and raged at his men, and drove them until they were ready to drop with exhaustion.

Then one day late in August, a superintendent ran into the place and shouted to Jurgis and his gang to drop their work and come. They followed him outside, to where, in the midst of a dense throng, they saw several two-horse trucks waiting, and three patrol-wagon loads of police. Jurgis and his men sprang upon one of the trucks, and the driver yelled to the crowd, and they went thundering away at a gallop. Some steers had just escaped from the yards, and the strikers had got hold of them, and there would be the chance of a scrap!

They went out at the Ashland Avenue gate, and over in the direction of the "dump." There was a yell as soon as they were sighted, men and women rushing out of houses and saloons as they galloped by. There were eight or ten policemen on the truck, however, and there was no disturbance until they came to a place where the street was blocked with a dense throng. Those on the flying truck yelled a warning and the crowd scattered pell-mell, disclosing one of the steers lying in its blood. There were a good many cattle-butchers about just then, with nothing much to do, and hungry children at home; and so some one had knocked out the steer—and as a first-class man can kill and dress one in a couple of minutes, there were a good many steaks and roasts already missing. This called for punishment, of course; and the police proceeded to administer it by leaping from the truck and cracking at every head they saw. There were yells of rage and pain, and the terrified people fled into houses and stores, or scattered helter-skelter down the street. Jurgis and his gang joined in the sport, every man singling out his victim, and striving to bring him to bay and punch him. If he fled into a house his pursuer would smash in the flimsy door and follow him up the stairs, hitting every one who came within reach, and finally dragging his squealing quarry from under a bed or a pile of old clothes in a closet.

Jurgis and two policemen chased some men into a bar-room. One of them took shelter behind the bar, where a policeman cornered him and proceeded to whack him over the back and shoulders, until he lay down and gave a chance at his head. The others leaped a fence in the rear, balking the second policeman, who was fat; and as he came back, furious and cursing, a big Polish woman, the owner of the saloon, rushed in screaming, and received a poke in the stomach that doubled her up on the floor. Meantime Jurgis, who was of a practical temper, was helping himself at the bar; and the first policeman, who had laid out his man, joined him, handing out several more bottles, and filling his pockets besides, and then, as he started to leave, cleaning off all the balance with a sweep of his club. The din of the glass crashing to the floor brought the fat Polish woman to her feet again, but another policeman came up behind her and put his knee into her back and his hands over her eyes— and then called to his companion, who went back and broke open the cash-drawer and filled his pockets with the contents. Then the three went outside, and the man who was holding the woman gave her a shove and dashed out himself. The gang having already got the carcass on to the truck, the party set out at a trot, followed by screams and curses, and a shower of bricks and stones from unseen enemies. These bricks and stones would figure in the accounts of the "riot" which would be sent out to a few thousand newspapers within an hour or two; but the episode of the cash-drawer would never be mentioned again, save only in the heartbreaking legends of Packingtown.

It was late in the afternoon when they got back, and they dressed out the remainder of the steer, and a couple of others that had been killed, and then knocked off for the day. Jurgis went down-town to supper, with three friends who had been on the other trucks, and they exchanged reminiscences on the way. Afterward they drifted into a roulette-parlor, and Jurgis, who was never lucky at gambling, dropped about fifteen dollars. To console himself he had to drink a good deal, and he went back to Packingtown about two o'clock in the morning, very much the worse for his excursion, and, it must be confessed, entirely deserving the calamity that was in store for him.

As he was going to the place where he slept, he met a painted-cheeked woman in a greasy "kimono," and she put her arm about his waist to steady him; they turned into a dark room they were passing— but scarcely had they taken two steps before suddenly a door swung open, and a man entered, carrying a lantern. "Who's there?" he called sharply. And Jurgis started to mutter some reply; but at the same instant the man raised his light, which flashed in his face, so that it was possible to recognize him. Jurgis stood stricken dumb, and his heart gave a leap like a mad thing. The man was Connor!

Connor, the boss of the loading gang! The man who had seduced his wife—who had sent him to prison, and wrecked his home, and ruined his life! He stood there, staring, with the light shining full upon him.

Jurgis had often thought of Connor since coming back to Packing-town, but it had been as of something far off, that no longer concerned him. Now, however, when he saw him, alive and in the flesh,

the same thing happened to him that had happened before—a flood
of rage boiled up in him, a blind frenzy seized him. And he flung
himself at the man, and smote him between the eyes—and then, as
he fell, seized him by the throat and began to pound his head upon
the stones.

The woman began screaming, and people came rushing in. The
lantern had been upset and extinguished, and it was so dark they
could not see a thing; but they could hear Jurgis panting, and hear
the thumping of his victim's skull, and they rushed there and tried
to pull him off. Precisely as before, Jurgis came away with a piece
of his enemy's flesh between his teeth; and, as before, he went on
fighting with those who had interfered with him, until a policeman
had come and beaten him into insensibility.

And so Jurgis spent the balance of the night in the stockyards station-
house. This time, however, he had money in his pocket, and when he
came to his senses he could get something to drink, and also a messenger to take word of his plight to "Bush" Harper. Harper did not
appear, however, until after the prisoner, feeling very weak and ill,
had been hauled into court and remanded at five hundred dollars'
bail to await the result of his victim's injuries. Jurgis was wild about
this, because a different magistrate had chanced to be on the bench,
and he had stated that he had never been arrested before, and also
that he had been attacked first—and if only some one had been there
to speak a good word for him, he could have been let off at once.

But Harper explained that he had been down-town, and had not
got the message. "What's happened to you?" he asked.

"I've been doing a fellow up," said Jurgis, "and I've got to get five
hundred dollars' bail."

"I can arrange that all right," said the other—"though it may cost
you a few dollars, of course. But what was the trouble?"

"It was a man that did me a mean trick once," answered Jurgis.

"Who is he?"

"He's a foreman in Brown's—or used to be. His name's Connor."

And the other gave a start. "Connor!" he cried. "Not Phil
Connor!"

"Yes," said Jurgis, "that's the fellow. Why?"

"Good God!" exclaimed the other, "then you're in for it, old man!
I can't help you!"

"Not help me! Why not?"

"Why, he's one of Scully's biggest men—he's a member of the War-
Whoop League, and they talked of sending him to the legislature!
Phil Connor! Great heavens!"

Jurgis sat dumb with dismay.

"Why, he can send you to Joliet,[9] if he wants to!" declared the other.

"Can't I have Scully get me off before he finds out about it?" asked Jurgis, at length.

"But Scully's out of town," the other answered. "I don't even know where he is—he's run away to dodge the strike."

That was a pretty mess, indeed. Poor Jurgis sat half-dazed. His pull had run up against a bigger pull, and he was down and out! "But what am I going to do?" he asked, weakly.

"How should I know?" said the other. "I shouldn't even dare to get bail for you—why, I might ruin myself for life!"

Again there was silence. "Can't you do it for me," Jurgis asked, "and pretend that you didn't know who I'd hit?"

"But what good would that do you when you came to stand trial?" asked Harper. Then he sat buried in thought for a minute or two. "There's nothing—unless it's this," he said. "I could have your bail reduced; and then if you had the money you could pay it and skip."

"How much will it be?" Jurgis asked, after he had had this explained more in detail.

"I don't know," said the other. "How much do you own?"

"I've got about three hundred dollars," was the answer.

"Well," was Harper's reply, "I'm not sure, but I'll try and get you off for that. I'll take the risk for friendship's sake—for I'd hate to see you sent to state's prison for a year or two."

And so finally Jurgis ripped out his bank-book—which was sewed up in his trousers—and signed an order, which "Bush" Harper wrote, for all the money to be paid out. Then the latter went and got it, and hurried to the court, and explained to the magistrate that Jurgis was a decent fellow and a friend of Scully's, who had been attacked by a strike-breaker. So the bail was reduced to three hundred dollars, and Harper went on it himself; he did not tell this to Jurgis, however— nor did he tell him that when the time for trial came it would be an easy matter for him to avoid the forfeiting of the bail, and pocket the three hundred dollars as his reward for the risk of offending Mike Scully! All that he told Jurgis was that he was now free, and that the best thing he could do was to clear out as quickly as possible; and so Jurgis, overwhelmed with gratitude and relief, took the dollar and fourteen cents that was left him out of all his bank account, and put it with the two dollars and a quarter that was left from his last night's celebration, and boarded a street-car and got off at the other end of Chicago.

9. The Illinois State Penitentiary in Joliet.

Chapter XXVII

Poor Jurgis was now an outcast and a tramp once more. He was crippled—he was as literally crippled as any wild animal which has lost its claws, or been torn out of its shell. He had been shorn, at one cut, of all those mysterious weapons whereby he had been able to make a living easily and to escape the consequences of his actions. He could no longer command a job when he wanted it; he could no longer steal with impunity—he must take his chances with the common herd. Nay worse, he dared not mingle with the herd—he must hide by himself, for he was one marked out for destruction. His old companions would betray him, for the sake of the influence they would gain thereby; and he would be made to suffer, not merely for the offence he had committed, but for others which would be laid at his door, just as had been done for some poor devil on the occasion of that assault upon the "country customer" by him and Duane.

And also he labored under another handicap now. He had acquired new standards of living, which were not easily to be altered. When he had been out of work before, he had been content if he could sleep in a doorway or under a truck out of the rain, and if he could get fifteen cents a day for saloon lunches. But now he desired all sorts of other things, and suffered because he had to do without them. He must have a drink now and then, a drink for its own sake, and apart from the food that came with it. The craving for it was strong enough to master every other consideration—he would have it, though it were his last nickel and he had to starve the balance of the day in consequence.

Jurgis became once more a besieger of factory gates. But never since he had been in Chicago had he stood less chance of getting a job than just then. For one thing, there was the economic crisis, the million or two of men who had been out of work in the spring and summer, and were not yet all back, by any means. And then there was the strike, with seventy thousand men and women all over the country idle for a couple of months—twenty thousand in Chicago, and many of them now seeking work throughout the city. It did not remedy matters that a few days later the strike was given up and about half the strikers went back to work; for every one taken on, there was a "scab" who gave up and fled. The ten or fifteen thousand "green" negroes, foreigners, and criminals were now being turned loose to shift for themselves. Everywhere Jurgis went he kept meeting them, and he was in an agony of fear least some one of them should know that he was "wanted." He would have left Chicago, only by the time he had realized his danger he was almost penniless; and it would be better to go to jail than to be caught out in the country in the winter-time.

At the end of about ten days Jurgis had only a few pennies left; and he had not yet found a job—not even a day's work at anything, not a chance to carry a satchel. Once again, as when he had come out of the hospital, he was bound hand and foot, and facing the grisly phantom of starvation. Raw, naked terror possessed him, a maddening passion that would never leave him, and that wore him down more quickly than the actual want of food. He was going to die of hunger! The fiend reached out its scaly arms for him—it touched him, its breath came into his face; and he would cry out for the awfulness of it, he would wake up in the night, shuddering, and bathed in perspiration, and start up and flee. He would walk, begging for work, until he was exhausted; he could not remain still— he would wander on, gaunt and haggard, gazing about him with restless eyes. Everywhere he went, from one end of the vast city to the other, there were hundreds of others like him; everywhere was the sight of plenty—and the merciless hand of authority waving them away. There is one kind of prison where the man is behind bars, and everything that he desires is outside; and there is another kind where the things are behind the bars, and the man is outside.

When he was down to his last quarter, Jurgis learned that before the bakeshops closed at night they sold out what was left at half price, and after that he would go and get two loaves of stale bread for a nickel, and break them up and stuff his pockets with them, munching a bit from time to time. He would not spend a penny save for this; and, after two or three days more, he even became sparing of the bread, and would stop and peer into the ash-barrels as he walked along the streets, and now and then rake out a bit of something, shake it free from dust, and count himself just so many minutes further from the end.

So for several days he had been going about, ravenous all the time, and growing weaker and weaker; and then one morning he had a hideous experience, that almost broke his heart. He was passing down a street lined with warehouses, and a boss offered him a job, and then, after he had started to work, turned him off because he was not strong enough. And he stood by and saw another man put into his place, and then picked up his coat, and walked off, doing all that he could to keep from breaking down and crying like a baby. He was lost! He was doomed! There was no hope for him! But then, with a sudden rush, his fear gave place to rage. He fell to cursing. He would come back there after dark, and he would show that scoundrel whether he was good for anything or not!

He was still muttering this when suddenly, at the corner, he came upon a green-grocery, with a tray full of cabbages in front of it. Jurgis, after one swift glance about him, stooped and seized the biggest of them, and darted round the corner with it. There was a hue and cry, and a score of men and boys started in chase of him; but he came to an alley, and then to another branching off from it and leading him into another street, where he fell into a walk, and slipped his cabbage under his coat and went off unsuspected in the crowd. When he had gotten a safe distance away he sat down and devoured half the cabbage raw, stowing the balance away in his pockets till the next day.

Just about this time one of the Chicago newspapers, which made much of the "common people," opened a "free-soup kitchen" for the benefit of the unemployed. Some people said that they did this for the sake of the advertising it gave them, and some others said that their motive was a fear lest all their readers should be starved off; but whatever the reason, the soup was thick and hot, and there was a bowl for every man, all night long. When Jurgis heard of this, from a fellow "hobo," he vowed that he would have half a dozen bowls before morning; but, as it proved, he was lucky to get one, for there was a line of men two blocks long before the stand, and there was just as long a line when the place was finally closed up.

This depot was within the danger-line for Jurgis—in the "Levée" district, where he was known; but he went there, all the same, for he was desperate, and beginning to think of even the Bridewell as a place of refuge. So far the weather had been fair, and he had slept out every night in a vacant lot; but now there fell suddenly a shadow of the advancing winter, a chill wind from the north and a driving storm of rain. That day Jurgis bought two drinks for the sake of the shelter, and at night he spent his last two pennies in a "stale-beer dive." This was a place kept by a negro, who went out and drew off the old dregs of beer that lay in barrels set outside of the saloons; and after he had doctored it with chemicals to make it "fizz," he sold it for two cents a can, the purchase of a can including the privilege of sleeping the night through upon the floor, with a mass of degraded outcasts, men and women.

All these horrors afflicted Jurgis all the more cruelly, because he was always contrasting them with the opportunities he had lost. For instance, just now it was election time again—within five or six weeks the voters of the country would select a President; and he heard the wretches with whom he associated discussing it, and saw the streets of the city decorated with placards and banners—and what words could describe the pangs of grief and despair that shot through him?

For instance, there was a night during this cold spell. He had begged all day, for his very life, and found not a soul to heed him, until toward evening he saw an old lady getting off a street-car and helped her down with her umbrellas and bundles, and then told her his "hard-luck story," and after answering all her suspicious questions satisfactorily, was taken to a restaurant and saw a quarter paid down for a meal. And so he had soup and bread, and boiled beef and potatoes and beans, and pie and coffee, and came out with his skin stuffed tight as a football. And then, through the rain and the darkness, far down the street he saw red lights flaring and heard the thumping of a bass-drum; and his heart gave a leap, and he made for the place on the run—knowing without the asking that it meant a political meeting.

The campaign had so far been characterized by what the newspapers termed "apathy." For some reason the people refused to get excited over the struggle, and it was almost impossible to get them to come to meetings, or to make any noise when they did come. Those which had been held in Chicago so far had proven most dismal failures, and to-night, the speaker being no less a personage than a candidate for the vice-presidency of the nation, the political managers had been trembling with anxiety. But a merciful Providence had sent this storm of cold rain—and now all it was necessary to do was to set off a few fireworks, and thump awhile on a drum, and all the homeless wretches from a mile around would pour in and fill the hall! And then on the morrow the newspapers would have a chance to report the tremendous ovation, and to add that it had been no "silk-stocking" audience, either, proving clearly that the high-tariff sentiments of the distinguished candidate were pleasing to the wage-earners of the nation.[1]

So Jurgis found himself in a large hall, elaborately decorated with flags and bunting; and after the chairman had made his little speech, and the orator of the evening rose up, amid an uproar from the band—only fancy the emotions of Jurgis upon making the discovery that the personage was none other than the famous and eloquent Senator Spareshanks, who had addressed the "Doyle Republican Association" at the stockyards, and helped to elect Mike Scully's ten-pin setter to the Chicago Board of Aldermen!

In truth, the sight of the senator almost brought the tears into Jurgis's eyes. What agony it was to him to look back upon those golden hours, when he, too, had a place beneath the shadow of the plum tree![2] When he, too, had been of the elect, through whom the country is governed—when he had had a bung in the campaign-barrel

---

1. "Silk stocking" or wealthy voters might be expected to favor, along with Republicans, high tariffs to protect American business from foreign competition.
2. A favorable position, perhaps alluding to Ella Wheeler Wilcox's 1873 poem "The Tale the Robin Told": "I walked to-day in the grassy dell / Where the cunning ground-bird hides her nest. / And just where the plum-tree's shadow fell / I sat me down for a while to rest."

for his own! And this was another election in which the Republicans had all the money; and but for that one hideous accident he might have had a share of it, instead of being where he was!

The eloquent senator was explaining the system of Protection;[3] an ingenious device whereby the working-man permitted the manufacturer to charge him higher prices, in order that he might receive higher wages; thus taking his money out of his pocket with one hand, and putting a part of it back with the other. To the senator this unique arrangement had somehow become identified with the higher verities of the universe. It was because of it that Columbia was the gem of the ocean;[4] and all her future triumphs, her power and good repute among the nations, depended upon the zeal and fidelity with which each citizen held up the hands of those who were toiling to maintain it. The name of this heroic company was "the Grand Old Party"—[5]

And here the band began to play, and Jurgis sat up with a violent start. Singular as it may seem, Jurgis was making a desperate effort to understand what the senator was saying—to comprehend the extent of American prosperity, the enormous expansion of American commerce, and the Republic's future in the Pacific and in South America, and wherever else the oppressed were groaning. The reason for it was that he wanted to keep awake. He knew that if he allowed himself to fall asleep he would begin to snore loudly; and so he must listen—he must be interested! But he had eaten such a big dinner, and he was so exhausted, and the hall was so warm, and his seat was so comfortable! The senator's gaunt form began to grow dim and hazy, to tower before him and dance about, with figures of exports and imports. Once his neighbor gave him a savage poke in the ribs, and he sat up with a start and tried to look innocent; but then he was at it again, and men began to stare at him with annoyance, and to call out in vexation. Finally one of them called a policeman, who came and grabbed Jurgis by the collar, and jerked him to his feet, bewildered and terrified. Some of the audience turned to see the commotion, and Senator Spareshanks faltered in his speech; but a voice shouted cheerily: "We're just firing a bum! Go ahead, old sport!" And so the crowd roared, and the senator smiled genially, and went on; and in a few seconds poor Jurgis found himself landed out in the rain, with a kick and a string of curses.

He got into the shelter of a doorway and took stock of himself. He was not hurt, and he was not arrested—more than he had any

---

3. Part of a slogan of William McKinley (1843–1901) in the 1896 presidential campaign, "Protection" refers to tariffs on imports, which the 1897 Dingley Tariff had raised to an average of 57 percent.
4. "Columbia" refers to America. Allusion to "O, Columbia! The Gem of the Ocean," patriotic 19th-century song by David T. Shaw (1813–1898).
5. Republican Party, still known as the GOP.

right to expect. He swore at himself and his luck for a while, and then turned his thoughts to practical matters. He had no money, and no place to sleep; he must begin begging again.

He went out, hunching his shoulders together and shivering at the touch of the icy rain. Coming down the street toward him was a lady, well-dressed, and protected by an umbrella; and he turned and walked beside her. "Please, ma'am," he began, "could you lend me the price of a night's lodging? I'm a poor working-man—"

Then, suddenly, he stopped short. By the light of a street lamp he had caught sight of the lady's face. He knew her.

It was Alena Jasaityte, who had been the belle of his wedding-feast! Alena Jasaityte, who had looked so beautiful, and danced with such a queenly air, with Juozas Raczius, the teamster! Jurgis had only seen her once or twice afterward, for Juozas had thrown her over for another girl, and Alena had gone away from Packing-town, no one knew where. And now he met her here!

She was as much surprised as he was. "Jurgis Rudkus!" she gasped. "And what in the world is the matter with you?"

"I—I've had hard luck," he stammered. "I'm out of work, and I've no home and no money. And you, Alena—are you married?"

"No," she answered, "I'm not married, but I've got a good place."

They stood staring at each other for a few moments longer. Finally Alena spoke again. "Jurgis," she said, "I'd help you if I could, upon my word I would, but it happens that I've come out without my purse, and I honestly haven't a penny with me. I can do something better for you, though—I can tell you how to get help. I can tell you where Marija is."

Jurgis gave a start. "Marija!" he gasped.

"Yes," said Alena; "and she'll help you. She's got a place, and she's doing well; she'll be glad to see you."

It was not much more than a year since Jurgis had left Packing-town, feeling like one escaped from jail; and it had been from Marija and Elzbieta that he was escaping. But now, at the mere mention of them, his whole being cried out with joy. He wanted to see them; he wanted to go home! They would help him—they would be kind to him. In a flash he had thought over the situation. He had a good excuse for running away—his grief at the death of his son; and also he had a good excuse for not returning—the fact that they had left Packingtown. "All right," he said, "I'll go."

So she gave him a number on Clark Street, adding, "There's no need to give you my address, because Marija knows it." And Jurgis set out, without further ado.

He found a large brown-stone house of aristocratic appearance, and rang the basement bell. A young colored girl came to the door, opening it about an inch, and gazing at him suspiciously.

"What do you want?" she demanded.

"Does Marija Berczynskas live here?" he inquired.

"I dunno," said the girl. "What you want wid her?"

"I want to see her," said he; "she's a relative of mine."

The girl hesitated a moment. Then she opened the door and said, "Come in." Jurgis came and stood in the hall, and she continued; "I'll go see. What's yo' name?"

"Tell her it's Jurgis," he answered, and the girl went upstairs. She came back at the end of a minute or two, and replied, "Dey ain't no sich person here."

Jurgis's heart went down into his boots. "I was told this was where she lived!" he cried.

But the girl only shook her head. "De lady says dey ain't no sich person here," she said.

And he stood for a moment, hesitating, helpless with dismay. Then he turned to go to the door. At the same instant, however, there came a knock upon it, and the girl went to open it. Jurgis heard the shuffling of feet, and then heard her give a cry; and the next moment she sprang back, and past him, her eyes shining white with terror, and bounded up the stairway, screaming at the top of her lungs: *"Police! Police! We're pinched!"*

Jurgis stood for a second, bewildered. Then, seeing blue-coated forms rushing upon him, he sprang after the negress. Her cries had been the signal for a wild uproar above; the house was full of people, and as he entered the hallway he saw them rushing hither and thither, crying and screaming with alarm. There were men and women, the latter clad for the most part in wrappers, the former in all stages of *déshabille*. At one side Jurgis caught a glimpse of a big apartment with plush-covered chairs, and tables covered with trays and glasses. There were playing-cards scattered all over the floor—one of the tables had been upset, and bottles of wine were rolling about, their contents running out upon the carpet. There was a young girl who had fainted, and two men who were supporting her; and there were a dozen others crowding toward the front-door.

Suddenly, however, there came a series of resounding blows upon it, causing the crowd to give back. At the same instant a stout woman, with painted cheeks and diamonds in her ears, came running down the stairs, panting breathlessly: "To the rear! Quick!"

She led the way to a back staircase, Jurgis following; in the kitchen she pressed a spring, and a cupboard gave way and opened, disclosing a dark passageway. "Go in!" she cried to the crowd, which now amounted to twenty or thirty, and they began to pass through. Scarcely had the last one disappeared, however, before there were cries from in front, and then the panic-stricken throng poured out again, exclaiming: "They're there too! We're trapped!"

"Upstairs!" cried the woman, and there was another rush of the mob, women and men cursing and screaming and fighting to be first. One flight, two, three—and then there was a ladder to the roof, with a crowd packed at the foot of it, and one man at the top, straining and struggling to lift the trap-door. It was not to be stirred, however, and when the woman shouted up to unhook it, he answered: "It's already unhooked. There's somebody sitting on it!"

And a moment later came a voice from downstairs: "You might as well quit, you people. We mean business, this time."

So the crowd subsided; and a few moments later several policemen came up, staring here and there, and leering at their victims. Of the latter the men were for the most part frightened and sheepish-looking. The women took it as a joke, as if they were used to it—though if they had been pale, one could not have told, for the paint on their cheeks. One black-eyed young girl perched herself upon the top of the balustrade, and began to kick with her slippered foot at the helmets of the policemen, until one of them caught her by the ankle and pulled her down. On the floor below four or five other girls sat upon trunks in the hall, making fun of the procession which filed by them. They were noisy and hilarious,[6] and had evidently been drinking; one of them, who wore a bright red kimono, shouted and screamed in a voice that drowned out all the other sounds in the hall—and Jurgis took a glance at her, and then gave a start, and a cry, "Marija!"

She heard him, and glanced around; then she shrank back and half sprang to her feet in amazement. "Jurgis!" she gasped.

For a second or two they stood staring at each other. "How did you come here?" Marija exclaimed.

"I came to see you," he answered.

"When?"

"Just now."

"But how did you know—who told you I was here?"

"Alena Jasaityte. I met her on the street."

Again there was a silence, while they gazed at each other. The rest of the crowd was watching them, and so Marija got up and came closer to him. "And you?" Jurgis asked. "You live here?"

"Yes," said Marija, "I live here."

Then suddenly came a hail from below: "Get your clothes on now, girls, and come along. You'd best begin, or you'll be sorry—it's raining outside."

"Br-r-r!" shivered some one, and the women got up and entered the various doors which lined the hallway.

6. Boisterously merry.

"Come," said Marija, and took Jurgis into her room, which was a tiny place about eight by six, with a cot and a chair and a dressing-stand and some dresses hanging behind the door. There were clothes scattered about on the floor, and hopeless confusion everywhere,—boxes of rouge and bottles of perfume mixed with hats and soiled dishes on the dresser, and a pair of slippers and a clock and a whiskey bottle on a chair.

Marija had nothing on but a kimono and a pair of stockings; yet she proceeded to dress before Jurgis, and without even taking the trouble to close the door. He had by this time divined what sort of a place he was in; and he had seen a great deal of the world since he had left home, and was not easy to shock—and yet it gave him a painful start that Marija should do this. They had always been decent people at home, and it seemed to him that the memory of old times ought to have ruled her. But then he laughed at himself for a fool. What was he, to be pretending to decency!

"How long have you been living here?" he asked.

"Nearly a year," she answered.

"Why did you come?"

"I had to live," she said; "and I couldn't see the children starve."

He paused for a moment, watching her. "You were out of work?" he asked, finally.

"I got sick," she replied, "and after that I had no money. And then Stanislovas died—"

"Stanislovas dead!"

"Yes," said Marija, "I forgot. You didn't know about it."

"How did he die?"

"Rats killed him," she answered.

Jurgis gave a gasp. "*Rats* killed him!"

"Yes," said the other; she was bending over, lacing her shoes as she spoke. "He was working in an oil factory—at least he was hired by the men to get their beer. He used to carry cans on a long pole; and he'd drink a little out of each can, and one day he drank too much, and fell asleep in a corner, and got locked up in the place all night. When they found him the rats had killed him and eaten him nearly all up."

Jurgis sat, frozen with horror. Marija went on lacing up her shoes. There was a long silence.

Suddenly a big policeman came to the door. "Hurry up, there," he said.

"As quick as I can," said Marija, and she stood up and began putting on her corsets with feverish haste.

"Are the rest of the people alive?" asked Jurgis, finally.

"Yes," she said.

"Where are they?"

"They live not far from here. They're all right now."

"They are working?" he inquired.

"Elzbieta is," said Marija, "when she can. I take care of them most of the time—I'm making plenty of money now."

Jurgis was silent for a moment. "Do they know you live here—how you live?" he asked.

"Elzbieta knows," answered Marija. "I couldn't lie to her. And maybe the children have found out by this time. It's nothing to be ashamed of—we can't help it."

"And Tamoszius?" he asked. "Does *he* know?"

Marija shrugged her shoulders. "How do I know?" she said. "I haven't seen him for over a year. He got blood-poisoning and lost one finger, and couldn't play the violin any more; and then he went away."

Marija was standing in front of the glass fastening her dress. Jurgis sat staring at her. He could hardly believe that she was the same woman he had known in the old days; she was so quiet—so hard! It struck fear to his heart to watch her.

Then suddenly she gave a glance at him. "You look as if you had been having a rough time of it yourself," she said.

"I have," he answered. "I haven't a cent in my pockets, and nothing to do."

"Where have you been?"

"All over. I've been hoboing it. Then I went back to the yards—just before the strike." He paused for a moment, hesitating. "I asked for you," he added. "I found you had gone away, no one knew where. Perhaps you think I did you a dirty trick, running away as I did, Marija—"

"No," she answered, "I don't blame you. We never have—any of us. You did your best—the job was too much for us." She paused a moment, then added: "We were too ignorant—that was the trouble. We didn't stand any chance. If I'd known what I know now we'd have won out."

"You'd have come here?" said Jurgis.

"Yes," she answered; "but that's not what I meant. I meant you—how differently you would have behaved—about Ona."

Jurgis was silent; he had never thought of that aspect of it.

"When people are starving," the other continued, "and they have anything with a price, they ought to sell it, I say. I guess you realize it now when it's too late. Ona could have taken care of us all, in the beginning." Marija spoke without emotion, as one who had come to regard things from the business point of view.

"I—yes, I guess so," Jurgis answered hesitatingly. He did not add that he had paid three hundred dollars, and a foreman's job, for the satisfaction of knocking down "Phil" Connor a second time.

The policeman came to the door again just then. "Come on, now," he said. "Lively!"

"All right," said Marija, reaching for her hat, which was big enough to be a drum-major's, and full of ostrich feathers. She went out into the hall and Jurgis followed, the policeman remaining to look under the bed and behind the door.

"What's going to come of this?" Jurgis asked, as they started down the steps.

"The raid, you mean? Oh, nothing—it happens to us every now and then. The madame's having some sort of time with the police; I don't know what it is, but maybe they'll come to terms before morning. Anyhow, they won't do anything to you. They always let the men off."

"Maybe so," he responded, "but not me—I'm afraid I'm in for it."

"How do you mean?"

"I'm wanted by the police," he said, lowering his voice, though of course their conversation was in Lithuanian. "They'll send me up for a year or two, I'm afraid."

"Hell!" said Marija. "That's too bad. I'll see if I can't get you off."

Downstairs, where the greater part of the prisoners were now massed, she sought out the stout personage with the diamond earrings, and had a few whispered words with her. The latter then approached the police sergeant who was in charge of the raid. "Billy," she said, pointing to Jurgis, "there's a fellow who came in to see his sister. He'd just got in the door when you knocked. You aren't taking hoboes, are you?"

The sergeant laughed as he looked at Jurgis. "Sorry," he said, "but the orders are every one but the servants."

So Jurgis slunk in among the rest of the men, who kept dodging behind each other like sheep that have smelt a wolf. There were old men and young men, college boys and graybeards old enough to be their grandfathers; some of them wore evening-dress—there was no one among them save Jurgis who showed any signs of poverty.

When the round-up was completed, the doors were opened and the party marched out. Three patrol-wagons were drawn up at the curb, and the whole neighborhood had turned out to see the sport; there was much chaffing, and a universal craning of necks. The women stared about them with defiant eyes, or laughed and joked, while the men kept their heads bowed, and their hats pulled over their faces. They were crowded into the patrol-wagons as if into street-cars, and then off they went amid a din of cheers. At the station-house Jurgis gave a Polish name and was put into a cell with half a dozen others; and while these sat and talked in whispers, he lay down in a corner and gave himself up to his thoughts.

Jurgis had looked into the deepest reaches of the social pit, and grown used to the sights in them. Yet when he had thought of all humanity as vile and hideous, he had somehow always excepted his own family, that he had loved; and now this sudden horrible discovery—Marija a whore, and Elzbieta and the children living off her shame! Jurgis might argue with himself all he chose, that he had done worse, and was a fool for caring—but still he could not get over the shock of that sudden unveiling, he could not help being sunk in grief because of it. The depths of him were troubled and shaken, memories were stirred in him that had been sleeping so long he had counted them dead. Memories of the old life—his old hopes and his old yearnings, his old dreams of decency and independence! He saw Ona again, he heard her gentle voice pleading with him. He saw little Antanas, whom he had meant to make a man. He saw his trembling old father, who had blessed them all with his wonderful love. He lived again through that day of horror when he had discovered Ona's shame—God, how he had suffered, what a madman he had been! How dreadful it had all seemed to him; and now, to-day, he had sat and listened, and half agreed when Marija told him he had been a fool! Yes—told him that he ought to have sold his wife's honor and lived by it!—And then there was Stanislovas and his awful fate—that brief story which Marija had narrated so calmly, with such dull indifference! The poor little fellow, with his frost-bitten fingers and his terror of the snow—his wailing voice rang in Jurgis's ears, as he lay there in the darkness, until the sweat started on his forehead. Now and then he would quiver with a sudden spasm of horror, at the picture of little Stanislovas shut up in the deserted building and fighting for his life with the rats!

All these emotions had become strangers to the soul of Jurgis; it was so long since they had troubled him that he had ceased to think they might ever trouble him again. Helpless, trapped, as he was, what good did they do him—why should he ever have allowed them to torment him? It had been the task of his recent life to fight them down, to crush them out of him; never in his life would he have suffered from them again, save that they had caught him unawares, and overwhelmed him before he could protect himself. He heard the old voices of his soul, he saw its old ghosts beckoning to him, stretching out their arms to him! But they were far-off and shadowy, and the gulf between them was black and bottomless; they would fade away into the mists of the past once more. Their voices would die, and never again would he hear them—and so the last faint spark of manhood in his soul would flicker out.

Chapter XXVIII

After breakfast Jurgis was driven to the court, which was crowded with the prisoners and those who had come out of curiosity or in the hope of recognizing one of the men and getting a case for blackmail. The men were called up first, and reprimanded in a bunch, and then dismissed; but Jurgis, to his terror, was called separately, as being a suspicious-looking case. It was in this very same court that he had been tried, that time when his sentence had been "suspended"; it was the same judge, and the same clerk. The latter now stared at Jurgis, as if he half thought that he knew him; but the judge had no suspicions—just then his thoughts were upon a telephone message he was expecting from a friend of the police captain of the district, telling what disposition he should make of the case of "Polly" Simpson, as the "madame" of the house was known. Meantime, he listened to the story of how Jurgis had been looking for his sister, and advised him dryly to keep his sister in a better place; then he let him go, and proceeded to fine each of the girls five dollars, which fines were paid in a bunch from a wad of bills which Madame Polly extracted from her stocking.

Jurgis waited outside and walked home with Marija. The police had left the house, and already there were a few visitors; by evening the place would be running again, exactly as if nothing had happened. Meantime, Marija took Jurgis upstairs to her room, and they sat and talked. By daylight, Jurgis was able to observe that the color on her cheeks was not the old natural one of abounding health; her complexion was in reality a parchment yellow, and there were black rings under her eyes.

"Have you been sick?" he asked.

"Sick?" she said. "Hell!" (Marija had learned to scatter her conversation with as many oaths as a longshoreman or a mule driver.) "How can I ever be anything but sick, at this life?"

She fell silent for a moment, staring ahead of her gloomily. "It's morphine," she said, at last. "I seem to take more of it every day."

"What's that for?" he asked.

"It's the way of it; I don't know why. If it isn't that, it's drink. If the girls didn't booze they couldn't stand it any time at all. And the madame always gives them dope when they first come, and they learn to like it; or else they take it for headaches and such things, and get the habit that way. I've got it, I know; I've tried to quit, but I never will while I'm here."

"How long are you going to stay?" he asked.

"I don't know," she said. "Always, I guess. What else could I do?"

"Don't you save any money?"

"Save!" said Marija. "Good Lord, no! I get enough, I suppose, but it all goes. I get a half share, two dollars and a half for each customer, and sometimes I make twenty-five or thirty dollars a night, and you'd think I ought to save something out of that! But then I am charged for my room and my meals—and such prices as you never heard of; and then for extras, and drinks—for everything I get, and some I don't. My laundry bill is nearly twenty dollars each week alone—think of that! Yet what can I do? I either have to stand it or quit, and it would be the same anywhere else. It's all I can do to save the fifteen dollars I give Elzbieta each week, so the children can go to school."

Marija sat brooding in silence for a while; then, seeing that Jurgis was interested, she went on: "That's the way they keep the girls—they let them run up debts, so they can't get away. A young girl comes from abroad, and she doesn't know a word of English, and she gets into a place like this, and when she wants to go the madame shows her that she is a couple of hundred dollars in debt, and takes all her clothes away, and threatens to have her arrested if she doesn't stay and do as she's told. So she stays, and the longer she stays, the more in debt she gets. Often, too, they are girls that didn't know what they were coming to, that had hired out for housework. Did you notice that little French girl with the yellow hair, that stood next to me in the court?"

Jurgis answered in the affirmative.

"Well, she came to America about a year ago. She was a store-clerk, and she hired herself to a man to be sent here to work in a factory. There were six of them, all together, and they were brought to a house just down the street from here, and this girl was put into a room alone, and they gave her some dope in her food, and when she came to she found that she had been ruined. She cried, and screamed, and tore her hair, but she had nothing but a wrapper, and couldn't get away, and they kept her half insensible with drugs all the time, until she gave up. She never got outside of that place for ten months, and then they sent her away, because she didn't suit. I guess they'll put her out of here, too—she's getting to have crazy fits, from drinking absinthe.[1] Only one of the girls that came out with her got away, and she jumped out of a second-story window one night. There was a great fuss about that—maybe you heard of it."

"I did," said Jurgis, "I heard of it afterward." (It had happened in the place where he and Duane had taken refuge from their "country customer." The girl had become insane, fortunately for the police.)

"There's lots of money in it," said Marija—"they get as much as forty dollars a head for girls, and they bring them from all over. There

---

1. Toxic liqueur, 70–80 percent alcohol, which had harmful neurological effects.

are seventeen in this place, and nine different countries among them. In some places you might find even more. We have half a dozen French girls—I suppose it's because the madame speaks the language. French girls are bad, too, the worst of all, except for the Japanese. There's a place next door that's full of Japanese women, but I wouldn't live in the same house with one of them."

Marija paused for a moment or two, and then she added: "Most of the women here are pretty decent—you'd be surprised. I used to think they did it because they liked to; but fancy a woman selling herself to every kind of man that comes, old or young, black or white—and doing it because she likes to!"

"Some of them say they do," said Jurgis.

"I know," said she; "they say anything. They're in, and they know they can't get out. But they didn't like it when they began—you'd find out—it's always misery! There's a little Jewish girl here who used to run errands for a milliner, and got sick and lost her place; and she was four days on the streets without a mouthful of food, and then she went to a place just around the corner and offered herself, and they made her give up her clothes before they would give her a bite to eat!"

Marija sat for a minute or two, brooding sombrely. "Tell me about yourself, Jurgis," she said, suddenly. "Where have you been?"

So he told her the long story of his adventures since his flight from home; his life as a tramp, and his work in the freight tunnels, and the accident; and then of Jack Duane, and of his political career in the stockyards, and his downfall and subsequent failures. Marija listened with sympathy; it was easy to believe the tale of his late starvation, for his face showed it all. "You found me just in the nick of time," she said. "I'll stand by you—I'll help you till you can get some work."

"I don't like to let you—" he began.

"Why not? Because I'm here?"

"No, not that," he said. "But I went off and left you—"

"Nonsense!" said Marija. "Don't think about it. I don't blame you."

"You must be hungry," she said, after a minute or two. "You stay here to lunch—I'll have something up in the room."

She pressed a button, and a colored woman came to the door and took her order. "It's nice to have somebody to wait on you," she observed, with a laugh, as she lay back on the bed.

As the prison breakfast had not been liberal, Jurgis had a good appetite, and they had a little feast together, talking meanwhile of Elzbieta and the children and old times. Shortly before they were through, there came another colored girl, with the message that the "madame" wanted Marija—"Lithuanian Mary," as they called her here.

"That means you have to go," she said to Jurgis.

So he got up, and she gave him the new address of the family, a tenement over in the Ghetto district. "You go there," she said. "They'll be glad to see you."

But Jurgis stood hesitating.

"I—I don't like to," he said. "Honest, Marija, why don't you just give me a little money and let me look for work first?"

"How do you need money?" was her reply. "All you want is something to eat and a place to sleep, isn't it?"

"Yes," he said; "but then I don't like to go there after I left them— and while I have nothing to do, and while you—you—"

"Go on!" said Marija, giving him a push. "What are you talking?—I won't give you money," she added, as she followed him to the door, "because you'll drink it up, and do yourself harm. Here's a quarter for you now, and go along, and they'll be so glad to have you back, you won't have time to feel ashamed. Good-by!"

So Jurgis went out, and walked down the street to think it over. He decided that he would first try to get work, and so he put in the rest of the day wandering here and there among factories and warehouses without success. Then, when it was nearly dark, he concluded to go home, and set out; but he came to a restaurant, and went in and spent his quarter for a meal; and when he came out he changed his mind—the night was pleasant, and he would sleep somewhere outside, and put in the morrow hunting, and so have one more chance of a job. So he started away again, when suddenly he chanced to look about him, and found that he was walking down the same street and past the same hall where he had listened to the political speech the night before. There was no red fire and no band now, but there was a sign out, announcing a meeting, and a stream of people pouring in through the entrance. In a flash Jurgis had decided that he would chance it once more, and sit down and rest while making up his mind what to do. There was no one taking tickets, so it must be a free show again.

He entered. There were no decorations in the hall this time; but there was quite a crowd upon the platform, and almost every seat in the place was filled. He took one of the last, far in the rear, and straightway forgot all about his surroundings. Would Elzbieta think that he had come to sponge off her, or would she understand that he meant to get to work again and do his share? Would she be decent to him, or would she scold him? If only he could get some sort of a job before he went—if that last boss had only been willing to try him!

—Then suddenly Jurgis looked up. A tremendous roar had burst from the throats of the crowd, which by this time had packed the hall to the very doors. Men and women were standing up, waving handkerchiefs, shouting, yelling. Evidently the speaker had arrived,

thought Jurgis; what fools they were making of themselves! What
were they expecting to get out of it anyhow—what had they to do
with elections, with governing the country? Jurgis had been behind
the scenes in politics.

He went back to his thoughts, but with one further fact to reckon
with—that he was caught here. The hall was now filled to the doors;
and after the meeting it would be too late for him to go home, so he
would have to make the best of it outside. Perhaps it would be better to go home in the morning, anyway, for the children would be at
school, and he and Elzbieta could have a quiet explanation. She
always had been a reasonable person; and he really did mean to do
right. He would manage to persuade her of it—and besides, Marija
was willing, and Marija was furnishing the money. If Elzbieta were
ugly, he would tell her that in so many words.

So Jurgis went on meditating; until finally, when he had been an
hour or two in the hall, there began to prepare itself a repetition of
the dismal catastrophe of the night before. Speaking had been going
on all the time, and the audience was clapping its hands and shouting, thrilling with excitement; and little by little the sounds were
beginning to blur in Jurgis's ears, and his thoughts were beginning
to run together, and his head to wobble and nod. He caught himself
many times, as usual, and made desperate resolutions; but the hall
was hot and close, and his long walk and his dinner were too much
for him—in the end his head sank forward and he went off again.

And then again some one nudged him, and he sat up with his old
terrified start! He had been snoring again, of course! And now what?
He fixed his eyes ahead of him, with painful intensity, staring at the
platform as if nothing else ever had interested him, or ever could
interest him, all his life. He imagined the angry exclamations, the
hostile glances; he imagined the policeman striding toward him—
reaching for his neck.—Or was he to have one more chance? Were
they going to let him alone this time? He sat trembling, waiting—

And then suddenly came a voice in his ear, a woman's voice, gentle and sweet, "If you would try to listen, comrade, perhaps you
would be interested."

Jurgis was more startled by that than he would have been by the
touch of a policeman. He still kept his eyes fixed ahead, and did not
stir; but his heart gave a great leap. Comrade! Who was it that called
him "comrade"?

He waited long, long; and at last, when he was sure that he was
no longer watched, he stole a glance out of the corner of his eyes at
the woman who sat beside him. She was young and beautiful; she
wore fine clothes, and was what is called a "lady." And she called
him "comrade"!

He turned a little, carefully, so that he could see her better; then he began to watch her, fascinated. She had apparently forgotten all about him, and was looking toward the platform. A man was speaking there—Jurgis heard his voice vaguely; but all his thoughts were for this woman's face. A feeling of alarm stole over him as he stared at her. It made his flesh creep. What was the matter with her, what could be going on, to affect any one like that? She sat as one turned to stone, her hands clenched tightly in her lap, so tightly that he could see the cords standing out in her wrists. There was a look of excitement upon her face, of tense effort, as of one struggling mightily, or witnessing a struggle. There was a faint quivering of her nostrils; and now and then she would moisten her lips with feverish haste. Her bosom rose and fell as she breathed, and her excitement seemed to mount higher and higher, and then to sink away again, like a boat tossing upon ocean surges. What was it? What was the matter? It must be something that the man was saying, up there on the platform. What sort of a man was he? And what sort of a thing was this, anyhow?—So all at once it occurred to Jurgis to look at the speaker.

It was like coming suddenly upon some wild sight of nature,—a mountain forest lashed by a tempest, a ship tossed about upon a stormy sea. Jurgis had an unpleasant sensation, a sense of confusion, of disorder, of wild and meaningless uproar. The man was tall and gaunt, as haggard as his auditor himself; a thin black beard covered half of his face, and one could see only two black hollows where the eyes were. He was speaking rapidly, in great excitement; he used many gestures—as he spoke he moved here and there upon the stage, reaching with his long arms as if to seize each person in his audience. His voice was deep, like an organ; it was some time, however, before Jurgis thought of the voice—he was too much occupied with his eyes to think of what the man was saying. But suddenly it seemed as if the speaker had begun pointing straight at him, as if he had singled him out particularly for his remarks; and so Jurgis became suddenly aware of the voice, trembling, vibrant with emotion, with pain and longing, with a burden of things unutterable, not to be compassed by words. To hear it was to be suddenly arrested, to be gripped, transfixed.

"You listen to these things," the man was saying, "and you say, 'Yes, they are true, but they have been that way always.' Or you say, 'Maybe it will come, but not in my time—it will not help me.' And so you return to your daily round of toil, you go back to be ground up for profits in the world-wide mill of economic might! To toil long hours for another's advantage; to live in mean and squalid homes, to work in dangerous and unhealthful places; to wrestle with the spectres of hunger and privation, to take your chances of accident, disease, and death. And each day the struggle becomes fiercer, the pace more cruel; each day you have to toil a little harder, and feel the iron hand of circumstance close upon you a little tighter. Months pass, years maybe—and then you come again; and again I am here to plead with you, to know if want and misery have yet done their work with you, if injustice and oppression have yet opened your eyes! I shall still be waiting—there is nothing else that I can do. There is no wilderness where I can hide from these things, there is no haven where I can escape them; though I travel to the ends of the earth, I find the same accursed system,—I find that all the fair and noble impulses of humanity, the dreams of poets and the agonies of martyrs, are shackled and bound in the service of organized and predatory Greed! And therefore I cannot rest, I cannot be silent; therefore I cast aside comfort and happiness, health and good repute—and go out into the world and cry out the pain of my spirit! Therefore I am not to be silenced by poverty and sickness, not by hatred and obloquy, by threats and ridicule—not by prison and persecution, if they should come—not by any power that is upon the earth or above the earth, that was, or is, or ever can be created. If I fail to-night, I can only try to-morrow; knowing that the fault must be mine—that if once the vision of my soul were spoken upon earth, if once the anguish of its defeat were uttered in human speech, it would break the stoutest barriers of prejudice, it would shake the most sluggish soul to action! It would abash the most cynical, it would terrify the most selfish; and the voice of mockery would be silenced, and fraud and falsehood would slink back into their dens, and the truth would stand forth alone! For I speak with the voice of the millions who are voiceless! Of them that are oppressed and have no comforter! Of the disinherited of life, for whom there is no respite and no deliverance, to whom the world is a prison, a dungeon of torture, a tomb! With the voice of the little child who toils to-night in a Southern cotton-mill, staggering with exhaustion, numb with agony, and knowing no hope but the grave! Of the mother who sews by candle-light in her tenement-garret, weary and weeping, smitten with the mortal hunger of her babes! Of the man who lies upon a bed of rags, wrestling in his last sickness and leaving his loved ones to perish! Of the young girl who, somewhere at this moment, is walking the streets of this horrible city, beaten and starving, and making her choice between the brothel and the lake! With the voice of those, whoever and wherever they may be, who are caught beneath the wheels of the juggernaut of Greed! With the voice of humanity, calling for deliverance! Of the everlasting soul of Man, arising from the dust; breaking its way out of its prison—rending the bands of oppression and ignorance—groping its way to the light!"

The speaker paused. There was an instant of silence, while men caught their breaths, and then like a single sound there came a cry from a thousand people.—Through it all Jurgis sat still, motionless and rigid, his eyes fixed upon the speaker; he was trembling, smitten with wonder.

Suddenly the man raised his hands, and silence fell, and he began again.

"I plead with you," he said, "whoever you may be, provided that you care about the truth; but most of all I plead with working-men, with those to whom the evils I portray are not mere matters of sentiment, to be dallied and toyed with, and then perhaps put aside and forgotten—to whom they are the grim and relentless realities of the daily grind, the chains upon their limbs, the lash upon their backs, the iron in their souls. To you, working-men! To you, the toilers, who have made this land, and have no voice in its councils! To you, whose lot it is to sow that others may reap, to labor and obey, and ask no more than the wages of a beast of burden, the food and shelter to keep you alive from day to day. It is to you that I come with my message of salvation, it is to you that I appeal. I know how much it is to ask of you—I know, for I have been in your place, I have lived your life, and there is no man before me here to-night who knows it better. I have known what it is to be a street-waif, a boot-black, living upon a crust of bread and sleeping in cellar stairways and under empty wagons. I have known what it is to dare and to aspire, to dream mighty dreams and to see them perish—to see all the fair flowers of my spirit trampled into the mire by the wild beast powers of life. I know what is the price that a working-man pays for knowledge—I have paid for it with food and sleep, with agony of body and mind, with health, almost with life itself; and so, when I come to you with a story of hope and freedom, with the vision of a new earth to be created, of a new labor to be dared, I am not surprised that I find you sordid and material,[2] sluggish and incredulous. That I do not despair is because I know also the forces that are driving behind you—because I know the raging lash of poverty, the sting of contempt and mastership, 'the insolence of office and the spurns.'[3] Because I feel sure that in the crowd that has come to me to-night, no matter how many may be dull and heedless, no matter how many may have come out of idle curiosity, or in order to ridicule—there will be some one man whom pain and suffering have made desperate, whom some chance vision of wrong and horror has startled and shocked into attention. And to him my

---

2. Concerned with physical rather than spiritual things; *sordid*: degraded, especially from poverty.
3. *Hamlet* III.i.72, from the "to be or not to be" soliloquy, in which Hamlet asks whether it is better to endure inequities or try to end them.

words will come like a sudden flash of lightning to one who travels in darkness—revealing the way before him, the perils and the obstacles—solving all problems, making all difficulties clear! The scales will fall from his eyes,[4] the shackles will be torn from his limbs—he will leap up with a cry of thankfulness, he will stride forth a free man at last! A man delivered from his self-created slavery! A man who will never more be trapped—whom no blandishments will cajole, whom no threats will frighten; who from to-night on will move forward, and not backward, who will study and understand, who will gird on his sword and take his place in the army of his comrades and brothers. Who will carry the good tidings to others, as I have carried them to him—the priceless gift of liberty and light that is neither mine nor his, but is the heritage of the soul of man! Working-men, working-men—comrades! open your eyes and look about you! You have lived so long in the toil and heat that your senses are dulled, your souls are numbed; but realize once in your lives this world in which you dwell—tear off the rags of its customs and conventions—behold it as it is, in all its hideous nakedness! Realize it, *realize it!* Realize that out upon the plains of Manchuria to-night two hostile armies are facing each other—that now, while we are seated here, a million human beings may be hurled at each other's throats, striving with the fury of maniacs to tear each other to pieces![5] And this in the twentieth century, nineteen hundred years since the Prince of Peace was born on earth! Nineteen hundred years that his words have been preached as divine, and here two armies of men are rending and tearing each other like the wild beasts of the forest! Philosophers have reasoned, prophets have denounced, poets have wept and pleaded—and still this hideous Monster roams at large! We have schools and colleges, newspapers and books; we have searched the heavens and the earth, we have weighed and probed and reasoned—and all to equip men to destroy each other! We call it War, and pass it by—but do not put me off with platitudes and conventions—come with me, come with me—*realize it!* See the bodies of men pierced by bullets, blown into pieces by bursting shells! Hear the crunching of the bayonet, plunged into human flesh; hear the groans and shrieks of agony, see the faces of men crazed by pain, turned into fiends by fury and hate! Put your hand upon that piece of flesh—it is hot and quivering—just now it was a part of a man! This blood is still steaming—it was driven by a human heart! Almighty God! and this goes on—it is systematic, organized, premeditated! And we know it, and read of it,

---

4. At Saul's conversion to Christianity, three days of blindness end when scales seem to fall from his eyes and he is baptized (Acts 9); hence an image of revelation and conversion.
5. Allusion to the Russo-Japanese War (1904–05), a conflict sparked by the two countries' rival imperial ambitions.

and take it for granted; our papers tell of it, and the presses are not stopped—our churches know of it, and do not close their doors— the people behold it, and do not rise up in horror and revolution!

"Or perhaps Manchuria is too far away for you—come home with me then, come here to Chicago. Here in this city to-night ten thousand women are shut up in foul pens, and driven by hunger to sell their bodies to live. And we know it, we make it a jest! And these women are made in the image of your mothers, they may be your sisters, your daughters; the child whom you left at home to-night, whose laughing eyes will greet you in the morning—that fate may be waiting for her! To-night in Chicago there are ten thousand men, homeless and wretched, willing to work and begging for a chance, yet starving, and fronting in terror the awful winter cold! To-night in Chicago there are a hundred thousand children wearing out their strength and blasting their lives in the effort to earn their bread! There are a hundred thousand mothers who are living in misery and squalor, struggling to earn enough to feed their little ones! There are a hundred thousand old people, cast off and helpless, waiting for death to take them from their torments! There are a million people, men and women and children, who share the curse of the wage-slave; who toil every hour they can stand and see, for just enough to keep them alive; who are condemned till the end of their days to monotony and weariness, to hunger and misery, to heat and cold, to dirt and disease, to ignorance and drunkenness and vice! And then turn over the page with me, and gaze upon the other side of the picture. There are a thousand—ten thousand, maybe—who are the masters of these slaves, who own their toil. They do nothing to earn what they receive, they do not even have to ask for it—it comes to them of itself, their only care is to dispose of it. They live in palaces, they riot in luxury and extravagance—such as no words can describe, as makes the imagination reel and stagger, makes the soul grow sick and faint. They spend hundreds of dollars for a pair of shoes, a handkerchief, a garter; they spend millions for horses and automobiles and yachts, for palaces and banquets, for little shiny stones with which to deck their bodies. Their life is a contest among themselves for supremacy in ostentation and recklessness, in the destroying of useful and necessary things, in the wasting of the labor and the lives of their fellow-creatures, the toil and anguish of the nations, the sweat and tears and blood of the human race! It is all theirs—it comes to them; just as all the springs pour into streamlets, and the streamlets into rivers, and the rivers into the ocean— so, automatically and inevitably, all the wealth of society comes to them. The farmer tills the soil, the miner digs in the earth, the weaver tends the loom, the mason carves the stone; the clever man invents, the shrewd man directs, the wise man studies, the inspired man sings—and all the result, the products of the labor of brain and muscle, are gathered into one stupendous stream and poured into their laps! The whole of society is in their grip, the whole labor of the world lies at their mercy—and like fierce wolves they rend and destroy, like ravening vultures they devour and tear! The whole power of mankind belongs to them, forever and beyond recall—do what it can, strive as it will, humanity lives for them and dies for them! They own not merely the labor of society, they have bought the governments; and everywhere they use their raped and stolen power to intrench themselves in their privileges, to dig wider and deeper the channels through which the river of profits flows to them!—And you, working-men, working-men! You have been brought up to it, you plod on like beasts of burden, thinking only of the day and its pain—yet is there a man among you who can believe that such a system will continue forever—is there a man here in this audience to-night so hardened and debased that he dare rise up before me and say that he believes it can continue forever; that the product of the labor of society, the means of existence of the human race, will always belong to idlers and parasites, to be spent for the gratification of vanity and lust—to be spent for any purpose whatever, to be at the disposal of any individual will whatever—that somehow, somewhen, the labor of humanity will not belong to humanity, to be used for the purposes of humanity, to be controlled by the will of humanity? And if this is ever to be, how is it to be—what power is there that will bring it about? Will it be the task of your masters, do you think—will they write the charter of your liberties? Will they forge you the sword of your deliverance, will they marshal you the army and lead it to the fray? Will their wealth be spent for the purpose—will they build colleges and churches to teach you, will they print papers to herald your progress, and organize political parties to guide and carry on the struggle? Can you not see that the task is your task—yours to dream, yours to resolve, yours to execute? That if ever it is carried out, it will be in the face of every obstacle that wealth and mastership can oppose—in the face of ridicule and slander, of hatred and persecution, of the bludgeon and the jail? That it will be by the power of your naked bosoms, opposed to the rage of oppression! By the grim and bitter teaching of blind and merciless affliction! By the painful gropings of the untutored mind, by the feeble stammerings of the uncultured voice! By the sad and lonely hunger of the spirit; by seeking and striving and yearning, by heartache and despairing, by agony and sweat of blood! It will be by money paid for with hunger, by knowledge stolen from sleep, by thoughts communicated under the shadow of the gallows! It will be a movement beginning in the far-off past, a thing obscure and unhonored, a thing easy to ridicule, easy to despise; a thing unlovely, wearing the aspect of vengeance and hate—but to you, the working-man, the wage-slave, calling with a voice insistent, imperious—with a voice that you cannot escape, wherever upon the earth you may be! With the voice of all your wrongs, with the voice of all your desires; with the voice of your duty and your hope—of everything in the world that is worth while to you! The voice of the poor, demanding that poverty shall cease! The voice of the oppressed, pronouncing the doom of oppression! The voice of power, wrought out of suffering—of resolution, crushed out of weakness—of joy and courage, born in the bottomless pit of anguish and despair! The voice of Labor, despised and outraged; a mighty giant, lying prostrate—mountainous, colossal, but blinded, bound, and ignorant of his strength. And now a dream of resistance haunts him, hope battling with fear; until suddenly he stirs, and a fetter snaps—and a thrill shoots through him, to the farthest ends of his huge body, and in a flash the dream becomes an act! He starts, he lifts himself; and the bands are shattered, the burdens roll off him; he rises—towering, gigantic; he springs to his feet, he shouts in his new-born exultation—"[6]

And the speaker's voice broke suddenly, with the stress of his feelings; he stood with his arms stretched out above him, and the power of his vision seemed to lift him from the floor. The audience came to its feet with a yell; men waved their arms, laughing aloud in their excitement. And Jurgis was with them, he was shouting to tear his throat; shouting because he could not help it, because the stress of his feeling was more than he could bear. It was not merely the man's words, the torrent of his eloquence. It was his presence, it was his voice: a voice with strange intonations that rang through the chambers of the soul like the clanging of a bell—that gripped the listener like a mighty hand about his body, that shook him and startled him with sudden fright, with a sense of things not of earth, of mysteries never spoken before, of presences of awe and terror! There was an unfolding of vistas before him, a breaking of the ground beneath him, an upheaving, a stirring, a trembling; he felt himself suddenly a mere man no longer—there were powers within him undreamed of, there were demon forces contending, age-long wonders struggling to be born; and he sat oppressed with pain and joy, while a tingling stole down into his finger-tips, and his breath came hard and fast. The sentences of this man were to Jurgis like the crashing of thunder in his soul; a flood of emotion surged up in him—all his old hopes and longings, his old griefs and rages and despairs. All that he had ever felt in his whole life seemed to come back to him at once, and with one new

6. Probably an allusion to the first voyage in *Gulliver's Travels* (1726), by the Anglo-Irish writer Jonathan Swift (1667–1745). When Gulliver awakes in the land of the tiny humans called Lilliputians, he finds they have tied him down with strings he can easily break.

emotion, hardly to be described. That he should have suffered such oppressions and such horrors was bad enough; but that he should have been crushed and beaten by them, that he should have submitted, and forgotten, and lived in peace—ah, truly that was a thing not to be put into words, a thing not to be borne by a human creature, a thing of terror and madness! "What," asks the prophet, "is the murder of them that kill the body, to the murder of them that kill the soul?"[7] And Jurgis was a man whose soul had been murdered, who had ceased to hope and to struggle—who had made terms with degradation and despair; and now, suddenly, in one awful convulsion, the black and hideous fact was made plain to him! There was a falling in of all the pillars of his soul, the sky seemed to split above him—he stood there, with his clenched hands upraised, his eyes bloodshot, and the veins standing out purple in his face, roaring in the voice of a wild beast, frantic, incoherent, maniacal. And when he could shout no more he still stood there, gasping, and whispering hoarsely to himself: "By God! By God! By God!"

7. The prophet is Jesus (Matthew 10:27–28).

Chapter XXIX

The man had gone back to a seat upon the platform, and Jurgis realized that his speech was over. The applause continued for several
minutes; and then some one started a song, and the crowd took it
up, and the place shook with it. Jurgis had never heard it, and he
could not make out the words, but the wild and wonderful spirit of
it seized upon him—it was the Marseillaise![1] As stanza after stanza
of it thundered forth, he sat with his hands clasped, trembling in
every nerve. He had never been so stirred in his life—it was a miracle that had been wrought in him. He could not think at all, he
was stunned; yet he knew that in the mighty upheaval that had taken
place in his soul, a new man had been born. He had been torn out
of the jaws of destruction, he had been delivered from the thraldom
of despair; the whole world had been changed for him—he was free,
he was free! Even if he were to suffer as he had before, even if he
were to beg and starve, nothing would be the same to him; he would
understand it, and bear it. He would no longer be the sport of circumstances, he would be a man, with a will and a purpose; he would
have something to fight for, something to die for, if need be! Here
were men who would show him and help him; and he would have
friends and allies, he would dwell in the sight of justice, and walk
arm in arm with power.

The audience subsided again, and Jurgis sat back. The chairman
of the meeting came forward and began to speak. His voice sounded
thin and futile after the other's, and to Jurgis it seemed a profana-
tion. Why should any one else speak, after that miraculous man—
why should they not all sit in silence? The chairman was explaining
that a collection would now be taken up to defray the expenses of
the meeting, and for the benefit of the campaign fund of the party.
Jurgis heard; but he had not a penny to give, and so his thoughts
went elsewhere again.

He kept his eyes fixed on the orator, who sat in an armchair, his
head leaning on his hand and his attitude indicating exhaustion. But
suddenly he stood up again, and Jurgis heard the chairman of the
meeting saying that the speaker would now answer any questions
which the audience might care to put to him. The man came forward, and some one—a woman—arose and asked about some
opinion the speaker had expressed concerning Tolstoi.[2] Jurgis had
never heard of Tolstoi, and did not care anything about him. Why

1. Hymn of the French Revolution (see below, p. 514, n. 6), written to commemorate the
taking of the Bastille, a state prison.
2. Leo Tolstoy (1828–1910), Russian novelist and philosopher whose ideas influenced
many reform movements. After converting to Christianity, he preached nonviolence

should any one want to ask such questions, after an address like that? The thing was not to talk, but to do; the thing was to get hold of others and rouse them, to organize them and prepare for the fight!

But still the discussion went on, in ordinary conversational tones, and it brought Jurgis back to the everyday world. A few minutes ago he had felt like seizing the hand of the beautiful lady by his side, and kissing it; he had felt like flinging his arms about the neck of the man on the other side of him. And now he began to realize again that he was a "hobo,"—that he was ragged and dirty, and smelt bad, and had no place to sleep that night!

And so, at last, when the meeting broke up, and the audience started to leave, poor Jurgis was in an agony of uncertainty. He had not thought of leaving—he had thought that the vision must last forever, that he had found comrades and brothers. But now he would go out, and the thing would fade away, and he would never be able to find it again! He sat in his seat, frightened and wondering; but others in the same row wanted to get out, and so he had to stand up and move along. As he was swept down the aisle he looked from one person to another, wistfully; they were all excitedly discussing the address—but there was nobody who offered to discuss it with him. He was near enough to the door to feel the night air, when desperation seized him. He knew nothing at all about that speech he had heard, not even the name of the orator; and he was to go away—no, no, it was preposterous, he must speak to some one; he must find that man himself and tell him. He would not despise him, tramp as he was!

So he stepped into an empty row of seats and watched, and when the crowd had thinned out, he started toward the platform. The speaker was gone; but there was a stage-door that stood open, with people passing in and out, and no one on guard. Jurgis summoned up his courage and went in, and down a hallway, and to the door of a room where many people were crowded. No one paid any attention to him, and he pushed in, and in a corner he saw the man he sought. The orator sat in a chair, with his shoulders sunk together and his eyes half closed; his face was ghastly pale, almost greenish in hue, and one arm lay limp at his side. A big man with spectacles on stood near him, and kept pushing back the crowd, saying, "Stand away a little, please, can't you see the comrade is worn out?"

So Jurgis stood watching, while five or ten minutes passed. Now and then the man would look up, and address a word or two to those who were near him; and, at last, on one of these occasions, his glance rested on Jurgis. There seemed to be a slight hint of inquiry about it, and a sudden impulse seized the other. He stepped forward.

---

and simplicity of life, insisting on putting beliefs into practice. Sinclair admired Tolstoy's belief that art was inherently moral.

"I wanted to thank you, sir!" he began, in breathless haste. "I could not go away without telling you how much—how glad I am I heard you. I—I didn't know anything about it all—"

The big man with the spectacles, who had moved away, came back at this moment. "The comrade is too tired to talk to any one—" he began; but the other held up his hand.

"Wait," he said. "He has something to say to me." And then he looked into Jurgis's face. "You want to know more about Socialism?" he asked.

Jurgis started. "I—I—" he stammered. "Is it Socialism? I didn't know. I want to know about what you spoke of—I want to help. I have been through all that."

"Where do you live?" asked the other.

"I have no home," said Jurgis, "I am out of work."

"You are a foreigner, are you not?"

"Lithuanian, sir."

The man thought for a moment, and then turned to his friend. "Who is there, Walters?" he asked. "There is Ostrinski—but he is a Pole—"

"Ostrinski speaks Lithuanian," said the other.

"All right, then; would you mind seeing if he has gone yet?"

The other started away, and the speaker looked at Jurgis again. He had deep, black eyes, and a face full of gentleness and pain. "You must excuse me, comrade," he said. "I am just tired out—I have spoken every day for the last month. I will introduce you to some one who will be able to help you as well as I could—"

The messenger had had to go no further than the door; he came back, followed by a man whom he introduced to Jurgis as "Comrade Ostrinski." Comrade Ostrinski was a little man, scarcely up to Jurgis's shoulder, wizened and wrinkled, very ugly, and slightly lame. He had on a long-tailed black coat, worn green at the seams and the buttonholes; his eyes must have been weak, for he wore green spectacles, that gave him a grotesque appearance. But his hand clasp was hearty, and he spoke in Lithuanian, which warmed Jurgis to him.

"You want to know about Socialism?" he said. "Surely. Let us go out and take a stroll, where we can be quiet and talk some."

And so Jurgis bade farewell to the master wizard, and went out. Ostrinski asked where he lived, offering to walk in that direction; and so he had to explain once more that he was without a home. At the other's request he told his story; how he had come to America, and what had happened to him in the stockyards, and how his family had been broken up, and how he had become a wanderer. So much the little man heard, and then he pressed Jurgis's arm tightly. "You have been through the mill, comrade!" he said. "We will make a fighter out of you!"

Then Ostrinski in turn explained his circumstances. He would have asked Jurgis to his home—but he had only two rooms, and had no bed to offer. He would have given up his own bed, but his wife was ill. Later on, when he understood that otherwise Jurgis would have to sleep in a hallway, he offered him his kitchen-floor, a chance which the other was only too glad to accept. "Perhaps tomorrow we can do better," said Ostrinski. "We try not to let a comrade starve."

Ostrinski's home was in the Ghetto district, where he had two rooms in the basement of a tenement. There was a baby crying as they entered, and he closed the door leading into the bedroom. He had three young children, he explained, and a baby had just come. He drew up two chairs near the kitchen stove, adding that Jurgis must excuse the disorder of the place, since at such a time one's domestic arrangements were upset. Half of the kitchen was given up to a work-bench, which was piled with clothing, and Ostrinski explained that he was a "pants-finisher." He brought great bundles of clothing here to his home, where he and his wife worked on them. He made a living at it, but it was getting harder all the time, because his eyes were failing. What would come when they gave out he could not tell; there had been no saving anything—a man could barely keep alive by twelve or fourteen hours' work a day. The finishing of pants did not take much skill, and anybody could learn it, and so the pay was forever getting less. That was the competitive wage system; and if Jurgis wanted to understand what Socialism was, it was there he had best begin. The workers were dependent upon a job to exist from day to day, and so they bid against each other, and no man could get more than the lowest man would consent to work for. And thus the mass of the people were always in a life-and-death struggle with poverty. That was "competition," so far as it concerned the wage-earner, the man who had only his labor to sell; to those on top, the exploiters, it appeared very differently, of course—there were few of them, and they could combine and dominate, and their power would be unbreakable. And so all over the world two classes were forming, with an unbridged chasm between them,—the capitalist class, with its enormous fortunes, and the proletariat, bound into slavery by unseen chains. The latter were a thousand to one in numbers, but they were ignorant and helpless, and they would remain at the mercy of their exploiters until they were organized—until they had become "class-conscious." It was a slow and weary process, but it would go on—it was like the movement of a glacier, once it was started it could never be stopped. Every Socialist did his share, and lived upon the vision of the "good time coming,"—when the working-class should go to the polls and seize the powers of government, and put an end to private property in the means of production. No matter how poor a man was, or how much he suffered, he could never be really unhappy while he knew of that future; even if he did not live to see it himself, his children would, and, to a Socialist, the victory of his class was his victory. Also he had always the progress to encourage him; here in Chicago, for instance, the movement was growing by leaps and bounds.[3] Chicago was the industrial centre of the country, and nowhere else were the unions so strong; but their organizations did the workers little good, for the employers were organized, also; and so the strikes generally failed, and as fast as the unions were broken up the men were coming over to the Socialists.

Ostrinski explained the organization of the party, the machinery by which the proletariat was educating itself. There were "locals" in every big city and town, and they were being organized rapidly in the smaller places; a local had anywhere from six to a thousand members, and there were fourteen hundred of them in all, with a total of about twenty-five thousand members, who paid dues to support the organization. "Local Cook County," as the city organization was called, had eighty branch locals, and it alone was spending several thousand dollars in the campaign. It published a weekly in English, and one each in Bohémian and German; also there was a monthly published in Chicago, and a cooperative publishing house, that issued a million and a half of Socialist books and pamphlets every year. All this was the growth of the last few years—there had been almost nothing of it when Ostrinski first came to Chicago.

Ostrinski was a Pole, about fifty years of age. He had lived in Silesia, a member of a despised and persecuted race, and had taken part in the proletarian movement in the early seventies, when Bismarck, having conquered France, had turned his policy of blood and iron upon the "International."[4] Ostrinski himself had twice been in jail, but he had been young then, and had not cared. He had had more of his share of the fight, though, for just when Socialism had broken all its barriers and become the great political force of the empire, he had come to America, and begun all over again. In America every one had laughed at the mere idea of Socialism then—in America all men were free. As if political liberty made wage-slavery any the more tolerable! said Ostrinski.

3. Due in part to its large immigrant population, Chicago was an early center of socialist activity in the U.S., hosting Socialist Party conventions (one of them in 1904) and socialist publications in many languages.
4. German statesman Otto von *Bismarck* (1858–1898), known as the Iron Chancellor, precipitated the Franco-Prussian War (1870–71), which led to the creation of the German empire, of which he became the first chancellor. Fearing opposition, Bismarck in 1878 banned socialist meetings such as those of the International Workingmen's Association (the First *International*), an organization uniting socialists, communists, and anarchists, founded in 1864. In 1872 the First International split into two factions, one led by Karl Marx (also known as the Red International) and the other by the Russian revolutionary anarchist Mikhail Bakunin (the Black International). The First International dissolved in 1876, and the Second International followed in 1889 (see below, p. 507 and p. 507, n. 2).

The little tailor sat tilted back in his stiff kitchen-chair, with his feet stretched out upon the empty stove, and speaking in low whispers, so as not to waken those in the next room. To Jurgis he seemed a scarcely less wonderful person than the speaker at the meeting; he was poor, the lowest of the low, hunger-driven and miserable—and yet how much he knew, how much he had dared and achieved, what a hero he had been! There were others like him, too—thousands like him, and all of them working-men! That all this wonderful machinery of progress had been created by his fellows—Jurgis could not believe it, it seemed too good to be true.

That was always the way, said Ostrinski; when a man was first converted to Socialism he was like a crazy person,—he could not understand how others could fail to see it, and he expected to con- vert all the world the first week. After a while he would realize how hard a task it was; and then it would be fortunate that other new hands kept coming, to save him from settling down into a rut. Just now Jurgis would have plenty of chance to vent his excitement, for a presidential campaign was on, and everybody was talking politics. Ostrinski would take him to the next meeting of the branch-local, and introduce him, and he might join the party. The dues were five cents a week, but any one who could not afford this might be excused from paying. The Socialist party was a really democratic political organization—it was controlled absolutely by its own membership, and had no bosses. All of these things Ostrinski explained, as also the principles of the party. You might say that there was really but one Socialist principle—that of "no compromise," which was the essence of the proletarian movement all over the world. When a Socialist was elected to office he voted with old party legislators for any measure that was likely to be of help to the working-class, but he never forgot that these concessions, whatever they might be, were trifles compared with the great purpose,—the organizing of the working-class for the revolution. So far, the rule in America had been that one Socialist made another Socialist once every two years; and if they should maintain the same rate they would carry the coun- try in 1912—though not all of them expected to succeed as quickly as that.

The Socialists were organized in every civilized nation; it was an international political party, said Ostrinski, the greatest the world had ever known. It numbered thirty millions of adherents, and it cast eight million votes. It had started its first newspaper in Japan, and elected its first deputy in Argentina; in France it named members of cabinets, and in Italy and Australia it held the balance of power and turned out ministries. In Germany, where its vote was more than a third of the total vote of the empire, all other parties and powers had united to fight it. It would not do, Ostrinski explained, for the proletariat of one nation to achieve the victory, for that nation would be crushed by the military power of the others; and so the Socialist movement was a world movement, an organization of all mankind to establish liberty and fraternity. It was the new religion of humanity—or you might say it was the fulfilment of the old religion, since it implied but the literal application of all the teachings of Christ.

Until long after midnight Jurgis sat lost in the conversation of his new acquaintance. It was a most wonderful experience to him—an almost supernatural experience. It was like encountering an inhabitant of the fourth dimension of space,[5] a being who was free from all one's own limitations. For four years, now, Jurgis had been wandering and blundering in the depths of a wilderness; and here, suddenly, a hand reached down and seized him, and lifted him out of it, and set him upon a mountain-top, from which he could survey it all,—could see the paths from which he had wandered, the morasses into which he had stumbled, the hiding-places of the beasts of prey that had fallen upon him. There were his Packingtown experiences, for instance—what was there about Packingtown that Ostrinski could not explain! To Jurgis the packers had been equivalent to fate; Ostrinski showed him that they were the Beef Trust. They were a gigantic combination of capital, which had crushed all opposition, and overthrown the laws of the land, and was preying upon the people. Jurgis recollected how, when he had first come to Packingtown, he had stood and watched the hog-killing, and thought how cruel and savage it was, and come away congratulating himself that he was not a hog; now his new acquaintance showed him that a hog was just what he had been—one of the packers' hogs. What they wanted from a hog was all the profits that could be got out of him; and that was what they wanted from the working-man, and also that was what they wanted from the public. What the hog thought of it, and what he suffered, were not considered; and no more was it with labor, and no more with the purchaser of meat. That was true everywhere in the world, but it was especially true in Packingtown; there seemed to be something about the work of slaughtering that tended to ruthlessness and ferocity—it was literally the fact that in the methods of the packers a hundred human lives did not balance a penny of profit. When Jurgis had made himself familiar with the Socialist literature, as he would very quickly, he would get glimpses of the Beef Trust from all sorts of aspects, and he would find it everywhere the same; it was the incarnation of blind and insensate

5. According to the theory of relativity elaborated just before Sinclair wrote *The Jungle*, space and time are joined together, making time the fourth dimension of space.

Greed. It was a monster devouring with a thousand mouths, trampling with a thousand hoofs; it was the Great Butcher—it was the spirit of Capitalism made flesh.[6] Upon the ocean of commerce it sailed as a pirate ship; it had hoisted the black flag and declared war upon civilization. Bribery and corruption were its everyday methods. In Chicago the city government was simply one of its branch-offices; it stole billions of gallons of city water openly, it dictated to the courts the sentences of disorderly strikers, it forbade the mayor to enforce the building laws against it. In the national capital it had power to prevent inspection of its product, and to falsify government reports; it violated the rebate laws, and when an investigation was threatened it burned its books and sent its criminal agents out of the country. In the commercial world it was a Juggernaut car; it wiped out thousands of businesses every year, it drove men to madness and suicide. It had forced the price of cattle so low as to destroy the stock-raising industry, an occupation upon which whole states existed; it had ruined thousands of butchers who had refused to handle its products. It divided the country into districts, and fixed the price of meat in all of them; and it owned all the refrigerator cars, and levied an enormous tribute upon all poultry and eggs and fruit and vegetables. With the millions of dollars a week that poured in upon it, it was reaching out for the control of other interests, railroads and trolley lines, gas and electric light franchises—it already owned the leather and the grain business of the country. The people were tremendously stirred up over its encroachments, but nobody had any remedy to suggest; it was the task of Socialists to teach and organize them, and prepare them for the time when they were to seize the huge machine called the Beef Trust, and use it to produce food for human beings and not to heap up fortunes for a band of pirates.—It was long after midnight when Jurgis lay down upon the floor of Ostrinski's kitchen; and yet it was an hour before he could get to sleep, for the glory of that joyful vision of the people of Packingtown marching in and taking possession of the Union Stockyards!

6. Allusion to Jesus as the word of God made flesh; see John 1:14.

Chapter XXX

Jurgis had breakfast with Ostrinski and his family, and then he went home to Elzbieta. He was no longer shy about it—when he went in, instead of saying all the things he had been planning to say, he started to tell Elzbieta about the revolution! At first she thought he was out of his mind, and it was hours before she could really feel certain that he was himself. When, however, she had satisfied herself that he was sane upon all subjects except politics, she troubled herself no further about it. Jurgis was destined to find that Elzbieta's armor was absolutely impervious to Socialism. Her soul had been baked hard in the fire of adversity, and there was no altering it now; life to her was the hunt for daily bread, and ideas existed for her only as they bore upon that. All that interested her in regard to this new frenzy which had seized hold of her son-in-law was whether or not it had a tendency to make him sober and industrious; and when she found he intended to look for work and to contribute his share to the family fund, she gave him full rein to convince her of anything. A wonderfully wise little woman was Elzbieta; she could think as quickly as a hunted rabbit, and in half an hour she had chosen her life-attitude to the Socialist movement. She agreed in everything with Jurgis, except the need of his paying his dues; and she would even go to a meeting with him now and then, and sit and plan her next day's dinner amid the storm.

For a week after he became a convert Jurgis continued to wander about all day, looking for work; until at last he met with a strange fortune. He was passing one of Chicago's innumerable small hotels, and after some hesitation he concluded to go in. A man he took for the proprietor was standing in the lobby, and he went up to him and tackled him for a job.

"What can you do?" the man asked.

"Anything, sir," said Jurgis, and added quickly: "I've been out of work for a long time, sir. I'm an honest man, and I'm strong and willing—"

The other was eying him narrowly. "Do you drink?" he asked.

"No, sir," said Jurgis.

"Well, I've been employing a man as a porter, and he drinks. I've discharged him seven times now, and I've about made up my mind that's enough. Would you be a porter?"

"Yes, sir."

"It's hard work. You'll have to clean floors and wash spittoons and fill lamps and handle trunks—"

"I'm willing, sir."

"All right. I'll pay you thirty a month and board, and you can begin now, if you feel like it. You can put on the other fellow's rig."

And so Jurgis fell to work, and toiled like a Trojan[1] till night. Then he went and told Elzbieta, and also, late as it was, he paid a visit to Ostrinski to let him know of his good fortune. Here he received a great surprise, for when he was describing the location of the hotel Ostrinski interrupted suddenly, "Not Hinds's!"

"Yes," said Jurgis, "that's the name."

To which the other replied, "Then you've got the best boss in Chicago—he's a state organizer of our party, and one of our best-known speakers!"

So the next morning Jurgis went to his employer and told him; and the man seized him by the hand and shook it. "By Jove!" he cried, "that lets me out. I didn't sleep all last night because I had discharged a good Socialist!"

So, after that, Jurgis was known to his "boss" as "Comrade Jurgis," and in return he was expected to call him "Comrade Hinds." "Tommy" Hinds, as he was known to his intimates, was a squat little man, with broad shoulders and a florid face, decorated with gray side-whiskers. He was the kindest-hearted man that ever lived, and the liveliest—inexhaustible in his enthusiasm, and talking Socialism all day and all night. He was a great fellow to jolly along a crowd, and would keep a meeting in an uproar; when once he got really waked up, the torrent of his eloquence could be compared with nothing save Niagara.[2]

Tommy Hinds had begun life as a blacksmith's helper, and had run away to join the Union army,[3] where he had made his first acquaintance with "graft," in the shape of rotten muskets and shoddy blankets. To a musket that broke in a crisis he always attributed the death of his only brother, and upon worthless blankets he blamed all the agonies of his own old age. Whenever it rained, the rheumatism would get into his joints, and then he would screw up his face and mutter: "Capitalism, my boy, Capitalism! '*Écrasez l'Infâme!*'"[4] He had one unfailing remedy for all the evils of this world, and he preached it to every one; no matter whether the person's trouble was failure in business, or dyspepsia, or a quarrelsome mother-in-law, a twinkle would come into his eyes and he would say, "You know what to do about it—vote the Socialist ticket!"

---

1. Worked very hard (idiom, derived from ancient Greek and Roman accounts of residents of ancient Troy as industrious).
2. Niagara Falls, waterfall that straddles the border between New York and Canada; here used as metaphor for "torrent" of speech.
3. Northern army in the American Civil War (see below, p. 333, n. 4).
4. "Crush the infamous thing," famous saying of French writer François-Marie Arouet Voltaire (1694–1778). In *Mammonart* (excerpted below, pp. 485–86), Sinclair explains that by "l'Infâme," Voltaire meant "Catholic absolutism," but claims that "Now America has its 'infâme,' which is capitalist absolutism."

Tommy Hinds had set out upon the trail of the Octopus[5] as soon as the war was over. He had gone into business, and found himself in competition with the fortunes of those who had been stealing while he had been fighting. The city government was in their hands and the railroads were in league with them, and honest business was driven to the wall; and so Hinds had put all his savings into Chicago real estate, and set out single-handed to dam the river of graft. He had been a reform member of the city council, he had been a Greenbacker, a Labor Unionist, a Populist, a Bryanite[6]—and after thirty years of fighting, the year 1896 had served to convince him that the power of concentrated wealth could never be controlled, but could only be destroyed. He had published a pamphlet about it, and set out to organize a party of his own, when a stray Socialist leaflet had revealed to him that others had been ahead of him. Now for eight years he had been fighting for the party, anywhere, everywhere— whether it was a G. A. R. reunion, or a hotel-keepers' convention, or an Afro-American business-men's banquet, or a Bible society picnic, Tommy Hinds would manage to get himself invited to explain the relations of Socialism to the subject in hand.[7] After that he would start off upon a tour of his own, ending at some place between New York and Oregon; and when he came back from there, he would go out to organize new locals for the state committee; and finally he would come home to rest—and talk Socialism in Chicago. Hinds's hotel was a very hot-bed of the propaganda; all the employees were party men, and if they were not when they came, they were quite certain to be before they went away. The proprietor would get into a discussion with some one in the lobby, and as the conversation grew animated, others would gather about to listen, until finally every one in the place would be crowded into a group, and a regular debate would be under way. This went on every night—when Tommy Hinds

---

5. A metaphor commonly invoked to describe the grasping power of large companies, as in the 1901 novel of that name by the American writer Frank Norris (1870–1902).

6. Late-nineteenth-century reform movements: *Greenbackers* opposed monopolies and advocated for "greenback" currency (paper money not backed by gold), believing it would raise profits for farmers. Initially an agrarian organization, Greenbackers later aligned with labor before fading out in the late 1880s. *Labor Unionists* advocated trade unions to protect workers. Much of the Greenbackers' agenda resurfaced as tenets of the left-wing, agrarian People's Party, better known as *Populists*. The Populist Party emerged in the 1890s, attacking finance capitalism and advocating free coinage of silver (to put more money into circulation so as to bring up depressed prices), a graduated income tax, and direct election of senators (elected by state legislatures until the ratification of the Seventeenth Amendment in 1913) and of the president. Many Populists became *Bryanites*, followers of renowned orator William Jennings Bryan (1860–1925), an unsuccessful presidential candidate in 1896, 1900, and 1908. Tommy Hinds probably turns to more radical solutions in 1896 in response to the defeat of Bryan.

7. Hinds addresses some audiences unlikely to be receptive, such as the Grand Army of the Republic, an overwhelmingly Republican group established in 1866 by Civil War veterans of the Union army and navy, and Black businessmen who, influenced by such leaders as Booker T. Washington (1856–1915), sought integration into U.S. society by making themselves integral to the economy.

was not there to do it, his clerk did it; and when his clerk was away campaigning, the assistant attended to it, while Mrs. Hinds sat behind the desk and did the work. The clerk was an old crony of the proprietor's, an awkward, raw-boned giant of a man, with a lean, sallow face, a broad mouth, and whiskers under his chin, the very type and body of a prairie farmer. He had been that all his life—he had fought the railroads in Kansas for fifty years, a Granger, a Farmers' Alliance man, a "middle-of-the-road" Populist.[8] Finally, Tommy Hinds had revealed to him the wonderful idea of using the trusts instead of destroying them, and he had sold his farm and come to Chicago.

That was Amos Struver; and then there was Harry Adams, the assistant clerk, a pale, scholarly-looking man, who came from Massachusetts, of Pilgrim stock. Adams had been a cotton operative in Fall River,[9] and the continued depression in the industry had worn him and his family out, and he had emigrated to South Carolina. In Massachusetts the percentage of white illiteracy is eight-tenths of one per cent, while in South Carolina it is thirteen and six-tenths per cent; also in South Carolina there is a property qualification for voters—and for these and other reasons child-labor is the rule, and so the cotton mills were driving those of Massachusetts out of the business.[1] Adams did not know this, he only knew that the Southern mills were running; but when he got there he found that if he was to live, all his family would have to work, and from six o'clock at night to six o'clock in the morning. So he had set to work to organize the mill-hands, after the fashion in Massachusetts, and had been discharged; but he had gotten other work, and stuck at it, and at last there had been a strike for shorter hours, and Harry Adams had attempted to address a street meeting, which was the end of him. In the states of the far South the labor of convicts is leased to contractors, and when there are not convicts enough they have to be supplied. Harry Adams was sent up by a judge who was a cousin of the mill-owner with whose business he had interfered; and though the life had nearly killed him, he had been wise enough not to murmur, and at the end of his term he and his family had left the state of South Carolina—hell's back yard, as he called it. He had no money for car-fare, but it was

8. Farmers banded together in the late 1860s to form the *Granger* movement, hoping to use their alliance to combat the exorbitant rates railroads charged for transporting crops and farm equipment. One of the *Farmers' Alliances*, which used cooperatives and advocacy to try to improve economic conditions for farmers, grew out of the Granger movement.
9. Southwestern Massachusetts town; once a leading cotton textile center and site of several strikes in the late nineteenth century, it became a center of union activity in New England.
1. During the 1880s, small textile mills began moving south, where wages were lower and more children worked; in part to disenfranchise freed slaves and their descendants, South Carolina allowed a man to vote only if he owned three hundred dollars' worth of property.

harvest-time, and they walked one day and worked the next; and so Adams got at last to Chicago, and joined the Socialist party. He was a studious man, reserved, and nothing of an orator; but he always had a pile of books under his desk in the hotel, and articles from his pen were beginning to attract attention in the party press.

Contrary to what one would have expected, all this radicalism did not hurt the hotel business; the radicals flocked to it, and the commercial travellers all found it diverting. Of late, also, the hotel had become a favorite stopping-place for Western cattlemen. Now that the Beef Trust had adopted the trick of raising prices to induce enormous shipments of cattle, and then dropping them again and scooping in all they needed, a stock-raiser was very apt to find himself in Chicago without money enough to pay his freight bill; and so he had to go to a cheap hotel, and it was no drawback to him if there was an agitator talking in the lobby. These Western fellows were just "meat" for Tommy Hinds—he would get a dozen of them around him and paint little pictures of "the System." Of course, it was not a week before he had heard Jurgis's story, and after that he would not have let his new porter go for the world. "See here," he would say, in the middle of an argument, "I've got a fellow right here in my place who's worked there and seen every bit of it!" And then Jurgis would drop his work, whatever it was, and come, and the other would say, "Comrade Jurgis, just tell these gentlemen what you saw on the killing-beds." At first this request caused poor Jurgis the most acute agony, and it was like pulling teeth to get him to talk; but gradually he found out what was wanted, and in the end he learned to stand up and speak his piece with enthusiasm. His employer would sit by and encourage him with exclamations and shakes of the head; when Jurgis would give the formula for "potted ham," or tell about the condemned hogs that were dropped into the "destructors" at the top and immediately taken out again at the bottom, to be shipped into another state and made into lard, Tommy Hinds would bang his knee and cry, "Do you think a man could make up a thing like that out of his head?"

And then the hotel-keeper would go on to show how the Socialists had the only real remedy for such evils, how they alone "meant business" with the Beef Trust. And when, in answer to this, the victim would say that the whole country was getting stirred up, that the newspapers were full of denunciations of it, and the government taking action against it, Tommy Hinds had a knock-out blow all ready. "Yes," he would say, "all that is true—but what do you suppose is the reason for it? Are you foolish enough to believe that it's done for the public? There are other trusts in the country just as illegal and extortionate as the Beef Trust: there is the Coal Trust, that freezes the poor in winter—there is the Steel Trust, that doubles the price of every nail in your shoes—there is the Oil Trust, that keeps you from reading at night—and why do you suppose it is that all the fury of the press and the government is directed against the Beef Trust?" And when to this the victim would reply that there was clamor enough over the Oil Trust, the other would continue: "Ten years ago Henry D. Lloyd told all the truth about the Standard Oil Company in his 'Wealth versus Commonwealth'; and the book was allowed to die, and you hardly ever hear of it. And now, at last, two magazines have the courage to tackle 'Standard Oil' again, and what happens?[2] The newspapers ridicule the authors, the churches defend the criminals, and the government—does nothing. And now, why is it all so different with the Beef Trust?"

Here the other would generally admit that he was "stuck"; and Tommy Hinds would explain to him, and it was fun to see his eyes open. "If you were a Socialist," the hotel-keeper would say, "you would understand that the power which really governs the United States to-day is the Railroad Trust. It is the Railroad Trust that runs your state government, wherever you live, and that runs the United States Senate. And all of the trusts that I have named are railroad trusts—save only the Beef Trust! The Beef Trust has defied the railroads—it is plundering them day by day through the Private Car; and so the public is roused to fury, and the papers clamor for action, and the government goes on the war-path! And you poor common people watch and applaud the job, and think it's all done for you, and never dream that it is really the grand climax of the century-long battle of commercial competition,—the final death-grapple between the chiefs of the Beef Trust and 'Standard Oil,' for the prize of the mastery and ownership of the United States of America!"

Such was the new home in which Jurgis lived and worked, and in which his education was completed. Perhaps you would imagine that he did not do much work there, but that would be a great mistake. He would have cut off one hand for Tommy Hinds; and to keep Hinds's hotel a thing of beauty was his joy in life. That he had a score of Socialist arguments chasing through his brain in the meantime did not interfere with this; on the contrary, Jurgis scrubbed the spittoons and polished the banisters all the more vehemently because at the same time he was wrestling inwardly with an imaginary recalcitrant. It would be pleasant to record that he swore off drinking immediately, and all the rest of his bad habits with it; but that would

2. *Wealth Against Commonwealth* (1894), a carefully researched exposé of the trusts, concentrating on John D. Rockefeller's Standard Oil, which the American journalist Henry Demarest Lloyd claimed was built out of graft, treachery, and corruption. The American writer Ida M. Tarbell's *A History of the Standard Oil Company* was originally published in *McClure's* magazine, a major outlet for muckraking, beginning in 1902, and appeared as a book in 1904.

hardly be exact. These revolutionists were not angels; they were men, and men who had come up from the social pit, and with the mire of it smeared over them. Some of them drank, and some of them swore, and some of them ate pie with their knives; there was only one difference between them and all the rest of the populace—that they were men with a hope, with a cause to fight for and suffer for. There came times to Jurgis when the vision seemed far-off and pale, and a glass of beer loomed large in comparison; but if the glass led to another glass, and to too many glasses, he had something to spur him to remorse and resolution on the morrow. It was so evidently a wicked thing to spend one's pennies for drink, when the working-class was wandering in darkness, and waiting to be delivered; the price of a glass of beer would buy fifty copies of a leaflet, and one could hand these out to the unregenerate, and then get drunk upon the thought of the good that was being accomplished. That was the way the movement had been made, and it was the only way it would progress; it availed nothing to know of it, without fighting for it—it was a thing for all, not for a few! A corollary of this proposition of course was, that any one who refused to receive the new gospel was personally responsible for keeping Jurgis from his heart's desire; and this, alas, made him uncomfortable as an acquaintance. He met some neighbors with whom Elzbieta had made friends in her neighborhood, and he set out to make Socialists of them by wholesale, and several times he all but got into a fight.

It was all so painfully obvious to Jurgis! It was so incomprehensible how a man could fail to see it! Here were all the opportunities of the country, the land, and the buildings upon the land, the railroads, the mines, the factories, and the stores, all in the hands of a few private individuals, called capitalists, for whom the people were obliged to work for wages. The whole balance of what the people produced went to heap up the fortunes of these capitalists, to heap, and heap again, and yet again—and that in spite of the fact that they, and every one about them, lived in unthinkable luxury! And was it not plain that if the people cut off the share of those who merely "owned," the share of those who worked would be much greater? That was as plain as two and two makes four; and it was the whole of it, absolutely the whole of it; and yet there were people who could not see it, who would argue about everything else in the world. They would tell you that governments could not manage things as economically as private individuals; they would repeat and repeat that, and think they were saying something! They could not see that "economical" management by masters meant simply that they, the people, were worked harder and ground closer and paid less! They were wage-earners and servants, at the mercy of exploiters whose one thought was to get as much out of them as possible; and they were taking an interest in the process, were anxious lest it should not be done thoroughly enough! Was it not honestly a trial to listen to an argument such as that?

And yet there were things even worse. You would begin talking to some poor devil who had worked in one shop for the last thirty years, and had never been able to save a penny; who left home every morning at six o'clock, to go and tend a machine, and come back at night too tired to take his clothes off; who had never had a week's vacation in his life, had never travelled, never had an adventure, never learned anything, never hoped anything—and when you started to tell him about Socialism he would sniff and say, "I'm not interested in that—I'm an individualist!" And then he would go on to tell you that Socialism was "Paternalism," and that if it ever had its way the world would stop progressing. It was enough to make a mule laugh, to hear arguments like that; and yet it was no laughing matter, as you found out—for how many millions of such poor deluded wretches there were, whose lives had been so stunted by Capitalism that they no longer knew what freedom was! And they really thought that it was "Individualism" for tens of thousands of them to herd together and obey the orders of a steel magnate, and produce hundreds of millions of dollars of wealth for him, and then let him give them libraries; while for them to take the industry, and run it to suit themselves, and build their own libraries—that would have been "Paternalism"!

Sometimes the agony of such things as this was almost more than Jurgis could bear; yet there was no way of escape from it, there was nothing to do but to dig away at the base of this mountain of ignorance and prejudice. You must keep at the poor fellow; you must hold your temper, and argue with him, and watch for your chance to stick an idea or two into his head. And the rest of the time you must sharpen up your weapons,—you must think out new replies to his objections, and provide yourself with new facts to prove to him the folly of his ways.

So Jurgis acquired the reading habit. He would carry in his pocket a tract or a pamphlet which some one had loaned him, and whenever he had an idle moment during the day he would plod through a paragraph, and then think about it while he worked. Also he read the newspapers, and asked questions about them. One of the other porters at Hinds's was a sharp little Irishman, who knew everything that Jurgis wanted to know; and while they were busy he would explain to him the geography of America, and its history, its constitution and its laws; also he gave him an idea of the business system of the country, the great railroads and corporations, and who owned them, and the labor unions, and the big strikes, and the men who had led them. Then at night, when he could get off, Jurgis would attend the Socialist meetings. During the campaign one was not dependent upon the street-corner affairs, where the weather and the quality of the orator were equally uncertain; there were hall meetings every night, and one could hear speakers of national prominence. These discussed the political situation from every point of view, and all that troubled Jurgis was the impossibility of carrying off but a small part of the treasures they offered him.

There was a man who was known in the party as the "Little Giant."[3] The Lord had used up so much material in the making of his head that there had not been enough to complete his legs; but he got about on the platform, and when he shook his raven whiskers the pillars of Capitalism rocked. He had written a veritable encyclopædia upon the subject, a book that was nearly as big as himself.—And then there was a young author, who came from California, and had been a salmon-fisher, an oyster-pirate, a longshoreman, a sailor; who had tramped the country and been sent to jail, had lived in the Whitechapel slums, and been to the Klondike in search of gold.[4] All these things he pictured in his books, and because he was a man of genius he forced the world to hear him. Now he was famous, but wherever he went he still preached the gospel of the poor.—And then there was one who was known as the "millionnaire Socialist." He had made a fortune in business, and spent nearly all of it in building up a magazine, which the post office department had tried to suppress, and had driven to Canada.[5] He was a quiet-mannered man, whom you would have taken for anything in the world but a Socialist agitator. His speech was simple and informal—he could not understand why any one should get excited about these things. It was a process of economic evolution, he said, and he exhibited its laws and methods. Life was a struggle for existence, and the strong overcame the weak, and in turn were overcome by the strongest. Those who lost in the struggle were generally exterminated; but now and then they had been known to save themselves by combination—which was a new and higher kind of strength. It was so that the gregarious animals had overcome the predaceous; it was so, in human history, that the people had mastered the kings. The workers were simply the citizens of industry, and the Socialist movement was the expression of their will to survive. The inevitability of the revolution depended upon this fact, that they had no choice but to unite or be exterminated; this fact, grim and inexorable, depended upon no human will, it was the law of the economic process, of which the editor showed the details with the most marvellous precision.

3. Probably Daniel De Leon (1852–1914), a leading figure in the Socialist Labor Party; also see below, p. 507; p. 507, n. 2; p. 509, n. 8; and p. 511.
4. Sinclair's fellow socialist novelist Jack London (1876–1916); *Klondike*: a gold mine in the Yukon, discovered in 1896.
5. When the U.S. post office denied *Wilshire's Magazine* second-class mail status, claiming it was propaganda, wealthy editor Gaylord Wilshire (1861–1927) moved its publication to Canada.

And later on came the evening of the great meeting of the campaign, when Jurgis heard the two standard-bearers of his party. Ten years before there had been in Chicago a strike of a hundred and fifty thousand railroad employees, and thugs had been hired by the railroads to commit violence, and the President of the United States had sent in troops to break the strike, by flinging the officers of the union into jail without trial. The president of the union came out of his cell a ruined man; but also he came out a Socialist; and now for just ten years he had been travelling up and down the country, standing face to face with the people, and pleading with them for justice. He was a man of electric presence, tall and gaunt, with a face worn thin by struggle and suffering. The fury of outraged manhood gleamed in it—and the tears of suffering little children pleaded in his voice. When he spoke he paced the stage, lithe and eager, like a panther. He leaned over, reaching out for his audience; he pointed into their souls with an insistent finger. His voice was husky from much speaking, but the great auditorium was as still as death, and every one heard him.[6]

And then, as Jurgis came out from this meeting, some one handed him a paper which he carried home with him and read; and so he became acquainted with the "Appeal to Reason." About twelve years previously a Colorado real-estate speculator had made up his mind that it was wrong to gamble in the necessities of life of human beings; and so he had retired and begun the publication of a Socialist weekly.[7] There had come a time when he had to set his own type, but he had held on and won out, and now his publication was an institution. It used a car-load of paper every week, and the mail-trains would be hours loading up at the depot of the little Kansas town. It was a four-page weekly, which sold for less than half a cent a copy; its regular subscription list was a quarter of a million, and it went to every cross-roads post-office in America.

The "Appeal" was a "propaganda" paper. It had a manner all its own,—it was full of ginger and spice, of Western slang and hustle.

---

6. Eugene V. Debs (1855–1926), charismatic hero of American socialism. In the summer of 1894, as president of the American Railway Union, Debs called a boycott of the Pullman Palace Car Company after George Pullman (1831–1897), inventor of the railroad sleeping car, fired one-third of his workers and slashed wages. The first nationwide strike followed, halting railway service throughout the country. Claiming interference with mail service, President Grover Cleveland (1837–1908) sent in federal troops, which provoked considerable violence, including rioting throughout Chicago's South Side. After serving six months in jail for contempt, Debs, who had initially supported the strike only reluctantly, embraced socialism. He became a symbolic figure, seen as one forced into socialism by the injustices of American capitalism.

7. It was the most widely read socialist newspaper in American history, founded in 1895 by Julius Augustus Wayland (1854–1912) and later taken over by Fred D. Warren (1872–1959), headquartered after 1897 in Girard, Kansas. The *Appeal* published the first version of *The Jungle*.

It collected news of the doings of the "plutes,"[8] and served it up for the benefit of the "American working-mule." It would have columns of the deadly parallel,[9]—the million dollars' worth of diamonds, or the fancy pet-poodle establishment of a society dame, beside the fate of Mrs. Murphy of San Francisco, who had starved to death on the streets, or of John Robinson, just out of the hospital, who had hanged himself in New York because he could not find work. It collected the stories of graft and misery from the daily press, and made little pungent paragraphs out of them. "Three banks of Bungtown, South Dakota, failed, and more savings of the workers swallowed up!" "The mayor of Sandy Creek, Oklahoma, has skipped with a hundred thousand dollars. That's the kind of rulers the old partyites give you!" "The president of the Florida Flying Machine Company is in jail for bigamy. He was a prominent opponent of Socialism, which he said would break up the home!" The "Appeal" had what it called its "Army," about thirty thousand of the faithful, who did things for it; and it was always exhorting the "Army" to keep its dander up, and occasionally encouraging it with a prize competition, for anything from a gold watch to a private yacht or an eighty-acre farm.[1] Its office helpers were all known to the "Army" by quaint titles—"Inky Ike," "the Bald-headed Man," "the Red-headed Girl," "the Bulldog," "the Office Goat," and "the One Hoss."

But sometimes, again, the "Appeal" would be desperately serious. It sent a correspondent to Colorado, and printed pages describing the overthrow of American institutions in that state. In a certain city of the country it had over forty of its "Army" in the headquarters of the Telegraph Trust, and no message of importance to Socialists ever went through that a copy of it did not go to the "Appeal." It would print great broadsides during the campaign; one copy that came to Jurgis was a manifesto addressed to striking working-men, of which nearly a million copies had been distributed in the industrial centres, wherever the employers' associations had been carrying out their "open shop" program. "You have lost the strike!" it was headed. "And now what are you going to do about it?" It was what is called an "incendiary" appeal,—it was written by a man into whose soul the iron had entered.[2] When this edition appeared, twenty thousand copies were sent to the stockyards district; and they were taken out and stowed away in the rear of a little cigar-store, and every evening, and on Sundays, the members of the Packingtown locals would

8. Plutocrats, those who rule by wealth (slang).
9. Comparison of two things (as in parallel newspaper columns) to suggest an underlying relationship.
1. Eighty thousand volunteers brought out various editions of the *Appeal*—as many as eighteen editions at one point.
2. The man with the iron soul is Sinclair, who on September 17, 1904, had published a manifesto under this title in the *Appeal*.

get armfuls and distribute them on the streets and in the houses. The people of Packingtown had lost their strike, if ever a people had, and so they read these papers gladly, and twenty thousand were hardly enough to go round. Jurgis had resolved not to go near his old home again, but when he heard of this it was too much for him, and every night for a week he would get on the car and ride out to the stock-yards, and help to undo his work of the previous year, when he had sent Mike Scully's ten-pin setter to the city Board of Aldermen.

It was quite marvellous to see what a difference twelve months had made in Packingtown—the eyes of the people were getting opened! The Socialists were literally sweeping everything before them that election, and Scully and the Cook County machine were at their wits' end for an "issue." At the very close of the campaign they bethought themselves of the fact that the strike had been broken by negroes, and so they sent for a South Carolina fire-eater, the "pitchfork senator," as he was called, a man who took off his coat when he talked to working-men, and damned and swore like a Hessian.[3] This meeting they adver-tised extensively, and the Socialists advertised it too—with the result that about a thousand of them were on hand that evening. The "pitchfork senator" stood their fusillade of questions for about an hour, and then went home in disgust, and the balance of the meeting was a strictly party affair. Jurgis, who had insisted upon coming, had the time of his life that night; he danced about and waved his arms in his excitement—and at the very climax he broke loose from his friends, and got out into the aisle, and proceeded to make a speech himself! The senator had been denying that the Democratic party was corrupt; it was always the Republicans who bought the votes, he said,—and here was Jurgis shouting furiously, "It's a lie! It's a lie!" After which he went on to tell them how he knew it—that he knew it because he had bought them himself! And he would have told the "pitchfork senator" all his experiences, had not Harry Adams and a friend grabbed him about the neck and shoved him into a seat.

3. German soldier hired by the British to fight against colonists during the American Revolution. South Carolina governor, U.S. senator, and demagogue Benjamin R. Tillman (1847–1918) became a Southern political boss by playing on white fears of a resurgence of African Americans at the polls. The moniker "Pitchfork Ben" reflects his public image as rural champion of the common farmer, but his rhetoric was full of hate and profanity.

Chapter XXXI

One of the first things that Jurgis had done after he got a job was to go and see Marija. She came down into the basement of the house to meet him, and he stood by the door with his hat in his hand, saying, "I've got work now, and so you can leave here."

But Marija only shook her head. There was nothing else for her to do, she said, and nobody to employ her. She could not keep her past a secret—girls had tried it, and they were always found out. There were thousands of men who came to this place, and sooner or later she would meet one of them. "And besides," Marija added, "I can't do anything, I'm no good—I take dope. What could you do with me?"

"Can't you stop?" Jurgis cried.

"No," she answered, "I'll never stop. What's the use of talking about it—I'll stay here till I die, I guess. It's all I'm fit for." And that was all that he could get her to say—there was no use trying. When he told her he would not let Elzbieta take her money, she answered indifferently: "Then it'll be wasted here—that's all." Her eyelids looked heavy and her face was red and swollen; he saw that he was annoying her, that she only wanted him to go away. So he went, disappointed and sad.

Poor Jurgis was not very happy in his home-life. Elzbieta was sick a good deal now, and the boys were wild and unruly, and very much the worse for their life upon the streets. But he stuck by the family nevertheless, for they reminded him of his old happiness; and when things went wrong he could solace himself with a plunge into the Socialist movement. Since his life had been caught up into the current of this great stream, things which had before been the whole of life to him came to seem of relatively slight importance; his interests were elsewhere, in the world of ideas. His outward life was commonplace and uninteresting; he was just a hotel-porter, and expected to remain one while he lived; but meantime, in the realm of thought, his life was a perpetual adventure. There was so much to know—so many wonders to be discovered! Never in all his life did Jurgis forget the day before election, when there came a telephone message from a friend of Harry Adams, asking him to bring Jurgis to see him that night; and Jurgis went, and met one of the minds of the movement.

The invitation was from a man named Fisher, a Chicago millionaire who had given up his life to settlement-work, and had a little home in the heart of the city's slums. He did not belong to the party, but he was in sympathy with it; and he said that he was to have as his guest that night the editor of a big Eastern magazine, who wrote against Socialism, but really did not know what it was. The millionnaire suggested that Adams bring Jurgis along, and then start up the subject of "pure food," in which the editor was interested.

Young Fisher's home was a little two-story brick house, dingy and weather-beaten outside, but attractive within. The room that Jurgis saw was half lined with books, and upon the walls were many pictures, dimly visible in the soft, yellow light; it was a cold, rainy night, so a log-fire was crackling in the open hearth. Seven or eight people were gathered about it when Adams and his friend arrived, and Jurgis saw to his dismay that three of them were ladies. He had never talked to people of this sort before, and he fell into an agony of embarrassment. He stood in the doorway clutching his hat tightly in his hands, and made a deep bow to each of the persons as he was introduced; then, when he was asked to have a seat, he took a chair in a dark corner, and sat down upon the edge of it, and wiped the perspiration off his forehead with his sleeve. He was terrified lest they should expect him to talk.

There was the host himself, a tall, athletic young man, clad in evening dress, as also was the editor, a dyspeptic-looking gentleman named Maynard. There was the former's frail young wife, and also an elderly lady, who taught kindergarten in the settlement, and a young college student, a beautiful girl with an intense and earnest face. She only spoke once or twice while Jurgis was there—the rest of the time she sat by the table in the centre of the room, resting her chin in her hands and drinking in the conversation. There were two other men, whom young Fisher had introduced to Jurgis as Mr. Lucas and Mr. Schliemann; he heard them address Adams as "Comrade," and so he knew that they were Socialists.

The one called Lucas was a mild and meek-looking little gentleman of clerical aspect; he had been an itinerant evangelist, it transpired, and had seen the light and become a prophet of the new dispensation. He travelled all over the country, living like the apostles of old, upon hospitality, and preaching upon street-corners when there was no hall. The other man had been in the midst of a discussion with the editor when Adams and Jurgis came in; and at the suggestion of the host they resumed it after the interruption. Jurgis was soon sitting spellbound, thinking that here was surely the strangest man that had ever lived in the world.

Nicholas Schliemann was a Swede, a tall, gaunt person, with hairy hands and bristling yellow beard; he was a university man, and had been a professor of philosophy—until, as he said, he had found that he was selling his character as well as his time. Instead he had come to America, where he lived in a garret-room in this slum district, and made volcanic energy take the place of fire. He studied the composition of food-stuffs, and knew exactly how many

proteids[1] and carbohydrates his body needed; and by scientific
chewing he said that he tripled the value of all he ate, so that it cost
him eleven cents a day. About the first of July he would leave Chicago for his vacation, on foot; and when he struck the harvest-fields
he would set to work for two dollars and a half a day, and come
home when he had another year's supply—a hundred and twenty-
five dollars. That was the nearest approach to independence a man
could make "under capitalism," he explained; he would never
marry, for no sane man would allow himself to fall in love until
after the revolution.

He sat in a big arm-chair, with his legs crossed, and his head so
far in the shadow that one saw only two glowing lights, reflected
from the fire on the hearth. He spoke simply, and utterly without
emotion; with the manner of a teacher setting forth to a group of
scholars an axiom in geometry, he would enunciate such propositions
as made the hair of an ordinary person rise on end. And when the
auditor had asserted his non-comprehension, he would proceed to
elucidate by some new proposition, yet more appalling. To Jurgis
the Herr Dr. Schliemann assumed the proportions of a thunder-
storm or an earthquake. And yet, strange as it might seem, there
was a subtle bond between them, and he could follow the argument
nearly all the time. He was carried over the difficult places in spite
of himself; and he went plunging away in mad career—a very
Mazeppa-ride upon the wild horse Speculation.[2]

Nicholas Schliemann was familiar with all the universe, and with
man as a small part of it. He understood human institutions, and
blew them about like soap-bubbles. It was surprising that so much
destructiveness could be contained in one human mind. Was it government? The purpose of government was the guarding of property-
rights, the perpetuation of ancient force and modern fraud. Or was it
marriage? Marriage and prostitution were two sides of one shield,
the predatory man's exploitation of the sex-pleasure. The difference
between them was a difference of class. If a woman had money
she might dictate her own terms: equality, a life-contract, and the
legitimacy—that is, the property-rights—of her children. If she had
no money, she was a proletarian, and sold herself for an existence.
And then the subject became Religion, which was the Arch-fiend's
deadliest weapon. Government oppressed the body of the wage-slave,
but Religion oppressed his mind, and poisoned the stream of progress
at its source. The working-man was to fix his hopes upon a future

1. An early variant of the word *protein*.
2. Cossack leader Ivan Mazeppa (1644–1709), lashed naked to a wild horse for courting
the wife of a count, was a favorite literary subject, popularized by the English Romantic poet George Gordon, Lord Byron (1788–1824), in an 1819 poem.

life, while his pockets were picked in this one; he was brought up to frugality, humility, obedience,—in short to all the pseudo-virtues of capitalism. The destiny of civilization would be decided in one final death-struggle between the Red International and the Black, between Socialism and the Roman Catholic Church; while here at home, "the stygian midnight of American evangelicalism—"[3]

And here the ex-preacher entered the field, and there was a lively tussle. "Comrade" Lucas was not what is called an educated man; he knew only the Bible, but it was the Bible interpreted by real experience. And what was the use, he asked, of confusing Religion with men's perversions of it? That the church was in the hands of the merchants at the moment was obvious enough; but already there were signs of rebellion, and if Comrade Schliemann could come back a few years from now—

"Ah, yes," said the other, "of course. I have no doubt that in a hundred years the Vatican will be denying that it ever opposed Socialism, just as at present it denies that it ever tortured Galileo."[4]

"I am not defending the Vatican," exclaimed Lucas, vehemently. "I am defending the word of God—which is one long cry of the human spirit for deliverance from the sway of oppression. Take the twenty-fourth chapter of the Book of Job, which I am accustomed to quote in my addresses as 'the Bible upon the Beef Trust'; or take the words of Isaiah—or of the Master himself![5] Not the elegant prince of our debauched and vicious art, not the jewelled idol of our society churches—but the Jesus of the awful reality, the man of sorrow and pain, the outcast, despised of the world, who had no where to lay his head—"

"I will grant you Jesus," interrupted the other.

"Well, then," cried Lucas, "and why should Jesus have nothing to do with his church—why should his words and his life be of no authority among those who profess to adore him? Here is a man who was the world's first revolutionist, the true founder of the Socialist movement; a man whose whole being was one flame of hatred for wealth, and all that wealth stands for,—for the pride of wealth, and

---

3. *Stygian* means something resembling or pertaining to the River Styx, which runs through the underworld in Greek mythology; the metaphor *stygian midnight* suggests a black night or nadir. On the Red and Black Internationals, see above, p. 287, n. 4. The ensuing debate illustrates that socialism has more than one face. Like many of Sinclair's socialist mentors, Lucas affirms Christian socialism, whereas Schliemann's perspective is anarchistic.

4. Italian astronomer and physicist *Galileo* Galilei (1564–1642) championed heliocentrism (the theory that the Earth revolves around the sun), which the Catholic Church proclaimed was heretical because it contradicted the Bible. Galileo was tried during the Inquisition, found guilty of heresy, and sentenced to imprisonment (immediately commuted to house arrest). The widely circulated story that the Vatican "tortured" him has been discredited as a myth.

5. Jesus; *twenty-fourth chapter of the Book of Job*: in which Job laments that God seems indifferent to the wicked; *words of Isaiah*: Hebrew Bible prophet; Lucas may have in mind the prophecies of destruction of the wicked (Isaiah 13–24).

the luxury of wealth, and the tyranny of wealth; who was himself a beggar and a tramp, a man of the people, an associate of saloon-keepers and women of the town; who again and again, in the most explicit language, denounced wealth and the holding of wealth: 'Lay not up for yourselves treasures on earth!'—'Sell that ye have and give alms!'—'Blessed are ye poor, for yours is the kingdom of Heaven!'—'Woe unto you that are rich, for ye have received your consolation!'—'Verily, I say unto you, that a rich man shall hardly enter into the kingdom of Heaven!' Who denounced in unmeasured terms the exploiters of his own time: 'Woe unto you, scribes and pharisees, hypocrites!'—'Woe unto you also, you lawyers!'—'Ye serpents, ye generation of vipers, how can ye escape the damnation of hell?'[6] Who drove out the business men and brokers from the temple with a whip! Who was crucified—think of it—for an incendiary and a disturber of the social order! And this man they have made into the high-priest of property and smug respectability, a divine sanction of all the horrors and abominations of modern commercial civilization! Jewelled images are made of him, sensual priests burn incense to him, and modern pirates of industry bring their dollars, wrung from the toil of helpless women and children, and build temples to him, and sit in cushioned seats and listen to his teachings expounded by doctors of dusty divinity—"

"Bravo!" cried Schliemann, laughing. But the other was in full career—he had talked this subject every day for five years, and had never yet let himself be stopped. "This Jesus of Nazareth!" he cried. "This class-conscious working-man! This union carpenter! This agitator, law-breaker, firebrand, anarchist! He, the sovereign lord and master of a world which grinds the bodies and souls of human beings into dollars—if he could come into the world this day and see the things that men have made in his name, would it not blast his soul with horror? Would he not go mad at the sight of it, he the Prince of Mercy and Love! That dreadful night when he lay in the Garden of Gethsemane[7] and writhed in agony until he sweat blood—do you think that he saw anything worse than he might see to-night upon the plains of Manchuria, where men march out with a jewelled image of him before them, to do wholesale murder for the benefit of foul monsters of sensuality and cruelty? Do you not know that if he were in St. Petersburg[8] now, he would take the whip with which he drove out the bankers from his temple—"[9]

6. These sayings, largely from the Sermon on the Mount (Matthew 5–7), suggest why Sinclair considered Jesus a misunderstood radical. In his *Autobiography*, Sinclair speaks of having "a real love, a personal affection for the historical Jesus; it seemed to me that he had been a social rebel who had been taken up and made into an object of superstition."
7. Where Judas Iscariot betrayed Jesus, leading to Jesus's arrest (Mark 14:43–46).
8. Former capital of Russia; the riot leading to the Russian Revolution of 1905 began here.
9. In Matthew 21:12, Jesus drives out from the temple all those who were conducting business there.

Here the speaker paused an instant for breath. "No, comrade," said the other, dryly, "for he was a practical man. He would take pretty little imitation-lemons,[1] such as are now being shipped into Russia, handy for carrying in the pockets, and strong enough to blow a whole temple out of sight."

Lucas waited until the company had stopped laughing over this; then he began again: "But look at it from the point of view of practical politics, comrade. Here is an historical figure whom all men reverence and love, whom some regard as divine; and who was one of us—who lived our life, and taught our doctrine. And now shall we leave him in the hands of his enemies—shall we allow them to stifle and stultify his example? We have his words, which no one can deny; and shall we not quote them to the people, and prove to them what he was, and what he taught, and what he did? No, no,—a thousand times no!—we shall use his authority to turn out the knaves and sluggards from his ministry, and we shall yet rouse the people to action!—"

Lucas halted again; and the other stretched out his hand to a paper on the table. "Here, comrade," he said, with a laugh, "here is a place for you to begin. A bishop whose wife has just been robbed of fifty thousand dollars' worth of diamonds! And a most unctuous and oily of bishops! An eminent and scholarly bishop! A philanthropist and friend of labor bishop—a Civic Federation[2] decoy-duck for the chloroforming of the wage-working-man!"

To this little passage of arms the rest of the company sat as spectators. But now Mr. Maynard, the editor, took occasion to remark, somewhat naïvely, that he had always understood that Socialists had a cut-and-dried programme for the future of civilization; whereas here were two active members of the party, who, from what he could make out, were agreed about nothing at all. Would the two, for his enlightenment, try to ascertain just what they had in common, and why they belonged to the same party? This resulted, after much debating, in the formulating of two carefully worded propositions: First, that a Socialist believes in the common ownership and democratic management of the means of producing the necessities of life; and, second, that a socialist believes that the means by which this is to be brought about is the class-conscious political organization of the wage-earners. Thus far they were at one; but no farther. To Lucas, the religious zealot, the cooperative commonwealth was the New Jerusalem, the kingdom of Heaven, which is "within you." To the other, Socialism was simply a necessary step toward a far-distant

---

1. Grenades.
2. National Civic Federation (NCF), a moderately progressive organization founded in 1900, which sought to resolve labor disputes by bringing together representatives from business and labor. NCF's approach was criticized by conservatives who objected to unions and also, as seen here through Lucas, by socialists who found it too friendly to capitalism. Hence Lucas's metaphor about *chloroforming* (anesthetizing) workers.

goal, a step to be tolerated with impatience. Schliemann called himself a "philosophic anarchist"; and he explained that an anarchist was one who believed that the end of human existence was the free development of every personality, unrestricted by laws save those of its own being. Since the same kind of match would light every one's fire and the same-shaped loaf of bread would fill every one's stomach, it would be perfectly feasible to submit industry to the control of a majority vote. There was only one earth, and the quantity of material things was limited. Of intellectual and moral things, on the other hand, there was no limit, and one could have more without another's having less; hence "Communism in material production, anarchism in intellectual," was the formula of modern proletarian thought. As soon as the birth-agony was over, and the wounds of society had been healed, there would be established a simple system whereby each man was credited with his labor and debited with his purchases; and after that the processes of production, exchange, and consumption would go on automatically, and without our being conscious of them, any more than a man is conscious of the beating of his heart. And then, explained Schliemann, society would break up into independent, self-governing communities of mutually congenial persons; examples of which at present were clubs, churches, and political parties. After the revolution, all the intellectual, artistic, and spiritual activities of men would be cared for by such "free associations"; romantic novelists would be supported by those who liked to read romantic novels, and impressionist painters would be supported by those who liked to look at impressionist pictures—and the same with preachers and scientists, editors and actors and musicians. If any one wanted to work or paint or pray, and could find no one to maintain him, he could support himself by working part of the time. That was the case at present, the only difference being that the competitive wage-system compelled a man to work all the time to live, while, after the abolition of privilege and exploitation, any one would be able to support himself by an hour's work a day. Also the artist's audience of the present was a small minority of people, all debased and vulgarized by the effort it had cost them to win in the commercial battle; of the intellectual and artistic activities which would result when the whole of mankind was set free from the nightmare of competition, we could at present form no conception whatever.

And then the editor wanted to know upon what ground Dr. Schliemann asserted that it might be possible for a society to exist upon an hour's toil by each of its members. "Just what," answered the other, "would be the productive capacity of society if the present resources of science were utilized, we have no means of ascertaining; but we may be sure it would exceed anything that would sound reasonable to minds inured to the ferocious barbarities of Capitalism. After the triumph of the international proletariat, war would of course be inconceivable; and who can figure the cost of war to humanity—not merely the value of the lives and the material that it destroys, not merely the cost of keeping millions of men in idleness, of arming and equipping them for battle and parade, but the drain upon the vital energies of society by the war-attitude and the war-terror, the brutality and ignorance, the drunkenness, prostitution, and crime it entails, the industrial impotence and the moral deadness? Do you think that it would be too much to say that two hours of the working time of every efficient member of a community goes to feed the red fiend of war?"

And then Schliemann went on to outline some of the wastes of competition; the losses of industrial warfare; the ceaseless worry and friction; the vices—such as drink, for instance, the use of which had nearly doubled in twenty years, as a consequence of the intensification of the economic struggle; the idle and unproductive members of the community, the frivolous rich and the pauperized poor; the law and the whole machinery of repression; the wastes of social ostentation, the milliners and tailors, the hairdressers, dancing masters, chefs and lackeys. "You understand," he said, "that in a society dominated by the fact of commercial competition, money is necessarily the test of prowess, and wastefulness the sole criterion of power. So we have, at the present moment, a society with, say, thirty per cent of the population occupied in producing useless articles, and one per cent occupied in destroying them. And this is not all; for the servants and panders of the parasites are also parasites, the milliners and the jewellers and the lackeys have also to be supported by the useful members of the community. And bear in mind also that this monstrous disease affects not merely the idlers and their menials, its poison penetrates the whole social body. Beneath the hundred thousand women of the élite are a million middle-class women, miserable because they are not of the élite, and trying to appear of it in public; and beneath them, in turn, are five million farmers' wives reading 'fashion papers' and trimming bonnets, and shop-girls and serving-maids selling themselves into brothels for cheap jewellery and imitation seal-skin robes. And then consider that, added to this competition in display, you have, like oil on the flames, a whole system of competition in selling! You have manufacturers contriving tens of thousands of catchpenny devices, storekeepers displaying them, and newspapers and magazines filled up with advertisements of them!"

"And don't forget the wastes of fraud," put in young Fisher.

"When one comes to the ultra-modern profession of advertising," responded Schliemann,—"the science of persuading people to buy what they do not want,—he is in the very centre of the ghastly charnel-house of capitalist destructiveness, and he scarcely knows which of a dozen horrors to point out first. But consider the waste in time and energy incidental to making ten thousand varieties of a thing for purposes of ostentation and snobbishness, where one variety would do for use! Consider all the waste incidental to the manufacture of cheap qualities of goods, of goods made to sell and deceive the ignorant; consider the wastes of adulteration,—the shoddy clothing, the cotton blankets, the unstable tenements, the ground-cork life-preservers,[3] the adulterated milk, the aniline soda-water, the potato-flour sausages—"

"And consider the moral aspects of the thing," put in the ex-preacher.

"Precisely," said Schliemann; "the low knavery and the ferocious cruelty incidental to them, the plotting and the lying and the bribing, the blustering and bragging, the screaming egotism, the hurrying and worrying. Of course, imitation and adulteration are the essence of competition—they are but another form of the phrase 'to buy in the cheapest market and sell in the dearest.' A government official has stated that the nation suffers a loss of a billion and a quarter dollars a year through adulterated foods; which means, of course, not only materials wasted that might have been useful outside of the human stomach, but doctors and nurses for people who would otherwise have been well, and undertakers for the whole human race ten or twenty years before the proper time. Then again, consider the waste of time and energy required to sell these things in a dozen stores, where one would do. There are a million or two of business firms in the country, and five or ten times as many clerks; and consider the handling and rehandling, the accounting and reaccounting, the planning and worrying, the balancing of petty profit and loss. Consider the whole machinery of the civil law made necessary by these processes; the libraries of ponderous tomes, the courts and juries to interpret them, the lawyers studying to circumvent them, the pettifogging and chicanery, the hatreds and lies! Consider the wastes incidental to the blind and haphazard production of commodities,—the factories closed, the workers idle, the goods spoiling in storage; consider the activities of the stock-manipulator, the paralyzing of whole industries, the over-stimulation of others, for speculative purposes; the assignments and bank-failures, the crises and panics, the deserted towns and the starving populations! Consider the energies wasted in the seeking of markets, the sterile trades, such as drummer,[4] solicitor, bill-poster, advertising agent.

3. While natural cork blocks were used in vests and belts to make effective life preservers, some of the binding agents used in manufactured (*ground*) cork, such as binders made from animal proteins, made the product denser than water and so it would sink.
4. Traveling salesperson, one who drums up business.

Consider the wastes incidental to the crowding into cities, made necessary by competition and by monopoly railroad-rates; consider the
slums, the bad air, the disease and the waste of vital energies; consider the office-buildings, the waste of time and material in the piling of story upon story, and the burrowing underground! Then take
the whole business of insurance, the enormous mass of administra-
tive and clerical labor it involves, and all utter waste—"

"I do not follow that," said the editor.

"The Coöperative Commonwealth[5] is a universal automatic insurance company and savings-bank for all its members. Capital being
the property of all, injury to it is shared by all and made up by all.
The bank is the universal government credit-account, the ledger in
which every individual's earnings and spendings are balanced. There
is also a universal government bulletin, in which are listed and precisely described everything which the commonwealth has for sale.
As no one makes any profit by the sale, there is no longer any stimulus
to extravagance, and no misrepresentation; no cheating, no adulteration or imitation, no bribery or 'grafting.'"

"How is the price of an article determined?"

"The price is the labor it has cost to make and deliver it, and it is
determined by the first principles of arithmetic. The million workers
in the nation's wheat-fields have worked a hundred days each, and
the total product of the labor is a billion bushels, so the value of a
bushel of wheat is the tenth part of a farm labor-day. If we employ
an arbitrary symbol, and pay, say, five dollars a day for farm-work,
then the cost of a bushel of wheat is fifty cents."

"You say 'for farm-work,'" said Mr. Maynard. "Then labor is not
to be paid alike?"

"Manifestly not, since some work is easy and some hard, and we
should have millions of rural mail-carriers, and no coal-miners. Of
course the wages may be left the same, and the hours varied; one or
the other will have to be varied continually, according as a greater
or less number of workers is needed in any particular industry. That
is precisely what is done at present, except that the transfer of the
workers is accomplished blindly and imperfectly, by rumors and
advertisements, instead of instantly and completely, by a universal
government bulletin."

"How about those occupations in which time is difficult to calculate? What is the labor cost of a book?"

"Obviously it is the labor cost of the paper, printing, and binding
of it—about a fifth of its present cost."

---

5. A society based on cooperative and socialist principles. The concept was popularized
   by the Danish-American writer Laurence Gronland's 1884 book by this name, which
   adapted Marx's socialism for an American audience.

"And the author?"

"I have already said that the state could not control intellectual production. The state might say that it had taken a year to write the book, and the author might say it had taken thirty. Goethe[6] said that every *bon mot* of his had cost a purse of gold. What I outline here is a national, or rather international, system for the providing of the material needs of men. Since a man has intellectual needs also, he will work longer, earn more, and provide for them to his own taste and in his own way. I live on the same earth as the majority, I wear the same kind of shoes and sleep in the same kind of bed; but I do not think the same kind of thoughts, and I do not wish to pay for such thinkers as the majority selects. I wish such things to be left to free effort, as at present. If people want to listen to a certain preacher, they get together and contribute what they please, and pay for a church and support the preacher, and then listen to him; I, who do not want to listen to him, stay away, and it costs me nothing. In the same way there are magazines about Egyptian coins, and Catholic saints, and flying machines, and athletic records, and I know nothing about any of them. On the other hand, if wage-slavery were abolished, and I could earn some spare money without paying tribute to an exploiting capitalist, then there would be a magazine for the purpose of interpreting and popularizing the gospel of Friedrich Nietzsche, the prophet of Evolution, and also of Horace Fletcher, the inventor of the noble science of clean eating; and incidentally, perhaps, for the discouraging of long skirts, and the scientific breeding of men and women, and the establishing of divorce by mutual consent."[7]

Dr. Schliemann paused for a moment. "That was a lecture," he said with a laugh, "and yet I am only begun!"

"What else is there?" asked Maynard.

"I have pointed out some of the negative wastes of competition," answered the other. "I have hardly mentioned the positive economies of cooperation. Allowing five to a family, there are fifteen million families in this country; and at least ten million of these live separately, the domestic drudge being either the wife or a wage-slave. Now set aside the modern system of pneumatic house-cleaning,[8] and the economies of cooperative cooking; and consider one single item, the washing of dishes. Surely it is moderate to say that the dish-washing

---

6. See above, p. 16, n. 5.
7. A series of then-popular reform ideas. At the time, divorce could be granted only if one spouse was proven guilty and the other innocent rather than the now-familiar practice of *mutual consent*. *Nietzsche* (1844–1900), German philosopher and critic, articulated the theory of the Übermensch ("overman" or "superman"), the exceptional being into which he hoped humans would evolve, thereby transcending the "slave morality" of Western bourgeois culture. *Fletcher* (1849–1919) popularized faddish eating practices, especially thorough chewing, which he claimed had cured him of chronic stomach trouble and general malaise. *Scientific breeding*: by eugenics.
8. By air pressure; blown-air vacuums were still a novelty.

for a family of five takes half an hour a day; with ten hours as a day's work, it takes, therefore, half a million able-bodied persons—mostly women—to do the dish-washing of the country. And note that this is most filthy and deadening and brutalizing work; that it is a cause of anæmia, nervousness, ugliness, and ill-temper; of prostitution, suicide, and insanity; of drunken husbands and degenerate children—for all of which things the community has naturally to pay. And now consider that in each of my little free communities there would be a machine which would wash and dry the dishes, and do it, not merely to the eye and the touch, but scientifically— sterilizing them—and do it at a saving of all of the drudgery and nine-tenths of the time! All of these things you may find in the books of Mrs. Gilman; and then take Kropotkin's 'Fields, Factories, and Workshops,'[9] and read about the new science of agriculture, which has been built up in the last ten years; by which, with made soils and intensive culture, a gardener can raise ten or twelve crops in a season, and two hundred tons of vegetables upon a single acre; by which the population of the whole globe could be supported on the soil now cultivated in the United States alone! It is impossible to apply such methods now, owing to the ignorance and poverty of our scattered farming population; but imagine the problem of providing the food supply of our nation once taken in hand systematically and rationally, by scientists! All the poor and rocky land set apart for a national timber-reserve, in which our children play, and our young men hunt, and our poets dwell! The most favorable climate and soil for each product selected; the exact requirements of the community known, and the acreage figured accordingly; the most improved machinery employed, under the direction of expert agricultural chemists! I was brought up on a farm, and I know the awful deadliness of farm-work; and I like to picture it all as it will be after the revolution. To picture the great potato-planting machine, drawn by four horses, or an electric motor, ploughing the furrow, cutting and dropping and covering the potatoes, and planting a score of acres a day! To picture the great potato-digging machine, run by electricity, perhaps, and moving across a thousand-acre field, scooping up earth and potatoes, and dropping the latter into sacks! To see every other kind of vegetable and fruit handled in the same way—apples and oranges picked by machinery, cows milked by electricity— things which are already done, as you may know. To picture the

9. In *Fields, Factories, and Workshops* (1899), the Russian anarcho-communist Peter *Kropotkin* (1842–1921) describes a harmonious way of life based on cooperation instead of competition, emphasizing local production, agriculture, and self-sufficient communities. In *Women and Economics* (1898), the American writer Charlotte Perkins *Gilman* (1860–1935) urges communal housekeeping, cooking, and childcare. With some of the proceeds from *The Jungle*, Sinclair founded a utopian cooperative (November 1906–March 1907), Helicon Hall, which practiced such communal ideas.

harvest-fields of the future, to which millions of happy men and women come for a summer holiday, brought by special trains, the exactly needful number to each place! And to contrast all this with our present agonizing system of independent small farming,—a stunted, haggard, ignorant man, mated with a yellow, lean, and sad-eyed drudge, and toiling from four o'clock in the morning until nine at night, working the children as soon as they are able to walk, scratching the soil with his primitive tools, and shut out from all knowledge and hope, from all the benefits of science and invention, and all the joys of the spirit—held to a bare existence by competition in labor, and boasting of his freedom because he is too blind to see his chains!"

Dr. Schliemann paused a moment. "And then," he continued, "place beside this fact of an unlimited food supply, the newest discovery of physiologists, that most of the ills of the human system are due to overfeeding! And then again, it has been proven that meat is unnecessary as a food; and meat is obviously more difficult to produce than vegetable food, less pleasant to prepare and handle, and more likely to be unclean. But what of that, so long as it tickles the palate more strongly?"

"How would Socialism change that?" asked the girl-student, quickly. It was the first time she had spoken.

"So long as we have wage-slavery," answered Schliemann, "it matters not in the least how debasing and repulsive a task may be, it is easy to find people to perform it. But just as soon as labor is set free, then the price of such work will begin to rise. So one by one the old, dingy, and unsanitary factories will come down—it will be cheaper to build new; and so the steamships will be provided with stoking-machinery, and so the dangerous trades will be made safe, or substitutes will be found for their products. In exactly the same way, as the citizens of our Industrial Republic become refined, year by year the cost of slaughter-house products will increase; until eventually those who want to eat meat will have to do their own killing—and how long do you think the custom would survive then?—To go on to another item—one of the necessary accompaniments of capitalism in a democracy is political corruption; and one of the consequences of civic administration by ignorant and vicious politicians, is that preventable diseases kill off half our population. And even if science were allowed to try, it could do little, because the majority of human beings are not yet human beings at all, but simply machines for the creating of wealth for others. They are penned up in filthy houses and left to rot and stew in misery, and the conditions of their life make them ill faster than all the doctors in the world could heal them; and so, of course, they remain as centres of contagion, poisoning the lives of all of us, and making happiness impossible for even the most selfish. For this reason I would seriously maintain that all the medical and surgical discoveries that science can make in the future will be of less importance than the application of the knowledge we already possess, when the disinherited of the earth have established their right to a human existence."

And here the Herr Doctor relapsed into silence again. Jurgis had noticed that the beautiful young girl who sat by the centre-table was listening with something of the same look that he himself had worn, the time when he had first discovered Socialism. Jurgis would have liked to talk to her, he felt sure that she would have understood him. Later on in the evening, when the group broke up, he heard Mrs. Fisher say to her, in a low voice, "I wonder if Mr. Maynard will still write the same things about Socialism"; to which she answered, "I don't know—but if he does we shall know that he is a knave!"

✻   ✻   ✻   ✻   ✻

And only a few hours after this came election day—when the long campaign was over, and the whole country seemed to stand still and hold its breath, awaiting the issue. Jurgis and the rest of the staff of Hinds's Hotel could hardly stop to finish their dinner, before they hurried off to the big hall which the party had hired for that evening.

But already there were people waiting, and already the telegraph instrument on the stage had begun clicking off the returns. When the final accounts were made up, the Socialist vote proved to be over four hundred thousand—an increase of something like three hundred and fifty per cent in four years.[1] And that was doing well; but the party was dependent for its early returns upon messages from the locals, and naturally those locals which had been most success-ful were the ones which felt most like reporting; and so that night every one in the hall believed that the vote was going to be six, or seven, or even eight hundred thousand. Just such an incredible increase had actually been made in Chicago, and in the state; the vote of the city had been 6,700 in 1900, and now it was 47,000; that of Illinois had been 9,600, and now it was 69,000! So, as the evening waxed, and the crowd piled in, the meeting was a sight to be seen. Bulletins would be read, and the people would shout themselves hoarse; and then some one would make a speech, and there would be more shouting; and then a brief silence, and more bulletins. There would come messages from the secretaries of neighboring states, reporting their achievements; the vote of Indiana had gone from 2300

1. Eugene Debs, who had garnered 100,000 votes when he ran for president on the socialist ticket in 1900, quadrupled that figure in 1904. Six years after publication of *The Jungle*, in 1912, Debs got 900,000 votes.

to 12,000; of Wisconsin from 7000 to 28,000; of Ohio from 4800 to 36,000! There were telegrams to the national office from enthusiastic individuals in little towns which had made amazing and unprecedented increases in a single year: Benedict, Kansas, from 26 to 260; Henderson, Kentucky, from 19 to 111; Holland, Michigan, from 14 to 208; Cleo, Oklahoma, from 0 to 104; Martin's Ferry, Ohio, from 0 to 296—and many more of the same kind. There were literally hundreds of such towns; there would be reports from half a dozen of them in a single batch of telegrams. And the men who read the despatches off to the audience were old campaigners, who had been to the places and helped to make the vote, and could make appropriate comments: Quincy, Illinois, from 189 to 831—that was where the mayor had arrested a Socialist speaker! Crawford County, Kansas, from 285 to 1975; that was the home of the "Appeal to Reason"! Battle Creek, Michigan, from 4261 to 10,184; that was the answer of labor to the Citizens' Alliance Movement![2]

And then there were official returns from the various precincts and wards of the city itself! Whether it was a factory district or one of the "silk-stocking" wards seemed to make no particular difference in the increase; but one of the things which surprised the party leaders most was the tremendous vote that came rolling in from the stockyards. Packingtown comprised three wards of the city, and the vote in the spring of 1903 had been five hundred, and in the fall of the same year, sixteen hundred. Now, only a year later, it was over sixty-three hundred—and the Democratic vote only eighty-eight hundred! There were other wards in which the Democratic vote had been actually surpassed, and in two districts, members of the state legislature had been elected. Thus Chicago now led the country; it had set a new standard for the party, it had shown the working-men the way!

—So spoke an orator upon the platform; and two thousand pairs of eyes were fixed upon him, and two thousand voices were cheering his every sentence. The orator had been the head of the city's relief bureau in the stockyards, until the sight of misery and corruption had made him sick. He was young, hungry-looking, full of fire; and as he swung his long arms and beat up the crowd, to Jurgis he seemed the very spirit of the revolution. "Organize! Organize! Organize!"— that was his cry. He was afraid of this tremendous vote, which his party had not expected, and which it had not earned. "These men are not Socialists!" he cried. "This election will pass, and the excitement will die, and people will forget about it; and if you forget about it, too, if you sink back and rest upon your oars, we shall lose this vote

2. Dedicated to ending unions, which they saw as un-American, these largely secret groups spread in the first decade of the 20th century.

that we have polled to-day, and our enemies will laugh us to scorn! It rests with you to take your resolution—now, in the flush of victory, to find these men who have voted for us, and bring them to our meetings, and organize them and bind them to us! We shall not find all our campaigns as easy as this one. Everywhere in the country to-night the old party politicians are studying this vote, and setting their sails by it; and nowhere will they be quicker or more cunning than here in our own city. Fifty thousand Socialist votes in Chicago means a municipal-ownership Democracy[3] in the spring! And then they will fool the voters once more, and all the powers of plunder and corruption will be swept into office again! But whatever they may do when they get in, there is one thing they will not do, and that will be the thing for which they were elected! They will not give the people of our city municipal ownership—they will not mean to do it, they will not try to do it; all that they will do is give our party in Chicago the greatest opportunity that has ever come to Socialism in America! We shall have the sham reformers self-stultified and self-convicted; we shall have the radical Democracy left without a lie with which to cover its nakedness! And then will begin the rush that will never be checked, the tide that will never turn till it has reached its flood—that will be irresistible, overwhelming—the rallying of the outraged working-men of Chicago to our standard! And we shall organize them, we shall drill them, we shall marshal them for the victory! We shall bear down the opposition, we shall sweep it before us—and Chicago will be ours! *Chicago will be ours!* CHICAGO WILL BE OURS!"

THE END

---

3. National ownership of the infrastructure, such as railroads and telephone and telegraph systems, which some considered the logical response to big business. Some Democrats also urged city ownership of public utilities, especially public transportation.

CONTEXTS AND BACKGROUNDS

While ancillary readings are grouped into four sections, there are many synergies among the readings and the sections. For instance, the food justice readings in the "Immigration and Labor" unit can be paired with any of the readings in the "Nature" section. The four sections can be read in any order, as can the individual pieces within each unit. Most sections begin with pieces written around the time of *The Jungle* before turning to recent works, many of which indicate the persistence of numerous issues of concern to Sinclair.

Division of labor among pork butchers, Swift & Company, Chicago (1905). Image courtesy of the Library of Congress.

"Everybody Welcome," reception room for visitors at Armour Packing Plant, Chicago. Armour claimed to welcome 100,000 guests a year (1909). Image courtesy of the Library of Congress.

Young sausage-fillers at Armour, Chicago (1893). Image courtesy of the Library of Congress.

Cattle at Union Stock Yards, the meatpacking district in Chicago, unaware of what is in store for them (1903). Image courtesy of the Library of Congress.

325

Capitalism

This unit begins with perspectives on the meatpacking industry written around the time of *The Jungle*. According to socialist A. M. Simons, by the turn into the twentieth century, meatpacking had become America's quintessential capitalist enterprise. Theodore Dreiser, before becoming a novelist, conducted interviews for popular magazines, including one of packer P. D. Armour that offers a view of entrepreneurial and merito-cratic capitalism quite different from the view in *The Jungle*. Harper Leech and John Charles Carroll discuss how Armour and other packers transformed abattoirs and village butcher shops into a national industry, in part by developing what later writers would describe as a *dis*assembly line. Muckraker Charles Edward Russell describes the packing indus-try as a secret monopoly that flouts the law. British journalist Adolphe Smith, who came to Chicago in 1904 to investigate work conditions at the slaughterhouses, discusses the industry's disconcerting treatment of animals as commodities. (Smith, Simons, and Russell were some of Sinclair's sources for *The Jungle*.) J. Ogden Armour, who took over the business after the death of his father in 1901, denies negative publicity (with his eye trained especially on *The Jungle*) in a series of ghostwritten articles originally published in *The Saturday Evening Post* and later compiled into a book.

The unit then turns to modern perspectives on the history of capital-ism in general and the meatpacking industry in particular. Martin J. Sklar describes the transformation of capitalism during the Progressive era, from an entrepreneurial to a corporate model, not as a natural evo-lution of economic laws, but rather as a strategy deliberately pursued by owners of corporations. Joshua Specht's history of the packing indus-try traces continuities between Sinclair's time and our own, from the difficulties in limiting the power of Big Food to the complicity of con-sumers, while also looking at how attitudes toward gender and race play out in what he calls a "red meat *republic*" (355). Marion Nestle shows that the imperative to turn a profit causes food companies—which continue to produce far more calories than people actually need—to promote a lifestyle of "*eat more*" (362) that endangers public health. Political economist Thomas Piketty's examination of income inequality over the last hundred years predicts that America in the twenty-first century is on track to record greater inequality than even what is seen in *The Jungle*.

A. M. [ALGIE] SIMONS

[The Perfection of Capitalism]†

Perhaps there is no one feature of the "Windy City" of which its ruling class are so proud as the Union Stock Yards and Packing Houses. Perhaps it is because from start to finish they are more nearly typical of the system in which they exist than anything else in the great city. From the general air of hoggishness that pervades everything from the general managers' offices down to the pens beneath the buildings and up to the smoke that hangs over it all, the whole thing is purely capitalistic. In fact, it is safe to say that in the entire world there is not another so perfect example of the capitalistic system in all its purity (or impurity, rather), as is furnished by this group of industries.

So it has become one of the "sights of the town," and no visitor thinks his tour of the World's Fair City[1] complete until he has been piloted through the mazes of "Packingtown" and seen the wondrous machinery that whirls the animal along in the transforming journey from pen to barrel. He gazes in amazement at the contrivances of iron and steel, whose variety, intricacy and humaneness are only equaled in marvelousness by the uniformity, simplicity and mechanicalness of their flesh and blood competitors. The interest and admiration of the visitor is divided between the iron and steel expression of human intelligence that follows all the curves of a hog's anatomy to remove the bristles, and the flesh and blood mechanism that removes all the meat from the bone with a single stroke of the knife. He is led into the great cooling rooms and gazes on acres of freezing hogs in course of preparation for journeys of perhaps half way around the world, and he is asked to admire the perfect machinery that carries the carcass along through all these various processes, with never a break or a slip. But his attention is never called to the gangs of workmen with bare arms rushing at headlong speed from this frigid atmosphere to the torrid heat of the "killing floor." Neither is he told that from the time he enters the confines of the "Yards" until he leaves, his every movement is noted by paid spies who dog his footsteps or note his presence as he passes their designated station. In fact, there are many things not on exhibition for the casual visitor, or pointed out by the affable uniformed guide who

---

† From *Packingtown* (Chicago: Charles H. Kerr, 1899), pp. 2–4, 21–23. Notes are by the editor of this Norton Critical Edition.

1. In May–October 1893, Chicago hosted the World's Columbian Exposition to commemorate the 400th anniversary of Christopher Columbus's voyage to the Americas. The spectacular exhibits brought millions of visitors to marvel at the displays of national power and opulence, making the fair a huge boon to Chicago.

leads the way. It is the purpose of this paper to take the visitor a
little behind the scenes and point out some of the conditions that
attach to this splendid development of capitalism.

As was stated above, the industry as a whole is probably the best
example of the completed product of capitalistic evolution to be found
in the world. The process of consolidation has about run its course.
All competing butchers were long ago destroyed, save in a few out-of-
the-way places, where their competition is unfelt. The process by
which this was carried out is familiar to the residents of almost every
small city or town in this country. At the beginning there are several
little competing butchers. Everything is going on lovely, with all the
wastes and weaknesses of competition. Some fine morning one of the
butchers, generally the strongest financially in the place, is approached
by an affable stranger, who introduces himself as a representative
of Swift's or Armour's packing house and makes a flattering offer to
the proprietor of the shop if he will handle their meats instead of his
own. If he accepts, he is immediately enabled to undersell all his previous competitors, and for a time he thinks he has stumbled upon a
Klondike.[2] The consumers of the town are also elated, for they now
get better meats at much lower prices, and they are apt to grow a
little bitter toward their fellow townsmen, who had "been cheating
them all these years." Finally, one by one these competitors disappear, and the victorious butcher becomes of much importance in
his little circle, and a great admirer of Armour and Swift.

One day there comes a change. The hitherto affable agent suddenly becomes stern. The wholesale price of meat is raised, the margin of profit is wiped out, and the independent merchant becomes a
commission agent for the great Chicago packing house. The price of
meat goes up again and everything is lovely—for the packer. If the
local butchers object, they are helpless—their slaughter houses are
dismantled and out of repair and their trade scattered, and besides
there is before them the certainty that no matter how successful they
might be for a short time there is nothing before them but absolute
ruin as soon as they grow large enough to again attract the attention
of the Chicago packers. Thousands of men have thus been robbed of
a life-long trade experience and had the inexorable law of monopoly,
"Thou shalt not produce," read to them. So far there has been no talk
of "compensation" to those whose property was "confiscated."

*　*　*

* * *Visitors as they watch the mechanical perfection with which
everything moves at the Yards, as they see the way in which each man

---

2. Allusion to the Klondike Gold Rush (1896–99), which drew an estimated 100,000
people to the Canadian Yukon territory and Alaska.

is but a cog in the great machine that runs on in wondrous smooth-ness, are apt to break out in fulsome praises of the tremendous intel-lects and marvelous generalship that marshals all these armies of industry for the service of society. Before we join in this chorus of admiration let us make sure that we bestow our praise where it is due. Let us examine one of these mammoth institutions and see if we can locate the organizing, directing, controlling force that preserves order and regularity throughout all its complex ramifications.

At the head we shall find a general superintendent, under him two or more division superintendents; then department superinten-dents and foremen; then overseers of floors, and finally bosses of gangs. Each little potentate is engaged in a fierce struggle to gain the favor of those above him and thus secure further advancement. Jealousies, intrigues and plots of all kinds flourish. Bribery, nepo-tism and diplomacy that would test the resources of an expert politi-cian are employed to gain one step nearer the coveted top. Aside from such methods, the surest way to rise is to reduce the margin of expenses relative to the product in a department. If one man can be thrown upon the streets by forcing the remaining poor wretches to further exertions, promotion is almost within the grasp of the little slave driver who has whipped his fellows on to more rapid death. If he can invent a machine that will send a whole gang of his brother workmen out to beg, starve, or steal, while their work is done by the cheaper labor of their wives and children, his promotion is certain and sure. All the evil effects of competition upon the laborer and consumer is present, and the only person always benefited is the owner of the plant.

But if the effect is damning upon those who are in the line of advancement, what is the condition of those who are condemned to remain forever at the bottom? For it must be remembered that for fully 90 per cent of those who begin work in the Yards there is no hope of ever becoming anything more than an ordinary laborer. Entering the establishment at 14, or if the pressure on the family income is very hard (and when is it light?), a year or two earlier through the use of easily obtained certificates, they have little edu-cation or preparation that would fit them for anything but the sim-plest tasks. Robbed of their birth-right to the development of the powers that are within them they are bound over to a terrible monot-onous slavery to some machine before which they will stand day after day until its rhythmic motions have burnt themselves into their brain and their thinking becomes as mechanical as their work. Or perhaps they stand at some bench and seize a piece of meat as it falls before them, and with that same machine-like regularity that marks everything in the Yards from its politics to its pork-packing, repeat the same motions over and over until they can perform the work equally well with eyes open or closed and until the motions of the hand have stamped their impress on the mind; and they move on in a dreary circle of common things through the day until very weariness at last stops the thinking and they creep away to a place called home, and drag off the great "Yard boots" that seem to hold mind as well as body down to the level of the mire in which they are steeped and throwing them into a corner seek the bed too tired to think, only to go on with the work in dreams until awakened to the reality of another day's unchanging toll.

THEODORE DREISER

[Interview with P. D. Armour][†]

I found Mr. Armour in his crowded office at 205 La Salle Street, Chicago, an office in which a snow storm of white letters falls thickly upon a mass of dark desks, and where brass and lamps and electrical instruments abound, yet not much more than do the hurrying men. Such a mobilization of energy, to promote the private affairs of one man, I had never seen.

"Is Mr. Armour within?" I asked, supposing, since it was but 9:30 A.M., that he had not arrived.

"He is," said the attendant, "and has been since half-past seven."

"Does he usually arrive so early?" I inquired.

"Always," was the significant reply.

I presented my letters, and was soon informed that they were of no avail there. Mr. Armour could see me only after the crush of the day's affairs,—that is, at 6 P.M., and then in the quiet of the Armour Institute, his great philanthropic school for young men and women. He was very courteous, and there was no delay. He took my hand with a firm grasp, evidently reading with his steady gaze such of my characteristics as interested him, and saying, at the same time, "Well, sir."

"Mr. Armour," I said, "will you answer enough questions concerning your life to illustrate for our readers what success means?"

The great Hercules[1] of American industry visibly recoiled at the thought of implied notoriety, having, until the present time, steadily veiled his personality and general affairs as much as possible from public gaze.

"I am only a plain merchant," he answered.

---

† From "Life Stories of Successful Men—No. 10," *Success* 1 (October 1898): 1–2. Notes are by the editor of this Norton Critical Edition.
1. Hero from Greek and Roman mythology known for great strength and endurance, for which he was rewarded with immortality.

A Boy's Chance To-Day

"Do you consider," I said, "that the average American boy of to-day has equally as good a chance to succeed in the world as you had, when you began life?"

"Every bit, and better. The affairs of life are larger. There are greater things to do. There was never before such a demand for able men."

"Were the conditions surrounding your youth especially difficult?"

"No. They were those common to every small New York town in 1832. I was born at Stockbridge, in Madison County. Our family had its roots in Scotland. My father's ancestors were the Robertsons, Watsons, and McGregors of Scotland; my mother came of the Puritans who settled in Connecticut."

"Dr. Gunsaulus[2] says," I ventured, "that all these streams of heredity set toward business affairs."

Inherited Qualities

"Perhaps so. I liked trading as well. My father was reasonably prosperous and independent for those times. My mother had been a school-teacher. There were six boys, and, of course, such a household had to be managed with the strictest economy in those days. My mother thought it her duty to bring to our home some of the rigid discipline of the school-room. We were all trained to work together, and everything was done as systematically as possible."

"Had you access to any books?"

"Yes, the Bible, 'Pilgrim's Progress,'[3] and a history of the United States."

It is said of the latter, by those closest to Mr. Armour, that it was as full of shouting Americanism as anything ever written, and that Mr. Armour's whole nature is yet colored by its stout American prejudices; also that it was read and re-read by the Armour children, though of this the great merchant would not speak.

* * *

"When did you begin to build up your Chicago interests?"

"They were really begun before the war, by my brother Herman. When he went to New York for us, we began adding a small packing-house to the Chicago commission branch. It gradually grew with the growth of the West."

"Is there any one thing that accounts for the immense growth of the packing industry here?" I asked.

2. Chicago minister and educator Frank W. Gunsaulus (1856–1921), founding president of the Armour Institute of Technology (now called the Illinois Institute of Technology).
3. See above, p. x, and below, p. 477, n. 3.

"System and the growth of the West did it. Things were changing at startling rates in those days. The West was growing fast. Its great areas of production offered good profits to men who would handle and ship the products. Railway lines were reaching out in new directions or increasing their capacities and lowering their rates of transportation. These changes and the growth of the country made the creation of a food-gathering and delivering system necessary. Other things helped. At that time (1863), a great many could see that the war was going to terminate favorably for the Union.[4] Farming operations had been enlarged by the war demand and war prices. The state banking system had been done away with, and we had a uniform currency, available everywhere, so that exchanges between the East and the West had become greatly simplified. Nothing more was needed than a steady watchfulness of the markets by competent men in continuous telegraphic communication with each other, and who knew the legitimate demand and supply, in order to sell all products quickly and with profit."

Qualities That Bring Success

"Do you believe that system does so much?" I ventured.

"System and good measure. Give a measure heaped full and running over and success is certain. That is what it means to be the intelligent servants of a great public need. We believed in thoughtfully adopting every attainable improvement, mechanical or otherwise, in the methods and appliances for handling every pound of grain or flesh. Right liberality and right economy will do everything where a public need is being served."

"Have your methods improved any with years?"

"All the time. There was a time when many parts of cattle were wasted, and the health of the city injured by the refuse. Now, by adopting the best known methods, nothing is wasted, and buttons, fertilizer, glue and other things are made cheaper and better for the world in general, out of material that was before a waste and a menace. I believe in finding out the truth about all things,—the very latest truth or discovery,—and applying it."

"You attribute nothing to good fortune?"

"Nothing!" Certainly the word came well from a man whose energy, integrity, and business ability made more money out of a ditch than other men were making out of rich placers in the gold region.[5]

---

4. The American Civil War (1861–65), in which eleven Southern states seceded from the Union to form the Confederate States of America. The Emancipation Proclamation, which freed all enslaved persons on January 1, 1863, deprived the Confederacy of much of its labor force and inspired international public support for the Union.
5. Allusion to the Klondike Gold Rush (see above, p. 329, n. 2). Placers were bits of gold dredge that had been washed away from the primary deposits, called nodes.

"May I ask what you consider the turning-point of your career?"

"The time when I began to save the money I earned at the goldfields."

"What trait do you consider most essential in young men?"

"Truth. Let them get that. Young men talk about getting capital to work with. Let them get truth on board, and capital follows. It's easy enough to get that."

*   *   *

"There is no need to ask you," I continued, "whether you believe in constant, hard labor?"

"I should not call it hard. I believe in close application, of course, while laboring. Overwork is not necessary to success. Every man should have plenty of rest. I have."

"You must rise early to be at your office at half past seven?"

"Yes, but I go to bed early. I am not burning the candle at both ends."

*   *   *

A Business King

And yet the business which this man forgets, when he gathers children about him and moves in his simple home circle, amounted, in 1897, to over $102,000,000 worth of food products, manufactured and distributed. The hogs killed were 1,750,000; the cattle were 1,080,000; the sheep, 625,000. Eleven thousand men were constantly employed, and the wages paid them were over $5,500,000; the railway cars owned and moving about all parts of the country, four thousand; the wagons of many kinds and of large number, drawn by 750 horses. The glue factory, employing 750 hands, made over twelve million pounds of glue! In his private office, it is he who takes care of all the general affairs of this immense world of industry, and yet at half past four he is done, and the whole subject is comfortably off his mind.

"Do you believe in inherited abilities, or that any boy can be taught and trained, and made a great and able man?"

"I recognize inherited ability. Some people have it, and only in a certain direction; but I think men can be taught and trained so that they become much better and more useful than they would be, otherwise. Some boys require more training and teaching than others. There is prosperity for everyone, according to his ability."

"What would you do with those who are naturally less competent than others?"

"Train them, and give them work according to their ability. I believe that life is all right, and that this difference which nature makes is all right. Everything is good, and is coming out satisfactorily, and we ought to make the most of conditions, and try to use and improve everything. The work needed is here, and everyone should set about doing it."

*   *   *

Some Secrets of Success

"Do you consider your financial decisions which you make quickly to be brilliant intuitions?" I asked.

"I never did anything worth doing by accident, nor did anything I have come that way. No, I never decide anything without knowing the conditions of the market, and never begin unless satisfied concerning the conclusion."

"Not everyone could do that," I said.

"I cannot do everything. Every man can do something, and there is plenty to do."

"You really believe the latter statement?"

"There was never more. The problems to be solved are greater now than ever before. Never was there more need of able men. I am looking for trained men all the time. More money is being offered for them everywhere than formerly."

"Do you consider that happiness consists in labor alone?"

"It consists in doing something for others. If you give the world better material, better measure, better opportunities for living respectably, there is happiness in that. You cannot give the world anything without labor, and there is no satisfaction in anything but labor that looks toward doing this, and does it."

HARPER LEECH AND
JOHN CHARLES CARROLL

[From Village Abattoirs to National Industry][†]

Philip Danforth Armour, greatest swine-slayer of the nineteenth century, is both label and folklore. To the extent that his spirit and methods sway the great corporate institution which he founded, Armour is yet present in the kitchens and pantries of a majority of

---

† From *Armour and His Time* (New York: D. Appleton-Century, 1938), pp. 1–2, 3, 4–7, 7–8. Notes are by the editor of this Norton Critical Edition.

American families. He is an intangible guest of millions of families overseas.

In Chicago's Packingtown, the great city of slaughter within the greater city which a poet of the prairies called "hog butcher for the world,"[1] Armour yet is "P.D."—a sandy-haired, red-whiskered demigod of stock-yards mythology.

In our budding national legend Armour bids fair to become the premier "pork baron" who taught mankind how to use "all the pig but the squeal."

The flesh and blood Armour was more merchant than butcher. He did kill more pigs than any other man in all history before him, but he slew his swine by proxy. There is no tradition, much less authentic record, that Armour ever stuck a pig, slit the throat of a sheep, or stunned a struggling steer with a hammer blow that piled its lifeless carcass upon the blood-soaked killing floor.

Armour became a packer of pork at Milwaukee, Wisconsin, because the trade in salted, smoked, and pickled pork had prospects of fat profit when he came to that port on Lake Michigan.

A farmer boy from upstate New York, who had acquired a stake by shrewd trading with the gold-diggers of California,[2] young Armour knew, of course, how hogs were slaughtered, dressed, and preserved on his father's farm. If he ever killed a hog, it was on that Madison County farm by the side of a brook, which drained away the porker's blood, as the carcass was scalded in a great kettle, and later hung from a tree so that the bristles might be scraped off the hide.

Knowing that much, Armour knew enough to be a packer in Milwaukee when he went into the provision business in partnership with Frederick B. Miles on March 1, 1859.

* * *

The work of Armour and the other packing pioneers was essentially fitting the primitive farm smoke-house and the village slaughter-house of pre-industrial America into the new and fast growing order of cities, steam-powered factories, and railroads.

In that process the growing of meat animals, the methods of slaughter and preserving the flesh were all revolutionized, but the key job was more commercial than industrial. It was in assembly and distribution rather than in manufacture that the packing industry, to which Armour contributed so much, made itself an indispensable part of our civilization.

1. The poem "Chicago" (1916), by the American writer Carl Sandburg (1878–1967), begins with this phrase.
2. During the California Gold Rush (1848–55), millions of dollars' worth of gold was extracted, most of it by everyday citizens.

Despite its imposing array of huge buildings filled with intricate machinery, turning out hundreds of specialized products, the packing business is fundamentally trading and transportation made necessary by widening gaps between the centers of human and animal population.

*   *   *

The country smoke-house, which the modern packing-plant has magnified and glorified with many contributions from chemistry and combustion engineering, was a clean place with pleasant acrid odors of hickory smoke, wood ashes, salt, and sodium nitrate. No modern packing-plant produces the equal of the properly aged hams of the farm. Interest on the money tied up militates against large-scale aging of meat and liquor alike. But men will pay more for age in liquor.

But in virtually ridding America of the old-time slaughter-house which supplied villages, small towns and cities, Armour and his sort did unqualified service to quality, cleanliness, and health. Few Americans of this day have ever seen the old-style abattoirs. Most of them were located on the outskirts of communities. Some were placed in spots that seemed chosen for concealment, like the site of the ancient "pest-house" where futile efforts were made at the beginning of epidemics to isolate victims of smallpox, cholera and yellow jack.[3] But the practiced eye could spot the slaughter-house by the carrion birds sailing overhead or by the polluted stream below it. Around some of the worst were bleaching ribs and piles of leg bones, with here and there a horned skull. Where the trees hid the thing, the nose could find it. The building was usually on the order of a low-class cow barn. The floors were covered with caked blood and offal. Flies and rats of fearful predacity abounded.

*   *   *

From those ancient arenas of pain, blood, and filth arose gruesome folk-tales about the slaughtering trade, which long survived to plague the packing industry. The lag of tradition behind technology is nowhere better illustrated than in the persistence of such habits of thought. From the first the packers were whipped into sanitation and ever more sanitation by self-interest.

The magnitude and growth of their killings made cleanliness ever more imperative, and the danger of loss from taint and spoilage greater. Soap, sal soda,[4] and disinfectants were an increasing item of expense for Armour every year of forty years, and scrubbing and

---

3. Yellow fever, a virus spread by mosquitos.
4. A sodium carbonate used in making soap.

scraping called for more and more labor. When packing entered its power age live steam came to the help of health.

Nevertheless, the increasing size of the slaughtering-plants served only to make the tall tales taller. The humble cattle pen and dirty killing floor of the village slaughter-house seemed bucolic, homey, and democratic. The gigantic packing-houses were castles of barons or giants in which all sorts of gruesome goings on were plausible.

From these origins one may trace much of the public distrust and fear of the packers and their products which later was to blossom into the "embalmed beef" scandal,[5] the embargo of American meats by European nations and muckraking crusades of which Upton Sinclair's *Jungle* was the supreme effort. A sincere zealot, Sinclair was a preordained victim for the "raw head and bloody bones" tales which came from the origins of packing. By compressing into one volume all the tales and actual instances of mistake, mishap, and horror which accumulated about Chicago's Packingtown for a generation, Sinclair was able to pen a lurid masterpiece of the sordid and dirty. Yet in the end, the effect of his attacks was undoubtedly good—both for the public and the packers, because it accelerated sanitation and by increasing the effectiveness of Federal inspection gave to the packers' products the prestige of the National Government itself.

Philip D. Armour and the packers of his time took the farm smoke-house and fitted it into national and international trade by organizing continuous processing of meats that were proof against spoilage, and fit for transportation over great distances. They later abolished the bulk of local slaughtering and substituted central slaughter and far flung shipment of both fresh and preserved beef, mutton, and pork. But they had to begin with the tools at hand, and could improve them only so fast as trial and error, later supplemented by scientific research and discovery, made betterment possible.

* * *

There is a paradox in the packing industry which the lay observer is apt to overlook. Unlike most modern large-scale industrial operations, packing is not the assembly of raw materials to be fabricated into one or more finished products. It is the tearing apart of elaborate organisms fashioned by biological forces and breaking them up into a large number of products. Many of the parts of the animals pass directly into consumption. A much smaller part pass into by-products which are then manufactured in much the same manner as the products of other industries.

Nevertheless it was in packing that the basic device of modern straight line production seems to have originated. The "assembly

5. See above, p. 208.

line" and "belt" of the modern motor car, chemical, or electrical equipment plant are merely an adaptation of the "chain" which came into packing-plants in 1865 or thereabouts. Before its introduction the carcass of the animal was cleaned and cut up much as one prepares and carves a chicken at dinner—only there were more carvers, more knives, more tables, more garbage cans and those were of far greater sizes.

CHARLES EDWARD RUSSELL

[The Secret Beef Monopoly][†]

In the free republic of the United States of America is a power greater than the government, greater than the courts or judges, greater than legislatures, superior to and independent of all authority of state or nation.

It is a greater power than in the history of men has been exercised by king, emperor, or irresponsible oligarchy. In a democracy it has established a practical empire more important than Tamerlaine's[1] and ruled with a sway as certain. In a country of law, it exists and proceeds in defiance of law. In a country historically proud of its institutions it establishes unchecked a condition that refutes and nullifies the significance of those institutions. We have grown familiar in this country with many phases of the mania of money-getting, and the evil it may work to mankind at large; we have seen none so strange and alarming as this of which I write. Names change, details change; but when the facts of these actual conditions are laid bare it will puzzle a thoughtful man to say wherein the rule of the great power now to be described differs in any essential from the rule of a feudal tyrant in the darkness of the Middle Ages.

Three times a day this power comes to the table of every household in America, rich or poor, great or small, known or unknown; it comes there and extorts its tribute. It crosses the ocean and makes its presence felt in multitudes of homes that would not know how to give it a name. It controls prices and regulates traffic in a thousand markets. It changes conditions and builds up and pulls down industries; it makes men poor or rich as it will; it controls or establishes or obliterates vast enterprises across the civilized circuit. Its lightest word affects men on the plains of Argentina or the by-streets of London.

---

† From *The Greatest Trust in the World* (New York: Ridgway-Thayer 1905), pp. 1–3, 89–94, 130–33. Unless otherwise indicated, notes are by the editor of this Norton Critical Edition.
1. Also known as Timur, 14th-century Turkic conqueror and founder of the Timurid Empire.

Of some of the most important industries of this country it has an absolute, iron-clad, infrangible monopoly; of others it has a control that for practical purposes of profit is not less complete. It fixes at its own will the price of every pound of fresh, salted, smoked, or preserved meat prepared and sold in the United States. It fixes the price of every ham, every pound of bacon, every pound of lard, every can of prepared soup. It has an absolute monopoly of our enormous meat exports, dressed and preserved. It has an absolute monopoly of the American trade in fertilizers, hides, bristles, horn and bone products. It owns or controls or dominates every slaughter-house except a few that have inconsiderable local or special trades. It owns steam and electric railroads, it owns the entire trolley-car service in several cities, and is acquiring the like property elsewhere. It owns factories, shops, stock-yards, mills, land and land companies, plants, warehouses, politicians, legislators, and Congressmen.

* * *

As I come to darker chapters in the history of the Beef Trust,[2] it seems fair to say that these papers have no object except to show what are the practical results to humanity of certain systems and ideals of business success that we in this country have tolerated and even cherished. The men that control the Beef Trust are not different from other men; the painful fact is, that their methods are not particularly different from other men's methods. They have merely followed to its logical conclusion the idea of the survival of the fittest, the right of the strong to annihilate the weak, the theory that in business any advantage is fair—the accepted creed of inordinate gain. By the aid of illegal rebates[3] they have built up a gigantic monopoly; but their distinctive offence in this respect has been only in its extent. We may as well face the plain truth, that if all the men that have taken or have tried to secure illegal rebates were to be imprisoned, some of our business streets would look lonely indeed.

We shall see here that up to the worshipped throne of our national deity of Success the trail of this evil thing lies through crime and lawlessness, through the monstrous losses of great populations, through business depression, cruel suffering, ruined lives, embezzlements, and suicides. It should not blind us to the fact that the system—not the individual—is essentially at fault. Engaged in managing this oppression are men that are models of business integrity,

2. "Trust" was a common word for monopoly in Sinclair's day; for more on the terminology, see above, p. 106, n. 3.
3. In effect, rebates allow a company to charge clients different prices, generally favoring the large customer at the expense of the small. The 1903 Elkins Act had made rebates illegal, but the huge packing companies continued to get them from the railroads (see above, p. 220, n. 8). On *survival of the fittest*, see above, p. 57, n. 6.

energy, application, diligence, and all other commercial virtues; so careful of their walk that they would scorn the slightest departure from their own standard of rectitude, so generous that they would not hear of any case of distress without trying to relieve it. In one of the Trust families are four young men, conspicuous examples of clean, wholesome, serious-minded American manhood; inheriting great wealth and yielding to no ordinary temptations of it. Here is no attack except on the system for which all of us are morally responsible with those that most benefit from it—the system and the standard of morality that holds it laudable to pile up great fortunes, by whatsoever means acquired. I am trying merely to show what this thing really is that we all have admired, clergymen have eulogized, and our young men have been inspired to seek.

* * *

* * * The four great packing-houses waxed apace in the fierce competitive strife, until they overshadowed and at last absorbed their competitors. Then as they drew together into the gentlemen's agreement and next into the Trust, the farmer, like the produce-dealer, found that he paid the price of the gentlemen's harmony. Instead of selling his cattle in the market, they were practically confiscated at a price arbitrarily fixed for him, at a price he had nothing to do with, at a price that actual market conditions did not govern.

For the first step of the Trust was to abolish competitive buying.

Naturally. There was no longer any reason for competition. All the great plants being in reality though not in name under one management, all were assured of all the supply the country produced.

* * *

Here then is the issue straitly drawn. Government, through its court, forbids certain men to do certain things. The forbidden things continue daily to be done. How does it come about that any citizens of this country are stronger than the country's laws and courts?

It comes about primarily in this way. The fact of the lawlessness is absolutely certain, the results are apparent, but its methods are devised with such cunning that the law can be baffled and its somnolent officers can have a perfect excuse for sleeping on.

To see this plainly we must go into the organization, real and apparent, of this combination of giants. And first we should understand clearly that here is something unique in corporation management, here is a system without a precedent in the history of monopolies. What do we understand by the word Trust? If we mean a central incorporated body controlling an industry, and having stockholders, officers, offices, records, and books; if we mean, in other words, only such an organization as the Standard Oil Trust has, or the Sugar Trust, or the Steel Trust, here is no Trust at all, and Mr. Lorimer was quite right when he solemnly assured President Roosevelt[4] that there is no such thing as a Beef Trust. In the packing-house industry there is no organization that resembles the Oil Trust, nor any other Trust; no central body, no control, no officers, no holding company, no stock, no books, no records, no president to subpoena, nothing to bring into court. The packing-house combination has no office, no designated meeting-place, no secretary, no stenographer, no minutes. It holds its meetings in cabs, on street corners, in private houses. It is as intangible as the air, as mysterious as destiny, as certain as a perfect machine. It represents the highest and most dangerous achievement in corporation management. Beyond this, human ingenuity has not gone.

Here are four houses, Armour & Co., Swift & Co., Morris & Co., the National Packing Company.[5] Nominally each maintains in business a flawless autonomy. No central organization binds together these great concerns. There is no common treasury, no legally definable management in common. A combination among them may be as close as wax, as obvious as sunlight—where are the documents to prove the compact? * * *

* * * Here are in fact two complete organizations. One, with its individual companies, its separate houses, its books, its reports, its dividends, is always on exhibition for grand juries and complaisant commissioners of corporations. The other, secret, intangible, without record and without form, without officers, without a scratch of a pen to mark its trail, without witnesses and without papers, almost infallibly screens the real operations of the real Trust.

Even this recounts but a part of the advantages of this wonderfully skilful plan. It has moral and sentimental as well as business strength. It enables any person that so desires to declare that there is no Beef Trust, and if by Trust we mean strictly such an organization as the Standard Oil, the assertion is tolerably true. It yields the flattering unction to the uneasy or ill-trained conscience. It soothes the casuist. It affords boundless support for the smooth attorneys that the Trust sends to all meetings of cattlemen to pat the aggrieved on the back and assure them that the Trust is a myth. It provides point and substance for the defence of the Trust, adroitly urged in reactionary newspapers. And it all but nullifies the law.

---

4. Theodore Roosevelt (1858–1919), U.S. president 1901–09. George Horace Lorimer (1867–1937), editor-in-chief of *The Saturday Evening Post*, remained loyal to his earlier employer P. D. Armour.
5. The Schwarzschild & Sulzberger and the Cudahy Companies mentioned in the Garfield report and commonly included in the Trust, while closely related to it and operated in harmony with it, are of less importance and have restricted fields. Cudahy does not buy in the Chicago market [*Author's note*].

A. [ADOLPHE] SMITH

[The Commodification of Animals]†

The first or most obvious defect of the stockyards is the absence of slaughter-houses. Here living animals are treated in exactly the same manner as is ordinary raw material. The Chicago stockyards therefore consist of a number of factories instead of slaughter-houses. These various enterprises are grouped together on the same spot and work not in opposition but as "a combine" one with the other. Here the evident desire is to treat living animals as if they were bales of cotton, of wool, or of any other kind of raw material. What would have happened but for the intervention from Washington of the Federal Government and the prohibitive laws enacted by European States against Chicago products, it is appalling to conjecture. Left to themselves the organisers of this vast industry were not likely to consider that animals, whether living or recently slaughtered, are more liable than inorganic raw material to convey or to absorb germs of disease. That what is intended for food should be prepared in especially clean places is also insufficiently taken into account. The sole object seems to be to convert each animal into saleable product in the quickest and cheapest manner possible. For this the work has to be organised on a wholesale scale so as to pay the cost of labour-saving machinery and there must be the greatest possible subdivision of labour. In a word, the principles of modern industrialism have to be applied and there is no business in the world, not even at the Krupp works,[1] where this [is] done on a larger scale. Of course, all the private butchers have been bought up or driven out of existence for many a mile round by this huge monopoly. Private slaughter-houses were, and generally are, very defective when judged from the sanitary point of view; still they are preferable to slaughtering in factories. The number of animals killed is much smaller than in factories and this is done not upstairs but on the ground and in a little building like a stable where there is no difficulty in obtaining air and light. * * *

* * * I saw bullocks slaughtered in the following manner. The animals are brought up to a huge building which looks more like a lofty prison than a slaughter-house. As they approach the outer wall men strike them on the head with a mallet. Then a sort of wooden partition gives way and lets the half-stunned animals fall into the

† From "Chicago: The Dark and Insanitary Premises Used for the Slaughtering of Cattle and Hogs—The Government Inspection," *The Lancet* (January 14, 1905): 120–22. Notes are by the editor of this Norton Critical Edition.

1. German munitions factory.

basement of the building beyond. As they come tumbling in men seize their hind legs, affix ropes, and they are strung up to some machinery above that moves them along with their heads hanging downwards. Sometimes, however, and before this can be done an animal jumps up and rushes about. It has then to be shot at the risk of the bullet striking an onlooker. When I inquired why a leather gear was not affixed to the bullock's head with a nail so placed in it that, however clumsy the stroke given, it would cause the nail to penetrate the brain and instantly kill the animal, I was told that such a process would take far too much time. Indeed, so great is the hurry that the unfortunate animals are frequently not given time to die. First, they are dropped into the building, though some of them may be insufficiently stunned. Then, when strung up, the machinery carries the living animal forwards and men have to run after it to cut its throat, while others follow with great pails to catch the blood; and all this without interrupting the dying animal's journey to the part of the factory where the next process of manufacture begins. Sometimes the cattle are struck down and stunned more quickly than the men can pick them up and cut their throats, so they are left to live some time suspended in the air by their hind feet. The machinery carries forwards the animals that are hooked on to it regardless of their agony. On they go from stage to stage of manufacture and the men have to keep pace with them whether dead or alive. Quickly the throats are cut, no time can be lost to let the animals bleed, a man with a pail must walk by their side to catch the blood. Much of the hot blood is spilt over the man or over the floor; that does not matter so long as a small section of a minute is economised.

J. OGDEN ARMOUR

[A Packer's Rebuttal]†

Government inspection is another important feature of the packers' business. To the general public, the meat-eating public, it ought to appeal as one of the *most important* features of any and all business in the whole country. It is the wall that stands between the meat-eating public and the sale of diseased meat.

This government inspection alone, if there were no other business or economic reasons, would be an all-sufficient reason for the existence of the packing and dressed-meat business on a mammoth

† From *The Packers, the Private Car Lines, and the People* (Philadelphia: Henry Altemus, 1906), pp. 60–63, 66, 358–64. Notes are by the editor of this Norton Critical Edition.

scale. It should, if understood, make the general public a partisan supporter of the large packers.

Strangely enough, in view of its vital importance, this government inspection has been the subject of almost endless misrepresentation—of *ignorantly or maliciously false statements*.

The public has been told that meat animals and carcasses condemned as diseased are afterwards secretly made use of by the packers and sold to the public for food in the form of both dressed meats and canned meats.

*　*　*

* * * In Armour & Co.'s business *not one atom of any condemned animal or carcass finds its way, directly or indirectly, from any source, into any food-product or food-ingredient.*

Every meat-animal and every carcass slaughtered in the Union Stock Yards, or stock-yards at any of the markets of the United States, is carefully inspected by the United States government. This inspection by the national government is supplemented, in practically all cases, by state or city inspection, or both. The live animals are inspected on the hoof and again when slaughtered.

The inspection by the United States government is not compulsory on the packers in the strict legal sense of the term; it is more binding than if it were compulsory. *It is business*. Attempt to evade it would be, from the purely commercial viewpoint, suicidal. *No packer can do an interstate or export business without government inspection.* Self-interest forces him to make use of it.

*　*　*

This government inspection thus becomes an important adjunct of the packer's business from two viewpoints. It puts the stamp of legitimacy and honesty upon the packer's product, and so is to him a business necessity. To the public it is an *insurance* against the sale of diseased meats.

*　*　*

There has been so much said lately about the lack of care for cleanliness in packing house processes, and about the wholesomeness of the meats and food products that come through the packing houses, that I feel constrained to add something to what I have already said about the way the public health is safeguarded from the time a meat animal comes to the stock yards until it leaves the packing house as a finished product. At every step in the conversion of animals into meat the public is protected, not only by rigid government inspection of every animal before slaughter and of every carcass after slaughter, but also by the common-sense business methods of the packers themselves.

Writers and publishers who have only the dollars-and-cents purpose to serve assume the tragic pose and unfold hair-raising tales about dark secrets of the packing industry. They make statements that should, if they were true, cause every packing house in America to be closed by law, and should convert the whole world to vegetarianism.

We are told of hidden chambers and mysterious cellars where nameless materials are worked up by secret processes into food. We are told, with a gravity that is intended to pass for sincerity, that "outsiders" are never permitted to see the inner workings of a packing house. These literary concoctions are served up with a garnishment of all the circumstantial detail that can be conceived by a dishonest mind and a feverish imagination working together. The very excess of detail, to the thinking mind, ought to be evidence of untruth.

*   *   *

* * * Unfortunately there is a serious side, a very serious side, to this performance. It does real harm, not only to the packer, but practically to the entire public.

It is a foul blow at the entire industry of raising meat animals and distributing meats and meat products, an industry that permeates every section of this country and engages, in one form or another, from farm to retail meat shop, the income producing work of a very large percentage of the population—a larger percentage probably than does any other industry in the land. It is an injustice to every man, woman or child who eats meat, because, utterly without justification, it plants in their minds a suspicion of the wholesomeness of their daily food.

The packers have nothing to hide. They hide nothing. The public knows this if it would but let itself remember facts. * * * Literally hundreds of thousands of people—I could, I believe, say millions, in truth—all meat eaters, have gone through these plants and have seen every process of converting animals into food.

Outside of the offices there is not a locked door in Chicago's Packing Town. Could the packers afford to throw their plants open to the world in this way if they had anything to conceal? Could they risk giving a bad impression of packing house processes and methods to hundreds of thousands of actual customers for their product? On the contrary, they have pursued the open house policy as good business policy. They have believed and have proved that the more the public knows about the inside of a modern packing house the less prejudice there will be against packing house food products.

But these facts, which the whole world knows when it stops to think about them, have no restraining influence on the makers of "yellow" literature.[1] * * *

Unfortunately a good many people will always believe anything that is persistently told them, particularly if it be about a corporation.

MARTIN J. SKLAR

From The Corporate Reconstruction of American Capitalism[†]

The period 1890–1916 in United States history, encompassing what is commonly called the Progressive Era, was both an age of reform and the age of the corporate reconstruction of American capitalism. * * * In one and the same period were laid down and intermeshed the foundations of the corporate-capitalist economy, of the regulatory state, of internationalist foreign policy, and of modern political liberalism, as they would develop in mutually reinforcing and conflicting ways over the next several decades in the United States.

　　　　　　✣　　✣　　✣

The corporate reorganization of industry that crystallized in the merger movement of 1898–1904 and developed thereafter to World War I marked the passage of a relatively mature American industrial capitalism from its proprietary-competitive stage to an early phase of its corporate-administered stage. It marked, that is, the emergence of the corporate reconstruction of American capitalism.[1]

---

1. Usually called yellow journalism; refers to newspapers that run sensationalistic and scandalous stories and use scare headings, fake interviews, and pseudoscience. The term dates from a circulation war in the 1890s between Joseph Pulitzer's *New York World* and William Randolph Hearst's *New York Journal.*

† From *The Corporate Reconstruction of American Capitalism, 1890–1916: The Market, the Law, and Politics* (New York: Cambridge UP, 1988), pp. 1, 4–5, 6, 9–11, 13–14, 15–16, 20–21, 33–34. © Martin J. Sklar 1988. Reprinted with permission of Cambridge UP through PLSclear. Unless otherwise indicated, notes are by the editor of this Norton Critical Edition. Some of the author's notes have been excerpted or omitted. Bibliographic information has been included.

1. The term "proprietary-competitive" in this study refers to capitalist property and market relations in which the dominant type of enterprise was headed by an owner-manager (or owner-managers), or a direct agent thereof, and in which such enterprise was a price-taker, rather than a price-maker, price being determined by conditions of supply and demand beyond the control of the enterprise short of anticompetitive inter-firm collusion. The term "corporate reorganization of industry," or "corporate reconstruction of capitalism," in this study, means not simply the *de jure* incorporation of a property otherwise managed *de facto* along proprietary lines, but the capitalization of the property in the form of negotiable securities relatively widely dispersed in ownership, a corresponding separation of ownership title and management function, and management of the enterprise by bureaucratic-administrative methods involving a division, or a specialization, of managerial function, and an integration, or at least a centralization, of financial control. The term is also meant to designate a process

The word "reconstruction" is meant to connote, as with the earlier era of the Civil War and its aftermath,[2] far-reaching and interrelated changes transpiring in the political, governmental, cultural, and intellectual spheres, as well as in the economy. The corporate reorganization of capitalist property and market relations substantially affected, or integrally related to, changes in intra-class and inter-class relations, in law and public policy, in party politics, in international relations, in prevalent modes of social thought, in education and philanthropy, in civic association, in the structure and role of government, and in the government-society relation in general. As Woodrow Wilson[3] put it at the end of the new century's first decade, "the world of business" had changed "and therefore the world of society and the world of politics." With the change in "our economic conditions from top to bottom," he noted, had also come the change in "the organization of our life," so that the great "economic questions" of the day were also "questions of the very structure and operation of society itself." Or, as historian Richard Hofstadter noted almost a half century later, in the corporation question—the trust question—"nothing less was at stake than the entire organization of American business and American politics, the very question of who was to control the country."[4] In speaking of a corporate reconstruction of American capitalism, then, as distinctively periodizing, or defining, the years 1890–1916, and the Progressive Era in particular, we may also speak of a corporate reconstruction of American society.

*   *   *

*　*　* [I]t will be helpful to conceive of capitalism not simply as economics, not simply as an "economic aspect" of society, but as a system of social relations expressed in characteristic class structures, modes of consciousness, patterns of authority, and relations of power. Hence, although not necessarily identical with society as a whole, capitalism may be viewed as a complex of social relations that

---

occurring not merely in a few notable firms, or in a sector of the economy (e.g., railroads or public utilities), but pervasively, and hence involving the change in the broader economy from price-competitive to administered, or "oligopolistic," markets. The terms (a) "corporate" or "corporate capitalism" and (b) "pro-corporate," as used throughout this study unless otherwise indicated, refer, respectively, (a) to the rise of large corporations and administered markets to dominance in the United States political economy, and (b) to the outlook of those who affirmed it, whether as desirable or as inevitable or unavoidable. The terms do not connote or imply some special "organicist" or "corporative" organization, outlook, or ideology. *　*　* [Author's note].

2. Reconstruction (1865–77), the period immediately following the end of the Civil War (1861–65, and see above, p. 333, n. 4), marked the federal effort to integrate newly freed Black people into American society. Congress passed several constitutional amendments to protect African Americans, but the period is now seen as one of the biggest failed experiments in U.S. history.

3. Thomas Woodrow Wilson (1856–1924), U.S. president 1913–21.

4. *　*　* Hofstadter, The Age of Reform (New York: Random House, Vintage Books, 1955), p. 252 [Author's note].

constitutes—where dominant over, or not subdued by, other social relations—the critical component of a distinct type of society, one that can be called, without undue violence to the empirical record and if left open to appropriate qualification, a capitalist society, as distinguished from, say, tribal hunting-gathering, slave, feudal, or state-socialist societies.

* * *

* * * [W]e should not take at face value the claims of pro-corporate leaders in the Progressive Era that they were doing no more than adapting law and policy, and seeking the adaptation of the people's thinking, habits, and expectations, to natural evolution dictated by indefeasible laws of economics. It was their way of explaining and justifying, to themselves and to the general public, the rise of corporate capitalism, in a society whose political culture placed great value on small-unit enterprise and the dispersal of economic power, and at the same time on improvement, development, and progress in accordance with "natural" laws. This was not a matter of premeditation or deliberate rationalization but rather of a way of thinking, strongly embedded in the late-nineteenth-century American mind, cutting across class and ideological lines, and receiving sanction from at least four venerable sources: (1) the older Protestant idea of predestination or its more modern, impersonal version of providential design manifested in the laws of nature; (2) principles of classical political economy that posited economic laws operating without reference to human will or preference and identifiable with the laws of nature and hence with providential design (if no longer the Invisible Hand of the old competitive market, then at least the Finger of God, as it were);[5] (3) the idea that in the same way that the just government was a government of laws, not of persons, so the just market was one that operated and evolved in accordance with laws, not the design of persons; and (4) the more recent, prestigious principles of evolution by natural selection, applying to human history laws of cumulative and progressive development similar to those presumably governing the natural world of biology.[6] From these premises, or some mixture of them, the demise of the older competitive capitalism at the hands of a rising corporate capitalism could be understood, with convincing cogency, as the necessary result of a progressive evolution governed by natural economic laws, not the work of willful human design, and therefore

5. In *An Inquiry into the Nature and Causes of the Wealth of Nations* (1776), the Scottish political economist Adam Smith (1723–1790) famously claims that the actions of individuals looking out for their own interests in the marketplace are coordinated by an "Invisible Hand" that ends up benefiting all of society. The metaphor has become a shorthand way of defending unregulated markets, although that misstates Smith's economic beliefs, which included the presupposition of a strong state.

6. See above, p. 57, n. 6.

as justified and ineluctable. As Wilson would put it, the large corporations were not hobgoblins, nor the work of the rascally rich; they were, rather, natural, and anything that was natural could not be called immoral.[7]

As American capitalism entered its transition from the competitive stage to the corporate stage, opinion among leaders in business, political, and intellectual spheres began shifting from the old classical economic laws of free competition and supply-demand equilibrium, to thinking centered on new economic laws of business cycles, crises, and disequilibrium, and on cooperation and administered markets as the progressively evolved alternative to "the wastes of competition." The elements of cooperation and administered markets in the new thinking would pose an inconsistency with the principle of natural evolution proceeding apart from human design, an inconsistency lying at the heart of pro-corporate thought and placing it in dialogue with—or at jeopardy to—both populist and socialist thought. In any case, among pro-corporate partisans, as among others, there is to be found by the opening years of the twentieth century increasingly enfeebled appeals to dog-eat-dog social Darwinism:[8] It was cooperation that now made firms, economics, and nations fit to survive; or, as Wilson phrased it in 1897, the American people were poised to realize "the triumphs of cooperation, the self-possession and calm choices of maturity."[9]

Something else, then, or at least something more, than suprahuman laws of economics, was at work in the rise of corporate capitalism: namely, movements of thought and social action. We have little trouble comprehending that the rise of capitalism in early modern Western history involved to some decisive degree a rising bourgeoisie,[1] a rising social class, and corresponding trends of social thought and sociopolitical movements. If that was the case with early capitalism and a rising bourgeoisie, so it was with a developing, maturing capitalism and a risen or regnant bourgeoisie. Capitalism as a mode of production and a set of social relations has a history, and so does the capitalist class, as do the other classes and the class relations, the property and market relations, associated with capitalism. If the establishment of the "natural" competitive marketplace took for its attainment powerful political movements and modes of thought suited to creating the necessary governmental,

---

7. [Woodrow] Wilson, "The Lawyer and the Community" (1910). *The Public Papers of Woodrow Wilson*, ed. Ray S. Baker and William E. Dodd. Vol. 2 (New York: Harper Brothers, 1925), 254, 258 [*Author's note*].
8. See above, p. 57, n. 6.
9. Woodrow Wilson, "The Making of the Nation." *The Public Papers of Woodrow Wilson*, Vol. 1, 328 [*Author's note*].
1. Can refer both to the middle class and to the class that owns most of the wealth as well as the means of production (such as factories) in a society.

legal, intellectual, and cultural conditions, no less so did the subsequent evolution of capitalist market relations, including their passage to the corporate-administered stage.

The history of capitalism, in its very property and market relations, involves not simply "economics" but also human agency in
such forms as associational activity, trends of thought, passage of
laws, and the shaping of government—in sum, in the form of social
movements and politics. * * *

The corporate reconstruction of capitalism in the United States,
accordingly, is a historical event that requires explanation and interpretation: It cannot simply be taken as a "natural" outcome of economic evolution, as an "objective" consequence of techno-economic
development, as a logical defensive reaction of capitalists to the
depression of the 1890s, or as an organizational aspect of some
broader search for order. Nor can the rise of corporate capitalism
be properly understood as a "business" aspect of a society's response
to industrialism. In dispelling parochialism with a comparative perspective, the concept "response to industrialism" has served a good
purpose, portraying Americans engaged in a historical experience
similar to that of other societies. In effect, however, the concept
applies to the United States thinking drawn from modernization
studies of twentieth-century nonindustrial societies; that is, it treats
industrialism as an external force to which Americans responded.
But industrialism was not only something Americans responded to;
since at least the early nineteenth century, it was also something
they were doing. Industrialism itself was, in an early phase, a
"response" of many Americans to their own republican[2] values; in
all phases, a response to nature, the market, and the opportunities
and insecurities of capitalism. Similarly, the corporate reorganization of industry was a way in which some Americans, particularly
capitalists, were making industrialism respond to their changing
position in, and to their changing ideas of, the market, or to their
perception of the requirements of preserving capitalist property relations, or at least their own position as capitalist property owners.

Both capitalist industrialism and its corporate reorganization, in
sum, are better understood not simply as an "external force" or an
"objective" economic or organizational phenomenon but as a social
movement, no less than populism, trade unionism, feminism, Afro-
American equalitarianism, or socialism. Just as we treat these latter
and their respective intellectual trends as political and social movements among farmers, workers, women, Afro-Americans, and others,

2. In distinction to the capital-R Republican Party, *republican* refers to an advocate of a
particular system of government, such as the U.S., in which citizens elect people to
represent them. Thus a republican might believe that citizens have the supreme power
and condemn aristocracies and monarchies.

so may we treat the corporate reconstruction of capitalism and the corresponding intellectual, legal, and legislative trends as political and social movements among capitalists and corresponding groups of intellectuals, reformers, politicians, and others. The tendency to regard "business" as economics or as economic history, or as consisting of "interests" and techno-economic structures and functions, in contrast to ideas and social movements, has obstructed the study of capitalists as a social class and as involved in social movements broader than, but directly related to, their property relations, no less than workers or farmers. It has largely confined the discipline of social history to noncapitalist classes and strata, and has narrowed the framework of research respecting capitalists to special studies of interest-group activity, business history, or the "business mind."

*   *   *

* * * Corporate capitalism, that is, had to be constructed. It did not come on the American scene as a finished "economic" product, or as a pure-ideal type; nor did it "take over" society and simply vanquish or blot out everything else. On the contrary, although tending toward relative decline and a permanent position of subordination, nevertheless, market relations, forms of thought, political movements, and cultural patterns associated with small-producer and proprietary enterprise remained widespread, influential, and strongly represented in party politics, Congress, and the judiciary, and at the state and local levels of politics and government. They continued to exert a large impact, moreover, in the national electoral arena and in national legislative forums. The large corporations and corporate-administered markets, for some time to come, lacked anything near full legitimacy in the minds of a considerable segment of the people and their political representatives.

The social relations, institutions, forms of thought, and policy preferences associated with corporate capitalism reached ascendancy in and through accommodations to, and modifications by, those on the decline and rooted in the past. Many corporations were themselves impregnated with attributes of the proprietary era—for example, in their being dominated by a strong personality, a "captain of industry" or "captain of finance," a figure like E. H. Harriman, John D. Rockefeller, Sr., J. P. Morgan, Sr., Elbert H. Gary, Henry Ford, or Henry O. Havemeyer.[3] In reaching the peak of their power,

---

3. All famous, and in some cases infamous, American capitalists of the time. *E. H. Harriman* (1848–1901), financier and railway tycoon; *John D. Rockefeller, Sr.* (1839–1931), founder of the Standard Oil Company, one of the first great trusts (and see p. 296, n. 2 and p. 510, n. 9); *J. P. Morgan, Sr.* (1837–1913), financier involved in deals leading to the creation of huge corporations including U.S. Steel, International Harvester, and General Electric; *Elbert H. Gary* (1846–1947), founder of U.S. Steel; *Henry Ford* (1863–1947), founder of the Ford Motor Company, who revolutionized factories through

however, at the head of large corporations (or investment banking houses specializing in corporate finance), these "Napoleons" of the market, as Cornell professor of political economy Jeremiah W. Jenks called them, prepared the way of their own decline as they exerted themselves on behalf of building bureaucratic organizations that rendered their style and authority increasingly dysfunctional and hence obsolete.[4] * * *

* * *

After the depression of the 1890s, the change in the organization of the capitalist property-production system crystallized quickly and involved massive amounts of property. Yet, for all the bitter and angry conflict it generated and for all its rapidity and hugeness of scale, it proceeded relatively peacefully and within the framework of the existing political institutions. How come? It has not ordinarily occurred to historians to raise this question. The peaceful transition to corporate capitalism is generally taken for granted. But changes in property organization and ownership on so large a scale are not routine occurrences in history, and violence is a not uncommon accompaniment of such changes, as the Indian wars of the preceding decades and the Civil War[5] scarcely four decades earlier had testified.

It must be said, first, that the nation's political life in the course of the change was not altogether peaceful or lacking in violence and coercive force. The disfranchisement, and the suppression of the citizenship rights, of Afro-Americans in the 1890s and early twentieth century,[6] attended by legal and extralegal violence, narrowed the range of political democracy and substantially weakened populist or anti-corporate forces in the body politic. To some considerable extent, racism and racist violence played a facilitative role in the emergence of corporate capitalism.

Second, the 1890s saw the weakening of such trade unionism in industry as existed, from the effects both of the depression and of legal and extralegal violence against striking workers, as at Homestead in 1892, in the Pullman and railway strike of 1894, and in the

---

assembly lines; *Henry O. Havemeyer* (1847–1907), with the help of his brothers, founded the Sugar Refinerics Company, seen by many as a Sugar Trust.

4. Jenks, *The Trust Problem* (New York: McClure, Phillips, 1900), pp. 73–74. * * * [*Author's note*].

5. The American Civil War (1861–65, and see above, p. 333, n. 4) ended the signature Southern economic system of the plantation, which was based on the exploitation of slave labor. Numerous *Indian wars* between the colonial or federal government and indigenous populations (intermittent between 1622–1924) resulted in the appropriation of most of the land that now forms the U.S. For instance, a series of battles called the Cherokee Wars (1759) forced the Cherokee to give up millions of acres to settlers.

6. While the Fifteenth Amendment (1870) affirmed the right of Black men to vote, by the 1890s, all Southern states had implemented restrictive voting laws to prohibit them from exercising that right. The system of Jim Crow segregation based on the idea of "separate but equal" took hold in the 1890s and lasted until the Civil Rights era.

western mining industry.[7] It would seem, until further study indicates differently, that the curtailment of industrial union strength in the 1890s, and a decline in industrial workers' market power, served as a precondition of the corporate reorganization of American capitalism, and not that the corporate reorganization was itself a strategic capitalist reaction to a presumably growing market power on the part of industrial workers.

Third, the Spanish-American War and the three-year war of conquest in the Philippines, in the years 1898–1902,[8] coinciding in time with most of the activity of the 1898–1904 merger wave, contributed to a political environment favorable to the corporate reorganization of industry. This effect was due in part to domestic economic expansion attributable to war-induced demand, and in part to the spread of chauvinistic or simply nationalistic sentiment, which strengthened the electoral hand of an incumbent president who favored the corporate reorganization of industry as a progressive national asset and was not inclined to turn the might of the national government against it.

* * *

The antitrust debates came to the center of national politics in the Progressive Era because they were, in essence, about the passage of American society from the proprietary-competitive stage to the corporate-administered stage of capitalism—whether the passage should be permitted, and if so, on what terms. The debates, that is, were about the very fundamentals of American society, not simply over particular interests as they might be affected by competition, consolidation, or restraint of trade. Hence, it was not merely coincidental that it took an extended length of time—about twenty-five years—to attain a resolution of the trust question, and that, by the same token, the end of what we call the Progressive Era virtually coincided with this resolution. The Progressive Era, in other words,

7. The *Homestead* strike (also known as the Homestead massacre), called at the Homestead Steel Works near Pittsburgh, resulted in a battle with private security agents. The defeat of labor was a major setback in the effort to unionize steelworkers. *Pullman . . . of 1894*: see above, p. 300, n. 6. *Western mining industry*: The Western Federation of Miners was involved in several famous strikes in the 1890s. In 1894, when owners of a mine in Cripple Creek, Colorado, increased the working day from eight to ten hours, the sheriff brought in thousands of armed deputies to support the owners against the strikers. A second event in Leadville, Colorado, was sparked when miners asked to have returned to them the fifty cents an hour that had been docked from their pay during the 1893 recession. Nearly 1,000 miners walked out, and the owners locked out an additional 1,000, as well as employing labor spies. This event led to the deaths of at least four miners and a fireman, as well as the summoning of the Colorado National Guard.
8. *Spanish-American War*: 1898 conflict between Spain and the U.S., in which the U.S. supported Cuban independence from Spain. The war was ended by the Treaty of Paris, which authorized the U.S. to take possession of the *Philippines* from Spain. When the First Philippine Republic objected to the treaty, the U.S. interpreted this move as insurrection, leading to the 1899–1902 Philippine-American War.

corresponded with the period that constituted the first phase in the corporate reconstruction of American capitalism.

٭ ٭ ٭

The antitrust debates, then, were about basics: Were the central principles of the American political tradition compatible with anything other than small-producer, competitive capitalism? In particular, could they be reconciled with corporate capitalism and administered markets? If large-scale industry in the form of corporate enterprise was the progressive outcome of socioeconomic evolution, were traditional American political principles compatible with progress? In essence, could corporate capitalism and the American liberal tradition be mutually adapted the one to the other?

JOSHUA SPECHT

[How Beef Transformed America into a Red Meat Republic]†

America made modern beef at the same time that beef made America modern. What emerged in the late nineteenth century was truly a red meat *republic;* beef production and distribution were tightly linked to the development of the federal state and the expansion of American power west of the Mississippi. During the 1870s, small-scale cattle ranchers supported as well as instigated and justified wars against the Plains Indians. In Wyoming and Montana, wealthy ranchers dominated state and territorial governments, shaping their early histories. Meanwhile, the emergence of the regulatory state was closely connected to beef production. Key federal bureaucracies, such as the Department of Agriculture, the Bureau of Animal Industry, and the Bureau of Corporations were in large part outgrowths of state attempts to regulate beef production and distribution. In Chicago, the "Big Four" meatpacking houses were some of the first large, integrated corporations, pioneering the assembly line, managing global distribution, maintaining complex supply chains, and growing into the largest private employers of their day. * * * The national market for fresh beef was the culmination of a technological revolution, but it was also the result of collusion and predatory pricing. The modern slaughterhouse was a triumph

† From *Red Meat Republic: A Hoof-to-Table History of How Beef Changed America* (Princeton, NJ: Princeton UP, 2019), pp. 2–6, 10–11, 235–240, 255–56. Reprinted with permission of Princeton UP; permission conveyed through Copyright Clearance Center, Inc. Unless otherwise indicated, notes are by the author. Some of the author's notes have been excerpted or omitted. Bibliographic information has been included.

of human ingenuity as well as a site of brutal labor exploitation. Industrial beef production, with all its troubling costs and undeniable benefits, reflected seemingly contradictory realities. * * *

* * * Technological advances and innovative management techniques made cheap beef possible, but they did little to determine who would benefit most from this new regime (meat-packers and investors) or bear its heaviest costs (workers, small ranchers, and American Indians). This new beef production system was the product of thousands of struggles, large and small, in places like the Texas Panhandle, the West's burgeoning stockyards, and butchers' shops nationwide. The story of modern beef, then, is fundamentally political.

* * * [W]hat might seem like structural features of the beef industry, such as the invisibility and brutality of slaughterhouse labor, were actually the outcome of individual choices and hard-fought policies. This view allows us to see possibilities when they were foreclosed—could today's struggling ranchers have dominated a system the meatpackers now control? In exploring the contingent reasons why meatpacker-dominated, low-cost beef production won out, this [approach] explains the ongoing resilience of a system that has remained in key ways unchanged since *The Jungle*'s publication.

* * *

* * * Starting around the time of the Civil War, a group of Chicago companies capitalized on sizable government contracts to dominate the beef and pork industries. Through an innovative system of refrigerator cars and distribution centers, these companies sold fresh beef nationwide. Millions of cattle were soon passing through Chicago's slaughterhouses each year. These companies did not want to replace local retailers, but aggressively and often coercively sought partnerships that bankrupted retailers' local wholesale supplier. By 1890, the Big Four meatpacking companies—Armour & Company, Swift & Company, Morris & Company, and Hammond & Company—directly or indirectly controlled the majority of the nation's beef and pork.

These changes in production accompanied a far-reaching democratization of beef consumption.[1] Despite the efforts of reformers, debates over industrial change and the growing concentration of capital were quite distant from consumers, for whom the real story was a bigger steak at a cheaper price. * * *

* * * Ranchers, meatpackers, politicians, and bureaucrats all sought to channel policy decisions to advance their own interests or undermine rivals' efforts.

---

1. By democratization, I mean widespread beef consumption and a pervasive belief that beef was something everyone should be able to eat.

These actors all framed their interests in a way that made them palatable to a wider audience. Often, the strategy was to portray industrialized food as inevitable. This way of framing changes in food production helped transform centralized, industrial food from strange and artificial to familiar and natural. * * * In response to his critics, Jonathan Ogden Armour characterized unfettered private control of meat, vegetable, and fruit shipping as "not only natural but inevitable."[2] According to this logic, it was better for regulators to accept centralized meatpacking, despite the cries of traditional butchers and populist ranchers, than try to stop the march of economic progress.

* * *

The cattle-beef complex's resilience also depended on beef's supreme importance to consumers. Because industrial production provided ever-cheaper beef, critics of the system in 1890, as today, faced—often rightfully—charges of elitism. When butchers sought regulation curtailing the Chicago meatpackers' power, they had to acknowledge to lawmakers that industry decentralization would increase prices. Lawmakers would ultimately side with industrial production. In contrast, charges that beef was not sanitary—such as during the US Army beef scandal of 1898[3]—spurred rapid consumer mobilization and state action. But once the Chicago packers resolved these sanitation issues, it merely strengthened their grip. While consumers' concerns about prices and sanitation seem self-evident, we have to understand the logic of consumers who demanded beef more than any other food, and were at times willing to riot for cheap beef rather than eat fish or chicken.

* * *

The democratization of beef sparked new debates about the meaning of beef consumption. Heightened expectations of quality and lower prices, for instance, sparked public conversations about the relationship between gender and food preparation. Elites began studying working-class eating habits. Union leaders celebrated beef consumption as a tangible marker of the labor movement's success. * * * Though in many ways eating is fundamentally about taste, one's dietary choices are always inseparable from broader questions of race, class, gender, and hierarchy.

* * *

2. J. Ogden Armour, *The Packers, the Private Car Lines, and the People* (Philadelphia: Henry Altemus Co., 1906), 38. [For a selection from this book, see above, pp. 344–47—*Editor.*]
3. See above, p. 93, n. 8 [*Editor*].

Though women were expected to purchase and prepare meat for home consumption, beef was nevertheless a man's domain, as evident in the variety of stories mocking women's purchases, cooking, and even dietary choices. In "The Masculine Way," a man instructs a woman buying beef. He boasts that "a man can buy and sell a cargo of wheat while a woman is ordering a pound of steak," and explains that she "ought to hear me give an order for meat, and profit thereby."[4] Elsewhere, a doctor chastises a woman for her "absurd" breakfast choices. He condemns new foods like "oatmeal . . . though it is said to be healthful, it has caused more dyspepsia than all the candy, pastry, and hot rolls ever made." Rather, "the best breakfast in the world for an ordinary healthy person is a steak or a chop, with good coffee, hot rolls, and eggs."[5] With regard to food, women were caught in a condescending trap: expected to purchase and prepare beef as well as mocked for being incapable of doing so.

A barrage of articles attacked women's inability to cook a good steak. A *New York Herald* article, reprinted in the *Philadelphia Inquirer* and elsewhere, wondered "that while there are plenty of men, professional and amateur, who can cook a beefsteak, it is an accomplishment which can be claimed by but few women." Apparently, the secret to a good beefsteak was the butcher, and "women have no taste for butchery and the science evolved from blood."[6] Women were nevertheless expected to provide high-quality meat. * * * The rise of dressed beef was changing expectations.

By the day's thinking, if beef was for men, the best beef was for educated white men. In the late 1860s, Dr. George Miller Beard, better known for his study of neurasthenia,[7] penned a lengthy analysis of "the diet of brain workers," that combined social Darwinism[8] (thoughts on the "barbarous races" are sprinkled liberally), quack nutritional analysis (fish is "pre-eminently adapted to nourish the brain"), and rambling monologue ("restaurants are an abomination").[9] The essay, first published in a self-help magazine called *Hours at Home,* placed food at the center of its racial theories, noting that "race, climate, and diet are the chief agencies which give character and development to a people." Addressing the world's "brain workers," the piece is an extended refutation of the idea that "brain-workers—especially literary men—needed less food and less sleep than those who handle the shovel and spade."

4. "The Masculine Way," *Aberdeen Daily News,* December 25, 1887.
5. "Beefsteak and Rolls," *Aberdeen Daily News,* December 1, 1887.
6. "Can Women Broil Beefsteak?" *Philadelphia Inquirer,* March 29, 1893.
7. A common diagnosis at the time, particularly for middle-class patients, neurasthenia was believed to be a debilitating nerve disorder caused by the stresses of modern life [Editor].
8. See above, p. 57, n. 6 [Editor].
9. [George Miller Beard,] "The Diet of Brain Workers," *Hours at Home* 9:5 (September 1869).

Following a vigorous defense of the idea that "even the most secluded book-worm" has greater dietary needs than "the uneducated and laboring classes," the author enters into an argument about the dietary needs of various historical civilizations. Apparently "the ruling people of the world, who have from time to time shaped the destiny of humanity, have always, so far as can be ascertained, been liberal feeders."[1] He contrasts the diets of the powerful English and Germans with those of the Italians and Spaniards, whose "brains are less active and original." The author is even more dismissive of "the rice-eating Hindoos" and other non–Northern European people and diets. Following a dig at the Irish, the author wonders "what have the natives of South America, the savages of Africa, the stupid Greenlander, the peasantry of Europe, all combined, done for civilization, in comparison with any single beef-eating class of Europe?" The essay oscillates between a discussion of classes and occupations and the discussion of race or nationality.[2]

As may be clear by now, Beard believed that meat is the key, for "experience tells us that the diet of brain-workers should consist largely of meat, with, of course, an agreeable variety of fruits and cereals." * * *

Discussions about diet often started with the assumption that a beef-heavy diet was essential to success. An 1887 article in the *Kansas City Star* and republished elsewhere mentioned several "brainworkers"—Goethe, Johnson, and Wordsworth[3]—who were "tremendous feeders," and provided a list of "best foods," at the top of which was beef.[4] This list could be compared with a much later article criticizing thinkers like Benjamin Franklin and Thomas Jefferson who had tried vegetarianism and failed. Tolstoy had become vegetarian late in life, but apparently his greatest works were behind him.[5]

This kind of social Darwinian thinking about food reflected the singular importance of meat, and particularly beef, to nineteenth-century consumers. Its importance ensured abundant demand for beef and explained why Americans rich and poor wanted ever-larger steaks at ever-lower prices. Further, the emphasis on the relationship between diet and social status would inform attitudes about food and class in the twentieth century. Although few thought about

1. Good eaters [*Editor*].
2. [Beard,] "The Diet of Brain Workers."
3. German writer Johann Wolfgang von *Goethe* (1749–1832), English writer Samuel *Johnson* (1709–1784), and English Romantic poet William *Wordsworth* (1770–1850) [*Editor*].
4. Charles Dana, "The Special Diets in Various Nervous Diseases," *Scientific American Supplement* 25:649 (June 1888).
5. "Vegetarianism No Diet for Brain Workers," *Salt Lake Telegram*, July 18, 1915. [American Founding Father, writer, and inventor *Benjamin Franklin* (1706–1790); American Founding Father and (third) U.S. president *Thomas Jefferson* (1743–1826); and Russian novelist Leo *Tolstoy* (1828–1910), who converted to vegetarianism around 1885—*Editor*.]

diet in these crude terms in the twentieth century, the general belief
that some people have less need for certain kinds of food is evident
even today in the simultaneous aestheticization of elite food and
obsession with reforming the eating habits of the poor.

To return to the nineteenth century, the obsession with diet and
civilizational accounts of carnivorousness was a reaction to the period's surging immigration. For many of these immigrants, fresh
meat may only have been consumed a few times per year. The abundance of fresh beef in the United States meant that a food for special occasions—generally, religious holidays—became daily fare.
While many of these poorer immigrants initially ate cheap cuts like
the round steak, they, too, eventually sought choicer cuts.

The class tensions over meat consumption and immigration were
most obvious in *Meat vs. Rice*, an American Federation of Labor
pamphlet calling for Chinese exclusion. The pamphlet's subtitle
expressed the close linkage between meat consumption and identity: *American Manhood against Asiatic Coolieism: Which Shall
Survive?*[6] Though the pamphlet contained a relatively broad analysis
of cost-of-living and labor questions, meat was the ultimate symbol of
the successful American worker, while rice represented the threat
of persistently low wages and the victory of capital. The pamphlet
links Chinese labor to the effects of slave labor throughout, and
relies on racist tropes of Chinese docility but also hard work and
ability to "live on nothing" to build concern about the American
worker's ability to compete.[7]

The pamphlet closes by quoting James G. Blaine,[8] a supporter of
Chinese exclusion, who argues that the effect of immigration will be
the further impoverishment of the American worker. Blaine argues
"in all such conflicts, and all such struggles, the result is not to bring
up the man who lives on rice to the beef-and-bread standard, but it is
to bring down the beef-and-bread man to the rice standard."[9] Though
Meat vs. Rice was a particularly egregious example, the connection
between meat and the manhood of American laborers was one that
workers and reformers reproduced again and again. * * *

* * *

6. Various treaties and congressional acts barred Chinese and other Asian immigrants,
   including the 1882 Chinese Exclusion Act (responding to white workers' fears that
   they were losing jobs to Chinese workers, as well as to a general panic over maintaining
   white "racial purity"), and the Johnson-Reed Act of 1924 (prohibiting all immigrants from
   Asia [see also p. 393, n. 2]). *Coolie* is a racist slur for a Chinese worker [*Editor*].
7. Gompers, Samuel, and Herman Gutstadt. *Meat vs. Rice: American Manhood against
   Asiatic Coolieism, Which Shall Survive?* (San Francisco: American Federation of Labor,
   1902), 8.
8. Prominent Republican who served in the U.S. House of Representatives, in the U.S.
   Senate, and two times as secretary of state [*Editor*].
9. Gompers and Gutstadt. *Meat vs. Rice*, 22.

The cattle-beef complex would evolve over the twentieth century. Thanks to trucking, beef processing moved out of midwestern cities and into rural areas closer to ranches and feedlots. The rise of the fast-food industry, particularly McDonald's, would revolutionize how people ate. Beef consumption crested in the 1970s and began a slow decline in the wake of health concerns. Nevertheless, the persistent association of red meat with manliness explains the continued popularity of eating regimes like the beef-heavy Atkins diet or the paradoxically industrial-agriculture friendly caveman/paleo diet.

Despite these changes, the system's broad strokes remain the same. The nineteenth century's four largest beef processors remained in business well into the twentieth century and survive in some form today. A small number of companies still dominate global beef production. Ranching remains decentralized and subordinate to meat processing. Slaughterhouse labor remains largely invisible immigrant labor, though now these workers are generally from Latin America, rather than Central or Eastern Europe.

Contemporary food politics still reflects its nineteenth-century origins. The obesity epidemic and the "foodie" cultural phenomenon suggest that food debates remain inflected with class and gender concerns. Similarly, the willingness to celebrate the aesthetic qualities of one's own food choices and neglect them when considering the diets of the poor or heavy continues. Vegetarianism—eschewing animal flesh—and veganism—rejecting animal products altogether—are popular for reasons ranging from health to animal rights.

MARION NESTLE

From Food Politics[†]

As an academic nutritionist, I grapple on a daily basis with what I see as a central contradiction between nutrition theory and practice. On the one hand, our advice about the health benefits of diets based largely on food plants—fruits, vegetables, and grains—has not changed in more than 50 years and is consistently supported by ongoing research. On the other hand, people seem increasingly confused about what they are supposed to eat to stay healthy. As a population, Americans are eating more animal-based foods—and more food in general—to the point where half of us are overweight, even our children are obese, and diseases related to diet are leading causes of death and disability. In thinking about this contradiction, I have

[†] From *Food Politics: How the Food Industry Influences Nutrition and Health* (Berkeley and Los Angeles: U of California P, 2013), pp. xvii–xviii, 1–3, 8, 11, 13, 16–18, 21. Reprinted with permission of U of California P; permission conveyed through Copyright Clearance Center, Inc. The author's notes have been omitted.

often wondered what role the food industry might play in creating an environment so conducive to overeating and poor nutritional practices and so confusing about basic principles of diet and health.

* * *

In thinking about such matters, I eventually came to the conclusion that food companies—just like companies that sell cigarettes, pharmaceuticals, or any other commodity—routinely place the needs of stockholders over considerations of public health. This conclusion may not surprise anyone who follows the political scene, but I had heard few discussions of its significance among my professional colleagues, despite its evident implications. Food companies will make and market any product that sells, regardless of its nutritional value or its effect on health. In this regard, food companies hardly differ from cigarette companies. They lobby Congress to eliminate regulations perceived as unfavorable; they press federal regulatory agencies not to enforce such regulations; and when they don't like regulatory decisions, they file lawsuits. Like cigarette companies, food companies co-opt food and nutrition experts by supporting professional organizations and research, and they expand sales by marketing directly to children, members of minority groups, and people in developing countries—whether or not the products are likely to improve people's diets.

* * *

* * * That diet affects health is beyond question. The food industry has given us a food supply so plentiful, so varied, so inexpensive, and so devoid of dependence on geography or season that all but the very poorest of Americans can obtain enough energy and nutrients to meet biological needs. Indeed, the U.S. food supply is so abundant that it contains enough to feed everyone in the country nearly twice over—even after exports are considered. The overly abundant food supply, combined with a society so affluent that most people can afford to buy more food than they need, sets the stage for competition. The food industry must compete fiercely for every dollar spent on food, and food companies expend extraordinary resources to develop and market products that will sell, regardless of their effect on nutritional status or waistlines. To satisfy stockholders, food companies must convince people to *eat more* of their products or to eat their products instead of those of competitors. They do so through advertising and public relations, of course, but also by working tirelessly to convince government officials, nutrition professionals, and the media that their products promote health—or at least do no harm. Much of this work is a virtually invisible part of contemporary culture that attracts only occasional notice.

* * *

* * * [T]he primary mission of food companies, like that of tobacco companies, is to sell products. Food companies are not health or social service agencies, and nutrition becomes a factor in corporate thinking only when it can help sell food. The ethical choices involved in such thinking are considered all too rarely.

Early in the twentieth century, when the principal causes of death and disability among Americans were infectious diseases related in part to inadequate intake of calories and nutrients, the goals of health officials, nutritionists, and the food industry were identical—to encourage people to eat more of all kinds of food. Throughout that century, improvements in the U.S. economy affected the way we eat in important ways: We obtained access to foods of greater variety, our diets improved, and nutrient deficiencies gradually declined. The principal nutritional problems among Americans shifted to those of *overnutrition*—eating too much food or too much of certain kinds of food. Overeating causes its own set of health problems; it deranges metabolism, makes people overweight, and increases the likelihood of "chronic" diseases—coronary heart disease, certain cancers, diabetes, hypertension, stroke, and others—that now are leading causes of illness and death in any overfed population.

People may believe that the effects of diet on chronic disease are less important than those of cigarette smoking, but each contributes to about one-fifth of annual deaths in the United States. * * *

* * *

Overweight itself constitutes ample evidence that many Americans consume more calories than they burn off, but other sources of information also confirm the idea that people are eating too much food. The calories provided by the U.S. food supply increased from 3,200 per capita in 1970 to 3,900 in the late 1990s, an increase of 700 per day. * * *

* * *

The U.S. food industry is the remarkably successful result of twentieth-century trends that led from small farms to giant corporations, from a society that cooked at home to one that buys nearly half its meals prepared and consumed elsewhere, and from a diet based on "whole" foods grown locally to one based largely on foods that have been processed in some way and transported long distances. * * *

The greater efficiency, specialization, and size of agriculture and food product manufacture have led to one of the great unspoken secrets about the American food system: overabundance. As already noted, the U.S. food supply—plus imports less exports—provides a daily average of 3,900 calories per capita. This level is nearly twice the amount needed to meet the energy requirements of most women, one-third more than that needed by most men, and much higher than that needed by babies, young children, and the sedentary elderly. Even if, as the USDA estimates, 1,100 of those calories might be wasted (as spoiled fruit, for example, or as oil for frying potatoes), the excess calories are a major problem for the food industry: they force competition. Even people who overindulge can eat only so much food, and choosing one food means rejecting others. * * *

*   *   *

* * * When food is plentiful and people can afford to buy it, basic biological needs become less compelling and the principal determinant of food choice is personal preference. In turn, personal preferences may be influenced by religion and other cultural factors, as well as by considerations of convenience, price, and nutritional value. To sell food in an economy of abundant food choices, companies must worry about those other determinants much more than about the nutritional value of their products—unless the nutrient content helps to entice buyers * * *. Thus the food industry's marketing imperatives principally concern four factors: taste, cost, convenience, and * * * public confusion.

*   *   *

One result of overabundance is pressure to add value to foods through processing. The producers of raw foods receive only a fraction of the price that consumers pay at the supermarket. In 1998, for example, an average of 20% of retail cost—the "farm value" of the food—was returned to its producers. This percentage, which has been declining for years, is unequally distributed. Producers of eggs, beef, and chicken receive 50% to 60% of retail cost, whereas producers of vegetables receive as little as 5%. Once foods get to the supermarket, the proportion represented by the farm value declines further in proportion to the extent of processing. The farm value of frozen peas is 13%, of canned tomatoes 9%, of oatmeal 7%, and of corn syrup just 4%.

* * * [T]he remaining 80% of the food dollar goes for labor, packaging, advertising, and other such value-enhancing activities. Conversion of potatoes (cheap) to potato chips (expensive) to those fried in artificial fats or coated in soybean flour or herbal supplements (even more expensive) is an example of how value is added to basic food commodities. Added value explains why the cost of the corn in Kellogg's Corn Flakes is less than 10% of the retail price. With this kind of pricing distribution, food companies are more likely to focus on developing added-value products than to promote consumption of fresh fruits and vegetables, particularly because opportunities for adding value to such foods are limited. Marketers can add value

to fruits and vegetables by selling them frozen, canned, or precut, but even the most successful of such products—prepackaged and branded "baby" carrots, salad mixes, and precut fruit—raise consumer concerns about freshness, safety, and price.

* * *

In a competitive food marketplace, food companies must satisfy stockholders by encouraging more people to eat more of their products. They seek new audiences among children, among members of minority groups, or internationally. They expand sales to existing as well as new audiences through advertising but also by developing new products designed to respond to consumer "demands." In recent years, they have embraced a new strategy: increasing the sizes of food portions. Advertising, new products, and larger portions all contribute to a food environment that promotes eating more, not less.

THOMAS PIKETTY

From Capital in the Twenty-First Century[†]

The distribution of wealth is one of today's most widely discussed and controversial issues. But what do we really know about its evolution over the long term? Do the dynamics of private capital accumulation inevitably lead to the concentration of wealth in ever fewer hands, as Karl Marx[1] believed in the nineteenth century? Or do the balancing forces of growth, competition, and technological progress lead in later stages of development to reduced inequality and greater harmony among the classes, as Simon Kuznets[2] thought in the twentieth century? What do we really know about how wealth and income have evolved since the eighteenth century, and what lessons can we derive from that knowledge for the century now under way?

* * * Modern economic growth and the diffusion of knowledge have made it possible to avoid the Marxist apocalypse[3] but have not

---

[†] From *Capital in the Twenty-First Century*, trans. Arthur Goldhammer (Cambridge, MA: Belknap P of Harvard UP, 2014), pp. 1, 152, 257–61, 264, 292–94, 309–10, 324, 347–79, 577. Copyright © 2014 by the President and Fellows of Harvard College. Reprinted with permission of the publisher. Notes are by the editor of this Norton Critical Edition. The author's notes have been omitted. Bibliographic information has been included.

1. German political economist, revolutionary, and advocate of communism (1818–1883). Trained as a philosopher, Marx is one of the most influential figures of the modern world, particularly for his championing of labor against capital. See also p. 287, n. 4; p. 497, n. 6; and p. 512, n. 6. For a sampling of Marx's writing, see below, pp. 406–11; for discussion of his influence, see below, pp. 506–12.

2. American economist (1901–1985), who believed that while economic growth increased income inequality in poor countries, growth increased equality in wealthier countries.

3. Marx believed capitalism was so exploitative and riddled with contradictions that its overthrow—metaphorically, an "apocalypse"—was inevitable.

modified the deep structures of capital and inequality—or in any case not as much as one might have imagined in the optimistic decades following World War II. When the rate of return on capital exceeds the rate of growth of output and income, as it did in the nineteenth century and seems quite likely to do again in the twenty-first, capitalism automatically generates arbitrary and unsustainable inequalities that radically undermine the meritocratic[4] values on which democratic societies are based. * * *

* * *

In 1840, Tocqueville[5] noted quite accurately that "the number of large fortunes [in the United States] is quite small, and capital is still scarce," and he saw this as one obvious reason for the democratic spirit that in his view dominated there. He added that, as his observations showed, all of this was a consequence of the low price of agricultural land: "In America, land costs little, and anyone can easily become a landowner." Here we can see at work the Jeffersonian[6] ideal of a society of small landowners, free and equal.

Things would change over the course of the nineteenth century. The share of agriculture in output decreased steadily, and the value of farmland also declined, as in Europe. But the United States accumulated a considerable stock of real estate and industrial capital, so that national capital was close to five years of national income in 1910, versus three in 1810. The gap with old Europe remained, but it had shrunk by half in one century. * * * The United States had become capitalist, but wealth continued to have less influence than in Belle Époque[7] Europe, at least if we consider the vast US territory as a whole. If we limit our gaze to the East Coast, the gap is smaller still. In the film *Titanic,* the director, James Cameron, depicted the social structure of 1912. He chose to make wealthy Americans appear just as prosperous—and arrogant—as their European counterparts: for instance, the detestable Hockley, who wants to bring young Rose to

---

4. Referring to an economic or other system in which winners and losers emerge solely based on their merit, not due to any privilege or advantage. Piketty's focus on the profits ("return") on capital is central to his analysis. Elsewhere in *Capital in the Twenty-First Century* he explains that capital is distinct from income or wages. Piketty defines capital as "the sum total of nonhuman assets that can be owned and exchanged on some market" (46). The layperson might think of capital as accumulated wealth, in distinction from income or a paycheck.
5. *Democracy in America* (1835 and 1840), by the French historian Alexis de Tocqueville (1805–1859), recounts the Frenchman's observations while traveling in America. The book remains a classic study not only of 19th-century conditions, but also of enduring American characteristics, beliefs, and values. The quotations are from the edition translated by Arthur Goldhammer (New York: Library of America, 2004), Vol. II, pp. 646, 679.
6. Pertaining to ideas of American Founding Father and (third) U.S. president Thomas Jefferson (1743–1826).
7. Beautiful epoch (French); a period of European and particularly French history from the late 19th century until World War I, characterized by relative prosperity, optimism, and artistic flourishing, and arguably also representing the pinnacle of European power and influence.

Philadelphia in order to marry her. (Heroically, she refuses to be treated as property and becomes Rose Dawson.) The novels of Henry James[8] that are set in Boston and New York between 1880 and 1910 also show social groups in which real estate and industrial and financial capital matter almost as much as in European novels: times had indeed changed since the Revolutionary War, when the United States was still a land without capital.

*   *   *

* * * Currently, in the early 2010s, the richest 10 percent own around 60 percent of national wealth in most European countries, and in particular in France, Germany, Britain, and Italy.

The most striking fact is no doubt that in all these societies, half of the population own virtually nothing: the poorest 50 percent invariably own less than 10 percent of national wealth, and generally less than 5 percent. In France, according to the latest available data (for 2010–2011), the richest 10 percent command 62 percent of total wealth, while the poorest 50 percent own only 4 percent. In the United States, the most recent survey by the Federal Reserve, which covers the same years, indicates that the top decile[9] own 72 percent of America's wealth, while the bottom half claim just 2 percent. Note, however, that this source, like most surveys in which wealth is self-reported, underestimates the largest fortunes. * * *

*   *   *

Concretely, in such a society, the poorest half of the population will generally comprise a large number of people—typically a quarter of the population—with no wealth at all or perhaps a few thousand euros[1] at most. Indeed, a nonnegligible number of people—perhaps one-twentieth to one-tenth of the population—will have slightly negative net wealth (their debts exceed their assets). * * *

For this [poorest] half of the population, the very notions of wealth and capital are relatively abstract. For millions of people, "wealth" amounts to little more than a few weeks' wages in a checking account or low-interest savings account, a car, and a few pieces of furniture. The inescapable reality is this: wealth is so concentrated that a large segment of society is virtually unaware of its existence, so that some people imagine that it belongs to surreal or mysterious entities. * * *

*   *   *

---

8. American-born novelist (1843–1916), who wrote extensively about wealthy characters.
9. Top 10 percent.
1. Currency of the European Union. The exchange rate varies, but at the time of Piketty's writing, one euro was worth about $1.20.

Make no mistake: the growth of a true "patrimonial (or propertied) middle class" was the principal structural transformation of the distribution of wealth in the developed countries in the twentieth century.

To go back a century in time, to the decade 1900–1910: in all the countries of Europe, the concentration of capital was then much more extreme than it is today. * * *

In other words, there was no middle class in the specific sense that the middle 40 percent of the wealth distribution were almost as poor as the bottom 50 percent. The vast majority of people owned virtually nothing, while the lion's share of society's assets belonged to a minority. * * *

The emergence of a patrimonial middle class was an important, if fragile, historical innovation, and it would be a serious mistake to underestimate it. To be sure, it is tempting to insist on the fact that wealth is still extremely concentrated today: the upper decile own 60 percent of Europe's wealth and more than 70 percent in the United States. And the poorer half of the population are as poor today as they were in the past, with barely 5 percent of total wealth in 2010, just as in 1910. Basically, all the middle class managed to get its hands on was a few crumbs: scarcely more than a third of Europe's wealth and barely a quarter in the United States. * * *

*   *   *

* * * [W]hether such extreme inequality is or is not sustainable depends not only on the effectiveness of the repressive apparatus but also, and perhaps primarily, on the effectiveness of the apparatus of justification. If inequalities are seen as justified, say because they seem to be a consequence of a choice by the rich to work harder or more efficiently than the poor, or because preventing the rich from earning more would inevitably harm the worst-off members of society, then it is perfectly possible for the concentration of income to set new historical records. * * *

*   *   *

* * * I shall begin by examining the overall evolution of the share of income going to the top decile (Figure [1]). The most striking fact is that the United States has become noticeably more inegalitarian than France (and Europe as a whole) from the turn of the twentieth century until now, even though the United States was more egalitarian at the beginning of this period. What makes the US case complex is that the end of the process did not simply mark a return to the situation that had existed at the beginning: US inequality in 2010 is quantitatively as extreme as in old Europe in the first decade of the twentieth century, but the structure of that inequality is rather clearly different.

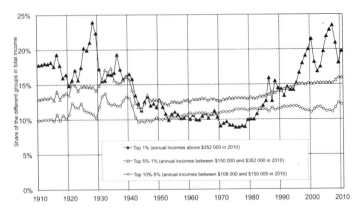

Figure [1]. Decomposition of the top decile, United States, 1910–2010

The rise of the top decile income share since the 1970s is mostly due to the top percentile. Sources and series: see piketty.pse.ens.fr/capital21c.

I will proceed systematically. First, European income inequality was significantly greater than US income inequality at the turn of the twentieth century. In 1900–1910, according to the data at our disposal, the top decile of the income hierarchy received a little more than 40 percent of total national income in the United States, compared with 45–50 percent in France (and very likely somewhat more in Britain). This reflects two differences. First, the capital/income ratio was higher in Europe, and so was capital's share of national income. Second, inequality of ownership of capital was somewhat less extreme in the New World. Clearly, this does not mean that American society in 1900–1910 embodied the mythical ideal of an egalitarian society of pioneers. In fact, American society was already highly inegalitarian, much more than Europe today, for example. One has only to reread Henry James or note that the dreadful Hockney who sailed in luxury on *Titanic* in 1912 existed in real life and not just in the imagination of James Cameron to convince oneself that a society of rentiers[2] existed not only in Paris and London but also in turn-of-the-century Boston, New York, and Philadelphia. Nevertheless, capital (and therefore the income derived from it) was distributed somewhat less unequally in the United States than in France or Britain. Concretely, US rentiers were fewer in number and not as rich (compared to the average US standard of living) as their European counterparts. * * *

2. People who earn money from property (including rent) or investments, as opposed to those who earn money from working.

* * *

Inequality reached its lowest ebb in the United States between 1950 and 1980: the top decile of the income hierarchy claimed 30 to 35 percent of US national income, or roughly the same level as in France today. This is what Paul Krugman nostalgically refers to as "the America we love"—the America of his childhood. In the 1960s, the period of the TV series *Mad Men* and General de Gaulle,[3] the United States was in fact a more egalitarian society than France (where the upper decile's share had increased dramatically to well above 35 percent), at least for those US citizens whose skin was white.

Since 1980, however, income inequality has exploded in the United States. The upper decile's share increased from 30–35 percent of national income in the 1970s to 45–50 percent in the 2000s—an increase of 15 points of national income * * *. The shape of the curve is rather impressively steep, and it is natural to wonder how long such a rapid increase can continue: if change continues at the same pace, for example, the upper decile will be raking in 60 percent of national income by 2030.

* * *

In the United States, a federal minimum wage was introduced in 1933, nearly twenty years earlier than in France. As in France, changes in the minimum wage played an important role in the evolution of wage inequalities in the United States. It is striking to learn that in terms of purchasing power, the minimum wage reached its maximum level nearly half a century ago, in 1969, at \$1.60 an hour (or \$10.10 in 2013 dollars, taking account of inflation between 1968 and 2013), at a time when the unemployment rate was below 4 percent. From 1980 to 1990, under the presidents Ronald Reagan and George H. W. Bush, the federal minimum wage remained stuck at \$3.35, which led to a significant decrease in purchasing power when inflation is factored in. It then rose to \$5.25 under Bill Clinton in the 1990s and was frozen at that level under George W. Bush before being increased several times by Barack Obama after 2008. At the beginning of 2013 it stood at \$7.25 an hour, or barely 6 euros, which is a third below the French minimum wage, the opposite of the situation that obtained in the early 1980s * * *. President Obama, in his State of the Union address in February 2013, announced his intention to raise the minimum wage to about \$9 an hour for the period 2013–2016.

---

3. Charles *de Gaulle* (1890–1970), French army officer, statesman, and president of France 1958–69. *Paul Krugman* (b. 1953): American economist, Nobel laureate, and *New York Times* columnist.

Inequalities at the bottom of the US wage distribution have closely followed the evolution of the minimum wage: the gap between the bottom 10 percent of the wage distribution and the overall average wage widened significantly in the 1980s, then narrowed in the 1990s, and finally increased again in the 2000s. Nevertheless, inequalities at the top of the distribution—for example, the share of total wages going to the top 10 percent—increased steadily throughout this period. Clearly, the minimum wage has an impact at the bottom of the distribution but much less influence at the top, where other forces are at work.

✳   ✳   ✳

If we calculate ✳ ✳ ✳ an average for Europe based on these four countries [Britain, Sweden, France, and Germany], we can make a very clear international comparison: the United States was less inegalitarian than Europe in 1900–1910, slightly more inegalitarian in 1950–1960, and much more inegalitarian in 2000–2010 ✳ ✳ ✳.

✳   ✳   ✳

It is a well-established fact that wealth in the United States became increasingly concentrated over the course of the nineteenth century. In 1910, capital inequality there was very high, though still markedly lower than in Europe: the top decile owned about 80 percent of total wealth and the top centile[4] around 45 percent ✳ ✳ ✳. Interestingly, the fact that inequality in the New World seemed to be catching up with inequality in old Europe greatly worried US economists at the time. Willford King's book on the distribution of wealth in the United States in 1915[5]—the first broad study of the question—is particularly illuminating in this regard. From today's perspective, this may seem surprising: we have been accustomed for several decades now to the fact that the United States is more inegalitarian than Europe and even that many Americans are proud of the fact (often arguing that inequality is a prerequisite of entrepreneurial dynamism and decrying Europe as a sanctuary of Soviet-style egalitarianism). A century ago, however, both the perception and the reality were strictly the opposite: it was obvious to everyone that the New World was by nature less inegalitarian than old Europe, and this difference was also a subject of pride. In the late nineteenth century, in the period known as the Gilded Age, when some US industrialists and financiers (for example John D. Rockefeller, Andrew Carnegie, and J. P. Morgan) accumulated unprecedented wealth, many US observers were alarmed by the thought that the

---

4. Top 1 percent.
5. *The Wealth and Income of the People of the United States* (New York: Macmillan, 1915).

country was losing its pioneering egalitarian spirit. To be sure, that spirit was partly a myth, but it was also partly justified by comparison with the concentration of wealth in Europe. * * * [T]his fear of growing to resemble Europe was part of the reason why the United States in 1910–1910 pioneered a very progressive estate tax on large fortunes, which were deemed to be incompatible with US values, as well as a progressive income tax[6] on incomes thought to be excessive. Perceptions of inequality, redistribution, and national identity changed a great deal over the course of the twentieth century, to put it mildly.

*   *   *

* * * [I]t seems to me that all social scientists, all journalists and commentators, all activists in the unions and in politics of whatever stripe, and especially all citizens should take a serious interest in money, its measurement, the facts surrounding it, and its history. Those who have a lot of it never fail to defend their interests. Refusing to deal with numbers rarely serves the interests of the least well-off.

6. The Sixteenth Amendment, ratified in 1913, granted Congress the power to collect income taxes. Initially the rate ranged from 1 percent on incomes up to $20,000 to 7 percent on incomes over $500,000. (A *progressive* tax is not a political term; it means one with graduated rates, charging a higher percentage to those making more money.) The Revenue Act of 1916 adjusted income tax rates, increasing the top bracket to 25 percent; the following year, the top bracket was raised to 77 percent. The 1916 Revenue Act also instituted the precursor of the modern estate tax, another progressive tax, with rates ranging from 1 percent for estates with a net value below $50,000 to 10 percent for estates over $5,000,000. These rates were increased in 1917 to 25 percent for estates over $10,000,000.

Immigration and Labor

Sinclair's intent in writing *The Jungle* was to expose not unhygienic food, but rather the brutal treatment of workers. Because his descriptions of meatpacking plants were based on intensive research, and because Packingtown employed so many immigrants, Sinclair's exposé of labor practices makes *The Jungle* necessarily also a study of immigrant life.

This unit begins with contemporaneous writings about various urban immigrant populations. Social reformer Jacob Riis's 1890 study of New York City famously presents immigrants as "the other half," the objects of concern, to be sure, but also of pity. Two studies by University of Chicago social scientists address the poverty of Packingtown's immigrant families: J. C. Kennedy examines family budgets, and Sophonisba P. Breckinridge and Edith Abbott look at housing conditions. A 1911 study by the Vice Commission of Chicago sounds an alarm over the sexual exploitation of immigrant women. Modern historian Matthew Frye Jacobson discusses the belief in Sinclair's era that there were multiple white races, as well as how shifting attitudes toward race have defined America's immigration policy.

To understand why Packingtown's immigrant workers were particularly vulnerable, it is important to see how the industry instituted a minute division of labor, as explained in a report by the U.S. Bureau of Corporations. Modern historian Rick Halpern explains why this labor segmentation was so profitable to packers, as were the racial and ethnic differences among workers, all of which packers used to obstruct the labor movement. Nineteenth-century political philosopher Karl Marx describes how capitalism turns labor into a commodity in order to make a profit.

The dangerous and unpleasant work performed disproportionally by immigrants as seen in *The Jungle* is not only a matter of historical interest. Donald D. Stull overviews the demographics of employees found in meat processing plants and the workplace hazards they face from Sinclair's time until our own. Eric Schlosser reveals that the meat processing industry continues to rely on immigrant as well as migrant employees who toil at great danger to their health and safety—and for wages that, adjusted for inflation, have declined significantly. Robert Gottlieb and Anupama Joshi describe food production—still, in the twenty-first century—as a form of slavery, and call for an equitable sharing of its benefits and risks, known as food justice. Alison Hope Alkon and Julian Agyeman characterize the entire food system as a racial project that reflects not individual bias but rather institutional racism, and show how food justice principles mirror those of the movement for environmental justice.

JACOB RIIS

From How the Other Half Lives[†]

Long ago it was said that "one half of the world does not know how the other half lives."[1] That was true then. It did not know because it did not care. The half that was on top cared little for the struggles, and less for the fate of those who were underneath, so long as it was able to hold them there and keep its own seat. There came a time when the discomfort and crowding below were so great, and the consequent upheavals so violent, that it was no longer an easy thing to do, and then the upper half fell to inquiring what was the matter. Information on the subject has been accumulating rapidly since, and the whole world has had its hands full answering for its old ignorance.

*　*　*

What the tenements are and how they grew to what they are, we shall see hereafter. The story is dark enough, drawn from the plain public records, to send a chill to any heart. If it shall appear that the sufferings and the sins of the "other half," and the evil they breed, are but as a just punishment upon the community that gave it no other choice, it will be because that is the truth. The boundary line lies there because, while the forces for good on one side vastly outweigh the bad—it were not well otherwise—in the tenements all the influences make for evil; because they are the hot-beds of the epidemics that carry death to rich and poor alike; the nurseries of pauperism and crime that fill our jails and police courts; that throw off a scum of forty thousand human wrecks to the island asylums and workhouses year by year; that turned out in the last eight years a round half million beggars to prey upon our charities; that maintain a standing army of ten thousand tramps with all that that implies; because, above all, they touch the family life with deadly moral contagion. This is their worst crime, inseparable from the system. That we have to own it the child of our own wrong does not excuse it, even though it gives it claim upon our utmost patience and tenderest charity.

What are you going to do about it? is the question of to-day. *　*　*

*　*　*

† From *How the Other Half Lives*, ed. Hasia R. Diner (New York: Norton, 2010), pp. 5, 6, 15–16, 46–47, 102–03, 105–06. Copyright © 2010 by W. W. Norton & Company. Used by permission of W. W. Norton & Company, Inc. Notes are by the editor of the original work. Some of the editor's notes have been omitted.
1. Riis may very well have gotten this quotation from Benjamin Franklin's *Poor Richard's Almanack*, in which Franklin wrote, "It is a common saying that one half of the world does not know how the other half lives."

When once I asked the agent of a notorious Fourth Ward alley how many people might be living in it I was told: One hundred and forty families, one hundred Irish, thirty-eight Italian, and two that spoke the German tongue. Barring the agent herself, there was not a native-born individual in the court. The answer was characteristic of the cosmopolitan character of lower New York, very nearly so of the whole of it, wherever it runs to alleys and courts. One may find for the asking an Italian, a German, a French, African, Spanish, Bohemian, Russian, Scandinavian, Jewish, and Chinese colony. Even the Arab, who peddles "holy earth" from the Battery as a direct importation from Jerusalem, has his exclusive preserves at the lower end of Washington Street. The one thing you shall vainly ask for in the chief city of America is a distinctively American community. There is none; certainly not among the tenements. Where have they gone to, the old inhabitants? I put the question to one who might fairly be presumed to be of the number, since I had found him sighing for the "good old days" when the legend "no Irish need apply" was familiar in the advertising columns of the newspapers. He looked at me with a puzzled air. "I don't know," he said. "I wish I did. Some went to California in '49, some to the war and never came back. The rest, I expect, have gone to heaven, or somewhere. I don't see them 'round here."

Whatever the merit of the good man's conjectures, his eyes did not deceive him. They are not here. In their place has come this queer conglomerate mass of heterogeneous elements, ever striving and working like whiskey and water in one glass, and with the like result: final union and a prevailing taint of whiskey. * * *

* * *

Grouped about a beer-keg that was propped on the wreck of a broken chair, a foul and ragged host of men and women, on boxes, benches, and stools. Tomato-cans filled at the keg were passed from hand to hand. In the centre of the group a sallow, wrinkled hag, evidently the ruler of the feast, dealt out the hideous stuff. A pile of copper coins rattled in her apron, the very pennies received with such showers of blessings upon the giver that afternoon; the faces of some of the women were familiar enough from the streets as those of beggars forever whining for a penny, "to keep a family from starving." Their whine and boisterous hilarity were alike hushed now. * * *

* * *

* * * Out in the street was heard the tramp of the hosts already pursuing that well-trodden path, as with a fresh complement of men we entered the next stale-beer alley. There were four dives in one cellar here. The filth and the stench were utterly unbearable; even

the sergeant turned his back and fled after scattering the crowd with his club and starting them toward the door. The very dog in the alley preferred the cold flags[2] for a berth to the stifling cellar. We found it lying outside. Seventy-five tramps, male and female, were arrested in the four small rooms. In one of them, where the air seemed thick enough to cut with a knife, we found a woman, a mother with a new-born babe on a heap of dirty straw. She was asleep and was left until an ambulance could be called to take her to the hospital.

*   *   *

As a thief never owns to his calling, however devoid of moral scruples, preferring to style himself a speculator, so this real home-product of the slums, the stale-beer dive, is known about "the Bend" by the more dignified name of the two-cent restaurant. Usually, as in this instance, it is in some cellar giving on a back alley. Doctored, unlicensed beer is its chief ware. Sometimes a cup of "coffee" and a stale roll may be had for two cents. The men pay the score. To the women—unutterable horror of the suggestion—the place is free. *   *   *

*   *   *

The problem of the children becomes, in these swarms, to the last degree perplexing. *   *   *

The old question, what to do with the boy, assumes a new and serious phase in the tenements. Under the best conditions found there, it is not easily answered. In nine cases out of ten he would make an excellent mechanic, if trained early to work at a trade, for he is neither dull nor slow, but the short-sighted despotism of the trades unions has practically closed that avenue to him. Trade-schools, however excellent, cannot supply the opportunity thus denied him, and at the outset the boy stands condemned by his own to low and ill-paid drudgery, held down by the hand that of all should labor to raise him. Home, the greatest factor of all in the training of the young, means nothing to him but a pigeon-hole in a coop along with so many other human animals. Its influence is scarcely of the elevating kind, if it have any. The very games at which he takes a hand in the street become polluting in its atmosphere. With no steady hand to guide him, the boy takes naturally to idle ways. Caught in the street by the truant officer, or by agents of the Children's Societies, peddling, perhaps, or begging, to help out the family resources, he runs the risk of being sent to a reformatory, where contact with vicious boys older than himself soon develops the latent possibilities for evil that lie hidden in him. The city has no Truant Home in which to keep him, and all efforts of the children's friends to enforce school attendance are paralyzed by this want. The risk of the reformatory is

2. I.e., flagstones.

too great. What is done in the end is to let him take chances—with the chances all against him. The result is the rough young savage, familiar from the street.* * *

* * *

Nothing is now better understood than that the rescue of the children is the key to the problem of city poverty, as presented for our solution to-day; that a character may be formed where to reform it would be a hopeless task. The concurrent testimony of all who have to undertake it at a later stage: that the young are naturally neither vicious nor hardened, simply weak and undeveloped, except by the bad influences of the street, makes this duty all the more urgent as well as hopeful. Helping hands are held out on every side. To private charity the municipality leaves the entire care of its proletariat of tender years, lulling its conscience to sleep with liberal appropriations of money to foot the bills. Indeed, it is held by those whose opinions are entitled to weight that it is far too liberal a paymaster for its own best interests and those of its wards. It deals with the evil in the seed to a limited extent in gathering in the outcast babies from the streets. To the ripe fruit the gates of its prisons, its reformatories, and its workhouses are opened wide the year round. What the showing would be at this end of the line were it not for the barriers wise charity has thrown across the broad highway to ruin—is building day by day—may be measured by such results as those quoted above in the span of a single life.

J. C. KENNEDY

[Immigrant Wages and Family Budgets]†

The packing industry has influenced more or less directly the life of the whole city of Chicago, but this study will be confined to the district extending half a mile west of the stockyards to Robey Street, and half a mile south of the stockyards to 51st Street. This district is commonly known as "Packingtown."

It is within this district that the majority of the packing-house workers, especially the unskilled, have their homes, and it is here that the University of Chicago Settlement[1] does its chief work.

* * *

---

† From *Wages and Family Budgets in the Chicago Stockyards District* (Chicago: U of Chicago P, 1914), pp. 4–10, 65–66, 68, 71–78, 80. Notes are by the editor of this Norton Critical Edition.

1. A settlement house operated by the University of Chicago. On settlement houses, see above, p. 189, n. 3.

Most of the people in this district are of foreign birth or parentage, but as the census figures on nationality are not yet available it is impossible to classify them accurately. Judging by the school census, it seems probable that the distribution of population is approximately as follows: Polish (including Slovaks), 18,000; Lithuanians, 12,000; German, 6,000; Bohemian, 5,000; Irish, 4,000; American, 2,000; others, 3,000.

During the past decade not only has there been a great increase of the population of this district—at least 75 per cent—but there has also been a decided change in its makeup. There has been a tendency for the English-speaking element, as well as the Bohemians and Germans, to seek employment in other industries and to move farther south and west, while in their place has come an influx of Poles (including Slovaks) and Lithuanians. * * *

* * *

The question arises here: Why is it that the Poles, Slovaks, and Lithuanians are supplanting other nationalities, especially English-speaking, [in] the packing industry, and consequently becoming the chief element in the community. * * *

* * * What is desired is the young, strong, willing worker who can do the work in a highly organized industrial machine. The vigorous Polish, Slovak, and Lithuanian peasants are well adapted to this demand and consequently they are filling the places in ever-increasing numbers.

Moreover, they are cheap, as will be shown by the wage tables printed later. The Lithuanians, Poles, and Slovaks will work for wages which would seem small to the average American workingman. The standards of living of these workers are comparatively low and over half of them are boarders without families to support, so they can easily underbid Americans, Germans, and Bohemians.

From the standpoint of the Poles, Slovaks, and Lithuanians the reasons for coming to "Packingtown" are obvious. Not only are economic opportunities in America superior to those of Europe, especially western Europe, but politically and socially there is much greater freedom and security. America has been, and still is, synonymous with opportunity in the minds of millions of European peasants—especially those who have been oppressed, such as the Poles and Lithuanians. Slavic immigrants pour into "Packingtown" in particular because it is a great market for unskilled labor. In the majority of cases they come at the suggestion of friends or relatives already established who can help them to get work and find homes. The newcomer may not find a job immediately but if he is young and strong he is sure to get work sooner or later. Moreover, now that the foreign colonies are well established, he is sure to find fellow-countrymen with whom he can live, a church of his own faith where he can hear the service in his own language, and various social institutions and organizations in which he is always welcome. Hence, even though the work may be poorly paid, and in many cases heavy and disagreeable, the Poles, Slovaks, and Lithuanians come to the stockyards district in large numbers and it seems probable that they will become increasingly important factors both in the packing industry and in the life of this community.

※ ※ ※

The average yearly wage of these 250 employees was $634.80, or $12.20 per week.※※※34 per cent of all the workers in this group secured incomes ranging between $500.00 and $600.00 per year.※※※

※ ※ ※

First in importance for a knowledge of working and living conditions in the stockyards district is an investigation of actual standards of living. The true significance of the prevailing rates of wages, for example, becomes apparent only when we know how these wages are spent and what they will buy. Previous to a discussion of wages and working conditions we must consider the cost of living. We must answer, if possible, the question: What is the least wage that will support a family of five, six, seven, or eight people decently in the stockyards district?

In order to answer the above and other questions, we have gathered family budgets from 184 typical stockyards families.※※※

※ ※ ※

※※※[The following table] will show the average income derived from each source by the families which were securing an income from that source.※※※

SOURCES OF INCOME[2]

	Husband	Children 14–15	Other Members of Family	Lodgers	Other Sources	Totals
Polish..............	$486.14	$185.57	$559.00	$159.01	$174.88	$869.39
Lithuanian.......	511.06	240.60	475.08	191.43	205.69	804.60
Miscellaneous..	541.71	207.83	564.19	189.53	138.69	926.46
All families	503.15	200.14	552.02	183.44	145.23	854.13

※ ※ ※

It is a significant fact that, considering all the families together, the husbands contributed on the average only $464.87, or

2. One dollar in 1904 would be worth approximately $30.51 in 2021 dollars.

54.4 per cent of the average family income. Here we have the chief explanation of the fact that in order to make ends meet it was necessary in most cases for the children or the mother to go to work or for the family to supplement its income by taking in lodgers or in some other way. In another part of this chapter we will show that it was very difficult for most of our families to live upon the income which they derived from all sources. It would have been almost impossible for them to live upon the income from the husband alone.

* * *

The gross expenditures may be analyzed as follows:

Rent

Of the 184 families, 131 were renters. The average annual rental per apartment paid by the various nationalities and the percentage of the average expenditure per family paid for rent are shown by the following table:

	Average Annual Rental per Apartment	Percentage of Average Annual Expenditure
Polish renters..	$ 91.55	10.9
Lithuanian renters...............................	123.36	15.9
Miscellaneous renters.........................	110.95	12.5
All renting families..............................	107.83	13.2

These figures show very clearly that the percentage of income spent for rent by stockyards families is not excessive when compared with the percentage spent by families in other sections of the city. The Lithuanian renters pay considerably more than other nationalities. This is due very largely to the fact that they crowd closely together and that the demand for houses in the Lithuanian district is very great. Most Lithuanian families would prefer to pay $12 per month for four rooms in the heart of the Lithuanian colony rather than $10 per month for four equally good rooms half a mile distant. The Lithuanians also take in a large number of lodgers, which is both a cause and an effect of relatively high rents.

* * *

Food-Stuffs

The average expenditure of each of the 184 families for food-stuffs and liquors was $441.83, or 53.62 per cent of all expenditures. In addition to this each family spent on an average $9.22 for meals out-side of the home. The percentage on food-stuffs spent by the vari-ous nationalities was as follows: Polish, 51.82; Lithuanian, 56.60; miscellaneous, 52.69 per cent. It will be noted that the expenditures for meat were relatively heavy. * * *

The next largest item in the outlay for food was the expenditure for bread, rolls, cakes, crackers, and other baked goods, including flour for home baking. Among the Polish families the expenditures on this item amounted to $96.09 per family, or 11.44 per cent of their total; among the Lithuanians $65.95, or 8.48 per cent of the total expendi-tures; among the others, $83.56, or 9.42 per cent of the total. The average for all families was $83.05, or 10.20 per cent of the total.

The expenditures for fruit and vegetables were comparatively low. For fruits each family spent, on an average, $16.94, or 2.06 per cent of the total expenditures; on vegetables, $31.59, or 3.84 per cent of the total expenditures. The expenditures for milk averaged $33.87 per family, 4.11 per cent of all expenditures, while those for beer and other alcoholic liquors averaged $36.42, or 4.42 per cent of the total. Out of the 184 families 180 listed expenditures for alcoholic liquors. All of the 184 families were coffee- or tea-users, the average being $15.92 per family, or 1.93 per cent of all expenditures.

* * *

Clothing

Next to food and rent the heaviest expenditures were those for clothing. The average expenditure for clothing for each of the 184 families was $95.41, or 11.58 per cent of their total expenditures. Of this amount, $55.78, or 6.74 per cent of the total family expenses, was spent for the childrens' clothing; $23.64, or 2.85 per cent, for the father's clothing, and $19.65, or 2.39 per cent, for the mother's clothing. * * *

* * *

Special Expenditures

As stated at the outset, the majority of families from whom we col-lected budgets had a small surplus above their annual expenditures. Fifty-six, however, had deficits, in some cases running into hundreds of dollars. In most cases these deficits were caused by unemployment and extraordinary expenditures. Long periods of illness, weddings, funerals, and moving nearly always ran the family into debt.

Wedding Expenses of Clara Z.

BRIDE'S OUTFIT		WEDDING DINNER	
Dress..................................	$29.00	3 doz. ducks........................	$13.00
Slippers..............................	1.50	5 doz. chickens..................	22.50
Stockings...........................	0.25	Wedding cake	10.00
Underwear, petticoat..........	8.75	Cakes and bread................	16.00
Gloves...............................	1.75	Fruit, fresh	10.00
Veil....................................	3.50	Fruit, canned.....................	3.25
Flowers	6.00	Meat and ham....................	8.63
Notions..............................	3.00	Candy and ice cream	2.10
Household linen, etc..........	35.00	Milk and coffee..................	3.38
Present..............................	10.00	Vegetables..........................	3.17
	$98.75	Sugar, 10 lbs	0.50
			$97.63
		Bride's outfit	98.75
			$196.38

The groom made a present of $50, which was used to defray the expenses in part. The remaining $156.38 was paid by the parents, who borrowed $150 of the amount from relatives.

*   *   *

Poverty

It goes without saying that in a district where 56 out of 184 families show a deficit in their annual accounts, there is a great deal of poverty. It must not be forgotten, moreover, that the poverty of material goods is often surpassed by the poverty of knowledge. This latter poverty becomes doubly significant when we try to ascertain the minimum income necessary to support a certain size family in this district. When we expect that every dollar of the income should be spent in the most intelligent way we expect too much. When we expect that foods should be chosen wisely from the standpoint of their relative values in nutriment, and that they should be cooked in the best possible way, we expect too much. In some ways the families of this district know how to economize, but in others they do not, as is only too well shown by the high expenditures for alcoholic liquors compared with the expenditures for the prime necessities of life.

The Cost of Living for a Family of Five

Perhaps the most important question to be answered by our study of family budgets is the minimum amount necessary to support a family of five, or any other size family, decently in the stockyards district. * * *

* * *

* * * In practically every case where the family income went below $600 there was a deficit. This does not mean, however, that a family of five can live on $600 a year. They may exist on that amount for a time, but they cannot live on it. The least misfortune will plunge them into debt and sooner or later they will become dependent on charity.

* * *

Summary of Significant Facts

One hundred and eighty-four families represented: 88 Polish, 68 Lithuanian, 28 miscellaneous.

Average size of family, 5.33. In addition, on an average, 1.09 lodgers per family.

In 94 families the father was the only wage-earner; in 52 families children fourteen to fifteen were at work; in 21 families wife was at work; 92 families obtained an income from lodgers.

The income of 110 families was $800 per year or less; the income of 74 families was over $800 per year; the average income of all families was $854.13.

The average wage of all the husbands was $503.15. Fifty-three husbands lost 580 solid weeks of work or on an average 10.9 weeks each per year.

In the 52 families where children were at work the average income derived from this source was $200.14 per year.

One hundred and thirty-one families rented their quarters. The average rental per family was $107.83, or 13.2 per cent of the total expenditure. One hundred of the 131 renting families occupied flats of four rooms.

The 68 Lithuanian families had on an average 4.12 lodgers per family. In one case 13 people were crowded together in four small basement rooms.

The average expenditure for food-stuffs and liquors was $441.83 per family, or 53.62 per cent of the total expenditure.

One hundred and eighty families used alcoholic liquors; the average expenditure per family was $36.42, or 4.42 per cent of the total expenditure.

The minimum amount necessary to support a family of five efficiently in the stockyards district is $800 per year, or $15.40 per week.

SOPHONISBA P. BRECKINRIDGE
AND EDITH ABBOTT

From Housing Conditions in Chicago, Ill: Back of the Yards[†]

In 1901, when a committee of the City Homes Association made an inquiry into housing conditions in Chicago, the Stockyards district was not one of those selected for intensive investigation. The appearance of the district showed it to be so neglected and conditions there were, in general, supposed to be so extraordinary that it was regarded as unsuitable for purposes of intensive investigation. On this account little attention was given to conditions prevailing within the houses, and only a superficial examination of these conditions was made. The unpaved streets, lack of sidewalks, indescribable accumulations of filth and rubbish, together with the absence of sewerage were said to make the so-called "outside insanitary conditions as bad as any in the world."

* * * No other neighborhood in this, or perhaps in any other, city is dominated by a single industry of so offensive a character. Large numbers of live animals assembled from all sections of the country, processes of slaughtering and packing, the disposition of offensive animal waste, constitute an almost unparalleled nuisance. South Chicago lies under the smoke-shadows of the steel mills, and in those mills are dangers to life and limb, blinding glare from the furnaces, magnificent exposure and terrible peril; but the influence upon the neighborhood is rather terrifying than degrading. In the Stockyards, on the other hand, are the mingled cries of the animals awaiting slaughter, the presence of uncared-for-waste, the sight of blood, the carcasses naked of flesh and skin, the suggestion of death and disintegration—all of which must react in a demoralizing way, not only upon the character of the people, but [upon] the conditions under which they live.

* * *

The fact of chief interest is that 1,167 out of 1,562 heads of households are Polish or Lithuanian. When the large numbers of Polish and Lithuanian lodgers are added to these family groups, it is clear that this is now a district almost exclusively made up of Slavic immigrants, many of them newly arrived and unable to speak any English. The problem of the adjustment of the newly arrived

† From *The American Journal of Sociology* 16:4 (January 1911): 433–35, 437–39, 442, 446, 450, 461–62, 464–66. Notes are by the editor of this Norton Critical Edition.

immigrant is very closely connected with the housing problem. It almost uniformly happens that the families which are most foreign are most exploited in the matter of their housing situation. They pay the highest rents for the poorest apartments, and they seem quite unable to understand that they have a right to insist on needed repairs or a decent standard of cleanliness. If a roof leaks, or the plumbing is out of order, they have no idea how to set about getting the landlord to attend to it. The student investigators who made the house-to-house canvass reported that their authority was rarely questioned among the less Americanized groups; the people were uniformly submissive, and apparently it never occurred to them that they had a right to ask why strangers could come in and measure their doors and windows.

✳ ✳ ✳

The primitive sanitary arrangements which still exist in this neighborhood are a result in part of the newness of the district, in part of the low standard of living that prevails among the people, and in greater part perhaps of their ignorance, poverty, and general helplessness. An ordinance passed in 1894 made it illegal for privy vaults[1] to be maintained on premises where sewers were possible, and this ordinance is still in force. In these few blocks, however, 44 privies with 21 separate vaults were found. The evil is greater than the number indicates, for 46 families and 248 persons used these miserable toilet accommodations which are so offensive and insanitary that they were outlawed fifteen years ago.

✳ ✳ ✳

✳ ✳ ✳ [I]n 1,981 cases the law against overcrowding was violated, and in many instances the number of cubic feet in the room was shockingly below the number of cubic feet required by law. Thus it appears that in 19 cases when rooms of 350 to 400 cubic feet were being illegally occupied, in two cases, 600 cubic feet, in ten cases 800, and in one case 1,000, and in another 1,400 were required by law. In 77 cases when 1,200 cubic feet of air were required, rooms containing less than 800 cubic feet were occupied. In one case four people slept in a room containing only 333 cubic feet, a room that could not have been legally occupied by even a single person over twelve years of age. In another case five people slept in a room containing 472 cubic feet, a room that could legally be occupied only

1. Pits without plumbing, used for human excrement. A 1902 *Journal of the American Medical Association* article speculates that flies feeding on "unclosed privy vaults and cesspools . . . in some of the most densely populated districts of Chicago" contributed to a serious typhoid outbreak in the "poorer quarters of the city" (Edwin Oakes Jordan, "Typhoid Fever and Water Supply," 39:25 [December 29, 1902]: 1564).

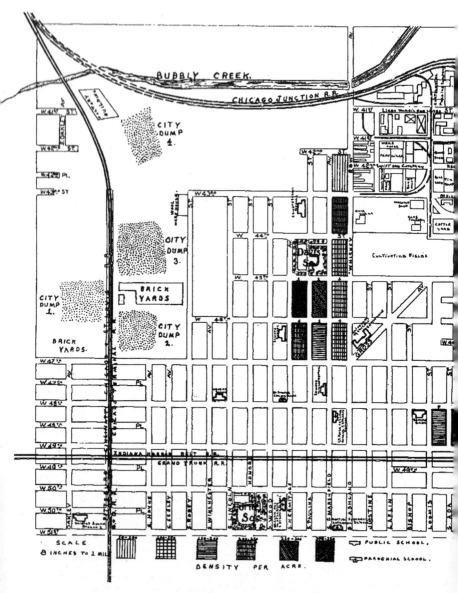

MAP SHOWING THE DISTRICT BETWEEN THE UNION
STOCKYARDS AND THE CITY DUMPS

In addition to the numbered blocks and those on the west side of
"Whiskey Row," the houses on the east side were also investigated.
(Map by Estelle B. Hunter.)

by a single person. In another case seven people, for whom 2,800 cubic feet would have been the legal minimum, slept in a room containing only 657 cubic feet.

One of the worst features of this overcrowding is the demoralizing lack of privacy. Grown brothers and sisters, for example, often occupy the same room. Sometimes the crowding is unnecessary; the family prefer, especially in the winter, to huddle into the rooms which are near the kitchen and in this way save the expense of extra fuel and an extra stove. In one apartment a bedroom which was light and sunny was left vacant, although the family were sleeping in a dark room which had only one window opening into a hall. The dark room was of course near the kitchen.

The secret of the overcrowding which prevails here is to be explained in part by the un-American standard of living. Polish and Slovak women, for example, told of conditions in their own homes where a large family often lived in one or two rooms.

* * *

In this as in most immigrant neighborhoods, a large number of families either own or are buying the house in which they live. It was found that 298 out of 613 premises were owned by people living on them. This 48 per cent of ownership is, however, likely to give a false impression of prosperity, for many of these places which the people claim to own are heavily encumbered and in many instances after a long struggle the house and all that has been paid slips away. The old idea of the prosperous workman owning a house of his own—usually a small cottage with a cheerful garden—fails of illustration in the immigrant tenement neighborhoods found in all large cities. * * *

* * *

There is, however, another feature of this neighborhood which is more offensive than the Stockyards and the saloons. Reference has already been made to the fact that conditions in the yards must be a demoralizing influence on the people who live near; but along with the influence of the Stockyards should be reckoned that of the great city "dump." A brief statement concerning the exact location and the extent of the "dump" as well as the way in which it is used by the city as a place of deposit for waste matter from distant wards will perhaps throw some further light upon conditions in this section of the city. In an open tract lying between Forty-seventh and Forty-second streets and near the Pittsburgh, Cincinnati, Chicago, & St. Louis Railroad are four places of deposit which are indicated on the accompanying map: the first, which is just north of Forty-seventh Street and west of the railroad, contains about seven acres; the second, north of Forty-seventh Street and east of the railroad, contains five acres; the third and fourth which are also east of the tracks contain respectively ten and six acres. These "dumps" are great holes from which the clay has been dug out for the neighboring brickyards. In the autumn of 1909, when our investigation was made, No. 1 (*see map*) had been filled with deposits of waste matter until it was almost level with the street; No. 2 had been nearly filled, but clay was still being removed so that the space continued to be enlarged; No. 3 which was still filled with water had been as yet only slightly used as a dumping-ground; while No. 4 was abandoned as a clay pit and was about half full of refuse.

* * *

These various kinds of waste tempt different kinds of persons to explore the dumps. On dumps Nos. 2 and 4 there are the professionals, who pay a regular stipend for the privilege of "picking" and who dispose of the articles collected in the regular course of trade. For the picking on dump No. 4, a payment of $15 a week is made by a man who employs five helpers. After these commercial pickers have taken their goods, the women and children, who have been watching the wagon unload and the picking take place, are allowed to hunt for the wood they want for kindling, the old mattresses which may serve on the bed at home, and the fragments of food. Of course the prospective find is most uncertain, but for both the women and children there is the excitement of exploration and the hope of a bit of silver or some other article of value, such as a lucky neighbor was rumored to have found. It is hardly necessary to say that the filthy condition of some of the household articles and the presence of decaying organic matter make this an obviously unfit place for children.

THE VICE COMMISSION OF CHICAGO

[Immigrant Women and Prostitution][†]

Sources of Supply. The investigation of the Commission on the sources of supply [for prostitution] has resulted in a large amount of illuminating data, sad and pitiful in its details. * * *

Wherever there is a demand, artificial or otherwise, there must be a supply. In another part of this report the conservative estimate is made that there are at least five thousand professional prostitutes in Chicago. Medical men affirm that the average life of these unfortunate women for service is from five to seven years. Thus it follows

---

† From *The Social Evil in Chicago* (Chicago: Gunthorp-Warren Printing Company, 1911), pp. 39–41, 227–28. Notes are by the editor of this Norton Critical Edition.

that fresh young girls must be continually supplied to take the place of those who die or are rendered useless by disease. Where do these new victims come from? Is the demand supplied?

From the mass of evidence we learn that the path which leads *down* to disease and death is constantly filled with young recruits who go stumbling on, blinded by the want of necessities of life, by a desire for some simple luxuries, by ignorance, by vain hopes, by broken promises, by the deceit and lust of men.

The Immigrant. The immigrant woman furnishes a large supply to the demand. Generally virtuous when she comes to this country, she is ruined and exploited because there is no adequate protection and assistance given her after she reaches the United States. That some prostitutes come from foreign countries is of course true, but the Federal Government, especially through its officials in Chicago, has done considerable to stop this importation. The White Slave Act,[1] recently passed by Congress, has been most effective in minimizing the traffic in foreign women. Much needs to be done, however, to protect the innocent immigrant who is betrayed and led into an immoral life after landing in New York or elsewhere. The care of immigrant women, upon their arrival in Chicago, needs supervision. Immigrant girls should not be left to private expressmen and cab drivers, to be lost to their relatives and friends in the city, because of incorrect addresses or the carelessness or vicious intent of the drivers.

Bad Home Conditions. The subject under consideration should bring forward most prominently, too, the fact that the supply comes largely from bad home conditions and lack of recreational privileges. In a large number of cases investigated, the home conditions have contributed to, if not caused, the downfall of many a wife and daughter. * * * [T]he perversion of the natural sex relationships by immorality of the guardian, by the evil example of a brother, sister, or other relative, and by the abuse of the marriage relation is the specific source of the ruin of many lives.

Statements are often made, and in some instances warranted by facts, that the excessive demands upon the mother because of a large family of children, without sufficient income or help to care for them, is also the occasion for many neglected children going astray. The statement is also made and supported by facts, learned from long and faithful experience in caring for dependent and delinquent children, that more delinquent girls come from small families where they are spoiled, than from large families where there may be poverty, but a

---

1. The White-Slave Traffic Act, also called the Mann Act (1910), making it a felony to engage in interstate or foreign transport of "any woman or girl for the purpose of prostitution or debauchery, or for any other immoral purpose." Because of its ambiguous language about "immorality," the act was also used to criminalize consensual sexual acts. Amended by Congress in 1978 and in 1986 to limit its application to transport for the purpose of prostitution or other illegal sexual acts.

sort of unconscious protective union of the children shielding one another.

White Slave Traffic. The subject of the so-called White Slave Traffic has attracted much attention throughout this and foreign countries. The term "white slave," is a misnomer. As a matter of fact the traffic is not confined to white girls, but to all unfortunate girls and women of all colors, races and nationalities. The use of this term, however, is authorized by the National Government and was incorporated in the international law on the subject. A "white slaver" in reality is a man who employs men or women or goes out himself to secure girls upon some false pretense, or misrepresentation, or when the girl, intoxicated or drugged, and not in possession of her senses, is conveyed to any place for immoral purposes.

If the girl is wayward and goes of her own free will she would not be a white slave in the true sense of the word; nor the man or woman who induced her to go or accompanied her to an immoral place a "white slaver." However, any man or woman who induces or accompanies any woman to enter an immoral place is guilty under the Illinois Pandering Act.

* * *

Investigations of the Immigrants' Protective League of Chicago on the Relation of Immigrant Women and Colonies of Foreign Laboring Men in Construction Camps, Lodging Houses in Cities, and Elsewhere

The investigation of the United States Immigration Commission into the relation of the immigrant woman to the social evil showed that very few prostitutes are brought into the United States. The great majority of young immigrant women who were found in resorts were virtuous when they came here, and were ruined because there was not adequate protection and assistance given them after they reached the United States. Such protection is especially needed on the journey to Chicago, and in the location of her relatives and friends, because of her ignorance of English and the country, a girl may through her own mistake or the carelessness of railroad officials be left at the wrong station or persuaded by some unscrupulous person to get off and see some town en route. * * * The delivery of immigrant women upon their arrival in Chicago also needs supervision. At present they are turned over to private expressmen and cabmen and as a result because of incorrect addresses and the carelessness or vicious intent of the drivers the Immigrants' Protective League finds that a good many girls do not find their relatives and friends in Chicago. These girls are nearly all from the country districts of eastern Europe and are therefore peculiarly helpless in such a situation. Better policing of the railroad stations which would keep runners from cheap and disreputable hotels from the neighborhood of the immigrant waiting rooms, more supervision of express and cabmen might do something but the situation can be properly handled only by the establishment of a Federal Protective Bureau under the Immigration Department which would have full authority to detain the immigrants and regulate their release in Chicago.

MATTHEW FRYE JACOBSON

[European Immigrants and the Alchemy of Race]†

As races are invented categories—designations coined for the sake of grouping and separating peoples along lines of presumed difference—Caucasians are made and not born. White privilege in various forms has been a constant in American political culture since colonial times, but whiteness itself has been subject to all kinds of contests and has gone through a series of historical vicissitudes. * * *

* * *

American scholarship on immigration has generally conflated race and color, and so has transported a late-twentieth-century understanding of "difference" into a period whose inhabitants recognized biologically based "races" rather than culturally based "ethnicities." But in the interest of an accurate historical rendering of race in the structure of U.S. culture and in the experience of those immigrant groups now called "Caucasians," we must listen more carefully to the historical sources than to the conventions of our own era; we must admit of a system of "difference" by which one might be both white *and* racially distinct from other whites.

* * *

The sociologists Michael Omi and Howard Winant assert that the contending forces of class formation and racial formation in American political culture produced "the institutionalization of a racial order that drew a color line *around* rather than *within* Europe."[1] True enough, and a useful corrective to those who would disavow their whiteness even while they live lives predicated upon its

---

† From *Whiteness of a Different Color: European Immigrants and the Alchemy of Race* (Cambridge, MA: Harvard UP, 1998), pp. 4, 6–10, 41–43. Copyright © 1998 by the President and Fellows of Harvard College. Reprinted by permission of the publisher. Unless otherwise indicated, notes are by the author. Some of the author's notes have been excerpted or omitted. Bibliographic information has been included.
1. Michael Oni and Howard Winant, *Racial Formation in the United States: From the 1960s to the 1980s* (New York: Routledge and Kegan Paul, 1986), p. 65.

privileges. But between the 1840s and the 1920s it was not altogether clear just where that line ultimately *would* be drawn. Just as it is crucial to recognize the legal whiteness undergirding the status of the white races in the United States, so is it crucial to reckon seriously with the racial othering that overlaid that whiteness. One way of doing that is to examine the relationship among competing ideas such as *white, Caucasian, Nordic, Anglo-Saxon, Celt, Slav, Alpine, Hebrew, Mediterranean, Iberic, Latin,* and so on.

The vicissitudes of race represent glacial, nonlinear cultural movements. Nonetheless, the history of whiteness in the United States is divisible into three great epochs. The nation's first naturalization law in 1790 (limiting naturalized citizenship to "free white persons") demonstrates the republican convergence of race and "fitness for self-government"; the law's wording denotes an unconflicted view of the presumed character and unambiguous boundaries of whiteness. Fifty years later, however, beginning with the massive influx of highly undesirable but nonetheless "white" persons from Ireland, whiteness was subject to new interpretations. The period of mass European immigration, from the 1840s to the restrictive legislation of 1924, witnessed a fracturing of whiteness into a hierarchy of plural and scientifically determined white races. Vigorous debate ensued over which of these was truly "fit for self-government" in the good old Anglo-Saxon sense. Finally, in the 1920s and after, partly because the crisis of over-inclusive whiteness had been solved by restrictive legislation and partly in response to a new racial alchemy generated by African-American migrations to the North and West, whiteness was reconsolidated: the late nineteenth century's probationary white groups were now remade and granted the scientific stamp of authenticity as the unitary Caucasian race—an earlier era's Celts, Slavs, Hebrews, Iberics, and Saracens, among others, had become the Caucasians so familiar to our own visual economy and racial lexicon.

*   *   *

Two premises guide my approach* * *. First, race is absolutely central to the history of European immigration and settlement. It was the racial appellation "white persons" in the nation's naturalization law that allowed the migrations from Europe in the first place; the problem this immigration posed to the polity was increasingly cast in terms of racial difference and assimilability; the most significant revision of immigration policy, the Johnson-Reed Act of 1924,[2] was founded upon a racial logic borrowed from biology and eugenics; and, consequently, the civic story of assimilation (the

---

2. Also known as the Immigration Act of 1924; implemented a national-origins quota system to limit number of immigrants allowed entry into the U.S. [*Editor*].

process by which the Irish, Russian Jews, Poles, and Greeks became Americans) is inseparable from the cultural story of racial alchemy (the process by which Celts, Hebrews, Slavs, and Mediterraneans became Caucasians). The European immigrants' experience was decisively shaped by their entering an arena where Europeanness— that is to say, whiteness—was among the most important possessions one could lay claim to. It was their *whiteness*, not any kind of New World magnanimity, that opened the Golden Door. And yet, for those who arrived between 1840 and 1924, New World experience was also decisively stamped by their entering an arena where race was the prevailing idiom for discussing citizenship and the relative merits of a given people.

The second premise * * * is that race resides not in nature but in politics and culture. One of the tasks before the historian is to discover which racial categories are useful to whom at a given moment, and why. Nor is this simply a case of immigrants' insisting upon their whiteness while nativists tarred them as "Hebrews" or "Slavs." Immigrants were often as quick to recognize their racial distance from the Anglo-Saxon as vice versa. Immigrant nationalisms were particularly prolific in generating and sustaining distinct racial identities—the Irish Race Conventions of the 1910s,[3] for example, represent another instance where "race" really meant "race." Racial categories themselves—their vicissitudes and the contests over them—reflect the competing notions of history, peoplehood, and collective destiny by which power has been organized and contested on the American scene.

*　　*　　*

And so this history of whiteness and its fluidity is very much a history of power and its disposition. But there is a second dimension: race is not just a conception; it is also a perception. The problem is not merely how races are comprehended, but how they are seen. * * * * * * The American eye sees a certain person as black, for instance, whom Haitian or Brazilian eyes might see as white. Similarly, an earlier generation of Americans *saw* Celtic, Hebrew, Anglo-Saxon, or Mediterranean physiognomies where today we see only subtly varying shades of a mostly undifferentiated whiteness. * * *

*　　*　　*

Whereas the salient feature of whiteness before the 1840s had been its powerful political and cultural contrast to nonwhiteness, now its internal divisions, too, took on a new and pressing significance.

---

3. Sponsored by the Friends of Irish Freedom, an Irish nationalist group, and held in various cities, including Philadelphia and New York in the 1910s [*Editor*].

The main currents in this period (c. 1840s–1920s) included, first, a spectacular rate of industrialization in the United States, whose voracious appetite for cheap labor—combined with political and economic dislocations across industrializing Europe—brought unprecedented numbers of migrants to New World shores; second, a growing nativist perception of these laborers themselves as a political threat to the smooth functioning of the republic; and third, consequently, a fracturing of monolithic whiteness by the popular marriage of scientific doctrines of race with political concerns over the newcomers' "fitness for self-government."

This increasing fragmentation and hierarchical ordering of distinct white *races* (now in the plural) was theorized in the ratified discourses of science, but it was also reflected in literature, visual arts, caricature, political oratory, penny journalism, and myriad other venues of popular culture. It was this notion of variegated whiteness that surfaced in 1863, for instance, when the New York *Tribune* characterized the rioting Irish in New York as a "savage mob," a "pack of savages," "savage foes," "demons," and "incarnate devils." It was this notion of variegated whiteness that undergirded Henry Cabot Lodge's[4] claim, in 1891, that Slovak immigrants "are not a good acquisition for us to make, since they appear to have so many items in common with the Chinese." * * *

* * *

Thus race is not tangential to the history of European immigration to the United States but absolutely central. "Fitness for self-government," a racial attribute whose outer property was whiteness, became encoded in a naturalization law that allowed Europeans' unrestricted immigration and their unhindered (male) civic participation. It is solely because of their race, in other words, that they were permitted entrance. But the massive influx borne of this "liberal" immigration policy, in its turn, generated a new perception of some Europeans' *un*fitness for self-government, now rendered racially in a series of subcategorical white groupings—Celt, Slav, Hebrew, Iberic, Mediterranean, and so on—white Others of a supreme Anglo-Saxondom. This does not simply represent a shift in American thinking "toward racism," as John Higham, still the premier historian of American nativism, would have it.[5] Rather, the political history of whiteness and its vicissitudes between the 1840s and the 1920s represents a shift from one brand of bedrock racism to another—from the unquestioned hegemony of a unified race of

---

4. At this point a Republican U.S. representative from Massachusetts; later a U.S. senator (1893–1924) [*Editor*].
5. John Higham, *Strangers in the Land: Patterns of American Nativism, 1865–1925* (New Brunswick, NJ: Rutgers UP, 1955), Chapter 6.

"white persons" to a contest over political "fitness" among a now fragmented, hierarchically arranged series of distinct "white races."
Race has been among the central organizers of the political life of
the republic all along, and the racial reclassification of various European immigrants as their numbers swelled is among the most
salient reminders of how powerful its sway has been.

U.S. BUREAU OF CORPORATIONS

[Division of Labor in the Meatpacking Industry]†

The most conspicuous fact which strikes one in observing the process of slaughtering and dressing is the remarkable extent to which
the division of labor is carried. In the old-fashioned small slaughterhouse one man, or at most a very few men, performed all the tasks
from the dealing of the death blow to the final preparation of the
carcass for sale. In the largest slaughtering plants of to-day will be
found hundreds, or even thousands, of workmen, each of whom performs but a very small, narrowly defined task, in which by innumerable repetitions he becomes adept.

A concrete illustration will serve to show more clearly this high
subdivision of labor. At one of the great abattoirs in Chicago 157
men are employed in one of the beef-killing gangs. All these men are
engaged in handling the cattle killed by two "knockers" and one
"sticker." The number includes all those conducting the processes
from the driving up of the cattle to the loading of beef into the cars,
but does not include the men who operate the power plants, refrigerating machinery, etc., nor those who handle by-products, even those
by-products which are sold in a fresh condition. These 157 represent
no less than 78 different occupations; that is, the work of killing and
dressing of cattle and refrigerating and loading beef is subdivided
into 78 distinct processes.[1] A gang of men thus organized can handle

---

† From *Report of the Commissioner of Corporations on the Beef Industry,* March 3, 1905
(Washington: Government Printing Office, 1905), pp. 17–18. Notes are by the author
of the original work.

1. The following 157 employees were required in slaughtering 1,050 cattle in a working day
of ten hours: 1 general foreman, 1 foreman over yard gang, 1 driving up cattle, 2 penning
cattle, 2 knocking cattle, 2 shackling cattle, 1 hanging off for shackler, 1 squeezing
blood from beds, 1 switching onto heading beds and putting up heads, 1 throwing down
heads, 1 pritching up, 1 dropping cattle, 1 pritching up helper, 1 sticker, 3 headers, 1
ripper, 4 leg breakers, 3 feet skinners, 1 gullet raiser, 7 floormen, 1 breast sawyer, 1 aitch
sawyer, 2½ cart pullers, 2 putting in hooks to hoists for fell cutter, 1 floor squeezer, 1
washing crutches and bellies, 4 fell cutters, 1 cutting out bladders, 2 rumpers, 1 rump
helper and drop hide feller, 2 backers, 4 splitters, 1 back and rump hand, 1 washing hind
shanks, 1 ripping tails and cutting out, 1 pulling tails, 2½ gutters, 2 throwing down guts
and paunches, 3 tail sawyers, 2 hanging off from splitter, 3 beating out fells, 1 helper
sawing tails and ripping open, 2 neck splitters, 1 tallow lot man, 1 trucking feet, 1 trucking up hooks, 1 hanging up hooks, 2 clearing out, 3 dropping hides.

more than a thousand cattle in a day of ten hours. Some of the packing houses have two or more such cattle-killing gangs. In the hog and sheep slaughtering departments the division of labor is carried to a similar degree of minuteness, and the same is true of those departments which can and cure meats, and which handle or manufacture the various by-products.

RICK HALPERN

[Capitalizing on Racial and Ethnic Divisions]†

Mass production in meatpacking depended as much upon the reorganization of work as it did upon technological and managerial innovation. Low profit margins, the desire to boost speed and output, and the need to bring down labor costs led packing companies to launch an assault upon the power of skilled butchers in their plants. By undermining these craftsmen, the packers gained the upper hand in the struggle for control of the production process. They also changed the character of the packinghouse workforce and the nature of the surrounding community, for their mastery of the shop floor depended upon thousands of unskilled, low-paid immigrants from central and eastern Europe. Moreover, the ways in which these newcomers interacted with one another and with established groups of workers depended in large measure on social dynamics originating in the

---

Washing gang: 1 foreman, 1 trimming bruises on rail, 1 wiping beef, 1 putting in neck and kidney cloths, 1 scribe sawyer, 1 hoseman, 1 washing shanks, 1 switchman, 3 washing ribs and necks inside, 1 squeezing beef, 1 pumping kidneys, 3 long brush washers, 1 washing rags, 2 wiping hinds, 2 ladder men (knife), 2 bruise trimmers, 1 cutting off cords and shanks, 1 tying veins, 2 trimming skirts and necks, 1 pumping necks.

Weighing beef and helpers: 1 scaler, 1 grader, 1 pushing on scale or tagger, 1 pulling off scale, 1 elevator man.

Refrigerating and car loading: 14 beef coolers, 5 trimmers, 7 carriers and loaders, 11 laborers.

The following 63 employees were engaged in handling by-products:

Hide gang: 1 hide inspector, 2 spreading out hides, 2 trucking to chute.

Laborers downstairs: 1 throwing down paunches, 3 truckers, 2 peck machine hands, 1 taking off toes, 1 sawing shin bones, 1 hanging livers, 1 sawing horns, 1 chopping brains, 1 offal lot hand, 1 ruffle man, 1 trimming glands (boy), 1 washing tongues, 1 washing weasands, 1 foreman, 1 bed tallow hand, 1 tripe washer, 1 squeezing, 1 sealer, 3 head boners.

Cooler department for offal, etc.: 12 cooler men, 1 scaler.

Knife men downstairs: 1 cutting off pecks, 1 cutting off peck butter, 3 trimming paunches, 1 opening paunches, 3 handling pecks and trimming deeds, 1 trimming heart casings, 1 trimming small bungs.

Offal department: 1 trimming livers, 1 cutting off tongues, 1 trimming tongues, 1 pulling weasands, 1 trimming plucks, 1 trimming hearts, 1 trimming cheek meat, 1 trimming small cheek meat, 1 trimming sweetbreads and tails, 1 cutting sinews.

† From *Down on the Killing Floor: Black and White Workers in Chicago's Packinghouses, 1904–54* (Chicago: U of Illinois P, 1997), pp. 21–31. Copyright © 1997 Board of Trustees of the University of Illinois. Used with permission of the University of Illinois Press. Unless otherwise indicated, notes are by the editor of this Norton Critical Edition. Some of the author's notes have been excerpted or omitted. Bibliographic information has been included.

packinghouses. The growth of Chicago's meatpacking industry entailed not just the emergence of new production techniques and business strategies but the formation of a new working class as well.

The introduction of mass production methods in meatpacking had profound social consequences. The industry's insatiable demand for cheap labor attracted thousands of immigrants to the neighborhood surrounding the stockyards. In the early twentieth century this was a community in flux. Older immigrant groups that provided muscle for the packing industry in its infancy increasingly gave way to newer arrivals. As early as 1900, the outlines of an ethnically stratified geographic unit started to take shape. The Irish and Germans still formed the most cohesive ethnic groupings, together accounting for nearly half of the families in the neighborhood, but Poles and Lithuanians continued to pour into the community during the first decade and a half of the century. By the time World War I arrested European immigration, one out of every two residents was a Pole; and by 1920, three-quarters of Packingtown's dwellers hailed from east of the Danube River.[1]

As the immigrant presence grew, the older, more acculturated families departed. Some Irish and Germans moved out to "better" neighborhoods, following the native Protestants to the new communities springing up on the city's southwestern edge. * * *

To an outsider, the Back-of-the-Yards neighborhood might have seemed homogeneous—solidly eastern European and decidedly foreign—but this impression belies a reality of social fragmentation. Each immigrant group built its own network of churches, fraternal organizations, and social clubs within which it attempted to re-create the old-world community left behind. Each institution was a declaration of a separate ethnic identity. "We pretty much kept to ourselves," remarked Gertie Kamarczyk, whose parents immigrated from Poland in 1900. She recalled that as a child her budding friendship with a Bohemian[2] girl met with the severe disapproval of her father, a beef lugger at Swift, who "never liked anyone who wasn't from the old country or whose parents weren't." The language, the culture, and even the style of dress set ethnic groups apart from one another. Back-of-the-Yards was not a single community. Rather, it was an industrial neighborhood honeycombed with dozens of ethnic enclaves.

The diversity of Packingtown's population was nowhere more apparent than at the workplace. The labor force in the stockyards was incredibly diverse, certainly more so than that working in the

1. Europe's second longest river, flowing through ten countries in Eastern and Central Europe. Countries to its east include Romania, Poland, Ukraine, Belarus, and the Czech Republic.
2. From the historical nation of Bohemia, located in what is now the western part of the Czech Republic.

steel mills to the south or the Harvester works[3] to the west. A 1909 survey found over forty distinct nationalities represented in the stockyards, while contemporary accounts rarely failed to remark upon the vast sea of humanity, speaking in different tongues and bidding against one another for jobs at the plant gates. Most departments in the packinghouses must have seemed like the proverbial Tower of Babel,[4] a hodgepodge of peoples and languages furiously working on discrete individual tasks.

Ethnic loyalties and nationalist identities complicated the project of working-class solidarity and provided the packing companies with a powerful weapon against organized labor. In facing the challenge of forging unity amongst a fragmented working class, union activists confronted deep divisions of culture accentuated by differences of skill. One veteran packinghouse worker, an Irish hog butcher who later served as a foreman, captured precisely this dynamic when he noted that his friends from work, the men with whom he regularly stopped at a nearby tavern before heading home, all spoke English, all worshiped at the same church, and all earned "top dollar, not like the rest of the Polacks and what have you workin' away in there."

Ethnic differences accentuated the division between the skilled minority of knifemen and the great mass of common laborers. The former group was comprised of German and Irish workers with small but significant sprinklings of Bohemians and native white Americans; recent immigrants from central and eastern Europe, especially Poland and Lithuania, filled the ranks of the latter group. Over the course of the early twentieth century, though, racial conflict supplemented and then supplanted ethnic tension as the major source of working-class fragmentation in the stockyards. Although black workers accounted for only 3 percent of the total workforce in 1909, they occupied a special and increasingly important position in the packers' calculations. Brought into the packinghouses in 1904 to replace striking workers, their continued presence made it impossible for whites to forget the relative ease with which their employers had bested them and, by extension, the tenuous nature of job security.

Labor Market Segmentation in Meatpacking

Chicago's meatpackers were among the first concerns to take advantage of what scholars recently have termed labor market segmentation. They tapped one market for skilled labor and another, larger

---

3. See above, p. 183, n. 5.
4. From Genesis 11:1–9, the biblical account of why people speak different languages: Before the Great Flood, everyone shared one language. But when people started building a tower tall enough to reach Heaven, God, to punish them, made them speak different languages so they could not communicate and thus could not complete the tower.

one for the remainder of their requirements. A third pool of workers, consisting of African Americans, was held in reserve for use
during periods of unrest or labor shortage. Although the three groups
might rub shoulders as they labored side by side within the plants,
the mechanisms through which they were hired and fired differed
greatly, as did the manner in which management treated them.
Beyond the world of work, their lives rarely overlapped. They lived
in different geographic areas, occupied different social spheres, and
pursued different cultural agendas. The maintenance and reproduction of a segmented labor market was crucial to the packers' ability
to operate profitably and central to the process of working-class
formation.

The packing companies benefited from this arrangement in two
major ways. First, they kept their wage bill to a minimum, hiring
cheap casual labor as needed and retaining only a small number of
highly paid workers with skills essential to production. Second,
despite considerable commonality of interest amongst packinghouse
workers, divisions of skill and ethnicity remained paramount. The
cultivation and utilization of a segmented labor market produced a
fragmented workforce unable to challenge the packers' authority
effectively. The packers' manipulation of deeply felt ethnic and racial
antagonisms fortified their structural control over production by
dividing workers from one another.

The packers felt it neither necessary nor prudent to conceal this
policy of divide and rule, as John R. Commons[5] discovered in 1904
when he traveled to Chicago to witness conditions in the stockyards
and meatpacking industry. Visiting Swift's employment office, he
noticed a surprising homogeneity amongst the morning's hirees.
Blond-haired, fair-skinned young men sat on benches waiting to be
assigned to various departments. "How comes it you are employing
only Swedes?" Commons queried. "Well, you see it is only for this
week," came the reply. "Last week we employed Slovaks. We change
among different nationalities and languages. It prevents them from
getting together. We have the thing systematized."

Philip Armour echoed this statement, candidly explaining to his
biographers that eastern European immigrants helped forestall
unionism "by displacing experienced and perhaps disillusioned
employees . . . who might have been contaminated by contacts with
union organizers." Moreover, he admitted pursuing policies intended
to "keep the races and nationalities apart after working hours, and
to foment suspicion, rivalry, and even enmity among such groups."[6]

5. American labor historian and author of "Labor Conditions in Slaughtering and Meatpacking," *Quarterly Journal of Economics* 19 (1904): 1–32.
6. Harper Leech and John Charles Carroll, *Armour and His Times* (New York: D.
   Appleton-Century, 1938), 232 [*Author's note*].

Labor market segmentation in meatpacking, and the resulting fragmentation of the workforce, arose from specific policies formulated and implemented by capital. Market forces undoubtedly played a role in this process by facilitating the packers' access to an abundant supply of cheap labor. But deliberate human decisions determined the precise ways in which labor power was recruited and allocated. This important dynamic is the key to understanding the failure of organizing drives in 1894, 1904, and 1917–22. Before turning to examine these campaigns, it is helpful to consider in greater detail the workings of the labor market and the anatomy of the packinghouse workforce.

By conceptualizing the workforce as a horizontally layered pyramid, we can discern a clear pattern—one which joined occupation, skill, and ethnicity in an elaborate hierarchy—amidst what appeared to contemporary observers as tumultuous chaos. A small triangle at the top of the pyramid represents the elite "butcher aristocracy"; and a broad hexagon at the bottom denotes the mass of common laborers. Multiple layers separating these two extremes signify sizeable ranks of semiskilled workers.

The butcher aristocracy formed the most homogenous group of workers in Chicago's packinghouses. In the first years of the twentieth century, Germans and Irishmen made up the bulk of skilled butchers, along with a small number of native whites and a larger sprinkling of recently arrived Bohemians. English speaking and well assimilated, many of these workers were able to move up into lower level management positions. As late as the 1930s most foremen were drawn from these two ethnic groups.

*   *   *

Most of these skilled workers labored on the killing floors. Even though much of the work was heavy and dirty, this butcher aristocracy enjoyed relatively high wages and regular work. A floorsman on the cattle kill, for example, performed the exacting task of removing the steer's hide. For this he received fifty cents an hour in 1904—the highest rate. In addition to great strength, this job required considerable skill. Floorsmen had to be ambidextrous, and capable of working quickly and cutting accurately for eight to ten hours at a time. The floorsman's superior position stemmed from the high cost of a mistake. A slip in one direction marred the valuable hide; an error in the other direction damaged the meat itself. Cattle splitters, who wielded heavy cleavers and cleanly separated the carcass into halves, received the same rate of pay. Backers and rumpers, charged with making precise cuts along the hide, received slightly less.

Skilled workers formed a small minority in their departments. In the large houses, a typical cattle-killing gang was made up of around two hundred men, only fourteen of whom were in the top pay brackets. * * *

* * *

The wages earned by skilled butchers * * * separated them from other packinghouse workers and placed them on par with some of the better paid craftsmen in the city. Their annual incomes of around $1500 compared favorably with machinists in the nearby Rock Island Railroad car shops and at the McCormick Harvester works. The highest paid knifemen earned considerably more than the male white-collar workers who staffed the packers' offices. But this butcher aristocracy was a small elite. By 1910 it made up no more than 20 percent of the total workforce; and their numbers were shrinking. Because their skills were essential to the process of production and not easily acquired, floorsmen and splitters enjoyed a kind of job security and income wholly foreign to the mass of workers in the stockyards.

* * *

Standing between the butcher aristocracy and the thousands of common laborers was a group of semiskilled workers who performed a wide array of jobs. The feature they shared was the use of a knife. Some of these jobs required considerable training and paid hourly rates just a few cents below that of the butchers. Others, however, could be picked up quickly and consisted of simple repetitive motions. These jobs were closer in pay to the common labor rate. * * *

This group of semiskilled workers was ethnically heterogeneous. It contained significant numbers of old stock immigrants but was dominated by newcomers, most notably Poles, who by 1905 comprised the largest foreign-born group in the packinghouse workforce. The Slovaks and Lithuanians who followed after the turn of the century had a more difficult time adjusting to the industrial setting, in part due to their smaller numbers and, consequently, greater isolation. Unattached and unsettled, isolated by the formidable language barrier, these ethnic groups occupied the lowest space on the social ladder.

* * *

Most of the newer immigrants worked not in semiskilled slots but as common laborers, earning between sixteen and eighteen cents an hour. By 1910, common labor accounted for two-thirds of the workforce, but even within these vast ranks a hierarchy existed. At the upper end of the scale were "regular" employees—workers who returned daily to the same departments and jobs. Most of these involved the application of brute muscle power—hauling, carting, trucking, or hoisting. Others called for some kind of decision making, but little skill or judgment. * * *

* * *

Common laborers constantly worried about job security. Whereas knifemen could count on employment throughout the fall and winter rush and were likely to see at least some work during the rest of the year, common laborers led a precarious economic existence. During slack periods, management preferred to keep part of a gang working full-time rather than employ the entire gang on reduced hours. When reduced livestock supply necessitated layoffs, those on the lower rungs of the job ladder were thrown out of work. Uncertainty was a constant part of life. * * * Packinghouse workers devised a number of strategies to maintain the solvency of their households. Most families counted more than one wage earner among their members, since even a child's small paycheck could spell the difference between hard times and ruin. Up until World War I, most families lodged at least one boarder; and in addition to presiding over this system, women took in washing, sold preserves, and served as midwives. Children scavenged for food and salvageable materials in the garbage dumps below Thirty-ninth Street; and men often traveled considerable distances in search of work when laid off. The boxcar journey of Jurgis, the fictional hero of Sinclair's *Jungle,* was one traveled in real life by countless Packingtown residents desperate for work.

At the bottom of the pyramidal job structure stood thousands of casual workers hired on a temporary basis. Between 20 and 30 percent of those laboring in the stockyards during the 1910s and 1920s were employed by the day, or even by the hour. Many of these workers were Packingtown residents; most probably lived in the Chicago area. Others were part of a transient population of laborers constantly on the move throughout the margins of the industrial economy. Because it served as the hub of the nation's railroad network, Chicago attracted a large number of casual workers. Employment agencies and flop houses dotted the streets and alleys in the vicinity around Union Station a few miles northeast of the stockyards. The surplus of casual labor in the city was more severe than elsewhere and kept wages at an absolute minimum.

The institution which serviced the packers' fluctuating labor needs was the morning "shape-up." Starting before dawn, hundreds of workers gathered outside the doors of the packinghouses hoping to secure employment. Foremen surveyed the assembled crowd and chose the dozen or so extra laborers required to round out their gangs. At other plants, operating on a more rationalized basis, employment officers received requests from the various departments and then hired those needed.

Job security was nonexistent for these laborers. "A man never knows if he is hired for an hour or for a week," an industry expert informed a congressional committee. While some workers succeeded in parlaying a day of work into regular employment, most soon found themselves on the other side of the gate. Unfettered by any constraint, management treated labor as a simple commodity. This was an essential component in the packers system of labor recruitment, allocation, and control. Since the supply of labor outstripped demand, the casual market helped the packers keep a ceiling on their wage bill.

The psychological impact of casual labor was profound. The crowds massing in search of work each morning loomed in the minds of packing house workers. With the exception of the skilled elite, workers were acutely aware of how easily they could be replaced. * * *

Of equal, if not greater, psychological importance was the presence of a small number of black workers in the stockyards. Even though they had worked in the industry since the 1880s, black workers were confined to the most menial positions and were concentrated in the most disagreeable departments. Unlike the Bohemians and Poles, who entered the stockyards at about the same time, black workers made negligible gains in promotion and advancement. Accounting for no more than 2 or 3 percent of the workforce, they nonetheless exerted an influence disproportionate to their minuscule numbers, serving as a visible, daily reminder of the inexhaustible supply of reserve labor to which the packers could turn if confronted with labor unrest. They introduced a powerful element of fear and mistrust into a situation already tense with ethnic frictions.

In responding to their African American co-workers, both on a daily basis and in times of strife, white packinghouse workers drew upon an historical legacy dating back to the initial entry of blacks into the industry as strikebreakers. A particularly vicious pattern of race relations was established as early as 1894, when the packing companies first used black labor to undermine a strike called by white workers. This pattern was given powerful reinforcement a decade later when the packers recruited thousands of southern blacks to put down the Amalgamated Meat Cutters.[7] Rooted in a distinct set of historical circumstances, white hostility toward blacks came to form the most formidable obstacle to workers' solidarity in the stockyards.

Early Unionism and the Origins of Racial Conflict

Before 1894 the few blacks working in the stockyards attracted little notice. Alma Herbst suggests that there was little friction between

---

7. As depicted in Chapter XXVI of *The Jungle*. Chartered by the American Federation of Labor (AFL) in 1897, the Amalgamated Meat Cutters and Butcher Workmen of North America was a labor union representing packinghouse workers.

these men and their white co-workers. "To stand beside a black man was an unfamiliar experience which at first created an element of curiosity and interest rather than conflict."[8] In a rapidly changing industry that was starting to absorb immigrants from the far reaches of the globe, it appeared that blacks might not be treated differently from the other ethnic groups drawn to the yards in search of work.

This promise was never realized. In the summer of 1894, striking workers at the Pullman car works[9] appealed for help. Several thousand butchers walked out of the packinghouses in sympathy with the rapidly spreading strike. Although unskilled workers joined the walkout, when the knifemen met to formulate a set of demands they made no effort to encompass the grievances of the common laborers. When they dispatched representatives to spread the strike to other midwestern packing centers, they instructed them to direct their appeals to skilled butchers rather than to the workforce as a whole. This strategy proved to be their undoing.

The Chicago packers responded swiftly and decisively. Brushing aside their employees' demands, they began recruiting replacement workers. With foremen and superintendents performing the skilled work, the packers utilized hundreds of Polish and black strikebreakers to maintain production. After several weeks desperation set in and violence erupted. Even though a far greater number of white immigrants crossed the butchers' lines, most of the strikers' hostility was directed against the black scabs. Crowds mercilessly harassed strikebreakers as they made their way to and from work, but a special animus was reserved for blacks. Effigies with the words "Nigger Scab" scrawled upon them hung from lampposts around the stockyards; and numerous attacks and assaults were recorded.

While the butchers remained solid, many other departments refused to take part in the strike. Once the larger Pullman conflict died down, hundreds of packinghouse workers trickled back to their jobs. When rail traffic resumed, the packers augmented their loyal core of butchers with skilled men from Kansas City, Omaha, and other packing centers. After nine weeks the effort was abandoned, a failure that had sown formidable seeds of discord.

Defeat underscored the obsolescence of craft unionism[1] in meatpacking. The extreme division of labor prevailing inside the plants not only undermined the bargaining power of the few highly skilled butchers but made them vulnerable to replacement by less-skilled knifemen whose own jobs could then be performed by workers

8. Alma Herbst, *The Negro in the Slaughtering and Meat-Packing Industry in Chicago* (New York: Houghton-Mifflin, 1932) [*Author's note*].
9. See above, p. 251, n. 1.
1. The model of labor organizing by specific trade or craft (such as electricians), as opposed to industrial unionism, which organizes labor by an entire industry (such as construction).

farther down the job ladder. Nonetheless, skilled butchers tenaciously clung to the craft model, declining to reach out to the growing mass of unskilled workers, thus ensuring their ineffectiveness in the face of the packers' superior power.

KARL MARX

[Labor Power as Commodity]†

Now, therefore, for the first question: *What are wages? How are they determined?*

If workers were asked: "How much are your wages?" one would reply: "I get a mark[1] a day from my employer"; another, "I get two marks," and so on. According to the different trades to which they belong, they would mention different sums of money which they receive from their respective employers for the performance of a particular piece of work, for example, weaving a yard of linen or typesetting a printed sheet. In spite of the variety of their statements, they would all agree on one point: wages are the sum of money paid by the capitalist for a particular labour time or for a particular output of labour.

The capitalist, it seems, therefore, *buys* their labour with money. They *sell* him their labour for money. But this is merely the appearance. In reality what they sell to the capitalist for money is their labour *power*. The capitalist buys this labour power for a day, a week, a month, etc. And after he has bought it, he uses it by having the workers work for the stipulated time. For the same sum with which the capitalist has bought their labour power, for example, two marks, he could have bought two pounds of sugar or a definite amount of any other commodity. The two marks, with which he bought two pounds of sugar, are the *price* of the two pounds of sugar. The two marks, with which he bought twelve hours' use of labour power, are the price of twelve hours' labour. Labour power, therefore, is a commodity, neither more nor less than sugar. The former is measured by the clock, the latter by the scales.

*   *   *

Labour power is, therefore, a commodity which its possessor, the wage-worker, sells to capital. Why does he sell it? In order to live.

But the exercise of labour power, labour, is the worker's own life-activity, the manifestation of his own life. And this *life-activity* he

† From "Wage Labour and Capital," *The Marx-Engels Reader*, ed. Robert C. Tucker (New York: Norton, 1972), pp. 169–71, 176, 178–79, 183–84, 187–90. Notes are by the editor of this Norton Critical Edition.
1. Former monetary unit in Germany.

sells to another person in order to secure the necessary *means of subsistence*. Thus his life-activity is for him only a means to enable him to exist. He works in order to live. He does not even reckon labour as part of his life, it is rather a sacrifice of his life. It is a commodity which he has made over to another. Hence, also, the product of his activity is not the object of his activity. What he produces for himself is not the silk that he weaves, not the gold that he draws from the mine, not the palace that he builds. What he produces for himself is *wages*, and silk, gold, palace resolve themselves for him into a definite quantity of the means of subsistence, perhaps into a cotton jacket, some copper coins and a lodging in a cellar. And the worker, who for twelve hours weaves, spins, drills, turns, builds, shovels, breaks stones, carries loads, etc.—does he consider this twelve hours' weaving, spinning, drilling, turning, building, shovelling, stone breaking as a manifestation of his life, as life? On the contrary, life begins for him where this activity ceases, at table, in the public house, in bed. The twelve hours' labour, on the other hand, has no meaning for him as weaving, spinning, drilling, etc., but as *earnings*, which bring him to the table, to the public house, into bed. If the silk worm were to spin in order to continue its existence as a caterpillar, it would be a complete wage-worker. Labour power was not always a *commodity*. Labour was not always wage labour, that is, *free labour*. The *slave* did not sell his labour power to the slave owner, any more than the ox sells its services to the peasant. The slave, together with his labour power, is sold once and for all to his owner. He is a commodity which can pass from the hand of one owner to that of another. He is *himself* a commodity, but the labour power is not *his* commodity. The *serf* sells only a part of his labour power. He does not receive a wage from the owner of the land; rather the owner of the land receives a tribute from him.

The serf belongs to the land and turns over to the owner of the land the fruits thereof. The *free labourer*, on the other hand, sells himself and, indeed, sells himself piecemeal. He sells at auction eight, ten, twelve, fifteen hours of his life, day after day, to the highest bidder, to the owner of the raw materials, instruments of labour and means of subsistence, that is, to the capitalist. The worker belongs neither to an owner nor to the land, but eight, ten, twelve, fifteen hours of his daily life belong to him who buys them. The worker leaves the capitalist to whom he hires himself whenever he likes, and the capitalist discharges him whenever he thinks fit, as soon as he no longer gets any profit out of him, or not the anticipated profit. But the worker, whose sole source of livelihood is the sale of his labour power, cannot leave the *whole class of purchasers, that is, the capitalist class*, without renouncing his existence. He belongs not to this or that capitalist but to the *capitalist class*, and, moreover, it is his business to dispose of himself, that is, to find a purchaser within this capitalist class.

✳ ✳ ✳

Another consideration, however, also comes in. The manufacturer in calculating his cost of production and, accordingly, the price of the products takes into account the wear and tear of the instruments of labour. If, for example, a machine costs him 1,000 marks and wears out in ten years, he adds 100 marks annually to the price of the commodities so as to be able to replace the worn-out machine by a new one at the end of ten years. In the same way, in calculating the cost of production of simple labour power, there must be included the cost of reproduction, whereby the race of workers is enabled to multiply and to replace worn-out workers by new ones. Thus the depreciation of the worker is taken into account in the same way as the depreciation of the machine.

✳ ✳ ✳

The worker receives means of subsistence in exchange for his labour power, but the capitalist receives in exchange for his means of subsistence labour, the productive activity of the worker, the creative power whereby the worker not only replaces what he consumes but *gives to the accumulated labour a greater value than it previously possessed.* The worker receives a part of the available means of subsistence from the capitalist. For what purpose do these means of subsistence serve him? For immediate consumption. As soon, however, as I consume the means of subsistence, they are irretrievably lost to me unless I use the time during which I am kept alive by them in order to produce new means of subsistence, in order during consumption to create by my labour new values in place of the values which perish in being consumed. But it is just this noble reproductive power that the worker surrenders to the capitalist in exchange for means of subsistence received. He has, therefore, lost it for himself.

Let us take an example: a tenant farmer gives his day labourer five silver groschen[2] a day. For these five silver groschen the labourer works all day on the farmer's field and thus secures him a return of ten silver groschen. The farmer not only gets the value replaced that he has to give the day labourer; he doubles it. He has therefore employed, consumed, the five silver groschen that he gave to the labourer in a fruitful, productive manner. He has bought with the five silver groschen just that labour and power of the labourer which produces agricultural products of double value and makes ten silver groschen out of five. The day labourer, on the other hand, receives

2. Former German coin.

in place of his productive power, the effect of which he has bargained away to the farmer, five silver groschen, which he exchanges for means of subsistence, and these he consumes with greater or less rapidity. The five silver groschen have, therefore, been consumed in a double way, *reproductively* for capital, for they have been exchanged for labour power which produced ten silver groschen, *unproductively* for the worker, for they have been exchanged for means of subsistence which have disappeared forever and the value of which he can only recover by repeating the same exchange with the farmer. *Thus capital presupposes wage labour; wage labour presupposes capital. They reciprocally condition the existence of each other; they reciprocally bring forth each other.*

*   *   *

A rapid increase of capital is equivalent to a rapid increase of profit. Profit can only increase rapidly if the price of labour, if relative wages, decrease just as rapidly. Relative wages can fall although real wages rise simultaneously with nominal wages, with the money value of labour, if they do not rise, however, in the same proportion as profit. If, for instance, in times when business is good, wages rise by five per cent, profit on the other hand by thirty per cent, then the comparative, the relative wages, have not *increased* but *decreased.*

Thus if the income of the worker increases with the rapid growth of capital, the social gulf that separates the worker from the capitalist increases at the same time, and the power of capital over labour, the dependence of labour on capital, likewise increases at the same time.

*   *   *

We have thus seen that:

Even the *most favourable situation* for the working class, the *most rapid possible growth of capital*, however much it may improve the material existence of the worker, does not remove the antagonism between his interests and the interests of the bourgeoisie, the interests of the capitalists. *Profit and wages* remain as before in *inverse porportion.*

If capital is growing rapidly, wages may rise; the profit of capital rises incomparably more rapidly. The material position of the worker has improved, but at the cost of his social position. The social gulf that divides him from the capitalist has widened.

*   *   *

The greater *division of labour* enables *one* worker to do the work of five, ten or twenty; it therefore multiplies competition among the workers fivefold, tenfold and twentyfold. The workers do not only compete by one selling himself cheaper than another; they compete by *one* doing the work of five, ten, twenty; and the *division of labour*, introduced by capital and continually increased, compels the workers to compete among themselves in this way.

Further, as the *division of labour* increases, labour *is simplified*. The special skill of the worker becomes worthless. He becomes transformed into a simple, monotonous productive force that does not have to use intense bodily or intellectual faculties. His labour becomes a labour that anyone can perform. Hence, competitors crowd upon him on all sides, and besides we remind the reader that the more simple and easily learned the labour is, the lower the cost of production needed to master it, the lower do wages sink, for, like the price of every other commodity, they are determined by the cost of production.

Therefore, as labour becomes more unsatisfying, more repulsive, competition increases and wages decrease. The worker tries to keep up the amount of his wages by working more, whether by working longer hours or by producing more in one hour. Driven by want, therefore, he still further increases the evil effects of the division of labour. The result is that *the more he works the less wages he receives*, and for the simple reason that he competes to that extent with his fellow workers, hence makes them into so many competitors who offer themselves on just the same bad terms as he does himself, and that, therefore, in the last resort he *competes with himself, with himself as a member of the working class*.

Machinery brings about the same results on a much greater scale, by replacing skilled workers by unskilled, men by women, adults by children. It brings about the same results, where it is newly introduced, by throwing the hand workers on to the streets in masses, and, where it is developed, improved and replaced by more productive machinery, by discharging workers in smaller batches. We have portrayed above, in a hasty sketch, the industrial war of the capitalists among themselves; *this war has the peculiarity that its battles are won less by recruiting than by discharging the army of labour. The generals, the capitalists, compete with one another as to who can discharge most soldiers of industry.*

✳   ✳   ✳

Finally, as the capitalists are compelled, by the movement described above, to exploit the already existing gigantic means of production on a larger scale and to set in motion all the mainsprings of credit to this end, there is a corresponding increase in industrial earthquakes, in which the trading world can only maintain itself by sacrificing a part of wealth, of products and even of productive forces to the gods of the nether world—in a word, *crises* increase. They become more frequent and more violent, if only because, as the mass of production, and consequently the need for extended markets, grows, the world market becomes more and more contracted, fewer and fewer new markets remain available for exploitation, since every preceding crisis has subjected to world trade a market hitherto unconquered or only superficially exploited. But capital does not *live* only on labour. A lord, at once aristocratic and barbarous, it drags with it into the grave the corpses of its slaves, whole hecatombs[3] of workers who perish in the crises. Thus we see: *if capital grows rapidly, competition among the workers grows incomparably more rapidly, that is, the means of employment, the means of subsistence, of the working class decrease proportionately so much the more, and, nevertheless, the rapid growth of capital is the most favourable condition for wage labour.*

DONALD D. STULL

[Meat Processing Employees and Working Conditions][†]

Packinghouses became the first American workplaces to fragment tasks and mechanically regulate output through conveyor systems that brought animals directly to workers. By the 1950s, the conveyor's endless chain had been refined to allow "on-the-rail dressing," which mechanically moves the animal along an overhead rail past stationary workers who kill, bleed, skin, gut, and cut up each carcass. Mechanization of the disassembly process also simplified—or deskilled—the work.

* * *

Conditions in American packinghouses were first brought to national attention by Upton Sinclair in *The Jungle*. Public outcry over the filthy packinghouses and tainted meat [that] Sinclair described in his 1906 novel led to passage of the Pure Food and Drug Act and the Meat Inspection Act later that year.

Low wages and horrid working conditions encouraged unions and spawned strikes. In the late 19th and early 20th centuries, meatpacking was the most strike-prone American industry, as workers fought for the 8-hour workday, the 40-hour workweek, and time-and-a-half pay for overtime. Immigrants, African Americans, and

---

3. Originally, ancient Greek or Roman sacrifices (usually of 100 oxen or cattle) to the gods; here used metaphorically to signify public, almost ceremonial, sacrifices of laborers to increase capital.

† From "Meat Processing," *The SAGE Encyclopedia of Food Issues*, ed. Ken Albala (Thousand Oaks, CA: SAGE, 2015), pp. 946–49. Reprinted with permission of Sage Publications, Inc.; permission conveyed through Copyright Clearance Center, Inc. Notes are by the editor of this Norton Critical Edition.

poor whites provided meatpacking's workforce. Deskilling and rigid division of labor on packinghouse floors opened opportunities for women, who entered meatpacking at the bottom of the pay scale. The National Labor Relations (Wagner) Act of 1935 established the National Labor Relations Board and guaranteed workers the right to organize and bargain collectively. By World War II, collective bargaining was accepted in the meat industry, and some companies signed "master contracts" covering workers in all their plants. But the 1947 Labor Management Relations (Taft-Hartley) Act required unions to bargain with management, outlawed sympathy strikes and secondary boycotts, and banned closed shops,[1] which made union membership a condition of employment. It did permit union shops, except in right-to-work states, where union membership as a prerequisite for employment is outlawed.

Union power in the meat industry peaked in the 1950s, as strikes and negotiations led to master contracts granting better wages and working conditions. By 1960, wages in meatpacking were 15% above the average manufacturing wage in the United States. Between 1960 and 1990, 46,000 meatpacking jobs were lost to plant closings and mechanization, as the industry restructured and relocated. In the process, meatpacking was transformed from an urban, unionized industry to a rural, nonunion one. Master contracts became a thing of the past, and by 1990, wages in meatpacking had fallen to 20% below the average for manufacturing. Meat and poultry line workers now earn less than half the hourly rate in manufacturing overall.

Meatpacking is one of the few remaining manufacturing jobs in North America where employers do not require workers to have a high school diploma, have previous work experience, or speak English. From 1980 to 2000, non-Hispanic whites dropped from 74% of the meat-processing labor force to under 50%, while Hispanics increased from under 10% to 30%, of which more than 80% were foreign-born. The majority of hourly workers in many meat and poultry plants are now immigrants and refugees.

Meat processing has a reputation for hiring unauthorized immigrants. Stricter worksite enforcement operations, such as the 2006 U.S. Immigration and Customs Enforcement raid on six Swift and Company packing plants in five states,[2] have altered industry hiring

1. Arrangements whereby employers agree to hire only persons who belong to unions. *"Master contracts"*: collective bargaining agreements covering all unionized workers in a given industry or company. *Sympathy strikes*: when unions without a grievance of their own strike to show support for another union. *Secondary boycotts*: efforts to prohibit doing business with a company that trades with another (secondary) company involved in a labor dispute.

2. In one of the largest immigration enforcement actions in U.S. history, ICE arrested 1,300 undocumented immigrants working at six plants owned by Swift & Co. Most of those arrested were deported, while other immigrant employees stopped going to work out of fear.

practices. Refugees from Asia and Africa, who have authorization to live and work in the United States, are a growing part of the industry's workforce.

Increased industry reliance on Latin American immigrants and refugees has altered the demographic, cultural, and linguistic characteristics of communities that are home to meat-processing plants. Beginning in the High Plains and Midwest in the 1980s and spreading to the Southeast in the 1990s, small towns that host meat- and poultry-processing plants have been transformed into multicultural boomtowns. In addition to rapid growth and dramatic increases in cultural and linguistic diversity, these communities also experience population mobility, housing shortages, soaring school enrollments, rising crime rates, and strains on infrastructure and social services. Many of the challenges faced by meat- and poultry-processing towns stem not so much from the influx of immigrants themselves as from the consequences of the low-wage jobs that attract them.

* * *

Meatpacking workers are prone to injury, given that they work with knives, saws, and heavy equipment in extreme temperatures on floors slick with blood and fat. Chicago's Armour plant reported that half of its workers were injured or became ill on the job in 1917. In 1970, meatpacking's annual injury rate stood at 47 per 100 fulltime workers, and until the end of the 20th century, it had the highest injury and illness rate of any industry in the United States, three times the average for manufacturing overall.

Fatalities, while they do occur in meat-processing plants, are rare. Instead, meatpacking workers are subject to frequent but less severe injuries, but their cumulative effect is often debilitating. In the first half of the 20th century, cuts, bruises, strains, and fractures made up the vast majority of reported injuries. In the 1950s, meatpacking unions brought greater attention to plant safety and forced reduction in line speeds. As a result, injury rates fell, but this decline was short lived. With industrial restructuring came increased mechanization, further simplifying tasks, and allowing plants to operate faster and boost worker productivity (output per hour). The Occupational Safety and Health Act of 1970 introduced new data collection methods and categories of workplace injury and illness. For the first time, repetitive motion disorders were reported even if workdays were not missed. Between 1970 and 1975, meatpacking's injury and illness rate declined from 46.9 to 31.2, but it climbed steadily thereafter, peaking at an annual rate of 45.5 in 1991. Fueling this dramatic rise were repetitive motion disorders, primarily carpal tunnel syndrome, which by 1991 made up one third of all meatpacking injuries.

ERIC SCHLOSSER

From Fast Food Nation[†]

[T]he growth of the fast food chains has encouraged consolidation in the meatpacking industry. McDonald's is the nation's largest purchaser of beef. In 1968, McDonald's bought ground beef from 175 local suppliers. A few years later, seeking to achieve greater product uniformity as it expanded, McDonald's reduced the number of beef suppliers to five. Much like the french fry industry, the meatpacking industry has been transformed by mergers and acquisitions over the last twenty years. Many ranchers now argue that a few large corporations have gained a stranglehold on the market, using unfair tactics to drive down the price of cattle. Anger toward the large meatpackers is growing, and a new range war threatens to erupt, one that will determine the social and economic structure of the rural West.

A century ago, American ranchers found themselves in a similar predicament. The leading sectors of the nation's economy were controlled by corporate alliances known as "trusts." There was a Sugar Trust, a Steel Trust, a Tobacco Trust—and a Beef Trust. It set the prices offered for cattle. Ranchers who spoke out against this monopoly power were often blackballed, unable to sell their cattle at any price. In 1917, at the height of the Beef Trust, the five largest meatpacking companies—Armour, Swift, Morris, Wilson, and Cudahy—controlled about 55 percent of the market. The early twentieth century had trusts, but it also had "trustbusters," progressive government officials who believed that concentrated economic power posed a grave threat to American democracy. The Sherman Antitrust Act had been passed in 1890 after a congressional investigation of price fixing in the meatpacking industry, and for the next two decades the federal government tried to break up the Beef Trust, with little success. In 1917 President Woodrow Wilson ordered the Federal Trade Commission to investigate the industry. The FTC inquiry concluded that the five major meatpacking firms had secretly fixed prices for years, had colluded to divide up markets, and had shared livestock information to guarantee that ranchers received the lowest possible price for their cattle. Afraid that an antitrust trial might end with an unfavorable verdict, the five meatpacking companies signed a consent decree in 1920 that forced them to sell off

† From *Fast Food Nation: The Dark Side of the All-American Meal* (Boston and New York: Houghton Mifflin, 2001), pp. 136–38, 159–60, 162–63, 178, 205–06. Copyright © 2001 by Eric Schlosser. Reprinted by permission of Houghton Mifflin Harcourt Company. All rights reserved. Notes are by the editor of this Norton Critical Edition.

their stockyards, retail meat stores, railway interests, and livestock journals. A year later Congress created the Packers and Stockyards Administration (P&SA), a federal agency with a broad authority to prevent price-fixing and monopolistic behavior in the beef industry.

For the next fifty years, ranchers sold their cattle in a relatively competitive marketplace. The price of cattle was set through open bidding at auctions. The large meatpackers competed with hundreds of small regional firms. In 1970 the top four meatpacking firms slaughtered only 21 percent of the nation's cattle. A decade later, the Reagan administration allowed these firms to merge and combine without fear of antitrust enforcement. The Justice Department and the P&SA's successor, the Grain Inspection, Packers and Stockyards Administration (GIPSA), stood aside as the large meatpackers gained control of one local cattle market after another. Today the top four meatpacking firms—ConAgra, IBP, Excel, and National Beef—slaughter about 84 percent of the nation's cattle. Market concentration in the beef industry is now at the highest level since record-keeping began in the early twentieth century.

* * *

You can smell Greeley, Colorado, long before you can see it. The smell is hard to forget but not easy to describe, a combination of live animals, manure, and dead animals being rendered into dog food. The smell is worst during the summer months, blanketing Greeley day and night like an invisible fog. Many people who live there no longer notice the smell; it recedes into the background, present but not present, like the sound of traffic for New Yorkers. Others can't stop thinking about the smell, even after years; it permeates everything, gives them headaches, makes them nauseous, interferes with their sleep. Greeley is a modern-day factory town where cattle are the main units of production, where workers and machines turn large steer into small, vacuum-sealed packages of meat. The billions of fast food hamburgers that Americans now eat every year come from places like Greeley. The industrialization of cattle-raising and meatpacking over the past two decades has completely altered how beef is produced—and the towns that produce it. Responding to the demands of the fast food and supermarket chains, the meatpacking giants have cut costs by cutting wages. They have turned one of the nation's best-paying manufacturing jobs into one of the lowest-paying, created a migrant industrial workforce of poor immigrants, tolerated high injury rates, and spawned rural ghettos in the American heartland. Crime, poverty, drug abuse, and homelessness have lately taken root in towns where you'd least expect to find them. The effects of this new meatpacking regime have become as inescapable

as the odors that drift from its feedlots, rendering plants, and pools
of slaughterhouse waste.

*   *   *

Having broken the union at the Greeley slaughterhouse, Monfort
began to employ a different sort of worker there: recent immigrants,
many of them illegals.[1] In the 1980s large numbers of young men and
women from Mexico, Central America, and Southeast Asia started
traveling to rural Colorado. Meatpacking jobs that had once provided
a middle-class American life now offered little more than poverty
wages. Instead of a waiting list, the slaughterhouse seemed to acquire
a revolving door, as Monfort plowed through new hires to fill the
roughly nine hundred jobs. During one eighteen-month period, more
than five thousand different people were employed at the Greeley
beef plant—an annual turnover rate of about 400 percent. The average worker quit or was fired every three months.

Today, roughly two-thirds of the workers at the beef plant in Greeley cannot speak English. Most of them are Mexican immigrants
who live in places like the River Park Mobile Court, a collection of
battered old trailers a quarter-mile down the road from the slaughterhouse. They share rooms in old motels, sleeping on mattresses that
cover the floor. The basic pay at the slaughterhouse is now $9.25 an
hour. Adjusted for inflation, today's hourly wage is more than a third
lower than what Monfort paid forty years ago when the plant opened.
Health insurance is now offered to workers after six months on the
job; vacation pay, after a year. But most of the workers will never get
that vacation. A spokesman for ConAgra recently acknowledged
that the turnover rate at the Greeley slaughterhouse is about
80 percent a year. That figure actually represents a decline from the
early 1990s.

*   *   *

As in so many other aspects of meatpacking, IBP was a trailblazer
in recruiting migrant labor. The company was among the first to recognize that recent immigrants would work for lower wages than
American citizens—and would be more reluctant to join unions. To
sustain the flow of new workers into IBP slaughterhouses, the company has for years dispatched recruiting teams to poor communities
throughout the United States. It has recruited refugees and asylum-
seekers from Laos and Bosnia. It has recruited homeless people living at shelters in New York, New Jersey, California, North Carolina,
and Rhode Island. It has hired buses to import these workers from

1. I.e., undocumented immigrants. *Monfort*: slaughterhouse in rural Greeley, Colorado,
named after its owner, who broke the union following a 1979 strike by closing the plant
and firing the workers. In 1982 Monfort reopened without a union.

thousands of miles away. IBP now maintains a labor office in Mexico City, runs ads on Mexican radio stations offering jobs in the United States, and operates a bus service from rural Mexico to the heartland of America.

The Immigration and Naturalization Service estimates that about one-quarter of all meatpacking workers in Iowa and Nebraska are illegal immigrants. The proportion at some slaughterhouses can be much higher. Spokesmen for IBP and the ConAgra Beef Company adamantly deny that they in any way seek illegal immigrants. "We do not knowingly hire undocumented workers," an IBP executive told me. "IBP supports INS efforts to enforce the law and do[es] not want to employ people who are not authorized to work in the United States." Nevertheless, the recruiting efforts of the American meatpacking industry now target some of the most impoverished and most vulnerable groups in the Western Hemisphere. "If they've got a pulse," one meatpacking executive joked to the *Omaha World-Herald* in 1998, "we'll take an application."

The real costs of this migrant industrial workforce are being borne not by the large meatpacking firms, but by the nation's meatpacking communities. Poor workers without health insurance drive up local medical costs. Drug dealers prey on recent immigrants, and the large, transient population usually brings more crime. At times, the meatpacking firms have been especially brazen in assuming that public funds will cover their routine business costs. In September of 1994, GFI America, Inc.—a leading supplier of frozen hamburger patties to Dairy Queen, Cracker Barrel Old Country Store, and the federal school lunch program—needed workers for a plant in Minneapolis, Minnesota. It sent recruiters to Eagle Pass, Texas, near the Mexican border, promising steady work and housing. The recruiters hired thirty-nine people, rented a bus, drove the new workers from Texas to Minnesota, and then dropped them off across the street from People Serving People, a homeless shelter in downtown Minneapolis. Because the workers had no money, the shelter agreed to house them. GFI America offered to pay the facility $17 for each worker and to donate some free hamburgers, but the offer was declined. The company's plan to use a homeless shelter as worker housing soon backfired. Most of the new recruits refused to stay at the shelter; they had been promised rental apartments and now felt tricked and misled. The story was soon picked up by the local media. Advocates for the homeless were especially angry about GFI America's attempt to misuse the largest homeless shelter in Minneapolis. "Our job is not to provide subsidies to corporations that are importing low-cost labor," said a county official.

* * *

A brief description of some cleaning-crew accidents over the past decade says more about the work and the danger than any set of statistics. At the Monfort plant in Grand Island, Nebraska, Richard Skala was beheaded by a dehiding machine. Carlos Vincente—an employee of T and G Service Company, a twenty-eight-year-old Guatemalan who'd been in the United States for only a week—was pulled into the cogs of a conveyer belt at an Excel plan in Fort Morgan, Colorado, and torn apart. Lorenzo Marin, Sr., an employee of DCS Sanitation, fell from the top of a skinning machine while cleaning it with a high-pressure hose, struck his head on the concrete floor of an IBP plant in Columbus Junction, Iowa, and died. Another employee of DCS Sanitation, Salvador Hernandez-Gonzalez, had his head crushed by a pork-loin processing machine at an IBP plant in Madison, Nebraska. The same machine had fatally crushed the head of another worker, Ben Barone, a few years earlier. At a National Beef plant in Liberal, Kansas, Homer Stull climbed into a blood-collection tank to clean it, a filthy tank thirty feet high. Stull was overcome by hydrogen sulfide fumes. Two coworkers climbed into the tank and tried to rescue him. All three men died. Eight years earlier, Henry Wolf had been overcome by hydrogen sulfide fumes while cleaning the very same tank; Gary Sanders had tried to rescue him; both men died; and the Occupational Safety and Health Administration (OSHA) later fined National Beef for its negligence. The fine was $480 for each man's death.

* * *

The meatpacking industry's response to *The Jungle* established a pattern that would be repeated throughout the twentieth century, whenever health concerns were raised about the nation's beef. The industry has repeatedly denied that problems exist, impugned the motives of its critics, fought vehemently against federal oversight, sought to avoid any responsibility for outbreaks of food poisoning, and worked hard to shift the costs of food safety efforts onto the general public. The industry's strategy has been driven by a profound antipathy to any government regulation that might lower profits. "There is no limit to the expense that might be put upon us," the Beef Trust's Wilson said in 1906, arguing against a federal inspection plan that would have cost meatpackers less than a dime per head of cattle. "[Our] contention is that in all reasonableness and fairness *we are paying all we care to pay.*"

During the 1980s, as the risks of widespread contamination increased, the meatpacking industry blocked the use of microbial testing in the federal meat inspection program. A panel appointed by the National Academy of Sciences warned in 1985 that the nation's meat inspection program was hopelessly outdated, still

relying on visual and olfactory clues to find disease while dangerous pathogens slipped past undetected. Three years later, another
National Academy of Sciences panel warned that the nation's public health infrastructure was in serious disarray, limiting its ability
to track or prevent the spread of newly emerging pathogens. Without additional funding for public health measures, outbreaks and
epidemics of new diseases were virtually inevitable. "Who knows
what crisis will be next?" said the chairman of the panel.

Nevertheless, the Reagan and Bush administrations cut spending
on public health measures and staffed the U.S. Department of Agriculture with officials far more interested in government deregulation
than in food safety. The USDA became largely indistinguishable from
the industries it was meant to police. President Reagan's first secretary of agriculture was in the hog business. His second was the president of the American Meat Institute (formerly known as the American
Meat Packers Association). And his choice to run the USDA's Food
Marketing and Inspection Service was a vice president of the National
Cattleman's Association. President Bush later appointed the president
of the National Cattleman's Association to the job.

ROBERT GOTTLIEB AND ANUPAMA JOSHI

From Food Justice†

Food justice, like environmental justice, is a powerful idea. It reso-
nates with many groups and can be invoked to expand the support
base for bringing about community change *and* a different kind of
food system. It has the potential to link different kinds of advocates,
including those concerned with health, the environment, food quality, globalization, workers' rights and working conditions, access to
fresh and affordable food, and more sustainable land use.

* * *

* * * [W]e identify food justice in two ways. First, and most simply, we characterize food justice as ensuring that the benefits and
risks of where, what, and how food is grown and produced, transported and distributed, and accessed and eaten are shared fairly.
Second, by elaborating what food justice means and how it is realized in various settings, we hope to identify a language and a set of
meanings, told through stories as well as analysis, that illuminate

† From *Food Justice* (Cambridge, MA: MIT P, 2013), pp. 5–6, 15–16, 17–18, 20–22. © 2010
Massachusetts Institute of Technology, by permission of the MIT Press. Unless otherwise
indicated, notes are by the authors. Some of the authors' notes have been excerpted or
omitted. Bibliographic information has been included.

how food injustices are experienced and how they can be challenged and overcome.

* * *

The idea of slavelike conditions seems as inconceivable today as it did fifty years ago. But stories of similar abuses continue to appear. Food researcher Eric Holt-Giménez recounted the case of labor contractors who had beaten, enslaved, and stolen the wages of twelve workers. These contractors were finally exposed and convicted of their crimes, but, as Holt-Giménez asserts, they were "just one of dozens of labor contractors that serve up poorly-paid day workers to the wealthy tomato growers of Florida . . . [who] supply over 90 percent of the U.S.'s winter tomatoes, and are the main suppliers for McDonalds, Subway, Taco Bell, Wendy's, Burger King, Kentucky Fried Chicken (KFC), Pizza Hut and other retailer and restaurant chains." Holt-Giménez also pointed out that the three main buyers of the state's tomato crop were Cargill, Tropicana . . . and Minute Maid.[1]

Holt-Giménez was describing conditions in Immokalee, a major center of agricultural production in Florida and ground zero for the modern-day slave trade. Immokalee is also where one of the most inspiring contemporary struggles centered on food justice has emerged. It was in Immokalee that a group of Latino, Mayan Indian, and Haitian workers, calling themselves the Coalition of Immokalee Workers (CIW), in early 1993 began exposing the horrendous farmworker abuses and organizing for change. Early in the organizing effort, the CIW also began to understand that bringing about change meant taking on some of the biggest players in the food system.

* * *

• In 1997, two agricultural employers were prosecuted by the Department of Justice on slavery, extortion, and firearms charges and sentenced to fifteen years each in federal prison. The slavers had held more than 400 men and women in debt bondage in Florida and South Carolina. The workers, mostly indigenous Mexicans and Guatemalans, were also forced to work ten- to twelve-hour days, six days a week, for as little as $20 per week, under the constant watch of armed guards. Those who attempted to escape were assaulted, pistol-whipped, and even shot. The case was brought to the attention of federal authorities after five years of investigation by escaped workers and CIW members.

1. Eric Holt-Giménez, "The Coalition of Immokalee Workers: Fighting Modern Day Slavery in the Industrial Food System," Institute for Food & Development Policy, *Food First*, March 12, 2009. Accessed online.

• In 2000, a South Florida employer was prosecuted by the Department of Justice on slavery charges and sentenced to three years in federal prison. He had held more than thirty tomato pickers in two trailers in the isolated swampland west of Immokalee, keeping them under constant watch. Three workers escaped the camp, only to be tracked down a few weeks later. The employer ran one of them down with his car, stating that he owned them. The workers sought help from the CIW and the police, and the CIW worked with the Justice Department in the ensuing investigation.

• In 2002, three Florida-based agricultural employers were convicted in federal court on slavery, extortion, and weapons charges. The men, who employed more than 700 farmworkers, had threatened workers with death if they tried to leave, and had pistol-whipped and assaulted at gunpoint passenger van service drivers who gave rides to farmworkers leaving the area. The case was brought to trial by federal authorities from the Department of Justice's Civil Rights Division after two years of investigation by the CIW.

Since 1997, seven slavery operations in Florida involving more than a thousand workers have been brought to light by the CIW. Exposing these episodes contributed to the development of the CIW's extraordinary national campaign. While similar in some ways to the heroic organizing in the vineyards of Delano in the 1960s,[2] the CIW's campaigns have focused on the role of the huge food industry players and fast food companies in influencing the wages, working conditions, and abuses experienced by farmworkers. The workers who picked the tomatoes for the large growers that supply the giant food companies and fast food chains are still subject to what Laura Germino, the co-founder of CIW, has called the "modern-day version of slavery; [working in] the only industry in America where employers have that level of power and those types of abuses take place."[3] Fifty years after the broadcast of "Harvest of Shame,"[4] it is shocking that such abuses still prevail. But as the CIW organizers have also learned, in order for significant change to happen in the fields, the entire range of food industry players needs to be challenged and new kinds of organizing strategies need to be developed.

* * *

2. California grape pickers protested low pay and poor working conditions through marches, hunger strikes, and calling for a boycott on grapes. After several years, they won a contract for better pay and benefits; their efforts also led to the passage of the California Agricultural Labor Relations Act of 1975 [Editor].
3. John Bowe, "Nobodies: Does Slavery Exist in America?," New Yorker, Annals of Labor, April 21, 2003.
4. A 1960 television documentary by the acclaimed American journalist Edward R. Murrow (1908–1965) about the plight of migrant agricultural workers [Editor].

The hazardous conditions of farmworkers in the United States are further worsened by the exploitation of the most vulnerable of those workers in the fields: children. Children as young as fourteen years are allowed by federal law to work in agriculture, and children as young as sixteen years are allowed to perform field work defined as particularly hazardous, whereas the minimum age for performing hazardous work in all other industries is eighteen (and sixteen for nonhazardous work). Often children as young as nine or ten accompany their parents to the fields, with the only restriction being that such work not occur during school hours. Since 1938, exemptions in the federal child labor law, the Fair Labor Standards Act, have excluded child agricultural workers from many of the protections afforded almost every other working child.

*   *   *

Where farmworkers are housed has also become part of the system of abuse and unhealthy living conditions. When employers have provided housing for farmworkers, the conditions have at times been scandalous, including barbed wire encampments and even five-by-five caves that the workers had to dig themselves, as a California Rural Legal Assistance lawyer documented. There continue to be problems of enormous overcrowding, leading to farmworkers' suffering from poor sanitation and proximity to pesticides. Such overcrowded units have included garages, sheds, barns, and various temporary structures. A California Agricultural Workers Health Survey (CAWHS) found that nearly half of the housing of California farmworkers was overcrowded and a quarter extremely overcrowded. In fact, nearly one-third of that housing was not even recognized by the local county assessor or by the U.S. Postal Service. "Many of these dwellings are irregular structures not intended for human habitation, and one-sixth (17 percent) lack either plumbing or food preparation facilities, or both," researchers Don Villarejo and Marc Schenker said of the CAWHS survey results. They also noted the handful of studies that have linked substandard or overcrowded conditions to such health problems as "gastro-intestinal illnesses associated with the lack of a refrigerator and significantly elevated levels of anxiety and depression associated with poor living conditions."[5]

The poor status of farmworkers and the hazards and abuses they are subjected to receive scant attention compared with the attention lavished, relatively speaking, on food quality, food safety, accessibility, and affordability concerns. When food is purchased for home

5. Don Villarejo and Marc Schenker, "Environmental Health Policy and California's Farm Labor Housing," Environmental Infrastructure Policy Papers Grant Program, John Muir Institute of the Environment, University of California, Davis (May 2007), 2.

consumption or ordered at a restaurant, the conditions experienced by the farmworkers are not a visible part of the consumer's experience. Even for food advocates who seek out local and organic foods and are willing to pay a higher price for those qualities, ensuring justice at all levels of the food system has not become as central as the UFW, the CIW, and other farmworker organizing campaigns would like. For example, at Slow Food Nation 2008, a first-of-its-kind event in the United States that drew thousands of food activists and other attendees to taste and advocate for what the slow foodies call "good food," advocacy for farmworkers still remained a marginal issue. While applauding the concept of good food and opportunities for food advocacy, *Fast Food Nation* author Eric Schlosser pointedly asked the audience, "Does it matter whether an heirloom tomato is local and organic if it was harvested with slave labor?"[6]

It is a question that lies at the core of food justice advocacy.

ALISON HOPE ALKON AND JULIAN AGYEMAN

From Cultivating Food Justice[†]

[W]e offer a variety of accounts that explore the ways that race and class are enmeshed in the food system. Such stories are rooted in the low-income communities and communities of color that are all too often absent from the dominant food movement narrative, and are disproportionately harmed by the current food system. From these communities' silenced histories, and from the framings deployed by activists seeking redress, we learn that race and class play a central role in organizing the production, distribution, and consumption of food. Time and again, communities of color have been subject to laws and policies that have taken away their ability to own and manage land for food production, though members of these communities continue to be exploited as farm laborers. Moreover, low-income communities and communities of color often lack access to locally available healthy food, and what food is available is often more expensive than similar purchases in wealthier areas.

6. Eric Schlosser, "Slow Food for Thought," *Nation*, September 22, 2008, 2.
† From *Cultivating Food Justice: Race, Class, and Sustainability* (Cambridge, MA: MIT P, 2011), pp. 4–10. © 2011 Massachusetts Institute of Technology, by permission of the MIT Press. Unless otherwise indicated, notes are by the authors. Some of the authors' notes have been excerpted or omitted. Bibliographic information has been included.

In these ways, the food system is implicated in many of what Omi and Winant[1] call *racial projects,* political and economic undertakings through which racial hierarchies are established and racialized subjectivities are created. Federal immigration laws, for example, act as racial projects when they define who is a legitimate subject deserving of workplace protections, and who is regarded as an alien "other." Similarly, urban planning and mortgage lending policies become racial projects when they serve to shape built environments that lack access to basic amenities, and to restrict communities of color to those areas. In another example, the appropriation of Native American lands by white settlers and past and present-day forced assimilation are examples of racial projects that have deprived some Native American tribes of both material wealth and cultural sovereignty. While these communities' circumstances are widely divergent, various chapters in this volume demonstrate the ways that racial projects have led to widespread hunger, exploitation, and environmental degradation.

In response, communities of color are beginning to engage in *food justice* activism in order to provide food for themselves while imagining new ecological and social relationships. * * * According to veteran organization Just Food, food justice is "communities exercising their right to grow, sell, and eat [food that is] fresh, nutritious, affordable, culturally appropriate, and grown locally with care for the well-being of the land, workers, and animals." Detroit's D-Town Farmers additionally emphasize that those communities that have been most marginalized by the agribusiness system need to "lead the movement to provide food for the members of their community."[2] Essential to the food justice movement is an analysis that recognizes the food system itself as a racial project and problematizes the influence of race and class on the production, distribution, and consumption of food. Communities of color and poor communities have time and again been denied access to the means of food production, and, due to both price and store location, often cannot access the diet advocated by the food movement. Through food justice activism, low-income communities and communities of color seek to create local food systems that meet their own food needs.

The movement for food justice has begun to take root between the cracks in busted sidewalks in some of the poorest neighborhoods in the United States. * * * According to food justice activists, local

---

1. Sociologists Michael Omi and Howard Winant developed an influential theory of the social construction of race, and how race functions in politics, culture, and society, in their *Racial Formation in the United States* (1986). Also referenced above, p. 392 [*Editor*].
2. https://www.justfood.org/; Monica Marie White, "Shouldering Responsibility for the Delivery of Human Rights: A Case Study of the D-Town Farmers of Detroit," *Race/Ethnicity: Multidisciplinary Global Perspectives* 3:2 (2010): 204.

food systems can help to create social justice in the form of stable, meaningful jobs in communities that have been decimated by the decline of the manufacturing industry. They can also contribute to sustainability by providing access to environmental benefits, such as healthy food, green space, and outdoor activities, that are often missing from the places inhabited by low-income people and people of color. Indeed, food justice activists often refer to these neighborhoods as *food deserts* because it is so difficult to find fresh food there.

The food justice movement combines an analysis of racial and economic injustice with practical support for environmentally sustainable alternatives that can provide economic empowerment and access to environmental benefits in marginalized communities. Its race- and class-conscious analysis expands that of the food movement to include not only ecological sustainability but also social justice. The commonly celebrated notion of *sustainability* indicates the mutual dependence and necessity of economic growth, environmental protection, and social equity. * * *

* * *

The environmental justice movement cohered around the well-substantiated claim that low-income people and people of color bear a disproportionate share of the burden of environmental degradation. Low-income people and people of color are more likely to live in neighborhoods dominated by toxic industries and diesel emissions, or in rural areas burdened by the pesticides and dust that result from agribusiness. * * *

* * * The environmental justice movement's early tactics reveal its roots in the civil rights movement. For example, one of its first notable campaigns, which took place in predominantly African American Warren County, North Carolina, in 1982, occurred when the local government issued permits for the construction of a hazardous waste landfill despite the concerns of local residents already beleaguered by other toxic land uses. While the activists' campaign was ultimately unsuccessful, the sympathetic publicity garnered by more than five hundred protestor arrests spurred a growing social movement. In addition to opposing the permitting of locally unwanted land uses, communities have also organized for procedural justice, which encompasses the rights of all affected communities to be included in environmental decision making. Although definitions of environmental justice vary, the two most common components are equal protection from environmental pollution and procedural justice.

The food justice movement mirrors these two key concerns through the concepts of *food access* and *food sovereignty*. Food access is the ability to produce and consume healthy food. While the environmental justice movement is primarily concerned with preventing disproportionate exposure to toxic environmental burdens, the food justice movement works to ensure equal access to the environmental benefit of healthy food. Food sovereignty is a community's "right to define their own food and agriculture systems."[3] Like procedural justice, food sovereignty moves beyond the distribution of benefits and burdens to call for a greater distribution of power in the management of food and environmental systems.

In addition, the food justice and environmental justice movements both rely on an institutional concept of racism consistent with those of antiracist activists and the academic literature. Popular approaches to racism in the United States tend to assume that an individual must consciously make a biased decision based on race. In contrast, *institutional racism* occurs when institutions such as government agencies, the military, or the prison system adopt policies that exclude or target people of color either overtly or in their effects. From the perspective of environmental justice scholars and activists, the disproportionate burden of toxics borne by low-income people and people of color need not be linked to intentional discrimination (though the U.S. Environmental Protection Agency has tried to define it in this limited way) if the outcome is a disproportionate burden borne by communities of color. Similarly, food justice activists point to a variety of institutional policies, such as the U.S. Department of Agriculture's discrimination against African American farmers or the supermarket industry's practice of charging lower prices in suburban versus urban locations, through which communities of color have been systematically disadvantaged. An institutional approach claims that racial and economic inequalities are built into the zoning ordinances, mortgage requirements, and other policies that determine how industries, human communities, and goods and services come to exist in particular places. Such institutional understandings of racism do not see it separable from class, but rather as producing and being produced by economic inequalities. Activists from both movements tend to highlight issues of race, although they do so with the knowledge that communities of color are disproportionately poor.

* * *

Studies of food justice offer an excellent opportunity to bring the environmental justice and just sustainability literatures together with contemporary social science approaches to race because food is deeply intertwined with both personal and cultural identities.

---

3. Via Campesina. 2002. Food Sovereignty. Flyer distributed at the World Food Summit +5, Rome. <http://viacampesina.org> (accessed June 5, 2009).

[Anthony] Winson refers to food as an "intimate commodity" that is literally taken inside the body and imbued with heightened significance.[4] Not only is it a physiological necessity, but food practices—what scholars often call *foodways*—are manifestations and symbols of cultural histories and proclivities. As individuals participate in culturally defined proper ways of eating, they perform their own identities and memberships in particular groups. Food informs individuals' identities, including their racial identities, in ways that other environmental justice and sustainability issues—energy, water, garbage and so on—do not.

4. Anthony Winson, *The Intimate Commodity: Food and the Development of the Agro-Industrial Complex in Canada* (Toronto: U of Toronto P, 1994) [*Editor*].

Nature

Producing and eating meat entails, as a matter of course, killing living creatures. Animal rights pioneer Peter Singer challenges what he calls "speciesism" and makes a case for the moral imperative for vegetarianism. Political scientist Timothy Pachirat goes undercover in an Omaha slaughterhouse from 2004 to 2006 to unmask the cruelty that industrialized slaughter deliberately hides from public view. Food writer Michael Pollan describes the economic rationale for raising steer on a diet of corn in a Concentrated Animal Feeding Operation (CAFO), as well as the hidden costs to animals, to humans, and to the environment of that practice. Feminist-vegetarian activist Carol J. Adams examines the connotations of the words we use to talk about meat, as well as what that language reveals about violence against women.

In addition to its unsettling treatment of animals, the meat industry harms the biosphere. For example, the website Project Drawdown (an organization devoted to reducing greenhouse gases to avert catastrophic climate change), notes that "[i]f cattle were their own nation, they would be the world's third-largest emitter of greenhouse gases." A pioneering study by William Cronon examines the ecological consequences of meat production in Sinclair's day. Environmentalists Denis Hayes and Gail Boyer Hayes spell out the consequences of eating from the top of the food chain. Writing fourteen years before the start of the COVID-19 pandemic, and taking West Africa and South China as case studies, Mike Davis warns of a different sort of pandemic caused by global agrocapitalism and the rising demand for meat worldwide.

PETER SINGER

From Animal Liberation[†]

"Animal Liberation" may sound more like a parody of other liberation movements than a serious objective. The idea of "The Rights of Animals" actually was once used to parody the case for women's

[†] From *Animal Liberation: The Definitive Classic of the Animal Movement*, updated ed. (New York: HarperCollins, 2009), pp. 1–9, 95, 159–62. © Peter Singer, 1975, 2009. Reprinted with permission of the author. Unless otherwise indicated, notes are by the editor of this Norton Critical Edition. Some of the author's notes have been excerpted or omitted. Bibliographic information has been included.

rights. When Mary Wollstonecraft,[1] a forerunner of today's feminists, published her *Vindication of the Rights of Woman* in 1792, her views were widely regarded as absurd, and before long an anonymous publication appeared entitled *A Vindication of the Rights of Brutes.* * * *

In order to explain the basis of the case for the equality of animals, it will be helpful to start with an examination of the case for the equality of women. * * *

* * *

* * * There are obviously important differences between humans and other animals, and these differences must give rise to some differences in the rights that each have. Recognizing this evident fact, however, is no barrier to the case for extending the basic principle of equality to nonhuman animals. The differences that exist between men and women are equally undeniable, and the supporters of Women's Liberation are aware that these differences may give rise to different rights. Many feminists hold that women have the right to an abortion on request. It does not follow that since these same feminists are campaigning for equality between men and women they must support the right of men to have abortions too. Since a man cannot have an abortion, it is meaningless to talk of his right to have one. Since dogs can't vote, it is meaningless to talk of their right to vote. There is no reason why either Women's Liberation or Animal Liberation should get involved in such nonsense. The extension of the basic principle of equality from one group to another does not imply that we must treat both groups in exactly the same way, or grant exactly the same rights to both groups. * * *

* * * [I]f we examine more deeply the basis on which our opposition to discrimination on grounds of race or sex ultimately rests, we will see that we would be on shaky ground if we were to demand equality for blacks, women, and other groups of oppressed humans while denying equal consideration to nonhumans. To make this clear we need to see, first, exactly why racism and sexism are wrong. * * *

* * *

* * * Equality is a moral idea, not an assertion of fact. There is no logically compelling reason for assuming that a factual difference in ability between two people justifies any difference in the amount of consideration we give to their needs and interests. *The principle of the equality of human beings is not a description of an alleged actual*

---

1. Moral and political philosopher (1759–1797), widely seen as the first English feminist.

equality among humans: it is a prescription of how we should treat human beings.

Jeremy Bentham,[2] the founder of the reforming utilitarian school of moral philosophy, incorporated the essential basis of moral equality into his system of ethics by means of the formula: "Each to count for one and none for more than one." In other words, the interests of every being affected by an action are to be taken into account and given the same weight as the like interests of any other being. * * *

It is an implication of this principle of equality that our concern for others and our readiness to consider their interests ought not to depend on what they are like or on what abilities they may possess. Precisely what our concern or consideration requires us to do may vary according to the characteristics of those affected by what we do: concern for the well-being of children growing up in America would require that we teach them to read; concern for the well-being of pigs may require no more than that we leave them with other pigs in a place where there is adequate food and room to run freely. But the basic element—the taking into account of the interests of the being, whatever those interests may be—must, according to the principle of equality, be extended to all beings, black or white, masculine or feminine, human or nonhuman.

Thomas Jefferson, who was responsible for writing the principle of the equality of men into the American Declaration of Independence, saw this point. It led him to oppose slavery even though he was unable to free himself fully from his slaveholding background. He wrote in a letter to the author of a book that emphasized the notable intellectual achievements of Negroes in order to refute the then common view that they had limited intellectual capacities:

> Be assured that no person living wishes more sincerely than I do, to see a complete refutation of the doubts I myself have entertained and expressed on the grade of understanding allotted to them by nature, and to find that they are on a par with ourselves . . . but whatever be their degree of talent it is no measure of their rights. Because Sir Isaac Newton was superior to others in understanding, he was not therefore lord of the property or persons of others.[3]

Similarly, when in the 1850s the call for women's rights was raised in the United States, a remarkable black feminist named Sojourner

2. English philosopher, jurist, and social reformer (1748–1832).
3. *Thomas Jefferson to Henri Gregoire.* 02-25, 1809. Manuscript/Mixed Material. Retrieved from the Library of Congress [*Author's note*]. [*Sir Isaac Newton*: English mathematician and physicist (1643–1727), leading figure in the scientific revolution of the 17th century—*Editor.*]

Truth[4] made the same point in more robust terms at a feminist convention:

> They talk about this thing in the head; what do they call it? ["Intellect," whispered someone nearby.] That's it. What's that got to do with women's rights or Negroes' rights? If my cup won't hold but a pint and yours holds a quart, wouldn't you be mean not to let me have my little half-measure full?

It is on this basis that the case against racism and the case against sexism must both ultimately rest; and it is in accordance with this principle that the attitude that we may call "speciesism," by analogy with racism, must also be condemned. Speciesism—the word is not an attractive one, but I can think of no better term—is a prejudice or attitude of bias in favor of the interests of members of one's own species and against those of members of other species. It should be obvious that the fundamental objections to racism and sexism made by Thomas Jefferson and Sojourner Truth apply equally to speciesism. If possessing a higher degree of intelligence does not entitle one human to use another for his or her own ends, how can it entitle humans to exploit nonhumans for the same purpose?

Many philosophers and other writers have proposed the principle of equal consideration of interests, in some form or other, as a basic moral principle; but not many of them have recognized that this principle applies to members of other species as well as to our own. Jeremy Bentham was one of the few who did realize this. In a forward-looking passage written at a time when black slaves had been freed by the French but in the British dominions were still being treated in the way we now treat animals, Bentham wrote:

> The day *may* come when the rest of the animal creation may acquire those rights which never could have been withholden from them but by the hand of tyranny. The French have already discovered that the blackness of the skin is no reason why a human being should be abandoned without redress to the caprice of a tormentor. It may one day come to be recognized that the number of the legs, the villosity of the skin, or the termination of the *os sacrum* are reasons equally insufficient for abandoning a sensitive being to the same fate. What else is it that should trace the insuperable[5] line? Is it the faculty of reason, or perhaps the

---

4. Born Isabella Bomfree, Sojourner Truth (1797–1883) renamed herself in 1843. She had been sold as a slave four times. After escaping from slavery in 1827, she became a preacher, abolitionist, women's rights advocate, and charismatic speaker. The quotation below comes from Truth's famous "Ain't I a Woman?" speech given at the Women's Convention in Akron, Ohio (1851).
5. Impossible to overcome. *Villosity*: quality of being covered with soft hairs. *Os sacrum*: triangular-shaped bone at the base of the spine.

faculty of discourse? But a full-grown horse or dog is beyond comparison a more rational, as well as a more conversable animal, than an infant of a day or a week or even a month, old. But suppose they were otherwise, what would it avail? The question is not, Can they *reason*? nor Can they *talk*? but, Can they *suffer*?[6]

In this passage Bentham points to the capacity for suffering as the vital characteristic that gives a being the right to equal consideration. * * *

Racists violate the principle of equality by giving greater weight to the interests of members of their own race when there is a clash between their interests and the interests of those of another race. Sexists violate the principle of equality by favoring the interests of their own sex. Similarly, speciesists allow the interests of their own species to override the greater interests of members of other species. The pattern is identical in each case.

* * *

For most human beings, especially those in modern urban and suburban communities, the most direct form of contact with non-human animals is at mealtime: we eat them. This simple fact is the key to our attitudes to other animals, and also the key to what each one of us can do about changing these attitudes. * * *

In general, we are ignorant of the abuse of living creatures that lies behind the food we eat. Buying food in a store or restaurant is the culmination of a long process, of which all but the end product is delicately screened from our eyes. We buy our meat and poultry in neat plastic packages. It hardly bleeds. There is no reason to associate this package with a living, breathing, walking, suffering animal. The very words we use conceal its origins: we eat beef, not bull, steer, or cow, and pork, not pig. * * *

* * *

* * * [T]here is one other thing we can do that is of supreme importance; it underpins, makes consistent, and gives meaning to all our other activities on behalf of animals. This one thing is that we take responsibility for our own lives, and make them as free of cruelty as we can. The first step is that we cease to eat animals. * * *

As a matter of strict logic, perhaps, there is no contradiction in taking an interest in animals on both compassionate and gastronomic grounds. If one is opposed to inflicting suffering on animals,

---

6. Jeremy Bentham, *Introduction to the Principles of Morals and Legislation*. First published 1789. A new edition, corrected by the author, 1823.

but not to the painless killing of animals, one could consistently eat animals who had lived free of all suffering and been instantly, painlessly slaughtered. Yet practically and psychologically it is impossible to be consistent in one's concern for nonhuman animals while continuing to dine on them. If we are prepared to take the life of another being merely in order to satisfy our taste for a particular type of food, then that being is no more than a means to our end. In time we will come to regard pigs, cattle, and chickens as things for us to use, no matter how strong our compassion may be; and when we find that to continue to obtain supplies of the bodies of these animals at a price we are able to pay it is necessary to change their living conditions a little, we will be unlikely to regard these changes too critically. The factory farm is nothing more than the application of technology to the idea that animals are means to our ends. * * *

*   *   *

Becoming a vegetarian is not merely a symbolic gesture. Nor is it an attempt to isolate oneself from the ugly realities of the world, to keep oneself pure and so without responsibility for the cruelty and carnage all around. Becoming a vegetarian is a highly practical and effective step one can take toward ending both the killing of nonhuman animals and the infliction of suffering upon them. * * *

*   *   *

The people who profit by exploiting large numbers of animals do not need our approval. They need our money. The purchase of the corpses of the animals they rear is the main support the factory farmers ask from the public (the other, in many countries, is big government subsidies). They will use intensive methods as long as they can sell what they produce by these methods; they will have the resources needed to fight reform politically; and they will be able to defend themselves against criticism with the reply that they are only providing the public with what it wants.

Hence the need for each one of us to stop buying the products of modern animal farming—even if we are not convinced that it would be wrong to eat animals who have lived pleasantly and died painlessly. Vegetarianism is a form of boycott. For most vegetarians the boycott is a permanent one, since once they have broken away from flesh-eating habits they can no longer approve of slaughtering animals in order to satisfy the trivial desires of their palates. But the moral obligation to boycott the meat available in butcher shops and supermarkets today is just as inescapable for those who disapprove only of inflicting suffering, and not of killing. Until we boycott meat, and all other products of animal factories, we are, each one of us, contributing to the continued existence, prosperity, and growth of factory farming and all the other cruel practices used in rearing animals for food.

It is at this point that the consequences of speciesism intrude directly into our lives, and we are forced to attest personally to the sincerity of our concern for nonhuman animals. Here we have an opportunity to do something, instead of merely talking and wishing the politicians would do something. It is easy to take a stand about a remote issue, but speciesists, like racists, reveal their true nature when the issue comes nearer home. To protest about bullfighting in Spain, the eating of dogs in South Korea, or the slaughter of baby seals in Canada while continuing to eat eggs from hens who have spent their lives crammed into cages, or veal from calves who have been deprived of their mothers, their proper diet, and the freedom to lie down with their legs extended, is like denouncing apartheid in South Africa while asking your neighbors not to sell their houses to blacks.

TIMOTHY PACHIRAT

[Undercover in a Twenty-First-Century Slaughterhouse]†

Like its more self-evidently political analogues—the prison, the hospital, the nursing home, the psychiatric ward, the refugee camp, the detention center, the interrogation room, the execution chamber, the extermination camp—the modern industrialized slaughterhouse is a "zone of confinement," a "segregated and isolated territory," in the words of sociologist Zygmunt Bauman, "invisible" and "on the whole inaccessible to ordinary members of society." Close attention to how the work of industrialized killing is performed might thus illuminate not only how the realities of industrialized animal slaughter are made tolerable but the ways distance and concealment operate in analogous social processes: war executed by volunteer armies; the subcontracting of organized terror to mercenaries; and the violence underlying the manufacture of thousands of items and components we make contact with in our everyday lives. Such scrutiny makes it possible, as social theorist Pierre Bourdieu puts it, "to think in a completely astonished and disconcerted way about things [we] thought [we] had always understood."[1]

† From *Every Twelve Seconds: Industrialized Slaughter and the Politics of Sight* (New Haven, CT: Yale UP, 2011), pp. 4–5, 23, 29–30, 39–40, 43–47, 53–57, 66–67, 234–36, 240, 245–47, 252–53. Reprinted with permission of Yale University Press through PLSclear. Unless otherwise indicated, notes are by the author. Some of the author's notes have been excerpted or omitted. Bibliographic information has been included.
1. Zygmunt Bauman, *Modernity and the Holocaust* (Ithaca, NY: Cornell UP, 1989), 97; Pierre Bourdieu, *Language and Symbolic Power* (Cambridge, Eng.: Polity, 1991), 207.

*　*　*

Those who profit directly from contemporary slaughterhouses also
actively seek to safeguard the distance and concealment that keep the
work of industrialized killing hidden from larger society. On March 17,
2011, the Iowa State House of Representatives passed, by a vote of 66
to 27, HF 589, "A Bill for an Act Relating to Offenses Involving
Agricultural Operations, and Providing Penalties and Remedies"
(a similar bill is also under consideration in the Florida legislature).
Supported by lobbyists for Monsanto,[2] the Iowa Farm Bureau Federation, and the Iowa Cattlemen's, Pork Producers, Poultry, and
Dairy Foods associations, the bill makes it a felony to gain access to
and record what takes place in slaughterhouses and other animal
and crop facilities without the consent of the facilities' owners. *　*　*
*　*　* I could not have precisely articulated what I had subcon-
sciously anticipated at a modern industrialized slaughterhouse: perhaps not quite rivulets of blood running through uncovered drains,
screams of distressed animals, decomposing kidneys and lungs floating in open cesspools of feces, or muscled white-clad butchers
drenched in blood, strutting about with gargantuan cleavers—but
nothing in my imagination had prepared me for the utter invisibility of the slaughter, the banal insidiousness of what hides in plain
sight. Facing outward, this industrialized slaughterhouse blends
seamlessly into the landscape of generic business parks ubiquitous
to Everyplace, U.S.A., in the early twenty-first century.

*　*　*

The front office's small square window and galvanized-steel door
allow visual and physical movement into the next compartment of
the industrialized slaughterhouse: its fabrication department. Here
hundreds of handheld knives and saws reinvent chilled half-carcasses
as steaks, rounds, and roasts that are then boxed and shipped to dis-
tributors and retailers around the world. The work requires manufacturing skill: it is a kind of construction, a kind of craftsmanship. But
it is also a work of making up, of framing and invention, an alchemy
of deception that authorizes mythical tales—lies, really—about
"meat" in contemporary industrialized societies. Cattle half-carcasses
enter the fabrication department from the cooler without head, hide,
hoofs, or internal organs, but the basic contours of a once-living creature are plain: there the legs, severed just above the hoofs; there
the neck and broad shoulders, eerily headless; there the ribs, the
back, the bisected spinal cord. By the time these half-carcasses

---

2. Agrochemical and biotechnological agricultural company. Monsanto was a pioneer in
   genetically modified seeds and the producer of Roundup, an herbicide that causes can-
   cer. In 2018 it was acquired by Bayer [Editor].

have made their circuit through the fabrication department, they will have been manufactured and constructed into "primal" and "subprimal" cuts, shrink-wrapped, and boxed in ways that render them unintelligible as animal, as a once-living creature. Here there occurs both linguistic and material manufacturing: the fabrication department is a site of production, a hidden workshop floor where the linguistic leap from *steer* to *steak*, from *heifer* to *hamburger* is enacted.

* * *

* * *The cooler and fabrication departments work with solids, which makes them more sanitary than the kill floor, where leaking fluids—from blood to urine to feces to vomit to bits of brain matter to bile—are a constant presence: on the floor, on the walls, on the machinery, and on the knives, clothes, and bodies of the workers themselves. In contrast to the crisp, cold air of fabrication, the air of the kill floor is steamy and humid; each time a carcass is split open, it emits more heat and humidity into the room. The smell on the kill floor varies from place to place, but it is always fiercely organic, a combination of feces, urine, vomit, brain matter, and blood in various stages, from fresh to congealed.

The homogenization of the animal that takes place in the fabrication department corresponds to a more disciplined, bureaucratized, and predictable production regime. The living creature, the *animal* that is herded off a truck and into the production sequence of the kill floor, in contrast, arrives in varied shapes and sizes, each distinct, each unique. Some balk when prodded up the chute leading to the kill box, some collapse from exhaustion or disease, some have horns that are especially difficult to cut off, some are pregnant and about to give birth, some are unusually large, and some are unexpectedly small. The kill floor must make concessions to this uniqueness, this regular irregularity. In tandem with the cooler, its function is to erase individuality and produce in its place a raw material, an input. Already stripped of all individuating characteristics of hide, horns, and sex, the carcass that reaches the cooler is further homogenized: the very texture of the flesh is reduced to one temperature, one consistency, one thing identical to the thing next to it, which is identical to the thousands of things next to it, all ready to be fabricated into a series of meat "products."

* * *

* * *Trace the path taken by the cattle on the kill floor* * *, and actively imagine the actions performed on them and how these transform the individual cow, steer, or heifer as it moves through the kill floor. At what point is the animal killed? Where does it lose its tail?

Its hoofs? Its hide? Its head? Its heart, lung, liver, and intestines? Consider also what each individual worker is able to see, from his or her particular vantage point on the kill floor. What does the animal look like to the individual worker as it passes? The "sticker," * * * for example, sees something radically different from what is seen by the "spinal cord removers," * * * and this is yet again completely distinct from what is seen by the "omasum and tripe washers and refiners." * * * There are 121 job functions, 121 perspectives, 121 experiences of industrialized killing.

*   *   *

Alive/Dead

Although the precise point that separates life from death in the slaughterhouse is located somewhere in the electrical stimulation and bleed pit area, * * * the actual killing begins just inside the walls of the slaughterhouse and continues for another fifty or so feet along the line. This killing process occurs in two stages, each stage located out of the direct line of sight of the other. The first stage is the knocking box, the second the presticker * * * and sticker * * *.

*   *   *

* * * The knocker pulls the trigger, which releases a retracting cylindrical steel bolt approximately five inches long and an inch in diameter. The bolt penetrates the cow's skull, then quickly retracts. The sound made by the firing of the bolt and its impact is a muted *pffft, pffft*. As the bolt retracts, gray brain matter often flies out of the hole in the cow's skull, sometimes splattering the clothing, arms, or face of the knocker. Seconds later, blood gushes out of the wound, bubbling up and out in a dark maroon stream as it oxygenates. Sometimes the cow's head will immediately drop, hitting the metal conveyor or (if the cattle are spaced closely together) falling onto the rump of the cow in front of it. At other times the cow's neck will stiffen, with its head locked unnaturally face up in the air. When this happens, the neck and head tremble at a high speed, as if in a seizure. Whether the head falls or the neck stiffens, the cow's eyes typically take on a glazed look, and its tongue often hangs limply from its mouth. Sometimes the power, angle, or location of the steel bolt shot is insufficient to render the cow unconscious, and it will bleed profusely and thrash about wildly while the knocker tries to shoot it again.

After the cow has been shot, the knocker advances the conveyor, and the cow drops onto another conveyor, of wide green plastic, about five feet under the metal conveyor. Because the cow is unconscious at this point, it often falls forward onto its head, sometimes breaking its teeth or biting its tongue. Once the animal is on the plastic conveyor, the shackler*** wraps a metal hook around its left hind leg. The hook is suspended from a chain connected via a wheel to an overhead rail. The rail moves the wheel forward, lifting the cow into the air by its left hind leg until it is suspended vertically, head down. The cow's right hind leg and front legs often begin to kick wildly at this point, creating the impression that the cow is still alive and conscious. Meat-industry publications state that these motions are purely reflexive and do not indicate consciousness; the key to establishing consciousness, they claim, lies in the tongue and the eyes. If it has not done so already, the cow will often vomit, depositing a rank greenish substance onto the floor that mixes with the blood flowing from its head wounds.

* * *

*** [T]he space separating life from death on the kill floor is an important one, a fact demonstrated by the problems that arise if the animal either dies too early or lives too long. Cows sometimes collapse in the serpentine chute leading to the kill box because of disease, exhaustion, or the nervous stress of being prodded repeatedly with electrical shockers. If the cow collapses in the chute after the point where the two parallel chutes have narrowed into a single one, the passageway where the live cows enter the slaughterhouse becomes completely blocked, causing a major crisis.

If a cow survives the knocker's bolt and the knocker does not stop the metal conveyor in time, the live cow can fall onto the green-plastic shackling conveyor before it has been stunned. If it does, it usually struggles off the belt and begins to run around the kill floor, panicked by the blood, vomit, and sight and smells of the stunned and shackled cows dangling overhead. ***

* * *

*** To watch the movement of a cow from the chute to the down puller is to witness the transformation of a creature from fully animal to carcass. In the chutes, each of the cattle has its own unique characteristics: breed, sex, height, width, hide pattern, level of curiosity, eyes, horns, sound of bellow. From a phenomenological standpoint, after the cattle are stunned, shackled, and suspended upside down in the air, the entire process seems geared to stripping them of these unique identifiers in order to begin the process of turning living animals into homogeneous raw material. ***

* * *

*** Although I had initially planned to work on the kill floor for up to twelve months, my movement from cooler to chutes to quality control has already afforded me a thoroughness of access that I could not have anticipated when I first applied for work five months earlier. The initial fear that I might spend an entire year hanging livers has been replaced by physical, emotional, and psychological exhaustion from the grueling physical demands and ethical conflicts of quality-control work. * * *

* * *

I quit at the end of the next day. * * * Noting the slaughterhouse's employment-at-will policy, which states, "Either you or the company may terminate employment at any time, with or without notice," I compose a brief letter of resignation to the kill floor manager and the human resources office, leaving a copy for each at the end of the work day. It states that I regret the abrupt nature of my resignation and lists the work equipment I have left behind in my locker: one employee identification card, one parking permit, four keys to various offices, two hard hats, one pair of leather boots, two pairs of rubber boots, one digital thermometer, one stopwatch, one black permanent ink marker, one flashlight, two knives, one sharpening steel, one orange hook, one plastic scabbard, one pair of safety gloves, one radio, and all uniforms not currently being cleaned.

The prosaic list belies the complexity of observing and participating in the massive, routinized work of killing, work that remains hidden from the majority of those who literally feed off such labor. It is a complexity that highlights the unexpected sympathy between concealment and surveillance in the social strategies that distance dirty, dangerous, and demeaning work such as this from those it benefits directly. What I have called a politics of sight—organized, concerted attempts to make visible what is hidden and to breach, literally or figuratively, zones of confinement in order to bring about social and political transformation—must be alert to this sympathy.

* * *

Let us now imagine, as an alternative, a world in which distance and concealment failed to operate, in which walls and checkpoints did not block sight, in which those who benefited from dirty, dangerous, and demeaning work had a visceral engagement with it, a world in which words explained rather than hid and in which those with legal, medical, scientific, and academic expertise immersed themselves in the lived experiences of those they claimed authority over. Imagine, that is, a world organized around the *removal*, rather than the creation, of physical, social, linguistic, and methodological distances.

* * *

But how might the work of killing fit into this society "where all is open to the eye and to the hand"?[3] Would children be permitted to wander the kill floor, to work with, say, the lower belly ripper or make mud pies out of eviscerated livers? As part of this impulse for transparency, the food writer Michael Pollan advances the powerful idea of the glass abattoir, which he developed after visiting an open-air chicken slaughterhouse in Virginia:

> This is going to sound quixotic, but maybe all we need to do to redeem industrial animal agriculture in this country is to pass a law requiring that the steel and concrete walls of the CAFO's [Concentrated Animal Feeding Operations] and slaughterhouses be replaced with . . . glass. If there's any new "right" we need to establish, maybe it's this one: the right to look. No other country raises and slaughters its food animals quite as intensively or brutally as we [in the United States] do. Were the walls of our meat industry to become transparent, literally or even figuratively, we would not long continue to do it this way. Tail-docking and sow crates and beak-clipping would disappear overnight, and the days of slaughtering 400 head of cattle an hour would come to an end. For who could stand the sight?[4]

Like the open shop fronts and factories of Le Guin's Anarres,[5] Pollan's glass-walled slaughterhouse is an attempt to counter distance and concealment as mechanisms of power by making all "open to the eye." The repugnant practices of the slaughterhouse (no other country slaughters its animals as brutally) continue only because they take place in a zone of confinement (the walls of the slaughterhouse), and these practices would come to a halt (disappear overnight) if there were a breach in the zone of confinement that made the repugnant visible (were the walls of the slaughterhouse to become transparent, literally or even figuratively). Reworded in this way, Pollan's glass-abattoir argument relies centrally on the assumption that simply making the repugnant visible is sufficient to generate a transformational politics: for who could stand the sight?

* * *

3. From *The Dispossessed* (1974), a science fiction classic by the American writer Ursula K. Le Guin (1929–2018) [*Editor*].
4. Michael Pollan, "An Animal's Place," *New York Times Sunday Magazine*, November 10, 2002. [The glass abattoir in the Polyface Farm in Virginia is also discussed in Pollan's *The Omnivore's Dilemma*, excerpted below, pp. 442–48—*Editor*].
5. In *The Dispossessed*, Anarres is a moon colony inhabited by utopian anarchists, in contrast with the militaristic and capitalistic inhabitants of neighboring planet Urras. Earlier, Pachirat describes Anarres as "a world in which physical, social, and linguistic mechanisms of distance and concealment are subverted" (245) [*Editor*].

* * * In a world characterized by the operation of physical, social, linguistic, and methodological distance and concealment as techniques of power, movements and organizations that seek to subvert or shorten this distance through a politics of sight are necessary and important. WikiLeaks, Transparency International, People for the Ethical Treatment of Animals, Operation Rescue, Human Rights Watch, Amnesty International, Doctors Without Borders, the Humane Society of the United States, the Humane Farming Association, Smile Train, the Open Society Institute—these are just a few of the vast number of movements that aim at the metaphorical equivalent of a world in which slaughterhouses are enclosed by walls of glass. Advancing dissimilar or even highly antagonistic political agendas, these movements nonetheless share a common politics of sight insofar as they deploy words, images, and social media to breach zones of confinement on the implicit or explicit assumption that once those breaches are created, a "reign of opinion" rooted in outrage, pity, disgust, sympathy, compassion, solidarity, shock, horror, or some other emotive response will lead to political action in the service of their desired goals. For who could stand the sight?

MICHAEL POLLAN

[The Short, Unnatural Life of a Steer]†

I'd traveled to Poky[1] early one January with the slightly improbable notion of visiting one particular resident, though as I nosed my rental car through the feedlot's rolling black sea of bovinity, I began to wonder if this was realistic. I was looking for a young black steer with three white blazes on his face that I'd met the previous fall on a ranch in Vale, South Dakota, five hundred miles due north of here. In fact, the steer I hoped to find belonged to me: I'd purchased him as an eight-month-old calf from the Blair Ranch for $598. I was paying Poky Feeders $1.60 a day for his room and board (all the corn he could eat) and meds.

My interest in this steer was not strictly financial, or even gustatory. No, my primary interest in this animal was educational. I wanted to learn how the industrial food chain transforms bushels of corn into steaks. How do you enlist so unlikely a creature—for the

---

† From *The Omnivore's Dilemma: A Natural History of Four Meals* (New York: Penguin, 2006), pp. 65–84. Copyright © 2006 by Michael Pollan. Used by permission of Penguin Press, an imprint of Penguin Publishing Group, a division of Penguin Random House LLC. All rights reserved. Notes are by the editor of this Norton Critical Edition.
1. Poky Feeders, a feedlot in western Kansas.

cow is a herbivore by nature—to help dispose of America's corn sur-plus? By far the biggest portion of a bushel of American commodity corn (about 60 percent of it, or some fifty-four thousand kernels) goes to feeding live-stock, and much of that goes to feeding America's 100 million beef cattle—cows and bulls and steers that in times past spent most of their lives grazing on grasses out on the prairie.

America's food animals have undergone a revolution in lifestyle in the years since World War II. At the same time as much of America's human population found itself leaving the city for the suburbs, our food animals found themselves traveling in the opposite direction, leaving widely dispersed farms in places like Iowa to live in densely populated new animal cities. These places are so different from farms and ranches that a new term was needed to denote them: CAFO—Concentrated Animal Feeding Operation. The new animal and human landscapes were both products of government policy. The postwar suburbs would never have been built if not for the interstate highway system, as well as the G.I. Bill[2] and federally subsidized mortgages. The urbanization of America's animal population would never have taken place if not for the advent of cheap, federally subsidized corn.

*   *   *

The economic logic of gathering so many animals together to feed them cheap corn in CAFOs is hard to argue with; it has made meat, which used to be a special occasion in most American homes, so cheap and abundant that many of us now eat it three times a day. Not so compelling is the biological logic behind this cheap meat. Already in their short history CAFOs have produced more than their share of environmental and health problems: polluted water and air, toxic wastes, novel and deadly pathogens.

Raising animals on old-fashioned mixed farms such as the Naylors'[3] used to make simple biological sense: You can feed them the waste products of your crops, and you can feed their waste products to your crops. In fact, when animals live on farms the very idea of waste ceases to exist; what you have instead is a closed ecological loop—what in retrospect you might call a solution. One of the most striking things that animal feedlots do (to paraphrase Wendell Berry)[4] is to take this elegant solution and neatly divide it into two new problems: a fertility problem on the farm (which must be remedied with

---

2. The Servicemen's Readjustment Act of 1944, commonly known as the G.I. Bill, pro-vided a range of benefits for World War II veterans. The original bill expired in 1956, but the term is still used to refer to programs that assist U.S. military veterans.

3. A farm in Iowa. When founded in 1919, the farm grew a dozen plants and animals and supported a family. When visited by Pollan nearly 100 years later, it grew only corn and soybeans, and George Naylor was struggling to make ends meet.

4. American writer and environmentalist (b. 1934).

chemical fertilizers) and a pollution problem on the feedlot (which seldom is remedied at all).

This biological absurdity, characteristic of all CAFOs, is compounded in the cattle feedyard by a second absurdity. Here animals exquisitely adapted by natural selection to live on grass must be adapted by us—at considerable cost to their health, to the health of the land, and ultimately to the health of their eaters—to live on corn, for no other reason than it offers the cheapest calories around and because the great pile must be consumed. This is why I decided to follow the trail of industrial corn through a single steer rather than, say, a chicken or a pig, which can get by just fine on a diet of grain: The short, unhappy life of a corn-fed feedlot steer represents the ultimate triumph of industrial thinking over the logic of evolution.

＊　＊　＊

＊＊＊Born on March 13, 2001, in the birthing shed across the road,[5] 534 and his mother were turned out on pasture just as soon as the eighty-pound calf stood up and began nursing. Within a few weeks the calf began supplementing his mother's milk by nibbling on a salad bar of mostly native grasses: western wheatgrass, little bluestem, buffalo grass, green needlegrass.

Apart from the trauma of the Saturday in April when he was branded and castrated, one could imagine 534 looking back on those six months as the good old days. It might be foolish for us to presume to know what a cow experiences, yet we can say that a calf grazing on grass is at least doing what he has been supremely well suited by evolution to do. Oddly enough, though, eating grass is something that after October my steer will never have the opportunity to do again.

The coevolutionary relationship between cows and grass is one of nature's underappreciated wonders; it also happens to be the key to understanding just about everything about modern meat. For the grasses, which have evolved to withstand the grazing of ruminants, the cow maintains and expands their habitat by preventing trees and shrubs from gaining a foothold and hogging the sunlight; the animal also spreads grass seed, plants it with his hooves, and then fertilizes it with his manure. In exchange for these services the grasses offer ruminants a plentiful and exclusive supply of lunch. For cows (like sheep, bison, and other ruminants) have evolved the special ability to convert grass—which single-stomached creatures like us can't digest—into high-quality protein. They can do this because they possess what is surely the most highly evolved digestive organ in nature:

---

5. The author is now talking about Blair Ranch, South Dakota, where his steer spent its first six months before being sent to Poky Feeders.

the rumen. About the size of a medicine ball, the organ is essentially a twenty-gallon fermentation tank in which a resident population of bacteria dines on grass. Living their unseen lives at the far end of the food chain that culminates in a hamburger, these bacteria have, like the grasses, coevolved with the cow, whom they feed.

Truly this is an excellent system for all concerned: for the grasses, for the bacteria, for the animals, and for us, the animals' eaters. * * *

* * *

So then why is it that steer number 534 hasn't tasted a blade of prairie grass since October? Speed, in a word, or, in the industry's preferred term, "efficiency." Cows raised on grass simply take longer to reach slaughter weight than cows raised on a richer diet, and for half a century now the industry has devoted itself to shortening a beef animal's allotted span on earth. "In my grandfather's time, cows were four or five years old at slaughter," Rich[6] explained. "In the fifties, when my father was ranching, it was two or three years old. Now we get there at fourteen to sixteen months." Fast food, indeed. What gets a steer from 80 to 1,100 pounds in fourteen months is tremendous quantities of corn, protein and fat supplements, and an arsenal of new drugs.

Weaning marks the fateful moment when the natural, evolutionary logic represented by a ruminant grazing on grass bumps up against the industrial logic that will propel the animal on the rest of its swift journey to a wholesale box of beef. This industrial logic is rational and even irresistible—after all, it has succeeded in making beef everyday fare for millions of people for whom it once represented a luxury. And yet the further you follow it, the more likely you are to begin wondering if that rational logic might not also be completely mad.

* * *

Traveling from the ranch to the feedyard, as 534 and I both did (in separate vehicles) the first week of January, feels a lot like going from the country to the big city. A feedlot is very much a premodern city, however, teeming and filthy and stinking, with open sewers, unpaved roads, and choking air rendered visible by dust.

The urbanization of the world's livestock being a fairly recent historical development, it makes a certain sense that cow towns like Poky Feeders would recall human cities centuries ago, in the days before modern sanitation. As in fourteenth-century London, say, the workings of the metropolitan digestion remain vividly on display, the foodstuffs coming in, the streams of waste going out. The crowding

---

6. Rich Blair, one of the owners of Blair Ranch.

into tight quarters of recent arrivals from all over, together with the lack of sanitation, has always been a recipe for disease. The only reason contemporary animal cities aren't as plague-ridden or pestilential as their medieval human counterparts is a single historical anomaly: the modern antibiotic.

*   *   *

We've come to think of "corn-fed" as some kind of old-fashioned virtue, which it may well be when you're referring to Midwestern children, but feeding large quantities of corn to cows for the greater part of their lives is a practice neither particularly old nor virtuous. Its chief advantage is that cows fed corn, a compact source of caloric energy, get fat quickly; their flesh also marbles well, giving it a taste and texture American consumers have come to like. Yet this corn-fed meat is demonstrably less healthy for us, since it contains more saturated fat and less omega-3 fatty acids than the meat of animals fed grass. * * * In the same way ruminants are ill adapted to eating corn, humans in turn may be poorly adapted to eating ruminants that eat corn.

*   *   *

The economic logic behind corn is unassailable, and on a factory farm there is no other kind. Calories are calories, and corn is the cheapest, most convenient source of calories on the market. Of course, it was the same industrial logic—protein is protein—that made feeding rendered cow parts back to cows seem like a sensible thing to do, until scientists figured out that this practice was spreading bovine spongiform encephalopathy (BSE), more commonly known as mad cow disease.[7] * * *

*   *   *

What keeps a feedlot animal healthy—or healthy enough—are antibiotics. Rumensin buffers acidity in the rumen, helping to prevent bloat and acidosis, and Tylosin, a form of erythromycin, lowers the incidence of liver infection. Most of the antibiotics sold in America today end up in animal feed, a practice that, it is now generally acknowledged (except in agriculture), is leading directly to the evolution of new antibiotic-resistant superbugs. In the debate over the use of antibiotics in agriculture, a distinction is usually made between their clinical and nonclinical uses. Public health advocates don't object to treating sick animals with antibiotics; they just don't

---

7. Disease that slowly destroys the brain and spinal cord in cattle. The human form, variant Creutzfeldt-Jakob disease, is a fatal degenerative disorder that attacks the brain and spinal cord.

want to see the drugs lose their effectiveness because factory farms are feeding them to healthy animals to promote growth. But the use of antibiotics in feedlot cattle confounds this distinction. Here the drugs are plainly being used to treat sick animals, yet the animals probably wouldn't be sick if not for the diet of grain we feed them.

✳ ✳ ✳

For one thing, the health of these animals is inextricably linked to our own by that web of relationships. The unnaturally rich diet of corn that undermines a steer's health fattens his flesh in a way that undermines the health of the humans who will eat it. The antibiotics these animals consume with their corn at this very moment are selecting, in their gut and wherever else in the environment they end up, for new strains of resistant bacteria that will someday infect us and withstand the drugs we depend on to treat that infection. We inhabit the same microbial ecosystem as the animals we eat, and whatever happens in it also happens to us.

Then there's the deep pile of manure on which I stand, in which 534 sleeps. We don't know much about the hormones in it—where they will end up, or what they might do once they get there—but we do know something about the bacteria, which can find their way from the manure on the ground to his hide and from there into our hamburgers. The speed at which these animals will be slaughtered and processed—four hundred an hour at the plant where 534 will go—means that sooner or later some of the manure caked on these hides gets into the meat we eat. One of the bacteria that almost certainly resides in the manure I'm standing in is particularly lethal to humans. *Escherichia coli* O157:H7[8] is a relatively new strain of the common intestinal bacteria (no one had seen it before 1980) that thrives in feedlot cattle, 40 percent of which carry it in their gut. Ingesting as few as ten of these microbes can cause a fatal infection; they produce a toxin that destroys human kidneys.

✳ ✳ ✳

So much comes back to corn, this cheap feed that turns out in so many ways to be not cheap at all. While I stood in pen 63 a dump truck pulled up alongside the feed bunk and released a golden stream of feed. The black mass of cowhide moved toward the trough for lunch. The $1.60 a day I'm paying for three meals a day here is a bargain only by the narrowest of calculations. It doesn't take into account, for example, the cost to the public health of antibiotic

---

8. A strain of bacterium better known as *e coli*. While many *Escherichia coli* harmlessly inhabit human and animal intestines, this strain can cause severe illness. One of the most common vehicles of transmission is eating undercooked contaminated meat.

resistance or food poisoning by *E. coli* O157:H7. It doesn't take into account the cost to taxpayers of the farm subsidies that keep Poky's raw materials cheap. And it certainly doesn't take into account all the many environmental costs incurred by cheap corn.

I stood alongside 534 as he lowered his big head into the stream of fresh grain. How absurd, I thought, the two of us standing hock-deep in manure in this godforsaken place, overlooking a manure lagoon in the middle of nowhere somewhere in Kansas. Godforsaken perhaps, and yet not apart, I realized, as I thought of the other places connected to this place by the river of commodity corn. Follow the corn from this bunk back to the fields where it grows and I'd find myself back in the middle of that 125,000-mile-square monoculture,[9] under a steady rain of pesticide and fertilizer. Keep going, and I could follow the nitrogen runoff from that fertilizer all the way down the Mississippi into the Gulf of Mexico, adding its poison to an eight-thousand-square-mile zone so starved of oxygen nothing but algae can live in it. And then go farther still, follow the fertilizer (and the diesel fuel and the petrochemical pesticides) needed to grow the corn all the way to the oil fields of the Persian Gulf.

I don't have a sufficiently vivid imagination to look at my steer and see a barrel of oil, but petroleum is one of the most important ingredients in the production of modern meat, and the Persian Gulf[1] is surely a link in the food chain that passes through this (or any) feedlot. Steer 534 started his life part of a food chain that derived all of its energy from the sun, which nourished the grasses that nourished him and his mother. When 534 moved from ranch to feedlot, from grass to corn, he joined an industrial food chain powered by fossil fuel—and therefore defended by the U.S. military, another never-counted cost of cheap food. (One-fifth of America's petroleum consumption goes to producing and transporting our food.) After I got home from Kansas, I asked an economist who specializes in agriculture and energy if it might be possible to calculate precisely how much petroleum it will take to grow my steer to slaughter weight. Assuming 534 continues to eat twenty-five pounds of corn a day and reaches a weight of twelve hundred pounds, he will have consumed in his lifetime the equivalent of thirty-five gallons of oil—nearly a barrel.

So this is what commodity corn can do to a cow: industrialize the miracle of nature that is a ruminant, taking this sunlight and prairie grass–powered organism and turning it into the last thing we need: another fossil fuel machine. This one, however, is able to suffer.

9. The cultivation of a single species (such as corn or cattle), unlike the more sustainable mixed farm of the original Naylor generation.
1. Between Iran and the Arabian peninsula, this area is the world's largest source of crude oil.

CAROL J. ADAMS

From The Sexual Politics of Meat[†]

Both the words "men" and "meat" have undergone lexicographical narrowing. Originally generic terms, they are now closely associated with their specific referents.[1] Meat no longer means all foods; the word *man*, we realize, no longer includes *women*. Meat represents *the essence or principal part of something*, according to the *American Heritage Dictionary*. Thus we have the "meat of the matter," "a meaty question." To "beef up" something is to improve it. Vegetable, on the other hand, represents the least desirable characteristics: *suggesting or like a vegetable, as in passivity or dullness of existence, monotonous, inactive*. Meat is *something one enjoys or excels in*, vegetable becomes representative of someone who does not enjoy anything: a *person who leads a monotonous, passive, or merely physical existence*.

* * *

* * * Of special concern will be the cultural representations of the butchering of animals because meat eating is the most frequent way in which we interact with animals. Butchering is the quintessential enabling act for meat eating. It enacts a literal dismemberment upon animals while proclaiming our intellectual and emotional separation from animals' desire to live. Butchering as a paradigm provides, as well, an entry for understanding exactly why a profusion of overlapping cultural images exists.

* * *

Through butchering, animals become absent referents. Animals in name and body are made absent *as animals* for meat to exist. Animals' lives precede and enable the existence of meat. If animals are alive they cannot be meat. Thus a dead body replaces the live animal. Without animals there would be no meat eating, yet they are absent from the act of eating meat because they have been transformed into food.

* * *

Generally, however, the absent referent, because of its absence, prevents our experiencing connections between oppressed groups.

† From *The Sexual Politics of Meat: A Feminist-Vegetarian Critical Theory*, 20th anniv. ed. (New York and London: Continuum, 2010), pp. 60, 66, 72–73, 78–80, 98–99, 113–15. © Carol J. Adams, 1990, 2000, 2010, 2015. Reprinted with permission of Bloomsbury Publishing Inc. Unless otherwise indicated, notes are by the author. Some of the author's notes have been excerpted or omitted. Bibliographic information has been included. Page references in brackets refer to this Norton Critical Edition.
1. In other words, the meaning of each word has narrowed. A *referent* is what a word stands for or refers to (for instance, the word "tree" can refer to an actual tree) [*Editor*].

Cultural images of butchering and sexual violence are so interpenetrated that animals act as the absent referent in radical feminist discourse. In this sense, radical feminist theory participates in the same set of representational structures it seeks to expose. We uphold the patriarchal structure of absent referents, appropriating the experience of animals to interpret our own violation. For instance, we learn of a woman who went to her doctor after being battered. The doctor told her her leg "was like a raw piece of meat hanging up in a butcher's window."[2] Feminists translate this literal description into a metaphor for women's oppression. Andrea Dworkin states that pornography depicts woman as a "female piece of meat" and Gena Corea observes that "women in brothels can be used like animals in cages."[3] * * * When one is matter without spirit, one is the raw material for exploitation and for metaphoric borrowing.

Despite this dependence on the *imagery* of butchering, radical feminist discourse has failed to integrate the *literal* oppression of animals into our analysis of patriarchal culture or to acknowledge the strong historical alliance between feminism and vegetarianism. Whereas women may feel like pieces of meat, and be treated like pieces of meat—emotionally butchered and physically battered— animals actually are made into pieces of meat. In radical feminist theory, the use of these metaphors alternates between a positive figurative activity and a negative activity of occlusion, negation, and omission in which the literal fate of the animal is elided. Could metaphor itself be the undergarment to the garb of oppression?

* * *

What we require is a theory that traces parallel trajectories: the common oppressions of women and animals, and the problems of metaphor and the absent referent. I propose a cycle of objectification, fragmentation, and consumption, which links butchering and sexual violence in our culture. Objectification permits an oppressor to view another being as an object. The oppressor then violates this being by object-like treatment: e.g., the rape of women that denies women freedom to say no, or the butchering of animals that converts animals from living breathing beings into dead objects. This process allows fragmentation, or brutal dismemberment, and finally consumption. While the occasional man may literally eat women, we all consume visual images of women all the time. Consumption is the fulfillment of oppression, the annihilation of will, of separate

---

2. R. Emerson Dobash and Russell Dobash, *Violence Against Wives: A Case Against the Patriarchy* (New York: Free P, Macmillan, 1979), p. 110.
3. Andrea Dworkin, *Pornography: Men Possessing Women* (New York: Perigee, 1981), p. 209; Gena Corea, *The Hidden Malpractice: How American Medicine Mistreats Women* (New York: William Morrow, 1977, New York: Jove–Harcourt Brace Jovanovich, 1978), p. 129.

identity. So too with language: a subject first is viewed, or objectified, through metaphor. Through fragmentation the object is severed from its ontological meaning. Finally, consumed, it exists only through what it represents. The consumption of the referent reiterates its annihilation as a subject of importance in itself.

✳ ✳ ✳

Generally, if we enter a slaughterhouse we do so through the writings of someone else who entered for us. Early in the century, Upton Sinclair entered the slaughterhouse for his readers. He seized the operations of the slaughterhouse as a metaphor for the fate of the worker in capitalism. Jurgis, the worker whose rising consciousness evolves in *The Jungle*, visits a slaughterhouse in the opening pages. A guide ushers him through the place and he experiences what "was like some horrible crime committed in a dungeon, all unseen and unheeded, buried out of sight and of memory" [36]. Hogs with their legs chained to a line that moves them forward hang upside down, squealing, grunting, wailing. The line moves them forward, their throats are slit, and then they vanish "with a splash into a huge vat of boiling water." Despite the businesslike aspect of the place, one "could not help thinking of the hogs; they were so innocent, they came so very trustingly; and they were so very human in their protests—and so perfectly within their rights!"

Then came the dismemberment: the scraping of the skin, beheading, cutting of the breastbone, removal of the entrails. Jurgis marvels at the speed, the automation, the machinelike way in which each man dispatched his job, and he congratulates himself that he is not a hog. The next three hundred pages trace the rising of his consciousness so that he realizes that a hog is exactly what he is— "one of the packer's hogs. What they wanted from a hog was all the profits that could be got out of him; and that was what they wanted from the working-man, and also that was what they wanted from the public. What the hog thought of it, and what he suffered, were not considered; and no more was it with labor, and no more with the purchaser of meat" [289].

In response to Sinclair's novel people could not help thinking of the hogs. The referent—those few initial pages describing butchering in a book of more than three hundred pages—overpowered the metaphor. Horrified by what they learned about meat production, people clamored for new laws, and for a short time, became, as humorist Finley Peter Dunne's "Mr. Dooley" described it, "viggytaryans."[4] As

4. Mr. Dooley is a fictional Irish bartender used in humorous columns created by the American journalist Finley Peter Dunne (1867–1936). Quoted in Robert B. Downs, afterword to Upton Sinclair, *The Jungle* (1906, New York: New American Library), p. 346 [*Editor*].

Upton Sinclair bemoaned, "I aimed at the public's heart and by accident hit it in the stomach."[5] Butchering failed as a metaphor for the fate of the worker in *The Jungle* because the novel carried too much information on how the animal was violently killed. To make the absent referent present—that is, describing exactly how an animal dies, kicking, screaming, and is fragmented—disables consumption and disables the power of metaphor.

*   *   *

One of the basic things that must happen on the disassembly line of a slaughterhouse is that the animal must be treated as an inert object, not as a living, breathing, being. Similarly the worker on the assembly line becomes treated as an inert, unthinking object, whose creative, bodily, emotional needs are ignored. For those people who work in the disassembly line of slaughterhouses, they, more than anyone, must accept on a grand scale the double annihilation of self: they are not only going to have to deny themselves, but they are going to have to accept the cultural absent referencing of animals as well. They must view the living animal as the meat that everyone outside the slaughterhouse accepts it as, while the animal is still alive. Thus they must be alienated from their own bodies and animals' bodies as well. Which may account for the fact that the "turnover rate among slaughterhouse workers is the highest of any occupation in the country."[6]

*   *   *

Language can make animals absent from a discussion of meat because the acts of slaughtering and butchering have already rendered the animal as absent through death and dismemberment. Through language we apply to animals' names the principles we have already enacted on their bodies. When an animal is called a "meat-bearing animal" we effect a misnomer, as though the meat is not the animal herself, as though the meat can be separated from the animal and the animal would still remain.

*   *   *

* * *Vegetarians choose words that parallel the effect of feminist terms such as *manglish* and *herstory,* which Varda One calls "reality-violators and consciousness-raisers."[7] To remind people that they are consuming dead animals, vegetarians create a variety of reality-violators and consciousness-raisers. Rather than call meat "complete protein," "iron-rich food," "life-giving food," "delectable,"

---

5. Upton Sinclair, "What Life Means to Me," below, p. 481 [*Editor*].
6. John Robbins, *Diet for a New America* (Walpole, NH: Stillpoint, 1987), p. 136.
7. Quoted in Cheris Kramarae and Paula A. Treichler, *A Feminist Dictionary* (Boston, London, and Henley: Pandora P, 1985), p. 33.

or "strength-inducing food" they refer to meat as "partly cremated portions of dead animals," or "slaughtered nonhumans," or in Bernard Shaw's words, "scorched corpses of animals." Like Benjamin Franklin, they consider fishing "un-provok'd murder" or refer, like Harriet Shelley to "murdered chicken."[8] (Buttons, T-shirts, posters, and stickers are now available announcing "meat is murder.")

*   *   *

New naming is required to identify the recent developments in the way animals animalize protein. Since World War II, a new way of treating animals has evolved that is named in euphemistic terms, "factory farming." I suggest we consider the development that incarcerates animals into these misnamed factory farms as the fourth stage of meat eating. The first stage in the development of people's meat eating was that of relying predominantly on vegetarian foods, and what little meat (from small animals or bugs) consumed was acquired with one's hands or sticks. * * *

Hunting is the second stage of meat eating. When meat is obtained through killing animals who are not domesticated, there is little reliance on feminized protein.[9] With the second stage, implemental violence is introduced, as well as the selection of some members of a community to be hunters. Distance from the animal is achieved through the implements used to kill the animal as well as from the division of a culture into hunters and nonhunters.

The third stage of meat eating is the domestication of animals, providing them with the trappings of care and security while planning their execution. With the third stage, meat consumption increases because meat is now from domesticated, easily available, animals. Domestication of animals provides another food resource: feminized protein.

The fourth stage of meat eating involves the imprisoning of animals. In the fourth stage we find the highest per capita consumption of animalized and feminized protein: 60 percent of the food Americans now eat is provided by the meat, dairy, and egg industries. Animals are separated from most people's everyday experience, except in their final fate as food. * * *

8. Geoffrey L. Rudd, *Why Kill for Food?* (Madras, India: Indian Vegetarian Congress, 1973), p. 77; Peter Singer, *Animal Liberation*, p. xii; Bernard Shaw quoted in Dudley Giehl, *Vegetarianism: A Way of Life* (New York: Harper & Row, 1979), p. 137; *The Autobiography of Benjamin Franklin*, ed. Leonard W. Labaree, Ralph L. Ketcham, Helene Boatfield, and Helene Fineman (New Haven: Yale University Press, 1964), p. 87; Richard Holmes, *Shelley: The Pursuit* (New York: E. P. Dutton, 1975), p. 129. [(George) *Bernard Shaw* (1856–1950), Irish playwright and activist; *Benjamin Franklin*: See above, p. 359, n. 5. *Harriet Shelley*: (1795–1816), first wife of Romantic poet Percy Bysshe Shelley—*Editor*.]

9. The author uses this term to emphasize what she calls "the exploitation of the reproductive processes of female animals: milk and eggs should be called *feminized protein*, that is, protein that was produced by a female body. The majority of animals eaten are adult females and children" (21) [*Editor*].

The changes in the stages of meat eating signal the increasing dependence of a culture on the structure of the absent referent. * * *

*   *   *

A model for alternative naming can be found in one of the most famous writers and weavers of webs: [the spider] Charlotte in E. B. White's *Charlotte's Web*. Charlotte weaves words into her web to prevent the butchering of Wilbur the pig. Rather than accede to the false naming of Wilbur the pig as pork, bacon, and ham, Charlotte effects new naming: Wilbur is "some pig," not a meat-bearing animal but rather "terrific."[1] Charlotte's words are a form of vegetarian protest literature. The alternative naming of this protest literature attempts to keep all Wilburs alive and whole, rather than dead, fragmented, and renamed.

WILLIAM CRONON

From Nature's Metropolis[†]

Like the progressive reformers who followed them, the packers worshiped at the altar of efficiency, seeking to conserve economic resources by making a war on waste. This was their most important break with the past. Chicago pork packers in the 1850s had relatively limited options in utilizing the nonmeat portions of the animals they killed. They could boil them down into tallow and lard, which a number of firms used for making candles, soap, and other products. They could feed packing wastes to scavenger pigs, practicing an early form of recycling in which pig flesh people were unwilling to eat was reconverted into pig flesh they were willing to eat. But whatever was left sooner or later made its way as refuse into the Chicago River. The stench that hung over the South Branch and the filthy ice harvested from it were clear signs of its pollution. Decaying organic matter, whether in the form of packing wastes, manure, or raw human sewage, was the chief water supply problem the city faced by midcentury. Seeing it as a threat to health and comfort alike, Chicagoans were trying to do something about it as early as the 1850s.

One solution was to try to send the filthy water elsewhere, out of sight, out of smell, out of mind. By 1871, city engineers had accomplished the extraordinary feat of reversing the Chicago River,

1. E. B. White, *Charlotte's Web* (New York: Harper & Row, 1952, 1973), pp. 78, 95.
† From *Nature's Metropolis: Chicago and the Great West* (New York: Norton, 1991), pp. 249–59. Copyright © 1991 by William Cronon. Used by permission of W. W. Norton & Company, Inc. Notes are by the editor of this Norton Critical Edition.

sending its ordinary flow via the Illinois and Michigan Canal south-west into the Illinois River rather than east into Lake Michigan. The city could thereby count on fresher drinking water from the two-mile tunnel it had built under the lake bottom just after the Civil War. Only during storms, spring runoffs, and other periods of heavy flow did meat-packing debris from the South Branch continue to threaten the urban water supply. Reversing the river did not, of course, mean that its pollution had vanished. It may have appeared less frequently in Chicago's tap water, but downstate residents had a clear idea of where it had gone. * * *

Since industrial wastes produced pollution wherever one threw them away, a better solution might be to avoid throwing them out in the first place. If the packers could devise ways of using meat-packing refuse for productive purposes, it would cease to be waste at all. The refuse would pollute the river less, and—better still—turn a tidy profit for its owner. "There was a time," remembered Philip Armour at the end of the century, "when many parts of cattle were wasted, and the health of the city injured by the refuse. Now, by adopting the best known methods, nothing is wasted, and buttons, fertilizer, glue, and other things are made cheaper and better for the world in general, out of material that was before a waste and a menace."

As the packers pushed the disassembly line toward its fullest possible development, they turned what had been a single creature—a hog or a steer—into dozens and then hundreds of commodities. In the new chemical research laboratories that the packers installed during the 1880s and 1890s, older by-products like lard and tallow were joined by more exotic items like oleomargarine, bouillon, brushes, combs, gut strings, stearin, pepsin, and even canned pork and beans. * * *

*   *   *

* * * For those like Upton Sinclair who saw in the city all that was most evil in capitalism, Packingtown represented the decline of cor-porate morality and the end of an earlier, more familiar and trust-worthy way of life. The stench in the Chicago River and the insidiously invisible substances that might make their way into a package of bologna appeared to be the product of companies so intent on their own profits that they were indifferent to the harm they did the public. Obsessed with turning waste into profit what-ever the noneconomic cost, they sold what they should have thrown away—and yet did little to prevent pollution from the wastes that finally washed down their sewers. * * *

*   *   *

* * * Nothing in Chicago at the end of the nineteenth century better symbolized the city's profoundly transformed relationship to the natural world than its gigantic meat-packing corporations. Although they joined the Board of Trade and the lumberyards in guidebooks that sought to impress visitors with the ways in which Chicago stood first among cities, the packers in fact represented the city's greatest break with nature and the past. At the Board of Trade, hundreds of grain traders vied with each other to profit from the sale of wheat and corn drawn from Chicago's broad western hinterland, but none of them could control the market for long. A handful of meat-packers, on the other hand, could do just that. By managing supply and demand, they effectively rearranged the meat trade of the entire world. * * *

* * * The very scale on which they operated made them increasingly susceptible to the same abstract logic which the railroads had first discovered in their balance sheets. Fixed costs meant an inescapable need to service debt. Unused capital—whether in the form of equipment, employees, or raw materials—meant waste. * * * It must be eliminated with every strategy and device that managerial ingenuity could muster against it. * * * Death's hand must be stayed to extend by hundreds and thousands of miles the distance between the place where an animal died and the place where people finally ate it. Prices must be standardized so that markets in distant places would fluctuate together if they fluctuated at all. An industry that had formerly done its work in thousands of small butcher shops around the country must be rationalized to bring it under the control of a few expert managers using the most modern and scientific techniques. The world must become Chicago's hinterland.

The combined effect of these many managerial strategies was to make meat seem less a product of first nature and more a product of human artifice. With the concentration of packing at Chicago, meat came increasingly to seem an urban product. Cows and cowboys might be symbols of a rugged natural life on the western range, but beef and pork were commodities of the city. Formerly, a person could not easily have forgotten that pork and beef were the creation of an intricate, symbiotic partnership between animals and human beings. One was not likely to forget that pigs and cattle had died so that people might eat, for one saw them grazing in familiar pastures, and regularly visited the barnyards and butcher shops where they gave up their lives in the service of one's daily meal. In a world of farms and small towns, the ties between field, pasture, butcher shop, and dinner table were everywhere apparent, constant reminders of the relationships that sustained one's own life. In a world of ranches, packing plants, and refrigerator cars, most such connections vanished from easy view.

The packing plants distanced their customers most of all from the act of killing. Those who visited the great slaughterhouses came away with vivid memories of death. Rudyard Kipling[1] described being impressed much more by the "slaying" he saw in Chicago than by the "dissecting." "They were so excessively alive, these pigs," he wrote. "And then they were so excessively dead, and the man in the dripping, clammy, hot passage did not seem to care, and ere the blood of such an one had ceased to foam on the floor, such another, and four friends with him, had shrieked and died." The more people became accustomed to the attractively cut, carefully wrapped, cunningly displayed packages that Swift had introduced to the trade, the more easily they could fail to remember that their purchase had once pulsed and breathed with a life much like their own. As time went on, fewer of those who ate meat could say that they had ever seen the living creature whose flesh they were chewing; fewer still could say they had actually killed the animal themselves. In the packers' world, it was easy not to remember that eating was a moral act inextricably bound to killing. Such was the second nature that a corporate order had imposed on the American landscape. Forgetfulness was among the least noticed and most important of its by-products.

The packers' triumph was to further the commodification of meat, to alienate still more its ties to the lives and ecosystems that had ultimately created it. Transmuted by the packing plants into countless shape-shifting forms, an animal's body might fill human stomachs, protect human feet, fasten human clothes, fertilize human gardens, wash human hands, play human music—do so many amazing things. The sheer variety of these new standardized uses testified to the packers' ingenuity in their war on waste, but in them the animal also died a second death. Severed from the form in which it had lived, severed from the act that had killed it, it vanished from human memory as one of nature's creatures. Its ties to the earth receded, and in forgetting the animal's life one also forgot the grasses and the prairie skies and the departed bison herds of a landscape that seemed more and more remote in space and time. The grasslands were so distant from the lives of those who bought what the packers sold that one hardly thought of the prairie or the plains while making one's purchase, any more than one thought about Packingtown, with its Bubbly Creek and its stinking air. Meat was a neatly wrapped package one bought at the market. Nature did not have much to do with it.

There was a final irony in this for Chicago itself. The new corporate order, by linking and integrating the products of so many ecosystems and communities, obscured the very connections it

---

1. English writer (1865–1936); the quotation is from *American Notes* (1891), in which Kipling says of Chicago, "Having seen it, I urgently desire never to see it again" (Chapter 5, Project Gutenberg).

helped create. Its tendency was to break free from space altogether, managing its activities with organizational charts that stressed function rather than geography. The traditional butcher shop had belonged very much to its particular place, bound to customers in the immediate neighborhood and farmers in the surrounding countryside. The packing companies had none of these ties, not even to the place that had nurtured their own birth. By the 1880s, their managers could already see that Chicago's advantages—its transportation facilities, its concentrated market, its closeness to western supplies of cattle—were by no means unique. Conditions at the Union Stockyards were crowded, there was little room for expansion, and the city was not as close to the chief grazing regions of the country as were certain other cities that lay still farther to the west. The sensible thing to do was not to invest more capital in Chicago but to set up new plants that could take advantage of more favorable conditions elsewhere.

All the major Chicago packers saw the logic of this analysis; it was, after all, the logic of capital. * * * [T]he major cities of the Great Plains began to rival Chicago for primacy in the cattle trade. By the end of the century, Omaha was butchering nearly a third as many steers as Chicago was, while Kansas City was packing more than half of the lakeside city's total volume.

It was the beginning of the end. * * * Chicago continued for the next half century to handle an immense number of animals, never fewer than thirteen million per year, but its relative share declined as the industry continued its steady westward movement onto the plains. The rise of the diesel truck eventually undermined the technological tendency toward centralization that the railroads had promoted, until finally Chicago lost its earlier advantages altogether. By the 1930s, the output of the stockyards was in steady decline; by 1960, all the major packers had shut down their Chicago factories. Ten years later, the stockyards finally closed altogether. The familiar odor of manure vanished, and the strange silence of abandonment fell over the old animal pens. Grass began to grow again amid the ruins.

The whole point of corporate meat-packing had been to systematize the market in animal flesh—to liberate it from nature and geography. Chicago had been the place to accomplish that feat, but the industry the city fostered ultimately exercised its independence even from the great Union Stockyard itself. * * * Once within the corporate system, places lost their particularity and became functional abstractions on organizational charts. Geography no longer mattered very much except as a problem in management: time had conspired with capital to annihilate space. The cattle might still graze amid forgotten buffalo wallows in central Montana, and the hogs might still devour their feedlot corn in Iowa, but from the corporate point of view they could just as well have been anywhere else. Abstract, standardized, and fungible, their lives were governed as much by the nature of capital as by the nature that gave them life. It was perhaps nothing more than simple justice that the city which had remade them in this way should be subject to the same alchemy. In losing control of its corporate meat-packing hinterland, Chicago's stockyard fulfilled the logic of its own birth.

DENIS HAYES AND GAIL BOYER HAYES

[The Environmental Costs of Meat]†

Overall, America has a fine temperate climate that serves us well and that should be counted as one of our important natural resources. The warming of Earth's atmosphere and oceans has begun to make that climate less benign.

Feed production and processing, the fermentation that goes on inside cows, and the decomposition of cow manure release three warming gases: carbon dioxide, methane, and nitrous oxide. A report issued by the Food and Agriculture Organization of the United Nations in 2013 concluded that livestock account for 14.5 percent of anthropogenic (human-caused) greenhouse gas emissions. Beef cattle are responsible for 41 percent of livestock emissions, milk cows for another 19 percent. It would be prudent to reduce those emissions.

Since the start of the Industrial Revolution, human activity has increased the amount of carbon dioxide (CO_2) in the atmosphere by 40 percent. University of Chicago oceanographer David Archer warns, in *The Long Thaw*, that humans are putting carbon dioxide into the air that could stay there for centuries, *a quarter of it lasting essentially forever*. Archer advises, "The next time you fill your tank, reflect upon this."[1] Think of it, too, the next time you bite into a cheeseburger. Because many aspects of climate change are now inevitable, scientists and planners have recently replaced the word "sustainability" with the word "resiliency" when speaking of their goals for many communities. Although still hoping to reduce even greater warming, they are also looking for ways for communities to adapt to those shocks now certain to come. (Unless, of course,

† From *Cowed: The Hidden Impact of 93 Million Cows on America's Health, Economy, Politics, Culture, and Environment* (New York: Norton, 2015), pp. 33–36, 74–76. Copyright © 2015 by Denis Hayes and Gail Boyer Hayes. Used by permission of W. W. Norton & Company, Inc. Notes are by the authors. Some of the authors' notes have been excerpted or omitted. Bibliographic information has been included.
1. David Archer, *The Long Thaw: How Humans Are Changing the Next 100,000 Years of Earth's Climate* (Princeton: Princeton UP, 2008), p. 11.

something strange and unforeseeable happens, such as the Yellowstone mega-volcano awakens or a big asteroid hits and kicks up a worldwide dust storm. If that happens we'll have more pressing concerns.)

Globally, the livestock sector accounts for 9 percent of human-caused warming that's due to increases in the gas carbon dioxide. Most of this comes indirectly, such as from cutting down forests to create pastures and growing feed for cattle. Carbon dioxide is also released during the manufacture of the fertilizers and pesticides that drench the crops used to feed confined cows. Burning fossil fuels to power farm machinery, and to transport cows, meat, feed, water, and cow waste, also creates this gas.

Methane (CH_4) is another powerful warming gas, one that hasn't received the public spotlight it deserves. Although it doesn't stay in the atmosphere nearly as long as carbon dioxide does, methane is far better at trapping heat. So over the course of a century, methane contributes more to warming than does carbon dioxide. Human activities have put more methane into the atmosphere today than it has contained for at least four hundred thousand years, and those emissions are accelerating worldwide. Globally, around 14.5 percent of all anthropogenic warming emissions are due to this gas, and around 37 percent of anthropogenic methane comes from livestock, mostly from cows. Methane is produced when cow manure breaks down. It also comes from cow burps (and a bit from cow farts).

A report issued in December 2013 by the National Academy of Sciences found that livestock operations in the States emitted twice as much methane in 2007 and 2008 as previously believed. The new study included measurements from actual samples of air, whereas earlier studies by the Environmental Protection Agency (EPA) and an international group had calculated emissions based on assumptions and models.

Methane emissions can be reduced by feeding cows higher-quality (and more expensive) forages such as flax and alfalfa seeds, or by providing cows with more fat, particular proteins, tannins, nutrient-laden salt licks, certain medications, fish oils, or a new "burpless grass." Canadian scientists came up with a diet for beef cows that balances starch, fat, sugar, cellulose, etc., and reportedly cuts methane emissions by a quarter. Cows will eat an astonishing variety of biowaste. Some are obligingly swallowing a weird array of foods like cashew-nut-shell liquid and whole cottonseed to see if doing so reduces their methane output. A by-product of winemaking, grape marc, reduces dairy-cow methane emissions by 20 percent. Cows don't normally eat their own bedding—but if the hay and straw are cut into pieces about three inches in length and tossed with a few goodies, cows will consume it. Milk yield goes up and methane burps are 20 percent fewer. A Penn State dairy scientist found our favorite partial solution: feeding cows the culinary herb oregano. This cut methane emissions by 40 percent, boosted milk production, and gave Clover the freshest breath in the barn.

Farmers won't adopt new feeds unless they are also affordable and reasonably easy to implement. Moreover, even with all these dietary tweaks, cows will still release massive amounts of methane.

Finally, cows' manure releases the warming gas nitrous oxide (N_2O). Your dentist may have offered you nitrous oxide before a painful procedure. "Laughing gas" induces a feeling of euphoria and brings on a dreamy mental state. Molecule for molecule, nitrous oxide is 310 times more potent than carbon dioxide as a greenhouse gas, and it has an impressive atmospheric lifetime of around 120 years. The livestock sector is responsible for 65 percent of the anthropogenic nitrous oxide in the air, most of which comes from the breakdown of cow manure.

❊   ❊   ❊

A food chain is a flow of energy from the eaten to the eater, usually from a little organism to a larger one. It starts with something green that harvests energy from the sun through photosynthesis. The green thing is often eaten by a herbivore, and the herbivore by a carnivore or omnivore. To survive, a predator must use less energy getting food than the food contains. Here's one simplified food chain: Corn > cow > you.

Because a great deal of energy is lost at each stage, food chains tend to be short. Some energy goes into making seeds and offspring. More energy is used for growth, movement, and reproduction, some [is used] for keeping an animal warm, and some remains in feces. This energy isn't really lost—it's still hanging around in some form as heat, chemical bonds, and such—but it isn't passed on up the food chain. *Typically, only about 10 percent of the energy at one stage moves on to the next.*

In November 2013, a leaked report by the Intergovernmental Panel on Climate Change said that climate change might cause a drop as big as 2 percent in global food production each decade. This is a grimmer prediction than earlier reports and is based on new research on how heat waves affect crops. At the same time, demand for food is expected to increase up to 14 percent per decade. This means humans (and cows) will have to become ever more efficient in getting the calories they need out of food.

Today, most American cows are finished (fattened) on grain, not grass. It takes roughly ten thousand pounds of corn to produce one thousand pounds of cow, so grain-fed cows will become expensive luxuries in a crowded, hungry world. For humans, a vegetarian diet that includes beans, lentils, peas, and chickpeas can be just as nutritious as one based on beef, while feeding perhaps ten times as many people per acre of farmland.

Grandma's and Grandpa's cows were benign beasts that transformed grass into protein, fertilized their own pastures, and provided agricultural muscle. Today's cows are more like energy-sucking black holes. How much energy they require depends on what you include in your calculations. But if you include all the fertilizer, pesticides, and fuel required by growing and harvesting cow feed, the total is daunting. David and Marcia Pimentel of Cornell University calculate that 40 calories of energy are used to produce 1 calorie of beef protein. The ratio for milk is 14 to 1.[2] And this calculation ignores the additional energy needed to process, refrigerate, transport, package, and cook the meat.

*   *   *

The higher you eat on a food chain, the greater your "carbon footprint." * * * [Y]our carbon footprint is the sum of the greenhouse gas emissions that your diet contributes to the atmosphere. According to the United Nations Food and Agriculture Organization, the average American's yearly beef consumption produces as much greenhouse gas as driving an automobile 1,800 miles.

There is no real dispute that, if you want to slow global warming, eating less red meat is critically important. From a financial, nutritional, and environmental perspective, protein is the most expensive component of our diet. Gorging on beef, as Americans do, wastes money and energy.

*   *   *

Eating less-processed, in-season foods that are grown close to your home will also reduce your carbon footprint, but it won't make as much of a difference as eating lower on the food chain. Eighty percent of the carbon footprint of food goes into the air before food leaves the farm. There are many important reasons, including freshness, to patronize small, local, organic farms. Eating locally reduces the energy used for transportation. But to reduce the climate impact of your diet, the most important shift is to reduce your red meat consumption.

---

2. David Pimentel and Marcia Pimentel, "Sustainability of Meat-Based and Plant-Based Diets and the Environment," *American Journal of Clinical Nutrition* 78:3 (September 2003): 6605–35.

MIKE DAVIS

[The Global Meat Market and the Coming Pandemic]†

In a time of plague, like the influenza pandemic that swept away my mother's little brother and 40 to 100 million other people in 1918, it is difficult to retain a clear image of individual suffering. Great epidemics, like world wars and famines, massify death into species-level events beyond our emotional comprehension. The afflicted, as a result, die twice: their physical agonies are redoubled by the submergence of their personalities in the black water of megatragedy. * * *

The essence of the avian flu threat, as we shall see, is that a mutant influenza of nightmarish virulence—evolved and now entrenched in ecological niches recently created by global agro-capitalism—is searching for the new gene or two that will enable it to travel at pandemic velocity through a densely urbanized and mostly poor humanity. This is a destiny, moreover, that we have largely forced upon influenza. Human-induced environmental shocks—overseas tourism, wetland destruction, a corporate "Livestock Revolution," and Third World urbanization with the attendant growth of megaslums— are responsible for turning influenza's extraordinary Darwinian mutability[1] into one of the most dangerous biological forces on our besieged planet. Likewise, our terrifying vulnerability to this and other emergent diseases has been shaped by concentrated urban poverty, the neglect of vaccine development by a pharmaceutical industry that finds infectious diseases "unprofitable," and the deterioration, even collapse, of public-health infrastructures in some rich as well as poor countries. * * *

* * *

* * * Written in the shadow of the AIDS pandemic and the Ebola outbreak in Africa, *Emerging Viruses* warned that global economic and environmental change were speeding the evolution and interspecies transmission of new viruses, some of which might be as

---

† From *The Monster at Our Door: The Global Threat of Avian Flu*, rev. and exp. ed. (New York: Henry Holt, 2006), pp. 3, 8, 55–60, 81–84, 89–90, 151–54. Copyright © 2005 by Mike Davis. Reprinted with permission of The New Press. Unless otherwise indicated, notes are by the author. Some of the author's notes have been excerpted or omitted. Bibliographic information has been included.

1. Tendency of species to change over time, as first theorized by the English naturalist Charles Darwin (1809–1882). Darwin's theory of natural selection holds that variation is inherent within each species, and that the traits enabling an organism to best adapt to its environment will help it survive and produce more offspring, thus leading to changes in the species over time. Darwin first formulated natural selection before the discovery of genes, and later scientists built on his work to establish that genetic mutation drives the evolution of species. Mutation can be random or result from exposure to something in the environment [*Editor*].

deadly as HIV. In his foreword, Richard Krause of the National Institutes of Health pointed to the new ecologies of disease resulting from globalization. "Microbes thrive in these 'undercurrents of opportunity' that arise through social economic change, changes in human behavior, and catastrophic events. . . . They may fan a minor outbreak into a widespread epidemic."[2]

One such catastrophic event is Third World urbanization, which is shifting the burden of global poverty from the countrysides to the slum peripheries of new megacities. Ninety-five percent of future world population growth will be in the poor cities of the South, with immense consequences for the ecology of disease. This concentration of the world population in deprived conditions, more than global population growth per se, undergirds what William McNeill calls the "Law of the Conservation of Catastrophe."[3]

McNeill is a well-known University of Chicago historian of disease ecology. He writes:

> It is obvious that as virus host populations (or potential host populations) increase, there is concomitant increase in the probability of major evolutionary changes in virus populations due to increased opportunities for replication, mutation, recombination, and selection. As the world population of humans (and of their domestic animals and plants) increase, the probability for new viral disease outbreaks must inevitably increase as well. AIDS is not the first 'new' virus disease of humans, and it will not be the last.[4]

"From the point of view of a hungry virus," McNeill writes in another piece, "we offer a magnificent feeding ground with all our billions of human bodies, where, in the very recent past, there were only half as many people."[5] (As we shall see later, this same relationship between population density and viral evolution obviously applies to industrial livestock as well.)

* * *

Explosive city growth in West Africa (where the urban population is expected to reach 60 million by 2025) drives an ever-growing demand for animal protein. Traditionally, West Africans, like many East Asians, have consumed fish as their principal source of protein; fishing, moreover, is a major industry, employing nearly a quarter of

2. Richard Krause, "Foreword," in *Emerging Viruses*, ed. Stephen S. Morse (Oxford: Oxford UP, 1993), p. vii.
3. William McNeill, "Control and Catastrophe in Human Affairs," *Daedalus* 118:1 (1989): 1–12.
4. McNeill, "Control and Catastrophe," pp. 1–12.
5. William McNeill, "Patterns of Disease Emergence in History," in *Emerging Viruses*, ed. Morse, p. 33.

the workforce in some countries. But local boats have been unable to compete with the modern, government-subsidized fleets from Europe that now trawl the Gulf of Guinea. These big factory fleets, along with foreign-flag pirate fishers, "illegally extract fish of the highest commercial value, while . . . dumping 70 to 90 percent of their haul as by-catch." As a result fish biomass has fallen by at least half since 1977, and fish has become scarcer and more expensive in local markets. Increasingly bushmeat (the generic name for the flesh of some 400 different species of terrestrial vertebrates) has been substituted for fish—yearly some 400,000 tons of wild game now end up on West African dinner plates. Like the practices that led to declining fish stocks, this level of hunting is unsustainable, and mammal biomass is now decreasing at a rate that fundamentally threatens wildlife diversity.[6]

The authors of this fascinating and troubling study, however, fail to connect a few all-important dots in the causal chain, although undoubtedly they are aware of their importance. One is deforestation, as largely foreign logging companies denude West Africa's remaining coastal rain forests. The bushmeat trade is indissolubly linked to this logging juggernaut and the food needs of its workers, although hunters also poach within official wildlife reserves as well, with the inevitable result being radically increased biological contact between humans and wild animals. The formerly isolated microbiological reservoirs of the rain forests and mountains have been inadvertently integrated into the food economy of the cities—and the result of this "under-current of opportunity" has been a series of viral leaps from animals to humans. The most infamous, of course, is HIV/AIDS: researchers believe that HIV-1 arose as a result of humans eating chimpanzees, while HIV-2 (specific to West Africa) has been linked to the consumption of sooty mangabeys. In the fall of 2004 a team headed by Nathan Wolfe of Johns Hopkins raised new fears with the isolation of a novel HIV-like retrovirus (possibly from gorillas) in the bushmeat trade in Cameroon.[7]

There is every reason to believe that the ecological impact of the recent urban-industrial revolution in south China has been just as profound and far-reaching as urban population growth in West Africa. Guangdong—long considered the epicenter of influenza evolution—has become the world's leading export-manufacturing

6. Justin Brashares et al., "Bushmeat Hunting, Wildlife Declines, and Fish Supply in West Africa," *Science* 306 (November 12, 2004): 1180–82.
7. "Bushmeat and the Origin of HIV/AIDS," conference abstract, Environmental and Energy Study Institute, Washington DC, February 2002; BBC News File, "AIDS Warning over Bushmeat Trade," October 26, 2004. [Cameroon is a country in East Africa—*Editor*.]

platform, a postmodern Manchester[8] whose toys, running shoes, sports clothing, and cheap electronics are consumed in every corner of the earth. From 1978 until 2002, the province's GDP[9] grew at an astonishing 13.4 percent per year, and the urban population of the Pearl River Delta area increased from 32 percent to 70 percent of the total population. This spectacular regional transformation, crowned by the return of Hong Kong to China in 1997,[1] has been accompanied by a series of socioeconomic developments that are also likely to reinforce Guangdong's primacy as a viral exporter.

Key parameters of influenza emergence include human and animal population densities, intensity of contact between different species, and the prevalence of chronic respiratory or immune disorders. Population densities are very high in the Delta, with about 1,273 persons per square kilometer. A large segment of the population (indeed, the majority in the industrial boomtown of Shenzhen) are rural immigrants or "floaters" in perpetual motion between city factories and thousands of rural villages. Without permanent residency permits, these workers live in overcrowded dormitories or slums and are less likely than the registered population to have access to modern medicine. Meanwhile, the state's share of healthcare spending has fallen sharply (from 34 percent in 1978 to less than 20 percent in 2003) since the advent of a market economy. "[A]bout 50 percent of people who are sick," explains Yanzhong Huang, "do not see a doctor because of the extremely high out-of-pocket payments."[2] And rampant industrialization has increased exposure to all sorts of environmental hazards and toxins. The Delta, for example, has monstrous air pollution: twenty-four times higher than the rest of China. The population accordingly suffers from all the classical respiratory problems (and, probably, cancers) associated with industrial smog and high sulfur dioxide omissions.

Thanks especially to the prevalence of wet markets[3] in the cities, the urbanization of Guangdong has probably intensified rather than decreased microbial traffic between humans and animals. As income has risen with industrial employment, the population is eating more meat and less rice and vegetables. The most dramatic increase has

8. Manchester, England, was an epicenter of the Industrial Revolution. *Guangdong* (also known as Canton) is a coastal province in South China [*Editor*].
9. Gross Domestic Product, a measure of the total market value of all goods and services produced in a country within a given time period [*Editor*].
1. In 1997, the United Kingdom returned sovereignty over what had been the British Territory of Hong Kong to China, ending 156 years of colonial rule [*Editor*].
2. Yanzhong Huang, "The SARS Epidemic and its Aftermath in China: A Political Perspective," in *Learning from SARS: Preparing for the Next Disease Outbreak*, ed. Stacey Knobler, Adel Mahmoud, Stanley Lemon, Alison Mack, Laura Sivitz, and Katherine Oberholtzer (Washington: National Academies P, 2004), p. 127.
3. Which sell perishable goods such as poultry and meat, in contrast with dry markets, which sell durable goods such as cloth or metal [*Editor*].

been in the consumption of poultry, which has more than doubled since 1980. Guangdong is one of China's three largest poultry producers and is home to more than *700 million* chickens. An extraordinary concentration of poultry, in other words, coexists with high human densities, large numbers of pigs, and ubiquitous wild birds. Battery chickens,[4] indeed, "are sometimes kept directly above pig pens, depositing their waste right into the pigs' food troughs."[5] Moreover, as the urban footprint has expanded and farm acreage has contracted, a fractal[6] pattern of garden plots next to dormitories and factories has brought urban population and livestock together in more intimate contact. Finally, Guangdong is also a huge market for wild meat. Unlike West Africa, where subsistence demand drives the bushmeat trade, the Chinese predilection for exotic animals stems from ancient homeopathic beliefs; the demand is inexorable, and Laos (via Vietnam) has become a major supplier of live game.

※   ※   ※

The SARS pandemic[7] ratified Guangdong's exceptional importance as a disease epicenter. But does Guangdong have a unique franchise? Some influenza experts believe that all pandemics originate in the mixed swine-and-poultry agriculture of south China, a near-dogma that makes them resist compelling evidence that the 1918 reassortant[8] first emerged in Kansas. Other researchers, however, argue that the environmental preconditions for the rapid interspecies evolution of influenza are now found elsewhere, and they point specifically to the ecological impacts of the export-led industrialization of poultry and pork production since the 1980s.

This so-called Livestock Revolution has been primarily driven by Third World urbanization and the rising demand in developing countries—above all, China—for poultry, pork, and dairy products. Although Third World urban dwellers are obviously poorer than their OECD[9] counterparts, a much larger percentage of income growth is expended on animal protein, and this is the demand engine that currently drives huge increases in chicken and swine populations. According to Australian researchers, "The [global] share of meat and

---

4. Which are confined to rows and columns of interconnected cages, often tiny [*Editor*].

5. *Sydney Morning Herald*, April 9, 2003.

6. Never-ending [*Editor*].

7. In 2003, over 8,000 people worldwide became sick with Severe Acute Respiratory Syndrome, a viral respiratory illness caused by a coronavirus, SARS-CoV-1–a different strain of coronavirus than SARS-COV-2, the one that caused COVID-19 in the 2020–21 pandemic [*Editor*].

8. Influenza A virus subtype H1N1, which caused the 1918 Spanish flu [*Editor*].

9. Organisation for Economic Co-operation and Development, an intergovernmental economic group with 37 member countries, including the U.S., Canada, most of Europe, Japan, Korea, Australia, New Zealand, Israel, Turkey, and several Central and South American countries [*Editor*].

milk consumed in developing countries rose from 37 to 53 percent
and from 34 to 44 percent, respectively, from 1983 to 1997. . . . By
contrast, both per capita and aggregate milk and meat consumption
stagnated in the developed world, where saturation levels of consumption have been reached and population growth is small." From
the standpoint of influenza ecology, moreover, it is striking that
pork and poultry constitute 76 percent of the developing world's
increased meat consumption, and poultry has accounted for almost
all of the small net increase in rich countries' food consumption.[1]
The viral "food supply"—poultry, swine, and humans—has been
dramatically enlarged.

Like the Green Revolution before it, the Livestock Revolution has
favored corporate producers rather than peasants and family farmers. As a recent UN report emphasizes, "large-scale, industrial production accounts already for roughly 80 percent of the total
production increase in livestock products in Asia since 1990. In the
future, most production, especially of pigs and poultry, is expected
not to come from traditional production systems that have characterized the region for centuries, but from industrial, large-scale
production."[2]

The world icon of industrialized poultry and livestock production
is giant Tyson Foods, which, like Wal-Mart, grew up in hardscrab-
ble Arkansas. Tyson, which kills 2.2 billion chickens annually, has
become globally synonymous with scaled-up, vertically coordinated
production; exploitation of contract growers; visceral antiunionism;
rampant industrial injury; downstream environmental dumping; and
political corruption. The global dominance of behemoths like Tyson
has forced local farmers to either integrate with large-scale chicken-
and pork-processing firms or perish. "These firms," write Donald
Stull and Michael Broadway, "owned not only the broilers they supplied to contract growers, but the eggs that hatched the birds, the
feed that went into them, and the plants that processed and then
sold them to grocery stores."[3] Whether in the Ozarks, Holland, or
Thailand, entire farming districts have been converted to the ware-
housing of poultry, with farmers serving as little more than chicken
custodians. At the same time, livestock has been disintegrated from

1. Christopher Delgado, Mark Rosegrant, and Nikolas Wada, "Meating and Milking
   Global Demand: Stakes for Small-Scale Farmers in Developing Countries," in *The
   Livestock Revolution: A Pathway from Poverty?*, ed. A. G. Brown. Proceedings of a conference held at Canberra, Australia, August 13, 2003 (Canberra, Australia: ATSE
   Crawford Fund, 2003), p. 14.
2. UNEP/GEF, "Protecting the Environment from the Impact of the Growing Industrialization of Livestock Production in East Asia," working paper, Phuket, Thailand, 2003,
   p. 1.
3. Donald Stull and Michael Broadway, *Slaughtering Blues: The Meat and Poultry Industry in North America* (Belmont, CA: Thompson/Wadsworth, 2004), p. 41.

agriculture; thus creating a new geography where grain and feed production is spatially separate from the raising of chickens and pigs.[4]

The result has been extraordinary population concentrations of poultry. A crucial requirement of the modern chicken industry, for example, is "production density," the compact location of broiler farms around a large processing plant.[5] As a result, there are now regions in North America, Brazil, western Europe, and South Asia with chicken populations in the hundreds of millions—in western Arkansas and northern Georgia, for example, more than 1 billion chickens are slaughtered annually. Similarly, the raising of swine is increasingly centralized in huge operations, often adjacent to poultry farms and migratory bird habitats. The superurbanization of the human population, in other words, has been paralleled by an equally dense urbanization of its meat supply. (One swine megafarm in Milford Valley, Utah, reputedly produces more sewage than the city of Los Angeles.) Might not one of these artificial Guangdongs be a pandemic crucible as well? Could production density become a synonym for viral density?

* * *

Several specific developments in the wake of the global Livestock Revolution have especially put scientists' nerves on edge. One is the sudden viral chaos on pig farms since 1997. For the previous sixty or seventy years, swine influenza—a lineage derived from the H1N1 of 1918—exhibited extraordinary genetic stability. Although individual pigs occasionally became mixing vessels for avian strains (as many believed happened in 1957 and again in 1968), the H1N1 dynasty was otherwise as unremitting as the Habsburgs.[6] Then in 1997, the hogs on one of North Carolina's megafarms caught H3N2, a human flu; this subtype soon reassorted with avian and classic swine viruses, and "by late 1999, the novel viruses could be found wherever there were pigs in North America and so were presumably spread by cross-country transport." The emergent menagerie includes an H1N2 that is the offspring of human and swine subtypes, as well as an H1N1 that preserves the classical outer proteins but whose internal proteins are human and avian. All novel subtypes are dangerous, but an H4N6 virus, a wholly avian strain that passed to Canadian hogs from ducks, is perhaps the most sinister, because it has "already acquired genetic mutations that give it the potential to bind to human cell

4. James Rhodes, "The Industrialization of Hog Production," *Review of Agricultural Economics* 17 (1995): 107–18.
5. William Boyd and Michael Watts, "Agro-Industrial Just-in-Time: The Chicken Industry and Postwar American Capitalism," in *Globalizing Food: Agrarian Questions and Global Restructuring*, ed. Michael Goodman and Michael Watts (London: Routledge, 1997), p. 209.
6. One of Europe's most powerful royal houses, producing monarchs of the Holy Roman Empire for 300 years without interruption; here used metaphorically [*Editor*].

receptors." "Such an event," warns one research team, "could be catastrophic, as humans have no immunity to H4 viruses."[7]

The new swine flu pandemic threat apparently has arisen directly from the increasing scale of hog production; researchers told *Science* that swine influenza's sudden burst of mutational energy has probably been stimulated by parallel changes in herd size, interstate transport of hogs, and vaccination practice. Since 1993, U.S. pork production has been restructured around the Tyson [model], or "poultry model," of very large, industrialized units. In a single decade, from 1993 to 2003, the percentage of hogs raised on factory farms with more than 5,000 animals increased from 18 percent to 53 percent. Such large herds maximize the opportunities for new viruses to replicate and develop epidemic momentum. "With a group of 5,000 animals," an agricultural statistician explained to *Science*, "if a novel virus shows up, it will have more opportunity to replicate and potentially spread than in a group of 100 pigs on a small farm."[8]

*   *   *

Scientific agreement about the imminent danger of an avian flu pandemic is almost as broad and all-encompassing as the consensus that humans are largely responsible for global warming. All the summit organizations responsible for world health, including the WHO and the CDC,[9] have warned that the coming viral hurricane might be even more deadly than the 1918 pandemic. * * *

* * * The 1918 pandemic dramatically grew in virulence between its initial spring outbreak and the deadly second wave in the early fall, so the key variables must have been crowded, often unsanitary conditions with large concentrations of sick victims able to transmit an evolving virus quickly to distant locations. Ewald[1] calls such an environment a "disease factory." He might also have called it a slum.

The Western Front of the world's first industrialized war recapitulated much of the disease ecology of the classic Victorian slum—the *locus classicus*[2] of most discourse about infectious disease. In the nineteenth century, the great slums of Europe, America, and Asia had a total population of perhaps 25 million; today, according to UN-Habitat, there are 1 billion slum-dwellers: a number expected to

7. Bernice Wuethrich, "Chasing the Fickle Swine Flu," *Science* 299 (March 7, 2003), 1502–05; Christopher Olsen, Gabriele Landolt, and Alexander Karasin, "The Emergence of Novel Influenza Viruses among Pigs in North America Due to Interspecies Transmission and Reassortment," in *Options for the Control of Influenza* V, ed. Y. Kawaoka (Amsterdam: Elsevier, 2004), pp. 196–198.
8. Rodger Ott quoted in Wuethrich, "Fickle Swine Flu," p. 1503.
9. Centers for Disease Control and Prevention, the U.S. health protection agency; *WHO*: World Health Organization [*Editor*].
1. Paul Ewald, *Evolution of Infectious Disease* (Oxford: Oxford UP, 1994), pp. 110–13.
2. Classic example, case, or passage. *Western Front*: term used for main military theaters of both world wars, especially the first; here used metaphorically [*Editor*].

Table [1]
Urban Density (1000s per km²)

(Slums in Italics)	
Dharavi (Mumbai—densest streets)	571.0
Delhi (densest slum)	300.0
Kibera (Nairobi)	200.0
Cite-Soleil (Port-au-Prince)	180.0
Lower East Side (1910)	145.0
City of Dead (Cairo)	116.0
Les Halles (Paris, 1850s)	100.0
Imbaba (Cairo)	84.0
Dhaka (old town)	80.0
Five Points (New York, 1850)	77.0
Nairobi slums (average)	63.0
Orangi (Karachi)	50.0
Manhattan (1910)	32.0
Cairo (greater) & Caracas *barrios*	25.0
Mumbai & Lagos	20.0
Colonias populares (Mex. City)	19.0
Shanghai	16.4
Manhattan & central Tokyo	13.4
Mexico City	11.7
World urban average	6.6
London	4.5
Los Angeles	2.4

double by 2020. Is there any reason to assume that today's *bustees, colonias*, and shantytowns[3] are any less efficient "disease factories" than Victorian slums or crowded 1918 army camps? If, according to Ewald, the *sine qua non* of a deadly airborne pandemic is "host density" in poor sanitary conditions, then—as Table [1] shows— today's megaslums are just as fetid and overcrowded as any of their notorious Victorian predecessors. With population densities as high as 200,000 residents per square kilometer, they offer perfect environments for the evolution of flu virulence. By such criteria, pandemic influenza and other deadly infections have a brilliant future.

3. Poor areas or slums, in India, Mexico, and the developed countries, respectively [*Editor*].

UPTON SINCLAIR AND
LITERARY PROGRESSIVISM

Upton Sinclair was his own best publicist, carefully crafting a public image and instructing readers about how to interpret his novels. His 1962 *Autobiography* hones a story that Sinclair often told about the origins of his literary and reform interests in his difficult childhood. In a revealing article written around the time of *The Jungle*, "What Life Means to Me," Sinclair describes how the discovery of socialism gave him direction and purpose, and he lays out his view of that doctrine in "What Socialism Means to Me" (a selection from his article "The Socialist Party in the United States"). "Art and Propaganda," excerpted from a book of Sinclair's that provides one of the first socialist interpretations of literary history published in the U.S., encapsulates his aesthetic principles.

The Jungle's reviewers reached opposing verdicts about its merits: While fellow socialist author Jack London praises the novel for its political message and command of facts, Edward Clark Marsh faults its politics and disputes its accuracy. Perhaps *The Jungle*'s most famous reviewer, Winston Churchill (at this time a member of the British Parliament and later the prime minister of Britain), commends the book but also identifies a flaw that will draw considerable criticism over the years: its implausible ending.

Robert M. Crunden uses Sinclair's complicated relationship to progressivism to explain the origins of *The Jungle*, and discusses how another progressive, President Theodore Roosevelt (TR), coined the derogatory term "muckraking" for investigative exposés such as Sinclair's. Crunden also documents *The Jungle*'s enormous role in spurring passage of the Pure Food and Drug Act of 1906—much to the surprise of its author. Mark M. Van Wienen examines what the ending of the novel reveals about the many faces of American socialism. Sandra M. Gustafson uses the work of two political theorists to examine *The Jungle*'s treatment of character formation, the relationship between identity and politics, and the role of debate and consensus within democracy.

UPTON SINCLAIR

[The Early Life of a Muckraker]†

III

My father was the youngest son of Captain Arthur Sinclair and was raised in Norfolk [Virginia]. In the days before the war, and after it, all Southern gentlemen "drank." My father became a wholesale whisky salesman, which made it easy and even necessary for him to follow the fashion. Later on he became a "drummer"[1] for straw-hat

---

† From *The Autobiography of Upton Sinclair* (New York: Harcourt, Brace & World, 1962), pp. 6–9. Notes are by the editor of this Norton Critical Edition.
1. Traveling salesman.

manufacturers, and then for manufacturers of men's clothing; but he could never get away from drink, for the beginning of every deal was a "treat," and the close of it was another. Whisky in its multiple forms—mint juleps, toddies, hot Scotches, egg-nogs, punch—was the most conspicuous single fact in my boyhood. I saw it and smelled it and heard it everywhere I turned, but I never tasted it.

The reason was my mother, whose whole married life was poisoned by alcohol, and who taught me a daily lesson in horror. It took my good and gentle-souled father thirty or forty years to kill himself, and I watched the process week by week and sometimes hour by hour. It made an indelible impression upon my childish soul, and is the reason why I am a prohibitionist, to the dismay of my "libertarian" friends.

*   *   *

When he was not under the influence of the Demon Rum, the little "drummer" dearly loved his family; so the thirty years during which I watched him were one long moral agony. He would make all sorts of pledges, with tears in his eyes; he would invent all sorts of devices to cheat his cruel master. He would not "touch a drop" until six o'clock in the evening; he would drink lemonade or ginger ale when he was treating the customers. But alas, he would change to beer, in order not to "excite comment"; and then after a week or a month of beer, we would smell whisky on his breath again, and the tears and wranglings and naggings would be resumed.

*   *   *

IV

Human beings are what life makes them, and there is no more fascinating subject of study than the origin of mental and moral qualities. My father's drinking accounted for other eccentricities of mine besides my belief in prohibition. It caused me to follow my mother in everything, and so to have a great respect for women; thus it came about that I walked in the first suffrage parade in New York, behind the snow-white charger of Inez Milholland.[2] My mother did not drink coffee, nor even tea; and so, when I visited in England, I made all my hostesses unhappy. No lady had ever been known to smoke in Baltimore—only old Negro women with pipes; therefore

2. American socialist labor lawyer (1886–1916), who became the face of the suffrage movement. The exact parade Sinclair remembers is unclear. New York's first unofficial suffrage parade, in February 1908, was quite small; Sinclair may have in mind a larger one such as the 1912 Fifth Avenue event, which drew 10,000 participants. Milholland led a number of suffrage parades but is particularly associated with the first one in Washington, D.C., in 1913, where she rode a *snow-white charger* (a horse).

I did not smoke—except once. When I was eight years old, a big boy on the street gave me a cigarette, and I started it; but another boy told me a policeman would arrest me, so I threw the cigarette away, and ran and hid in an alley, and have never yet recovered from this fear. It has saved me a great deal of money, and some health also, I am sure.

The sordid surroundings in which I was forced to live as a child made me a dreamer. I took to literature, because that was the easiest refuge. * * *

My mother would read books to me, and everything I heard I remembered. I taught myself to read at the age of five, before anyone realized what was happening. I would ask what this letter was, and that, and go away and learn it, and make the sounds, and very soon I was able to take care of myself. I asked my numerous uncles and aunts and cousins to send me only books for Christmas; and now, three quarters of a century later, traces of their gifts are still in my head. * * *

While arguments between my father and my mother were going on, I was with Gulliver in Lilliput, or on the way to the Celestial City with Christian, or in the shop with the little tailor who killed "seven at one blow." I had Grimm and Andersen and *The Story of the Bible*, and Henty and Alger and Captain Mayne Reid.[3] I would be missing at a party and be discovered behind the sofa with a book. At the home of my Uncle Bland there was an encyclopedia, and my kind uncle was greatly impressed to find me absorbed in the article on gunpowder. Of course, I was pleased to have my zeal for learning admired—but also I really did want to know about gunpowder.

Readers of my novels know that I have one favorite theme, the contrast between the social classes; there are characters from both worlds, the rich and the poor, and the plots are contrived to carry you from one to the other. The explanation is that as far back as I can remember, my life was a series of Cinderella transformations; one

---

3. Thomas Mayne Reid (1818–1883), American author of adventure novels. In *Gulliver's Travels* (1726), by the Anglo-Irish writer Jonathan Swift (1667–1745), the title character visits fantastical lands including Lilliput, which is populated by tiny but bellicose humans. *Celestial City with Christian*: Written by the English Puritan John Bunyan (1628–1688), *The Pilgrim's Progress* (1678) follows the journey of the main character, Christian, to the Celestial City (Heaven), as he faces many temptations along the way; the story is an allegory for the life of all Christians; see also above, p. x, and below, p. 520. *Little tailor*: In a fairy tale collected by the Grimm brothers, a brave little tailor tricks giants and a ruthless king into believing fanciful accounts of his bravery, including that he killed seven flies at one blow. *Grimm and Andersen*: The Grimm brothers (Jacob Ludwig Carl Grimm [1785–1863] and Wilhelm Carl Grimm [1786–1859] collected and published now-famous European folk and fairy tales, such as "Cinderella," which Sinclair mentions in the next paragraph; Danish author Hans Christian Andersen (1805–1875) also published celebrated fairy tales. *Henty*: G. A. Henty (1832–1902), English author of popular historical adventure stories. *Alger*: Horatio Alger Jr. (1832–1899), American author who popularized rags-to-riches stories about poor boys who succeed because of hard work and honesty.

night I would be sleeping on a vermin-ridden sofa in a lodging house, and the next night under silken coverlets in a fashionable home. It all depended on whether my father had the money for that week's board. If he didn't, my mother paid a visit to her father, the railroad official in Baltimore. No Cophetua or Aladdin[4] in fairy lore ever stepped back and forth between the hovel and the palace as frequently as I.

From What Life Means to Me[†]

I was born in what is called the upper middle-class; my parents were members of the ruined aristocracy of the South. I was brought up in a very secluded way, with high traditions and delicate sensibilities, and then turned loose in our modern commercial inferno to shift for myself. I went to college, but I did not take many degrees, because I did not fit into the molds. But I loved the libraries, and I would begin all the courses, find out what the professors had to give me, and then quit. I did this for nine years, in the meantime reading the world's literature and practicing the violin sometimes fourteen hours a day.

I was enabled to do this because of a happy knack which I possessed—that of composing (and marketing) boys' adventure stories. For a considerable period I used to talk these off to a stenographer, grinding them out at the rate of six or eight thousand words a day; in which manner I took care of myself from the age of sixteen. * * *

At the age of twenty, I received a conviction of inspiration, and went away into the woods to write the "great American novel."[1] I was so anxious to begin that I went in the month of April. I was in a tent, and the second night the thermometer dropped to seventeen; in trying to get warm I set fire to my tent, and nearly ended my adventure then and there. A little later in the summer I was storm-bound for three days (I was on an island), and lived on fried crow. Toward the end I went short on money, and then I lived entirely on fish and moldy soda-biscuit.

At the conclusion of the summer, having finished the novel, and considering that I had secured myself a place in literature, and was assured of an income thereby, I was married[2]—my earthly possessions at that moment amounting to eight dollars. I soon made

---

4. *Cophetua*: in legend, an African king who fell in love with and married a beggar girl. *Aladdin*: in a folk tale, a boy who made a genie appear by rubbing a lamp [*Editor*].
† From *Cosmopolitan* 41 (October 1906): 591–95. Unless otherwise indicated, notes are by the editor of this Norton Critical Edition.
1. Sinclair's work would become *Springtime and Harvest* (1901), later titled *King Midas*.
2. In 1900, to Meta Fuller (1883–1964), who also had ambitions of becoming a writer.

the appalling discovery that my novel was not wanted, that my inspiration was not believed in, and that I was out of touch with the entire civilized world—an outcast and a tramp. I could no longer write entertaining dime-novels—the effort to do so simply tore me to pieces, and the publishers of the dime-novels soon found out that something was wrong, and passed me by. I had all the burden and the travail of the future humanity in my soul, but I was powerless to express my vision; I had only incoherent protests and cries of despair. I had no friends; I had no one to advise me or help me or guide me to the light. My rich relations did no more than send me their old clothes occasionally, and offer me a position in the family banking-establishment.

Not caring for this, I had no alternative but to go away into the woods, and live in tents and shanties, and wash the dishes, and tend the baby, and nurse an invalid wife, and write literature. Some of the rage and bitterness of this experience I put into a book called "The Journal of Arthur Stirling,"[3] which was the diary of a young poet who starved in a garret, and finally committed suicide. It created something of a sensation in England, as well as in America; but it was a book about my own soul—and the world has not yet time to pay any attention to individual souls. My nightmare experience had to continue until I discovered the Socialist movement, until I had learned to identify my own struggle for life with the struggle for life of humanity.

※　※　※

It was a wonderful discovery when I made it, for it gave me the key to all my problems. I discovered that I did not have to carry the whole burden of the world's woe upon my own shoulders; that I had comrades and allies in the fight. I was no longer obliged to think of civilization as a place where wild beasts fought and tore one another without purpose and without end; I saw the anguish of the hour as the first pang of the great world-birth that is coming.

And at the same time I discovered my own place in the world, and the purpose and meaning of my experience. Down in the bottom of the social pit were millions of human beings, rotting in squalor and vice, and spreading a slow contagion that was infecting the whole of civilization. But these wretches were ignorant; they did not know what was the matter with them. They were also voiceless, and could not have told even had they known. On the other hand those who had voices—they did not know! They were sitting at ease and speculating about it; they had been born to success themselves, and were prattling that the individual was to blame for failure. I, alone of all

3. Published in 1903; discussed above, p. vii.

men who had education and a voice, had been down into the social pit, and had lived the life of the proletarian; so that I, a boy of twenty-five or six, knew, of my own experience, things of which all the doctors and wise men, the scholars and statesmen of the world, were ignorant. I had tested upon my own person the effects of cold and hunger, of misery and disease and despair. I had tried to the full the power of the individual will, and had found its impotence; I had watched the beginning and the swift progress of degeneration—in body and mind and soul—in myself, and, more horrible yet, in those I loved; I had "fronted the blood-red eyes of the old primeval terror of life." And so I knew, with a knowledge that no man could impeach, the cause and the meaning of all the evils that are raging in modern society—of neurasthenia,[4] melancholia, and hysteria; of drunkenness, insanity, and suicide; of prostitution, war, and crime.

The immediate cause of the writing of "The Jungle" was a request from a Socialist paper, the "Appeal to Reason," that I write them a serial. I had on hand a trilogy[5] which I was anxious to complete—an American historical series, which America did not seem to want very anxiously. I saw that I was at the end of my tether, and had better give the world the lesson of my experience while I could.

I began to plan a novel which should portray modern industrial conditions, and show how they were driving the workingman into socialism. It was just after the big strike in Packingtown, and the newspapers had contained some account of the situation, which had attracted my attention to it. I knew that this was a place where modern commercial forces held complete sway, and had the making of the entire environment. I went out there and lived among the people for seven weeks; I being a socialist, they took me in and told me all they knew. I would sit in their homes at night, and talk with them, and then in the daytime they would lay off their work, and take me around, and show me whatever I wished to see. I studied every detail of their lives, and took notes enough to fill a volume. I talked, not merely with workingmen and their families, but with bosses and superintendents, with night-watchmen and saloon-keepers and policemen, with doctors and lawyers and merchants, with politicians and clergymen and settlement-workers.[6] I spared no pains to get every detail exact, and I know that in this respect "The Jungle" will stand the severest test—it is as authoritative as if it were a statistical compilation.

---

4. Literally "nerve weakness," a common diagnosis for many ailments at the turn of the century.
5. Sinclair planned to write a trilogy about the Civil War, but only completed the first volume, *Manassas* (1904), before turning to other projects—most notably, *The Jungle*.
6. See above, p. 189, n. 3.

In many respects I had "Uncle Tom's Cabin"[7] in mind as a model of what I wished to do. First of all I was an artist, and I wished to write a piece of literature; but I wished also if possible to make a popular book, one that would be read by the people and would shake the country out of its slumber. In this I am afraid that I failed. I might have succeeded if I had had as good an opportunity as Mrs. Stowe had; but my task was so much harder—the life of the modern wage-slave is so much more mechanical and so much less picturesque than that of the chattel-slave of fifty years ago. The black slave was a scarce article; he was worth three hundred dollars the day he was born, and if he were taken care of he would be worth five times as much when he had attained his full growth. As a consequence he had a bright and happy childhood. On the other hand, there is a superfluity of unskilled labor all over the world, and it is nobody's business whether the child of the modern industrial slum ever attains its full growth or not. Also the black slave generally lived in the country, and might be loved by his master; while the wage-slave knows nothing but a tenement-room and a factory, and his master is a machine.

All of which made it infinitely harder for a novelist; it gave him so much less opportunity for color and brightness, for humor and adventure, such as a popular book must have. I was warned by my friends that the sheer horror of "The Jungle" would kill it; but I could only answer that I had to make it *true*. * * *

Perhaps you will be surprised to be told that I failed in my purpose, when you know of all the uproar that "The Jungle" has been creating. But then that uproar is all accidental, and was due to an entirely different cause. I wished to frighten the country by a picture of what its industrial masters were doing to their victims; entirely by chance I had stumbled on another discovery—what they were doing to the meat-supply of the civilized world. In other words, I aimed at the public's heart, and by accident I hit it in the stomach.

I smile whenever I think of it now; I was so unpractical that I did not realize the bearing of this discovery. I really paid very little attention to the meat-question while I was in Chicago. When I had once studied out the universal system of graft which prevails in the place, the meat-graft seemed to me simply a natural and obvious part of it. I saw a great deal of it, of course; but I did not see half as much as I might have seen had I tried harder. I do not eat much meat myself,

7. The 1852 antislavery novel by the American writer Harriet Beecher Stowe (1811–1896), so influential that President Abraham Lincoln is reputed to have said to its author, "So you're the little lady who wrote the book that made this great [civil] war."

and my general attitude toward the matter was one of indifference; I was of the opinion (and I am still of the opinion) that any man who takes into his stomach food which has been prepared under the direction of unscrupulous commercial pirates such as the Chicago packers, deserves all the poisoning he gets.

Just now "The Jungle" is the sensation of the hour; its publishers got rid of seven thousand copies in one day of June. And I have no particular objection to that—the public might as well be looking at my picture in the newspapers as at the picture of any murderer or prize-fighter. But I protest mildly to those academic critics who think that the book is nothing but the sensation of a moment. I do not think that we have any book in American literature, with the possible exception of "Uncle Tom's Cabin," into the making of which more human anguish has entered. Its publication marks the beginning of a proletarian literature in America; we have had nothing before it excepting sugar-coated sentimentality like "Mrs. Wiggs of the Cabbage Patch."[8]

"The Jungle" differs from most of the work of the realists in that it is written from the inside. It is the result of an attempt to combine the best of two widely different schools; to put the content of Shelley into the form of Zola—a method which I believe will come more into favor as the revolutionary Socialist movement finds its voice. The realists of the French school, of which George Moore[9] is the English representative, are middle-class writers. They assemble their material with infinite skill, and are expert psychologists; but it is no part of their programme to live the life which they portray, and they do not feel obliged to share in the emotions of their characters. They do their work from the outside, and they resemble a doctor who is too much absorbed in his study of the case to sympathize with the patient's desire to escape from his agony.

But now there is a stirring of life within the masses themselves. The proletarian writer is beginning to find a voice, and also an audience and a means of support. And he does not find the life of his fellows a fascinating opportunity for feats of artistry; he finds it a nightmare inferno, a thing whose one conceivable excellence is that it drives men to rebellion and to mutual aid in escaping. The proletarian writer is a writer with a purpose; he thinks no more of

8. The 1901 novel by the American writer Alice Caldwell Hegan Rice (1870–1942).
9. Irish writer (1852–1933), some of whose novels were banned for what critics alleged to be immoral subjects such as extramarital sex, lesbianism, and prostitution. The English Romantic poet Percy Bysshe *Shelley* (1792–1822) was a personal hero of Sinclair's; *Zola:* See above, p. 92. By "put[ting] the content of Shelley into the form of Zola," Sinclair means creating protest literature—for he saw Shelley as above all a protest writer—in the form of a naturalistic novel.

"art for art's sake"[1] than a man on a sinking ship thinks of painting a beautiful picture in the cabin; he thinks of getting ashore, and of getting his brothers and comrades ashore—and then there will be time enough for art.

And that is what life means to me. * * *

* * * The curtain is going up on a world-drama the like of which history has never shown before; and it is your privilege to be a spectator—it is a privilege that I would not exchange for a ticket of admission to all that has gone before since the human race began. And alas for you if you are one of those unfortunates who sit cold and inattentive, because they do not understand the language in which the great drama is played!

The name of the language is Socialism. It is a world-language; it is spoken in Russia and Japan, in Germany and Argentina, in America and Australia. It is spoken wherever men are herded together in masses, and made the slaves of machines; it is a language of brotherhood and comradeship, of mutual service and of mutual escape, of liberty and justice and humanity.

Perhaps you are one of those unfortunates who live shut up in a little class of their own, and do not think that there is anything interesting in the world outside of it. You think that men who tend machines are dirty and stupid and all alike, and that what they suffer does not matter, nor whether they live or die. And just now they are dreaming the mightiest dream and fighting the mightiest battle that history has ever told; and you know and care nothing about it! But I have been down into the workshop where the swords are being forged; I have seen the troops being marshaled, and heard the trumpets calling—and I am a captain in the fight!

What, for instance, does the great Russian upheaval[2] mean to you, if you do not understand the Socialist movement? What can you do but watch it in perplexity and dismay, and marvel that men should be so perverse as to do something which you had declared they could not do? And when the same birth-pangs seize upon France and Germany, when the same crisis comes to England and to America—what will you do but run about, crying out in fright like children in a burning house? And this when you might have played the part of thinking men, and have understood and guided the change; and all for lack of taking the trouble to look into the social pit, and realize that they down there are men like yourself, and that the life they live is not to be endured by men, and that it is only a question of the time it takes them to find out the way of deliverance!

1. Associated particularly with the Irish writer Oscar Wilde (1854–1900) and the aestheticism movement, the belief that the sole purpose of art was beauty, not political or didactic purpose.
2. The 1905 Revolution.

[What Socialism Means to Me][†]

* * *The Socialist doctrine is, that the evils of present-day society are the consequences of industrial competition nearing its end and collapse. The economic struggle has resulted in the survival of the Rockefellers and Armours. There is no longer competition in prices, there is competition only in labour; and the result of this condition is, that the surplus product of industry goes to the big capitalist. This wealth he invests in new industries; and to sell his surplus he seeks foreign markets. When new markets are no longer to be had, there is over-production, and an insoluble problem of unemployment—a condition now chronic in England and Germany. Its effect is cumulative; for the unemployed compete and cause reductions of wages, and this is a diminution of the purchasing power of the community and the cause of a still further shrinkage in markets. These causes operate universally, and the issue of them can only be a world-wide industrial revolution. Just as in France when monarchy became no longer endurable the people seized the powers of government, the Socialists desire the people to seize, by means of the ballot, the industrial machinery of the country, and to establish an industrial republic. This involves the confiscation, gift, or purchase—for a small sum, in time of panic—of all capital, and its democratic administration for the equal benefit of all. "Capital," as here used, is to be distinguished from "private property"; the latter is houses, lands, machinery, &c., owned and used by an individual for his own benefit; while "capital" is houses, land, machinery, &c., not used, but rented to others, or operated by others for wages. The Socialists anticipate that the actual managers of these latter will become government officers, that prices will be reduced to abolish dividends, the plants being operated as the post office is now operated, at cost. Ultimately this change would make industrial equality a fundamental principle of government, as political equality has already become. This would mean the abolishing of poverty, and consequently of prostitution and crime; and it would put an end to war, which is now caused by competition for markets, not by race animosities.

"Utopian Socialism" which believed that the co-operative commonwealth could be established at once upon a small scale is now almost extinct. The modern "Scientific Socialist" believes that the end of the competitive wage system will come by a revolutionary change affecting the whole of society at once, and coming as the end of a long process of industrial evolution.

† From "The Socialist Party in the United States," *World's Work* 8 (July 1906): 140–41.

[Art and Propaganda]†

Since childhood the writer has lived most of his life in the world's art. For thirty years he has been studying it consciously, and for twenty-five years he has been shaping in his mind the opinions here recorded; testing and revising them by the art-works which he has produced, and by the stream of other men's work which has flowed through his mind. His decisions are those of a working artist, one who has been willing to experiment and blunder for himself, but who has also made it his business to know and judge the world's best achievements.

The conclusion to which he has come is that mankind is today under the spell of utterly false conceptions of what art is and should be; of utterly vicious and perverted standards of beauty and dignity. We list six great art lies now prevailing in the world, which this book will discuss:

Lie Number One: the Art for Art's Sake[1] lie; the notion that the end of art is in the art work, and that the artist's sole task is perfection of form. It will be demonstrated that this lie is a defensive mechanism of artists run to seed, and that its prevalence means degeneracy, not merely in art, but in the society where such art appears.

Lie Number Two: the lie of Art Snobbery; the notion that art is something esoteric, for the few, outside the grasp of the masses. It will be demonstrated that with few exceptions of a special nature, great art has always been popular art, and great artists have swayed the people.

Lie Number Three: the lie of Art Tradition; the notion that new artists must follow old models, and learn from the classics how to work. It will be demonstrated that vital artists make their own technique; and that present-day technique is far and away superior to the technique of any art period preceding.

Lie Number Four: the lie of Art Dilettantism; the notion that the purpose of art is entertainment and diversion, an escape from reality. It will be demonstrated that this lie is a product of mental inferiority, and that the true purpose of art is to alter reality.

Lie Number Five: the lie of the Art Pervert; the notion that art has nothing to do with moral questions. It will be demonstrated that all art deals with moral questions; since there are no other questions.

---

† From *Mammonart: An Essay in Economic Interpretation* (Pasadena, CA: Published by the Author, 1925), pp. 8–10. Note is by the editor of this Norton Critical Edition.
1. See above, p. 483, n. 1.

Lie Number Six: the lie of Vested Interest; the notion that art excludes propaganda and has nothing to do with freedom and justice. Meeting that issue without equivocation, we assert:

All art is propaganda. It is universally and inescapably propaganda; sometimes unconsciously, but often deliberately, propaganda.

As commentary on the above, we add, that when artists or art critics make the assertion that art excludes propaganda, what they are saying is that their kind of propaganda is art, and other kinds of propaganda are not art. Orthodoxy is my doxy, and heterodoxy is the other fellow's doxy.

JACK LONDON

[What Jack London Says of *The Jungle*]†

Dear Comrades:

Here it is at last! The book we have been waiting for these many years! The *Uncle Tom's Cabin*[1] of wage slavery! Comrade Sinclair's book, *The Jungle!* And what *Uncle Tom's Cabin* did for black slaves, *The Jungle* has a large chance to do for the wage slaves of to-day.

It is essentially a book of to-day. The beautiful theoretics of Bellamy's *Looking Backward*[2] are all very good. They served a purpose and served it well. *Looking Backward* was a great book. But I dare to say that *The Jungle*, which has no beautiful theoretics, is even a greater book.

It is alive and warm. It is brutal with life. It is written of sweat and blood and groans and tears. It depicts, not what man ought to be, but what man is compelled to be in this our world in the twentieth century. It depicts, not what our country ought to be, or what it seems to be in the fancies of Fourth-of-July spellbinders, the home of liberty and equality of opportunity; but it depicts what our country really is, the home of oppression and injustice, a nightmare of misery, an inferno of suffering, a human hell, a jungle of wild beasts.

And there you have the very essence of Comrade Sinclair's book—the jungle! And that is what he has named it. This book must go. And you, comrades, must make it go. It is a labor of love on the part of the man who wrote it. It must be a labor of love on your part to distribute it.

And take notice and remember, comrades, this book is straight proletarian. And straight proletarian it must be throughout. It is written

---

† From *Chicago Socialist* 6:351 (November 25, 1905): 2. Notes are by the editor of this Norton Critical Edition.

1. See above, p. ix, and p. 481, n. 7, and below, p. 499.

2. Best-selling utopian novel (1888), by the American writer Edward Bellamy (1850–1898), about a future socialist America in which the country's productive capacity is collectively owned and the goods of society are equally shared by all citizens.

by an intellectual proletarian. It is written for the proletariat. It is published by a proletarian publishing house. It is to be read by the proletariat. And depend upon it, if it is not circulated by the proletariat it will
not be circulated at all. In short, it must be a supreme proletarian effort.

Remember, this book must go out in the face of the enemy. No capitalist publishing house would dare to publish it. It will be laughed
at—some; jeered at—some; abused some; but most of all, worst of all,
the most dangerous treatment it will receive is that of silence. For that
is the way of capitalism.

Comrades, do not forget the conspiracy of silence. Silence is the
deadliest danger this book has to face. The book stands on its own
merits. You have read it and you know. All that it requires is a hearing.
This hearing you must get for it. You must not permit this silence. You
must shout out this book from the housetops; at all times; and at all
places. You must talk about it, howl about it, do everything but keep
quiet about it. Open your mouths and let out your lungs, raise such a
clamor that those in the high places will wonder what all the row is
about and perchance to feel tottering under them the edifice of greed
they have reared.

All you have to do is to give this book a start. You have read the
book yourselves, and you will vouch for it. Once it gets its start it
will run away from you. The printers will be worked to death getting out larger and larger editions. It will go out by the hundreds of
thousands. It will be read by every workingman. It will open countless ears that have been deaf to Socialism. It will plough the soil for
the seed of our propaganda. It will wake thousands of converts to
our cause. Comrades, it is up to you!

Yours for the revolution,
JACK LONDON

EDWARD CLARK MARSH

[*The Jungle*]†

Our twentieth century philosopher, Bernard Shaw,[1] tells us that "up
to a certain point illusion—or, as it is commonly called by Socialists,
enthusiasm—is more or less precious and indispensable; but beyond
that point it gives us more trouble than it is worth." It is a sage remark,
and nicely applicable to the queer document of Socialist propaganda
which Mr. Sinclair has promulgated under the inappropriate title,
The Jungle. The author has enthusiasm; and up to a certain point—to

---

† From *Bookman* 23 (April 1906): 195–97. Notes are by the editor of this Norton Critical
Edition.
1. (George) Bernard Shaw (1856–1950), an Irish writer and socialist who advocated gradual change rather than revolution.

be precise, up to page 252—it is, as the philosopher avers, precious and indispensable. It has enabled Mr. Sinclair to present, in the first half of his book, a study of social conditions which, if substantially true, should have been made long ago; but it has also carried him off into the wildest rhapsodizing concerning an alleged remedy for these conditions. The faults of *The Jungle*, like those of most writings designed to tell us how evil is the world in which we live, are multitudinous and plain; its great possible virtue is solely dependent on the question of its truth.

Of so much of the book as has any serious significance, the truth or falsity is at least ascertainable. It purports to be a plain, straightforward statement of the lives of workers in the Chicago packing houses, and of the methods by which those enterprises flourish. It is not a pretty story. Those amateur critics who have amused themselves and bored others by taking Mrs. Wharton[2] to task for uncovering plague spots in the body of "high society" ought to find in Mr. Sinclair's book an occupation for many days and nights. It would be unfair to the book to cite only a few of the least offensive details of the "exposé." Their effect is cumulative, and simple justice to Mr. Sinclair demands that you read him at first hand—so long as you can stomach him. Here is our first thorough-going American disciple, on one side at least, of Zola:[3] a novelist with little of the insight and imagination the Frenchman possessed at his best, but with all his industry and no little of his ingenuity in gaining an effect by piling detail on detail, directing attention so persistently to parts that the whole loses all perspective.

There is too much of it to be wholly true. Undoubtedly the impression that persists is that the horrors of the life are exaggerated, that the catalogue of crimes laid at the door of the packers is carried beyond the limits of mere strict, prosaic justice. But another impression remains with equal persistence: that even with very liberal allowances made for the prejudiced statements of a partisan observer, the conditions here described are intolerable, a disgrace to everyone who contributes, directly or indirectly, to their perpetuation.

This, of course, provided the indictment is substantially true. In the end it must be accepted as such or thoroughly, searchingly explained. For the present opinion must rest mainly on internal evidence. And the evidence would be more conclusive if the author had been less ambitious. So long as Mr. Sinclair writes about the stock-yards it is difficult to escape the conviction that he has informed himself of his subject; when he betakes himself to other

2. Edith Wharton (1862–1937), American author of novels critical of high society, such as *The House of Mirth* (1905).
3. See above, p. 92, n. 7.

scenes, and attempts to let his characters breathe the air of a more familiar life, it is impossible not to recognize his ignorance. About the middle of the book the leading character, a young Lithuanian, runs away from the hopeless struggle for existence in the stock-yards. In turn he becomes "hobo," thief, political "heeler," strike-breaker and street beggar. Whether or not with intention on the part of the author, the emphasis shifts from *milieu* to character; it is no longer the story of the stockyards, but the story of Jurgis Rudkus. Nor is it any longer Zolaesque, in spite of a delusion to that effect apparently existent in the mind of the author. A mere fondness for speaking of rather disgusting matters, and particularly for discussing the most sordid facts concerning prostitution in extremely plain terms, scarcely entitles an author to a place beside the French exponent of naturalism. No, Mr. Sinclair's most obvious literary affinity here is the gentleman who once wrote a book entitled "If Christ Came to Chicago."[4]

Yet all of Mr. Sinclair's plain speaking would be justified and even welcomed if it signified anything. Unfortunately it all comes to naught. We do not need to be told that thievery, and prostitution, and political jobbery, and economic slavery exist in Chicago. So long as these truths are before us only as abstactions they are meaningless. Mr. Sinclair has pretended to reduce them to concrete experience, but the pretence is too shallow. His chief character is a mere puppet. He is too obviously manipulated, his experiences are too palpably made to order, to signify anything one way or the other. Jurgis Rudkus is neither individual nor type. He is a mere jumble of impossible qualities labelled a man, and put through certain jerky motions at the hands of an author with a theory to prove. The whole performance shows how much Mr. Sinclair has yet to learn. And the worst of it is that his large ignorance of life throws doubt even on his competence as an observer and recorder of conditions in a special field.

And after all this there is yet a third section of the book—happily a brief one—which adds the crowning touch of unreality. Probably the author would describe it as the third period in the life of Jurgis Rudkus. The young man strays into a Socialist mass meeting one night and hears one of their great orators. He "gets Socialism" exactly as a backsliding brother in a Methodist camp meeting "gets religion," and the effect is equally revolutionary as to character. At last the true purpose of the book comes to light. Unlike Mr. Lawson[5] of Boston, Mr. Sinclair gives his "exposé" and his remedy in a single volume. For forty or fifty pages he discourses of Socialism as the

---

4. The 1894 exposé of Chicago's political corruption and the underground economy of vice by the English newspaper editor and investigative journalist William Thomas Stead (1849–1912).
5. See p. 106, n. 4.

social panacea, and quotes statistics of the voting strength of political parties to show how near the millenium is. It is impossible to withhold admiration of Mr. Sinclair's enthusiasm; and yet many socialists will regret his mistaken advocacy of their cause. His reasoning is so false, his disregard of human nature so naive, his statement of facts so biassed, his conclusions so perverted, that the effect can be only to disgust many honest, sensible folk with the very terms he uses so glibly. It is a misfortune that a book which displays genuine talent, and which is likely to be widely read, should contain so much error to nullify the effect of its merits.

WINSTON SPENCER CHURCHILL

The Chicago Scandals:
The Novel Which Is Making History[†]

When I promised to write a few notes on this book for the first number of Mr. O'Connor's new paper, I had an object—I hoped to make it better known. In the weeks that have passed that object has disappeared. The book has become famous. It has arrested the eye of a warm-hearted autocrat; it has agitated the machinery of a State department; and having passed out of the sedate columns of the reviewer into leading articles and "latest intelligence," has disturbed in the Old World and the New the digestions, and perhaps the consciences, of mankind.

* * * Nothing can exceed the skill and determination with which the author has marshalled his arguments. He is one of those debaters who stand no nonsense from their facts. He finds a place for each—even for the most contrary—in ingenious sequences which steadily approach his goal. All conditions of life—social, moral, political, economic, commercial, climatic, bacteriological—are assembled, drilled into order, arranged under their proper standards, and led by converging roads to the assault. No undisciplined statement is allowed to weaken the stability of their line. One purpose and one purpose alone animates the mind of the commander, and inspires his army down to the humblest item which marches silently in the ranks—to make the great Beef Trust stink in the nostrils of the world, and so to contaminate the system upon which it has grown to strength. Here in the compass of a few hundred pages has been collected all that can be said against the canning industry, all that will damage it before its servants and expose it to its customers.

---

† From *P.T.O.* (June 16, 1905): 25, (June 23, 1905): 66. Notes are by the editor of this Norton Critical Edition.

The "packers" are brought to the bar. The goods they sell, the materials they use, the city they dwell in, the wages they pay—every circumstance, great and small, of their business, together with its consequences, direct or remote, are subjected to a pitiless and malevolent scrutiny.

The worst has been told, and only the worst; it has been told in the most effective way; and the reader is confronted—nay, overwhelmed—by concatenations of filthy, tragic, detestable details, which reduce him, however combative or incredulous, to a kind of horror-struck docility.

Let me say at once that people have no right to hold their noses and shut their eyes. If these things are true, all honour to him who has the power and skill to fasten world-wide attention upon them. If they be only half true, a great public service has been rendered. If only one-tenth part be true, there would still, I fancy, be some debt owing by society to Mr. Upton Sinclair. And there is, unhappily, good reason to believe—scarcely, indeed, any reason to doubt—that a very considerable body of undeniable and easily ascertainable truth sustains the charges that are made. Mr. Upton Sinclair has done for the "packers" what Mr. Henry Lloyd did some years ago in "Wealth against Commonwealth"[1] for the Standard Oil Trust. The mood and the motive of both books are the same: but in one respect Mr. Sinclair's method has a great advantage over his forerunner. "Wealth against Commonwealth" was a laborious compilation. "The Jungle" is a human tragedy.

II

The thread on which all is strung is the gradual ruin, moral and physical, of a strong, brave, honest man. We are introduced abruptly to a family of Lithuanian peasants who have migrated to Chicago. The family is numerous. All relationships and all ages are included. There is Jurgis the hero, a mighty man, a Titan among workers. There is Ona, the girl to whom he is pledged, and for whose sake the great adventure of the ocean voyage has been made. There are her father and aunt, and his brother and his sister Marija, and four or five small children of varying ages. All the grown-ups are thrifty, industrious, simple Lithuanian folk who, having massed their savings, have sailed for the United States, and after being fleeced by every official into whose clutches their journey has led them, have arrived at length at Chicago, asking nothing better than to work from dawn to dusk at an honest trade.

The characters are drawn with care and feeling. We get to know them all. We get to like them all. We become swiftly interested in

1. See p. 296, n. 2.

their domestic economy. How much is left to them of their slender stock of money, what are their prospects of employment, what wages are they bringing in each week, what debts and expenses have they to meet, what perils are in their path—all these petty, everyday matters are made real and important to us by a hundred pages of lively and elaborate art. Once this has been accomplished, Mr. Upton Sinclair has the reader very much at his mercy. He uses his advantage to the full. The utter destruction of this whole family in circumstances of misery and horrid degradation is the plan on which he proceeds, and which he carries out in an exquisite detail and with a ruthlessness of purpose which certainly leave nothing to be desired from an artistic point of view.

✻   ✻   ✻

VI

The reader will not, I think, be satisfied with [the] conclusion. After all that has happened, after all that has been suffered, he will look for some more complete consolation. Not so Mr. Upton Sinclair. This shrewd delineator of character, this painstaking and careful exponent of detail, appears sincerely unconscious of our disappointment. Consolation?—have we not the Socialist orator? Regeneration?—is not Jurgis fully instructed? Salvation?—who can doubt the earnestness of his convictions? What more can anyone require? Let us rejoice that through all this filth and agony one heart at least has been saved from error. There is one man more in Chicago who may be trusted to vote straight for the Socialist ticket. Hurrah!

In writing thus I do not mean to carp at the really excellent and valuable piece of work which this terrible[2] book contains. It pierces the thickest skull and the most leathery heart. It forces people who never think about the foundations of society to pause and wonder. It enables those who sometimes think to understand. The justification of that vast and intricate fabric of Factory Law, of Health Acts, of Workmen's Compensation, upon which Parliament is swiftly and laboriously building year by year and month by month, is made plain, so that a child may see it, so that a fool may see it, so that a knave may see it. But I must frankly say that if the conditions of society in Chicago are such as Mr. Upton Sinclair depicts, no mere economic revolution would in itself suffice to purify and ennoble. A National or Municipal Beef Trust, with the United States Treasury at its back, might indeed give more regular employment at higher wages to its servants, and might sell cleaner food to its customers—at a price. But if evil systems corrupt good men, it is no less true that base men will

---

2. Inspiring terror in the reader.

dishonour any system, and while no bond of duty more exacting than that of material recompense regulates the relations of man and man, while no motion more lofty than that of self-interest animates the exertions of every class, and no hope beyond the limits of this fleeting world lights the struggles of humanity, the most admirable systems will merely succeed in transferring, under different forms and pretexts, the burden of toil, misery, and injustice from one set of human shoulders to another.

It is possible that this remarkable book may come to be considered a factor in far-reaching events. The indignation of millions of Americans has been aroused. That is a fire which has more than once burnt with a consuming flame. There are in the Great Republic in plentiful abundance all the moral forces necessary to such a purging process. The issue between Capital and Labour is far more cleanly cut to-day in the United States than in other communities or in any other age. It may be that in the next few years we shall be furnished with Transatlantic answers to many of the outstanding questions of economics and sociology upon whose verge British political parties stand in perplexity and hesitation. And that is, after all, an additional reason why English readers should not shrink from the malodorous recesses of Mr. Upton Sinclair's "Jungle."

✲　✲　✲

ROBERT M. CRUNDEN

[Progressivism, Muckraking, and the Origins of *The Jungle*]†

Next to political activity, journalism was the most visible progressive profession. Progressive journalists have been congratulated for inclining Presidents toward reform and attacked for not advocating radical social change. Scholars have frequently recognized the evils that progressive writers exposed and wondered at the way many of those evils seemed to persist long after reform laws were enacted to end them. The subsequent careers of a number of writers, as they joined the service of the very economic institutions they once condemned, have brought charges of bad faith, inconsistency, naïveté, and economic self-interest. Some later students of the period seem to have implied that a desire for inflated magazine sales, a need to

† From *Ministers of Reform: The Progressives' Achievement in American Civilization 1889–1920* (New York: Basic, 1982), pp. 163–68, 170–74, 182–83, 187–92, 195–96. Copyright © 1982 by Basic Books, Inc. Reprinted by permission of Basic Books, an imprint of Hachette Book Group, Inc. Unless otherwise indicated, notes are by the editor of this Norton Critical Edition. Some of the author's notes have been excerpted or omitted. Bibliographic information has been included.

achieve personal celebrity, and even a desire to deflect real reform all played their parts in the careers of progressive journalists.

* * *

Within progressivism one important group of writers were "muckrakers," a term President [Theodore] Roosevelt used in a mood of hostility when he felt that they had gone too far in their criticism of American life and its politicians. About forty journalists have been subsequently identified as muckrakers; about twenty of these were consistently active. As a rule they were attached, at one time or another, to several large-circulation magazines, although working for newspapers and writing fiction also attracted many of them. Any understanding of the progressive world, its laws, and its successes and failures, requires a thorough knowledge of muckrakers, their ambivalent relationship to several eminent progressive politicians, and their central role in the writing of progressive legislation. The key to any such understanding of the muckrakers, as with other progressives, lies in the pervasive Protestantism that was so much a part of their childhoods.

* * *

The muckrakers generally acquired their values in the Middle West. Most were born between 1857 and 1878, with 1868 about the median. They grew up in small towns and were vicarious if not always actual farmers. Chiefly of English, Scots-Irish, or German backgrounds, muckrakers were a racially homogeneous group. About 72 percent were native Americans. They came from families that had long been settled in America, sometimes with roots in colonial New England, and from families whose fathers were well-educated and sometimes professional men. They took great pride in their pioneer backgrounds. Their religious values were comparable to those of other progressives. Many were nominally Presbyterians and Methodists, but few were serious churchgoers.

They thus found themselves equipped intellectually with religious categories when they had to confront economic, social, and political problems. This is where much of the modern problem of analysis lies. Because of the muckrakers' backgrounds, they tended to regard exposure of an evil as an end in itself. Once a sin was recognized, surely decent citizens would repent and a good world could develop. Likewise, public agreement was important: if the public agreed with the preacher/journalist, then it was converted, and to the descendants of the Puritans, conversion was a self-justifying event. Good works would presumably follow, but few worried nearly as much about good works as about conversion. Here, too, was the birthplace of so many of the red herrings of progressivism: the drive for prohibition, for control of prostitution, for the regulation of human behavior. Here, too, was a faith in mechanism for its own sake, as if the initiative, referendum, and recall were self-fulfilling, good things. After all, the good puritan was more interested in being a saint than in performing good works. If the heart of the body politic were pure, then its actual achievements were often of minor interest.

* * * [O]ne piece of legislation conspicuously stands out as an archetype of how moral indignation could lead to progressive legislation. The background of the enactment of the Pure Food and Drug Act of 1906 shows muckraking in all its variety and detail: it includes the best piece of literary progressivism, Upton Sinclair's *The Jungle*; it includes muckrakers' feuds with their progressive president, Theodore Roosevelt; it shows how public opinion could be aroused, shaped, and used to force the enactment of a law, thus demonstrating how much a part of their culture the muckrakers were, and why they should not be separated from the body of average voters; and it shows, unfortunately, why progressive laws so often accomplished so little: honesty became a substitute for effective medicine, and inspected meat all too often became a substitute for pure, wholesome meat.

II

Any attempt to establish a "typical" muckraker or "typical" progressive encounters problems with Upton Sinclair. Even though most students of the Progressive Era acknowledge that Sinclair had great impact on American public opinion, legislation, and on the image of America in the minds of foreign readers, they often refuse to see him as a genuine progressive. He was a socialist, a food faddist, and [a] believer in various forms of mental telepathy. Unfriendly journalists made his private life into an object of public scorn, especially on matters of sex. He was not from the Midwest, but from the South. His father was not an old, abolitionist yankee, but rather, a frank sympathizer with the Confederacy whose family was deeply involved in the Confederate navy, and who cursed Republicans[1] until the day he died. Furthermore, Sinclair never lived for long in any small town: he was born in Baltimore, spent much of his early adulthood in New York City, and took occasional retreats to isolated cabins, farms, and

---

1. When the Republican Party was founded in 1854, one of its original principles was opposition to the extension of slavery into western territories. President Lincoln was a Republican, and during Reconstruction (see above, p. 348, n. 2) his party defended the rights of African Americans and sought to redress the legacy of slavery. During the 19th century the Democratic Party, in contrast, tolerated and often supported slavery. To retain the support of white Southern voters, the Democratic Party opposed civil rights for African Americans until the party's realignment toward progressive reform and minority rights by the mid-20th century.

a utopian colony. Born in 1878, he was ten to twenty years younger than his more important colleagues. Even odder, the family religion was a genteel, class-conscious Episcopalianism, on the surface innocent of any of the evangelicalism so obvious in other nurseries of progressivism. But with Upton Sinclair, the surface is most misleading; because of the peculiarities of his upbringing and his remarkable progress toward radicalism, he proves to be the exception that establishes the rule.

*　*　*

In the fall of 1902, Sinclair's life suddenly changed. He met Leonard D. Abbott on a visit to the offices of the *Literary Digest*, and then John Spargo,[2] the editor of *The Comrade*. Pleasant, and committed socialists, they quickly attracted Sinclair to their cause. Through them Sinclair met Gaylord Wilshire, the wealthy Los Angeles entrepreneur and editor of the socialist *Wilshire's Magazine*, and George D. Herron,[3] by this time a notorious ex-minister, whose divorce and remarriage had made him one of the best-known and most viciously attacked socialists in the country. Herron's charm of character and his suffering appealed to Sinclair, who had severe marital problems of his own. When William Moir died suddenly, Herron replaced him as the chief father-figure in Sinclair's life.[4] Herron explained the new religion of socialism to him and suggested that Sinclair's work had not been properly appreciated in America because capitalism had made the people blind to art and beauty. When Sinclair told him how poor he was and how desperate to write his next book, Herron offered to advance him enough money to survive. Sinclair not only remained true to Herron's ideas, he also remained grateful to Herron for this material aid.

The book Sinclair wrote while living on Herron's money was *Manassas*, projected to be the first volume of a Civil War trilogy. In it he followed a crooked path toward the progressivism that came more easily to those born within a conventionally northern, evangelical heritage. Sinclair abandoned the personal world of his earlier novels, discovered a heritage worthy of his new socialist ideas, and in the process, renounced forever the mint-julep Southernism of his inebriated father. The plot took a Southern slave plantation heir to Boston, where he was exposed to abolitionism and literate Negroes; it then returned him to the South, where he became convinced of

2. English writer (1876–1966) who moved to America, a socialist lecturer and early biographer of Marx. *Leonard D. Abbott*: (1878–1953), American journalist and anarchist-socialist.
3. Socialist clergyman and lecturer (1962–1925), whose second marriage, to the daughter of a wealthy patron, scandalized polite society; *Gaylord Wilshire*: See above, p. 299.
4. Sinclair's early mentor the Reverend William Wilmerding Moir (1857–1902) counseled abstaining from sex, contributing to the Sinclairs' marital difficulties.

the iniquity of slavery, the corruption of Southern whites, and his own estrangement from his people. Naturally, given Sinclair's own past, the most horrible of the curses brought by slavery were sexual license, especially between white men and black women, and excessive drinking. The plantation, he found, "was simply a house of shame," and every slave woman on the place was a harlot bidding for favor. Half-naked girls were everywhere, most of them pregnant by the time they reached fifteen. The boys grew up "steeped in vice to their very eyes." The hero became associated with a Quaker abolitionist, met Frederick Douglass and John Brown, joined the Union army, and by the end of the book, had gone through the battle at Manassas[5] with a socialist German freedom fighter at his side. The writing of the book in effect joined abolitionism and socialism for Sinclair, and enabled him to write his most successful fiction to date.

Indeed, while most progressives tended to find their historical roots in abolitionism, the Union, and the North in the Civil War, Sinclair characteristically carried the tendency to extremes. He decided that chattel slavery and wage slavery had a historical parallel, and that, therefore, abolitionism was another kind of progressivism and socialism. * * *

Once initiated into socialism, Sinclair scarcely paused for breath. He began to read omnivorously the most significant radical writers: Europeans like Karl Marx, Karl Kautsky, and Peter Kropotkin and Americans like Edmund Kelly, Jack London, and Edward Bellamy.[6] He became fascinated by the *Appeal to Reason*, a populist weekly published in Girard, Kansas. Socialist ideology gave him a doctrinal substitute for his old religious views, and he swallowed it whole. Fred D. Warren, editor of the *Appeal*, was impressed by *Manassas*, and offered Sinclair another subsidy to do for wage slavery what he had already done for chattel slavery. The offer appealed to Sinclair, who was desperate for the money and eager to tie literature to

5. The first major battle of the American Civil War, and a Confederate victory; called Manassas by the Confederacy, the First Battle of Bull Run by the Union. *Frederick Douglass*: African American (1818–1895) who escaped from slavery to become one of the most famous abolitionists, known for his eloquent speeches and writing. *John Brown*: white American abolitionist (1800–1859), whose raid on a federal arsenal in Harper's Ferry, Virginia (now West Virginia), made him a hero to the antislavery cause.
6. Sinclair's readings represent a variety of socialist views. *Karl Marx*: the preeminent socialist theoretician; defines history as unending class struggle and advocates revolution to overthrow capitalism; coauthor, with Friedrich Engels (1820–1895), of *The Communist Manifesto* (1848). See also p. 365, n. 1. For a sample of Marx's writing, see above, pp. 406–11. *Karl Kautsky*: Czech-Austrian philosopher (1854–1938) and leading theoretician of Orthodox Marxism (the official philosophy of the socialist movement as represented in the Second International [see below, p. 507, n. 2] until 1914), who edited Marx's *Theories of Surplus Value*. *Peter Kropotkin*: See above, p. 314, n. 9. *Edmund Kelly*: American reformer (1851–1901), who advocated socialism but opposed Marx's ideas of class struggle and revolution, advocating instead the gradual, peaceful evolution of society in deference to scientific experts. *Jack London*: See above, p. 299. *Edward Bellamy*: See above, p. 486, n. 2 and below, p. 507, n. 1.

socialism. A recent strike in the Chicago stockyards had drawn the attention of many socialists to Packingtown, so Sinclair decided to go there and study meat-packing the way he had studied slavery. He also formally joined the Socialist Party. Even so, he never abandoned his old religious vision; over a decade later, in a book almost unremittingly hostile to organized religion, he could still write: "I count myself among the followers of Jesus of Nazareth. His example has meant more to me than that of any other man, and all the experiences of my revolutionary life have brought me nearer to him."[7]

*   *   *

In gathering material for this propagandistic art, Sinclair soon learned of other progressive currents that helped to shape his own perceptions and prepared public opinion for his own writing. Chicago political corruption was already legendary. The traction industry had been particularly obnoxious, and the machinations of Charles T. Yerkes were even then in the process of exciting Theodore Dreiser to the writing of *The Titan*. Other food investigators, like Charles E. Russell and Algie M. Simons,[8] had fingered some of the unlovely products of the meat industry, with little obvious public impact. Sinclair was already familiar with much of this story; he knew of Russell's work in particular, and congratulated him for one of his articles in January 1905. He heard much more during the few weeks he spent exploring the industry and interviewing everyone available about working conditions, sanitation, and government inspection methods. He roomed at Mary McDowell's University Settlement House, where he met a constant flow of informed visitors. He visited Jane Addams at Hull-House and discovered what he could from her infinite supply of data on urban problems. Perhaps most significant for his insights and his self-confidence, he also met another man on a similar mission: Adolphe Smith,[9] an investigator from the respected and influential British medical journal, the *Lancet*. Smith not only confirmed much of what Sinclair discovered, but he assured Sinclair that the unsanitary conditions were all unnecessary, and that in Europe under state regulation, conditions were

---

7. Upton Sinclair, *The Profits of Religion* (Pasadena, CA: Published by the Author, 1918), pp. 176, 290 [*Author's note*].
8. American socialist and journalist (1870–1950). *Charles T. Yerkes*: See above, p. 185, n. 8. *Theodore Dreiser*: American novelist (1871–1945), who published a fictional trilogy based on Yerkes's life, the second volume of which, *The Titan* (1914), was set in Chicago. *Charles [Edward] Russell*: American journalist and activist (1860–1941).
9. On settlement houses, see above, p. 189, n. 3. The University of Chicago established a *settlement house* in the Stock Yard District in 1894 and hired social reformer Mary McDowell (1854–1936), who came to be known as "the Angel of the Stockyards" for all she did to support the workers, to head a larger Back of the Yards project. *Hull-House*, founded in 1899 by activist, sociologist, and later Nobel Laureate *Jane Addams* (1860–1935) and reformer Ellen Gates Starr (1859–1940), was the most famous settlement house. Addams introduced Sinclair to *Adolphe Smith* (1846–1924), British investigative journalist, photographer, and radical, who took him on at least one tour of the Armour plant.

different. Sinclair wrote frantically for about three months and serial publication of *The Jungle* in the *Appeal to Reason* began even before he was finished writing.

Sinclair's announced intentions in writing the book differed in some detail from the result, and enormously from the impact on most readers. He had wanted to "set forth the breaking of human hearts by a system which exploits the labor of men and women for profits." He planned a book with an implicit socialist message that would be fundamentally "identical with" *Uncle Tom's Cabin* in what it tried to do. It would depict an exploitative system "slaughtering women and children." The action would turn on a Chicago stockyards strike, with workers, employers' associations, grafting politicians, and foreign laborers all entangled in the scramble for survival and profit. It would include the white-slave traffic and impure food; the impact these make on the hero would drive him to socialism. Sinclair, in short, did not seek federal legislation. Now converted to the new religion of socialism, Sinclair planned to write a socialist tract in the form of a novel. His goals were the conversion of the reader through empathy with the workers of Packingtown, votes for socialist candidates, and ultimately, a socialist America. Pure food and drug laws received one unstressed sentence.

❊   ❊   ❊

The book's instant fame gave it a life of its own. Once he published it, Sinclair could not control it. It became a source of poetry, jokes, and indignation. It affected pending legislation, foreign relations, and, of course, the nation's eating habits. It showed how moral indignation about alcohol, sexual relations, and their Christian meaning could be translated into progressive ideas and, ultimately, into progressive legislation—even without the cooperation of the author. To Sinclair the brouhaha was distressing. "I aimed at the public's heart, and by accident I hit it in the stomach,"[1] was his famous lament. ❊ ❊ ❊

❊   ❊   ❊

IV

❊   ❊   ❊

During the year before the enactment of the Pure Food and Drug Act, two discrete influences tended to flow together, joining the many weaker ones that had been building for years. On the one hand, the muckrakers joined to form what amounted to an indignant and aroused moral lobby, pressuring every politican from

1. Sinclair, "What Life Means to Me," above, p. 481.

President Theodore Roosevelt to the local alderman. On the other a dedicated group of government officials, led by Harvey W. Wiley,[2] the highest ranking scientific bureaucrat in Washington, finally perfected their own case for reform, supported it with adroit publicity and hard data, and provided the political savvy essential to see the legislation through and then administer it.

Between 1879 and 1906, 190 measures connected to pure food or drugs were introduced into the Congress, but only 8 ever became law. Most bills died after their introduction. * * *

* * *

In the Fifty-ninth Congress, no fewer than eleven bills were introduced on the issue in the early days of the session. In the House William Peters Hepburn of Iowa and James R. Mann of Illinois led the fight, while in the Senate Porter J. McCumber of North Dakota and Weldon Heyburn of Idaho persistently pressed for action. Things were stalled, as they usually had been in previous years, when in the middle of February 1906, The Jungle landed on the dinner tables of the nation. The resulting outcry was so great that Senator Albert Beveridge of Indiana, then moving toward a progressivism greater than he had previously shown, seized the issue. He told the President [i.e., Theodore Roosevelt] about the book and then introduced in Congress a meat-inspection bill of his own as a rider to a pending agricultural appropriation bill. Beveridge's rider, and the essential parts of the bills supported by Heyburn and Hepburn, all survived to become law in May and June of 1906.

The sources that survive are more meager than one would expect for such a major piece of legislation, but they nevertheless reveal two fascinating aspects of progressive lawmaking in action. On the one hand, Harvey Wiley seems to have been ubiquitous in Washington. He helped Senator Heyburn write the bill, which, in altered form, became the key law. He was in constant contact, in person and in writing, with members of Congress. He supplied enormous quantities of data. He spoke to public meetings and helped to arouse the women's clubs and the AMA.[3] He was even the chief contact for lobbies from the packers, rectifiers, and others who felt they would be damaged by possible legislation. They understood that if they could persuade Wiley to compromise, he could probably persuade Congress. If ever a man were a vehicle for the transmission of an aroused public opinion, it was Harvey Wiley between late 1903 and the middle of 1906.

2. In 1883, appointed chemist of the U.S. Department of Agriculture (USDA) Chemical Division, later renamed Bureau of Chemistry; Wiley (1844–1930) was known for his work fighting food and drug adulteration.
3. American Medical Association.

Such influences were essential, because on the other hand, Theodore Roosevelt was preoccupied with other matters. The President was concerned with the issues that were in the headlines: the Russo-Japanese War and the possible menace of Japan, the Algeciras Conference, the tariff, and above all, railroad regulation.[4] The issue of pure food and drugs seemed tinged with fanaticism and journalistic excess, and the President was unclear about his commitment to the issue. Thus, following him as he slowly perceived the seriousness of the problem not only provides an excellent case study of progressive legislative change, it shows how public opinion could galvanize a president to moral indignation and result in progressive legislation.

Roosevelt was the consummate politician, but his motives, as a rule, were honest and decent. As the articles of the muckrakers had their impact, members of Congress and finally the President sensed the increased public concern and came to recognize the stakes. Just as Wiley worked closely with Congressional leaders like Heyburn, so, too, did Adams.[5] Indeed, it was apparently Adams' influence on Heyburn, and Heyburn's on Roosevelt, that led Roosevelt to commit himself on the issue. The President also was already in close personal contact with Lincoln Steffens and Ray Baker.[6] Soon this network of influences had their effect. Despite his preference for railroad regulation and foreign affairs, Roosevelt found the space to include the following commitment in his annual message to Congress on 5 December 1905: "I recommend that a law be enacted to regulate interstate commerce in misbranded and adulterated food, drinks, and drugs. Such law would protect legitimate manufacture and commerce, and would tend to secure the health and welfare of the consuming public. Traffic in food-stuffs which have been debased or adulterated so as to injure health or to deceive purchasers should be forbidden."[7] Having adopted such a position, Roosevelt found it attracted attention, focused public opinion, and seemed a sensible part of his own reform package. He had nothing to do with

---

4. Curbing the enormously powerful railroads was one of Roosevelt's major goals, and the Hepburn Act (1906) extended the authority of the recently created Interstate Commerce Commission (ICC) to set maximum rates that railroads could charge. *Russo-Japanese War*: See above, p. 278, n. 5. Roosevelt's success in brokering peace between Russia and Japan resulted in his winning the 1906 Nobel Peace Prize. *Algeciras Conference*: held in Algeciras, Spain, in 1906 to seek a solution to the First Moroccan Crisis between France and Germany. *Tariff*: Attitudes toward tariffs were divisive during Roosevelt's presidency, with Republicans supporting steep tariffs and Democrats denouncing them for resulting in what they saw as government-sponsored monopolies.

5. American writer Samuel Hopkins Adams (1871–1958), who exposed fraudulent claims of the patent medicine industry in a series of 1905 articles.

6. Leading American muckrakers; Steffens (1866–1936) exposed corruption in municipal governments, and Baker (1870–1946) was among the first white journalists to study racial discrimination and segregation in America.

7. *The Works of Theodore Roosevelt*, ed. Hermann Hagedorn (New York: C. Scribner's Sons, 1926), Vol. 15, p. 326 [*Author's note*].

the food and drug reform movement at its conception, but he was willing to adopt it when the times were ripe.

Roosevelt continued to dwell on railroad problems until late January 1906, when Attorney General William H. Moody informed him that legal counsel for the beefpackers, then under an antitrust indictment in Chicago, had attempted to bribe local reporters into giving the public news that was slanted favorably toward the packers. The government could pursue no legal remedy, but Moody thought that some distorted news had been printed that could have shaped local opinion more favorably toward the packers than they deserved. Roosevelt was predictably upset at this violation of ethics, and the next day ordered all relevant documents published so that public opinion could have more accurate information.

The Jungle appeared in the middle of February. Secretary Garfield[8] called Roosevelt's attention to the book and shortly thereafter Senator Beveridge did as well. Garfield thought the book "too pessimistic," but was generally sympathetic; Beveridge immediately spotted a popular issue. Roosevelt's reaction was complex. He disliked the "ridiculous socialistic rant" in the book, and tried to pressure F. N. Doubleday, its publisher, to make Sinclair cut much of the blatant propaganda. Doubleday replied that they already had succeeded in excising 30,000 words from the original manuscript, but that the rest of the "unfortunate sermonizing" had to remain because Sinclair would budge no farther.

Whatever his skepticisms about socialism or his distaste for reformers like Sinclair, Roosevelt was clearly aroused in the same way that the general public was aroused. Filthy meat was disgusting, its packers unethical, and the consequences possibly lethal. He wrote to Sinclair suggesting a meeting with Secretary Garfield. He instructed Secretary of Agriculture James Wilson to begin an investigation that would go well beyond what had already been done in Chicago. * * *

At this point Roosevelt assumed a sincere and characteristic pose, that of the interested and aroused citizen holding off the radicals and lecturing them while trying in all honesty to get the facts so he could act sanely. He often found Sinclair petulant and irritating. Sinclair gave the impression of being a hysteric even at a distance, as he peppered the White House with his doubts, fears, and intuitions about the packers and the government. He was especially perturbed at the thought that the government investigation would examine only meat—a white, middle-class, respectable concern—and entirely avoid the condition of the workers so important to Sinclair and the

---

8. James Rudolph Garfield (1865–1950), politician, lawyer, and secretary of the interior.

socialists. Roosevelt assured him that the working conditions would also be investigated, and he did issue instructions to that end.

On 10 April, to cite only the most extraordinary day, Sinclair sent one telegram and two separate letters, in an agony of distress over rumors he had heard about a possible "whitewashing" of the packing industry. He claimed to have "perfect confidence" in Roosevelt's appointees, but he clearly thought them vulnerable to easy deception. He also claimed to have confidence in Roosevelt's "sincerity and fairness"—a confidence unexpressed in the tone of his letters. The next day his confidence further expressed itself with a personal phone call to the White House. For his part Roosevelt could be equally moralistic and censorious. In one letter, he preached, for example, about his literary peeves—Tolstoy, Zola and Gorki—and lectured Sinclair about the superiority of individual initiative to socialism. His true attitude came out more clearly in a letter of a day earlier to Ray Baker, where he talked in a way that covered not only the railroads and pure food, but his whole orientation toward reform: "I want to let in light and air, but I do not want to let in sewer gas. If a room is fetid and the windows are bolted I am perfectly contented to knock out the window, but I would not knock a hole into the drain pipe."

The individuals Roosevelt appointed to make his own investigation of Packingtown were Charles P. Neill, the United States labor commissioner, and James B. Reynolds, a New York reformer. * * *

Sinclair's suspicions about Roosevelt's commitment to reform had more basis than Roosevelt was willing to admit. The two progressive moralists disagreed on many levels of tone and substance, and the disagreement would soon be public. Word began to filter out to the muckrakers that Roosevelt was about to turn on them, in spite of his having worked closely with a number of them, and in spite of the impact they had had on his and the public's perceptions of reform. Roosevelt would forever deny that this was the case: there were good and bad journalists, just as there were good and bad trusts, and journalists who were serious, moderate, and responsible were not muckrakers. But since Roosevelt never made public lists of his targets, many muckrakers could be forgiven if they felt their powerful friend had suddenly turned away. In all probability Roosevelt did not have them in mind; he had Sinclair in mind, along with Thomas Lawson of the "Frenzied Finance" series and David Graham Phillips of "The Treason of the Senate" articles.[9] These articles not only tended to attack the very roots of American capitalism and democracy, but they came uncomfortably close to men who were

9. These articles by American novelist and journalist David Graham Phillips (1816–1911) exposed the corruption of individual U.S. senators, spurring passage of the Seventeenth Amendment, which provides for the direct election of senators. *"Frenzied Finance"*: See above, p. 106, n. 4.

personal friends and supporters of Roosevelt and of the Republican
Party. If they were guilty, then by implication Roosevelt himself
might be covered with muck, and that to him was inconceivable. It
may be, as Roosevelt once suggested to William Howard Taft,[1] that
certain writers worked with a revolutionary spirit—although few
were even as socialistic as Upton Sinclair, and none were violent—
but it certainly was not true that they had done much evil and little
good. They had forced both Roosevelt and America to face hard
problems, and their tone was hardly more passionate than that of
Roosevelt himself on many issues. They were clergymen, as it were,
of different faiths, but all were preachers within an evangelical
Christian moral environment.

Roosevelt's imagery and message in the speech, finally given on
14 April in Washington, were replete with his Manichean vision of
the forces of good fighting the forces of evil. The man with the
muckrake, regrettably, helped the forces of evil because of the violence of tone and the lack of discrimination in his attacks. He set a
tone, in other words, that created an immoral climate. In discussing it, Roosevelt took a tradition dear to the McClure band,[2] and in
effect, tried to turn it against them:

> In Bunyan's "Pilgrim's Progress"[3] you may recall the descrip-
> tion of the Man with the Muck-rake, the man who could look
> no way but downward, with the muck-rake in his hand; who was
> offered a celestial crown for his muck-rake, but who would nei-
> ther look up nor regard the crown he was offered, but contin-
> ued to rake to himself the filth of the floor.
>
> In "Pilgrim's Progress" the Man with the Muck-rake is set
> forth as an example of him whose vision is fixed on carnal
> instead of on spiritual things. Yet he also typifies the man who
> in this life consistently refuses to see aught that is lofty, and
> fixes his eyes with solemn intentness on that which is vile and
> debasing. Now, it is very necessary that we should not flinch
> from seeing what is vile and debasing. There is filth on the floor,
> and it must be scraped up with the muck-rake; and there are
> times and places where this service is the most needed of all
> the services that can be performed. But the man who never does
> anything else, who never thinks or speaks or writes, save his
> feats with the muck-rake, speedily becomes, not a help to society,
> not an incitement to good, but one of the most potent forces
> for evil.

1. The 27th president (1857–1930) of the U.S. (1909–1913), immediately following Theodore Roosevelt.
2. *McClure's* magazine was a major outlet for muckraking journalism; *band* in the sense
of group, here a group of authors.
3. See above, p. x and p. 477, n. 3.

Roosevelt then went on to detail what this interpretation of a classic meant. To anyone familiar with the past lives of most muckrakers, his indictment was ludicrous. Here were people whose lives had been devoted to religion, to writing novels, to exalting poetry and love, who had been so conservative as to have been more favorable to William McKinley than to Theodore Roosevelt; McKinley's own vice-presidential running-mate![4] To Roosevelt these reform journalists exaggerated; they did not discriminate; and words such as "hysterical," "sensational," and "lurid" categorized their work. As a result, public opinion became numbed, and so color-blind that it could not distinguish good from evil. It also became cynical, and nothing made Roosevelt himself verge closer on hysteria than cynicism about democracy, patriotism, or his own righteousness.

Despite the injustice of this indictment, the muckrakers were never the same after Roosevelt's speech. The progressive president with wide popular following had called reform journalism extremist, and any further exposures could be dismissed as mere "muckraking." Reform journalists sensed immediately that they had received a possibly fatal blow. * * *

Even as they received the fatal wound, the muckrakers triumphed in Congress and in the very White House that had so hurt them. Even as Roosevelt dismissed them, he began to work with redoubled energy to push the investigations to a close and see remedial legislation enacted quickly. Because of his personal affection for Senator Beveridge, Beveridge's meat inspection rider received Roosevelt's closest attention and support. Given Roosevelt's dislike for Harvey Wiley, food and drug legislation on matters other than meat might well have been allowed to die. But in practice both the public and Congress seemed to identify the various measures as being part of a single effort, and the force behind the Beveridge rider was enough to carry the entire Pure Food and Drug Law.

* * *

The resulting law both limited the rights of food and drug manufacturers and expanded the power of the federal government. At the time these issues seemed paramount, and in a purely medical or legislative sense, they also remain paramount to later historians. But in terms of the bill as a document of progressivism, it also stands as a fine example of institutionalized moral indignation. It was *wrong*

---

4. Both were Republicans but *McKinley* (1843–1901), 25th president of the U.S. (1897–1901), was more conservative. He was pro-business and oversaw territorial expansion that has been described by some historians as the beginning of a U.S. empire. Following McKinley's 1901 assassination, his vice president, Roosevelt, assumed the presidency. Often described as a "trust-buster," Roosevelt was not anti-business but did believe that government needed to play a larger role in regulating it.

as well as unhealthy to include certain preservatives in food packages; it was *unethical* to claim efficacy for drugs that were really ineffectual compounds of water or alcohol; it was *immoral* to include drugs in a compound that might damage the heart or cause unpredictable addiction. The resulting law was moral in the sense that it did not require that drugs work, or that food taste good or keep for any specified period of time. It merely required that manufacturers tell the truth on their labels. They could not claim that their drugs did something they could not be proven to do; they must not claim ingredients if those ingredients were not present. They were not forbidden to include harmful ingredients, but if they did so, they must say so plainly. The United States Pharmacopoeia or National Formulary established standards for the use of certain terms, and the terms on the labels must coincide with these national standards unless there was clear indication of the way in which the given medicine was different or substandard. No one could mix or pack so as to deceive purchasers, and no use of chemicals, powders, or other ingredients could camouflage spoilage or inferiority. Filthy or putrid animals or vegetables were unacceptable. Misbranding or mislabeling was forbidden. Officials in the government would make uniform rules and regulations as the need arose; the Bureau of Chemistry would make the needed scientific analyses; and the Secretary of Agriculture would work through the appropriate United States district attorney to obtain enforcement. The overriding assumption was that honest businessmen would make, label, and sell what they wished to competent, progressive, decent citizens. As long as everyone behaved correctly, society functioned successfully.

MARK W. VAN WIENEN

[*The Jungle* and the Many Faces of American Socialism][†]

For all of the hopeful indications of the rising tide of progressivism, the American socialist movement ended the nineteenth century and began the twentieth at a critical juncture. The popular organizations that had espoused socialist and socialistic measures in the 1890s,

---

† From *American Socialist Triptych: The Literary-Political Work of Charlotte Perkins Gilman, Upton Sinclair, and W. E. B. Du Bois* (Ann Arbor, MI: U of Michigan P, 2012), pp. 64, 66–67, 75–81. Copyright © by the U of Michigan 2012. Reprinted with permission of the U of Michigan P; permission conveyed through Copyright Clearance Center, Inc. Unless otherwise indicated, notes are by the editor of this Norton Critical Edition. Some of the author's notes have been excerpted or omitted. Bibliographic information has been included. Page references in brackets refer to this Norton Critical Edition.

especially the Nationalists and the Populists,[1] had either lost their momentum or been co-opted by the mainstream parties. The more militant parties, De Leon's Socialist Labor Party for example, had never gained anything like a national following. Into the breach stepped the Socialist Party, formed in 1901 when the splinters of several disintegrating, smaller Marxian parties determined to present a united front, adopted the parliamentary style of the Second Internationale, and found a charismatic, coalition-building leader in Eugene Debs.[2]

❊   ❊   ❊

❊ ❊ ❊ [T]he diversity of American socialism between the turn of the century and the beginning of World War I was such that Sinclair, in trying to assimilate its breadth and intricacies, was led to attempt an almost Whitmanian synthesis of contraries, extending even to the anarchist "propaganda of the deed."[3] That he emerged with a functional socialist praxis at all—and with some definite results to show for his effort—is a testament to the dialectical work of socialism within U.S. culture as well as to Sinclair's own personal intellectual accomplishment.

❊   ❊   ❊

For some critics of Sinclair, an account of the author's views on socialism is closely connected with the profession of authorship itself, particularly as conditioned by the higher social status of writers as compared to working-class people whom socialist writers purport to represent. In the 1930s, the distinguished critic and then-Communist fellow traveler Granville Hicks averred that Sinclair's novels are often told "from the point of view of the middle-class convert to radicalism" and concludes that "he has never eradicated the

1. See above, p. 293, n. 6. In this context, Nationalists refers to members of organized socialist groups who sought to make America look like the vision put forward in Edward Bellamy's utopian novel Looking Backward, in which all industry is nationalized, all citizens receive the same pay, and everyone retires at age 45 (also see above, p. 486, n. 2 and p. 497, n. 6).
2. Advocating a gradual and peaceful transition to socialism, Debs was the Socialist Party's (SP's) presidential candidate five times (see also above, pp. 300 and 316). Critical of the trade unionists (see craft unionism above, p. 405, n. 1), which he saw as too accommodating and reformist, Daniel De Leon (1852–1914) became one of the leading members of the U.S. Socialist Labor Party (SLP). The Socialist Party of America was created when disaffected elements of the SLP and other organizations came together. Flourishing in the years before World War I, the SP had a wide base, appealing to immigrants, trade unionists, progressives, and populists. At its peak, the SP had 100,000 members; Sinclair became one of them in 1904. Second Internationale: or Second International, also called the Socialist International (1889–1916), a federation of socialist and labor parties; it continued the work of the dissolved First International (see above, p. 287, n. 4), but excluding anarcho-syndicalists and trade unions.
3. Late-19th-century anarchist concept, intended to bring about the fall of the state through acts of symbolic violence. Whitmanian synthesis of contraries: American poet Walt Whitman (1819–1892) is known for proclaiming sympathy for (and even identity with) seemingly opposed persons and beliefs.

effects of his bourgeois upbringing. Though his aim had been social-istic, his psychology has remained that of the liberal.[4] In what has remained for over thirty years the definitive description of Sinclair's creation of *The Jungle*, Michael Folsom also points to a bourgeois psychology. The novel's infamous ending seems to Folsom to reveal that Sinclair was interested most of all in his own fate as a professional writer: "Sinclair, who had spent a whole book immersed in the lives of laboring people, was ultimately most interested in the intelligentsia and its problems. A Socialist was, for him, someone who could make or write an argument."[5] Recent Sinclair biographer Kevin Mattson goes so far as to characterize the entire American Socialist Party as aligned with Sinclair's literary caste. "The Socialist Party that Sinclair would join was composed largely of lawyers, journalists, and teachers," Mattson reports, making it a relatively genteel and timid organization, "derided" by "some who were more revolutionary" as "slowcialism."[6]

✻　✻　✻

✻ ✻ ✻ The polemical and didactic passages toward the ending of the novel, which seem to lend substance to Folsom's and other critics' claims that Sinclair's socialism is for intellectuals only, are in fact the very passages that illustrate the means by which a regular pro-letarian, Jurgis, gains an intellectual mastery of his social circum-stances and of their remedy through socialist transformation. They are also the means by which Sinclair, however cumbersomely, ensured that the novel would introduce its readership of various classes to the core principles of socialism. Immediately after the speech in which Jurgis is first acquainted with socialism, he is handed over to one of the party's organizers, a Polish tailor named Comrade Ostrinski who can explain socialism to Jurgis in his own language. Thereafter, while in the current order of things he remains a menial laborer, his mind grows: "he was just a hotel-porter, and expected to remain one while he lived," but "in the realm of thought, his life was a perpetual adventure. There was so much to know—so many wonders to be discovered!" [303].

The Jungle does not in any way suggest that Jurgis, the former stockyard worker and current hotel service worker, occupies the same role within the socialist movement as the party intellectuals

4. Granville Hicks, [from *The Great Tradition*], in *Critics on Upton Sinclair: Readings in Literary Criticism*, ed. Abraham Blinderman (Coral Gables, FL: U of Miami P, 1975), p. 62 [*Author's note*].

5. Michael Brewster Folsom, "Upton Sinclair's Escape from *The Jungle*: The Narrative Strategy and Suppressed Conclusion of America's First Proletarian Novel," *Prospects* 4 (1979): 248, 261 [*Author's note*].

6. Kevin Mattson, *Upton Sinclair and the Other American Century* (Hoboken, NJ: Wiley, 2006), pp. 46, 47 [*Author's note*].

and itinerant party organizers. The novel pointedly shows, however, that their roles are not mutually exclusive. In the closing scene of *The Jungle*, in which the election results of 1904 are reported before a Socialist meeting in Chicago, the roles of intellectual and rank-and-file are portrayed as complementary to one another. The oratory of the speaker helps his hearers to envision the actions of individual voters as a coherent mass movement: "as he swung his long arms and beat up the crowd, to Jurgis he seemed the very spirit of the revolution" [317]. But it is the casting of Socialist votes by the rank-and-file that constitutes the fundamental political act, and each voter must in turn take up the task of party building and political education: "It rests with you to take your resolution—now, in the flush of victory, to find these men who have voted for us, and bring them to our meetings, and organize them and bind them to us!" [318]. Hence intellectual development along the lines of class analysis is fundamental to the socialist identity of a proletarian such as Jurgis Rudkus, just as it is necessary for intellectuals like Sinclair. * * *

* * *

* * * The election of 1904 described in the closing pages of *The Jungle* marked the beginning of what has been called the "golden age" of the socialist movement in America, a period lasting until the beginning of the Great War, in which the party made steady gains in the popular vote, placed a representative in the U.S. Congress, elected mayors in Milwaukee, Schenectady, and over fifty other municipalities, and gained majorities on the councils of many of these cities. It was also a period of remarkable diversity in the socialist movement. One commentator notes that "the Party was far from homogeneous or orthodox in the present sense of that word, although before 1920 such differences were generally accepted as normal and desirable aspects of the process of developing a viable mass party."[7] And this is considering only the Socialist Party proper. The American socialist movement also included, further to the left, a persistent cadre of anarchists and a steadily growing anarcho-syndicalist union, the Industrial Workers of the World. On the right, there were significant numbers of adherents to the Social Gospel,[8] and socialist ideas were manifest, perhaps unsystematically but nonetheless tangibly,

---

7. The summary is of socialist historian James Weinstein by Isabel González Díaz, "Whose Chicago, Anyway? 'Aesthetics' vs. 'Propaganda' in Upton Sinclair's Ending for *The Jungle*," *Revista Canaria de Estudios Ingleses* 32–33 (1996): 102 [*Author's note*].

8. Socialist-leaning reform movement that called for applying biblical principles to industrialized society; among the movement's concerns were abolishing child labor, shortening the work week, regulating factories, and establishing a living wage. *Industrial Workers of the World*: founded in 1905 by De Leon and Debs, among others, the IWW (also known as "the Wobblies") criticized the AFL for, in their view, accepting capitalism while the IWW urged revolution instead.

among the Progressives of both major parties. Most of these varieties of socialist activity are evident in Upton Sinclair's writing and activism beginning with *The Jungle* and continuing through his campaign on behalf of the victims of the Ludlow Massacre.[9] Broad as his sympathies and intellectual curiosity were, Sinclair developed in his work a compelling case that the various forms of socialism did, in fact, work effectively together—even when the various factions might sincerely distrust each other.

✳   ✳   ✳

The diversity of American socialism is practically flaunted in the closing pages of *The Jungle*, the infamously didactic monologues and dialogues upon socialist theory and praxis. Once apologizing for the rambling and expository style of these chapters, Sinclair confessed, "I ran wild at the end, attempting to solve all the problems of America; I put in the Moyer-Haywood case, everything I knew and thought my readers ought to know."[1] This very effort at comprehensiveness and didacticism, however, is a boon to our effort to describe American socialism near the beginning of its ascent into political prominence. To begin with, socialist variety is on display in Sinclair's cast of characters, both fictional and nonfictional. Comrade Ostrinski, Jurgis's tutor, presents the party-building and electoral strategies that were the main line pursued by the Socialist Party of America throughout its major period, 1901–20. As we have seen, the electoral strategy is subsequently dramatized in the closing, election-day scene as well. But Sinclair's interest in socialist leaders and philosophies ranges far and wide, as indicated by his brief character sketches of real-life socialists whom he generally does not name but describes with enough detail for readers to identify. There is Eugene Debs, of course, who is identified as one of the "two standard-bearers of the party" whom Jurgis hears during the 1904 election season, and described as "a man of electric presence, tall and gaunt, with a face worn thin by struggle and suffering" [300]. Besides pointed allusions to the radical publishers Wayland and Wilshire, ✳ ✳ ✳ characters that suggest the leftward extension of the socialist movement include Jack London, described as someone "who had tramped the

9. The 1914 attack by agents of a Standard Oil–affiliated coal company in Ludlow, Colorado, on striking miners and their families, resulting in 23 deaths, including those of 11 children. Sinclair spent three nights in jail for organizing a protest against John D. Rockefeller Sr. (owner of Standard Oil; see above, p. 352, n. 3) in New York.
1. Quoted in Folsom, "Upton Sinclair's Escape from *The Jungle*," p. 250 [*Author's note*]. [*Moyer-Haywood case*: During a 1905 strike of the Western Federation of Miners, three American labor leaders (Charles H. Moyer [1866–1929], William ["Big Bill"] Haywood [1869–1928], and George A. Pettibone [1862–1908]) were illegally extradited, accused of assassinating a former Idaho governor even though they were in another state at the time of the murder, and imprisoned for eighteen months. Haywood and Pettibone were acquitted, and Moyer released without trial—*Editor*.]

country and been sent to jail, had lived in the Whitechapel slums, and been to the Klondike in search of gold," and Daniel De Leon,[2] readily recognizable to socialist readers in the figure of the "Little Giant" who Sinclair says had "written a veritable encyclopedia upon the subject [of capitalism], a book that was nearly as big as himself" [299]. To broaden the socialist spectrum still further, Sinclair elsewhere includes reference to "Mrs. Gilman"—Charlotte Perkins Gilman, of course—as the author of books on women's economics and domestic cooperatives.[3]

The Jungle portrays the polyglot[4] nature of the socialist movement most fully, perhaps, through the fictional comrades Schliemann and Lucas, the contrasting characters who generate the long dialogue in the novel's penultimate scene. * * *

Notably, *neither* of these major spokesmen for socialism is typical of the Socialist Party line. Both are introduced as "Socialists." But as a Christian minister advocating the Social Gospel, Lucas would not be typical of the party with its resolutely secular ideology. And Schliemann *should* not, in point of fact, be a member of the party, although it is conceivable that he might be "one of the minds of the movement" without being a card-carrying party member. Schliemann openly declares himself to be a "philosophic anarchist," a point of view evident also from his [conviction] that "socialism was simply a necessary step toward a far-distant goal, a step to be tolerated with impatience" [303, 308–09]. * * * For holding such views openly—as well as sympathizing with the Russian direct-actionists—Schliemann ought to have been among the anarchists barred from the party from its inception.

* * *

That Sinclair was aware of tensions within the party stemming from its diversity is clear enough from the minimal common ground that the novel describes as binding the socialist movement together. There appear to be just three planks that might be agreed upon as a shared socialist platform. The first is the principle of "no compromise" [288] articulated by Comrade Ostrinski and reinforced by the election-day speaker, which seems to allow for a variety of means to socialist ends (including especially parliamentarianism) so long as all socialist parties remain united in their opposition to capitalism. The second and third are the "two carefully worded propositions" upon which the sparring debaters Lucas and Schliemann can agree. One is a statement of the socialist goal broad enough to include state

2. *Wayland and Wilshire, Jack London, De Leon:* See above, pp. 300, 299.
3. See above, p. 314.
4. Literally, speaking many languages; here *polyglot* is used metaphorically to capture the range of socialist positions.

socialism[5] as well [as] Schliemann's favored communes: "common ownership and democratic management of the means of producing the necessities of life" [308]. Another articulates with slightly more detail the means to this end, "the class-conscious political organization of the wage-earners" [308]. It is an articulation that shows some influence of Marxism upon Sinclair and the post-1900 socialist movement, although by using the term "wage-earners" instead of the "proletariat" Sinclair offers a formulation broad enough to accommodate the full range of pre-1900 producerist[6] thinkers and to include, with minimal friction, brain-laboring, piecework writers such as himself * * *.

For the most part, though, *The Jungle* envisages the tensions as productive. Implicitly as well as explicitly, *The Jungle* is all about inclusiveness, about entertaining all kinds of socialist philosophy and praxis and about contemplating the possibility that most of them would, in the end, be compatible with the aim of progress toward social democracy.

SANDRA M. GUSTAFSON

Rethinking Literature and Democracy: [*The Jungle* and Political Theory][†]

What does it mean today to be a democrat and to believe in the value of democratic self-governance? How are notions of democracy changing in the light of political, social, and economic transformations? To what extent is democracy tied up with matters of symbolization and language? And how might it resonate with the literature of the United States, understood in a transnational context? * * * I explore these questions via a comparative analysis of the work of political theorists Pierre Rosanvallon and Danielle Allen, who offer complementary insights into developments in

---

5. Centralized economy in which the state owns means of production.
6. Belief that workers engaged in producing goods or services are more socially useful than those living on accumulated or inherited wealth. *Influence of Marxism*: Class consciousness is a central premise for Marx, who declared in *The Communist Manifesto* (see above, p. 497, n. 6) that "the history of all hitherto existing society is the history of class struggles" ("Manifesto of the Communist Party," *The Marx-Engels Reader*, edited by Robert C. Tucker, Norton, 1972, p. 335). The term "proletarian" is also associated with Marx. On Marx, see also p. 287, n. 4, and p. 365, n. 1. For a sample of Marx's writing, see above, pp. 406–11 [*Editor*].
† From "Equality as Singularity: Rethinking Literature and Democracy," *New Literary History* 45:4 (Autumn 2014): 595–607, 609–610. © 2014 *New Literary History*, The University of Virginia. Reprinted with permission of Johns Hopkins University Press. Unless otherwise indicated, notes are by the author. Some of the author's notes have been excerpted or omitted. Bibliographic information has been included.

democratic thought and practice, focused on the emergent meaning of "equality." * * *

* * *

After developing this framework, I consider two authors from the United States whose fiction has not been well served by recent developments in political and literary theory: Saul Bellow and Upton Sinclair.[1] Rosanvallon's approach to equality-as-singularity and Allen's emphasis on political judgment help us to understand the contributions that the fiction of these authors make to the transnational unfolding of democratic thought and practice. * * *

Upton Sinclair's The Jungle earned its enduring literary success with vital writing and vividly realized descriptions of industrial exploitation in turn-of-the-century Chicago. Few novels written and published in the United States have had the global impact of Sinclair's novel. Yet while The Jungle continues to command an international readership, its status as a work of classic American fiction remains oddly insecure. Criticized in his own day for being too openly committed to the socialist cause or insufficiently orthodox in his Marxism, Sinclair today is often overlooked by theoretically minded critics who reject the melodrama and sentiment of the protest novel tradition influenced by Uncle Tom's Cabin.[2] By shifting our attention to Sinclair's depiction of character formation in the Lithuanian immigrant Jurgis Rudkus, we can see how he brings into sharp focus the complex relationship between egalitarian politics and identity that Rosanvallon reconfigures via the concept of singularity. Sinclair's novel also offers unusually well-developed scenes of debate and consensus formation that effectively illustrate Allen's approach to political judgment. * * *

* * *

The idea of democracy is closely associated with language, as the classic image of orators in the Athenian agora[3] suggests. In 1941 the leftist critic F. O. Matthiessen made the meanings of democracy central to his study of the American Renaissance writers. "The one common denominator of my five writers," Matthiessen noted, referring to Ralph Waldo Emerson, Nathaniel Hawthorne, Herman Melville, Henry David Thoreau, and Walt Whitman, "was their devotion to the possibilities of democracy."[4] * * *

1. The author's discussion of Saul Bellow, omitted here, can be found in "Equality as Singularity" [Editor].
2. See above, p. 481, n. 7 [Editor].
3. Marketplace in ancient Athens, where orators, who were greatly esteemed in Greek society, delivered speeches to the public [Editor].
4. F. O. Matthiessen, American Renaissance: Art and Expression in the Age of Emerson and Whitman (New York: Oxford UP, 1941), p. ix. [Matthiessen's term "American

Even as Matthiessen wrote *American Renaissance*, "democracy" was emerging as a god-term[5] in political discourse, where it has been used to describe a variety of practices and regimes, to cover a range of achievements and to cloak a multitude of sins. This is a dramatic and, in historical terms, quite sudden transformation. For over two millennia, from Plato's day until the age of revolution,[6] democracy occupied a marginal place within western political theory.

The study of democracy as a process of "endless enquiry"[7] is a prominent element in the recent work of Rosanvallon * * *. Historicism is another distinctive characteristic of his work. * * * Rather than simply having a history, he claimed, "democracy *is* a history. It has been a work irreducibly involving exploration and experimentation, in its attempt to understand and elaborate itself."[8] He offers an approach to democratic theory that is historically grounded and institutionally savvy; informed by philosophical pragmatism, notably the work of John Dewey;[9] and attentive to the place of language and the arts in democracy's elaboration. His treatment of singularity as an updating of the revolutionary concept of equality offers especially rich potential for the interrogation of the relationship between literature and democratic politics.

Rosanvallon's approach to democratic theory overlaps with recent work by Danielle Allen. * * * In her scholarship Allen moves between

---

Renaissance"—suggesting that literature flourished in the 19th century U.S. on par with the artistic accomplishments of the European Renaissance (14th through 17th centuries)—has deeply informed judgments about American literary history. The five writers Matthiessen studies have also been described as comprising a tradition of American Romanticism or of literary transcendentalism: popular philosopher, essayist, and poet *Ralph Waldo Emerson* (1803–1882); novelists drawn to dark themes *Nathaniel Hawthorne* (1804–1864) and *Herman Melville* (1819–1891); nature writer and popular philosopher *Henry David Thoreau* (1817–1862); and poet and journalist *Walt Whitman* (1819–1892)—*Editor*.]

5. Word reflecting a core value in a given culture. A god-term is often more expressive of feelings and beliefs than useful for conveying precise information [*Editor*].
6. Period of history, approximately 1775–1848, which saw numerous revolutions to overturn monarchies and establish constitutional states and republics. These revolutions include the American (1775–83), in which thirteen North American colonies overthrew British rule to establish the sovereign United States of America, founded with the Declaration of Independence in 1776; the French (1789–99), which overturned the absolute monarchy and feudal system and established many principles seen as central to Western democracies; the Haitian (1791–1804), in which self-liberated slaves overthrew French colonial rule to establish the sovereign state of Haiti; and numerous revolutions across Europe in 1848. *Plato's day*: the period in which the preeminent Athenian philosopher Plato lived (428–347 BCE); the term is often used as shorthand for the high point of the Classical period in ancient Greece, widely characterized as the origin of democracy [*Editor*].
7. John Dunn, *Democracy: A History* (New York: Atlantic Monthly Books, 2005), p. 37.
8. Pierre Rosanvallon, "Inaugural Lecture, Collège de France," in *Democracy Past and Future*, ed. Samuel Moyn (New York: Columbia UP, 2006), p. 38.
9. Prominent American philosopher (1859–1952), who believed philosophy had become overly technical and disconnected from the pressing problems of life. As one of the founders of *philosophical pragmatism*, Dewey sought to reorient philosophy toward issues of wide moral and practical significance, such as human freedom, the goals of education, and the meaning of democracy [*Editor*].

ancient Greece and the United States, with a focus on what the Greek example can teach modern democrats and an eye to the ways that race-based slavery constitutes a deforming legacy for American democracy. * * *

Both Rosanvallon and Allen build on the pragmatist revival[1] that brought philosophers into debates about the place and value of literature in a democratic society. That revival has been a largely U.S.-based phenomenon, which makes Rosanvallon's engagement with Dewey so striking and his interest in language and literature so intriguing. * * * Richard Rorty[2] proposed the instigation of "social hope" as a central task for the arts and humanities in *Achieving Our Country: Leftist Thought in Twentieth-Century America*, where he speculated that "it is only those who still read for inspiration who are likely to be of much use in building a cooperative commonwealth." Citing the influence of Whitman and Dewey, Rorty locates a connection between art and democracy in art's ability to "provide examples of the kind of courageous self-transformation of which we hope democratic societies will become increasingly capable—transformation which is conscious and willed, rather than semi-consciously endured."[3]

Martha Nussbaum is another reader of Dewey who finds in his work an understanding of self and community that revolves around the arts and humanities. In *Not For Profit: Why Democracy Needs the Humanities*, she builds on her earlier work about the ethical potential of literature to argue that for heterogeneous modern democracies to succeed, the human ability "to imagine the experience of another . . . needs to be greatly enhanced and refined." Literature has a major role to play in expanding the imagination. As Nussbaum notes in *Poetic Justice: The Literary Imagination and Public Life*, literature is not a sufficient basis for public reasoning in a democratic society, but it is a necessary one * * *.[4] This pragmatist strain in contemporary democratic theory sees possibilities in literary works other than those forms of critique offered by poststructuralist, postcolonial, and Marxist theories.[5] * * *

---

1. Building on the work of Dewey and other founders of pragmatism, a *pragmatist revival* in philosophy began in the 1970s and is ongoing [*Editor*].
2. One of best-known and most controversial philosophers (1931–2007) in the pragmatist revival [*Editor*].
3. Richard Rorty, *Achieving Our Country: Leftist Thought in Twentieth-Century America* (Cambridge, MA: Harvard UP, 1998), pp. 140, 122.
4. Martha C. Nussbaum, *Not for Profit: Why Democracy Needs the Humanities* (Princeton, NJ: Princeton UP, 2010), p. 10; Martha C. Nussbaum, *Poetic Justice: The Literary Imagination and Public Life* (Boston: Beacon, 1995), p. xvi.
5. Deriving from the writings of Marx and emphasizing power differentials among different social groups, particularly the exploitation of those who create economic value (labor) by those who own the instruments of economic production (capital); on Marx, also see above, p. 287, n. 4, and p. 365, n. 1, and for a selection of Marx's writing, see pp. 406–11. *Poststructuralist* theories (deriving from a movement in literary criticism and

Frustrations with what goes by the name of democracy shadow its modern evolution, and since 1968[6] these tensions have congealed in a protest-oriented oppositional stance that plays a major role in democratic theory and politics. * * * Rosanvallon addresses democratic disenchantment as a political phenomenon in *Counter-Democracy: Politics in an Age of Distrust*, where he defines "counter-democracy" not as opposition to democracy, but rather as "a form of democracy that reinforces the usual electoral democracy" by exposing and questioning its limits. Counter-democracy manifests "a durable democracy of distrust" and supplements democratic elections by enhancing the limited opportunities that the ballot makes available for expressing dissent and seeking accountability. Rosanvallon emphasizes that this "counter-democracy" is already well "disseminated throughout society" and provides mechanisms for "institutionalizing distrust in a positive way," with the "three primary modes of oversight" being *"vigilance, denunciation,* and *evaluation."*[7]

*   *   *

While Rosanvallon emphasizes that counter-democracy serves essential functions, he also notes that it has a "dark side: the unpolitical." The depoliticization that can accompany counter-democracy has given rise today to "a vague but persistent feeling of malaise, which paradoxically has grown even as civil society has become more active, better informed, and more capable of intervening in political decisions than ever before." Rosanvallon emphasizes the need to dispel the apathy that counter-democracy can generate by restoring "a vision of a common world, a sense that it is possible to overcome fragmentation and disintegration," which he believes calls for three types of "democratic works": the production of a political world that is legible to ordinary people, the symbolization of collective power, and the testing of social differences.[8] * * *

* * * In *Democratic Legitimacy*, Rosanvallon [discusses] the rise of political parties during the nineteenth century that led, within a few

---

philosophy originating in France in the late 1960s) hold that meaning is unstable and that it is therefore impossible to discern purposeful underlying structures or codes, whether in society, in the mind, or in language. *Postcolonial*: ideas associated with postcolonialism, an interdisciplinary critical theory that emerged in the U.S. and U.K. in the 1980s, which examines the enduring impact of colonialism and imperialism (even after the official end of empires), and which seeks to locate the voice and agency of peoples who have been colonized [*Editor*].

6. A year of worldwide social protests, including in France, where students joined forces with some 10 million striking workers, nearly toppling the government. In the U.S., protests followed the assassination of civil rights leader and advocate of nonviolent direct action Martin Luther King, Jr. (1929–1968), while the 1968 Democratic National Convention, held in Chicago, became the site of massive demonstrations against the Vietnam War, resulting in retaliatory violence against protesters by the police [*Editor*].

7. Pierre Rosanvallon, *Counter-Democracy: Politics in an Age of Distrust*, trans. Arthur Goldhammer (Cambridge, Eng.: Cambridge UP, 2008), pp. 9, 8–9, 13.

8. Rosanvallon, *Counter-Democracy*, pp. 306, 306–07.

decades, to a pervasive disenchantment with democracy. This disenchantment was registered as a relation to political language. By the latter part of that century, "the words *people* and *nation,* which had previously fed expectations and imaginations, were somehow diminished, drowned as they were in partisan squabbling and electioneering. The party system, which none of the early theorists of democracy had foreseen or analyzed, established itself everywhere as the actual center of political life, and government became enmeshed in the rivalries of personalities and clans." Rosanvallon goes on to note that "throughout the period 1890–1920, which saw the publication of countless books aimed at explaining 'the crisis of democracy,' the idea that a majoritarian electoral system could somehow express the interests of the whole of society lost all credibility."[9] * * *

* * * Rosanvallon's focus on political language as a barometer of democratic change leads him to identify a crisis that is conceptual in nature: we lack a set of ideas about democracy that correspond to our expectations and experiences, and it is his aim in *Democratic Legitimacy* to begin resolving the crisis by providing the missing concepts that make sense of decentered forms of democracy. Once we have come to recognize how democracy has changed, we can make better use of its potentialities.

Rosanvallon shines a light on language as a register of change in *Society of Equals,* tracking the evolution of the revolutionary slogan "Liberté, Égalité, Fraternité,"[1] with a close focus on the central term. The ideal of equality that emerged during the age of revolution rejected the aristocratic spirit of distinction. * * * Similarity became the basis of the Enlightenment[2] conception of equality. The American Revolution brought this ideal forward in a context where hierarchies among white men were relatively modest. * * * Meanwhile, vernacularized American English became the language of politics, as "democratic eloquence" became the new public idiom between the Revolution and the Civil War.[3] The contrast between American equality and European hierarchy was a staple of nationalist discourse in the nineteenth-century United States. * * *

Rosanvallon finds the similarity that underpinned postrevolutionary notions of equality to be an inadequate basis for our contemporary

9. Pierre Rosanvallon, *Democratic Legitimacy: Impartiality, Reflexivity, Proximity,* trans. Arthur Goldhammer (Princeton,: Princeton UP, 2011), pp. 2, 3.
1. "Liberty, Equality, Fraternity," slogan of the French Revolution, advocating principles that have come to be understood as central to Western liberal democracies [*Editor*].
2. Period of Western history (1685–1815), also known as the Age of Reason, in which philosophers questioned traditional centers of authority and affirmed that human life could be improved by embracing reason and science. Associated as well with political revolutions, Enlightenment ideals inspired the American and French revolutions [*Editor*].
3. Kenneth Cmiel, *Democratic Eloquence: The Fight over Popular Speech in Nineteenth-Century America* (New York: William Morrow 1990), esp. chap. 2. [On the American Civil War, see above, p. 333, n. 4 and p. 353, n. 5—*Editor*.]

understanding, and he puts heterogeneity at the core of his revised concept. The proliferation of identities made possible by contemporary social movements has undermined equality-as-similarity as a tenable ground for democratic engagement. In recent years, Marxist and other class-oriented forms of politics have been pitted against the identity politics of race and ethnicity, gender, and sexuality. * * * To address this schism, Rosanvallon recasts equality via an emphasis on "singularity," a theme he finds well expressed in Emerson's "Self-Reliance," which he describes as a "vibrant ode to individualism and autonomy" that treats "nonconformity as the essential condition of a true society of equals."[4] * * *

* * * Rosanvallon * * * stresses that singularity is a relational concept. * * * Rosanvallon similarly emphasizes that one becomes singular in one's orientation toward others. In contrast to revolutionary theories of equality that were rendered obsolete by industrial capitalism, "equality of singularities does not imply 'sameness.' Rather, each individual seeks to stand out by virtue of the unique qualities that he or she alone possesses."[5] * * *

* * * A similar interest in equality, understood as human flourishing, and a related set of questions about democracy and its relationship to writing animate Danielle Allen's book on the Declaration of Independence. In *Our Declaration*, Allen performs what she calls a "slow reading" of that founding document in order to draw out the meaning of equality, which she relates to political processes focused on democratic deliberation and writing. These processes require "scripts," leading to new "habits" (an Aristotelian[6] concept also foregrounded by Dewey) that allow "a moral idea to become real in the world."[7] Her goal is to help readers perceive and understand the scripts for democratic action present in the Declaration that have been obscured by the passage of time and the historical contradictions in which this founding document is involved. The focus, in short, is on democracy as an essentially textual and symbolic creation.

Allen attends to the contradiction that looms large in any reading of the Declaration: the words "all men are created equal" were penned by one slave owner and endorsed by others. * * * Many of the people who signed on to the Declaration endorsed its broadly egalitarian values, she argues, but they failed to develop "new scripts for

---

4. Pierre Rosanvallon, *The Society of Equals*, trans. Arthur Goldhammer (Cambridge, MA: Harvard UP, 2013), p. 68.
5. Rosanvallon, *Society of Equals*, pp. 260–61.
6. Associated with the ancient Greek philosopher Aristotle (385–322 BCE), who believed that habituation determines the course of a person's life, and that good habits form the foundation of moral virtue [Editor].
7. Danielle Allen, *Our Declaration: A Reading of the Declaration of Independence in Defense of Equality* (New York: Liveright/Norton, 2014), pp. 242, 243.

interacting with slaves or Native Americans,"[8] scripts that would be based on reciprocity rather than domination.

From the language of the document, Allen draws five interconnected facets of the ideal of equality: equality as freedom from domination, for both states and individuals; equality that involves "recognizing and enabling the general human capacity for political judgment" coupled with "access to the tool of government"; equality derived from the Aristotelian "potluck method" whereby individuals contribute their special forms of knowledge to foster social good; reciprocity or mutual responsiveness, which contributes to equality of agency; and equality as "co-creation, where many people participate equally in creating a world together."[9] * * *

The most expansive facet of equality, as Allen defines it, is the universal capacity for political judgment and access to government, which requires an appreciation for what she terms "democratic writings."[1] * * *

* * * How have writers negotiated the relationship between aesthetic practice and democratic politics—and how do we assess their efforts? Which literary works serve as political actors, and what (if anything) distinguishes them from propaganda? How do works of literature register or even catalyze the transformation of politically charged words as they acquire and shed meanings over time? * * * In the discussion of * * * Upton Sinclair that follows, I provide initial responses to many of these questions * * *.

One thing that these questions have in common is a shift away from generalized critique, and from a utopian view of "democracy to come" as pure potential divorced from present circumstances, toward a more nuanced view that seeks to identify both the achievements and limitations of our own time and to better understand the place of language and literature in democracy's unfolding. * * * By formulating equality not as sameness but as an other-oriented distinctiveness, equality-as-singularity provides a conceptual reorientation of one of the central dilemmas of modern democratic thought. Allen, meanwhile, suggests the egalitarian potential in the radical and decentered modes of political engagement authorized by the Declaration of Independence. * * * Rosanvallon and Allen emphasize the prospective dynamic within democratic thought, while focusing attention on its rich symbolic, linguistic, and literary sources and processes.

* * *

The relationship between democratic politics and character is central to Upton Sinclair's *The Jungle*. * * * Sinclair's novel is popular

8. Allen, *Our Declaration*, p. 28.
9. Allen, *Our Declaration*, pp. 268, 269.
1. Allen, *Our Declaration*, p. 145.

and sentimental and so direct in its anti-capitalist critique that it often verges on propaganda. The works of Rosanvallon and Allen help to bring forward several additional dimensions that enhance the novel's literary claims and expand the range of its contributions to democratic thought. In a plot modeled on John Bunyan's *Pilgrim's Progress*, *The Jungle* charts the formation of Protestant character in Jurgis Rudkus, a Catholic immigrant from Lithuania[2] who finds that the social institutions of his home country prove tragically inadequate to the circumstances of industrial capitalism in the United States. The character that emerges over the course of the novel is individual rather than corporate, mobile not rooted, and ideological instead of sacramental.[3] As Jurgis separates from his family and begins to hold something like a singular self-conception,[4] he finds his aspirations toward equality best represented by the Socialist party, which he comes to in a process that follows the stages of Protestant conversion. His political conversion leads to an extended scene late in the novel that exemplifies many of Allen's ideals: Jurgis attends an extended debate between a Christian socialist and an anarchist, which produces a limited but significant consensus and ushers the Socialists to electoral success. The scene can be difficult to engage because of its detailed representation of ideological contestation,[5] but it takes on greater resonance as a depiction of political deliberation and consensus formation.

The novel also illustrates the exclusion of women and African Americans from both the deliberations and the voting process, manifesting what, following Allen, we might point to as the need for the fashioning of new democratic scripts. And in fact, such scripts make a preliminary appearance in the version of *The Jungle* that appeared in the Socialist periodical *Appeal to Reason*.[6] This version includes a scene in which a character modeled on the race-baiting senator

2. The Christian allegory in *Pilgrim's Progress* (see above, p. x and p. 477, n. 3) encapsulates a Protestant worldview. The author is saying that while Sinclair's character Jurgis is technically Catholic, he converts to socialism in a manner that resembles a conversion to Protestantism. On the role of secularized Protestant views in shaping Sinclair, see above, pp. 494–99 [*Editor*].

3. Formed by ideology (specifically, by socialism), rather than by religious belief; sacraments are ceremonies central to Christian faith [*Editor*].

4. A conception of himself as a unique individual rather than as the member of a group [*Editor*].

5. The lengthy debate in *The Jungle*'s final chapter between Lucas and Schliemann, which dramatizes two different theories (or "ideologies") of socialism (pp. 304–16) [*Editor*].

6. In this paragraph, the author compares the endings of two different versions of *The Jungle*: an earlier variant appearing in installments in a periodical, and the legendary 1906 book published by Doubleday, Page & Company featured in this volume. While Senator Tillman (see next note) is mentioned in passing in the book version, the extended scene with Tillman discussed here appeared only in the periodical version. On the relationship between the two versions of *The Jungle*, see above, pp. xiii–xiv [*Editor*].

from South Carolina, Benjamin "Pitchfork Ben" Tillman,[7] confronts Socialists who are calling for an interracial coalition of workingmen. Sinclair portrays a confident and well-spoken woman who challenges Tillman and stands her ground in the face of his disparagement. Mirroring historical exclusions, this scene was excised from the book. The reasons for the differences between the book and the periodical version remain speculative. With Allen's approach to the Declaration in mind, we might ask if Sinclair's process of revision constitutes democratic writing. Was he pressured to eliminate this scene, and if so, by whom and to what end? What is clear is that Sinclair was not happy with either of the ways that he concluded his narrative: the book version that ends with the promising election results and a prophecy of Socialist triumph, or the periodical version that concludes with a deflating postscript in which Jurgis goes to jail. The book absorbs Jurgis in the political movement so completely that he disappears from the narrative, while the periodical version retains his singular identity but in a punitive context. Rosanvallon's work allows us to see how equality-as-singularity is incipiently present, though not fully articulated or accommodated, in Sinclair's novel, while Allen helps frame an approach to the novel's form that draws out the need for new social scripts to foster democratic inclusion.

7. A white supremacist who spoke on the floor of the U.S. Senate defending the lynching of African Americans, Tillman (1847–1918) was a member of the Democratic Party. On the racial politics of the major U.S. political parties at this time, see above, p. 495, n. 1 [*Editor*].

Upton Sinclair: A Chronology

Sinclair published nearly 90 books, only some of which are mentioned here.

1878	Upton Beall Sinclair Jr. is born in Baltimore, Maryland, the only child of Upton Beall Sinclair Sr., a salesman and alcoholic, and Priscilla Harden Sinclair, a strict Episcopalian who detests liquor, coffee, and tea.
1890	After completing the first eight grades in two years, begins high school.
1893	Begins as one of the youngest freshmen at City College of New York.
1897	Finishes City College and begins graduate studies at Columbia, initially studying law, and supporting himself by writing novels for boys.
1900	Decides to give up writing for money and sets out to become a literary artist. Moves into a log cabin on Lake Massawippi, near the Vermont-Quebec border, with plans for a novel about a woman redeemed by love (first published as *Springtime and Harvest*). While at the lake, becomes reacquainted with Meta Fuller, a young woman with literary aspirations. They marry in October.
1901	After several publishers reject *Springtime and Harvest*, borrows $200 from an uncle to print 1,000 copies himself, earning just enough from sales to repay the debt. Funk & Wagnalls republishes the novel as *King Midas*. Only child, David, born.
1902	Gets *The New York Times* to print an obituary of a made-up poet named

Stirling, an aesthete who killed himself. Less than a year later, publishes the novel *The Journal of Arthur Stirling*, reputedly by the fictitious suicide.

Meets the prominent socialists George Herron and Gaylord Wilshire.

1903   Announces big ambitions: projected trilogy of novels about the Civil War; establishment of the Sinclair Press, a publishing company; and creation of "My Cause," a foundation to liberate writers from the need for money. Herron fronts money for the first Civil War novel (published a year later as *Manassas*, to some strong reviews but little commercial success).

Reads socialist authors recommended by Herron and Wilshire.

1904   Joins the Socialist Party of America.

Immediate background of *The Jungle*:

Publishes an article supporting the 1904 strike of Chicago stockyard workers against meat packers in the popular socialist journal the *Appeal to Reason* (for reference to this article in *The Jungle*, see above, pp. 301–02).

Sends a copy of *Manassas* to the editor of the *Appeal*, explaining his belief that "wage slavery" in the North recapitulates chattel slavery in the South. Invited by the editor to write a novel demonstrating that thesis, to be published serially.

Also lines up the commercial press Macmillan to publish his as-yet unwritten novel.

Goes to Chicago for seven weeks of research in Packingtown. Jane Addams, the founder of Chicago's most famous settlement house, Hull-House, introduces him to Adolphe Smith, a British journalist who had been commissioned by the medical journal *The Lancet* to write a series of articles on Chicago's slaughterhouses. Smith takes Sinclair on a tour of the Armour plant.

By November, has background material for the novel but no story to hang it on—until he stumbles upon a Lithuanian wedding.

Christmas morning, starts writing *The Jungle*.

1905 February First chapter of *The Jungle* appears in the *Appeal*.

Macmillan reluctant to publish the novel as previously agreed; demands cuts.

August Launches the Intercollegiate Socialist Society, with the writer Jack London as the first president.

November After the *Appeal* declines to serialize additional chapters of *The Jungle*, Sinclair announces a forthcoming hardcover version—the "Sustainer's Edition"—to be published by himself.

December Doubleday, Page, which had recently published controversial novels such as Theodore Dreiser's *Sister Carrie* (1900, about a young woman who has sexual relations outside of marriage and ends up a wealthy actress) and Thomas Dixon's *The Clansman* (1905, which mythologizes the origins of the Ku Klux Klan), agrees to publish *The Jungle*.

1906 February *The Jungle* published; within months it is translated into seventeen languages. With help of an outstanding publicity campaign developed by Doubleday's Isaac Marcosson, Sinclair becomes famous virtually overnight.

April After Sinclair sends a copy of *The Jungle* to Theodore Roosevelt (TR), the president invites the author to the White House.

TR gives his "the man with the muckrake" speech, coining the term "muckraker" to denounce investigative writing that he believes goes too far (for excerpt, see above, p. 504).

In part because of *The Jungle*, TR authorizes a study of Chicago meatpackers.

June 23 Landmark Pure Food and Drug Bill passes.

	November	Using proceeds from *The Jungle*, Sinclair opens Helicon Hall, a cooperative commune.
1907	March	Helicon Hall burns down under suspicious circumstances.
	April	Upton Sinclair Sr. dies at age 54.
	September	Sinclair joins his wife, Meta, for the first of several health visits to Battle Creek, Michigan, this time to a famous sanatarium run by Dr. John Harvey Kellogg.
1909		With Michael Williams, publishes *Good Health, and How We Won It*.
	August	During his second health visit to Battle Creek, this time to Bernarr Macfadden's Health Home, meets Mary ("Craig") Kimbrough, from Mississippi.
	Fall	Lives in an artist's community in Fairhope, Alabama.
1910	April	With Meta, moves to an experimental single-tax community (where all members pay rent and share land collectively) on a 160-acre farm in Arden, Delaware.
1911	Summer	Craig and "tramp poet" Harry Kemp, who considers Sinclair his literary mentor, visit Arden. Sinclair walks in on Kemp and Meta making love; files for divorce in August. Sinclair, Meta, and Kemp hold a press conference at a Manhattan hotel to discuss their love triangle.
1911		Publishes *Love's Pilgrimage*, a semiautobiographical novel about the disintegration of his marriage and his efforts to establish himself as a writer.
1912	February	His divorce suit is denied due to the court's finding Sinclair complicit in Meta's adultery. (In the years before no-fault divorce, state laws required one innocent as well as one guilty party in order to grant a divorce.) He goes to Europe, visiting England, Italy, Switzerland, and Germany—and initiates divorce proceedings in Holland.
	May	Divorce finalized in Holland; Sinclair and Craig begin traveling together openly.
1913	April	Marries Craig.

	October	Sinclair and Craig move to Bermuda for six months, where he works on novels based on her Mississippi remembrances, *Sylvia* (1913) and *Sylvia's Marriage* (1914).
	Spring '13	Supports striking steelworkers in Paterson, New Jersey.
1913– 14	Sept. '13	A 3,000-person strike is called at Colorado Fuel and Iron Company, a Rockefeller holding.
	April '14	The governor of Colorado sends in the state militia, leading to the 1914 Ludlow Massacre. Sinclair organizes a protest against Rockefeller at the Standard Oil offices in New York and is jailed for three days.
	May '14	Delivers a talk, "Shall We Murder Rockefeller?"
1914	Summer	Proposes an anthology of socialist writings, *The Cry for Justice* (published 1915).
	June	Appears in the silent movie version of *The Jungle*, playing Eugene Debs, the beloved historical socialist (and in the novel, the man who converts Jurgis to socialism).
1916		The Sinclairs buy a house in Pasadena, California; they live in it for 25 years.
1917	April	Supports President Woodrow Wilson's decision for the U.S. to enter World War I. For doing so, Sinclair is denounced by fellow socialists as a traitor. (He later grows disillusioned with Wilson and declares he never should have supported the war.)
	July	Resigns from the American Socialist Party, though most of his views and principles remain socialist for the rest of his life.
	September	Publishes *King Coal*, a novel that confronts Rockefeller and his role in the Ludlow Massacre.
1918		In response to media outlets closing him out, launches monthly magazine, *Upton Sinclair's*, consisting largely of pieces supporting the war, many of which reappear

in the novel *Jimmie Higgins* (1919), written to demonstrate that a socialist can support war.

Publishes *The Profits of Religion*, a nonfiction book arguing that religion operates to serve capitalism.

1919   April   Newly launched successor to the *Appeal to Reason*, *The New Appeal*, commissions Sinclair to write a weekly column through 1925.

Sinclair becomes friendly with automobile magnate Henry Ford, who has rented a house in Pasadena; the unlikely pair discuss capitalism while hiking.

1920   Publishes *The Brass Check*, which Sinclair calls "the most important and most dangerous book I have ever written." This exposé of how big money corrupts the press also castigates yellow journalism for scandalmongering (including for how the press portrayed Sinclair's split from his first wife). It becomes his biggest hit since *The Jungle*.

1922   Publishes *They Call Me Carpenter*, about Jesus as a revolutionary.

1923   May   While supporting a strike by waterfront workers in the San Pedro community of Los Angeles, arrested for reading the Constitution in public, under the charge that he was "obstructing traffic."

1926   Nominated for governor of California, on the American Socialist Party ticket.

1927   Publishes *Oil!*, based on the Teapot Dome scandal of 1922, involving the secret leasing of federal oil reserves and resulting in the imprisonment of presidential Cabinet member Albert Bacon Fall. When the novel is banned in Boston, Sinclair publishes and markets a "fig leaf" edition, with offending passages covered by fig leaves. (In 2007, *Oil!* serves as the basis for the Academy Award–winning film *There Will Be Blood*.)

Novelist Floyd Dell publishes *Upton Sinclair: A Study in Social Protest*, which interprets Sinclair's life in terms of Sigmund Freud's psychoanalytic theories.

1928   Publishes *Boston*, a novel based on the execution of two real-life anarchists, Nicola Sacco and Bartolomeo Vanzetti, convicted of murder (their conviction and sentence are widely seen as travesties of justice).

1930   Publishes *Mental Radio*, based on Craig's experiences with telepathy and spiritualism. Physicist Albert Einstein agrees to write the introduction for the German edition.

1930– '30   Sinclair and Craig agree to sponsor *Que*
33   *Viva Mexico!*, a documentary about Indians in Mexico directed by the Soviet-emigré filmmaker Sergei Eisenstein (*Battleship Potemkin*, *Ten Days that Shook the World*).

'31   Sinclair receives a telegram from the Soviet dictator Josef Stalin, informing him that Eisenstein is seen as a deserter. Eisenstein leaves the Sinclairs with miles of footage, which Sinclair turns over to a Hollywood producer, who makes *Thunder Over Mexico* (1933).

1930–31   Campaigns unsuccessfully for the Nobel Prize in Literature.

1931   Publishes *The Wet Parade*, a novel in favor of prohibition, made into a Hollywood film in 1932.

1932   Publishes first autobiography, *American Outpost*, delaying it until after his mother's death, in 1931.

1933–35   In preparation for his second bid for governor, publishes *I, Governor of California, and How I Ended Poverty* (1933), a novel that sells over a million copies. Unveils 12-step End Poverty in California (EPIC) program and makes the cover of *Time* magazine. Deciding to run not as a socialist but as a Democrat, while lacking support from the party in California, Sinclair seeks national backing, visiting President Franklin Delano Roosevelt and

		many of his program directors in Washington. A vast and many-pronged promotional campaign is unveiled to defeat him, yet Sinclair receives nearly 38 percent of the vote. Publishes *I, Candidate for Governor, and How I Got Licked* (1935).
1937		Publishes *The Flivver King*, a novel that attacks the Ford empire.
1940–53		Publishes the eleven-volume Lanny Budd Series (also called *World's End* series, after the title of the first novel), considered by many to be Sinclair's best writing. Described by Sinclair as "contemporary history," the novels span 1913–53, putting the fictional Lanny Budd into contact with world-historical figures.
1943		The third book in the Lanny Budd series, *Dragon's Teeth* (1942), about the rise of German fascist leader Adolf Hitler, wins the Pulitzer Prize for Fiction.
1957		Craig publishes her autobiography, *Southern Belle*, with considerable help from Sinclair.
1961	April	Craig dies; Sinclair soon begins proposing to various women, including one by mail whom he has never met.
	October	At age 83, marries Mary Elizabeth ("Mae") Willis, whom he proposes to on the day they meet. After his years of estrangement from his son, David, Mae helps bring about a reconciliation.
1963		Dedicates his vast collection of personal and professional papers to the Lilly Library at Indiana University.
1967		In recognition of the continuing importance of *The Jungle*, invited to the White House to meet President Lyndon Johnson on the occasion of the president's signing the Wholesome Meat Act.
1968	November 25	Sinclair dies. He is buried at Rock Creek Cemetery in Washington, D.C.

Selected Bibliography

• indicates works included or excerpted in this Norton Critical Edition.

Historical Contexts: Writings from around the Time of *The Jungle*

Addams, Jane. *Twenty Years at Hull-House*. 1910. New York: New American Library, 1981.
• Armour, J. Ogden. *The Packers, the Private Car Lines, and the People*. Philadelphia: Henry Altemus, 1906.
• Breckinridge, Sophonisba P., and Edith Abbott. "Housing Conditions in Chicago, Ill.: Back of the Yards." *The American Journal of Sociology* 16:4 (1911): 433–68.
Bushnell, Charles J. *The Social Problem at the Chicago Stock Yards*. Chicago: U of Chicago P, 1902.
Commons, John R. "Labor Conditions in Slaughtering and Meat Packing." *Quarterly Journal of Economics* 19 (1904): 1–32. Reprinted in John R. Commons, ed., *Trade Unionism and Labor Problems*. Ginn, 1905, 222–49.
• Dreiser, Theodore. "Life Stories of Successful Men—No. 10." *Success* 1 (October 1898): 3–4.
Grand, W. Joseph. *Illustrated History of the Union Stockyards: Sketch-Book of Familiar Faces and Places at the Yards*. Chicago: T. Knapp, 1896.
Kaztauskis, Antanas. [Poole, Ernest]. "From Lithuania to the Chicago Stockyards—An Autobiography." *Independent* 57 (August 4, 1904): 241–48.
• Kennedy, J. C., et al. *Wages and Family Budgets in the Chicago Stockyards District*. Chicago: U of Chicago P, 1914.
• Leech, Harper, and John Charles Carroll. *Armour and His Times*. New York: D. Appleton-Century, 1938.
• Marx, Karl, and Friedrich Engels. *The Marx-Engels Reader*, ed. Robert C. Tucker. New York: Norton, 1972.
Poole, Ernest. "The Meat Strike." *The Independent*, July 8, 1904, 179–84.
• Riis, Jacob. *How the Other Half Lives*. 1890. Norton Critical Edition, ed. Hasia R. Diner. New York: Norton, 2010.
• Russell, Charles Edward. *The Greatest Trust in the World*. New York: Ridgway-Thayer, 1905.
• Simons, A. M. *Packingtown*. Chicago: Charles H. Kerr, 1899.
• Smith, A. [Adolphe]. "Chicago: The Dark and Insanitary Premises Used for the Slaughtering of Cattle and Hogs—The Government Inspection." *The Lancet*, January 14, 1905, 120–23.
———. "Chicago: The Stockyards and Packing Town: Insanitary Conditions of the World's Largest Meat Market." *The Lancet*, January 7, 1905, 49–52.
———. "Chicago: Tuberculosis among the Stockyard Workers—Sanitation in Packingtown—The Police and the Dumping of Refuse—Vital Statistics." *The Lancet*, January 21, 1905, 183–85.

————. "Chicago: Unhealthy Work in the Stockyards—Shameless Indifference to the Insanitary Condition of the Buildings and the Cattle Pens—Pollution of the Subsoil—The Need for Legislative Interference." *The Lancet*, January 28, 1905, 258–60.
• U. S. Bureau of Corporations. *Report of the Commissioner of Corporations on the Beef Industry, March 3, 1905*. Washington: Government Printing Office, 1905.
• Vice Commission of Chicago. *The Social Evil in Chicago*. 1911.

Historical Scholarship

Barrett, James R. "Women's Work, Family Economy and Labor Militancy: The Case of Chicago's Packing-House Workers, 1900–1922." *Labor Divided: Race and Ethnicity in United States Labor Struggles, 1835–1960*, ed. Robert Asher and Charles Stephenson. Albany: State UP of New York, 1990, pp. 246–66.
Bederman, Gail. *Manliness and Civilization: A Cultural History of Gender and Race in the United States, 1880–1917*. Chicago: U of Chicago P, 1966.
Braeman, John. "The Square Deal in Action: A Case Study in the Growth of a 'National Police Power.'" *Change and Continuity in Twentieth-Century America*, ed. John Braeman, Robert Bremner, and Everett Walters. Columbus: Ohio State UP, 1964, pp. 35–80.
Connelly, Mark Thomas. *The Response to Prostitution in the Progressive Era*. Chapel Hill: U of North Carolina P, 1918.
• Cronon, William. *Nature's Metropolis: Chicago and the Great West*. New York: Norton, 1991.
• Crunden, Robert M. *Ministers of Reform: The Progressives' Achievement in American Civilization 1889–1920*. New York: Basic, 1982.
Fainhauz, David. *Lithuanians in Multi-Ethnic Chicago until World War II*. Chicago: Lithuanian Library P and Loyal UP, 1977.
• Halpern, Rick. *Down on the Killing Floor: Black and White Workers in Chicago's Packinghouses, 1905–1954*. Urbana: U of Illinois P, 1997.
Handlin, Oscar. *The Uprooted: The Epic Story of the Great Migrations that Made the American People*. New York: Grosset & Dunlap, 1951.
Hofstadter, Richard. *The Age of Reform*. New York: Vintage, 1955.
Horowitz, Roger. *Putting Meat on the American Table: Taste, Technology, Transformation*. Balitmore: Johns Hopkins UP, 2005.
• Jacobson, Matthew Frye. *Whiteness of a Different Color: European Immigrants and the Alchemy of Race*. Cambridge, MA: Harvard UP, 1998.
Kolko, Gabriel. *The Triumph of Conservatism: A Reinterpretation of American History, 1900–1916*. New York: The Free P, 1963.
Mitchell, Okun. *Fair Play in the Marketplace: The First Battle for Pure Food and Drugs*. Dekalb: Northern Illinois UP, 1986.
Painter, Nell Irvin. *Standing at Armageddon: The United States, 1877–1919*. New York: Norton, 1989.
Pliley, Jessica R. *Policing Sexuality: The Mann Act and the Making of the FBI*. Cambridge, MA: Harvard UP, 2014.
Skaggs, Jimmy. *Prime Cut: Livestock Raising and Meatpacking in the United States 1607–1983*. College Station: Texas A & M UP, 1986.
• Sklar, Martin J. *The Corporate Reconstruction of American Capitalism, 1890–1916: The Market, the Law, and Politics*. Cambridge, Eng.: Cambridge UP, 1988.
• Specht, Joshua. *Red Meat Republic: A Hoof to Table History of How Beef Changed America*. Princeton: Princeton UP, 2019.
Stromquist, Shelton, and Marvin Bergman. *Unionizing the Jungle: Labor and Community in the Twentieth Century Meatpacking Industry*. Iowa City: U of Iowa P, 1997.
Thomas, Courtney I. P. *In Food We Trust: The Politics of Purity in American Food Regulation*. Lincoln: U of Nebraska P, 2014.

Wade, Louise Carroll. *Chicago's Pride: The Stockyards, Packingtown, and Environs in the Nineteenth Century.* Urbana: U of Illinois P, 1987.

Yeager, Mary. *Competition and Regulation: The Development of Oligopoly in the Meat Packing Industry.* Greenwich, CT: JAI P, 1981.

Young, James Harvey. *Pure Food: Securing the Federal Food and Drugs Act of 1906.* Princeton: Princeton UP, 1989.

Further Backgrounds and Contexts

Aaron, Daniel. *Writers on the Left: Episodes in American Literary Communism.* New York: Octagon, 1974.

• Adams, Carol J. *The Sexual Politics of Meat: A Feminist-Vegetarian Critical Theory.* 20th anniv. ed. New York and London: Continuum, 2010.

• Alkon, Alison Hope, and Julian Agyeman. *Cultivating Food Justice: Race, Class, and Sustainability.* Cambridge, MA: MIT P, 2011.

Cook, Fred J. *The Muckrakers: Crusading Journalists Who Changed America.* Garden City, NY: Doubleday, 1972.

• Davis, Mike. *The Monster at Our Door: The Global Threat of Avian Flu.* Rev. and exp. ed. New York: Henry Holt, 2006.

Denning, Michael. *Mechanic Accents: Dime Novels and Working Class Culture in America.* London: Verso, 1987.

Encyclopedia of Chicago. Ed. Janice L. Rieff, Ann Durkin Keating, and James R. Grossman. http://encyclopedia.chicagohistory.org

Filler, Louis. *Muckraking and Progressivism in the American Tradition.* Boston: Routledge, 2018. (Originally published as *Appointment at Armageddon*, 1976.)

Foer, Jonathan Safran. *Eating Animals.* New York: Little, Brown, 2009.

Foley, Barbara. *Telling the Truth: The Theory and Practice of Documentary Fiction.* Ithaca: Cornell UP, 1986.

• Gottlieb, Robert, and Anupama Joshi. *Food Justice.* Cambridge, MA: MIT P, 2010.

• Hayes, Denis, and Gail Boyer Hayes. *Cowed: The Hidden Impact of 93 Million Cows on America's Health, Economy, Politics, Culture, and Environment.* New York: Norton, 2015.

Imhoff, Daniel, ed. *The CAFO Reader: The Tragedy of Industrial Animal Factories.* Berkeley: Watershed, 2010.

Kingsdale, Jon M. "The 'Poor Man's Club': Social Functions of the Urban Working-Class Saloon." *American Quarterly* 24:4 (1973): 472–89.

Michaels, Walter Benn. *The Gold Standard and the Logic of Naturalism.* Berkeley: U of California P, 1987.

• Nestle, Marion. *Food Politics: How the Food Industry Influences Nutrition and Health.* Berkeley: U of California P, 2013.

• Pachirat, Timothy. *Every Twelve Seconds: Industrialized Slaughter and the Politics of Sight.* New Haven: Yale UP, 2011.

• Piketty, Thomas. *Capital in the Twenty-First Century.* Trans. Arthur Goldhammer. Cambridge, MA: Belknap P of Harvard UP, 2014.

• Pollan, Michael. *The Omnivore's Dilemma: A Natural History of Four Meals.* New York: Penguin, 2006.

Rosen, Ruth. *The Lost Sisterhood: Prostitution in America, 1900–1918.* Baltimore: Johns Hopkins UP, 1982.

• Schlosser, Eric. *Fast Food Nation: The Dark Side of the All-American Meal.* New York: Houghton Mifflin, 2001.

Seltzer, Mark. *Bodies and Machines.* New York and London: Routledge, 1992.

• Singer, Peter. *Animal Liberation.* Updated ed. New York: HarperCollins, 2009.

• Stull, Donald D. "Meat Processing." *Sage Encyclopedia of Food Issues,* ed. Ken Albala. http://dx.doi.org/10.4135/9781483346304.n285

Tichi, Cecelia. *Exposés and Excess: Muckraking in America, 1900/2000*. Philadelphia: U of Pennsylvania P, 2004.

Tietz, Jeff. "Boss Hog: The Dark Side of America's Top Pork Producer." *Rolling Stone*, December 14, 2006. https://www.rollingstone.com/culture/culture-news/boss-hog-the-dark-side-of-americas-top-pork-producer-68087/

Trachtenberg, Alan. *The Incorporation of America: Culture and Society in the Gilded Age*. New York: Hill and Wang, 1982.

Weinberg, Arthur, and Lila Weinberg, eds. *The Muckrakers*. Urbana: U of Illinois P, 2001.

Upton Sinclair: Biographies and Wide-Angled Studies

Arthur, Anthony. *Radical Innocent: Upton Sinclair*. New York: Random House, 2006.

Blinderman, Abraham, ed. *Critics on Upton Sinclair*. Coral Gables: U of Miami P, 1975.

Coodley, Lauren. *Upton Sinclair: California Socialist, Celebrity Intellectual*. Lincoln: U of Nebraska P, 2013.

Dell, Floyd. *Upton Sinclair: A Study in Social Protest*. New York: George H. Doran, 1927.

Eby, Clare Virginia. *Until Choice Do Us Part: Marriage Reform in the Progressive Era*. Chicago: U of Chicago P, 2014.

Gilenson, Boris. "A Socialist of the Emotions: Upton Sinclair." *American Literature: A Soviet View*, trans. Ronald Vroon. Moscow: Progress, 1976, 199–222.

Gottesman, Ronald, and Charles L. P. Silet. *The Literary Manuscripts of Upton Sinclair*. Columbus: Ohio State UP, 1972.

Harris, Leon. *Upton Sinclair: American Rebel*. New York: Thomas Y. Crowell, 1975.

Herms, Dieter, ed. *Upton Sinclair: Literature and Social Reform*. Frankfurt am Main, Germany, and New York: Peter Lang, 1990.

Homberger, Eric. *American Writers and Radical Politics, 1900–39*. London: Palgrave Macmillan, 1986.

Mattson, Kevin. *Upton Sinclair and the Other American Century*. Hoboken, NJ: Wiley, 2006.

Mookherjee, R. N. *Art for Social Justice: The Major Novels of Upton Sinclair*. Metuchen, NJ: Scarecrow P, 1988.

• Sinclair, Upton. *The Autobiography of Upton Sinclair*. New York: Harcourt, Brace & World, 1962. [An expanded and slightly revised version of Sinclair's *American Outpost: A Book of Reminiscences*, published by the author in 1932.]

• ———. *Mammonart: An Essay in Economic Interpretation*. Pasadena, Published by the Author, 1925.

———. *My Lifetime in Letters*. Columbia: U of Missouri P, 1960.

• ———. "The Socialist Party in the United States." *World's Work* 8 (July 1906): 40–41.

• ———. "What Life Means to Me." *Cosmopolitan* 44 (October 1906): 591–95.

Smith, Carl. *Chicago in the American Literary Imagination*. Chicago: U of Chicago P, 1984.

Wilson, Christopher P. *The Labor of Words: Literary Professionalism in the Progressive Era*. Athens: U of Georgia P, 1985.

Upton Sinclair: Includes Sustained Discussion
of *The Jungle*

Banerjee, Mita. *Color Me White: Naturalism/Naturalization in American Literature*. Heidelberg, Germany: Universitätsverlag Winter, 2013.

Bloodworth, William A., Jr. "From *The Jungle* to *The Fasting Cure*: Upton Sinclair on American Food." *Journal of American Culture* 2 (1979): 444–53.

Bracher, Mark. *Literature and Social Justice: Protest Novels, Cognitive Politics, and Schema Criticism.* Austin: U of Texas P, 2013.

Castronovo, Russ. "Teaching the Good." *Journal of Narrative Theory* 41:2 (2011): 167–174.

• Churchill, Winston Spencer. "The Chicago Scandals: The Novel Which Is Making History." *P.T.O.*, June 16, 1905, 25–26, and June 23, 1906, 65–66.

Derrick, Scott. "What a Beating Feels Like: Authorship, Dissolution, and Masculinity in Sinclair's *The Jungle*." *Studies in American Fiction* 23:1 (1995): 85–100.

Duvall, J. Michael. "Processes of Elimination: Progressive-Era Ideology, Waste, and Upton Sinclair's *The Jungle*." *American Studies* 43:2 (2002): 29–56.

Folsom, Michael Brewster. "Upton Sinclair's Escape from *The Jungle*: The Narrative Strategy and Suppressed Conclusion of America's First Proletarian Novel." *Prospects* 4 (1979): 237–66.

• Gustafson, Sandra M. "Equality as Singularity: Rethinking Literature and Democracy," *New Literary History* 45:4 (Autumn 2014): 595–614.

Howard, June. *Form and History in American Literary Naturalism.* Chapel Hill: U of North Carolina P, 1985.

• London, Jack. "What Jack London Says of 'The Jungle.'" *Chicago Socialist* 6 (November 25, 1905): 2.

Lundblad, Michael. *The Birth of a Jungle: Animality in Progressive-Era U.S. Literature and Culture.* Oxford: Oxford UP, 2013.

Marcosson, Isaac F. "The Story of *The Jungle*." *Adventures in Interviewing.* New York: John Lane, 1919, pp. 280–89.

• Marsh, Edward Clark. "The Jungle," *Bookman* 23 (April 1906): 195–97.

Morris, Matthew J. "The Two Lives of Jurgis Rudkus." *American Literary Realism* 29:2 (1997): 50–67.

Pickavance, Jason. "Gastronomic Realism: Upton Sinclair's *The Jungle*, the Fight for Pure Food, and the Magic of Mastication." *Food and Foodways* 11:2–3 (2003): 87–112.

Rideout, Walter. *The Radical Novel in the United States 1900–1954.* Cambridge, MA: Harvard UP, 1956.

Rosendale, Steven. "In Search of Left Ecology's Usable Past: *The Jungle*, Social Change, and the Class Character of Environmental Impairment." *The Greening of Literary Scholarship: Literature, Theory, and the Environment*, ed. Steven Rosendale. Iowa City: U of Iowa P, 2002, pp. 59–76.

Scriabine, Christine. "Upton Sinclair and the Writing of *The Jungle*." *Chicago History* 59 (1985): 27–37.

Scott, William. "The Powerless Worker and the Failure of Political Representation: 'The lowest and most degraded of human beasts.'" *Troublemakers: Power, Representation, and the Fiction of the Mass Worker.* New Brunswick, NJ: Rutgers UP, 2011.

Sinclair, Upton. *The Lost First Edition of Upton Sinclair's* The Jungle, ed. Gene DeGruson. Memphis: Peachtree, 1988.

Tavernier-Courbin, Jacqueline. "*The Call of the Wild* and *The Jungle*: Jack London's and Upton Sinclair's Animal and Human Jungles." *The Cambridge Companion to American Realism and Naturalism: Howells to London*, ed. Donald Pizer. Cambridge, Eng.: Cambridge UP, 1995, pp. 236–62.

• Van Wienen, Mark W. *American Socialist Triptych: The Literary-Political Work of Charlotte Perkins Gilman, Upton Sinclair, and W. E. B. Du Bois.* Ann Arbor: U of Michigan P, 2012.

Wade, Louise Carroll. "The Problem with Classroom Use of Upton Sinclair's *The Jungle*." *American Studies* 32:2 (1991): 79–101.

Wardell, Nicole. "Exploitation of the Fittest: Critique of Social Darwinism in Upton Sinclair's *The Jungle*." *CEAMAGazine* 23 (2014): 49–58.